Hanratty

THE FINAL VERDICT

Bob Woffinden is a journalist and independent television producer. His documentary, *Hanratty: The Mystery of Deadman's Hill*, which first went out in 1992 and was updated in 1994 and 1995, has formed the basis for the evidence submitted to the Home Office requesting that the case be referred to appeal. He has written one previous book, *Miscarriages of Justice* (Hodder & Stoughton, 1987).

Hanratty

THE FINAL VERDICT

Bob Woffinden

PAN BOOKS

In Memoriam

JEAN JUSTICE
(6 October 1930 – 2 July 1990)

First published 1997 by Macmillan

This edition published 1999 by Pan Books
an imprint of Macmillan Publishers Ltd
25 Eccleston Place, London SW1W 9NF
Basingstoke and Oxford
Associated companies throughout the world
www.macmillan.co.uk

ISBN 0 330 35301 2

A CIP catalogue record for this book is available from
the British Library.

Typeset by SetSystems Ltd, Saffron Walden, Essex
Printed and bound in Great Britain by
Mackays of Chatham plc, Chatham, Kent

CONTENTS

INTRODUCTION

JAMES HANRATTY was hanged on 4 April 1962. His was one of the last executions to take place in Britain, and has always been one of the most controversial. The crime he was found guilty of, the A6 Murder, remains to this day the most fascinating case there has ever been in British criminal history. The majority of contentious prosecutions turn on one or two disputed points of evidence. The A6 case has a rich abundance of material capable of varying interpretations. Most crimes have brief spells of notoriety and then pass into legal history the moment the verdict is given and sentence passed. The A6 case is not like that. It has evolved bit by bit over the past thirty-five years, providing fresh revelations at every turn.

Of course, an outstanding book about the case has already been written: Paul Foot's *Who Killed Hanratty?* Anyone would be wary of risking comparison with that masterpiece, so why am I being so foolhardy?

Unbelievably, Foot's book was published in 1971, over a quarter of a century ago, and much has happened in the interim. This current book developed out of a television programme that I produced for Channel 4's *True Stories* series. It was first broadcast in April 1992, the week of the thirtieth anniversary of Hanratty's execution.

In the course of research for that, I obtained access to all the case files held by Bedfordshire police. These had not previously been disclosed, and they soon threw a fresh light on many areas of this perplexing case.

After the programme had been transmitted, the next step was to prepare a submission on the case, based largely on all this newly acquired material. That turned into a work of over 400 pages. It was completed in 1994 and sent by courier to the Home Office. During 1996 all the signs were promising; at last it seemed as though the case was getting somewhere. Then, in March 1997, the Home Office suddenly announced that it had proved impossible to reach a decision on whether or not to refer it back to the Appeal Court.

By then it was evident that public interest in the case, far from abating after all this time, was continuing only to grow. After the documentary was transmitted, I started a 'current' file, to set alongside the stacks of those containing evidence and other original case material. I thought there might, with luck, be an occasional press-cutting to place in it. Now that file has grown to several bulging volumes, as the case seems to gather more and more attention. In view of all that had happened, it was desirable that all the available material should be placed on public record. In any event, there was clearly a need for a fresh work, to provide something approximating a complete history of this extraordinary affair. Four books predated Paul Foot's, so this is the sixth specifically written about the case. That in itself is one indication of its absolute pre-eminence in the long annals of English criminal justice.

There are many, many people for me to thank. Michael Hanratty has been wonderfully loyal to his brother's memory, and has provided me with consistent support, offering many perceptive insights into the case. Geoffrey Bindman, the Hanratty family solicitor, has overseen the whole progress of the case for more than twenty years, so he more than anyone must take credit for the fact that it now stands, finally, on the verge of rectification. He has given me unstinting and unselfish assistance whenever I required it. Michael Sherrard, too, Hanratty's counsel at his trial and appeal, who subsequently pleaded for his life at the Home Office, always gave characteristically courteous support to my endeavours.

Paul Foot has been consistently helpful, and always ready to offer advice and encouragement when I needed it. He is one of the rocks on which this case is founded; no cause could ever hope to attract a more passionate or persuasive champion.

We are all enormously grateful to the Bedfordshire police for, without their decision to allow us access to their material, the truth would not have been uncovered.

Graham Swanwick, the Crown P.C., who subsequently became Mr Justice Swanwick, was kind enough to discuss the case with me and prepare lunch for me, even though his own firmly-held view – that Hanratty was guilty as charged – remained unchanged. Valerie Storie did not wish to go over it all again, and no one would blame her for that. Former Superintendent Bob Acott also declined, though with great courtesy, to say anything at all about the case.

Janet Gregsten, however, was happy to be interviewed, over several hours, about the case and its aftermath.

During the making of the documentary and the subsequent further research for this book, I have spoken to as many of the surviving witnesses as possible. Not all wished to be quoted on the record, but I am especially grateful to those who freely allowed me to incorporate their testimony into this manuscript. Of those not mentioned in the text, I would like to thank Janet Freer, lifelong friend of Janet Gregsten, whose assistance, even from her present home in Canada, has been of great benefit. I am grateful, too, to Alan Williams, once of the *Daily Express*, now a prolific author, for sharing his always engaging and colourful reminiscences of the case with me, and to Brian Hilliard for his expert advice and assistance.

In January 1997 an extraordinary and very sad coincidence occurred. Within a few hours of the *Independent*'s front-page headline story, 'Wrongly Hanged: Hanratty is Found Innocent' (a story that, as it turned out, was another of the false dawns in the history of the case), two of those who played important roles in this long saga passed away. The first was Brenda Harris, daughter of Grace Jones, the landlady of Ingledene, where Hanratty stayed when he was in Rhyl. She died suddenly, only three years after her mother. Over the years since 1962 she had become more than used to strangers knocking on her door, making inquiries about the case, and asking to inspect the green bath in the attic. Never did she tire of acting as unofficial custodian of the Hanratty alibi. Her own belief in Hanratty's innocence was more than fervid; it was absolute. After all, she knew that he was there. When we called on her, she was still willing to go through the whole story yet again, and was uncomplainingly kind and patient as another film crew disrupted her guest-house around her.

At that same moment, in January 1997, David Lines also died. He was one of my most priceless discoveries: the last surviving witness to Hanratty's execution. When I asked him to tell me what had happened, I was astonished at the vivid power and narrative strength of his recollections. He came up to London so that we could interview him in a hotel by the British Museum. By then I'd convinced myself that he couldn't possibly be as compelling on camera. But he was. He was superb. What I especially admired was his commitment to historical truth. As a man steeped in the legal profession, he had never believed that Hanratty was wrongly convicted (although he did believe that he should not have been found guilty on the evidence presented at court). There was no ulterior motive in his saying what he did; he did it just to place on record what actually happened, and I was always immensely grateful to him for his fierce intellectual honesty.

That same afternoon, we interviewed Peter Woods, BBC crime correspondent at the time of the case, but best remembered as a news-reader. He lent willing assistance for which, again, we were particularly grateful; sadly, he too has since died.

Jean Justice, to whom this book is dedicated, died, as mentioned in the dedication, in 1990. All this – the film and the book – is to some extent his legacy, because it would not have happened without him. Since his death, Jeremy Fox, sole survivor of the Half Moon Street Irregulars, has continued Justice's work in ensuring that the case is pressed to a just resolution. He, too, has given every assistance that we have ever asked of him, and, I confess, there have been times when we asked much of him; but he remained unfailingly courteous and affable at all times. Likewise, we will always remember the earnest support and solicitousness of Dr David Lewes and his wife Daphne.

I should like to thank all those who helped to make *Hanratty – The Mystery of Deadman's Hill* a success. In particular, I am indebted to Peter Moore, who commissioned the documentary for Channel 4 and whose advice, encouragement and continuing interest have been of immense value; and also to those at Yorkshire Television whose expertise was evident in the finished film, in particular film editor Clive Trist and cameramen Andrew Hartley and Alan Wilson.

There are three people in particular, however, to whom I owe an enormous amount, for both their boundless professional generosity and continuing personal friendship: Grant McKee, my editor on *First Tuesday*, who could invariably be relied upon to work the old alchemist's trick of turning your own base material into something much more precious; Ros Franey, whose sage advice and inexhaustible enthusiasm I was always able to call upon; and Mike Cocker, whose brilliant vision and constant support were invaluable, and who has shared it all from start to finish, always assuming we ever get there.

None of those mentioned above are, of course, in any way responsible for either the views expressed or any mistakes there may be.

I also want to thank Richard Webster and David Godwin; and I'm especially grateful to Catherine Hurley and Richard Milner for their enormous hard work. And Anne, Kate and Eddie: for being just wonderful.

Finally, this book is for all those Hanratty supporters across the nation. There are lots of you out there. Those of you who have become – as which of us haven't – utterly obsessed with this case, who ponder it day and night, and try to reconcile and comprehend its intricacies and inexplicable features. Those of you who constantly write and telephone, and enquire about progress. Your dedication and support has been more valuable than you realize. And it has almost paid off. It has been a long dark tunnel, but we can see light at the end of it.

INTRODUCTION
TO PAN EDITION

On 29 March 1999, the Hanratty case was finally referred back to the Court of Appeal, after the Criminal Cases Review Commission had considered it for two years. The CCRC had been able to re-examine the case in its entirety, having had access to all the available material. Thankfully, the volume of documentation and exhibits that had survived the passage of time was considerable.

Fresh interpretations of some aspects of the case were indicated by newly uncovered statements. In particular, there is one area of the case which is now dramatically changed. I have not attempted to incorporate this fresh perspective into the general narrative. Our understanding of the case has naturally evolved over the years, as pieces of information have trickled into the public domain, notwithstanding the endeavours of the authorities to suppress them. So, apart from a few minor emendations, the narrative remains as it originally was. The fresh material is considered in its appropriate place, at the end.

Bob Woffinden, London, June 1999

• I •
THE SUSPECT

CHAPTER ONE

ON TUESDAY, 22 AUGUST 1961, two civil servants employed at the Road Research Laboratory at Langley, near Slough, Michael Gregsten and Valerie Storie, drew up in their Morris Minor car outside the Old Station Inn, a public house just outside the village of Taplow.

Taplow, though itself up-market and attractive, lies in a rather featureless and untidy part of the Thames Valley in Buckinghamshire. It is 4 miles west of Slough, which in turn is just over 20 miles west of London. In the early 1960s the area was dominated by the A4, the main London to Bristol trunk road; a parallel route, the M4 motorway, was under construction, and had already reached this far west. The region could also boast a first-class rail service, as well as the magnet of the fast-expanding London Airport. Inevitably, such excellent communications attracted sprawling commercial growth. Today, that part of the A4 is littered with the high-tech industries of the 1980s, the international hotels of the 1990s, and the incongruous remnants of the ribbon developments of the 1930s and 1950s.

In 1961 (and still today) the Old Station Inn was set well back from the A4, too far back to catch the attention of many motorists. The isolated inn had a sombre appearance. Earlier that year, the film producer George Brown had used it as a setting for a murder mystery, *Meet Miss Marple*, starring the redoubtable Margaret Rutherford. His wife had spotted it while driving past, and thought it an appropriate location.[1]

When they arrived that Tuesday evening, Valerie Storie and Michael Gregsten were recognized straightaway as regulars by the landlady, Mary Lanz. Storie drank gin and Pepsi Cola, Gregsten had Double Diamond. They left, at about 9.20 – or so the landlady recalled – in their Morris Minor, and headed back along the A4 before taking the third turning on the right, Huntercombe Lane. They parked down there a little while, before moving off. After going over the newly constructed M4 motorway, they forked right into Court Lane, and followed the road round to a cornfield at Dorney Reach.

The field was vast, stretching down to the banks of the Thames, although you could not see the river from where they parked. Afterwards Valerie Storie told Detective Superintendent Acott that she and Gregsten had been to that spot together a number of times over the previous twelve months, parking in the same place each time, 'usually always just inside the gate'.[2]

She remarked to Gregsten that the last time they had been in the field they saw a sputnik go across the sky. They were just talking when a man tapped at the driver's window.

Although obviously startled, they immediately supposed it to be the farmer who owned the land. However, as Gregsten wound down the window, the intruder stuck a gun through and said, 'This is a hold-up, I am a desperate man.'[3]

He asked for the ignition key which Storie, a plucky woman, wanted to refuse to give him. Gregsten, realizing the futility of their position, handed it over and acceded to the gunman's next request, opening the rear door for him. The man got in and sat in the rear off-side seat, with his gun pointing at Gregsten's back. Storie explained what happened then.

'The man said, "Lock all the doors." He kept the ignition keys, and said, "Are all the doors locked?"'

'We were both very scared, and asked the man what he wanted. He said, "Keep facing the front and don't look round. You'll be all right if you do as I tell you."'

'The gun was in the man's right hand, and he kept pointing it at Mike. He said it was loaded. He said, "This is a real gun and I haven't had it very long. It's like a cowboy's gun. I feel like a cowboy." He said it was a .38, whatever that may mean.

'At one stage he tapped his pockets. There was a rattle, and he said, "These are all bullets." It sounded like the rattle of marbles.

'I thought he was a burglar and he was waiting for someone.'[4]

After the three had sat there for a short while, the gunman returned the key to Gregsten and told him to drive further into the field. He made them drive along the track, swing out and back, and then park alongside what Gregsten and Storie assumed was a haystack covered by tarpaulin, with the car's nose facing the entrance, ready to go out. Even though it was late August, the corn had not yet been harvested (the 'haystack' was actually a harvester), and some was flattened in the manoeuvrings, enabling the police later to establish exactly where the car had been.

They stayed there for some time. Every time Storie or Gregsten started to turn round, the gunman ordered them to face the front.

'When he got into the back of the car, we had some conversation,' she recalled. 'He told us certain things about himself. We asked him where he had been and he said, "In the Oxford area." He said he had been living rough for two days. He said he had woken up the previous morning wet through because it had been raining, and I wondered how he had got himself so clean and tidy in the meantime. One would never believe he had been sleeping out in the open the previous night. This man, as far as we could see, was immaculately dressed.

'He asked Mike who he lived with, and whether I lived with my parents. He asked us if we were married, and we said, "No."'

He made them hand over their watches (though he later returned them) and also Gregsten's wallet, which contained £3, and the purse from Storie's shopping basket. Before handing it over, however, she adroitly removed the money – £7 – and put it in her bra. The gunman did not notice.

At about 10.30, an outside light went on at a cottage adjoining the field, to the north. They had the impression that someone was putting a bicycle away in a shed. The gunman became momentarily agitated, but there was no prospect of anyone at that distance divining the couple's predicament.

The gunman now decided that they should go for something to eat, and then return to the field. He at first resolved to put Gregsten in the boot, and they both got out of the car. However, Valerie Storie managed to persuade the man that as there was a crack in the exhaust-pipe, there was a danger of Gregsten being asphyxiated. The man changed his mind and said that Gregsten could drive. While the two of them were outside, Storie saw that the gunman was wearing a handkerchief, outlaw-style, to cover the bottom half of his face.

They then retraced their route back up to the A4. When they reached the T-junction, they asked the gunman which way: left to Maidenhead, or right to Slough? The gunman responded that he'd had enough of Maidenhead, so they turned right.

Outside Nevill & Griffin's dairy, they stopped at a milk machine, but found that none of them had a sixpence. The gunman said that he knew a café near Northolt where they could get some food, so they pressed on. As they drove down Slough High Street, Storie noticed by the clock in the Post Office that it was 11.45 p.m.

'We drove on through Slough,' Valerie Storie recalled, 'and [the gunman] said, "How much petrol has the car got?" Although it had in fact got two gallons in the tank, we told him it had only got one gallon and would only go for 20 miles, so he said, "We had better get some petrol." '[5]

In the circumstances, this was hardly straightforward. In those days, of course, petrol stations were not self-service.

'Near London Airport we saw a Regent garage on the left-hand side of the road,' continued Storie. 'He said to Mike, "I want you to go in and get two gallons of petrol. You are to stay in the car. You can wind down the window and ask the man for two gallons only. I have got the gun pointing at you and if you try to say anything else or give the man any indication that anything is wrong, I will shoot." He handed Mike £1 of the money which he had previously taken from him.

'Mike did as he was told. When the attendant had put two gallons in, he gave Mike back a 10-shilling note and a 3d piece ... The man took the note and gave the 3d piece to me and said, "You can have that as a wedding present." '[6]

Valerie Storie was unable to say what he might have meant by this last remark.

They continued in the direction of London before turning left to go through Hayes. They crossed what was then the A4010, and came out on Western Avenue. At the Greenford intersection, the gunman directed them straight on; apparently the idea of going to Northolt had been abandoned. Equally obviously, there was no prospect of returning to the cornfield.

'He was by this time giving instructions as to where we should go,' related Storie. 'He was a very nervous passenger. He kept saying, "What gear are you in? Why did you change gear there? Mind that car. Be careful of those traffic lights." He was definitely a back-seat driver. We said, "Do you drive?", and he said, "Oh, yes," but it still didn't make him any better a passenger.'

At some point they noticed some roadworks, which were to have an enduring significance. They took a north-easterly course through the outer suburbs of London. Storie recalled the major junction with Kenton Road, where they went straight on, northwards now, to Brooks Hill, west of Stanmore. They stopped for cigarettes – Valerie wasn't sure where, 'somewhere in the Harrow region' – and Gregsten got ten Nelson tipped out of a machine. The gunman said he'd have one, though they got the impression he wasn't a regular smoker. Storie lit one for Gregsten and one for him. When she handed him the cigarette, she noticed that he was wearing black gloves.

The gunman told them he'd never had a chance in life. 'He said he'd been locked up in a cellar for days, and been beaten and had bread and water,' recalled Storie. 'He said he had been in institutions since he was eight. He'd been to a remand home, he'd been to Borstal.' Despite the conversation, however, the gunman was shrewd enough to offer no tangible clue to his identity. Even when he did vouchsafe information, it was not necessarily helpful. 'We didn't know whether he was telling the truth or not,' explained Storie. 'He seemed to contradict himself most of the time.'

They left London behind, heading through Watford, Aldenham and Park Street, before picking up the A5 to St Albans. On a stretch of derestricted road (where no speed limit was in force), Gregsten tried flashing his reversing light to attract attention. At one point, a car did pull up alongside, and its occupants gestured towards the back. The gunman and Gregsten got out to check the rear lights.

This was 'my big chance', Valerie Storie wrote later. 'I was in the car. I was a good driver. I could easily have slipped into the driving seat and made a break for it. But I simply could not bring myself to run out on Mike like that.'[7]

In the centre of St Albans, the A5 branched off to the left. By carrying straight on, they found themselves on the A6. Gregsten tried various ruses to attract attention – flashing the headlights, going slowly in built-up areas – but to no avail. They also sometimes picked up speed, which perturbed the gunman. 'I kept telling Mike to go quickly,' said Storie. 'If we went above 50 miles an hour, the man usually said, "Do not go too fast," so Mike would drop his speed.'[8]

Gregsten and Storie talked to each other in undertones – the man didn't seem to mind. He didn't refer again to feeling hungry, but after they had been through Luton he started to mention that he was tired and needed 'a kip'.

Storie recalled that, still on the A6, they passed through the villages of Barton-le-Clay and Silsoe. On the gunman's instructions, they twice attempted to stop. The first time, they turned into a lane where she noticed a Private: No Parking sign. That was no good. They moved on, and turned off again, but there were houses down that lane, so they rejoined the main road. The third time, one mile north of the village of Clophill, they turned off into what seemed to be a lay-by, with a strip of parking space parallel to the main road. When they reached the far end, the man ordered Gregsten to turn the car round, so that it was pointing south, and then to switch off all the lights.

Throughout, they had been asking him to take what he wanted but just to leave and not shoot them. When they finally stopped, he said, 'If I was going to shoot you, I would have done it before now.'

As he'd decided he needed 'a kip', he thought he should tie them both up. There was a rug in the car; he thought about cutting that up. Then he looked in the boot with Gregsten and discovered a small piece of rope in the tool kit. They got back into the car. Then he made Gregsten take off his tie, which he used to bind Storie's wrists, none too successfully. He then tied them again with the piece of rope, equally ineptly.

He needed something for Gregsten's hands. There didn't seem to be anything else available. In the front passenger footwell there was a green and white duffel-bag containing laundry. The man told Gregsten to pass it back.

As Storie recalled, 'Mike half-turned towards the middle of the car with the washing.' Gregsten lifted the bag over his left shoulder, towards the back seat. It was probably a desperate last-ditch attempt to disarm the gunman; certainly, he appeared to regard it as a threatening gesture. He instantaneously fired two shots. 'There was a terrific noise and a smell of gunpowder or something,' said Storie. 'Mike fell forward over the steering-wheel and I could see the blood pouring out of his head.'[9]

Storie screamed, 'You shot him, you bastard, why did you do that?'

The man replied, 'He frightened me, he moved too quick.'[10]

Storie pressed him to allow her to fetch a doctor. The man replied, 'Be quiet, will you, I am thinking.'[11] For about fifteen or twenty minutes they argued about whether Gregsten was dead, or whether help should be sought. Finally, the gunman seemed to accept that Gregsten was dead. He took a piece of laundry from the bag – a pair of pyjama trousers – and put it over Gregsten's face.

Storie continued: 'I said, "I will drive to where we meet an oncoming vehicle and I will get you a lift and see to Mike." He did not think much of that and still kept contradicting himself. I thought he was slightly round the twist. He asked me my name and told me to get in the back of the car with him. I said, "No." I was playing for time.'

Then he said to Storie, 'I know your hands are free. Kiss me.'

She refused. He indicated that if she didn't, he would shoot. In the circumstances, she relented and he briefly kissed her. He then asked her to go and sit in the back with him. Again she refused; again he pressed her, finally making the same threat: 'I will count five and if you have not got in I will shoot.' She had no choice. He raped her.

Valerie Storie thought that it was about 2.30 by then. They continued talking and arguing. 'He kept looking at his watch, and the final time he said it was 2.50.

'He could never remember my name,' she continued. 'Whilst we were in the lay-by, he asked me at least six times, "What is your name?" He never seemed to remember what it was.' At this point she asked what his name was. 'I said, "Well, look, I must call you something." I don't know why I said this, one never knows why one says these things. I said, "What shall I call you?" and he sort of said, "Jim." That's the only name, obviously not his proper name I shouldn't think.'

She then said, 'For goodness' sake, take the car and go, it is almost daybreak.' But first he needed to get Gregsten's body out of the car. He told her, 'You will have to get him out. I must not get blood on me.' In fact, the corpse was too heavy for her, so the man had to help in getting Gregsten's legs out from between the pedals. She dragged the body around the car and to the edge of the concrete strip. Then with the gunman's permission, she took a few things out of the car – her basket, the duffel bag, one of the two paperback books (*Blackboard Jungle* and *The Life of Suzie Wong*) and whatever she could grab out of the glove compartment.

He took the rug out of the boot of the car and placed it over the driver's seat, reiterating that he could not get blood on him. He also wiped the steering-wheel. He asked her to start the car for him and show him how it worked. The car stalled and she restarted it for him, then went to sit on the ground beside Gregsten's body. The gunman seemed indecisive. He came back up to her, saying, 'I think I had better knock you on the head or something, or else you will go for help.' She said that she would not do so and held out a £1 note, saying, 'You can have that if you go quickly.' He momentarily seemed to wonder where she had got it from, then took it and walked away.

When a few feet from her, he suddenly turned round and fired a number of shots into her body. He then reloaded the gun and fired a further three times; Storie thought those passed over her head.

'I lay there not daring to breathe, not daring to moan,' she wrote. 'My mind focused on one point: I must pretend I am dead. He came up to me. Could I really make him think I was dead? Then he kicked me and walked away.'

He walked back to the car, got in, put the headlights on and drove off in the direction of Luton.[12]

Astonishingly, all this had occurred on a concrete service road that was divided from the main A6 only by a small bank. A disused road, which was screened off by hedges, looped behind it; that was the real lay-by.

There was a chilling irony. At that stage, none of them would have been aware precisely where their extraordinary journey, which had started on the A4 and proceeded by way of the A5 to the A6, had concluded: the scene of the crime was Maulden, Bedfordshire, on a stretch of road known as Deadman's Hill.

Storie was, inevitably, critically injured – and, indeed, paralysed for life – but, incredibly, she was not dead. She screamed and shouted for help. Resourceful even in those circumstances, she thought of constructing a scanty description of the man with stones, but couldn't find sufficient to hand. She tried vainly to attract attention by waving her petticoat, but there was little passing traffic and she was not seen. Not surprisingly, she lost consciousness.

In her wretched state, she was first spotted by an elderly farm labourer, Sydney Burton, at about 6.30 a.m. – probably a little more than three hours after the gunman had driven off.

'As I was passing the lay-by I heard a groan,' said Burton, 'it was the young lady.' He lacked the initiative to do anything more himself than to walk down to the other end of the concrete strip, where eighteen-year-old John Kerr, doing a two-week holiday job before going up to Magdalen College, Oxford, was conducting a traffic survey.

'I'd been picked up at home, and delivered to the census point at 5.40. I started my shift at 6.00. At about 6.35, this old farm labourer – I'd seen him before – came walking towards me, and said, "There's some woman up there in a terrible state." He wandered off, so I went up to have a look.

'It was a woman, with somebody else lying beside her. They would have been in vision all the time, but they were lying on the ground and until you got closer you couldn't discern anything that wouldn't have been, well, some debris.'

He could see that Gregsten was dead, and spoke to Storie. 'I said – can you believe it? – "Are you all right?" She said, "No, I've been shot." I ran across the road, flagged down a car, and asked them to go and get the police.'[13]

The car was driven by Thomas Reay, a machinist at Vauxhall Motors in Dunstable. He went down to the RAC telephone box at the southern end of the concrete strip and dialled 999.

The first police report was recorded by Inspector Edward Milborrow, and timed at 6.55 a.m.: 'We have received a 999 call that there are two bodies in the ditch near RAC box at Deadman's Hill, A6. I am attending, send ambulance.'

Meanwhile, John Kerr went back and covered Storie with his leather jacket. 'I had a short conversation with her, asking her what had happened. She said, "We picked up a man near Slough" – she actually did say that, which is why it was originally thought to be a hitch-hiker killing.

'She gave me certain details which I then wrote down. I had a clipboard, with various pages of the census form, so I turned one over. I wrote down the number of the car, and her name – I remember this especially, because she said to me, as I thought, that her name was Mary Storie.'

According to the statement which John Kerr made that afternoon, 'I asked her what the man was like and she said, "He had big staring eyes, fairish brown hair, slightly taller than I am, and I am 5 feet $3\frac{1}{2}$ inches."

'I can remember the hair,' Kerr recollected in 1991, 'because I said to her, "Do you mean like mine?" – amazingly, my hair is still the same colour today – and she said, "Yes."'

Reay returned, with his two passengers, having telephoned the emergency services. They spoke to the distressed woman, then went up to John Kerr, and said, 'She says her name's Valerie.' Kerr returned to her, and she clarified for him that her name was Valerie.

Storie could recall the arrival of the ambulance men, running down the grass verge, and, she thought, a police inspector. She was carefully placed on a stretcher, put into an ambulance, and taken to Bedford General Hospital.

Less than two hours later, at about 8.50, Janet Gregsten telephoned the Road Research Laboratory, asking if her husband had arrived at work. He hadn't been home all night, and she was worried about him.

CHAPTER TWO

MICHAEL GREGSTEN WAS born on 28 December 1924, the only child of Alan and Jeannie May Gregsten. Their marriage was not a happy one, and they divorced in 1929. Michael was thereafter raised in north London by his grandmother, mother and aunt, who were Christian Scientists.

After attending Barnet Grammar School, he joined the RAF in March 1943, becoming a navigator. His superiors decided that what was termed 'bad social behaviour' made him unsuitable officer material, so he didn't fulfil his wish of becoming a pilot. On leaving the RAF in September 1946, however, he got a grant to study physics at University College, London.

Despite his obvious high level of intelligence, he failed his finals – partly because of difficulties in concentrating; partly, he later admitted, because of his 'compulsive desire to pick up women' – and afterwards had a nervous breakdown.

In 1949 he was working as a clerk for NALGO (National and Local Government Officers), an unfulfilling job for someone of his aptitude, when he met the eighteen-year-old Janet Phillips.

Her upbringing had been scarcely less emotionally fraught than his. She was born on 10 January 1931. Her father left her mother when she was very young, and she was temporarily placed in a Barnardo's home. When her mother found another man, Janet moved into his large Hampstead house, named Far End, with her half-sister Valerie, elder sister Toni, and younger brother John. For a few months in about 1943, Valerie lived in a large room at the top of the house with her husband, a man named William Ewer.

'I left home when I was fourteen,' Janet Gregsten remembered, 'or rather I was kicked out – not because I'd done anything wrong, but because my mother was having her own difficulties with my stepfather (by then, they had a young baby, Cherie) and we kids were in the way. Toni had moved out the year before. John was at boarding school. I'd expected to go back to school after Christmas

1945, but instead found I had to get myself a job, which I did, in a library in Holborn, and I found a bed-sit in Hampstead.'[1]

Michael and Janet had much in common. They were both intelligent, articulate and attractive; Janet was petite, dark and strikingly pretty. Their – for the time – unconventional backgrounds had left them with some distinct advantages (a relative sophistication and acuity), but also crippling emotional insecurities. It would have been hard to determine who was the more psychologically fragile.

Janet first attempted suicide on 17 July 1949, taking an overdose of barbiturates, in response to the suicide of her boyfriend, Carl Schwarz. She bounced from this straight into the romance with Gregsten. When he announced, after they had been engaged for fifteen months, that he wanted to terminate their relationship, she reacted by again attempting suicide, taking phenobarbitone tablets.

At that time suicide was still a criminal offence, and the authorities felt unable to overlook this second transgression. Janet had to answer to the charge at Highbury Magistrates' Court. On 15 August 1951 she was found guilty and placed on probation for twelve months. Gregsten, however, responded compassionately to the trauma, and they married almost immediately on 8 September 1951.

They lived in Muswell Hill, north London, at first in Collingwood Avenue before finding a flat in Alexandra Road. Michael then found more rewarding work with the Scientific Civil Service, as a research physicist with the Fire Research Laboratories in Borehamwood; but, shortly after the birth of their first child, Simon, on 13 March 1953, his mental problems surfaced. While on a cycling tour on his own, he experienced painful sensations in his head. With his Christian Scientist background, he declined to consult a doctor.

The following year, the Gregstens took a flat 30 miles outside London, at Sabine House, Shirley Road, Abbot's Langley. The Building Research Station, a part of the Ministry of Works, had taken over this small estate as part of a post-war project to undertake research into all aspects of housing and domestic life. A large mobile laboratory would go round, taking various measurements. The intention was that the estate should be demolished once the experiments were complete. At a time of acute housing shortage, however, that began to seem a less than logical idea.

It was accordingly decided to offer the flats to civil servants working at one of the nearby research establishments (although adverts placed in local papers enabled others to apply). Prospective tenants had to be young married couples, with at least one child under five. The rents were set lower than those in the commercial rented sector, and tenants further benefited from an additional rebate of 10 shillings a week, on account of the experiments that were still being conducted.

Every flat in each block would contain certain differences from the neighbouring ones – different ceiling heights, work surfaces, plumbing systems, ventilation, and suchlike. Every time the toilet flushed, a meter would register the amount of water used – all in the cause of trying to determine the optimum size of toilet-pan. The principal experiment in the Sabine House block was concerned with sound insulation. Tenants would also be questioned about the social aspects of living there, including how they were getting on with their neighbours.

At the outset, the Gregstens' neighbours were Roy and Jean Catton, who took occupancy of No. 14 a week before Michael and Janet moved into No. 13. They became friends immediately; the Cattons' eldest child, Alastair, was almost the same age as Simon. At that stage, only twelve of the twenty-four apartments were occupied, so that everyone could be moved around. Those moving in had to agree to move a minimum of three times, to compare the accommodation. Although the Cattons finished up at the opposite end of the block to Michael and Janet, the families remained close.

'We were all of us very poor,' recalled Jean Catton. 'I remember Janet telling me just how desperate they had been to get the flat. We worked out that Janet could stay at home and look after Simon and Alastair while I went out to work, and we shared what I earned. Janet was also able to do a little work at home, airbrushing pictures and colouring photographs.'

The Gregsten marriage was not going well, however. Sexually, they were poles apart. Janet confessed to a certain frigidity (according to Michael, she was 'completely unresponsive to any emotional stimulus'); while one of his colleagues recognized that Michael had the opposite problem: 'He suffered from an over-developed sexual drive.'

Roy Bigmore, also employed at the Fire Research Laboratory, related that, 'While Mike was working here, he became involved with a girl employed as an assistant scientific officer. Eventually he confided to me that he was in love with her and even contemplating leaving home to go and live with her and would probably have done so if it had not been for his strong attachment to his son Simon.'[2] That affair lasted eighteen months, and was concluded when the woman broke it off because she wanted a more settled relationship.

Janet did see a solicitor about a divorce, and this alarmed Michael, who remembered the bitterness of his own parents' separation. They decided to try to make a fresh start, though such resolutions were a continuing feature of their stop–go marriage.

'They were always under emotional stress, both of them,' confirmed Roy Catton, 'long before the affair with Valerie. They were either on a high or a big low.'

'But Janet was very self-contained,' added Jean Catton, 'she wasn't a gossip, so we never knew what was going on.'

'To us, they seemed to move in sophisticated, Bohemian circles,' said Roy, 'going to car-rallies and parties – they once took us to one, but only, I think, because you had to take a bottle, and they couldn't afford one. We knew that Mike was often away, but didn't think more of it than that he was popular at work.

'We did know that Mike's mother and aunt sometimes caused problems. Mike was brought up, really, by maiden ladies – you never heard about his father – and they thought their Mike could have done a lot better for himself. To them, Janet was the silly neurotic little girl who'd taken away their darling Michael.'[3]

On 1 October 1956 Michael transferred to the Road Research Laboratory in Langley, just outside Slough. The department investigated accidents and road safety, amongst other things, and analysed traffic patterns.[4]

Despite finding himself in a job which suited and satisfied him, Gregsten's mental state was deteriorating. He was subject to depression, severe headaches, and much worse; by now, he was consulting doctors. In October 1957 his psychological problems were acute. He had a month off work. His doctor attributed his condition to 'psychoneurosis' and referred him to the renowned Tavistock Clinic in Beaumont Street, London. On 4 November he was seen there by the Tavistock's director, Dr John Sutherland, who reported that Gregsten was worried about financial matters and 'had a general feeling that he ought to be dead'.

Gregsten himself complained of 'depersonalization syndrome'. The Tavistock considered his problem 'more hysterical than schizophrenic', but serious enough, and recommended that he should become an in-patient. In the event, this didn't happen. It was arranged instead that he should attend the out-patients psychiatric clinic of Watford Peace Memorial Hospital.

By December 1958 it was clear that the Watford clinic could not provide adequate assistance, but the Tavistock, despite acknowledging 'a severe character disorder', could find no place for Gregsten. So his difficulties continued. Until 1960 he continued to pay regular monthly visits to his doctor, who did what little he could for his condition; he prescribed tranquillizers.

Valerie Storie, who was born on 24 November 1938, had been employed at the Road Research Laboratory since leaving Slough High School for Girls in 1955. She met Gregsten because both were members of the canteen committee. He and Valerie went out together for the first time in December 1957, to the Pineapple pub in Dorney. A year later they went to the Christmas dance together, an evening she later described as 'the most wonderful of my life'.[5]

Valerie acknowledged Michael's more cosmopolitan background ('He loved continental food and Indian curry – I didn't know very much about that sort of thing'), and shared his 'liking for cars, concerts and the theatre, and serious music' (Michael was an accomplished pianist, and often played at social functions).

Opportunities of seeing each other were limited. In the late summer of 1959 they did go to Devon together for a week's holiday, although – such were the social conventions of the day – they took separate digs.

Michael left Janet shortly afterwards, to live near Windsor. It was an especially insensitive time to do so: she was pregnant again. He did return shortly before the birth of their second son, Anthony, on 12 October.

Gregsten was a member of the Civil Service Motoring Association. He and Valerie began to enter car rallies, and won the Novices' Award in a race in June 1960. Thus encouraged, they joined the de Havilland car club, and took part together in about fifteen rallies.

Janet knew about Michael's relationship with Valerie. Believing that her own lack of carnal appetite was responsible for their marital difficulties, she was frequently content to let his nature take its course.

'It wasn't the first affair Mike had had,' Janet Gregsten confirmed. 'I won't say I wasn't affected by them. I was, but I wasn't jealous. Sexually, we weren't that marvellous together. I knew I wasn't giving Mike the sex he needed. So I understood why he was going elsewhere.

'We were just two people getting on with our lives as best we could, with Mike having his bit on the side. That's all Valerie Storie was to me, a bit on the side.'[6]

Whether or not it disconcerted Janet, the affair certainly offended against contemporary codes of Civil Service conduct. Gregsten and Storie's immediate superiors attempted to warn the couple that 'No good will come of it.' One officer told Gregsten that 'If I cannot trust you with young women, it will reduce your usefulness to the laboratory.' Storie was told bluntly by her superior officer that 'Your association with Mr Gregsten will have a harmful effect on his career.'

Another of the civil servants in the Road Research Laboratory office recalled what he had learned of the situation: 'Miss Storie said she would see less of Mr Gregsten if I took her out once a week. She pestered me, and eventually I took her out to the cinema on two or three occasions.

'On one of these occasions, she told me about Mr Gregsten's marriage, and that he had, as far as I can remember, married his wife at a time following a court action. Gregsten had married her in a moment of pity, but had regretted it since.

'Following one of these visits to the cinema, as I was driving her home, she suggested carrying on to Huntercombe Lane. We stopped eventually on Dorney Common and she said that this was where she and Gregsten usually stopped.'[7]

Some of the senior officers consulted the Civil Service Staff Section at Harmondsworth, with a view to having one of them transferred to another division: 'But we were told there were no grounds for this,' according to the principal scientific officer. Ronald Moore, Gregsten's section leader, was so concerned that he and his wife went to Abbot's Langley to try to impress upon Janet the need to resolve her differences with her husband.

'Typical civil servants they were,' recalled Janet Gregsten, 'very nice, sweet people, saying the two of you have got to do something about your marriage. I told them that our relationship was up to Mike and myself to deal with.

'They went away, leaving me a book, *Vivere in Pace* – Live in Peace – you know, a spiritual book.'

In the wake of this, Valerie herself went to the Gregstens' home. According to Valerie, 'We met on several occasions to try to reach a solution between the three of us. She didn't want to divorce Mike because of the children';[8] according to Janet – who referred only to one meeting between them – she had to tell Storie that she would never divorce Michael, because he wanted it to come from her: 'In other words, it wasn't his fault if he didn't get a divorce, it was mine – but that was OK by me.'

Doctors believed that Michael's mental disorder could be at least partly attributed to his domestic difficulties. There wasn't just the marital chaos; there were the enduring financial problems. Valerie Storie referred to him graphically as 'the type of man who if he had 10d in his pocket would spend a shilling' (in today's currency, having 4p and spending 5p): the Micawber recipe for misery.

This was an additional burden on an already distressed domestic situation. Michael was forever running up small debts, from which his mother usually rescued him. In a vain attempt to make ends meet, he took on evening work, teaching maths twice weekly at St Albans Technical College.

Michael again left Janet for a brief spell in 1960, returning just before Christmas. By this time his relationship with Valerie was also under strain. 'We used to have terrific arguments,' she recalled, 'but we always made it up, and always parted good friends. We had difficulties over his family life. He was very attached to his children. He was very attached to his wife, although he was attached to me in a different kind of way.'[9]

Gregsten also took out another colleague at Road Research. In a statement two weeks after the murder, she said: 'He asked me to meet him away from the laboratory in order that Miss Storie should not find out. He told me before I agreed to see him that he just wanted someone to talk to about his problems. He would then drive me in his car to one of the quieter roads in the Langley area, where he would tell me about his wife and his association with Miss Storie.

'I liked him a great deal, but he was very moody and always seemed to feel sorry for himself. He was always in financial difficulties too.'[10]

To raise urgently needed household funds, Janet, without consulting Michael, one day sold his beloved piano; but by March 1961 their financial straits were so desperate that Michael also had to sell his green Morris Minor. He couldn't get to work without a car, so once again his family had to bail him out. His aunt, Hilda Oulet, owned a car – another Morris Minor, a grey one – but her eyesight was failing. So she loaned the car to Michael until he could afford another of his own.

In June Valerie went on a week's holiday to Majorca with her friend Ann Binks. Gregsten started his annual leave on Monday, 7 August. Prior to that, at the beginning of the month, he had taken what he might have seen as the irrevocable step to ending the marriage. He got digs at 68 St Mark's Road, Maidenhead, and told Janet that he would be moving in on Sunday, 27 August.

Before parting from his family, he took Janet and the children for a caravan holiday in Swanage, Dorset, though he left half-way through to paint the flat.[11] He went back to Dorset for them, and they returned from Swanage on Saturday, 19 August. He spent most of the following day with Valerie. He had been due to return to work on the Monday, but instead rang in to say that he wouldn't be in on either the Monday or the Tuesday. (The woman who took the call 'presumed he was taking extra leave'.)

On Tuesday 22nd, he turned up at the Cattons' at lunchtime, and took Simon and Alastair to Cassiobury Park, in Watford, to play with their boats. He brought them back, then said goodbye to Janet at about 4.00 p.m., saying he was off to see Valerie. He picked up the family laundry from the launderette, and was waiting for Valerie when she finished work. They stopped in Cippenham, where she lived. Mike had a haircut, and they then went on to her house. She made tea. They ate it and washed up. It was about 7.45 when they arrived at the Old Station Inn.

CHAPTER THREE

SHORTLY AFTER 7.00 A.M. on the morning of Wednesday, 23
August, Gwen Woodin, who had served in the police for ten years
and become the very first woman detective constable appointed in
a provincial force, was woken by a police colleague knocking at the
door of her flat.

'He asked if I could get to Bedford Hospital as soon as possible,'
she recalled, 'because there had been a murder and a rape. I
thought he was joking, and said something about, "Pull the other
one." He said, "No, it's true."'[1]

When she arrived, there was already intense activity at the
hospital. Valerie Storie had been admitted to casualty, and Woodin
went with her when she was moved into Charteris Ward. Andrew
Pollen, a consultant orthopaedic surgeon, saw her at 9.45, at which
point Storie was receiving a blood transfusion. He made an
immediate assessment of the wounds she had suffered:

> My examination revealed a bullet entry wound on the left side of
> the neck, and an exit wound on the right side of the neck, at a
> slightly higher angle. I next saw five bullet holes in the region of the
> left shoulder, of which four were in a vertical line from the tip of the
> shoulder downwards, the fifth was situated high up on the left side
> of the chest. I was unable at this stage to say which were entry or
> exit wounds.[2]

Even at that early stage, however, it was clear that the hail of
bullets had paralysed the lower half of Valerie Storie's body.

Pollen recorded that 'Police officers were present at hospital the
whole of the time, and from time to time they spoke to Miss Storie;
but owing to her condition I would not allow the interviews to be
other than of short duration.'

However, he did firmly state that at this time Storie was compos
mentis. This opinion appeared to be unanimous. Woodin said that

Storie was 'very clear in her own mind'. Detective Chief Inspector Whiffen, who saw her later in the day, concurred that she was 'perfectly conscious and had complete control of her faculties'.

About 11.00 a.m., there was a panic when it seemed as though Storie might die, but she pulled through. 'I think Valerie Storie's about the only person who would have lived,' said Woodin. 'She had an awful lot of courage. Her main concern was to give the description of the person who had done this. She was very angry, and wanted to get the information across. She was really just so determined to live, and pulled through because she wanted this man caught so much.'

Gwen Woodin thus became the first in a succession of police officers who were solemnly to say to Storie words along the lines of 'We'll catch whoever did this, I promise you.'

Woodin stayed by her bedside for much of the day, and dutifully recorded whatever Storie recollected. Woodin passed her notes to Detective Sergeant Douglas Rees, who had joined her at the hospital at about 8.45 a.m., and he telephoned everything through to the incident room. ('We were in constant communication,' she later recalled.) On the basis of this information the police message incorporating the first full description of the wanted man was issued:

> The suspect is described as follows: man aged about 25 years, smooth face, big eyes, smartly dressed in a dark grey or black suit. When speaking says 'fings' instead of 'things'. Is believed still in possession of the revolver (murder weapon).
>
> If car is found please preserve for fingerprints and detain suspect if with the vehicle. He should not be questioned regarding the murder. It is believed the suspect forced the deceased and the woman to give him a lift in the car at about 9.30 p.m. at Dorney, Bucks, and travelled along the A5 and A6 roads to the scene of the crime. It is alleged that suspect gave his name as Brown.
>
> Inquiries are requested at all garages and filling stations. Any information leading to identity of suspect would be appreciated.

Bedfordshire received the message at 10.50 a.m. and wired it through at 11.27.

Tony Mason was a freelance journalist living in Slough who supplied stories mainly to the *Times*, *Express* and *Mail* and the capital's two evening papers. With London Airport on his patch, he was kept busy. Like any successful reporter, he always had an ear to the ground. On 23 August he soon gleaned that something had happened to a local couple overnight. He telephoned his Scotland Yard contact, who confirmed what he'd heard. Mason telephoned the *Evening Standard*, and was asked to visit the Stories' home. He traced the address and went round straightaway. On arriving, he was appalled to discover that Mr and Mrs Storie had no inkling of what had befallen their daughter.

'When I found Valerie's bed empty, I telephoned her office,' Marjorie Storie told the *Daily Telegraph*. 'They told me neither she nor Michael was at work. I telephoned the police twice, but they knew nothing.'

John and Marjorie Storie, a hospitable couple, invited Mason in. 'They said they couldn't understand why Valerie hadn't returned home,' recalled Mason. 'So, I had to tell them. They appeared to take it calmly, but I don't really think they were able to take it in at all.'[3]

Mason next saw one of Valerie's close friends. He filed reports to the London evening papers, and still reached the Old Station Inn before opening time.

There was increasing activity at the scene of the crime. Those who had played some peripheral part in the drama, and those who had turned up merely to stand and watch, were herded to the far side of the A6 as police arrived and screened off the murder area.

It was then that something of integral significance in the case occurred. John Kerr, the census taker, fell into conversation with a policeman. 'He said, "What did you see?" He wasn't interviewing me, we were just talking. I told him I'd made some notes. He responded, "Have you? You'd better let me have them."

'I unclipped the paper and gave it to him. It was written, I am sure, on the back of an unused sheet, so there was no problem about giving him census information that I'd been collecting.

'So, he took it away, and that's the last that's ever been seen of it.'

Just how the police managed to mislay the very first piece of documentary evidence in the case was a matter which would tax legal minds in the months to come.

Kerr finished his shift at 2.00 p.m. 'When the supervisor came, I tried to explain why there was a missing hour in my schedule. He certainly thought it was an interesting excuse; he hadn't heard that one before.'[4]

In fact Kerr's census duty had suffered a second interruption. He was asked to give a television interview as a contribution to the on-the-spot report for the ITN lunchtime news bulletin. Throughout the morning, news editors were dispatching their correspondents to Deadman's Hill.

The media did not then have the omnipresence it now enjoys. In fact, at that time – Marshall McLuhan had yet to publish his significant works – 'the media' was not a term that would have been generally understood in Britain. There was radio and television. The BBC administered 100 per cent of the former and 50 per cent of the latter (there were just two channels, ITV being responsible for the other). Then there were, in effect, seven national newspaper dailies – the *Mirror, Sketch, Express, Mail, Herald, Times* and *Telegraph*. The *News Chronicle* had closed the previous year, together with its stablemate, the *Star*, the London evening paper – which left just two of those, the *Evening Standard* and the *Evening News*. Even the Sunday press, traditionally regarded as thriving, had latterly shed three titles: the *Sunday Graphic, Sunday Dispatch* and the (Manchester-published) *Empire News*.

There were also daily and weekly local newspapers of a high editorial standard. The strength of the regional press had lately been depleted, however; the *Manchester Guardian* had slipped its provincial shackles, dropped the 'Manchester', and begun publishing in London – the emergent eighth national daily.

The interrelationship between the sections of the media in the early 1960s was utterly different from the situation today. Although the rivalry of the popular dailies with each other was cut-throat, there were few considerations of competition between, say, newspapers and television. They coexisted, serving audiences in their separate ways. Neither threatened, or barely even impinged on, the other.

For example, although crime was a staple of the majority of the national newspaper titles, and especially of the Sundays, it had not hitherto been regarded as a bona fide news topic by the BBC. Still subject to Reithian precepts, the Corporation maintained an aloofness from journalistic material as transitory and sordid as crime reporting. The *Guardian*'s editorial remit was similarly circumscribed. Views such as these ensured that crime was confined to the outer limits of the national debate – as discrete patches of lurid incident rather than the seamless shroud that it appears today.

The situation was changing, however. The BBC was only too aware that ITV's populist instincts were forcing it to rethink its high moral tone. In any case, the coincidence earlier that year of two notable spy trials – those of George Blake, and Gordon Lonsdale and the Portland spy ring – suggested that what went on in courtrooms was very much a matter of legitimate public concern.

This murder thus occurred at a critical juncture, and became a pivotal case which changed the nature of the media's response to crime. ITN (the news-gathering and -disseminating company within ITV) had reported straightaway from the crime scene. In turn, the BBC assigned its reporter Peter Woods to follow events. He became, in actuality if not in name, the BBC's first crime correspondent and the A6 Murder the first criminal case assiduously covered by the BBC.

There were more orthodox reasons why the A6 Murder should have become the most high-profile crime of its era. For everyone in the news business, its timing was perfect. It occurred in August, the ineffable 'silly season' for news when genuine stories are few and far between.

As it happened, there was a serious enough situation still unfolding at that time – the international tension between East and West over the construction of the Berlin Wall, which had begun the weekend before the crime – but the British media were always more comfortable retailing home rather than foreign stories, however globally important. Also, Berlin had been dominating the news for some days, so editors were looking for something fresh. The A6 Murder provided the opportunity to reinstate a domestic agenda with a compelling crime story.

With regard to daily deadlines, the timing couldn't have been better. The crime was uncovered at the very beginning of the working day. It led radio bulletins throughout the day. The country's major regional newspapers had ample time to ponder the headline alternatives for the late afternoon final editions; and the film footage could be leisurely edited for the evening news bulletins on television. Then the national newspapers, having had all day to prepare their coverage, blazed it across their front pages the following morning.

Even without any of these considerations, the special characteristics of this case would have ensured that it gripped the public consciousness. It seemed so unusual, so inexplicable, so utterly malevolent. People were tempted to play it over in their minds – what would they themselves have done on that terrifying car journey, in those baleful circumstances?

Yet however closely they scoured the press reports, however

attentively they studied the TV news bulletins, members of the public would have been able to gather little reliable information from those early reports. This, for instance, is part of the first ITN lunchtime report: 'Michael Gregsten and Valerie Storie set off from Slough last night to organize the Bedfordshire checkpoints in a motor rally for the staff of the Road Research Laboratory where they worked. They picked up a hitch-hiker.'

Apart from the identity of the couple involved and their place of work, everything there is inaccurate. Moreover, one would hardly blame the reporter, confronted with an illogical scenario and no time or sources to make sense of it. From the outset, the crime itself was bewildering.

Two aspects of the misreporting stood out as of particular interest. The lunchtime edition of that day's *Evening News* was headlined: 'HUNT FOR HITCH-HIKE MURDERER'.

The *Daily Telegraph* reported the following day: 'All policemen in the Metropolitan area were searching last night for a hitch-hiking gunman who, having "thumbed" a lift in a car, killed its driver and wounded the woman passenger.'[5]

The suggestion that the couple had picked up a hitch-hiker was scotched almost immediately. Yet it remained popular currency for some years. Many members of the public continued to think of the case as the hitch-hike murder and, not unnaturally, were loath to offer lifts to hitch-hikers.[6]

Valerie Storie herself denied that the idea had originated with her. She was cross-examined on the point in court: 'I do not think I said we gave him a lift – hardly that.'[7]

However, John Kerr firmly believed that to have been the case; and in fact there would seem to have been no other possible source. If she did indeed say it, it would have been pardonable. At that time, extra-marital relationships were still, hypocritically perhaps, regarded with public disapprobation. Valerie Storie was in an unhappily compromised position: were gratuitous insults to be heaped on top of her appalling injuries? So she may just have been instinctively, almost involuntarily, trying to shield her reputation.

As it transpired, there would have been no need for even momentary worries on that score. The second instructive aspect of the misinformed reports is that the newspapers were prepared, in a situation where overwhelming public sympathy for the torment suffered by Valerie Storie quickly emerged, to fetter their usually well-honed muck-raking instincts.

No doubt only those born yesterday actually believed that

Michael Gregsten and Valerie Storie had been in their car in a cornfield on a summer's evening to draw up plans for motor-rallies; but that is what the reports stated. No other explanation was even obliquely suggested; there was no hint of what the public at large doubtless suspected. Philip Larkin famously identified this very period in British life – between the end of the *Lady Chatterley's Lover* trial (November 1960) and the release of the Beatles' first LP (March 1963) – as the time when the notion of British sex was born. In August 1961, to judge from this episode, parturition had yet to take place. The liaison between Gregsten and Storie remained a matter which even the *News of the World* and the *People* forbore to pursue.

Some would doubtless perceive this as responsible journalism. In other circumstances, perhaps, it could have been. In this instance, the papers merely acquiesced in the misrepresentation of events from the outset – hardly an ideal grounding for a complex criminal case around which rumour and falsehood would accrete so virulently.

It was almost midday when a policeman arrived at Janet Gregsten's flat in Abbot's Langley to deliver the awful news. She just had time to leave her children with Roy and Jean Catton, and was then driven to the murder scene at Deadman's Hill, where she arrived at about 1.45 p.m. As though to compound her distress, she had to identify the body *in situ*.

Asking Janet Gregsten to identify the body of her husband at the murder scene was heartless but, in contemporary policing terms, unavoidable. A major murder inquiry was about to begin; a most serious crime had been committed; there was no motive or suspect; and, to all appearances, it was not a local matter. The Bedford force had only one option: to call in Scotland Yard.

At that time, policing had undergone but little evolution since its inception. There were about 250 separate police forces in the United Kingdom, with several in each county. Some were so small they had probably never had to deal with even a domestic murder. Even for larger forces, murder remained a blessedly rare crime. So when one did occur, was it an ideal opportunity for ambitious local police to prove their mettle? Alas not; most forces simply had no acumen, no experience and no resources to deal with major crime.

A local force, however, would not have wanted to call in police from a neighbouring area or from the nearest regional centre – that would have represented a severe blow to their pride. Calling in supposed experts from London involved no such loss of face. Nor was there any charge for assistance rendered by Scotland Yard: it came out of the Home Office budget. If manpower had been recruited from a neighbouring force, the local watch committee would have insisted on payment.

In spite of the way in which, seventy years earlier, the mental capacities of the capital's detectives had been mocked in Conan Doyle's Sherlock Holmes stories, there was still a certain kudos for local police in being involved, however peripherally, in an investigation that was so important it merited the attention of Scotland Yard.

A number of chief constables across the country were not local men, but had been recruited from outside – in many cases, from the Metropolitan Police. So they would be perfectly at ease about drawing on the assistance of former colleagues. At the same time, they could boost their standing in their own community by showing off their high-powered associations.

(After the amalgamation of the country's police forces between 1967 and 1969, with 250 being slimmed down to 43, the deference of local forces towards London underwent a complete transformation. After revelations of widespread corruption in the Metropolitan Police, provincial forces became wary of passing on information to the Met, assuming that if they did it would quickly be leaked to the villains they were trying to apprehend.)

So Scotland Yard – the Murder Squad of the Metropolitan Police – would be asked to assist. Officers there knew that they had to accept cases away from home. On the whole, they could assume that they'd spend two or three days in a pleasant country hotel and achieve a measure of glory, having identified the supposedly guilty party. Nevertheless, such work was not sought after. Most major crime tended to be in the London area, and so Scotland Yard's premier detectives were generally already assigned to those cases. There was a wooden frame on the wall in the office. In it would be written the name of the detective next in line to be called out. It was a sort of 'buggins' turn' rota. Whoever was named had to go wherever he was summoned. He was never chosen because he was the right man for a particular job but simply because his name was in the frame. This was where the term 'in the frame' originated: it referred first of all not to criminals, but to police.

That Wednesday morning, the name in the frame belonged to Detective Superintendent Basil Acott. Colleagues all called him

Bob: 'Perhaps they think that Basil doesn't sound right', wrote Pearson Phillips in a eulogistic piece for the *Daily Mail*, 'for one of the sharpest detective superintendents in the business.'

Acott had joined the Metropolitan Police in 1933, walking the beat in Harlesden, north London, and later distinguished himself as a bomber pilot during the war, flying thirty-five missions over Germany, for which he was awarded the DFC. After the war, he resumed his police career, joining the Flying Squad. Among his more celebrated investigations, he helped to ambush a gang trying to steal bullion from London Airport; and also arrested Victor Terry, who committed murder during the course of a bank robbery in Worthing, Sussex.

He was also the officer in charge when Gunther Podola was apprehended. This was popularly regarded as a less than honourable operation. Podola, a thirty-year-old German photographer, was convicted of the murder of Detective Sergeant Raymond Purdy in the foyer of a private apartment block in Kensington, west London. Arthur Koestler and C. H. Rolph wrote in 1961 of 'the widespread belief, based upon his appearance in court, that he was beaten up by the police after arrest. [These views were] in circulation for ten weeks, with no word of official explanation.'[8] Despite representations from, amongst others, the German Embassy and twenty Swedish professors, Podola was executed in November 1959.

The man whose name was in the frame would take an assistant, whom he chose, and the murder-bag. This was literally a bag containing the tools of the trade – a magnifying-glass (Sherlock Holmes's techniques still being in vogue), and also a fingerprint set. To the assistant would fall the task of carrying the murder-bag; thus he was the bagman. Acott's bagman was Detective Sergeant Kenneth Oxford, later to become Chief Constable of Merseyside.

The Bedfordshire police needed to preserve the murder scene until Acott and Oxford arrived. At the same time, they had to be able to tell them who the victim was, and only Janet Gregsten was able to make the authoritative identification. So she had the unbearable task of seeing the body at the murder spot. Thirty years later, in 1991, she still broke down when revisualizing this moment: 'It was the first time I'd ever seen a dead person. It just didn't seem possible it was Mike – and it still doesn't. Unbelievable, utterly unbelievable. For years after, I used to have dreams about his hands, because he had lovely hands.'

Even then, thirty years later, she still professed incomprehension:

'I just don't understand it. I mean, the whole thing just doesn't seem credible. We were such ordinary people, just jogging on. Yes, Mike might have been having an affair, but people don't get killed for having affairs.'[9]

This sense of bafflement was apparent at the time, in 1961, and was shared by all those engaged in the investigation. Detective Superintendent Acott's subsequent case report provides some insight into police attitudes at this initial stage: 'When the first account of her experiences during the night of 22/23 August was received from Valerie Storie,' he wrote, 'it sounded so fantastic that from the start it was treated as highly suspect – like the majority of accounts given by women who have made allegations of rape.'[10]

This may have explained the dilatory start to the inquiry. Acott and Detective Inspector John McCafferty, who undertook the scenes-of-crime and ballistics work, and also Detective Sergeant Harry Heavens, as well as Detective Superintendent Barron of Bedfordshire police, arrived at the murder scene at about 2.35 p.m. Dr Keith Simpson, the eminent pathologist, joined them shortly afterwards.

At Bedford General Hospital, Gwen Woodin was not impressed when the inquiry police turned up late in the afternoon, at 5.00 p.m., to see Valerie Storie (displacing her parents, who had reached the hospital at about 3.30). The party included the Scotland Yard team, who did not stay long, and also local officers.

'I thought it was a very strange way of running an investigation,' recalled Woodin. 'They'd all been out at the scene, right? But Gregsten was dead. In hospital, there was a witness to murder – and how often do you get that? She wasn't expected to live – so why leave it to late afternoon to come to interview her?

'The men were all smoking – I remember that. The hospital staff weren't pleased when they walked in. The sister was quite angry, she was rude to them. The doctors were annoyed because by that stage they just wanted to sedate Valerie Storie and let her sleep.

'I said to them, "Are you taking over? Do you want my notes?" and they said, "No, we're going to take a statement." A doctor said to them, "A statement's been taken continuously all day."

'No one even glanced at my notes. I walked out with them in my hand.'

The notes, nevertheless, were to play a major role in the case. They were written up the following year, in order to help clarify a point for prosecution purposes during the trial; and had a dramatic effect when they were publicly disclosed in 1974.

In the event, Bedfordshire police were able to make a start on taking what became a nine-page statement. After several interruptions by nursing staff, the questioning ceased at 7.15 p.m., and the statement was completed the following day.

After the first description of the wanted man issued at 11.27 a.m., an amended description was put out at 5.20 p.m. and sent to all forces. It was this description which appeared in the following morning's papers: 'Man aged about 30, height 5'6", proportionate build, dark brown hair, clean-shaven, brown eyes, fairly pale face, has a distinct East End of London accent. Wearing dark lounge suit and believed dark tie and shirt.'

The Scotland Yard team had travelled up from London to Bedford; but the next development in the case occurred squarely on their home patch. The car in which the gunman had made his getaway was a 1956 grey Morris Minor saloon, with a split windscreen, registration number 847 BHN. It was further characterized by three strips of illuminated tape on the rear bumper.

It was found at 6.45 p.m. by Allan Madwar, described in the press as an oil company representative. It was badly parked, partly on the pavement, in Avondale Crescent, a side street in the east London borough of Ilford, just off Eastern Avenue and behind Redbridge underground station. The three strips were still plainly visible. However, the front number-plate had been bent back under the vehicle, so that it was barely visible; and there was a dent in the centre of the rear bumper. Needless to say, the car had not been in that condition when it was driven away from Deadman's Hill.

From 5.30 until 6.45 p.m., Dr Simpson carried out the post-mortem on Gregsten at Bedford Mortuary. 'From the fall in temperature, rigor mortis and other conditions', he wrote, 'I estimated that Gregsten had died between 3.00 and 4.00 a.m. He had two bullet wounds of the head, shot "through and through" from left ear to right cheek. The skin was tattooed round the entry wounds, and the range could not have been more than an inch or two; the shots had evidently been fired in rapid succession, before the head had moved.'[11]

Janet Gregsten, back home in Abbot's Langley, was seen by a doctor who prescribed a sedative. She and the children spent the night with the Cattons.

CHAPTER FOUR

IN SEPTEMBER 1961 Roy Bigmore, reflecting on Gregsten's death, commented: 'I would say that Mike was my closest friend. My observations on his character are that he was a person who made friends easily, was fond of the opposite sex, and a very hard and conscientious worker. He was never flush with money, having borrowed small amounts of money from me in the past, and I knew that recently he had some debts. He was more than devoted to his son Simon and carried no ill-will against his wife. I can think of no enemies he might have.'[1]

It was this last point which baffled the police. There was no immediately discernible motive for the crime. Motiveless murders may be commonplace today but they were almost unheard of in those days.

Thus the identity of the gunman was an absolute mystery. There was perhaps one bona fide clue: the murderer's ignorance of cars and driving. Otherwise, even the most perspicacious detective would have been able to glean little from the analysis of those harrowing six hours.

Fortune is proverbially held to favour the brave – so why does it always seem to shine on the contemptible? The gunman might, could, should have been observed at a number of junctures; but seemed to ride his luck from start to finish.

First of all, he might have been seen when making his way to the cornfield. It was not especially warm, but it was an August evening. There were a number of houses scattered round the cornfield. Wouldn't there have been people out and about? How had the gunman reached that particular spot? Someone must have noticed something – unless, of course, it was dark.

These are Valerie Storie's timings: 'I should say we left the Old Station Inn at about a quarter to nine.' This would mean they should have arrived at the cornfield by 9.00 p.m.

'How long had you been sitting in the car', Detective Superintendent Acott asked her, 'before you heard the tap on the window?'

'I suppose it must have been about twenty to twenty-five minutes.'[2]

She said that when they parked the car, 'I don't think it was dark, it was twilight,'[3] but reckoned that it became 'dark' shortly after they arrived.

Unfortunately, her timings are probably incorrect. The landlady of the Old Station Inn, Mrs Mary Lanz, said, 'I think it was about 9.20 or 9.30 when the couple left the bar and went outside.'[4] This seems likely to have been a more accurate estimation of the time. There is a compelling statement to this effect from nineteen-year-old David Henderson, an apprentice plumber who left his girlfriend's house at about 9.45 to motor-cycle home to Burnham, which dovetails with the Lanz timing.

Henderson seems to have been the kind of observant passer-by that every police inquiry would welcome.

'When I came to the "S" bends in Huntercombe Lane South, I saw a motor-car parked in a field on the offside of the road. There is a gap in the hedge right on the left bend when travelling towards the Bath Road. The car was definitely a Morris, I think a Morris 1000 [i.e. a Morris Minor]. It was facing into the field and about eight yards from the road. It was dark and I had the headlights of my motor-cycle on. I can only say that the car was a lightish colour.

'There was a light on inside the car, I think it was a fitted interior light. I could not see into the car because the rear window was misted. I did not think anything unusual and continued on my way home.'[5]

Henderson's statement seems one to be relied upon. It is of great importance for two reasons. It shows that, from the outset, Valerie Storie misled everyone about precisely what happened after she and Gregsten left the Old Station Inn. Here was the car, parked up, but not in the cornfield. It explains one minor aspect of the case which has always baffled everyone: why did they take the *third* turning on the right from the pub when they could have reached the cornfield by taking the *first* right?

Clearly, the cornfield was just one of a number of options. They first of all stopped in Huntercombe Lane South. No doubt they were disturbed, and thus moved on. Had they been discussing a rally, of course, they would not have needed to move from one discreet parking-place to an even more discreet parking-place.

Henderson was precise about the timing – 'I know I left Margaret [his girlfriend] at about 9.45.' So this statement also demonstrates that Valerie Storie erred in her timings. It puts back the beginning of the crime by a critical 30 minutes or so, from approximately 9.30

to 10.00 – critical because the gunman would have been able to approach the car under cover of darkness.

Nevertheless, it remains bewildering that no one seemed to have caught even a glimpse of this man as he made his way to the field. One policeman diligently drew on statements taken from local residents, of sightings of strangers in the vicinity, to assemble a detailed chart. (He rather spoiled his handiwork, however, by heading it: 'Man Sitings'.)

There were, in all, twenty-six statements referring to a purported stranger. Of these, five clearly referred to the same person, who had been observed either at or close to the Pineapple pub, and who was safely eliminated from inquiries. Another three referred to a fancy leather worker who motor-cycled home on his NSU Quickly from Windsor Station and then took the dog out for a walk.

It is impossible to discern a common thread amongst the rest. Many simply did not correspond to the known facts of the case, scanty as those were.

One statement, made by Ruby Philpotts, a housewife, was rather tantalizing: 'At about 8.15 p.m., during our journey in the Dorney area, we went on a bridge over the new motorway. We noticed a sports car parked off the road in the entrance to a field and at right angles to the road. As I passed I saw a man sitting at the driving wheel and we commented on the fact that it seemed an odd place to park. About thirty minutes later we returned the same way and he was still sitting in the car. There was no other person in sight and certainly no other person in the car. The car was a fawny-pink colour with, I believe, black mudguards.

'I would describe the driver as about twenty-seven years, black hair, palish complexion, plain-looking jacket, white shirt and tie, smart appearance.'[6]

Interesting statement; but I am afraid I can take it no further. The gunman presumably hadn't driven himself to the field (even if he had been a capable driver). If he had arrived by car, then someone else must have dropped him off – a scenario which the police and prosecution case, from first to last, precluded. Like so much else, this was just an assumption for which the police had no evidence whatever; but, on this one occasion, their assumption was probably the right one.

Perhaps the most pertinent statements were provided by Stanley Cobb, his wife Elsie and their neighbour, Frederick Newell. Elsie said: 'On Tuesday, 22 August 1961, I saw a man passing the gate.

I went outside the house and called to my dog which was still barking at the man. I went up to the man and said, "It's all right, he probably wants your bag." The man said, "Oh, his bark is worse than his bite." It was a normal voice with no distinctive accent. It wasn't a cultured type of voice. The man was wearing a dark-coloured suit. I would put his age at between twenty-seven and thirty, height 5 feet 6 inches. He had dark hair brushed back. He had very dark eyes but I wouldn't say they were sunken. His nose was thin.'[7]

Stanley provided some additional information: 'He was respectably dressed and didn't look like a labourer type. Medium build, very pale complexion. His hair was dark brown or black, brushed back and inclined to recede at the temples. He was carrying a white carrier bag by the top which had been rolled over.'[8]

Their next-door neighbour, Frederick Newell, simultaneously noticed this man: 'I would describe him as twenty-five to thirty, very sallow complexion with dark eyes. His hair was very dark, brushed back but not tidy. It seemed to be receding from his forehead.'

Even more intriguingly, Newell had seen the man on two previous occasions: 'The first was about three weeks before 22 August, but I can't say which day, only that it was midweek. On this occasion, he was wearing a red pullover under a dark jacket. The next time would have been roughly a week later. He had this red-coloured garment under his coat, and each time he walked quite casually. He didn't seem to live locally to me.'[9]

It is of further significance that the Cobbs and Frederick Newell took the initiative in contacting police because they were struck by the similarity of the photofits publicly released on 29 August to the man they had seen a week earlier. In fact, their sightings of the man on 22 August occurred at 2.30 in the afternoon. It was presumably for this reason that the police discounted the statements. Yet it was very slack thinking to discount the possibility that the gunman might have got there much earlier in the day.

In my view, the police here spurned statements that may well have been gold-dust. It would certainly have been intriguing to know what was inside that rolled-over carrier bag in which the dog showed an interest; and it was a grievous shame that Newell and the Cobbs were not asked to attend the subsequent identity parades.[10] The consequence was that the police managed to amass no information whatever about when or how the man arrived in the area. There never has been any evidence placing any suspect in the vicinity of Dorney Reach on that particular day: an astounding omission.

From the outset, the overall police investigation was in disarray. In the circumstances, this should not have been surprising. The crime began in Buckinghamshire, but reached its savage conclusion in Bedfordshire. The latter force assumed nominal control, but immediately transferred it to Scotland Yard. Straightaway, therefore, the Buckinghamshire force was at two removes from the inquiry proper.

Nor was there any coordination or avenue of communication between all the disparate forces. There were no personal radios; and wavebands for police car radios only covered a force's own area. Moreover, police were constrained from trespassing on to neighbouring forces' turf. 'It sounds like a paradox,' said Brian Hilliard, former editor of *Police Review*, 'but police would routinely sidestep rules relating to perjury and the collecting of evidence, but they would abide by discipline regulations. One of the basic rules was that you didn't leave your own force area.'[11]

So no one was going to interview witnesses in the Buckinghamshire area except Buckinghamshire police; and they had neither the personnel to take the initiative themselves nor any incentive to do so. Indeed, there were positive disincentives, as they wouldn't wish to usurp the investigative functions of Scotland Yard.

Although the layman might have anticipated that in the aftermath of such a notorious crime the area surrounding the cornfield would have been flooded with police searching out possible witnesses and taking statements, there was in fact a minimum of police activity. (In fact, Acott and his team wanted to keep to themselves the location of the cornfield, and the fact that the murder originated there. It was always considered good practice by the police to keep information to themselves, to give them the opportunity of enticing the suspect into revealing something that only the murderer could know.) Elsie and Stanley Cobb and Frederick Newell had to contact the police themselves on 30 August (a week after the crime), because they hadn't seen a policeman in the neighbourhood.

The majority of the statements from other locals are all dated in September, when local police were belatedly asked to carry out inquiries. The *Slough Observer* of 15 September reported that 'Slough police are undertaking a marathon house-to-house check in the hope that someone may have seen the killer.' Clearly, this criminal investigation believed in striking when the iron was stone-cold.

The second danger-point for the gunman lay in the subsequent journey to Bedford. The stop for petrol, in particular, created potential difficulties, but again the gunman was a beneficiary of good fortune.

Michael Gregsten did try to attract attention by flashing his reversing light. Rex Mead, an engineer, was on the road between 12.15 and 12.45 a.m. He saw the 'light flashing at the back' and drew in behind, slowing right down to the same speed, which he estimated as 25–30 miles per hour, or even slower. Eventually, once he'd decided that the driver was 'doing nothing silly', he overtook the car, and in doing so noticed that it had three occupants, two in the front and one in the back. Although alerted to something odd, he wasn't unduly inquisitive – fortunately for the gunman.[12]

Ronald Chiodo, an American airman, finished work at 12.30 a.m. but did not start for home in Luton until 1.20. He drove south down the A6, and about 1.30 saw a car travelling in the opposite direction with its reversing light on. As he ascended Warden Hill, he watched in his rear-view mirror as it travelled away from him, the light on all the time.[13] Apart from these alert drivers, the journey was remarkably untroubled for the gunman, presumably because Gregsten didn't try anything 'silly'.

The third point of maximum danger was when the car came to a halt at the end of the journey. It was ironic that, at this stage, Gregsten and Storie's professional preoccupation – road traffic research – came close to rescuing them. In that August week, along that stretch of the A6, a twenty-four-hour traffic survey was in progress. A census point was at the further end of the concrete strip, beside the RAC telephone box. John Kerr began his stint at 6.00 a.m. A youngster named John Smith was one of two men doing the 10.00 p.m.–6.00 a.m. shift.

The police became momentarily excited by this discovery, according to a message to the incident room timed at 4.55 p.m. on 5 September. Disappointingly, however, Smith could add nothing to the story. For some extraordinary reason, which no one could now recall, during the night-time the traffic census was taken at a different point, back down the A6, half a mile south of Silsoe. So John Smith had seen or heard nothing of significance at the appropriate time: 'There was so little traffic between 2 and 4 a.m. that I spent most of the time reading and didn't notice any particular vehicle passing.'

He did, however, notice what may have been the murder car accelerating away from the vicinity: 'Towards 4.00 a.m., a saloon car passed our post travelling south at a fairly fast speed. I told Michael [Black, his colleague] I thought it was a Morris Minor.'[14]

The fourth area of danger for the gunman was in driving the car away himself. With his evident lack of experience, he could well have been apprehended straightaway. There were obviously difficulties – after all, the car had sustained damage at the front and back, in what must have been separate incidents. Yet his luck held. With just one possible exception, there were again no valuable witnesses.

There was a handful of statements from people who saw the car being driven in the early hours of that Wednesday morning. No one, sadly, noticed the driver; no one could provide even a rudimentary description. One of these statements was interesting. A milkman saw the car in Bedford, and gave a particular reason for remembering the number-plate precisely. Bedford, however, was further north from the murder scene, along the A6; and the gunman had driven away back down the A6 – southwards.

The fifth stage of potential danger for the gunman lay in his disposal of the Morris Minor. He had pushed his luck just too far and here, finally, it ran out – largely because the car was being driven ineptly at a time when the roads were getting busy as people set off for work.

Just after 7.00 a.m., John Skillett and Edward Blackhall saw the Morris Minor. They were driving to work in Skillett's car from the eastern outer suburbs of London; Skillett had picked Blackhall up at Brentwood. They travelled west along Eastern Avenue and approached the traffic lights at Ley Street at about 7.00 a.m. The lights were on red. They slowed down behind an Austin A40. Suddenly, in Blackhall's words, 'A grey Morris Minor came speeding on the inside of us, swerved in front of our car and practically hit us. He put his brakes on and did a back skid. He pulled up between us and the A40.'[15]

The lights turned green. The Morris Minor 'shot off' in the nearside lane, but got wedged in behind a Greenline bus. 'By the time we reached Gant's Hill roundabout, he came out from behind the bus and shot in front of us again. The car was being driven very erratically. He was swerving in his own lane and kept trying to come into our lane as if he was in a hurry.'

At the roundabout they managed to pull up on his offside. Skillett asked Blackhall to wind down the passenger window so that he could shout a few choice words across to the driver. Skillett swore at him; Blackhall ventured that he himself was 'probably more controlled'. The errant driver was not in the least contrite: 'The man just had a horrible smile on his face.'

Subsequently the car accelerated down Eastern Avenue. It was a few cars ahead of them when Blackhall noticed the driver cross the lanes of traffic to the offside lane, and turn right towards Redbridge underground station. They then lost sight of him.

Blackhall estimated that they had been behind or alongside the car for five to ten minutes, during which the driver had made no signals at all or given any indication of his intention to change lanes. After the morning newspapers of 24 August carried news of the recovery of the Morris Minor the previous evening, Blackhall straightaway reported the incident to police. He was taken to New Scotland Yard, and was easily able to identify the car. He had noticed the three strips of red tape on the back bumper, as well as a torn green label on the back window.

Skillett's account broadly corroborated Blackhall's.

There was an additional witness. James Trower also gave a colleague a lift to work. The colleague, Paddy Hogan, lived over Green's Stores in Redbridge Lane. According to Trower, he arrived to pick him up at about 7.05 a.m., and knocked at his door. As he did so, he heard the crunching sound that occurs when a driver tries to change gears without de-clutching properly, and looked up to see a Morris Minor going past. As the car pulled level, the driver momentarily looked across at him. He went on, and turned left almost immediately into Avondale Crescent.

Trower made his statement after being stopped and questioned by police making routine inquiries twenty-four hours after the car was abandoned.

As the car was left so close to an underground station, a reasonable assumption might have been made that the fleeing driver would head for Redbridge, a station on the Central Line giving rapid access to central London. The sixth and final point of danger would therefore have been at the underground, before he was swallowed up in the early-morning London rush-hour. The ticket-collector at Redbridge station that morning was Ada White:

'At about 7.00, I remember seeing a man in a brown suit, with staring eyes and he had a pale complexion. This man came from the street, and went through the barrier down on to the platform. I do not know where he was going, as I did not ask to see his ticket, as I should have done, but he looked so peculiar and frightening that I just let him go straight through.'

Unfortunately, the potential importance of this statement is vitiated by its date: 1 December 1961. Ada White had not previously mentioned all this to police when she was questioned immediately afterwards, as she confirmed in this fresh statement: 'The day following [24 August], I was on duty when I was seen by Detective Sergeant Arnold. I remember that I told him that at that time of morning at Redbridge things were very quiet, with very few passengers. The only two I could recall were two young Irish fellows with suitcases, who were studying the map and wanted to get to Epping.

'I did not mention to the sergeant about the man in the brown suit, it must have just gone right out of my mind.'[16]

What was going on here? The later statement was made in the wake of the magistrates' court hearing. Were the police, perhaps too aware that witness testimony was not forthcoming in areas where one would have expected it to be available, trying to bolster the all too scanty identification evidence? In the event, the White statement was never tendered as Crown evidence, which is just as well bearing in mind that it's as fishy as Brixham trawlers were in those days.

In summary, there were six significant areas of danger for the gunman but he surmounted the potential pitfalls with invidious ease. From all that happened the police managed to derive almost nothing by way of hard evidence. There was just a little bit of identification to set alongside whatever Valerie Storie would be able to recollect; and the reasonable deduction, reinforcing what they would have been able to glean from Storie's first-hand account, that the gunman had little experience of cars or driving skills.

That much was evident not only from the direct testimony of Blackhall, Skillett and Trower; but could equally be inferred from the location of the car. Had the gunman set a reasonable course from Deadman's Hill, he would have been able to dispose of the car before potential witnesses were up and about, and before the heavier early-morning traffic exacerbated the inadequacies of his driving. Yet the car, which left the murder scene travelling south, was subsequently seen north of it; when seen towards the end of the journey, it was travelling in a westerly direction along Eastern Avenue. The route had been anything but direct.

CHAPTER FIVE

THE DISCOVERY OF the murder car in the early evening of Wednesday, 23 August was swiftly followed by further developments the following day. Another express message was telexed to all police forces from the Bedfordshire inquiry centre: 'The suspect's clothing is undoubtedly bloodstained. Please cause inquiries to be made at laundries and dry-cleaners.'

On seeing the Morris Minor, police were immediately struck by the amount of blood in it: hence the telex. The murderer had more than once insisted that he must not get blood on him; but even a cursory inspection of the car revealed that he could hardly have been successful. His clothing was 'undoubtedly' bloodstained.

Early on Thursday morning two men were observant enough to notice suspicious strangers, and conscientious enough to make statements about them to the police. At 7.20, William Halcro, a carpenter, arrived on site at a block of flats under construction in New Wanstead, east London. All the flats were complete except one, which had no front door. On entering this flat, Halcro disturbed a man asleep on the floor. The latter – speaking with a slight cockney accent – said that he had missed the last bus home. He wandered off in the direction of Snaresbrook. Halcro described him as having 'brown eyes, dark wavy hair and a sallow complexion'. He wore a brown jacket and dark gabardine trousers.[1]

An hour-and-a-half later Alfred Hance, a sales rep who lived in Ilford, saw a man walking out of an alleyway from behind a row of shops in Eastern Avenue. The man caught his attention because 'the back of his jacket was all creased and there were strands of sacking on his back', which suggested that he had been sleeping rough.

Hance caught up with and passed him, and was able to give a full description: 'He was about 5 feet 6 inches, in his early thirties, round-faced, dark brown hair brushed back with no parting, large, very light blue eyes, straight nose, thin lips and pale complexion.'

He wore a 'reasonably clean' white shirt and dark tie, and carried a brown paper parcel.[2]

The Halcro–Hance sightings were singled out from the hundreds that were dutifully reported to police stations up and down the country in the first two weeks of the inquiry. Detectives regarded them as of potential importance. They seemed to believe that their suspect may have been sleeping rough. The descriptions could have tallied with the others that were being drawn up, and the sightings occurred in the area where the car had been abandoned. Accordingly, these two statements remained part of the core documentation throughout the inquiry. They are both referred to in Detective Superintendent Acott's final report.

Nevertheless, both were certainly red herrings. There was no tangible evidence to associate either of the men spotted by Halcro and Hance with the crime. However, the third possible sighting that day was in a different category altogether.

At about 11.00 a.m., twenty-three-year-old Audrey Willis was at home in Old Knebworth, Hertfordshire. There was a knock at the back door. A man asked for her husband. When she replied that he was not in, and that she was alone, he produced a 'short, black' gun and forced his way into the house.

She described him as having a long, thin pale face with a sallow complexion and deep-set brown eyes. His hair was dark brown, smoothed back and receding at the sides. He was, she thought, about thirty years old. He wore a pale grey knee-length raincoat with epaulettes, dark trousers and brown shoes.

He said 'words to the effect that if I did as he told me to do I should not be hurt, but that I had to do as I was told'.[3]

He asked her to take his shoes off, which she did, and then followed her into the kitchen. He said he wanted a drink, and asked for milk. 'This meant I had to go into the larder, a walk-in larder,' she recalled. 'I went in and saw my rolling-pin. He wasn't very big, he was a weedy fellow, and I remember thinking, I wonder. Anyway, I didn't. I don't know what I would have done if Hugh [her twenty-two-month-old son] hadn't been there – all my instincts were saying do as he says and perhaps he will go away.'[4]

She gave him a glass of milk; he also needed food, and she gave him a packet of biscuits. At that point he heard Hugh crying from the drawing-room. He told her to bring him in, and to put him on the floor. He then pointed the gun at the child rather than her.

He next demanded money. 'I went to go and get it. My bag was upstairs in our bedroom; there was a telephone there. I went to pick Hugh up – he said, "Leave the child there." So I went on winged feet, got the money and came back. I gave him £4, which was an awful lot of money in those days.'

He returned the empty glass, telling her to wash it up, which she did. He then told her to follow him to the back door, and left. 'He said I must not telephone the police, and that he'd watch the house. So I locked all the doors, took Hugh in my arms, got down behind the sofa with him, where the man wouldn't be able to see us through the window, and dialled 999.'

With police throughout London and the Home Counties on a major alert for a gunman, and with this incident having occurred not too far from Deadman's Hill, the matter was taken extremely seriously. Mrs Willis had not been aware of any sounds of a car, there were no buses, and it was a little distance to the railway station – which was on the main north-east line out of London, from King's Cross, through Finsbury Park and Alexandra Palace. The police put her in a car straightaway, and drove her round the area in case the gunman was still on foot, but there was no sign of him.

On any level, it was a curious episode. News cameramen and reporters rushed immediately to the scene. 'I think what upset me most', recalled Audrey Willis, 'was that my parents heard all about it from the television news bulletins before I'd had a chance to tell them.

'I hadn't followed the news, and hadn't been aware of the A6 murder, so if anything I was more frightened afterwards than I had been at the time. My husband wanted to install new security devices. I dissuaded him, saying it would all be unnecessary. I said, "It's a once-in-a-lifetime event." '

Was the gun that Audrey Willis was threatened with the murder weapon? If so, it was taken to London, because it was recovered that evening from a 36A bus at the Rye Lane depot in Peckham, south London.

London Transport employed Edwin Cooke on cleaning duties as a pick-up man. After a bus was garaged for the night, he picked up 'all the stuff which will not go through the vac pipe'.[5] A .38 Enfield revolver and five boxes of ammunition fell squarely into that category.

The back seat on the top deck was the only one which had a recess. When Cooke lifted it to check, he noticed a handkerchief and a couple of stray bullets. The gun and boxes of ammunition –

there were sixty rounds altogether – were under the handkerchief. The police arrived within ten minutes.

It was a matter of routine ballistics the following day to establish that the gun was the one used at the A6 shooting. Thus Scotland Yard was suddenly provided with a potential breakthrough they could hardly have anticipated. The detachment of Royal Engineers from Cambridge using mine detectors to search for the weapon in the woods on Deadman's Hill were told they could resume normal duties.

Cooke had been clocking on for London Transport since 1945 and was, happily, assiduous in his work. He was able to state categorically that it was part of his daily routine to lift the back seat, and that nothing had been there the previous evening.

That Thursday, the bus left Rye Lane at 5.40 a.m., making the short journey to its southern terminus at Brockley Rise, where it arrived just after 6.00. The complete 36A service ran from Brockley Rise to Kilburn, a south-east to north-west axis across London, passing through Victoria at the centre. The bus went there and back, reaching Brockley Rise again at 7.49. It was the only time that day that the full route was covered.

At 3.43 p.m. the bus went to Brockley Rise, arriving at 4.01. It then ran to Victoria and back again. Then, instead of returning to Victoria, it was diverted to Camberwell Green. From 6.10 until 6.36 it was left unattended in Walworth garage while the driver and conductor had a cup of tea. The driver, Sydney Moorcroft, emphasized that 'No unauthorized person could have boarded the vehicle during our absence because it had been parked in the garage behind other buses.'[6] The 36A went back to Brockley Rise, and returned to Rye Lane at 7.23. Moorcroft left the bus parked in the entrance to the washing-bay.

The police took statements from the two drivers and the two conductors. On the morning journey, the bus was crowded as far as Victoria, and relatively empty on its subsequent route up to Kilburn, where it arrived at 6.32 a.m. It was busier throughout the rest of the morning; and much busier for the afternoon runs. The conductor, Ernest Brine, explained that 'we were quite busy nearly all of the time' and that altogether he had 'issued 300 tickets'.[7]

It was assumed that no member of the public could have had access to the bus while it was in Rye Lane garage. The police, presumably believing that villains did not rise at a godly hour, seemed to discount the possibility that the gun could have been disposed of during the early-morning runs (and if the man involved in the Audrey Willis incident was indeed the murderer, then the gun wouldn't have been back in London before midday). At the outset, the police inclined to the view that the gun and ammunition must have been disposed of during the afternoon journeys:

'They appealed to anyone who travelled in the bus on Thursday night and saw anything suspicious happening on the back seat of the top deck to get in touch with any police station.'[8]

The four-minute period between 4.40 and 4.44, when the bus stood idle at Victoria, may have been the significant one. Passengers would have been able to board while waiting for the bus's departure. Someone may have been able to jump on before other passengers, and quickly conceal the gun without anyone noticing. It was an ideal opportunity, probably the only one that day, and would have been easier to do when the bus was not in motion. The person would not even have needed to travel on the bus.

This is scarcely a watertight theory. There would obviously have been a number of people around at that hour – although not so many as might be immediately supposed. This was 1961, when there were high levels of employment, and people worked rigid 9–5 or 9.30–5.30 hours. Four forty-five would have been a comparatively quiet time just prior to the end of the working-day. Moreover, someone could have waited a long time at Victoria for a bus which stood empty for a few minutes. Taking the available information into account, this seems the most cogent of the various possibilities.

It was, however, one which Scotland Yard neglected to consider. Nor was there even an adequate attempt to locate and interview those who would have been passengers at the critical times. The police merely appealed for people to come forward. A number indeed did, although none of the resulting statements were of any assistance. The 36A bus can be set alongside the cornfield as a significant aspect of the crime which yielded no evidence whatsoever.

The case was only two days old, and already the police seemed hopelessly baffled. The *Daily Telegraph*, which had very good sources at Scotland Yard, reported:

Detectives are wondering what sort of man they are dealing with who could commit such a strange, ruthless murder. They are at a loss to understand why he should have forced Gregsten to drive for almost six hours with the possibility that he might have been caught on the journey.

He made no attempt to rob the couple saying he simply wanted the car. But when it was offered to him, he refused. Again, why did he abandon the gun in such a conspicuous place as a London bus, knowing it must be discovered?[9]

While the police were pondering this problem – that the crime must have been committed by an unusually sinister man, working to his own ruthless logic – Peter Louis Alphon was taken in for questioning.

Among the many appeals which the police had made was the customary one asking whether there had been anyone behaving suspiciously in hotels or guest-houses: 'Landladies: Do you have a lodger', asked Scotland Yard, 'who has not stirred out for the past few days?'

At the Alexandra Court Hotel in Finsbury Park, north London, they thought they did. Guests considered very odd the behaviour of a man who seemed to have spent the time since the murder locked in his room, pacing up and down. Mary Perkins, the lady in the next room, described him as 'about thirty years, 5 feet 6 inches tall, medium build, fresh complexion, dark hair, with either a cockney or south country accent'.[10] The man was registered as Frederick Durrant, of 7 Hurst Avenue, Horsham, Sussex; and the hotel manager, Peter Sims, contacted the local police about him at about 11 a.m. on Sunday, 27 August.

Detective Sergeant Arthur Kilner and Detective Constable Anthony Dean carried out a routine check with Sussex police, and were interested to learn that the name and address were false. It was 1.45 p.m. when they got to the hotel. Durrant was not in, so they went back in the evening. They were already there, waiting, when Durrant returned at about 7.00 p.m.

Durrant at first persisted with his false name and address, and Kilner and Dean took him to Blackstock Road police station for further questioning. He then admitted that his name was Peter Louis Alphon. He gave his address as 142 Gleneagle Road, Streatham, London SW16. His father actually worked at Scotland Yard, in a clerical capacity.

At this stage, Alphon had failed to allay suspicions. Kilner, taking the opportunity to give his professional efficiency a gloss it did not entirely merit, contacted the A6 inquiry team in Bedford:

'We have been checking hotels in this area for your suspect and have found a man named Peter Louis Alphon, CRO 40238/53, staying at Alexandra Court Hotel under a false name. He has been there since Wednesday, 24 August. Apart from height (5'10"), he is similar to your description and I have him here.'[11] (CRO referred to the Criminal Record Office; the number indicated that Alphon had a previous conviction, in 1953.)

The reply was received almost straightaway: 'Examine clothing and obtain a statement including full details of his movements from 21–23 August, and verify.' Kilner was asked to forward his report and the statement through Detective Inspector Holmes at Scotland Yard.[12]

Pressed to explain himself further, Alphon said that he used a false name because he had previously left hotels without paying. He described himself as a student of philosophy. Kilner's statement continued:

'I asked him what university he was attending and he said he was not attending any at the moment, but was going to enrol in November at London University. I asked him what he was doing for a living and he said he sold *Old Moore's Almanac*, which he bought wholesale from Moore & Dewar, Little Brittain, near St Martin-le-Grand. I asked him where he sold them and how far he travelled in selling them and he said he went all over London, but the farthest place was about Wembley, Harrow and Northolt.'[13]

Kilner and Dean asked to search Alphon's case. After protesting, Alphon grudgingly allowed them to do so. Dean recorded:

'The contents of the case were wrapped up and placed neatly in the suitcase. They were all wrapped in either brown paper or newspaper. There were four or five, containing his personal papers, a note-book, some dirty underclothes, and literature on the League of Empire Loyalists, the Fascist movement and racial propaganda.'[14]

At the very bottom of the case, Kilner found a recent copy of the *Daily Express*. 'The front page, which was what I first saw, contained headlines of the A6 Murder and a photograph, taking up two-thirds of the top half of the page, of a lay-by.'[15]

When asked to account for his movements during the previous week, Alphon said that he had spent the weekend of the 19th/20th at Southend, and slept under the pier. On the Monday, he had come into London to go to the dog-track, but had then returned to Southend and slept under the pier again.

He had been at the Alexandra Court since Wednesday – so where had he been on the Tuesday, the critical date?

'He said, at first, the Great Western or the Great Eastern,' recorded Kilner. 'Then he said he had stayed for one night at the Vienna Hotel.'

Alphon said that he'd left Southend at about 11 a.m. on the Tuesday to return to London. At about 1 p.m., he'd met his mother where she worked in Ebury Street, Victoria, and she had given him a cheque for £2 which he'd cashed at her branch of the Westminster Bank in Upper Richmond Road. In the afternoon he saw a film entitled *The Last Sunset*, and about 8 p.m. went to the Broadway House Hotel in Dorset Square. They had no room there, but booked one for him at a hotel under the same ownership, the Vienna, in Sutherland Avenue, Maida Vale. Thereafter, he went again to his mother. Strangely, he met her in the street on the corner of Gleneagle Road – 'as I do not get on with my father'. He then returned to Victoria station, where he had to pick up something from the left luggage office. He then went to the Vienna Hotel, arriving just after 11.00 p.m.

He stayed in Room 6 and left the following morning at about 11.45 a.m. He then returned to Victoria, saw his mother again, and went back to Upper Richmond Road to get some more money. He arrived at the Alexandra Court Hotel at about 5 p.m., having previously telephoned to reserve a room. The following day, Thursday, he went to Hammersmith at about 11.30, and spent the entire afternoon at the cinema, although he couldn't remember which films he saw. He then walked along Upper Richmond Road to Putney: 'I think I stopped in a couple of pubs on the way.' He got back to the hotel at about 11.30. On the Friday, he left the hotel at noon, and again went to Victoria station to meet his mother. He went back to Finsbury Park, and went to the Astoria cinema. In the evening, he went to the dog-track at Harringay. Invited to give a description of himself, he said, 'I am aged thirty, about 5 feet 10 inches, dark brown hair, brushed back and greased without a parting, slim build, brown eyes, fresh complexion, round face.'[16]

At about 9.15 Dean had to leave to attend an incident in Holloway. Kilner continued taking the statement, and Alphon left about 10.00 p.m.

His statement was taken on a Sunday evening, and covered events of the previous week, when they would have been fresh in his mind. As Paul Foot has written, it was an extraordinary narrative. By his own account, Alphon, a thirty-year-old man, had wandered round London, doing nothing in particular, sponging off his mother, and seeing only her. His movements seemed to be as vague as they were capricious. Apart from his mother, there was no one – not even his father – who could possibly verify them.

However, it was apparently confirmed that Alphon had stayed the night of 22/23 August at the Vienna Hotel. He was allowed to leave after completing his statement. Kilner, however, told Alphon that he must re-register at the hotel in his correct name and address, and return to the police station the following day at 7.00 p.m. Alphon did so, and confirmed that he had now registered correctly. Kilner said it might be necessary to speak to him again 'to clear up certain things in his statement'. The latter responded that he would be staying at the Alexandra Court until Wednesday 30th, but that afterwards he would look for somewhere cheaper.

With that, the first man to have been questioned in connection with the A6 Murder left the police station.

In these early days of the investigation, the main objective of the police team appeared to be to release a photofit picture of the gunman.

The photofit was a pseudo-photographic technique that, although employed in the United States for some years, had only been introduced to Britain six months earlier. An identikit consisted of a series of transparent sheets, covering almost all facial features, which were laid one on another until a witness was satisfied with a particular completed image. 'I don't know of anybody who was ever identified from a photofit,' commented Brian Hilliard, former editor of *Police Review*. 'The technique came in in a blaze of technological glory, and about a year later everyone realized it wasn't of any real assistance.'

In this instance, there were two photofits, which was confusing, especially as they appeared to be impressions of different men. 'They differ considerably in general features,' the *Daily Telegraph* pointed out, not especially helpfully. One was constructed from what Valerie Storie remembered of the man's face. She spent the afternoon of Saturday 26th helping Detective Sergeant Jock Mackle, Britain's photofit expert, to compose it. The other was a composite drawn from the fleeting impressions of Blackhall and Trower.

Naturally, the police would have preferred to issue one distinct portrait. The only conceivable explanation for the release of two is that they found them at such variance with each other they were impossible to reconcile.

They initially refused to disclose which impression was provided by Valerie Storie; but it was quickly established that she had composed the one on the left.

The photofits were officially released on Tuesday, 29 August. They were shown on the BBC and ITN News and appeared in all the following day's newspapers. In addition, 500 police stopped motorists along the whole of the route the Morris Minor was presumed to have taken, and asked drivers if they could put names to the anaemic faces.

This intensive campaign appeared to bring immediate results:

> The response has been so great that more than twenty police officers and detectives are working on day and night shifts at Bedford analysing and classifying information.
>
> Calls have been received from all parts of the Home Counties, and detectives took statements from people in Portsmouth who believe they saw the man.
>
> At each place or town where the killer might have been seen, flags are put on a map. This gives officers a picture of where to make further inquiries. Much of the information is likely to prove of little or no value, but all of it will be carefully sifted ... Reports resulting from inquiries were being sent to Scotland Yard, and the relevant ones will be passed to Bedford.[17]

Among statements which were obtained at this juncture, those from Halcro and Hance were passed on as of particular interest. Those provided by Newell and Stanley and Elsie Cobb, of the sighting of a strange man in the cornfield area on the afternoon of the crime, which were potentially of such value, sadly slipped through and were not put to further use.

At 12.30 p.m. on 31 August Valerie Storie, in need of more specialist treatment, was moved from Bedford to Guy's Hospital, London. She was then placed in the care of Dr Ian Rennie. His examination revealed a bullet wound on the left of the neck, with an exit wound on the right; and four bullet holes in the area of the left shoulder. Two bullets remained in her body. He recommended that they should, for the time being, be left there. He noted that her spinal cord was irretrievably damaged. Despite her massive wounds, however, he found her 'fully able to talk' and 'remarkably cheerful ... Her memory is good, as is her intelligence'.[18]

Her arrival at Guy's Hospital coincided with another puzzling development. Police issued what the papers excitedly termed a 'fresh description' of the killer: he had 'large, icy-blue, saucer-like eyes'. Previous descriptions had referred to 'brown eyes'. Moreover, the two photofits, which did not have much in common, were at least in harmony in depicting the suspect as having dark eyes.

The 'new' description issued by Bedfordshire police was carried in most newspapers. The *Bedfordshire Times*, which was always reliably informed, reported that the eyes were the gunman's 'most striking feature'.

An analysis of Valerie Storie's statements reveals that she first told police about this on Monday, 28 August, while she was still at Bedford: 'The description of the man is aged between twenty-five and thirty, about 5 feet 6 inches, proportionately built, slender, brown hair, clean-shaven, a very smooth, pale face, with icy-blue large saucer-like eyes.'[19]

So the photofits – to the preparation of which the police had given such diligent attention – were known to be misleading before they were publicly released. Valerie Storie never at any stage described the murderer as having 'brown' eyes. So where did this misconception originate?

In the very first television report from the scene, broadcast in ITN's Wednesday lunchtime edition, Superintendent Morgan of Biggleswade said: 'We are anxious to trace a man of the following description: aged about thirty years, 5 feet 6 inches, proportionate build, dark brown hair, palish face, erm, brown eyes, deep-set, not very deep-set . . .'

The long hesitation before 'brown eyes' is unmistakable, as is the confusion over whether or not the eyes were deep-set. He seemed to be trying to make sense of hastily scribbled and probably confusing notes. The mistake over brown eyes may well have occurred at this moment.[20]

The 'brown' idea muddied the waters from the outset. As has already been recorded, the very first police telex incorporated the suggestion that the suspect's name was Brown. Janet Gregsten, too, recollected this: 'I remember one thing they asked me, and that was about Brown. Did I know anything about Brown? Anybody called Brown? Or anybody with brown hair, or brown eyes – it was all to do with brown. I didn't know anybody called Brown.'[21]

The police quickly recognized this error, and corrected it via a special message twenty-four hours later ('The name Brown is now to be disregarded'). Yet the word itself must have been used by Valerie Storie. It wasn't the name; it wasn't the eyes; it must have been the hair. Storie herself cautiously accepted this: 'I do not recall ever saying to anyone the name "Brown". I may have said the man had brown hair.'[22]

This would confirm John Kerr's recollections. Nevertheless, at this early juncture, reservations about Valerie Storie's ability to identify her assailant should have emerged. She recalled that the man had 'icy-blue' eyes after sanctioning a photofit showing him with dark eyes; and she now recollected this as 'his most striking feature' after having previously failed to accord it any overriding significance.

Detective Superintendent Acott's other priority, in these early stages, was to piece together the complete course of that fateful journey – from Dorney to the murder scene and then back into London – in the hope that this might elicit further information. Accordingly, on 4 September, he and three members of his team, in their green Jaguar police car, tried to track the exact route which the Morris Minor had taken:

> [They] drove to the cornfield entrance at Dorney Common ... The murder squad, driving until the early hours, visited villages in Buckinghamshire, Hertfordshire and Bedfordshire and part of the Metropolitan Police district ... Then they went back to Bedford, passing Deadman's Hill on the way.[23]

They were subsequently able to inform the media that they had now found the attendant at the garage where the car stopped for petrol:

> Harry Hirons, of Hendon, has told police he remembers the three people involved and the car calling at the filling-station between 12.15 and 12.30 on the morning of the murder. He has accurately described the car, has identified Mr Gregsten and Miss Storie and has examined an identikit picture of the murderer ...[24]

This was a prime example of news management by the police. The sixty-four-year-old Hirons came into the case not as a by-product of the police team's drive in the country on 4 September but on his own initiative. He made two statements on 30 August and a further one on 2 September. He worked at the 584, a Shell garage at Kingsbury Circle, London NW9.

He recalled that one man got out of the car. When the police showed him the photofits, he said that he'd looked like the right-hand one. He thought that one of the car's numbers was a '7', and that he may have written it down although, when examining the till-roll for that night, he couldn't find the 847 BHN registration number. On 1 September he was driven to Scotland Yard and shown the Morris Minor: 'I am positive that it was the same car as there were greenish-grey smears on the rear window and there was also a figure "7" in the index number.'[25]

Clearly, his information was taken very seriously:

> A statement made to police by Mr Hirons was discussed at a conference at Bedfordshire police headquarters yesterday. After the conference, which lasted about an hour, a number of lines of inquiry were discarded and a new plan of investigation was drawn up. During the next few days, senior officers are expected to visit witnesses at various parts of the route to re-question them in view of information which has been obtained during the past seven days of inquiries.
>
> The public response to appeals by police has been considerable and as a result police have definite information now on the car's movements both before and after the murder.[26]

More news management here. To this day, the police have no 'definite' information on what happened to the car when the gunman drove off in it. At this stage of the inquiry, they were assiduously cultivating the impression that leads were being followed up, and that the inquiry was going well. In actual fact, the detectives were groping in the dark. An examination of the police files makes it clear that at this time all the usual investigative channels were being pursued. Gangsters and their associates, informers, small-time criminals, prisoners: those with underworld associations were asked what they knew about this crime. No one knew anything. This approach – the traditional route one of crime detection – yielded nothing at all.

There was a flurry of interest in some of the more credulous dailies when one suspect was apparently being smoked out, until the *Daily Express* disclosed apologetically that an 'East End man has been ruled out'. On 5 September, the *Evening Standard* reported that

The Yard believe that . . .
SADIST GUNMAN IS ROAMING LONDON
. . . He may kill again.

It was hard to tell who was getting the more itchy: the police or the press. Neither – despite the bizarre incidents, and various clues that had already emerged – had any genuine news to report.

However, on Thursday, 7 September, there suddenly appeared to be a breakthrough. In the first edition of the *Evening News*, their crime reporter George Hollingbery reported an interesting story:

A6: MAN HELPS THE YARD
He is Questioned for Hours by the Murder Team

According to the story, a man had walked into Cannon Row police station and was 'still helping detectives with their inquiries'. The man went into the police station in Whitehall at 10.00 p.m. on Wednesday, and was still there at 2.00 p.m. the following day – sixteen hours later, so the whole matter must have been taken seriously. Bob Acott, together with Detective Superintendent Charles Barron and Detective Sergeant Harry Heavens, had driven down from Bedford – still in the green Jaguar – to question him.

Although the London evening papers, which were always on sale from mid-morning, were creating the impression that it was all over, nothing more was heard of this suspect. The importance of the matter lay in what happened immediately afterwards.

At about 1.30 p.m., a twenty-three-year-old Swedish housewife, Meike Dalal, was attacked by a man who called to look at some accommodation. Mrs Dalal and her husband Zahir owned a large terraced house on Upper Richmond Road West, where they lived with their two small children. The three rooms on the first floor were let off as furnished accommodation, which was usually advertised at Hammersmith and Earl's Court underground stations. For the first time Mrs Dalal had also advertised this room in the local paper, the *Weekly Advertiser*. She had received an inquiry about the room the previous day; but when she told the caller the rent, he muttered something about 'robbing bastards' and hung up.

She received a second call at about 11.00 a.m. on the Thursday, from someone who could have been the same man. He asked to see the room, and she gave him the address. (The advertisement carried only the telephone number.) Some time later he telephoned again from Putney station, to say he was having difficulty in finding the address. (It subsequently emerged that he'd called by mistake at a house along a different part of Upper Richmond Road.) She gave him fresh directions from there, and he arrived at 1.30.

She invited him in and took him to see the room to let. 'I started showing him around, we were talking about the room and its amenities, and suddenly he closed the door.' He struck her a violent blow on the left temple with something hard, she didn't see what. She collapsed on the floor beside the bed. He lifted her up, and laid her face-down on the bed. He tied her wrists behind her back with some flex which he'd taken from his coat pocket. As he was doing so, he said to her, 'Listen, I am the A6 murderer and I want some money.'

She pretended to be unconscious and didn't reply. He then struck her twice more on the head, gagged her mouth with a silk scarf, and tied her ankles with a piece of blue ribbon. 'Whilst I was lying on my face, he wiped the blood off the back of my head with a pillow and then he turned me over on my back and lifted up my skirts.'[27]

At this point she began to struggle, but in fact he made no attempt to touch her under her clothing. Once again – if this was the same man – his efforts at binding hands were unsuccessful. Mrs Dalal got hers free, and managed to parry another blow which he aimed at her head. She then got the gag out of her mouth and screamed twice, very loudly. As he escaped downstairs and out into the street, she ran out of the room, along the landing and into the front room. She opened the window on to the main road and screamed to wake the dead.

Two women and a man were passing by. The latter, Philip Dyerson (who thought she'd screamed, 'He's the Essex murderer') came into the house and dialled for an ambulance and the police, while the two women comforted Mrs Dalal. The police received the message at 1.45 and arrived within ten minutes. They found Mrs Dalal 'bleeding freely' from her injuries, which were quickly treated at Richmond Royal Hospital. She was detained there for a few days – although, happily, suffered no lasting damage.

The actions of all concerned had been commendably prompt; but they weren't prompt enough. The attacker made off, turning right along Upper Richmond Road and right again down Grosvenor Gardens. This road led into a Post Office depot. He ran into the yard there, where he was seen by GPO engineers who left their office to try to accost him. However, the man climbed the wall at the end of the yard and dropped down into Mortlake Cemetery. Half-way across, he took off his 'shortie' raincoat, folded it carefully inside out, and tucked it under his arm. He left the cemetery at South Worple Way, and crossed the footbridge over the railway into North Worple Way, Mortlake. His escape was complete.

There did seem to be two promising clues. First, scene-of-crime officers arrived at the Dalal property and found four good finger-prints. Three of those were eliminated immediately by checking them against the other residents; the fourth wasn't. Second, Detective Sergeant Jock Mackle visited Mrs Dalal in hospital the following day and, with her assistance, prepared another photofit.

Yet despite the prodigious investigations of Detective Inspector W. Lewis of Richmond police, separate lines of inquiry were being pursued. Acott showed not the slightest interest in seeing Mrs Dalal. The detectives on the A6 team were experienced men – among the best the country could provide – and they weren't going to allow themselves to be sidetracked by an irrelevance. They instinctively ruled out the possibility that there could be any link between the Dalal incident and the A6 Murder itself: 'Police believe he said [that he was the A6 killer] merely to frighten her into giving him money.'[28]

Some observers might have been struck by quite the opposite point: in both the murder and the Dalal attack the assailant put himself in a position where he could have obtained money and possessions, but had not actually seemed interested in taking anything.

The police quietly ran a check on all London families who'd been rehoused in the Slough area as part of the post-war overspill programme. It was completely unproductive. As one baffling incident succeeded another, the police were now being much more cautious about publicity. John Storie told the press, 'I cannot tell you how my daughter is because we have been told not to say anything.'[29]

The detectives continued to be preoccupied with the find on the 36A bus, so much so that they promised an amnesty to unlicensed gun-owners – in case any unlicensed gun had been stolen – and, for the first time, released details to the press of what had been discovered under the back seat: 'a .38 Webley revolver . . . and seven or eight boxes containing about 100 rounds'.[30]

The police always felt it helped them to withhold precise information which could become critical evidence, so all of this detail was incorrect: the revolver was an Enfield and there were five boxes, containing about sixty rounds. Nevertheless, this was an extraordinary – and extraordinarily bulky – amount of material for

someone to dispose of in a hurry. The questions remained
unanswered: how had someone managed this, and why had they
done it at all when it would have seemed the safer, more sensible
option to have hurled it all into the River Thames?

The more mental energy that was expended on this case, the
more its mysteries seemed to multiply. The concentration on the
ballistics, however, appeared to be vindicated when two cartridge
cases from the murder weapon were suddenly discovered in a
shabby hotel in Maida Vale.

SHORTLY AFTER 8.00 A.M. on Monday, 11 September, Robert Crocker went to the Vienna Hotel in Sutherland Avenue, Maida Vale. The Vienna was one of two hotels owned by an Austrian businessman, Frederick Pichler, who had fled central Europe in the 1930s. Crocker was the overall manager.

His was not the most rewarding of jobs. He only started there on 8 August, and left before September was out, 'dissatisfied with the conditions'. By the time of the magistrates' court hearing in November he was working as a trainee telephonist for the GPO. During the few weeks that he was in Mr Pichler's employment, Crocker was usually kept busy at the main hotel, the Broadway House in Dorset Square. He was summoned to the Vienna after the theft of £5.

The Vienna Hotel was run by a staff of just four: a Spanish couple – Juliana Galves, who was effectively in charge, and her husband; and another couple – the egregious William Glickberg and his wife, Florence Snell.

Snell wasn't actually his wife, although this was the least disturbing of Glickberg's deceits. He wasn't called Glickberg either, at least not all of the time. He was more routinely known as William Nudds, the kind of name that Charles Dickens might have chosen for him had he been etched from that unusually resourceful imagination. Unhappily Nudds/Glickberg was instead a figment of real life, one of its least sympathetic creations: an odious man, constant only in his inconstancy, whose company all would have been advised to shun.

One wouldn't have wanted to run a deck-chair concession in February with him, let alone a guest-house on the edge of central London at the peak of the tourist season. He and Snell had only started there on 12 August but that was ample time for Juliana and her husband to become well acquainted with their indolence and dishonesty. She recalled catching a glimpse of a horse-racing broadcast on television one afternoon. As the camera panned across the crowd, she suddenly saw Nudds; he'd told her he was too ill to work that day.[1] Crocker asserted that Nudds and his wife 'did practically nothing'[2]. He was adamant that he hadn't appointed them. They must have been recruited by Herr Pichler himself.

Faced with this latest incident, however – no one had any doubt who was responsible – Crocker had no hesitation in sacking them on the spot. While Nudds protested in the only way he knew – with a string of obscenities – Crocker told them they had to be out of the hotel by 9.00 a.m. Their live-in accommodation wasn't luxurious but it was all they'd got, so they did persuade Crocker to allow them to return to sleep for one night. They also received one week's wages in lieu of notice.

That unpleasantness over with, Crocker decided to check all the rooms. It was something he'd intended to do, but hadn't previously found time for. No doubt, he also wanted to ensure that Nudds and Snell hadn't wreaked further mischief. So early that Monday morning, he and Mrs Galves went round the rooms together.

No. 24 was the third on their little tour of inspection. It was one of the larger rooms, containing one double and three single beds. Although from the street it was at basement level, French windows opened at the back on to the hotel garden. Beyond that, there were public gardens.

On entering the room, Crocker noticed a strip of material hanging untidily underneath a dark-brown upholstered chair in the alcove. As he moved the chair to try to conceal its need of repair, something fell off: a .38 cartridge case. Running her hand over the seat, Mrs Galves immediately discovered a second – on the top of the seat, towards the back.

Crocker had been a gunner during the war, so he knew spent cartridge cases when he saw them. Even so, in the normal course of events he might perhaps have taken simply a momentary interest and then discarded them. At this juncture, however, special circumstances prevailed. The hotel had lately been the subject of police inquiries. On 27 August the Vienna had been contacted by Highbury Vale police station, asking about one of its guests, Frederick Durrant. Subsequently, the police needed a written record of the telephone verification. As a result, Juliana Galves went to Harrow Road police station on 6 September to make a statement.

Staff therefore knew, if only obscurely, that the hotel was being mentioned in connection with the A6 Murder inquiry. Crocker accordingly rang the police at Highbury, who had left their telephone number. They contacted Harrow Road police station, and PC John Copp arrived to convey the cartridge cases to the Metropolitan Police forensic laboratory. Detective Inspector John McCafferty was able to say that they could be positively associated with the gun used at Deadman's Hill.[3]

That particular day – Monday, 11 September – was the most critical in the A6 inquiry. Detective Inspector Robson, of South-wark police station, had the previous week reported to Detective Superintendent Acott from Guy's Hospital, saying there had been a slight improvement in Valerie Storie's condition, and that she would be able to undertake a long interview from that Saturday (9 September) onwards. He addded that Storie had asked the surgeon – Dr Rennie – if she could specifically speak to Acott about the crime. The hospital laid no conditions on the interview, other than that it should take place between 12.30 and 7.00 p.m.

Acott made immediate arrangements to conduct a lengthy conversation with Storie. It took place on the Monday, in Ruth Ward of Guy's Hospital, and lasted from 2.10 to 7.30 p.m. Also present were Detective Superintendent Charles Barron, head of Bedfordshire CID, and Woman Detective Sergeant Walters, a shorthand typist. Notwithstanding her presence, the conversation was, exceptionally, tape-recorded in its entirety. 'There were many occasions during that interview', wrote Acott, 'when the patient's failing voice made it quite impossible for me or the shorthand writer to hear what she had said, but when the tape recording was played over it was discovered that every single word spoken by Miss Storie that afternoon had been faithfully reproduced.'[4]

Acott had told journalists that this interview was going to take place, so he was afterwards obliged to say something about what had transpired. During this five-hour conversation with Storie, the papers reported the next day, Acott learned that the gunman, while sitting talking with his victims in the car, had provided a clue which could lead to his identity being established. The police, according to the *Daily Telegraph*, 'are keeping the information secret, but it is considered vital'. The report added that 'Miss Storie has told police that she would easily recognize the murderer.'[5]

Neither of these points was true. The gunman was careful enough not to drop any direct clue to his identity while talking in the car. What the police may have had in mind was what subsequently became known as the 'done the lot' point. Nor had Valerie Storie told police that she 'would easily recognize the gunman'.

The police had their own motive for releasing erroneous details: to keep up what they desperately hoped was the pressure on the gunman. Yet the most interesting aspect of this disinformation is not the extent to which they were deluding the public but the extent to which they were deluding themselves. It was clear even at this stage that a genuine prosecution, resting on points like an identification by Storie and 'done the lot', would be hard to sustain; the police apparently persuaded themselves otherwise.

They were completely justified, however, in assuming an air of optimism at this juncture. They had a major breakthrough: the discovery of the cartridge cases. Acott did not tell the press about that. Now that the murder inquiry at last seemed to be on the rails, the press became no longer an aid but an inconvenience. Acott had no compunction about freezing them out. For the next ten days, they had very little to report.

On the morning of the 11th, Acott, who'd based himself from the outset in Bedford, conferred with colleagues at Scotland Yard. A special information centre had been set up there to coordinate London inquiries into the murder. From this juncture, the Bedford base was discontinued. The investigation was run entirely from London – either from Scotland Yard or at the Broadway House and the Vienna, where Acott now established a police presence.

There was now one overriding suspect – as the full statement of Robert Crocker, made immediately after the cartridge cases were found, made clear. In his statement, Crocker referred solely to Durrant/Alphon, pointed out that he was booked in at the hotel for the night of 22/23 August, and suggested that the cartridge cases 'may have some connection' with him.[6]

However, according to the statement which Juliana Galves had made five days earlier, Alphon had a cast-iron alibi at the Vienna.

'About 11.30 a.m. on 22 August, a man phoned up the Vienna and asked for a room for the one night and said he would be late coming in. We told him we would save him the room and waited up for him. He arrived at about 11.30 p.m. and said he was the man who had phoned up in the morning for a room in the name of Durrant. He was shown to his room and in the morning he declined breakfast and left about 12.10 p.m.

'I would describe him as about 5 feet 8 or 9 inches, with straight black hair, greased back. He had a dark suit on and a white shirt. He had a darkish complexion and spoke with a cockney accent. When he arrived he looked unshaven and grubby. He signed the book as Durrant.

'The only luggage he had was a small brown suitcase, almost an attaché case, and when I looked into his room to ask when he was leaving, it was open and contained very dirty clothing.'[7]

So did Alphon have an alibi or not? In a second statement, on 13 September, Mrs Galves clarified the position: 'The only time I saw the man about whom I have already been asked by police, was about 11.45 a.m. on the day he left . . . I did not see Durrant on his arrival. According to the register, he stayed for one night on 22 August.'[8]

Seen in this fresh light, Juliana Galves's original statement can be regarded as a sort of composite, made on behalf of the Vienna staff. It contained little that was first-hand information, but much that was second-hand, doubtless from Nudds. This was certainly not her fault. She had not long been in the country, and no doubt did what she thought was required. (There is no reason to doubt this interpretation of these two statements. Tuesdays was the one day in the week that Mr and Mrs Galves had off, and they usually went to the cinema. Unusually they were in the hotel that evening, but were not on duty to see who arrived.) The police who took the first statement should have appreciated that it contained almost no personal testimony. The second one did; and that gave Alphon no alibi at all.

Inquiries were now focused in one direction only. At 8.00 p.m. that Wednesday evening, Acott went to south London, to 142 Gleneagle Road, where Felix and Gladys Alphon lived in the top two rooms of a house named St Elmo Villa, running behind Streatham Common railway station. The following day, detectives began a serious and detailed investigation of Alphon's character and background, questioning and taking statements from those who had known him for some time or had come into contact with him since the murder. Almost all those questioned were taken in to Scotland Yard.

On the 14th, however, a small snag arose. Alphon himself had not actually stayed in Room 24 at the Vienna Hotel. In fact, neither Crocker nor Galves suggested that he had; nor, according to them, had anyone else – not, at least, for the night. The second Galves statement had contained intriguing additional information about Room 24:

'Room 24 was not occupied from 16 August till today, 13 September. The hotel register shows that Room 25, a single room, was occupied on the night of 30 August for one night by R. Heppenstall of 86 Outer Circle Drive, Lincoln, and that Room 24 was occupied by Vigan Rapur, of Delhi, India. Mr Heppenstall had booked the room during the morning. About 8 p.m., Mr Pichler telephoned and told me to put up the Indian gentleman who was going to stay three nights, for that night in Room 24 and then move him to Room 25. Rapur came with a waiter from the Broadway House and signed in for Room 24. Shortly afterwards, Heppenstall said he was leaving, and the Indian was put into Room 25. He was actually in Room 24 for about five minutes before being transferred.'[9]

However, after a closer examination of the books, it now emerged that the room was occupied. Someone called J. Ryan slept in Room 24 on Monday, 21 August, the night before the murder.

The detectives investigating the case never deviated from their certainty that the Vienna Hotel held the key to the murder. No doubt at some point they tried to account for everyone who stayed there around the material time. That process of elimination would have left question marks concerning two guests, neither of whom had given a correct address, neither of whom had used their real name. Alphon remained the one and only suspect; but this Ryan character muddied the waters.[10]

If police had been hoping for someone to shed light on this little difficulty, then William Nudds was the very last person to consult.

Nudds made a statement on 15 September. It is notable for two reasons: it is the first occasion on which Alphon is given a concrete alibi; and it is the first time that the name of J. Ryan is brought into the case. In a lengthy statement, Nudds described how he started work at the Vienna, and explained the procedures for booking people in and collecting their payments. Then:

'I have been shown an entry in the register dated 21 August, signed J. Ryan, 72 Wood Lane, Kingsbury, who was allocated Room 24. I remember this booking quite well. It was one which came from the Broadway Hotel and the man was brought over by one of the waiters in the company's vehicle. It was between 9 and 11.00 p.m. I showed him into his room. There are a number of beds in the room and he occupied the bed on the left-hand side as you go in the door.

'At about 7.45 a.m. Mr Ryan came up to the dining room and was served with breakfast. He left soon after. It would be about

8.30 when he left. He returned a few minutes later and said he had forgotten something in his room. He asked if he could return there and I allowed him to go, and didn't go with him. He was gone a few minutes and re-appeared from the basement and asked me how he could get to Queensway. I told him to walk to Harrow Road, which is about half a mile away, and get a No. 36 bus . . .

'I have been shown another entry in the hotel register, signed F. Durrant. I remember this particular man. He arrived very late in the evening, I think about 11.30 to midnight. He was dealt with by my wife but I saw him and stood by whilst my wife dealt with him. My wife took him to his room. I didn't see him again until the following morning when I went to his room to see if he wanted breakfast. He was in Room 6, which is on the second floor. He told me he didn't want breakfast and he stayed in his room as far as I know until about noon.'[11]

In making this statement, Nudds managed to give his name, occupation – he grandly described himself as the manager of the Vienna – and date of birth incorrectly. In fact, he'd lie so automatically that even determining when he was born is fraught with difficulty. On this occasion, he said 4 February 1915. That's obviously wrong because his criminal record begins in 1917. The main entry in his CRO (Criminal Record Office) file gives his birth-date, probably accurately, as 16 January 1908. Since he is demonstrably wrong on all basic points where his veracity can be checked, it is reasonable to wonder what credibility can be attached to anything else he said.

His criminal record, prolix as it is, almost achieves the status of a unique historical document. He was first convicted, of truancy, at Lambeth Juvenile Court on 29 September 1917. Other convictions at Lambeth followed, for stealing bicycles; and then he was found guilty of being 'on premises' – breaking and entering – for which he received two months' detention. On 24 April 1926 he was given three months, this time at Greenwich, again for theft of a bicycle – it seems a harsh sentence, but he had been let off the previous time – and, within weeks of his release, was arrested for a jewellery theft. This time, the sentence was three years. He served exactly two, and was released on 14 September 1928.

The following year he repeated the offence, but, strangely, received only fifteen months. He was charged under a different name, in a different jurisdiction (Kent), so perhaps the files containing his lengthening record hadn't caught up with him.

In 1931 he was convicted – under yet another name, and again in a different part of the country (Sheffield) – of taking a motor-car. He got away with three months on that occasion. Within weeks, however, he was also convicted of a similar offence in the West Country. For that, he received six months, to run concurrently with the previous sentence. Back in London, in April 1932, at what was then Marylebone police court, he received six months for receiving stolen goods. Exactly six months after that – i.e. virtually as soon as he was released – he was convicted of shopbreaking and larceny.

He was released in June 1933, and convicted again in November – this time, of stealing an overcoat, an offence for which he was sentenced to five months' hard labour. He then managed to steer clear of trouble for almost twelve months, from March 1934 until March the following year, when he was convicted at Bow Street and given nine months' hard labour for attempted car theft and assault.

He spent Christmas 1935 as a free man, but was back inside by January 1936, serving two concurrent three-year sentences for shopbreaking and larceny.

So what did William Nudds do in the war? He continued thieving, of course. At the quarter sessions in Taunton, Somerset, in October 1942, he was convicted of theft, and asked for another seven cases of larceny and three of false pretences to be taken into consideration. Three years' penal servitude was the sentence on that occasion.

He was released in 1944, and managed to be outside long enough to celebrate the end of the war. By October 1945 he was back inside, again convicted of jewellery thefts, this time in Wakefield, in what was then the West Riding of Yorkshire: another three-year sentence.

In November 1950 he was convicted of a string of offences, including larceny, motor-car thefts and acting under false pretences. On this occasion, it seemed as though his previous record had been collated in all its shabby villainy. He went down for a nine-year stretch.

During the A6 Murder trial, Michael Sherrard, defence counsel, asked Nudds if he recognized a number of names: David Beaumont, David Stuart Beaumont, Jazzer Beaumont, Edward Baker, Edward Bartlett, George Knight, William George Itter – not to mention Jack Glickberg and, finally, William Nudds (sometimes, William George Richard Nudds). All, it seemed, were aliases of one and the same person.

Sherrard: Do you remember which is the right one?
Nudds: I do.
Sherrard: Which one?
Nudds: The one I am standing here under.
Sherrard: The last one we have just mentioned?
Nudds: Nudds.
Sherrard: Do you remember, when you were using the name
Beaumont and were known as Jazzer Beaumont, how it came
about that you got that nickname, Jazzer?
Nudds: Yes. Years ago I used to do quite a lot of dancing.
Sherrard: Someone would play a tune and you would dance. Is that
it?
Nudds: No.[12]

Paul Foot researched Nudds's background, and discovered that
he had no scruples about dancing to any tune.[13] He had long been
a notorious police informer, which probably explained the relative
leniency with which he was treated during his long criminal career.
He had given controversial evidence in a number of trials. On one
celebrated occasion he had got prison officers at Parkhurst arrested,
convicted and sacked after planting compromising letters. Within
three weeks of his release on 14 July 1958, the *Empire News*
documented his life-story, with particular reference to his record as
a prison grass, and dubbed him 'the most hated man in Britain'.

This, then, was the man who brought 'J. Ryan' into the A6
drama. Not merely introduced him, but straightaway placed him
centre-stage. The reference in his statement to Ryan's return to his
hotel room offered the occasion for the cartridge cases to have been
inadvertently dropped; and the mention of the 36A bus was
gratuitously damaging. It is inconceivable that such a scheming
mischief-maker as Nudds wasn't aware of its reverberating significance. At a stroke, Ryan, who had received no previous attention
in police inquiries, was linked four-square with the two most vital
pieces of evidence – the gun abandoned on the bus, and the
cartridge cases discarded in the hotel.

Nevertheless, the police didn't have a clue who 'J. Ryan' was.
But did it matter? For the moment, they ignored this statement. It
seemed immaterial: their attention was firmly fixed elsewhere.
Inquiries with regard to Durrant/Alphon were making smooth
headway. The more they learned, the more confident the police
became. A picture emerged of a man who was possibly an unstable
character and emphatically a loner.

In fact it soon became clear that the case for Alphon's defence hung by one shoddy thread: the statement of William Nudds, supported by his partner, Florence Snell, whose statement echoed his. Nor had she led a blameless life. She was twice prosecuted in 1945 for shopbreaking and larceny, receiving a three-month sentence on the second occasion; and in June 1947 was found guilty of the delightfully antiquated crime of 'wandering abroad'.[14]

It may have been significant that Florence Snell's vagrancy offence occurred at exactly the same time as she was divorced from her husband, Norman Doyle. She subsequently remarried, in June 1958, to Leonard Snell, whom she left in January 1959 to move in with Nudds.

The initial Nudds and Snell statements were made at their digs. Now Acott had Nudds brought into Scotland Yard so that a fresh statement could be made to Detective Sergeant Oxford and himself. The thread was cut. With some minor abbreviations, this is the bulk of Nudds's important second statement:

'Since I made my statement to you on 15 September, I realize that what I told you in that was wrong. I was confused and made an honest mistake about the booking and arrival of the man named Durrant that I then told you about. I am now perfectly clear about everything that happened at the Vienna Hotel in regard to Durrant.

'At about 11.00 a.m. on Tuesday, 22 August, my wife told me she had just received a booking from a man who gave the name of Durrant and asked for a room for one night. I made an entry in the hotel diary: "Mr Durrant, 1 night".

'I saw Durrant arrive at 1.00 p.m. My wife and I were together at the reception desk. We had no single or small rooms to offer him. We never turn a guest away if it is at all possible to accommodate him. In accordance with general practice I allocated him Room 24, which is a large room, in the basement. I pointed out to him that although the normal charge for bed and breakfast for a single person for one night was £1 7s 6d, the charge for occupying a room like 24 was £2 15s 0d; and also that, if other guests arrived later that day, he would have to agree to others sharing with him.

'When we entered Room 24, Durrant chose the single bed which is in the alcove immediately to the left as one enters the room, and he put his suitcase on the seat of the armchair, which is at the foot of that bed, behind a narrow partition which prevents the chair being seen from the doorway.

'This basement room is level with a park, which looks like an ordinary garden when one looks out of the window. Durrant walked round the room, and then said, "I don't like a basement. I prefer a room upstairs." I said, "All our single rooms are booked, but if one should become vacant, I'll let you have it."

'Durrant left his case in Room 24, the key of which he had already been given, and we all went back to the reception desk. He paid me £1 7s 6d and agreed that if he had to spend the night in the large room, he would pay the extra money. To cover myself with the hotel accounts, I added "Deposit £1 7s 6d" to the previous entry, "Mr Durrant, 1 night" . . .

'I noticed that Durrant had a smart appearance, something like a commercial traveller, wore neat clothes and clean white shirt, was well-shaven, and had hair neatly smoothed down with grease. He was, however, in a bit of a flurry and certainly in a hurry to get out of the hotel.

'Durrant told me that he was going out and wouldn't be back until late. When I asked how late, he said, "I may be very late. Don't wait up for me."

'When we had finished this business at the desk, Durrant left us to go to his Room 24, but I remember now that he came up shortly afterwards and went straight out of the hotel, and he was not wearing a hat or overcoat, and I don't think he was carrying anything at the time.

'Sometime that evening, Mr Pichler telephoned me from the Broadway House and told me that the booking for Mr Bell could now be cancelled. This left me then with Room 6, a single room, free for Mr Durrant when he returned.

'My wife and I sat up late, as was our usual custom, watching television and talking while we waited in case there were any late guests arriving.

'At 2.00 a.m., we decided to go to bed. Durrant was the only guest who had not returned to the hotel. We decided to leave a note for him notifying him of the change of room. I took a sheet of pale blue paper from a scribbling pad and wrote "Mr Durrant, I have been able to change your room to a single, No. 6. Herewith the key to the door. Manager." I placed this where it could not be missed by anybody coming to the reception desk. I and my wife went to our room in the basement and retired to bed.

'We got up at 7.00 that morning, and spent the next hour in the kitchen preparing breakfasts for the guests. At about 9.50, I asked my wife whether there were any more breakfasts wanted. She told me there was only one who had not had breakfast, Mr

Durrant in Room 6. I went up to ask whether he was going to have breakfast.

'I knocked but got no reply, so I opened the door with my pass-key. I saw Mr Durrant standing by the bed pulling on his trousers. A suitcase lay open on the bed, and I remember that it contained dirty linen. I asked him if he wanted any breakfast and he appeared to be agitated when he said, "No, no, I don't want any." He appeared dishevelled. His hair was ruffled and he was in need of a shave, and very different from the Durrant of the previous day. I said to him, "Did you sleep well?" and he said, "Yes." I said, "What time did you get in last night?" He said, "Eleven o'clock."

'I left the room and went back to my wife. I said to her, "Number 6 doesn't want any breakfast. It looks as if he's been drinking last night. He told me he came in at eleven o'clock." She said, "He couldn't or we would have seen him. He couldn't have got our note then, and wouldn't have been in No. 6 now."

'At about 11.45 that morning I asked my wife and Mrs Galves if they had finished with the rooms. My wife replied, "We've got one more, No. 6, he's still in his room." I told them to go to No. 6 and tell him that unless he vacated his room he would be charged for another night.

'I did not see Mr Durrant again and I was told later by my wife that he had left the hotel.

'This statement I have now made is a true account. The statements I have made to you before have been inaccurate as to detail because I was confused as to the comings and goings of the many guests that were using the hotel at that period, but what I have told you now is correct.

'In order to clear up any confusion, I want to point out the dfference between [Ryan] and Durrant, who entered Room 24 at about 1.00 p.m. on 22 August, after Ryan had vacated it at about 8.30 that morning.

'Durrant is five or six years older than Ryan; he is about two inches taller; he is bigger in build; although they both had dark-coloured hair, Ryan had a quiff; whereas Ryan had an accent, possibly Irish, Durrant had no accent and was better-spoken; though they were more or less dressed in equivalent clothes, Ryan was dressed in the style of a younger man; while Durrant carried a suitcase, Ryan carried a brown hold-all and a portable radio with a shoulder strap.

'The most important difference between the two was that Ryan was at all times cool, calm and composed, and left our hotel like a normal man who had had a breakfast after a full night's sleep and was leaving for work; whereas Durrant was flurried, hurried and agitated.

'This statement has been read to me and is true.

'I should add that ... I did not know until this moment when you mentioned it that two empty cartridge cases had been found by other members of staff in Room 24.'[15]

Florence Snell was taken in to Scotland Yard the following morning, 22 September. At 1.30 p.m., she made a statement which matched Nudds's in all essential details.

That's right – *the following morning*. Where witnesses are suspected of having colluded in making false statements (and especially when they already have criminal records), it would be standard practice, not to say basic common sense, to interview them separately but simultaneously. On this occasion, Acott gave Nudds the opportunity to go home and discuss his revised statement with his wife overnight, thereby ensuring that she would be word-perfect on the details for the next day. Accordingly, the statements might be true, or they might not be; the investigators deprived themselves of the ready-made opportunity of determining which.

There was just one additional detail of interest in Snell's new statement: 'I remember going up to the dining-room about 8.00 a.m. that morning and recall looking at the reception desk and noticing that the note had gone which we had left for Durrant. I feel sure that I noticed this.'[16]

Once Snell had left, at about 2.30 p.m., Felix Alphon was summoned to Acott's office. A police car took him home, and they picked up his wife. They returned immediately to Scotland Yard, where Gladys Alphon learned to her distress that her son had become the country's most wanted man.

However, she had no idea where he was. Nor did the police. It was time to bring the media in from the cold. That afternoon, Acott held a major press conference, making what the *Daily Telegraph* described as 'the most detailed appeal ever made by Scotland Yard'.[17] He told the assembled reporters and photographers the name of the man police wished to interview in connection with the A6 Murder: Peter Alphon.

The appeal was also carried on radio; and 'to stress the importance of finding this witness', as the *Telegraph* explained, on television. The BBC's Peter Woods spoke to Acott:

Woods: Mr Acott, I gather that you now have a man in mind who might be able to help you in your inquiries?

Acott: Yes. He is Peter Louis Alphon, who uses the alias of Frederick Durrant. He is thirty-one years of age, and 5 feet 9 inches. His hair is brushed straight back, rather dark and greased down.

Woods: How is he likely to be dressed?

Acott: A double-breasted dark blazer, a white shirt and dark clerical grey trousers. He may be in possession of an off-white, three-quarter-length raincoat which has a red lining and a cape effect on back and front of shoulders.

Woods: What sort of work does he do?

Acott: He hasn't done any work for the last four years or more, but we know he has been a casual barman or a casual waiter.

Woods: Is he likely to be in London?

Acott: Yes. We know that he roams most parts of London.

Woods: Have you got any recent address for him at all?

Acott: Yes. He has been giving the address of 7 Hurst Avenue, Horsham, Sussex.

Woods: Is that his actual address?

Acott: No, it isn't.

Woods: Now, what about pastimes? Do you know if he has any particular pastimes?

Acott: Yes. He is a very keen student of theosophy, theology and astrology and we know that he has been a frequent visitor to London reference libraries and borrowed books on those subjects.[18]

Thirty years later, Woods recalled that unprecedented interview: 'I'd been ten years in Fleet Street even before I went to the BBC, but I'd never known the police actually to name the person they wanted, in such a positive way, ruling out any doubt. He was the man they wanted, he had to be apprehended at all costs.

'There were legal implications, of course. We all felt it was going too far. The BBC lawyers were very worried about transmitting what Acott had said; but we did put it out on air.'[19]

Directly after issuing the appeal, Acott went to Guy's Hospital to see Valerie Storie. There is, unfortunately, no record of this meeting. But why would he have interrupted his busy schedule to visit her then? And what did he say to her? It is hard to believe he conveyed anything other than the message that the hunt for the A6 murderer was nearing its conclusion.

He was the second visitor of particular note that Storie had had that week. On Wednesday, Janet Gregsten had arrived. Just forty-eight hours later, following Acott's visit, Janet returned. Perhaps the family was doing a bit of public relations work on its own behalf. There had so far been no mention of an extra-marital affair, and this would help to perpetuate the charade.

Janet Gregsten had originally requested police permission to visit her on 6 September. At that stage, she was told that the hospital considered such a visit 'inadvisable'. Having thus sanctioned the visit, the police probably arranged for a photographer to be present and informed the press (thereby throwing it a sprat and leaving the inquiry undisturbed to concentrate on harpooning the whale).

The two women had previously met 'once' (according to Janet Gregsten), or 'on several occasions' (according to Valerie Storie). They had scant time or respect for each other, and little in common other than a heartbreaking bereavement, so it must have been a strained meeting. The photograph that was used in several papers shows them, well, not exactly engaged in earnest conversation.

After the first of her visits, Janet Gregsten spoke to reporters outside the hospital. Her comments were reported in Thursday's papers, and Friday's, when additional material was added once the photo became available:

'The whole thing seems without rhyme or reason. It can only be the work of a maniac. Mike and Val got the impression that he might have been committing a burglary somewhere and wanted a getaway car.

'The most important feature was his eyes. They were blue and staring.'[20]

When Acott left Valerie Storie, having spent forty-five minutes at her bedside, the media offensive which he had launched was already in full spate. The nation's attention was focused on the search for one man: a man with hazel eyes.

The *Evening News* reported the matter as follows:

Scotland Yard this afternoon issued the name and description of a man they wish to interview in connection with the murder of Michael Gregsten ... He is Peter Louis Alphon, alias Frederick Durrant, born at Croydon, Surrey on 30 August 1930. He is 5 feet 9 inches to 10 inches, slim build, complexion pale, dark brown hair brushed back and flat, hazel eyes, small round nose, thin lips, rounded chin, well-spoken and speaks like a Londoner in a quiet voice.[21]

The *Evening News* also explained that Alphon had been evacuated to Horsham during the war. Inquiries had been made there by both the police and press. The real Frederick Durrant, the brother of Joan Durrant, whose house Alphon had stayed at, had been found. He was a butcher.

In later years, Jean Justice, whom we will meet in due course, searched assiduously for a copy of an early edition of the *Daily Mail* of Saturday 23 September. His pertinacity was boundless and eventually, twenty-eight years later, he found it, happily bestowing a £10 note on the startled proprietor of a vintage newspaper stall in Brighton.

The newspaper edition was not merely an obscure object of desire for those fascinated by the case. It is a critically important document. The *Mail* ran an up-to-date headline news story; and, alongside, a lengthy profile of Alphon, who was dubbed (despite being thirty-one at the time) 'The Boy with his eyes on the stars'.

Alphon was the only child of Felix and Gladys. Felix Alphonse dropped the 'se' when he emigrated to Britain from Bordeaux at the turn of the century; Gladys Ives came from Dorset. The *Mail* reported:

> Alphon was a shy and lonely boy. He was quiet, studious, reserved: a dreamer who could not mix with classmates. He grew up a man who liked to be alone with a passion for astrology and religion. In hotels and boarding-houses where he stayed he left evidence of his craving for books on theology and theosophy.
>
> He was always a great reader. He gained a scholarship to Mercer's – oldest of London's public schools until it closed two years ago – [and] preferred a book to games.

In 1941 the school was evacuated to Horsham and Alphon was billeted with the Durrant family at 7 Hurst Avenue. The *Mail* had tracked down Joan Durrant, by then Mrs Joan Buckman, to Hamworthy, Poole, Dorset. She recalled that four boys from Mercer's stayed at her home. Three of the four remained for some time; it was the fourth in whom the police were interested. 'He did not settle down and appeared to be always on edge,' she told the *Mail*. 'He was pale, and just didn't fit in with Frederick and Robert, my two brothers, and the other evacuees. He was unhappy and, after about three weeks or a month, asked to be moved to another family. I can't remember ever seeing him again.'

His new billet was with Theresa Jeal in Gladstone Road, where he stayed for about a year. Mrs Jeal, still in the same terraced house in Horsham, told the *Mail*:

I remember Peter well. I can see him sitting at the table doing his homework. He was a nice, quiet little boy. He was rather thin, and when he first came to me he was very nervy. I remember a master from the school bringing him. I didn't want to have him. Mercer's was an exclusive school. None of their other boys were billeted in this road, and I didn't think my little home would be good enough.

He did not go out very much. He wasn't allowed by the school to play with the local children, and he always seemed to have a lot of homework. He used to come home, have his tea, do his homework and go to bed. He studied very hard. At weekends he would have to go to church and to Sunday school with the other boys.

His mother came to see him several times. Peter told me his father was a teacher of languages and that his grandmother was French.

Peter spoke beautifully. He was always telling me off, politely, for not speaking properly. He would often correct me and remind me when I dropped an 'h'.

After Peter left, his mother wrote to me several times. Just after the war she asked if he could come and stay for a week. He was still quiet and very well-behaved. He stayed indoors reading a lot during that week.

I have not seen him since. His mother continued to write to me occasionally. I wrote and asked her about Peter, what he was doing and whether he had got married. I did not receive an answer or any more letters. But I still get a Christmas card every year from his mother. She always signs them 'From Mrs Alphon and Peter with love'.

When the police came to see me they told me that if Peter came to the house I was in no circumstances to let him in.

Others contacted by the *Mail* had somewhat less cherished memories. Ron Knight, who lodged with Alphon at Hurst Avenue, said, 'I remember him as a misfit. He wasn't in the same pattern as the rest of us.' Mr H. Fyson, who taught Alphon maths, recalled, 'I remember him quite well. He was a quiet little chap. I always got the impression he wasn't very robust. He was not outstanding in any way either at his work or at games. He didn't make friends easily.'

His chemistry master, Mr H. G. Andrew, said, 'He seemed lonely and always wanted to draw attention to himself. He was always the boy in trouble. When he left school at the end of the war he didn't join the Old Boys' Club.'

The *Mail*'s lengthy piece was illustrated with photographs of Mrs Jeal, Robert Durrant, the house in Delamere Terrace, Paddington, where the Alphons lived when Peter was born; and the one in Agate Road, Hammersmith, where the couple lived when Peter was away at school. There was even a copy of Alphon's birth certificate.[22]

The front page featured a caricature of Alphon, a large picture of him with his shortie raincoat over his arm, and a smaller one showing him wearing it. The illustrations were by the *Mail*'s leading cartoonist, Illingworth.

All the papers reported that Alphon attended greyhound tracks regularly, so 'Squads of detectives were planning to mingle with the crowds at this evening's meetings at all greyhound tracks in London and the Home Counties.'[23]

This activity proved to be superfluous. Alphon grasped the nettle himself. That up-to-date headline in the *Mail* read as follows:

Murder Hunt Police Question Man Early Today
A6 SEARCH DRAMA
Midnight Caller at Yard Says: I'm Alphon

The story, by Arthur Tietjen, began:

A man giving the name of Peter Louis Alphon, whom police want to question about the A6 murder, walked into Scotland Yard just before midnight.

A check was begun to establish if in fact the man was Alphon. Early today a Scotland Yard spokesman said: 'The man is being questioned, but we cannot say any more at the moment.'

The man was indeed Alphon.

He telephoned the *Daily Express* and the *Daily Mirror* from outside Charing Cross station to say that he was going to Scotland Yard. *Mirror* reporter Hugh Curnow wrote, 'He phoned at 10.57. I was at the gates of Scotland Yard eighteen minutes later when he arrived. Under his arm was a well-thumbed evening paper.' Alphon explained to him that he had been reading all about himself, and 'wanted to know what it was all about'.[24]

Alphon seemed to have a shrewd understanding of both the police and the media. There are probably three reasons why he contacted newspapers, ensuring that his surrender to police was as public as possible. First, he would have wanted to make it clear that he was going voluntarily, to reinforce his claims of innocence. Second, as the country's most high-profile and widely denigrated suspect, he would have wanted to guard against physical maltreatment in police custody. Having credible witnesses to his condition immediately prior to giving himself up was a good insurance policy. Third, as subsequent events proved, he was simply a glutton for publicity.

'It took me half an hour to convince them I wasn't a hoaxer,' Alphon later told the *Express*. 'Then, a plain-clothes man told me that Acott had been contacted and was driving down to see me.'[25] The *Mirror* timed Acott's arrival at the Yard at 12.40.

The copy of the *Mail* that Justice had so sedulously sought was priceless because it was an intermediate edition. The first editions would have been on the trains before Alphon's dramatic appearance at Scotland Yard; later editions contained none of the discursive background material. Once Alphon had surrendered, and was being questioned, and the questions were thought likely to presage charges, then the window of opportunity for newspapers was closed and shuttered. In those days, contempt of court was taken very seriously.

This edition had obviously gone to press at about midnight – after Alphon's arrival, but before the police had established that he was who he said he was. It thus bears out both what Alphon said (that he first had to persuade them he wasn't a hoaxer), and that the police were instantly wrong-footed. They had hardly expected him to turn up so suddenly and so quixotically. Nor, indeed, had the press. The *Mail* must have been primed by the police, and its staff had gone to exhaustive lengths to compile their material. Down the years, Alphon would be guaranteed to provide good copy; on this one occasion, he ruined it.

The Metropolitan Police, which only hours earlier had alerted every force in the country, circulated a cancellation message to 'all districts and all ports'. At 2.00 a.m. Acott and Oxford began interviewing Alphon, a process they concluded at 5.15.

Early that Saturday morning, Detective Inspector McCafferty
arrived to examine Alphon's clothing. At 1.30 p.m., Dr Lewis
Nicholls, director of the Metropolitan Police forensic science laboratory, and Dr John Gavin, the local police surgeon, arrived to take
blood samples and specimens of Alphon's pubic hair.

That afternoon, Alphon was placed on two identity parades. At
3.10, the first took place outside, in the quadrangle in front of the
Commissioner's office. There were six witnesses. Harry Hirons, the
garage attendant, could identify no one. Nor could James Trower,
one of the Redbridge witnesses who saw the car in the early
morning. Another of these, Edward Blackhall, made an incorrect
identification; so did Florence Snell. William Nudds, perverse as
ever, picked out two men, one of whom was Alphon.

The upshot was that Alphon, who took up a position second
from the left in a line of ten men, was properly identified by only
one of the witnesses, Paul Alexander. As the latter had merely sold
Alphon a shortie raincoat from a branch of Burton's in the Seven
Sisters Road three days after the murder, he was hardly a crucial
witness. In any case, even he said that he 'wasn't 100 per cent sure'.
Not only was all this highly encouraging for Alphon, but it was
useful experience ahead of the main event.

Immediately, however, there was a second parade, which took
place at 3.27. Then, Mrs Dalal did identify him to police ('I think
it's the second from the left ... I think it is him') as the man who
had attacked her. However, she declined to identify him by tapping
him on the shoulder, as the police requested, explaining that she
was too frightened. The inspector in charge of the parade, Kenneth
Mayer, described her as 'distressed and trembling'.

At Guy's Hospital, the last two bullets were being removed from
Valerie Storie's body so, as the *News of the World* disclosed, doctors
'forbade' an identification parade on Saturday. Later on, however,
her condition was reported as 'very satisfactory'. Thus the main
event occurred the following morning. Two police vans left Scotland Yard and called at the Union Jack Club in Waterloo. Nine
volunteers were sought – they were not told what for – and divided
between the two vans, one of which already held Alphon.

They shortly arrived at Guy's Hospital, where full security was
in place. The parade in Ruth Ward before Valerie Storie, who was
the only patient there, took place at 11.07. Her bed was screened
off. As hospital staff went towards the screens, someone pointed out
that one of the men (Alphon, assuredly) had no tie, so all the others
had to remove theirs. The ten men formed a diagonal line across

the ward. Each was given a numbered card to hold. Alphon took up a position on the extreme left. He was No. 10.

Then Cyril Canham, the police inspector in charge of this parade, removed the screens. According to Canham's statement, Valerie Storie 'looked along the line in each direction for about five minutes'. She reached her decision: 'No. 4 is the man.'

In that instant, the case against Alphon that had looked so watertight only hours earlier collapsed. The day before, the *Evening News* had reported that Alphon was 'expected to travel to Ampthill this evening': the carefully coded way of saying that he was expected to be charged with the A6 Murder. Without Storie's identification, this could not realistically happen. (She was, according to Alan Bainbridge, one of the identity parade volunteers, sobbing as the screens were put back in place.) Alphon was taken not to Ampthill but to Richmond where – the police salvaging what they could from the calamitous turn of events – he was charged with causing grievous bodily harm to Mrs Dalal.

That Tuesday, so the *Slough Observer* reported, the police made loudspeaker appeals to the crowd at Slough's dog-racing stadium to ask whether anyone could assist their inquiries regarding a man in custody, dog-racing enthusiast Peter Alphon. Whether these farcically belated appeals concerned the A6 offence, of which he'd by now been cleared, or whether they related to the Dalal incident, is not clear; but one would logically suppose that, to warrant such prominence, it must have been the former.

Alphon was out of the woods on that matter, and about to get out of jail on the latter also. At 11.00 a.m. on Friday, 29 September he was placed on another identity parade, this time in Brixton prison. Two men from the City of London made positive identifications that he had been in their shop, picking up a supply of almanacs, on a Thursday lunchtime just over three weeks earlier – precisely the time at which Mrs Dalal suffered her unnerving attack.

Of all the identification parades in the whole A6 affair, this was certainly the most curious. Alphon had not thought to mention the alibi until the day after he was charged. The two men would have had no difficulty recognizing him, as he regularly went to their shop; how they could have been so certain that he was there at that exact time on that exact day is somewhat nebulous. Yet wouldn't their evidence have needed to be as solid as concrete? After all, the police already had a positive identification by Mrs Dalal. In normal circumstances, that should have been sufficient evidence to bring charges against Alphon.

The outcome was that this business redounded entirely to Alphon's advantage. Immediately following the Brixton identity parade he was granted bail by Mortlake magistrates. Then he returned to court the following Tuesday, 3 October, to hear the prosecution request his discharge. Alphon walked from court a free man. The magistrates awarded him 50 guineas (£50, 50 shillings; £52 10s) out of public funds, though this was to pay his legal costs. However, he was able to make money on his own account by selling his story to the *Daily Express*.

On 24 September, senior officers on the A6 inquiry team held a meeting with officials from the Director of Public Prosecutions, doubtless to rethink their strategy. It must have been a very black Monday morning. After the identification parade at Guy's Hospital concluded with Valerie Storie not only failing to pick out Alphon, but actually 'identifying' one of the parade volunteers, police embarrassment must have been acute. This was Scotland Yard; if the detectives believed their own mythology, they'd have thought themselves part of the finest police force in the world. Amid lively public interest and intense media scrutiny, they'd revealed their hand by publicizing the name of the man they wished to interview. 'The problem with naming a suspect', explained Brian Hilliard, 'is that if he turns out not to be the right man, then it's egg all over.' It indeed now seemed that Alphon had nothing to do with it. It *was* egg all over.

There were three reasons, it seemed, why Acott now believed that Alphon was in the clear. It was partly because Alphon had confounded police expectations by turning himself in; partly because Acott seemed to believe (though on precisely what basis remains a total mystery) that Alphon had disarmed suspicions during interview; and mostly because Storie was unable to identify him (yet it was less than two weeks since she had told Acott directly that she 'may not be able to pick him out').

For all their efforts over the previous month, the police had unearthed only one bona fide clue: the cartridge cases at the Vienna Hotel. But inquiries there had thrown up another name arousing suspicion.

So Detective Superintendent Acott went back to the Vienna Hotel – or at least had the key staff brought to him at Scotland Yard. Robert Crocker could do little more than look over the books again. Acott re-interviewed Juliana Galves, who seemed to have nothing of substance to add to her earlier statements. This was a pity, as she was a palpably honest witness.

Acott was left with Nudds and Snell. His aim was to establish the truth, so this was an elementary example of trying to make bricks without straw. This time, he decided to interrogate Florence Snell first. At 11.15 in the morning, she was shown to his office. With two short breaks, the interview lasted until 2.15 p.m. An hour later, Nudds was summoned. On this occasion, however, the two were given no opportunity to coordinate their stories.

By the end of the day, both had given fresh witness evidence in which they withdrew their second statements and re-affirmed the testimony of their original ones. This accordingly meant that Alphon now had what Acott termed 'a perfect alibi' to add to the other factors exculpating him; and that Acott was handed a genuine alternative suspect: a man named Ryan.

Ryan was first brought into the case by William Nudds; neither Galves nor Crocker had mentioned him. Suddenly, his was the only name in the frame. But who was he? And where was he?

• II •
THE ARREST

THE MAN WHO entered this case as Jim Ryan was born James Francis Hanratty on 4 October 1936. At that time his parents were living in Farnborough, near Orpington, in what was then Kent but has since become part of Greater London. James Hanratty senior had left Drogheda in Ireland, at the age of fourteen, to come to England. He was employed as a labourer on building sites and worked on the construction of Wembley Stadium. His wife Mary came from Durham. They had three more sons after James. Michael followed, on 5 February 1939; Peter and Richard were born after the end of the war, in 1945 and 1947 respectively.

Soon after James's birth the family moved diagonally across London, from south-east to north-west, to 29 Hillfield Avenue, Wembley. The family always remembered one particular incident at that house: during an air-raid, the four-year-old James was being carried to safety by his father but they weren't quite quick enough. A bomb dropped next door. The force from the blast blew them both into the garden shelter, with the father landing heavily on top of his son.

In July 1944, with the war dragging on longer than anticipated, and London and the south-east coming under sustained attack from the V1 pilot-less flying bombs (the so-called doodlebugs), there was a fresh exodus of children from the capital. James and Michael Hanratty were evacuated to the north-west of the country.

'Our mum put us on the train at King's Cross,' recollected Michael, 'with our sandwich-boxes and the labels pinned to our coats saying who we were. We had to stand all the way. It was completely packed – entirely with children. There were just a few adult supervisors.

'We were taken to Barrow-in-Furness, in Cumberland, and arrived late in the evening after an all-day journey. We were all put in a big hall. Then the public came round and inspected us and picked out the children they wanted. This couple, Mr and Mrs

Everside, chose Jimmy. He said, "You can't have me without my brother, we're a pair." They said they only wanted one, so they took him away. I was very upset. But then they came back for me. Jimmy had told them he wouldn't go with them unless I went too. I've always remembered that.'[1]

They stayed for about a year. When they returned, it was to a small council flat, at Elthorne Court, Church Lane, Kingsbury. Then their father, who had been serving in the Navy, came home and, in 1947, the family moved to a semi-detached council house, 12 Sycamore Grove.

Once back in London, James was enrolled at St James's Catholic School, Orange Hill Road, Burnt Oak. There the headmistress, Sister Catherine, had him examined by a school doctor. The latter recommended that the young James should be sent to a special school for children whom administrators then termed backward. James's parents did not agree, however, and so he completed his schooling, such as it was, at St James's. He left in July 1951.

His father was then employed as a dustman. By December, his son was also working for the public cleansing department of Wembley Borough Council. His job was to sort refuse, and he loathed it. However, he stuck at it until, in July 1952, he fell off his bicycle. He landed on his head, and remained unconscious for ten hours. He was kept under observation for a few days at Wembley hospital.

He was supposed to go back a week after his discharge, to get signed off so that he could return to work, but he never did. Instead, he went out one morning with Michael to the corner-shop. They took the ration-book and bought some sweets, but James gave them to Michael and sent him back home alone. It was the first sign of James's itineracy. 'He was forever looking for something,' said Michael, 'always searching for adventure, always chasing an elusive dream.'

'We saw no more of him for a month,' recalled his father, 'until the police came and told us they thought they'd traced him. He was in the Royal Sussex Hospital in Brighton. Would I go down and identify him?'[2]

In the month that he had been missing, James had found work with a Mr Smith in Brighton, loading logs on to lorries. He would come into London with the driver to deliver them. 'He used to sleep in the lorry. He had very little food, and collapsed. He was found in Brighton, unconscious and suffering from exposure,' explained his father. 'That was how he came to be in hospital.'

Doctors wondered whether James had suffered a brain hae-morrhage, and carried out a craniotomy (an exploratory brain operation). Incisions were made in each side of the skull, but there were no indications of haemorrhage. It seems, however, that when doctors concluded their reports, they wrote that they considered James to be mentally defective.

The surgeon who performed the operation told the family that there was nothing to worry about. Apart from his shaved head, James appeared normal when he returned home. At the suggestion of the Royal Sussex's neurological registrar, he spent two weeks recuperating with an aunt, Mary's sister, in Bedford, where in earlier years he and Michael had spent some summer holidays.

After that, James got a job in Wembley Park, driving a mechani-cal shovel for Green Brothers, a company that made breeze-blocks. It was a time of full employment, a baby boom, and a post-war housing shortage. The breeze-block trade was especially buoyant. James worked there for the next three years, until all thoughts of steady work were overwhelmed by successive terms of imprisonment.

His criminal career started in a small way, at Harrow magistrates' court on 7 September 1954. James was convicted of taking and driving away a motor-cycle without the owner's consent. Neither did he have insurance, nor a driving licence. He was placed on probation for twelve months, and disqualified from driving for the same period.

Shortly afterwards, in November, he underwent his medical examination for National Service. He failed. He was classified Grade III, unfit for service, on the grounds of illiteracy.

Hanratty had succumbed early to the superficial glamour of Soho in London's West End. 'He couldn't earn money fast enough,' explained Michael. 'When he was working on the shovel, making breeze-blocks, he'd be getting £6–£7 for a fifty-hour week. Once he started going down the West End as a teenager, he found he could get ready money. That's what led him astray.

'We both used to go up to Solomon's gym in Great Windmill Street. The gym was upstairs. Downstairs, there was an all-night billiard hall. Jimmy knew everybody there, they were all villains, dressed in sharp Italian suits and expensive shoes.'

Just round the corner, in Archer Street, was the Rehearsal Club, a drinking club and gathering-place for small-time (and not so small-time) criminals. 'You could play cards or snooker, and it had girlie shows. There were some beautiful women there: the girls, the clothes, the easy money. It was one hell of an attractive lifestyle.

'He loved gambling. We all used to go to the dogs regularly at Wembley. You know the feeling: before the races, you're in a good mood. By the end of the night, you've lost everything, you feel sick, and you know it's going to take another week's work to make up what you've lost. But Jimmy would be able to slip down to Soho, and someone would give him money. He'd say, "Wait here, I'll nip down the Rehearsal, someone owes me." He'd come back with £20. I didn't ask too many questions.'

In August 1955 Hanratty was charged with housebreaking and remanded in custody. While there, he tried to commit suicide by slashing his wrists. The prison medical officer came to the conclusion that he was a potential psychopath with hysterical tendencies. This opinion was, as far as can be ascertained, shared by no one else who ever examined Hanratty.

Because of the delay for hospital treatment, the case was not heard until 6 October. James was then convicted at Middlesex sessions, on two counts of housebreaking and theft. Four other cases of housebreaking and one of burglary were taken into consideration. The upshot was a first custodial sentence: two years' imprisonment.

He was released on 2 February 1957, but by 3 July was back in the dock. He later explained what had happened: 'I met a man called Bill, from Bloxwich, Walsall, who taught me how to drive. We nicked a car from the West End [of London]. It was a Ford Zephyr, with continental plates. After two days, we abandoned it in Leighton Buzzard. Then we took a Morris Oxford 10. I took Bill to Brighton, where I left him with the car. I took a Humber Hawk, but I got caught.'

He was charged with stealing a motor-car, driving without insurance and without a driving licence. A further case of taking without the owner's consent was taken into consideration. This was his third court appearance. Once arrested, he always behaved with complete openness, pleading guilty and coming clean about further offences. He was given six months, with a second sentence of three months to run concurrently. Additionally, he was fined 10 shillings and disqualified from driving for two years – although that was already becoming an irrelevant sanction in Hanratty's case, since he'd shown no inclination to become qualified.

He served four months in Walton Prison, Liverpool, but was soon in more serious trouble. Again, the offences involved cars. On

26 March 1958 he was convicted at the London sessions of two cases of stealing a car and two cases of driving while disqualified. With characteristic candour, he asked for another case of stealing to be taken into consideration. The sentence was severe: three years' corrective training (C.T.).

Hanratty began his time in Wandsworth. On being transferred to Maidstone, he met Laurence Lanigan, who was serving time for grievous bodily harm, with whom he became 'firm friends'. On 2 October, however, just before Lanigan was released, Hanratty was transferred from Maidstone to Camp Hill on the Isle of Wight, as punishment for twice trying to escape. However, he also made two escape attempts while at Camp Hill, one in November 1958 and the other on New Year's Day 1959. From Camp Hill he wrote to his brother, Michael, then doing National Service in Cyprus:

> *Dear Mick,*
> *I was very pleased when you came down and visited me just before you went away. You don't know how pleased I was to see you as at that time I was in a lot of trouble with the prison authorities. After you had seen me, soon after, I got a transfer to Camp Hill. I can assure you that it isn't no camp, Mick.*
>
> *As you know, I was supposed to come out on 24 March 1960, but now there has been a few alterations and it is twelve months later. I haven't told anyone at home yet. I don't know how Mum will take it. You know how she worries. Now you know why I haven't been writing, Mick, because it is a bit of a surprise to me and I haven't got over it yet.*
>
> *Mum told me that you have got a young lady, and it's quite a love affair, so Mum says. As for my own, Mick, I am not really keen. As you know, Gladys is a nice girl, and it's an awful long time to wait.*
>
> *Perhaps you would break the news to Mum sometime, but don't let her be upset about it because apart from that everything is alright.*
> *Mick, keep your chin up,*
> *Your brother, Jim*

From Camp Hill, Hanratty was sent to Strangeways, Manchester, and then, in January 1960, to Durham, where he again met Lanigan, by now serving a different sentence, this time for storebreaking. Hanratty told him he'd been transferred there to give him one last chance to learn a trade while he was doing his C.T. He was working in the blacksmith's shop.

His conduct was not satisfactory, and on 4 November 1960 he was returned to Strangeways as a recalcitrant. He was released from there on 24 March, having served every last day of his original three-year sentence. He had spent fifty-eight of the sixty-six months that had elapsed since his nineteenth birthday in prison. He was desperate not to return.

'No sooner had Jimmy arrived back home from prison than he disappeared,' recalled Michael. It turned out that he had found work with the British Steel company in Middlesbrough. However, after just a week, he abruptly quit the job, without even bothering to go and pick up his cards. On Thursday, 13 April, without prior warning, he arrived home and announced to his surprised but delighted family that he'd come back to make a real attempt to settle down.

There was nothing that James and Mary Hanratty wanted more. They thought nothing of re-arranging their lives to accommodate their eldest son. Ten years earlier, his father had helped to find him work in his own council department. Now he resolved that his best course of action was to leave work himself so that he and James could go into business together. Hanratty and Son: Window-Cleaners.

The wisdom of trying to wean a recidivist cat-burglar away from the temptations of his trade by setting him up in the window-cleaning business may have been debatable. The immediate signs, however, were encouraging. To purchase the essential materials Mr Hanratty had cashed his pension contributions, and they picked up steady work in their local vicinity of Kingsbury, north-west London. They laboured together for almost three months.

James was beginning to reap some of the benefits of regular work in a secure family environment. One hot weekend in June, he and Michael joined the tide of London youth – those in their late teens and early twenties – heading for the seaside at Southend.

That particular trip was highly successful. They arrived late on Saturday afternoon to join the youths thronging the seaside resort. Along with hundreds of others, they spent what remained of Saturday night and Sunday morning sleeping underneath the pier. On Sunday, they had a wash-and-brush-up, picked up a couple of girls, went for a drink with them and then took them to the famous Kursaal Fun-fair. In some ways, Jimmy was the ideal elder brother. 'He was all charm,' said Michael. 'He had the talent. He could always – as we used to call it – chat a girl up.'

On Saturday, 8 July, James took Michael along with him to Burnt Oak. He went to Hepworth's, the well-established men's outfitters, to be measured for a new bespoke suit. He chose a blue and black herringbone pattern and the most fashionable, Italian-style design. He ordered a double-breasted jacket, box-fitting (as the term was), a double-breasted waistcoat with an additional pocket for a wad of notes, and tapered trousers without turn-ups. It was, he admitted, 'rather flashy'.

That Saturday was profoundly significant. It was the day that James and Mary went on holiday to Southsea. The father thought the business would be capably looked after in his absence by James. For a few days it was; he kept on with the appointments in an unenthusiastic fashion. Then, without warning, it all came to an end. On the Thursday morning, Michael noticed the ladders leaning against the side of a customer's house. James had flown. 'I had no particular reason for leaving,' he later admitted, 'except that I was rather fed up with window-cleaning.'[3] His family never saw him again as a free man.

James couldn't cope with the humdrum. Window-cleaning didn't set the adrenalin pumping. He headed back to central London and the diverse attractions of Soho. He resumed his burglaries. From a succession of house-breakings in some of the well-to-do outlying districts of north London – Harrow, Wembley, Stanmore and Edgware – he accumulated significant sums of money. He would be needing that extra waistcoat pocket on the suit.

He explained his modus operandi: 'I never use gloves. I carry a spare handkerchief and use it to pick up articles or clean off fingerprints afterwards. Gloves give you away. I never carry anything which can pull me in for suspicion.

'Friday is the best day for business – people are out shopping and the children are at school. I always work on my own. I often change my area. I usually do night jobs, but sometimes work during the day as well. All my jobs are big ones.'

Nor was this mere braggadocio. He was, by contemporary standards, very well rewarded. For his few short months of freedom he often had quantities of cash at his disposal. 'I always get good stuff. I specialize in jewellery and silver, and have also taken furs. The most money I have got is £450. I have given a lot away.'

Then there were the car thefts. He had an obsessive interest in cars, and was very knowledgeable about them. He'd learned the basics of driving on the fork-lift truck and lorries in the builder's yard. Bill from Bloxwich taught him the rest. James quickly became adept. He initially started stealing cars purely for the pleasure he got from driving. Then he began stealing to order. 'He did once tell me the procedure involved,' recalled Michael. 'Someone would ask for a certain car. He'd go out and look for it, and take it and then park it in a pre-arranged place. They'd pick it up a few days afterwards.'

At the age of twenty-four, Hanratty was a prime example of someone for whom prison acts only as a training-ground in crime. He had no skills other than illicit ones. His background, connections, experiences: all were indelibly criminal. His record and lifestyle appeared to tell its own story; he had been found guilty in four separate trials, and sentenced to three separate terms of imprisonment. He would generally have been regarded as a habitual criminal. In several respects, however, James remained an innocent abroad. With his fair auburn hair, wide-open blue eyes and ready smile, he looked naive and innocuous. Adult vices like smoking and drinking were, well, for adults; he did neither.

Nor was he prone to violence. No one had even seen him involved in a fight. 'In his view, he never hurt anybody,' explained Michael. 'He only stole from rich people. It didn't matter, they'd got insurance: we know it's wrong, but that's the way he thought.'

His illiteracy remained a constant handicap, a source of great personal embarrassment. 'I can read and write,' he told his solicitors, 'although I admit I am not fluent. I cannot spell very well and I find difficulty in pronouncing hard words and reading them.' To be able to gauge his competence, the lawyers set him a series of basic spelling and mental arithmetic tests. They discovered he could cope with neither. Not only could he not spell; he had no conception of how to set about the task. Solicitor? 'SLETER,' he essayed. Excursion? 'EXCHNER' was the best he could do. And so on. 'I used to write all his letters for him,' revealed Laurence Lanigan, 'because he was unable to do it himself.'[4]

Socially, therefore, he was often ill-at-ease. He was punching well above his weight by trying to fraternize in some of London's more unscrupulous circles, where he was regarded merely with condescension. The owner of the Rehearsal Club, Mrs Roberts, described him as 'so quiet and polite – he was naive, you know, and people would take liberties with him'.[5]

In one other vital regard he was self-deluded. Like others before him, he interpreted his resolution to stay out of prison in terms not of giving up crime but of not getting caught. For Hanratty, this was destined to be another elusive dream.

*

For his first few days in the West End after abandoning the window-cleaning business he stayed in comfortable hotels like the Imperial in Russell Square and the Adelphi in Cromwell Road. Then, in Soho, as he was going into the Rehearsal Club, he literally bumped into an old acquaintance.

Charles Frederick Franz (a surname which, if it's not a contradiction, he anglicized to France) was born on 13 June 1919. He, too, had a chequered past. He was just twenty when war broke out in 1939, but by that time he had already acquired five criminal convictions: two for larceny, one for selling fruit in a restricted place, one for being in unlawful possession of an overcoat and one for stealing lead from the roof of a block of unoccupied dwellings.

During the war he collected six further convictions, two for theft and three for 'frequenting a common gaming house'. There were additionally three post-war convictions, all for gambling offences.

Although he had not seen him since his release from prison, and had not kept in touch while inside, Hanratty did know France from several years earlier. He knew him as 'Dixie'. They'd probably become acquainted sometime in 1955, when Hanratty's exploits as a burglar were just getting underway. He explained that France had, to some extent, taken him under his wing: 'I met him when I was a teenager and didn't know the ropes. I had lots of dealings in bits and pieces. He was more experienced.' Characteristically, the inarticulate Hanratty faltered in trying to find words to describe their relationship. All he could muster in summary was, 'He learned me previous occasions when I was younger.'

Here was the doomed Hanratty receiving tutelage from this abject man: a man just about as guileless and feckless as he; a man whose lack of moral fibre did not even enable him to make a success out of being a criminal. Ultimately, Hanratty himself came to regard France almost with contempt: 'I have often given him sums of money. He has been out of work since I have known him. He is a general layabout.'

On this occasion, France at least offered the prospect of companionship. They went for a cup of tea together. 'He told me he'd had a row with his family,' France testified. 'I invited him home for some supper. We talked until one in the morning. He stayed the night, sleeping on the sofa in the front room, and left the next day.'[6]

France had a flat in Boundary Road, just off the Finchley Road, very close to Swiss Cottage. It seems that he had at least managed to keep his family in ignorance of his petty criminal ways. His wife,

Charlotte, and three daughters of whom Carole was the eldest, seemed to have no inkling of the 'business' he conducted when he went up to town. At home he was Charles, the well-loved father of the family; in Soho he was Dixie, the small-time crook and gofer.

The France family came to regard Hanratty with some fondness. He stayed with them on several occasions. They offered him hospitality and came to accept him as almost an extra member of the family. Carole referred to him as 'Uncle Jim'. Sometime around this time, possibly in the middle of July, she dyed his hair. Hanratty apparently observed Carole applying mascara, and remarked that he needed something like that for his hair. The real reason for this was his concern that his light auburn hair made him too conspicuous when he was committing burglaries during daylight. He was well known to acquaintances as 'Ginger' Hanratty. He felt, probably correctly, that if the police heard of any burglary being committed by a light-haired man, they'd automatically associate it with him. So Carole, who was an apprentice hairdresser and perhaps grateful for the opportunity to demonstrate her tyro skills, turned his hair black. Hanratty, delighted with the results, gave her £2.[7]

Then he disappeared again. On Friday, 21 July, he embarked on a fresh adventure, initially with a friend called Terry. 'We stole a black Ford Consul from Park Road running alongside Hendon Cottage Hospital. Half-way down there is an estate, the car was parked just there. It had a radio, and there was a straw sunhat on the back seat. We stole it at night, between midnight and 1.00 a.m.

'We drove north. We ran short of money, so we sold the spare wheel in Birmingham for £3 so we could get some petrol. We went to Shrewsbury, but there we had a puncture. We were parked in the town centre, near the hospital. It was about 11.00 p.m. A policeman came over to ask me if we were having trouble. It was obvious the tyre was flat. He became suspicious and eventually asked for my driving licence.

'It was a warm evening and I had my coat off. It was in the car. I went round to the driver's door while the constable stood on the pavement with my mate. I just leaned over the steering-column, but didn't bother to get my coat. I just ran off. I left the constable holding my friend.' Hanratty, recognizing some measure of personal shame, added: 'It was not a very good gesture on my behalf.'

While the policeman held on to Terry, Hanratty tried to make good his escape. 'Ten minutes later, I was walking back through the centre, looking for a lorry to give me a lift so I could get out of town. As I came to a bridge, a police car pulled up about ten yards in front of me. I ran down some steps at the side of the bridge, and then along the embankment. One PC gave chase, while another ran across the bridge to block me off on the other side. But I had a start on them, and managed to hide where some old trucks were. I hid in one of them. I could hear them searching, but they didn't find me. I stayed there until daybreak.

'I didn't know where I was going to go. I was frightened my mate would have given a full description of me. Eventually, a lorry came along and I got on it.'

The lorry was going to Cardiff, but the driver dropped Hanratty off at Newport because he was not allowed to carry passengers. Another truck-driver took him into Cardiff, and Hanratty spent the night at the Salvation Army hostel in Bute Street. By now, he was so short of money that he was ready to consider anything, even work. First thing in the morning, he went along to the Labour Exchange, where he obtained a fresh National Insurance card. He then walked out of Cardiff for some distance, before being picked up by a lorry travelling north.

Where he spent that evening is not clear. The following day, he got another lift with a lorry that took him to the outskirts of Liverpool.

'I only had a few shillings left. I knew the only way I could get back to London was to break into a house and steal something. At about three o'clock in the afternoon, I got a Red Ribble bus to Crosby. On the Southport Road, we passed an Odeon picture house, and there was a church with a small brick wall. I got off at the bus-stop on the other side of the church. Two turnings past that there was a drive with a white board saying "PRIVATE". The houses were well-to-do. The trees were big, there was a gardener sweeping up, and a large clubhouse for tennis or golf. I walked past that and broke into the next house I came to.

'I took a large amount of silver which I put in my pockets, including silver serviette rings, and a silver cigarette box. I also got a big Ronson table-lighter. Downstairs in the living-room, on one of those little tables you write letters on, there were two little money-boxes full of sixpences. I took those. I also took a clean shirt.

'It was getting late. I got a paper bag and put all the silver into it. At about 5.00 in the afternoon, I went into a jeweller's in Liverpool, one on a corner at the back of the dance-hall. He weighed it and gave me 25 shillings. He also gave me a book to sign. This took me by surprise' – clearly Hanratty wasn't accustomed to dealing with such scrupulous traders – 'so I used my own name and address.'

At a wash-and-brush-up in Liverpool, he changed into the stolen clean shirt and threw away his dirty one. He took a bus to Rhyl, and arrived there sometime after 6.00, on what was now the early evening of Tuesday, 25 July.

With his predilection for fun-fairs, he immediately set off towards the bright lights and vivacity of the Ocean Beach amusement park. There he met Terry Evans, a man of almost his own age and very similar inclinations. Evans was well known locally, both because of the distinctive old black London taxi (a 1935 or 1936 model, according to Hanratty) which he owned and usually parked prominently at the top of the fairground; and because of the black star tattooed between his eyebrows. Terry Starr, some called him. He had convictions for a number of minor offences, including driving without due care and attention, failing to stop after an accident, and poaching. He was regarded as a man of some ill-repute; someone, like Hanratty and France, on the fringes of criminality. If anyone would have known how to dispose of stolen property in Rhyl, Evans would have.

However, Hanratty momentarily had something more above-board in mind. He asked if there was any work going. Evans consulted his boss, Arthur Webber, and Hanratty was taken on immediately. He was even able to give Webber his newly obtained National Insurance card.

For the remainder of the evening, about three or four hours, Hanratty worked as an attendant on the dodgems, with Terry Evans trying to give him on-the-job instruction. At the end of the night, Evans offered to put up Hanratty in his council house. They sat up for some time talking. Evans kindly loaned him a pair of shoes that he'd just bought for £3 15s. After the wear-and-tear of recent days in Shrewsbury, Cardiff and Liverpool, Hanratty's own shoes were falling apart. Then, in what was becoming a familiar routine, Hanratty bedded down on the sofa in the front room.

In the morning they had breakfast before Evans gave Hanratty a lift to the fairground. Evans himself could not go straight in to work because he had a pressing engagement elsewhere: in court. He was charged with the theft of sparking-plugs valued at £2 10s. The hearing went well for him – he was conditionally discharged – but when he arrived at Ocean Beach later that morning, he learned that Hanratty had not turned up for work. It seemed that the latter wasn't thrilled with that occupation, either: 'It was very draughty being on the sea-front. It was a bad night that night, and I did not like the job.' Hanratty, still wearing Evans's shoes, had moved on again.

He returned to Liverpool. Later that evening, as he was coming out of a café, he was approached by two men who said aggressively, 'We've had nothing to eat all day. How about buying us a meal?' Hanratty indicated that he couldn't: 'I'm short myself.' One of them said, 'Don't tell lies – give us your money.' Hanratty had noticed the knuckleduster in the hand of the other, so he knew a fight was about to start. He punched the one who'd spoken to him. They quickly overpowered him, knocking him to the ground. By a stroke of fortune, some people came round the corner at that moment, and the attackers made off.

The police were called. Hanratty was carried into a police-box on Lime Street. His knee was injured in the scuffle, he couldn't walk properly. An ambulance was called to take him to hospital. 'I used the name "Hanratty",' he recollected, 'there was no point in using any other name. The police wanted me to give a description of the men who jumped me.'

Hanratty couldn't help much. He just about managed to fill in, as sketchily as possible, a few details about who he was and what he was doing there ('I said I'd just come back from Rhyl where I'd been working on the fairground'). After his wounds were dressed, Hanratty paid 4s for a bed in a hostel. The following morning, he sold the lighter and a few other items left over from the Crosby burglary. It was enough to provide him with the train fare back to London.

On his return to London, Hanratty reappeared on the Frances' doorstep. He would have been welcomed anyway, but just to make sure he'd bought flowers and chocolates for Charlotte and he took the children out to buy them some sweets. He accepted their hospitality on a number of occasions, and certainly stayed with them over the bank holiday weekend. (In those days, the August bank holiday was the first, not the last, Monday in the month.) Carole got the black dye out and set to work on his hair again.

Then, in a matter which became the subject of intriguing dispute, Dixie and Hanratty went out together. The former's version of what occurred went as follows:

'On holiday Monday morning, he said, "Would you like to come to Hendon dog track with me?" and I said, "Yes." We went together to Hendon. I think it was about 10.00 a.m. We did not have any luck. When we left, we waited about half-an-hour for a bus. The sun was shining. It was hot, and he sat on the grass verge. When the bus came, it was empty, and we went upstairs. I went to go towards the front seat, and he pulled me back towards the rear seat and made a remark something like, "This is the only seat on the bus that lifts up and it is a good hiding-place." [8]

Two-and-a-half weeks later that, coincidentally or not, was where the murder weapon was found. Hanratty, while never denying the thrust of the conversation, always maintained that it occurred in different circumstances.

Prior to this, Hanratty had made the acquaintance of another of the Soho *demi-monde*, Louise Anderson. A forty-eight-year-old widow, she kept an antique shop, Juna Antiques, at 57 Greek Street, Soho. One day in July Hanratty, who clearly understood which line of business she was really in, went in and offered her various articles for sale – for instance, a silver Georgian plate and a silver-plated, brand-new coffee service.

In her early statements to police, she affirmed vehemently that she had always declined to buy anything from Hanratty. This was completely false. On the contrary, it seemed that a relationship – though not a sexual one – developed between them; and very soon Hanratty was taking the spoils from all his housebreakings direct to her, despite the fact that she appeared to give him particularly poor prices. Later, on 20 October, the police seized from her shop over fifty expensive items of doubtful provenance. These included many pieces of jewellery, as well as cine-cameras, binoculars and an electric razor. They seem to have represented some of the booty from numerous burglaries in the London area. Not all of these, of course, would have been committed by Hanratty: Louise Anderson was known to all as a fence, and doubtless had dealings with a variety of crooks. (A 'fence' was argot for a middleman, who received stolen items and then sold them on quasi-legitimately. The fence thus took the least amount of risk and the lion's share of the profits.)

On Sunday, 13 August, Hanratty took Louise out for dinner. Afterwards, they went back to her flat in Sussex Gardens, and he was able to give her first refusal of the takings from a robbery he'd carried out just the previous day, in broad daylight, in the Harrow area.

Altogether, it was a more than satisfactory haul: a solitaire ring; seven eternity rings, some ruby with surrounding pearls; a gentleman's ring; six sets of gold cuff-links with the initial 'E' on them; £14 in cash from a woman's purse in the bedroom; a three-quarter-length fur coat – 'not mink, I think it was ermine' – and a brand-new German Bolex cine-camera, in a leather pigskin case, which Hanratty noticed in the living-room on his way out.

Louise gave Hanratty £45 for the fur coat, and £15 for the cine-camera, a price he accepted, he later confessed, 'because I didn't know what it was worth then'.

After their meal on the Sunday, Hanratty stayed the night at Louise's flat, albeit not in any great comfort. He slept straddled across two chairs. From this juncture, however, whenever he was in London, he invariably bedded down for the night either on the Frances' sofa or Louise's two chairs.

Eileen Cunningham, Hanratty's cousin, was startled to see him in Willesden on Thursday, 17 August. They had a close relationship, but she hadn't seen him for some time. 'He called over to me across the street. I did not recognize him. His hair was dyed, absolutely jet-black. You would not have been able to tell he was really ginger.'[9]

Hanratty told Eileen that he was trying to arrange a date with a girl. 'He phoned her twice, at two different numbers,' Eileen said. 'I know, I had to dial for him – he finds difficulty in dialling phone numbers.' (The London phone numbers of that era were always three letters followed by four numerals.)

It is not clear who this girl was. However, around this time he asked Ann Pryce to go out with him. She was hardly a girl, being much older than he (she'd been born in Jamaica on 5 April 1918), and was employed at the Rehearsal Club. Dixie introduced them, probably in July.

'He said his name was Jimmy Ryan,' she recalled. 'I asked him what he did for a living. He said he did not work, but sometimes went thieving – just enough to live by. I asked him if he had ever been to prison and he said, "Yes." I told him he should get a job. He said I would not understand and left the club shortly afterwards.'[10]

When he next showed up, he asked Ann to go out with him and she agreed to go to the pictures with him. He took her to the cartoon cinema in Charing Cross Road, just round the corner from Old Compton Street. They only stayed about half-an-hour. While they were there, he told her that he soon had to go to Liverpool.

Friday, 18 August was a red-letter day. Hanratty picked up his suit – it cost £13 5s – from Hepworth's in Burnt Oak. Throughout that weekend, he stayed with Louise Anderson; but on the Saturday at lunchtime he called in to see the France family. He was carrying a suitcase full of dirty clothing. He asked Charlotte if she could do his washing for him, and pack his case. On Monday, he said, he had to go to Liverpool.

Now that he was proudly wearing his new suit he was able to take another, a green check suit – the pillage of yet another burglary – to be cleaned. On Monday morning, he went to Burtol's Cleaners in the arcade at Swiss Cottage. He gave his name as Ryan, his address as the non-existent 72 Boundary Road, and asked for the suit to be cleaned and altered; he wanted the trousers tapered.

He then walked the short distance to the Frances', to collect his suitcase. Charlotte had done everything for him. In his brown pigskin suitcase, she'd packed five clean shirts, all plain white with collars attached, four or five ties, some socks, pyjamas and toiletries. When he arrived, Carole was lying drowsily on the settee, having just had a tooth removed at the dentist's. He stayed a few hours. Charlotte gave him some tea, and he left soon after 5.00. He gave her £15 so that she could get her sewing-machine and clock out of pawn. He left another £15 for Dixie. They wished him well. 'Send us a postcard,' cried Charlotte. Then he was gone.

He'd told Ann Pryce he had to go to Liverpool to visit a friend in prison. He'd told the Frances he was going to visit an aunt who lived there. (He did indeed have an aunt in Liverpool, albeit one whom he hadn't seen for ten years.) He later explained to his lawyers that he hadn't been able to tell Charlotte the real reason for his visit: 'I was going to get rid of stolen rings. Three men with whom I stayed in Liverpool had connections, I thought they could get me the best price. I didn't want to tell Mrs France that I was going to Liverpool to dispose of stolen property.'

He said he hadn't been able to sell the rings in London. Although one fence had told him the jewellery was fake, Hanratty was sure it was all genuine. Louise, he said, had run out of money at that time. So he thought of Aspinall, whom he'd known in prison, although Hanratty couldn't quite remember where he lived. It was Talbot or Carlton or Tarleton Road – something like that – in Liverpool. That was his primary reason for going. Of course, the other reason for going was simply his wanderlust; he never liked staying any-where for very long.

Louise was able to purchase some of the takings from the Harrow robbery and he sold other small pieces of jewellery and trinkets to a jeweller in Kilburn. That left him with four rings, which he thought quite valuable, and which he kept in a handkerchief in his pocket. He also carried a gold Omega wrist-watch, which bore the inscription: 'To Tony, from Mother, with Love'. He estimated its value at £170, and thought he might be able to get £40 for it. Accordingly, he resolved to sell these in Liverpool; although, as with everything Hanratty did, what was notionally a hard-and-fast scheme became desultory and half-hearted in execution.

After leaving the Frances, Hanratty went to the left-luggage office at Leicester Square. He kept a second, smaller case there. It contained money, jewellery, and yet more items of dirty laundry. He left a sixpenny tip, and took out the case. He went to the wash-and-brush-up next door. In one of the cubicles, he took out the jewellery and the money, putting the jewellery into the pigskin case, and the money into the waistcoat pocket of his suit. He left the small case in the toilets, leaving the door ajar. He went back to the left-luggage counter, and paid sixpence to leave the pigskin case. Then he went back for the little case, still containing three dirty shirts, and several pairs of soiled socks. He dumped it in a dustbin, in the alley by the side of the Empire cinema.

Then he walked on to the Rehearsal Club, where he saw Ann Pryce again. He bought her a drink and chatted briefly to her. 'You look smart,' Ann commented. He left after about thirty minutes. He walked along Archer Street and into Windmill Street. He had a beef sandwich, and bought a racing paper. He saw the runners for the evening meeting at Hendon dog track. It was then about 6.45. On the spur of the moment, he decided to go.

He got a taxi and arrived in time: the meeting was about fifteen minutes behind schedule, and started at 7.45 instead of 7.30. He went into the main grandstand, sat at a table on his own, and ordered steak and chips. A woman went around the tables collecting bets. He bet on all the races and lost heavily. He did have two winners, but ended up about £70 out of pocket. That left him, he estimated, with about £12–14.

He left in a rush, before the last race, because he'd suddenly remembered his case at the left-luggage office, which he thought might close at 10.30. He took another taxi back to Leicester Square and retrieved his suitcase.

Still he didn't go to the station to set off to Liverpool. Instead, he went to have 'a short time' with a prostitute. She had a room over a club just behind the Palace Theatre, probably in Romilly Street. She knew him well. He was a regular client, and she had seen him 'probably two or three times a week for nearly two months'.

Afterwards, he went back to the Rehearsal again, where he had a Babycham. By this time, Hanratty, having spent several hours procrastinating, realized that it was too late to go to Liverpool.

He called another taxi, and told the driver to take him to a hotel. 'I had no particular place in mind,' he recalled afterwards. The cabbie took him to a hotel which Hanratty remembered as being close to Baker Street station. From the description he gave, however, and from their subsequent inquiries, the lawyers were able to establish that it was definitely the Broadway House Hotel in Portman Square. (In fact, it was just off Baker Street, but not especially close to the station.) The hotel was full. The owner – whom Hanratty described, succinctly if not charitably, as 'a foreigner, about fifty, he's fat' – did have a room available at another hotel that he owned. He arranged a room for Hanratty there, and advised him to take a cab. Hanratty, of course, would have considered nothing less.

He again hailed a taxi. He told the driver to take him to Maida Vale, to the Vienna Hotel. It was almost midnight on Monday, 21 August, the night before the A6 Murder.

ON THE MORNING of Tuesday, 26 September, Detective Superintendent Acott and Detective Sergeant Oxford embarked on their quest to find Ryan. Two days earlier, the case against Alphon had collapsed when Valerie Storie did not identify him; the previous day, Monday, the policemen had spent interviewing those refractory Vienna Hotel employees, William Nudds and Florence Snell.

They went to the address Ryan had given in the Vienna Hotel register, 72 Wood Lane, Kingsbury. There they spoke to George Pratt, a respectable toolmaker who had lived in the house for twenty-five years. As far as he knew, no one called Ryan had ever lived there. However, he could help the police because he had recently received a letter addressed to Mr Ryan. Acott opened it and saw that it came from a car-hire firm in Dublin (also called Ryan's), enclosing paperwork connected with a car rental.

That afternoon, Acott and Oxford went to Hanratty's home at 12 Sycamore Grove and told his parents that their son was wanted for car theft. James and Mary were, of course, unable to assist in any way, not having heard from him since early July. They took the view that Jimmy had to take whatever punishment was coming to him, and agreed to tell Acott as soon as they heard from him; Acott likewise promised to let them know if he traced him first.

Between those two separate inquiries lies much that needs to be explained. How did the police get from A (the visit to Pratt, checking on Ryan) to B (the family home, checking on Hanratty)? In other words, how did they discover that Ryan was Hanratty? The question is absolutely pivotal in the case; yet it has never been conclusively answered.

The police – behaving, perhaps, like scrupulous journalists – have always refused to reveal their sources. At the trial, Detective Sergeant Oxford said that 'actually on the 25th September, we had in fact identified the man Ryan as being possibly Hanratty'; but no additional information was elicited from him.[1]

Years later, in 1974, the then retired Bob Acott gave an account, through his solicitors, of how the critical link was made. According to this, it was provided by Gerrard Leonard, a commercial traveller with whom Hanratty spent an evening and shared a room at O'Flynn's hotel in Cork earlier in September. In the morning, Hanratty asked Leonard if he'd mind writing some postcards for him, 'as my handwriting isn't too good'. Leonard obliged, and found himself writing six postcards in all, two each to Mrs Hanratty, the France family, and Louise Anderson. Hanratty was grateful, and gave Leonard a packet of twenty cigarettes.

This was what Acott's solicitor wrote:

> The first time that Mr Acott heard of the name 'Hanratty' was at 6.00 p.m. on 25 September when, in consequence of the extraordinary memory of Gerrard Leonard, he learned from Dublin police that Mr Leonard had shared a room with James Ryan at Flynn's Hotel, Cork, and had written postcards to Mrs Louise Anderson, 'Dixie' France and to his mother Mrs Hanratty. Leonard remembered the name and address of Mrs Hanratty because he noted that the mother's name dictated by 'Ryan' was not Ryan but Hanratty; also because he was interested in the address as he had a friend in Kingsbury ... Mr and Mrs Hanratty, Mrs Anderson and 'Dixie' France were, in fact, interviewed the day after Mr Acott received the information and the lead from Eire, namely 26 September.[2]

This account cannot possibly be true. On Monday, 25 September, Gerrard Leonard would have needed not just an extraordinary memory but psychic powers to appreciate that police in London were searching for a man called Ryan. Scotland Yard didn't know that themselves, which is why they spent most of the day hammering it out in interviews with Florence Snell and William Nudds. The transcript of the interview with the former indicates that the police were still thrashing around in the dark:

Acott: What are you hiding, Mrs Glickberg?
Snell: I have nothing to cover up.
Acott: Are you covering up Ryan?
Snell: No.
Acott: Who is Ryan?
Snell: Ryan is the man who came in on 21 August, and stayed in Room 24, with a portable radio.
Acott: Do you know Durrant?

Snell: No.

Acott: What is your husband covering up?

Snell: I don't know. He is not my husband.

Acott: Did he commit the murder?

Snell: No, he was in bed all night with me.

Acott: Who's Glickberg covering? Did he give someone a gun?

Snell: That I couldn't tell you.

In the afternoon, Acott interviewed Nudds (Glickberg) and that concluded at 4.45 p.m. By then, the police knew their suspect was Ryan. There is nothing to suggest that they had any idea who he was, and no reason why the aid of police in Dublin would have been enlisted.

Secondly, Leonard, however prodigious his memory, couldn't possibly have told police that Hanratty had sent postcards to Louise Anderson because Hanratty hadn't – not exactly. He had mis-remembered her surname, and had asked Leonard to address them to Louise Andrew. When Hanratty later mentioned 'Louise' to Acott in his telephone conversation of 6 October, it is clear the police had no clear idea who she was. (On 7 October, the *Daily Telegraph* reported, 'The search continues for a woman, known only as Louise, to whom a postcard was sent from Ireland to London.') She was certainly not interviewed by police on 26 September.

So how were the police informed? According to an article in the *Sunday Times* published in December 1966, the police found out when Charles France went to Scotland Yard with one of the postcards which Hanratty had sent the family from Ireland.

Although there is nothing directly to substantiate this, it is a highly persuasive suggestion. If, on the Tuesday morning, the police actually knew that Ryan was Hanratty, then there would have been no point in two such senior officers undertaking the visit to George Pratt themselves. If, alternatively, they had no inkling that Ryan was Hanratty, they were unlikely to have bridged the gap at lunchtime. So the circumstances suggest that they did have some information, which must have been provided after the conclusion of the Nudds/Snell interviews, but which, being from a possibly unreliable source, they were initially treating with some caution. Once the visit to Pratt, however, appeared to corroborate the evidence of the postcard, they then felt confident enough to visit the Hanratty family.

The information they had to link Hanratty to the murder, however, was nebulous in the extreme. Hence they told his parents that their son was wanted for car thefts and running cars over to Ireland. At this stage, they would have been pooling the information they'd obtained from George Pratt, from the postcard to France and from Hanratty's own criminal record. They had nothing else to go on.

During this visit, they also mentioned the name of Dixie France. It meant nothing to James and Mary (in fact, they automatically understood it to be a reference to one of Jimmy's girlfriends), but it is near enough clinching evidence that the postcard theory is correct. Finally, if France did go to Scotland Yard with the postcard, then what Oxford said in court would have been wholly accurate.

Why, however, would France have wanted to provide this information? And how, in any case, would he have known that the police were searching for Ryan at all?

The traditional view, which I do not entirely share, is that this formed part of a conspiracy to frame Hanratty. Whatever did happen, Nudds obviously played a key part, as it was he who first mentioned Ryan and gave incriminating nuances to his conduct. One may speculate that, after leaving Scotland Yard, Nudds contacted Durrant (Alphon), or perhaps France himself, saying, 'They're after Ryan now.' If France went to Scotland Yard at 6.00 p.m., then at least one aspect of the Acott version would be correct – although for that to be true, France would have needed to act with particular haste.

Like virtually all other criminal moves in this case, it was probably a panic reaction. Just as the motive in bringing Ryan in at all had been to throw the scent off Durrant, so now there was a need to take the heat off Ryan. It was certainly no part of a plan to frame Hanratty. After all, France knew well enough where he was: in London. So where did his intervention send the police? On a wild-goose chase across Ireland. On Friday, 29 September Acott and Oxford flew to Dublin in pursuit of their suspect.

Of all the inglorious episodes in this whole saga, the hunt across Ireland was perhaps the most ridiculous. The *Evening News* in London carried a fittingly absurd report: 'Scotland Yard followed the trail in Ireland of a man who dresses as a woman. It is believed that within a day or so of the murder the mystery man boarded the Irish Mail train at Euston dressed as a woman and that was how he broke through the London police cordon.'[3]

Despite the high level of farce, several journalists flew out in the wake of Acott and Oxford, so convinced had everybody become that the trail was hot. Acott enlisted the support of the Garda, and arranged for checks to be carried out at the airports in London and Dublin. Over the weekend in Dublin, Acott and Oxford interviewed witnesses who might have seen Hanratty. They then drove west to Limerick. The reporters dogging the detectives' every move reported excitedly that they were on a '700-mile trail'. On the Monday, following a tip-off, they drove back east, past the Galty mountains, to Clonmel, County Tipperary. There they discovered two runaway lovers, one of whom, a seventeen-year-old girl from Derbyshire, had been made a ward of court. It was a poor return from such high expectations.

They were all still in Ireland when James Hanratty senior, who was fifty-four on 3 October, took one of his birthday cards in to Scotland Yard. Jimmy had remembered the occasion and, characteristically, sent him an expensive card. It was postmarked London. Mr Hanratty said to the officer on duty, 'It is time that Acott stopped fooling around in Ireland and came back to London.'[4]

James Hanratty senior wanted to trace his son as much as Acott did, albeit for an entirely different reason. He'd been at home on his own the previous Friday, the day that Acott went to Ireland, when, at about 8.30 in the evening, the first reporter arrived at his house. It was John King of the *Daily Express*. He had stolen a march on his rivals by discovering the identity of the Yard's second A6 suspect. He was therefore able to impress upon a shaken Hanratty the precise reason why his son was such a wanted man. Of course, Hanratty now understood, it all made sense. Two days after their first visit, Acott and Oxford had returned, catching Mr Hanratty as he arrived home from work. Senior detectives would be unlikely to arrive twice in three days if they were concerned merely about car theft. His aim accordingly became to find Jimmy as speedily as possible so that the whole matter could be cleared up.

The *Express* team now kept the Hanratty family regular company. On Tuesday, 3 October they drove Mr Hanratty and Michael to Scotland Yard; and then to Archer Street, Soho. While the father and the reporters waited outside in the car, Michael went down the stairs and spoke to Ann Pryce. No, she hadn't seen Jimmy; but she did say that Dixie France was expected in shortly. Michael bought a drink and sat down to wait.

'After about an hour, he came in. He had a slim build, and was older than I expected. I could see him talking to Ann Pryce, and her gesturing to me. He seemed to want to go straight back out, but I caught him. He turned white, and said to me, "You're

Jimmy's brother." I said, "There's been a terrible mistake, they're after him for this A6 business." He said, "Don't worry, he's got nothing to do with that." I said, "Do you know where he is?" He said he didn't; but he couldn't get away fast enough. He just said, "I've got to go," and ran up the stairs.'

Two days later, France was telephoned by Hanratty, who was in some anxiety, to say he understood that he was wanted for the A6 Murder. France advised him to give himself up. It seemed, though, that giving himself up was just about the last thing Hanratty had in mind.

The hunt for the A6 murderer was already one of the most protracted high-profile criminal investigations there had ever been. In the wake of the débâcle surrounding the first suspect, the newspaper reports betrayed signs of increasing desperation: the desperation of the journalists in needing to report some authentically fresh development; and the desperation of the police in needing to reconcile September's misapprehension with October's fresh line of inquiry.

This led to some bizarre results. The police tried to excuse their initial interest in Alphon by suggesting that, as the press reported, 'The A6 murderer had a double.' Alphon bore a 'close physical resemblance' to the actual gunman. 'The eyes, nose and hair are almost identical,' added the *Daily Mail*. Nor was that all, as the *Daily Telegraph* reported: 'The paths of the murderer and his double crossed. They stayed in similar locations at the same time, although they do not know each other and, it is believed, have never met. The murderer's route was hidden behind inquiries about his double.'[5]

On Thursday, 5 October, Acott and Oxford returned from Ireland and the police told reporters that a new description of the murder suspect would be issued the following day. That day, Friday, they abruptly changed their minds and said that no fresh description would be issued. The primary reason for this was probably mature reflection among senior officials – once bitten, twice shy – at Scotland Yard. There was, however, another pressing reason. As the *Evening News* explained, the promised announcement was cancelled because 'Acott is understood to have been given a vital clue' just before it was due to be made.

The vital clue? Whereas the first suspect had, following the public announcement, turned up at Scotland Yard in person, the second suspect had, even without any public announcement, done the next best thing. He had telephoned Detective Superintendent Acott.

Just after 11.30 in the morning, Hanratty dialled what was in those days the most famous telephone number in the country – Whitehall 1212 – and got put through to Acott's office. Detective Sergeant Arthur Howard answered the phone. Hanratty said to him, 'I want to explain some things about Ireland. I am who you are looking for, and some embarrassing things are happening for my family and friends.' Hanratty then told Detective Inspector William Holmes that 'I know the police are after me for the A6 Murder, but I didn't do it.'

'Who is speaking? Give me your name.'

'Ryan,' replied Hanratty.

'Have you another name?'

'Yes, Hanratty. I can't come forward. I have been doing other little things, but I'd like to get this other business cleared up.'

The line went dead. Half an hour later, at 12.15 p.m., Hanratty called back. This time, he got put straight through to Acott. The conversation, in abbreviated form, went as follows:

'I'm Jim Hanratty.'

'I'm Superintendent Acott.'

'I'm very worried and don't know what to do. I know you are the only one who can help me . . . I'd like to see you, but I've just come out from doing three and if I'm caught I'll get at least five. I had to ring off last time because I saw a policeman go by on the other side of the road.'

'Why don't you phone your mother? I've seen her and she's very worried. I've promised her I will do all I can for you.'

'I can't ring her because I've upset her. I don't know what to do or who to talk to, but I must get this off my chest. I know I've left my fingerprints at different places and done different things and the police want me, but I want to tell you, Mr Acott, that I didn't do that A6 murder.

'I think I'll ring a paper and ask them what to do. I'll think about it. I'll phone you tonight between 10.00 and midnight and tell you what I've decided. I must go now. My head's bad and I've got to think.'

He promised Acott to ring back that evening. Meanwhile, in the afternoon, he did indeed ring the *Daily Mirror*, and spoke to Barrie Harding, the assistant news editor. The brief conversation was considerably more rewarding for the *Mirror*, which landed a good splash story for its next edition, than for Hanratty: 'They told me to give myself up. They couldn't help me and I won't try them again.'

Over that weekend, the papers were straining at the leash, anticipating a swift end to the manhunt. The *Evening News* reported that 'a man may be traced during the weekend'; and the *Daily Telegraph* colluded in the air of optimism:

HUNT FOR A6 SUSPECT CLOSES IN
Police Expect Quick Trace

The problem for the press was that although journalists could sense a denouement, they were very restricted in what they were able to print. Thus they had to report as allusively as possible. Gradually, however, more information about the wanted man was reaching the public. Some of it was accurate: 'The man is believed to have red hair, which he may have dyed. He was known to his friends as Ginger' – *Daily Mirror*; some of it not: 'the man the police are seeking has the word "snake" tattooed on one arm and the word "Bert" on the other' – *Daily Herald*; the *Daily Telegraph* reported that the tattoos were of a picture of a snake and the word, more plausibly, was 'Bett', an abbreviation of 'Betty'.

At this stage, the police were enjoying some flattering publicity. The *Daily Telegraph* described 'a weekend of intensive investigations', which led to a breakthrough: the finding of a suitcase. This resulted 'from police tracing a woman known only as Louise. This was established by Detective Superintendent Acott during his recent investigations in Southern Ireland. No one knew who Louise was, but detectives, working to a special plan put into operation on Friday night, found her.'

No doubt all this helped to justify Acott's Irish expenses. In actual fact, the 'special plan put into operation on Friday night' was simplicity itself. It consisted of Superintendent Acott sitting at his desk in his office, waiting for the phone to ring. At four minutes past eleven, it did. James Hanratty was as good as his word.

'This is Jimmy Ryan.'

'How are you now, Jimmy? Tired?'

'No, I'm feeling fine now. I rang my mum, but I couldn't get any answer.'

'I know,' replied Acott. 'I've rung her number this evening but I can't get a reply. Perhaps they've all gone out.'

'Yes, they're looking for me. Look, I'll have to go soon, Mr Acott, because you'll have me caught in this box if I'm not careful. You nearly caught me this afternoon when I went to collect my car at a garage.'

'What garage was that, Jimmy? I didn't know you had a car.'

'One of the gears went, and I put it in a garage for repair. I went to collect it this afternoon, but as I got near it two plain-clothes men saw me and chased me up the street. I got away but it was a near squeak.'

'I think you've made a mistake, Jimmy. They couldn't have been policemen or I would have known about it. I haven't heard anything about you having a car or any policemen at a garage.'

'I'm going to try to phone Mum again.'

'By the way, Jimmy, when I saw your parents the other day, your mother told me you had sent her some flowers and she was very pleased and wanted me to thank you for them if I should see you. She also showed me a card you had sent her from Ireland and she was very pleased with that. If I were you, Jimmy, I would send her another card or some more flowers.'

'Yes, I'll try to write to her and send her some flowers if I can't get her on the phone.'

'How are you feeling, Jimmy?'

'I'm very worried and I don't know what to do. I saw in the papers this morning you're looking for a friend of mine, Louise. I can tell you who she is. I left my luggage with her. You ought to see her. She knows a lot about me.'

'What is her name, Jimmy?'

'Louise and she lives at 23 Cambridge Court, Sussex Gardens.'

'What is her surname?'

'I can't remember that, but she is a widow about fifty years old. See her and get my luggage. It will help you. Now I must go, Mr Acott. I can't stay any longer. I want to talk to you, but you'll catch me. I'm going, Mr Acott.'

The police tried desperately to trace the calls while the line was open, but failed on each occasion. However, they wasted little time in visiting Louise Anderson. They arrived at 2.30 in the morning. From her flat they collected Hanratty's two suitcases, which contained a quantity of clothing. In one was the waistcoat and trousers of his favourite Hepworth's suit; the jacket was missing. The police also traced the garage where Hanratty's Sunbeam Alpine was in for repair, and took from it what they thought were stolen articles.

The following day, there was another telephone call.

'Superintendent Acott speaking.'

'This is Jimmy Ryan again. You'll never guess where I'm speaking from. Liverpool.'

'How did you get up there, Jimmy?'

'I caught the night train to Liverpool from Euston. I read in the paper this morning that you and your mate slept at the Yard all night on a couple of camp beds. I'm sorry I'm causing you so much trouble, Mr Acott.'

'That's all right, Jimmy. I bet you slept well last night.'

'Yes, I slept all night on the train. It was very comfortable. I can't stay long, Mr Acott, as I haven't any more money for the phone.'

'Don't worry, Jimmy, when the pips go, I'll get the call reversed to me.'

The pips went. Acott gave the operator his rank, name and the Scotland Yard number and got the charges reversed.

'That's all right. What did you want to speak to me about this time, Jimmy?'

'Mr Acott, I'm in trouble and I know you are the only one who can help me. I've come up to Liverpool to see some friends, but they can't help me. I asked them to say I couldn't have committed your murder, but they wouldn't listen and wouldn't let me stay with them, as they said I'd bring the police down on them. You can't blame them because they're fences – you know what I mean – they receive jewellery. I don't know what to do. I want you to help me, but you'll only charge me and get me at least five.'

'Let me get this clear, Jimmy. Are you telling me that these three friends of yours in Liverpool can clear you of the murder by giving you an alibi?'

'Yes, but they don't want to know.'

'Listen to me carefully, Jimmy. My duty is to investigate this murder and find out the truth. If you are innocent it is my job to try and prove you are innocent. It is not my job just to charge you and get you convicted. If I can help you I will do my best for you. Is that clear, Jimmy?'

'Yes, I understand, Mr Acott, but there's nothing you can do for me.'

'I'm ready to listen. Tell me how you think your three friends in Liverpool can prove you didn't commit the murder.'

'All right, I'll tell you. On 21 August – that was a Monday, wasn't it? – I went to the Vienna Hotel and booked a room for the night, a basement room. I only stayed one night and next morning after breakfast I left and went to Paddington by mistake. When I got there I found the train to Liverpool went from Euston, so I caught a cab to Euston and caught a train to Liverpool, Lime Street Station. I caught the 11.55 a.m. – or was it the 10.55 – no, I think it was the 11.55 – anyway, you can find out what it was. Now that was Tuesday, and the murder was Tuesday and Wednesday, wasn't it? Well, I went to Liverpool and stayed five days with these three friends I told you about there. I came back to London on Friday and stayed with friends at St John's Wood. There you are, you see, I couldn't have committed the murder, could I? But you'll never believe me.'

'I cannot accept your story, Jimmy, without some corroboration from another witness. Now, as I understand it, you are telling me that at the time of the murder you were staying with these three friends in Liverpool. If they support your story, you won't have anything to worry about. Give me their names and addresses, Jimmy, and I'll see them as quickly as possible.'

'No, that won't do. They couldn't get mixed up with the police and they don't want to know anything about me or this murder. One of them is wanted on a warrant for non-payment of a fine or something. I've told them I'll pay this for him and give them all some money – I have plenty now, Mr Acott – but they won't listen. They say I embarrass them and they've kicked me out today and told me not to come back again.'

'Jimmy, I can't tell you how important it is for you that I should see these three men. How did you know [them], Jimmy?'

'I was in detention in Liverpool with one of them and I've been selling them gear from screwings.'

'Is there any other person who could say he saw you in Liverpool after you travelled there from the Vienna?'

'No.'

'Can you tell me any place you went to during those five days in Liverpool, or anything you did or anything you bought that might help me to check your story?'

'No. I'm on my own now, Mr Acott. Tomorrow, I'm going to do what you said and send [my mum] some flowers. I'm going to write and send her the papers for the car and tell her to go and collect the deposit. I paid out £105 for it. Mum can have that from me. That will help her. Now I must go, Mr Acott, before you catch me. One day, when all my money has gone, you'll get the cuffs on me, and I'll tell you the whole story then, but until then

I'm going to give you a good run, Mr Acott. I stuck a few hundred away for a rainy day and it will last me a good few months. I'm a bit fly, you know. Now I must go.'

This conversation was significant in two respects: Hanratty confirmed that he had taken a room at the Vienna Hotel; and also vouchsafed for the first time the rudiments of an alibi for the murder.

That Monday morning, Acott handed over the suitcases to Lewis Nicholls, director of the Metropolitan Police forensic science laboratory. In the afternoon, he and Oxford returned to Sycamore Grove, and between 3.45 and 5.30 re-interviewed Hanratty's parents. While they were doing so they missed another call from Hanratty, which was taken instead by Detective Constable Donald Langton. Hanratty was upset about what he was reading in the newspapers.

'I am very disgusted in what I have read in the papers today. I thought [Acott] was a very fair man. What he told the press about me giving the police a hard chase is all false. Tell him it is worrying my mother.'[6]

The police established that the call was from Liverpool, but could get no further as Hanratty had given a non-existent number.

After Acott's visit, James Hanratty senior was left in no doubt that his son would soon be traced; and something he would need straightaway would be a solicitor. He asked the family doctor for advice. The latter recommended a friend of his, Emmanuel Kleinman, whose practice was in Hendon. Kleinman arrived to meet the family at 7.00 that evening.

'We were all there when he arrived,' recalled Michael. 'The first thing he said was, "Before I can speak to you, I must ask you for £100."'

For someone whose weekly wage was less than £10, that was indeed a great deal of money. The Hanratty family simply didn't have it. However, the *Express* reporter John King, who'd already made himself a family fixture, intervened. He said, 'Well, look, we'll pay you for the story.' Mr Hanratty had already told him several times that he wasn't interested in money, only in getting the whole matter straightened out.

So a crude deal was quickly agreed. The *Express* would pay Kleinman what he was asking for, and would meet other legal costs which might be incurred. They would also provide the family, who did not have their own car, with transport as and when they needed it. They guaranteed the family relative privacy over what promised to be a trying period. 'Look outside,' said King, 'there's fifty reporters there already. You don't want everyone pestering you.' Indeed they didn't. But it was a wonderful deal for the *Express*: in return for a tiny outlay, they got exclusive access to the Hanratty family. No other reporters would be allowed near them.

It was also satisfactory for Kleinman, who got his money and agreed to take on the case.

The following day, Mary received nineteen artificial carnations, together with a note which read: 'I hope you will like this token. I am sorry to have caused you this trouble. You must have faith in me and I will work it out in my own time. I won't phone you again. If I do, it will only upset you and me. Give my love to Dad and the boys. Your loving son – Jim.'

He also sent her by mail the paperwork relating to the purchase of his car. He realized that he was not going to be able to continue the payments and keep it, so he hoped his mother would be able to reclaim the deposit. As it happened, his parents handed the note to Kleinman, who advised that it should be passed on to Acott; and the family ended up paying for and keeping the car.

It didn't take the press long to discover who Louise was. Nor did the short trip from Fleet Street to Greek Street present any difficulties. A picture of Louise in her antique shop appeared in several of Tuesday's papers. She gave a brief account of her friendship with Jim, and said, 'I soon discovered that he could not read or write, but that didn't matter to me.' She said she had last seen him about ten days earlier.[7]

She also mentioned that she had tried to fix Jimmy up with a girlfriend, Mary Meaden, who was tracked down the following day. She said she first met Hanratty about two weeks ago. 'Mrs Anderson thought what he needed was a nice, steady girlfriend, so she introduced us,' she told the *Daily Express*. 'He was only my second boyfriend and he seemed so gentle.'[8]

And then suddenly, inevitably and without melodrama, it was all over for the gentle fugitive. At the Stevonia Café in Central Drive, Blackpool, on Wednesday, 11 October, nineteen-year-old Bernard Daley was preparing to close for the night. Two policemen on patrol, Detective Constable James Williams and Detective Constable Albert Stillings, looked in, noted a youthful-looking man in a blue suit drinking coffee, and then left. They waited outside. When the man in the blue suit came out, he was arrested. He briefly protested that they were making a serious mistake: 'I'm Peter Bates.' However, he had to acknowledge a feeling of relief. 'I'm glad because now I can straighten things out.' He agreed to accompany them to the police station. 'I must say you have been very cooperative,' said Williams. 'I wish they were all like you.'

For the second time, Acott's quarry had been flushed out; for the second time Acott and Oxford drove through the night to interview him. This time the journey was considerably longer, and they arrived at Blackpool police station just after 7.00 a.m. By 7.45, they were confronting their suspect.

'Are you James Hanratty?' asked Acott.

'Yes,' he replied, 'but I want you to keep calling me Jimmy Ryan because I don't want to embarrass my parents.'

Acott then cautioned him: 'You are not obliged to say anything unless you wish to do so, but anything you do say will be taken down in writing and may be given in evidence.' Hanratty maintained an air of confidence: 'Fire away and ask me any questions you like. I'll answer them and you'll see I had nothing to do with that murder.'

The interview was concluded at 9.30, although there was a second interview, for forty-five minutes, after lunch.

The family heard of the arrest much later that day. 'The press told us he'd been picked up,' said Michael. 'We'd heard nothing from Acott.' Together with his parents, Michael set off immediately for Blackpool. They arrived at about 4.00 a.m. on Friday morning.

The police wouldn't allow them to speak to Jimmy, or see him at all. They did catch sight of him being escorted out through a side corridor, a blanket over his head, and bundled into a police car. At that point he'd just been cautioned by Detective Superintendent Charles Barron, head of Bedfordshire CID, and told that he was under arrest for the murder of Michael Gregsten. He was driven to Bedford, with the family chasing after them. When they arrived, Bedfordshire police did allow them to see him. 'He was very shaken,' said Michael, 'but he just said, "This has been a terrible mistake, I've had nothing to do with it, and it will turn out all right."'

Hanratty had his fingerprints taken and straightaway volunteered to provide forensic samples. Dr John Tree, the local police doctor, took samples of Hanratty's blood, scalp hair, pubic hair and saliva. Tree handed them to Detective Inspector John McCafferty, the Metropolitan Police's liaison officer with the forensic science laboratory.

An identity parade took place at Bedford county police headquarters on Goldington Road at 4.00 p.m. There were four witnesses: Edward Blackhall, John Skillett and James Trower, who had all caught glimpses of the gunman driving the car in Redbridge on the morning of the murder; and Harry Hirons, the garage attendant. Detective Superintendent Acott and Detective Superintendent Barron were present throughout, as was Emmanuel Kleinman, Hanratty's solicitor, who had just met his client for the first time. Blackhall and Hirons picked out parade extras; Trower and Skillett picked out Hanratty. The latter, though showing no real emotion, did go very red. He also raised with some exasperation the fact everyone was dressed in light clothing, except him. He said he had wanted to change because 'they know I wear a dark suit'. He was right: virtually all that morning's national newspapers had reported that the suspect arrested in Blackpool was wearing a blue suit. However, Kleinman registered no objection, and indeed assented to the parade.

The second parade was held the following day at Stoke Mandeville Hospital in Buckinghamshire. Valerie Storie had been transferred to its spinal injuries unit for specialized treatment on Monday, 25 September, the day after her previous identity parade. This time, the line-up was organized by officers from Aylesbury police station. Early that Saturday morning, they recruited men to make up the parade from local RAF stations at Halton and High Wycombe. They chose men whose natural hair-colouring was gingerish. Antony Luxemburg from Hertfordshire was one of those selected: 'We were picked up in a police van to be taken to the hospital. I'd actually been in the van for two or three minutes when I realized that Hanratty was in the van with us. I was taken aback. He had this extraordinary tension, he was the most tense human being I've ever seen in my life.'[9]

Jack Braybrook, one of the police constables guarding Hanratty, gave a statement indicating how nervous Hanratty was. 'He remarked several times that morning he would be leaving Bedford for Aylesbury. He was most concerned that he should not be late for the parade, and continually asked the time, and if the persons taking him had yet arrived.'[10]

One of those who had not yet arrived was Emmanuel Kleinman. The start of this crucial second parade was delayed by almost an hour while everyone waited for him to arrive. The delay further increased Hanratty's already manifest nervous tension.

This time, Hanratty insisted on changing his clothing. He wore a greenish sports jacket, a reddish tie, fawn cord trousers and suede shoes. These weren't his own clothes, so he must have looked ill-at-ease in them. He was also now the only one wearing flannel trousers and suede shoes. There were twelve others in the line. They were arranged across the medical inspection room, and each held a card numbered 1 to 13. Hanratty took up his position sixth from the right, so he was No. 6.

Kleinman said that he was satisfied with the arrangements. At 11.14 Valerie Storie was wheeled into the room, propped up in her bed. There were a large number of police officers present, including Acott, Barron, Oxford, Detective Sergeant Heavens and Detective Superintendent Fewtrell of Buckinghamshire police. Storie was wheeled up and down, up and down, and up and down again. About nine times in all. She asked them all to say: 'Be quiet, will you, I am thinking.' She was listening for a cockney accent, someone who said 'finking'. Then she asked them all to say it again. The parade took an extraordinarily long time. 'My impression', said Luxemburg, 'is that she took fifteen or twenty minutes'; in his report, Kleinman estimated the time at twenty minutes; and Valerie Storie herself wrote that it took a full twenty minutes.

Finally, she announced her decision: No. 6.

It had been an extremely tense time for everybody, as another of the parade members, Brian Oliver from Nottingham, remembered. 'We were all given half-a-crown, but I was just a bag of nerves after it was all over. I went straight down the pub and had a pint.'[11]

Detective Superintendent Barron took Hanratty to Ampthill police station and, at 6.15, charged him with the murder of Michael Gregsten. 'He said to me, "Have you anything to say?" I said "No." He said, "Sign here."'

Some hours earlier, at 11.04, indeed just before the critical identity parade had started, the inquiry team at Bedford had received the report on the fingerprints from Scotland Yard. In the course of the investigation, police had amassed quite a number of fingerprints and palm prints – from the 36A bus, from Upper Richmond Road and, most importantly, from the Morris Minor car and its contents. As a result of their analysis, Scotland Yard experts were able to report categorically that none of the prints was Hanratty's.[12]

CHAPTER NINE

ON MONDAY, 16 OCTOBER, the *Daily Express* carried a bleak half-page story with a large photograph of Mary Hanratty sitting beside her vase of nineteen artificial carnations and re-reading to herself the card that came with them. The report described the emptiness of that strange Sunday. 'It is not the usual Sunday at the Hanrattys' home, not the usual day when they can all relax. The neighbours called to ask about their son, to offer help. The family sat – restless, talking, wondering.'[1]

Then James took Mary out for a walk. 'They met no one in the misty streets, and were glad; they do not like fuss. And beyond the streets, they walked on wooded Barn Hill, where they had often taken Jimmy, playing hide-and-seek with him among the poplars and oaks. The trees were grey with mist now, and sad with autumn. And the boy who had played there was a man, in prison, and charged with murder.'

Hanratty was appearing in court that very morning charged with one of the most callous crimes in recent memory. Yet the piece was written without any trace of the abhorrence, vengefulness or moral outrage that one would now expect to find in similar circumstances in newspaper reports. Today, it would doubtless be indicated that such a family was shunned by neighbours and right-thinking members of society; in this instance, in 1961, 'The neighbours called . . . *to offer help.*'

The most transparent observation that could be drawn from this is that the journalists assigned to accompany the family had instantly warmed to their straightforward honesty and friendliness. Possibly also implied in the piece is a reluctance to believe that this man could have committed that murder. Certainly, the article today conveys a rare poignancy, evoking distant memories of a society – and, of course, a national press – that was less swift to condemn, more ready to bestow sympathy and understanding.

In Ampthill that morning, Hanratty was driven the short distance from the newly built police station up the hill to the courthouse. He wore his blue suit with a white shirt and yellow tie, and was flanked by Detective Chief Inspector Harold Whiffen and Detective Sergeant Harry Heavens. Hanratty's father and brother, Michael, sat in the public seats in court. Guy Owen, a local farmer who was chairman of the magistrates, remanded Hanratty in custody for a week. He also granted Kleinman legal aid. With that secured, Kleinman appointed a barrister to begin organizing the defence case for the magistrates' court. He chose Michael Sherrard, a young and talented lawyer of considerable promise.

Sherrard was plunged into the country's most high-profile criminal case, and straightaway had to deal with another of those bewildering developments that characterized it from start to finish. Someone had been trying to contact Valerie Storie by telephone, and making threats against her. The saga had started at the beginning of the month. At about ten past six on the evening of Sunday, 1 October – which was, intriguingly, the weekend that Peter Alphon was released from custody – the telephone operator at Stoke Mandeville hospital had received a strange call. The caller said, 'I am the man who shot Valerie Storie.' He added, 'I will be there at 11.30 to finish her off.'[2]

He said he was calling from Windsor. This turned out to be correct; the call was traced to a public call box in Windsor. Shortly afterwards, Windsor police received a call informing them that the A6 murderer would be in Aylesbury (the nearest town to Stoke Mandeville) at 11.00 that night. This call was also traced to a public call box in Windsor. The following day, the operator at Stoke Mandeville received a second call. She recognized the voice and was sure it was the same man. He said, 'I rang the hospital yesterday about Valerie Storie. I was unable to come last night, but will be there tonight.'

The police wanted to check such calls more quickly but the Post Office told them that, as they were then in the early days of the STD telephone system, it was almost impossible to trace calls while they were being made.

That Tuesday, the hospital received the third call in as many days: 'You know the call you had from Windsor? Tonight may be the night.' On this occasion a different operator was on duty, so no comparison could be made with the previous calls.

No more was heard from the mystery caller until Sunday, 22 October at 5.45. A man telephoned and asked whether Storie was still in the hospital, or whether she had been moved. Later that day, two newspapers contacted Scotland Yard to say they had received calls consisting of further threats against Valerie Storie, from a man saying that 'If anything happens to Jim Hanratty, his mates will be up at Stoke Mandeville to do her in.'

On Monday, 23 October, as almost his first public comment on the case, Sherrard had to say something about this situation: 'I learned today from the press, and the information is reliable, that there have been serious threats to kill Valerie Storie. It is perfectly obvious that these are the threats of somebody of an unhinged mentality, to say the least. I would appeal to that person to give himself up to the police, or to desist.

'From our point of view, it is absolutely vital that nothing is done which can interfere with the witnesses, intimidate them or blur their memories in any way.'[3]

Even after he had made his appeal, the *Daily Herald* received a further call. The unknown caller said, 'Tell Bob Traini [the *Herald*'s crime correspondent] I am going to kill Valerie Storie tonight.'

Sherrard was particularly concerned that nothing should contaminate the case because he then knew little more than that Hanratty adamantly denied any knowledge of the crime. The first time he saw him, at that 23 October court hearing, Hanratty told Sherrard that he would be pleading not guilty, irrespective of whether it turned out to be a capital charge, or a 'nut case' (i.e. one where the death sentence would be commuted on the grounds of diminished responsibility).

Hanratty insisted that he knew nothing at all about it: 'The charge is ridiculous,' he told Sherrard. 'I am not that kind of person. I don't even like talking about it. It upsets me. If I had done it, I would have taken my own life rather than do this to my mother.' He did admit to one slight area of concern – 'What worries me is that Acott is out for promotion.' Otherwise, he was merely apprehensive about the prospect of photographs of himself appearing in the press. He thought that 'might injure me when it is all over'.

On 31 October Hanratty made his third court appearance. Sherrard asked whether he might be remanded to a London prison, as this would facilitate the task of the defence in preparing its case. Although the crime had occurred just outside Bedford, most of the participants in the case lived in London; and the majority of developments in the case had occurred in London. The magistrates granted this request. On Friday, 3 November, Hanratty was moved to Brixton Prison in south London. The defence team now had a better opportunity of assembling their case, but less than three weeks in which to do so. The magistrates' court hearing was scheduled to begin on 22 November.

The defence team then began to assemble from Hanratty's own account a complete picture of his movements from the moment he left the Broadway House Hotel, on Monday, 21 August, until the time of his arrest. The critical time was obviously the period during which the crime occurred, and on Saturday, 14 October, immediately after Hanratty was charged, Kleinman had given the police details of his client's alibi for this period. But in building up a picture of his client's behaviour, his movements not only at the time of the murder but in the days and weeks following it were very important.

In the late evening of Monday, 21 August, after Hanratty left the Broadway House by taxi, the driver had some difficulty finding the Vienna. When they arrived, Hanratty understood why. The Vienna didn't meet his expectations of a proper hotel. There was no spacious and well-carpeted vestibule. It didn't have its name in lights; indeed, it didn't even have its name displayed at all. The hotel had few virtues, but one of these was discretion; as well as tourists seeking cheap accommodation, it was often used by businessmen staying overnight with girls, and sometimes by male couples who wished to spend the night together. 'I had never been to the hotel before, or gone there since,' Hanratty told his lawyers. 'I would not have gone there at all except that the other hotel had sent me.'

Hanratty was expected. A man and a woman were waiting for him at the front door. Hanratty said the couple were English, so they must have been Nudds and Florence Snell. Mr Pichler had telephoned to let them know he'd be arriving. Hanratty was given a book to sign and then Nudds showed him to his room, downstairs in the basement. He noticed the big French windows. There were four beds in the room, a double and three singles. Although it was late – about midnight, he estimated – he was told that he would have to share the room if anyone else turned up, and indeed that a woman was expected. Hanratty had his money and jewellery in the waistcoat pocket of his suit, and paid in advance (he thought it was 17s 6d), and in the event no one did share the room with him. He slept in the nearest single bed, which had a chair at the foot, and passed a peaceful night.

He woke up at about nine o'clock, and got down to breakfast about 9.30: 'I was in no hurry.' There were about six in the dining room. Hanratty sat alone and ate cornflakes, bacon and eggs and toast and marmalade. He was served by the 'oldish' woman who had met him when he arrived. (This would be the thirty-seven-year-old Snell, so presumably living with Nudds had put years on her age.) After breakfast Hanratty looked in the mirror and decided to have a shave. He then got his case, walked upstairs, said 'Cheerio' and left.

Leaving aside the highly contentious statements of Nudds and Snell, there was nothing at all in this account that was contradicted by any evidence, and there was obviously supporting documentation to confirm his stay at the hotel.

It was a lovely morning, so Hanratty, who was wearing his flashy, striped double-breasted suit, decided to walk: up Sutherland Avenue, down Edgware Road, and then down Praed Street to Paddington Station. On arriving, he realized straightaway that he was at the wrong station. He'd been to Liverpool about five times in the past five years; he'd even been discharged from Walton Prison in Liverpool; so he knew that the Liverpool trains ran to and from Euston. 'I do not know why I made this mistake. Perhaps I was excited by the jewellery and the deal I was going to do.' Similarly, Hanratty gave the stolen jewellery he was carrying as the reason why, on this occasion, he decided to take the train rather than risk stealing a car and driving north.

He called a black cab off the taxi rank and asked the driver to take him to Euston. He would probably have arrived at about 10.45, and had a long wait for the next train. He purchased a single ticket, which cost him just under £3. He bought some magazines from a newspaper stall at the front, and looked through them while having a coffee on the station. When he finished, Hanratty walked down to the platform. The train still wasn't in, so he went back and had another drink, tea this time. He bought a tube of toothpaste and spoke to a porter. By the time he returned to the platform the train was not only in, but rapidly filling up. He had difficulty finding a seat.

'I always like to sit next to the window. I had to go to the far end, near the engine. I got into a compartment and tried to get a window-seat, but someone had got there first. A man, like a college boy, was kissing his girl goodbye, but he had reserved the seat by leaving his books and papers there. There was another man in the opposite seat, though I didn't pay too much attention to him.'

One man who looked like a 'clerky gent' attracted Hanratty's attention partly because he thought he was the sort who normally should have been travelling first-class. 'I watched him, and studied his dress closely, as I am interested in the way people dress. He had very fine nylon stockings, and shiny shoes, with pinstripe trousers and a brief-case like Mr Kleinman's. He had very fine reading glasses which he put over his ordinary spectacles to read some papers. He had a gold pen, too, and a gold watch, a beautiful watch, which he wore on his right arm. He had initialled gold cuff-links too. He smoked a black pipe. He had the inside seat. First I sat on the other side, then I changed seats so that I was sitting next to him.'

The train was completely full, with many people standing in the corridors.

'I did not speak to anyone. Most of the men got up and went to the restaurant car. The train stopped at Crewe, but no one got in. We got into Liverpool at about 3.30 in the afternoon.'

At Lime Street Station Hanratty went into the wash-and-brush-up in the lavatory under the buffet. He exchanged a few words about horse-racing with the attendant. He had a cup of tea in the buffet and then put his pigskin case in the left-luggage office. 'The man who took it had a turned or withered hand. I said to him, "How much?" He said a shilling. I said, "It's usually sixpence." He said, "We charge a shilling for all bags." I said, "Well, it's only sixpence in London." I asked what time they closed, and he said they were open until the last train went.'

He then asked a woman outside the station where Carlton Avenue was. 'I was looking for Aspinall, to sell him the rings.' She said it was a twopenny bus ride away, up the Scotland Road. Hanratty caught the bus, and got out by a picture-house, the Regal, he thought. He asked a couple of pedestrians, but they did not know. So, he went into a sweet-shop and tobacconist, opposite the picture-house. There was a lady serving, and a small girl also serving with her in the shop. Hanratty asked the lady in there whether she knew where Carlton or Tarleton Avenue was. She said there wasn't a Carlton Avenue round there. 'This is Bank Hall,' she said to Hanratty. She explained to him that he needed to go back into town. She went to the shop door with him to show him the nearest bus stop.

'When the woman told me I had to go back into town, I abandoned my intention of going to the road, which I think is called Talbot Road.'

In fact, he walked back to the station. With his plans to sell the jewellery thwarted for the moment, he realized he needed some cash. 'I only had £8–9 on me, to me that is not a lot of money.' He went towards the billiard hall on the other side of Lime Street. Hanratty said that a man who owned it usually stood outside on the steps. He asked him if he would be interested in buying a gold watch. The man said no. Hanratty accordingly went up the entrance steps of the hall. The man called after him, saying, 'You can't go in there, those are licensed premises.' 'What difference does that make?' asked Hanratty. The man, fully comprehending that the watch was stolen property, replied, 'It makes a lot of difference. I don't want you to go in there with it.'

So according to his own account Hanratty was in Liverpool between approximately 4.00 and 6.00 p.m. on Tuesday afternoon. Even apart from all other considerations, this, if accurate, gave him a watertight alibi. If he was there then, he could not logically have been in a cornfield near Slough by 9.30 that evening. There were three witnesses in particular who might possibly buttress the alibi.

Hanratty's problem was that on the evening of Saturday, 14 October, immediately after he had been charged, his lawyer, Kleinman, passed to the police details of the alibi. This action, although scrupulous, was misguided. Kleinman should instead have instigated immediate inquiries himself. By leaving the investigations to the police, he allowed the waters to become muddied from the very start. Kempt, the man on the billiard-hall steps, for example, could indeed remember the incident, yet his evidence was of little value. This is what he subsequently told defence agents:

'I am the managing licensee of Reynold's Billiard Hall. It is my custom during the summer evenings when the hall is quiet to stand at the entrance to have a breath of fresh air. That is any time between 6.00 and 7.30 p.m. One evening when I was standing at the door a young fellow in his early twenties came to me and said, "Will you buy a watch?" I replied, "No." He said, "It's mine, I want some cash to go to the dogs." I still refused and he went to go up the stairs. I told him he could not go in there to sell that watch, "It's not a sale-room, it's licensed premises." He said, "I'm only going to the toilet," and went up and was down again in two minutes and he went away. I have no idea of the day, date or month, except that it was in the evening time. He was small and young and I might know him again.'

Here was a witness who recollected the incident in very much the way Hanratty had related it. The essence of Hanratty's story was therefore powerfully confirmed. There were a couple of variations, but even those only enhanced its ring of truth. Hanratty apparently said he wanted to sell the watch in order 'to go to the dogs'. Although Hanratty himself had not mentioned this, it would have been entirely characteristic of him to have said it.

From the defence point of view, however, Kempt's inability to recall the particular day was frustrating. But no one from the defence contacted him until December; had he been seen immediately, in October, he might have been better able to pinpoint the date. On the other hand, it obviously suited the police that he was unable to be specific. Nor did they, at this stage, even bother to investigate the part of the alibi which concerned the left-luggage office.

The sweet-shop alibi was, however, tantalizing from the outset.

On Monday, 16 October, the Chief Constable of Bedfordshire police wrote to the Chief Constable of Liverpool City police, asking if his force would be kind enough to inquire into the alibi. Liverpool police received the request on Tuesday morning and, to their credit, set to work immediately. They sent a detective constable to make inquiries at all the sweet-shops along Scotland Road. By lunchtime, he'd uncovered evidence that went some way towards supporting Hanratty's story.

That morning, Stella Cowley was serving in the confectioner's shop that she ran with her husband, David, who was a city councillor. Detective Constable Pugh called in, to say that they were inquiring about a man who may have called at a sweet-shop to ask for directions, possibly to Talbot or Tarleton Road. Mrs Cowley could not help him; she had been away at the time on holiday. DC Pugh left. Shortly afterwards, Mrs Olive Dinwoodie, a family friend, happened to call into the shop. Mrs Cowley naturally related the police visit to her. According to Mrs Cowley's statement, 'She [Mrs Dinwoodie] immediately said, "I can remember a man asking for Tarleton Road."' In view of this, Mrs Cowley conscientiously telephoned Liverpool police. DC Pugh returned to the shop and took a statement from Mrs Dinwoodie. This is what she said:

'On Monday, 21 August, I was engaged as assistant for two days. I was accompanied in the shop by my thirteen-year-old granddaughter, Barbara Ford.

'Between 3.30 and 4.00 p.m. on the Monday, a chap came into

the shop and asked me to direct him to Tarleton Road. I did not know where Tarleton Road was, though I knew Tarleton Street. I asked him if it was Tarleton Street, and he said, "No, Road."

'It was definitely the Monday, because I was alone on the Tuesday, my grand-daughter was only with me on the Monday.

'The photograph you have shown me is one of the man who came in on Monday, 21 August, asking for Tarleton Road.'

Superficially, this may have seemed of little or no use to Hanratty's defence. After all, although Mrs Dinwoodie recollected the incident, she testified that it had occurred on a different day.

On closer evaluation, however, the statement could justly be considered sensational. Mrs Dinwoodie had said she would take over in the shop as holiday relief. Even on the Monday, the first day, she was starting to feel unwell. She asked if her grand-daughter, Barbara Ford, could come along to assist her. Late on Tuesday afternoon, she became ill. She went to the doctor's that evening, and was unable to continue. David Cowley had to keep the shop open himself, and so couldn't join his wife on holiday.

In this context, there are three points of immense significance in Olive Dinwoodie's statement. First, she confirmed Hanratty's account of the incident; second, she recognized the photograph of Hanratty and identified him as the man concerned. Finally, and most importantly, the incident could only have happened on Monday, 21 or Tuesday, 22 August – because those were the only two days (during this period) in which Olive Dinwoodie served in the shop. All that has always been incontestable.

The police took a continuing interest in this statement. Olive Dinwoodie was asked to go over it all again, many, many times. There was little more she could add; such a fleeting encounter could hardly be embellished. She did just mention that 'I could hardly understand him,' which does not undermine in any sense the contention that the man was Hanratty.

No doubt the officers felt satisfied with this. Policemen believed that criminals, in concocting alibis, often tried to 'shift' events from one day to another. In this instance, the Liverpool police had examined the alibi of the suspect in the country's major murder investigation; by establishing that it occurred on the 'wrong' day, they had created no problems for their London colleagues.

Or so they probably imagined. In fact, Acott became so concerned about the situation that he telephoned Liverpool CID on Wednesday, 1 November to ask if they could investigate the matter further. His problem was a simple one: as a result of Liverpool police inquiries, Hanratty was placed in Liverpool in the late afternoon of 21 August; and as a result of Scotland Yard inquiries, Hanratty was placed in London at exactly the same time. Acott told Liverpool police 'to pursue inquiries to establish the accuracy or otherwise of Mrs Dinwoodie's statement'.[4]

So they went over it all again: with Mrs Dinwoodie; with David and Stella Cowley; with John Cowley, David's brother; and, for the first time, they took a statement from the thirteen-year-old grand-daughter, Barbara Ford. This is what she said:

'Sometime whilst I was on my holidays, I don't know when it was, but Mrs Cowley had just started her own holidays, Mrs Dinwoodie came one morning and said she was going to serve in Mr Cowley's shop. She asked me to meet her in the shop and I think I went shortly after lunch, I think that would be about 1.45.

'During the afternoon, a man called in the shop and asked my grandmother if she could direct him to a street or road, but I can't remember the name he asked for. My grandmother asked me if I knew it, but I don't know where it was . . .

'I am certain that the day I was in the shop was the Monday of the week Mrs Cowley started her holidays.'

Thus Barbara, too, had a precise recollection of the incident.

Having gone over the ground again, Liverpool police came up with the same result. Detective Chief Inspector T. Elliott concluded, 'Mrs Dinwoodie, although confident that the man who called at the shop asked for Tarleton Road, would not have known which particular day it was when the man called at the shop, but the day is pinpointed [because] it was said she was accompanied by a child.'[5]

Inquiries were thus proceeding promisingly for the defence, but neither Kleinman nor anyone else on the defence team knew that. No one from the prosecution side saw fit to tell them anything about this.

What, then, of the remainder of Hanratty's alibi? After the sole ostensible purpose of his trip to Liverpool, to raise money by selling some jewellery, had not been realized, what did he do then? Hanratty said he went to find some people he knew.

'They live in a block of flats called the Bull Ring in Scotland Road. The three men live close together. One has a sister who looks after the lot of them. McNally is the man I associated with in Liverpool. I met him in 1957 in prison. I have also met him in London. During the three days I was in Liverpool, I stayed with McNally in a block of flats known as the Bull Ring or the Gardens in Scotland Road, or a road just off it, Skellone Road. McNally lives there with a married couple, John and Lil, who have three young children. It is a second-floor flat.

'I think I stayed in on 22 August all evening. They were not expecting me to sleep there for three days. I slept on a couch in the living-room. The wife of the man is a sister of McNally.

'With regard to the three men I stayed with in Liverpool, I am sure I can establish an alibi without them. If I felt I could not prove my innocence otherwise, then I might have to involve them. But they have been so good to me and stood by me, I do not want to grass on them. I am not going to involve them.'

On Thursday, 24 August McNally sold some jewellery for him. 'That is why I waited three days. If I had got the money earlier, I would have come back sooner.'

That was Hanratty's account of the vital alibi period. That was what Hanratty said he'd done. Unfortunately, it wasn't what he'd actually done. In fact, at the critical time, he hadn't been in Liverpool at all.

After failing to sell any jewellery, he had, on the spur of the moment it seems, abandoned Liverpool and caught a coach to Rhyl. A Crosville bus – the only service available – left Liverpool at 6.00 and arrived in Rhyl at 8.19. Hanratty thought that perhaps the man whom he knew only as 'John' (Terry Evans) would be able to sell his stuff for him. He wasn't able to contact him, not surprisingly as he was initially reluctant to return to the one place he would have expected to find him – the fairground – after having walked out on his employment there the previous month. (Hanratty, however, had always regarded the shoes he'd taken from Evans as a gift, and thus conceived of no problem on that score.) Abandoning his search for Terry, he found a room for the night at a guest-house.

On the Wednesday, after breakfast, he went into a barber's for a shave, and then had a midday meal at a café called Dixie's, which he knew that Evans used. He even inquired about him there, though again without luck. During the afternoon he spent some time in the amusement arcades along the front, and wandered into Woolworth's ('which I never had a chance to do before'). In the evening, when it was getting dark, he was unable to resist the lure of the fairground, but still couldn't find Evans. Then he returned to Dixie's for a coffee, before returning to spend a second night at the guest-house.

On Thursday, he adjudged that he'd been long enough away

from London to enable him to return in ersatz triumph, pretending that he'd just spent a successful time 'on business' in the north. In the morning, he caught the bus back to Liverpool.

At that point the pretence was discarded and Hanratty could tell the actual truth. He put his case in the left-luggage, had a meal and then went to the pictures. He originally intended to see *Ben Hur*, but the woman at the box office told him they only had 15-shilling seats left. Hanratty considered this a bit steep, so, having considered and rejected Elvis Presley's *Wild in the Country*, he opted for *The Guns of Navarone*.

On the evening of his departure, he sent a telegram by phone. 'The porter at the GPO wrote the telegram out for me and told me to phone it through.' Hanratty did so, from a phone box on the forecourt of St George's Hall in Lime Street. The telegram was timed at 8.40 p.m. It read: *Having a nice time, be home early Friday morning for business. Yours sincerely, Jim.* It was sent to *Mr France at Boundary Road, Finchley Road, London.* The sender's name and address was *Mr P. Ryan, Imperial Hotel, Russell Square, London.* Hanratty was told that the telegram could not be delivered until the following morning. It cost 2s 6d.

While walking round, Hanratty found himself at the Liverpool stadium. There was a boxing programme on, the main attraction being a contest between Howard Winstone and Aryee Jackson. He tried to get in, but it was already sold out. Instead, he went over on the ferry to New Brighton, where he went to the fun-fair. He was disappointed that many of the side-shows were closed.

'I was on my own. I came back about 10 o'clock. I went back to the flat, picked up my luggage and took a large sum of cash with me. I went to the station about 10.15. I again put my case in the left-luggage – it was a different man – I gave him a 6d tip. I had an hour to kill. I stood on the corner of Lime Street. I went to the snack bar on the corner near the station and hung about there for an hour.'

He retrieved his case from the left-luggage, and bought a ticket costing £2 19s 7d. The train pulled in at about 11.30, and left just after midnight. Once again, it was packed and not easy to get a seat. Hanratty found a compartment occupied by a woman with two young daughters. After a while, two men got on at a place which Hanratty remembered particularly, and perhaps not unnaturally, because of its large prison. That would have been Stafford. The men were plumbers – 'two right cockneys' – and it seems they enjoyed animated conversation all the way to London. Hanratty was especially pleased that they complimented him on his suit. They also discussed the A6 Murder, which had occurred less than forty-eight hours earlier: 'We said what a shocking thing it was.'

There was plenty of detail here in Hanratty's account. At an early stage, the defence should have assembled a mountain of alibi evidence for this entire period. In fact, Kleinman ignored these possibilities – none of Hanratty's fellow train passengers was ever traced – on the grounds that what occurred outside the Tuesday/Wednesday night-time period could not constitute a direct alibi for the crime. Nevertheless, all this could have been valuable incidental evidence to underline the accuracy of Hanratty's testimony, especially bearing in mind that no one (other than the identification parade witnesses) ever placed him anywhere other than where he said he'd been. Of course, a greater emphasis on this may also have extracted the full truth from Hanratty at an earlier stage.

The journey from Liverpool to Euston was not particularly fast, as the train had stopped at every station en route. They got in at 5.20 a.m. As leisurely as he could manage, Hanratty took a bus from the station to Baker Street, and walked from there to St John's Wood. He managed to delay his arrival at the Frances' to about 8.30–9.00, by which time Carole had gone to work and the family were getting up. Hanratty always maintained that France showed him the telegram when he arrived. The postman had just delivered it.

They were pleased to see him, asking if he'd had a good time. He replied that he'd had a wonderful time. It seems that Charles and Charlotte asked him what he'd done, and Hanratty lied, saying he had seen his aunt and taken her to the dogs. Charles said to him, 'You went to the Club on Monday?' and Hanratty admitted that he hadn't, after all, gone straight to Liverpool. He showed them the bill from the Vienna Hotel.

That weekend, Carole again remarked that she thought the dye was beginning to fade from his hair, so he asked her to touch it up, and again she set to work and redyed it. Carole remembered the date with certainty, again because it fell just before another dental appointment that coming Monday.

Hanratty stayed most of the week with Louise Anderson, however. On the Thursday, he called in at the cleaners in Swiss Cottage arcade, and was disappointed to be told his suit wasn't yet ready. On Saturday, 2 September, he burgled a house near the lake in Edgware.

'I have done quite a few jobs round there. This was a large white house. It was ten o'clock in the morning, but I went round the back and could see that the house was empty. The windows had insurance locks on – this shows that the people are well-to-do. There were French windows with little leaded panes. I snapped the lead, so there was just enough room for me to squeeze through. I wiped the glass with my handkerchief. I could see straightaway that the place was full of silver, at least £200-worth.

'Silver, though, is not a perfect haul. I was looking for jewellery. I'd been there quite a while, but hadn't been able to find any. In a room upstairs there were two large cases, so I took these downstairs and started filling them with silver. I needed something to stop the silver clinking, so I went upstairs to the bathroom for some towels. On my way down again, I saw a woman coming down the path towards the front door.

'I'd already noticed that they were all oak doors, and there wasn't a key in the back door, so there was no easy way out except through the front door. I ran and hid in a downstairs toilet. I heard the key in the front door. The silver was scattered all over the place in the room. The door opened. I waited for it to shut, but it didn't. I got frightened, and came out of the bathroom. The woman was out at the front, bringing in the milk. So I shut the front door, thinking I could escape out of the back. As I went into the kitchen, though, she looked through a window in the hall and saw me. So I opened the front door. She said, "Who are you?" I just said, "Come in." She said, "No, I would know if you were a friend of my husband's. What do you want?" Then she ran off up the drive. I went straight to the back, and kicked open the French windows. I ran down the back garden, and out by the lake. Luckily, a bus came almost straightaway.'

Hanratty thought he had about £300 in cash at that time; a good burglar always works steadily, and doesn't wait until he is desperate. He hadn't accomplished anything that time, but the following morning he went down to Petticoat Lane and paid £14 for another suit, a blue one this time. He also bought two shirts and a pair of shoes. He needed them, he told Charles France, because he had to go to Ireland. Once again, Charlotte obliged by doing his washing. At some time over that weekend, when he was at the Frances' house, they saw on television the police photofits of the man wanted for the A6 Murder, and Charlotte seems to have remarked to Hanratty, 'Oh, doesn't that look like you?'

On Monday, 4 September, Hanratty booked a BEA flight to

Dublin in the name of Ryan from the Frances'. He then went to Swiss Cottage to collect his suit, which was now ready, although he complained about the length of time they had kept it. The suit had some bloodstains on it, which the cleaning had not removed. Hanratty was adamant that this was his own blood, after he had cut his hand during a burglary. (Hanratty was mistaken. The stains were probably paint, because when the clothes were subsequently analysed, the laboratory found no bloodstaining at all.)

He went to the airport in the afternoon to catch what should have been the 4.55 BEA flight. The plane was delayed for two hours (there was fog in Dublin) and he phoned Charlotte from the airport: 'I don't know why, no real reason, just to say I thought there was a man watching me.'

He arrived safely in Dublin later that evening. Although he generally travelled on a whim, this time he did have a particular reason for going. He now had enough money to be able to fulfil a long-held personal ambition and buy a car. However, he had never taken a driving test and had absolutely nothing by way of documentation. He knew it was easy to pick up a one-year driving licence in Ireland. The following morning, with an uncharacteristic sense of purpose, he went to the town hall, where a policeman helped him fill in the form, and he was given a licence.

He went to Limerick. There, he hired a car from the local branch office of Ryan's, the biggest car-hire firm in Dublin. It cost him about £21, rather a lot of money (the return air fare was only £14 2s.). He spent the night there, at the Thormond, but was disappointed not to be able to stay in a hotel called Hanratty's; it was full.

On Wednesday, he drove south-west from Limerick to Tralee, to see the races and have a flutter, and in the early evening drove south-east to Cork, where he arrived just before nine o'clock. As ever, finding a room was not easy. At O'Flynn's Hotel, he was told that there were no single rooms left, but they could put him up if he didn't mind sharing.

Thus he introduced himself to Gerrard Leonard, a commercial traveller. Hanratty had a wash, and then said he was going to a dance, and asked if Leonard wanted to go with him. Leonard replied that he would, but said he'd like a drink first. That was something which never occurred to Hanratty, who did not drink as a rule. So they got in his car and drove round Cork looking for a dance-hall. They found one within about five minutes' walk of the hotel. In a neighbouring bar, Leonard had a couple of drinks (and Hanratty just one lager-and-lime) and they then arrived at the dance-hall at about 9.30, and stayed until 11.25.

It was in the morning, when they again met up at breakfast, that Hanratty asked Leonard if he'd write some postcards for him. The police were always impressed by Leonard's clear memory of what had happened, so it must be emphasized that his account dovetailed precisely with Hanratty's own; and that Leonard recalled precisely what Hanratty was wearing: his grey/blue-and-black striped Hepworth's suit, and his pointed-toe shoes.

On Thursday morning, 7 September, Hanratty drove east out of Cork. Entering a village called Castlemartyr, he collided side-on with a car travelling in the opposite direction. Hanratty had damaged the offside front wing and both offside doors of the other car. He accepted full responsibility, saying that he had driven too fast on entering the village and gone over the white line in the middle of the road. As it happened, both cars were hired and both were being driven by Englishmen. The other driver was Arthur Sindall, from Sarratt in Hertfordshire. Hanratty was taken along to Castlemartyr police station, originally with the intention that he should make a statement. However, the officer concerned with the matter, John Dowling, decided not to bother: 'As the damage to both cars was slight, and as they had been removed before I reached the scene, and as Ryan accepted full responsibility for any damage to the other driver's car, I formed the opinion that it was not a case for investigation and consequently did not report the matter.'[6]

The whole affair was, or rather should have been, inconsequential. It did, however, constitute the most impregnable of alibis for Hanratty for the Meike Dalal incident: at the exact time that she was attacked in south London by a man claiming to be the A6 murderer, Hanratty was in a police station in southern Ireland explaining a minor traffic accident.

He drove north to Tipperary, then went to Killarney, back to Limerick and back to Dublin, where he arrived on Friday evening. He stayed there for two more nights, and left Ireland on Sunday evening. It was the early hours of Monday morning before he got back to the air terminus in Cromwell Road. He said it was midday when he arrived at the Frances'.

That Monday morning, Louise Anderson received both her cards from Ireland. In the evening, Hanratty bumped into Laurence Lanigan outside the Essoldo in Burnt Oak. The latter vividly remembered Hanratty's hair – 'You could see it was dyed because it seemed to have two shades.' Hanratty told him that he was on his way to Hendon dogs. Lanigan remembered, 'He told me he was going screwing [house-breaking] the next day because it was a Jewish holiday and they would all be at the synagogue.'[7]

During that week, Louise gave Hanratty £120 for stolen items which he'd sold to her. Altogether, in just over three weeks, she gave him about £360. To show his gratitude, he sent her eighteen carnations, with a card saying 'Love from Jim'.

It was possibly that Saturday, 16 September, when he was still wearing his favourite suit, that he took Carole France to Battersea Funfair. He'd been at the France house during the afternoon. As he was taking a taxi to the West End, she asked if he'd mind dropping her off as she wanted to go to Chelsea. It was a rare opportunity for him. Carole was an attractive girl, but he'd never been able to see her on her own: 'Dixie is very strict with her, he tried to keep me away from her.'

In the cab, Hanratty asked what she was going to do, and she replied that she had nothing particular in mind. She readily agreed to go out for the evening with him. He first had to go to Louise's, 'to show her some stones'. He did that quickly, while Carole waited outside. They then went for a coffee, before Hanratty hailed another cab and they went to the fair. They managed to fit in all the major attractions: the Big Splash, the Big Dipper, the Switchback, the Big Wheel and, of course, the dodgems.

They walked back across Chelsea Bridge and made it to a pub on the Embankment just before it closed. They had 'a kiss and a cuddle' there, and then Hanratty took her along one of the deserted side-streets behind Victoria coach station. 'I was intimate with her,' is how he put it. 'I had no Durex. Her father would go potty if he knew.'

Afterwards Hanratty called a taxi for her, and gave her the money for the fare home.

On 20 September Hanratty at last bought his car, making a down-payment of £113 on a cream 1953 Sunbeam Alpine, priced at £375. It was the type that would in those days have been described as a sports coupé. He got Louise and Ann Pryce to act as guarantors for him.

Whether he should have bought it was a different matter. This had nothing to do with financial or legal considerations; but rather that, in his enthusiasm to purchase the car, Hanratty had overlooked some glaring mechanical defects. The rear back bumper was dented, and the nearside rear light had been knocked out. More importantly, the car had a tendency to jump out of third gear; if you didn't hold it carefully on the clutch, it would stall.

Hanratty, however, was simply delighted and quite unperturbed. He was told that it had a six-month guarantee, and he could take it back to have any problems rectified. He was completely trusting: 'The man at the garage gave me a note.'

It wasn't too long before he was stopped by police – the following day, as it happened, when he was driving through Colindale. He produced his Irish driving licence, gave his name and address as James Ryan of 46 Mildenhall Road, Lower Clapton, E5 (which was actually Ann Pryce's address), and was soon on his way again.

He proudly showed the Sunbeam Alpine off to everyone. He took Louise out in it almost every day, ferrying her between her flat in Sussex Gardens and her shop in Greek Street, Soho. He allowed Dixie to drive it, although only close to his home as 'Dixie is not a careful driver.' France also had understandable problems in holding the car in gear. Still, he helped Hanratty remove a paint stain from the wing, and Charlotte (who else?) cleaned it for him.

The second day after he got it, he again saw Eileen Cunningham, his cousin. He gave her a lift, but she had some unsettling news for him. A few weeks earlier, the police had been to see his parents.

Detective Sergeant Douglas Elliott, from Ruislip police station, had been investigating burglaries in the area. On the night of 2/3 August, there was a break-in at a house named Vallan, in Hills Lane, Northwood. A Voightlander camera, valued at £110, and £42 in cash were stolen. Entry had been easily effected – a window was left open – but the burglar had left his fingerprints on the window-sill. On 22 August, the fingerprint branch informed DS Elliott that the prints from that robbery, as well as those from a break-in in Ruislip at the beginning of April, had been matched with James Hanratty's. Accordingly, DS Elliott went round to the family home on 27 August.

Hanratty didn't allow the news to quell his soaring spirits. In fact, he'd never been able to think through the consequences of any train of events; and this development wouldn't have been more than momentarily troubling. Those were heady days for him. There's every indication that in this brief period he was at his happiest and most confident. He had money to spare, a soft-topped two-seater sports car of his own to drive, and a choice of girls to accompany him.

On Saturday, 23 September, at about 1.00 p.m., he drew up

outside Gladys Deacon's house. Still only eighteen, she was the girl he'd known longest, and with whom he'd had a necessarily intermittent relationship. She hadn't expected him, so by the time she had agreed to go out with him, and got ready, it was about 3.00 when they left. Hanratty, still wearing his best suit, had chatted to her father while he waited.

He took Gladys for a drive in the country. They headed north to Bedford, an area he knew reasonably well. After tea at the restaurant in the Granada cinema in Bedford, he left Gladys sitting in the car alone in a car park. Predictably, Hanratty was hoping to combine pleasure with business. He knew of a contact, in Ashburnham Road, who he thought might be interested in buying some pieces of jewellery. Equally predictably, Hanratty wasn't sure of the address, couldn't find the man, and quickly gave up.

They drove back to London. After having a drink and a sandwich near Piccadilly, he took Gladys to what was, for him, always the main attraction, a funfair; he took her to Battersea. They left about midnight. He drove her back to north London, and parked just off Brockley Hill in Stanmore. They had sex in the car, though it must have been a more than usually messy business: Hanratty ended up with semen stains down his trousers. It was after one in the morning when he dropped her home.

He returned the following day, and took her to Richmond. (Ironically, Alphon was in Richmond that afternoon – being charged at the local police station with the assault on Meike Dalal.) They took a boat out on the Thames, stopped for a snack in a Wimpy bar, went to the pictures in Edgware, had a drink at what Gladys described as a 'nautical' public-house, and finally dined at an Italian restaurant in Hendon. It had been a wonderful weekend.

On the Monday, Hanratty stayed at the Pembury Hotel, one of the cluster of hotels along Seven Sisters Road opposite Finsbury Park, where the Alexandra Court, in which Alphon had stayed, was also situated. He stayed the remainder of the week with Louise. She had decided that he needed a steady girlfriend, and accordingly introduced him to Mary Meaden, a twenty-two-year-old who sometimes helped Louise out at her shop in the evenings, but whose regular work was as a dress-shop assistant in Stockwell, south London.

They hit it off. When Mary described him later to the press, she mentioned that he blushed easily; and didn't drink, smoke or dance; and that his hair, which was obviously ginger, had been dyed black. The second time they met, on the Wednesday, he asked her out.

He got tickets for the following night for Harry Secombe, one of Britain's major entertainment stars at that time, at the London Palladium.

He was clearly so thrilled by the prospect of this date, and also so concerned about the condition of his suit after Saturday night's performance with Gladys Deacon, that he took his suit in to be cleaned at a twenty-four-hour cleaners opposite the Twentieth Century Fox offices in Wardour Street.

There were only a few seats left for Secombe, so they sat in the gods. The following day, he took Mary out again, to the pictures in Golders Green. As they came out, he abruptly asked her to marry him. 'I told him you don't just fall head over heels in one week,' she testified. 'He seemed to accept that and said he would wait a bit.'[8]

Perhaps feeling slightly abashed, Hanratty did not stay at Louise's on the Saturday, although Mary was there waiting for him. He did, however, telephone to apologize. That Saturday night he was back at work, and back in familiar territory. He broke into houses by the recreation ground in Stanmore, just off Dennis Lane – and just the other side of Brockley Hill where, exactly a week earlier, he'd spent a rather different Saturday evening.

There were three houses together, in fairly open ground, and Hanratty broke into two of them. At the first, Trevone, he smashed some leaded lights in the windows downstairs to get in, but their interior locks were sound. He had to go outside again and climb a trellis to reach the bedrooms on the first floor. Here, he broke two windows to gain access, but it was awkward and dangerous. He did get in, but succeeded also in snagging his jacket, tearing it badly. Wearing your best suit for this kind of work may have helped in allaying suspicions before and afterwards, but there were clearly drawbacks.

He couldn't see anything he wanted here either, so he took the opportunity to go through the man's wardrobe. He found a barathea, a long coat worn with striped trousers on formal occasions. He decided he liked it, and threw it down to the garden. He then checked the other property, The Wheelhouse, a bungalow. The electricity was off, so he assumed, correctly, that the occupants were on holiday. He wandered round with a coloured candle which he'd taken from the bedroom dressing-table; the householder found its remains in a wash-hand basin when he returned. 'There was no jewellery or cash. I would not bother with anything else.' He left, picked up the barathea from the garden of the first house, and put it on. 'It fitted me excellent. I thought it went all right with the suit trousers, and made me look like a doctor.' He discarded his suit jacket in bushes on the recreation ground as he made good his escape.

He saw Mary again briefly on the Sunday, and gave her a compact as a present. They talked about his hair, which must by now have looked at best unsightly and at worst ridiculous. 'He said he had dyed it black', commented Mary, 'because he was tired of being fair, but that if I didn't like it he would go back to his original colour.'

Whether she said so or not, he seems to have assumed that she would prefer it in its natural state. On Tuesday he called in at a men's barber's shop in Kilburn for a shave. Hanratty then asked the hairdresser if he could remove the dye. Not altogether surprisingly, he couldn't; local barbers were hardly likely to be equipped with the necessary materials. He had to call in assistance from Jean Rice, who ran a ladies' salon above his premises. Mrs Rice described Hanratty's hair as 'black at the front, brown on the sides, mixed with deep auburn'.[9] Whether it was much improved by her valiant efforts at removing the tint is difficult to say.

The previous day Hanratty had remembered, despite his long absence from home, to post his father's birthday card. So, on the Tuesday, as Jimmy was trying to shed his disguise, his father was at Scotland Yard, telling police that they were looking for his son in the wrong country. The following day, Wednesday, was Jimmy's own birthday: he was twenty-five. He took his suitcases round to Louise Anderson's, probably because he wanted to leave them somewhere more permanently; and then telephoned Mary Meaden. Would she go out with him on his birthday? She explained she wouldn't be able to until 8.30; he considered that too late, but she did agree to see him on Friday. They arranged a meeting: 7.30 p.m. outside the Astoria in Charing Cross Road. He told her that he hoped to have his car back by then; the previous week, he'd had to put it back in the garage to get the problem with the gears sorted out. He only had the use of it for just over a week.

It was on Thursday, 5 October that Hanratty learned the dreadful situation. He was not being sought by police for a few desultory burglaries. He was not just one among hundreds in a second-division rogues' gallery; but the country's No.1 wanted man. It is assumed that he found out by going to the Rehearsal Club. He would have got all the confirmation he needed from the morning's papers, with their references to a man named Ryan, who had abandoned a hired car at Dublin Airport. Hanratty knew it had to be him. He rang Charles France in distress. It was a brief conversation. Hanratty had only just registered the shock, and France was constrained as he knew that the police were watching his house and tapping his phone. Hanratty immediately suspected that would be the case, and so told France he would be unable to go round to see him.

On Friday, Hanratty again bought the newspapers to read the latest reports. He tried to think through his perilous situation. 'I did want to come forward to clear the matter up, but I felt I could not as I knew the police were looking for me for burglary charges. I had only just come out in March from doing three years. I thought I would get a long sentence this time and I didn't want to go inside again. I knew that Superintendent Acott was in charge of the case and therefore decided to telephone him to explain my position.'

First, Hanratty went to a garage in Poland Street to purchase a Jaguar 'Fan 5' key. (With his specialized knowledge of cars, he appreciated precisely which models of Jaguar the key would fit.) 'Two men in white coats were there. They asked me for a driving licence. I showed them my Irish licence. They said, "You can buy as many keys as you like for 3s 6d."' Then he telephoned Acott from Warren Street underground station and, after coming out, walked down Tottenham Court Road and bought a pair of spectacles that he hoped might act as a disguise.

The reasoning was wretchedly misguided, hopelessly naive, but, given Hanratty's personality, utterly plausible. He was, as ever, thinking very short-term. Doubtless, his mind was in turmoil. Yet nothing would stand in the way of his important social engagement: his meeting with Mary Meaden outside the Astoria at 7.30. He arrived on time. She stood him up. He must have been utterly crestfallen. Only a week earlier, Hanratty had been riding high; now, he had lost everything that made him feel good: his suit, his car, his girl.

(Mary Meaden had no idea that he was a suspect. She subsequently explained, 'I was ill and did not turn up.' Even after Hanratty's conviction, she continued to have the highest regard for him, describing him as 'a perfect gentleman'.)[10]

Hanratty went in alone to see the film – it was *South Pacific* – and afterwards had fish-and-chips before ringing Acott from Leicester Square, and telling him where he could collect his belongings. Then he rang Charles France again. In this conversation, Hanratty stated that he had stayed at the Vienna hotel for one night, and that he had an alibi for the murder. He mentioned that he had £250 put aside, and he was going to 'give the police a good run for their money'. He also promised to ring again, but said that next time it would be long-distance.

He had hit upon a plan of action: 'I decided to go to Liverpool to straighten things out.'

Shortly after midnight, he stole a black Mark VII Jaguar from near Portland Place, just behind BBC Broadcasting House. 'The car was standing in front of a block of flats. I knew it would be there because the block had no garage space. I think it was a 1956 model. It had a red interior, and a floor gear-change with overdrive. The petrol gauge on the dashboard wasn't working – I noticed that because it was so unusual.'

To be on the safe side, therefore, Hanratty had to fill up the tank, putting 16 gallons of petrol in the car at a cost, he remembered, of £4 10s. He then went north up the M1 motorway, and from there to Manchester, where he abandoned the car. When it was found by police, it had several crates of Chester's beer in the boot. How they came to be there is, now, an unsolvable mystery.

Hanratty then caught a train to Liverpool. He phoned Scotland Yard on the Saturday; and again on the Monday. That day, he had taken up Acott's suggestion, and decided to send flowers to his mother. It is a measure of Hanratty's trusting and ductile nature that he did exactly as Acott had suggested. At about 4.45 p.m., he went into a flower shop along the Scotland Road, and asked for a bowl of artificial carnations.

He paid 35s, and left the shop; but Acott had, of course, ensured that a police warning was issued to florists in the Liverpool area. The shop assistant said, 'I'm sure that's the man they're looking for over the A6 Murder.' She saw a policeman coming up the street and told him. He telephoned the station. They didn't catch him, but the visit was recounted in detail in Tuesday morning's papers. Hanratty, who considered that he was being straight with Acott, felt betrayed: 'I read it all in the papers, and saw a photo of her shop. I rang up Acott and told him it was not fair to do that.'

Having read a full description of himself in the morning papers, however, he thought it imperative to adopt an immediate disguise. He was described as having dark auburn hair, wearing a dark suit, black pointed-toe shoes and an open V-necked T-shirt. So he changed into brown shoes and a sports jacket, with a white shirt and tie. Then, failing to distinguish the suitably cautionary from the utterly foolhardy, he went into a barber's and asked to have his hair bleached – at least the fourth time that he'd had his hair colour treated in less than three months, and the second time within a week.

Gladys Deacon was another who received a telephone call from him, though he was not so much concerned with reassuring her as with reassuring his mother. He asked if Gladys could go round to see her, to emphasize that everything was all right, to tell her – that old refrain with him – not to worry, and especially not to believe everything that she read in the papers.

He went to Blackpool on Wednesday, 11 October, and arrived at about 5.00 p.m. He wandered round for a while, then noticed queues forming for the early evening performance of the Yana show at the Queen's Theatre, with special guest Al Read. Hanratty bought a ticket. After coming out he went to the Winter Gardens, where a dance was in progress. He came out about 10.00 and looked around the amusement arcades. Then he booked a room at Hope House, a guest-house on Central Drive run by Jean Skellito and her parents. After booking he said something about his car being parked awkwardly, and they directed him to a car park. He left and went across the road for a late supper at the Stevonia Café.

Once Sherrard was appointed to head the defence team, he straightaway ensured, on 23 October, that the defence engaged a proper private investigator, Joe Gillbanks, a retired detective sergeant who had served with the Liverpool City police for thirty-three years, to carry out investigations there.

Not knowing anything about the police inquiries which (had the defence known about them) would have been regarded as encouraging, Gillbanks determined that the main thrust of his efforts must be to discover the contacts in Liverpool with whom Hanratty had spent the all-important night of 22/23 August.

When interviewed on 12 October, Hanratty had told Acott that, when he had returned to see his friends the previous weekend to ask them to confirm his alibi, they had thrown him out. 'They got really choked when they heard I was wanted for the A6 Murder. They don't want to know now.

'You can't blame them, Mr Acott. They're already in trouble with the police. The flat's full up with jewellery and they've a load of jelly there. Another thing, one of them's wanted on a warrant for non-payment of a fine for having TVs on HP.'

Gillbanks spoke to two likely people. Terence McNally, whom

Hanratty had mentioned and whose home was searched by police on the night of Hanratty's arrest (the *Daily Telegraph* had reported that police were checking 'a warren of tenements'), agreed that he did know Hanratty. However, he declined to be more forthcoming, arguing that if Hanratty was not willing to open up, why should he? Then Gillbanks interviewed Francis Healey, who met Hanratty in Walton Prison. He lived in the 'Bull Ring' flats with his parents, sister and two brothers; but there was nothing to indicate that Hanratty may have stayed there. Gillbanks concluded pessimistically, 'I have also interviewed a considerable number of other persons in an effort to trace the house where Hanratty stayed during his visit to Liverpool, but the details as supplied would fit so many places, that without some further information this task will take some considerable time.' In this vital area, not surprisingly, his inquiries came to naught.

If the defence was active in trying to gather fresh information, so too were the police, in taking statements about Hanratty's various criminal exploits from various criminal (and other) associates. One by one, Acott interviewed those who were connected in some way with Hanratty. Most could add nothing to his inquiries. However, he did enjoy some success with Charles France, Louise Anderson and Donald Slack.

Hanratty used to place bets with Slack. He'd known him for about five years, having met him in the billiard hall at Solomon's gym. He clearly looked up to him, and had even kept in touch while in prison. (Laurence Lanigan recalled having written these letters for Hanratty.) At about 6.00 p.m. on the day of his release in March, Hanratty went to see him at his home in Ealing. Slack gave him a meal and £25. Hanratty entrusted to him a private folder, containing photographs, letters and other mementoes which he said had great sentimental value. Slack promised to look after it for him.

After Hanratty's arrest, Acott went to see Slack, and took away this file of personal memorabilia. (No one knows what became of it.) The rest of the meeting is shrouded in some controversy. What is clear is that Acott later told Hanratty that he had been to see Slack, who had told him that he (Hanratty) had spoken to Slack about getting a gun when he (Hanratty) had gone to see him on his release from prison earlier that year.

Remarkably, the substance of this conversation was confirmed, not by Slack, but by Hanratty himself. He told his solicitor how he remembered it: 'He asked me what I had in mind. I said that screwing [house-breaking] was all played out. "If you want to get rich these days", I said, "you've got to have a shooter and go after cash."'

He said he made the remark out of a kind of childish bravado. He was dismayed to realize that idle talk of months earlier was now being listed in the inventory of his incriminating behaviour. 'I said that as I wanted to make an impression after coming out after three years. It was just a silly statement. Once, I broke into a house, years ago, and found a gun, possibly a woman's small gun, perhaps a derringer. I gave that away. If I'd wanted a shooter, I could have got one easily from the clubs. You can get one at the Rehearsal, easy, they stack them up there. I've seen any number of people with guns under their coats at Solomon's Billiard Hall. But it never entered my mind to get a gun.'

Hanratty wrote to Slack:

Dear Don,
Mr Acott mentioned to me that I asked you for a gun, or did I ever mention buying a gun, and you told him that I enquired about a gun. You know yourself it was only a matter of conversation and you know if I had had a gun, I would not be in the same line of business as at present. I am worried about this matter and I'd like you to drop me a line and let me know the details.

Unknown to Hanratty – unknown to anyone until thirty years later – Slack's statement created no problems whatever. In it, Slack said: 'I have certainly never spoken to him [Hanratty] about firearms or given him weapons of any kind.'[11]

It seems that Hanratty had fallen for Acott's bluff. The latter now had a 'gun' conversation in his cache of evidence against Hanratty.

For a strong personality like Slack, police questioning held few dangers; for weak ones like France or Louise Anderson, it was a petrifying prospect. Both, being on the fringes of criminality, were vulnerable to threats of facing charges themselves if they did not cooperate; both agreed to become prosecution witnesses. Louise Anderson must have undergone a torrid time in her police interviews. Each time they saw her, she seemed to become more and more antipathetic towards Hanratty. Poor France tried hard to muster as much integrity as possible in the circumstances. The substance of what he said was, again, confirmed by Hanratty himself, who merely disputed the interpretation placed upon it.

In essence, France's testimony was very damaging. It concerned the conversation he'd had with Hanratty about the back seat of a bus. Hanratty, in some exasperation, said that the conversation occurred not when they were coming back from the dog-track, but when they were going to a betting-shop in Chalk Farm. Hanratty was explaining some of the mechanics of housebreaking to France: 'I am telling him the burglar alarms on houses are always on the front so the burglar can know it's belled. I then said, "If you've got any rubbish you don't want, you put it under the back seat on a bus."'

In other words, Hanratty was referring to his own particular way of sorting through the proceeds of his robberies, separating the valuable items from the baubles and trinkets, and disposing of the latter, which he knew he would not able to sell, under the back seat. Nothing more would then be heard of them. So although he disagreed about the circumstances and the import of the dialogue, he did accept, as he did with Slack, that the substance of what was being used against him was broadly accurate.

Hanratty also wrote to Dixie France:

Dear Dixie,
I'm surprised over this difficulty that I'm in although it makes no difference to me, whatever you say will be the truth. In a way I am very glad that you are giving evidence against me as now my solicitor can have facts. You will not think much of me for what I'm about to do and I don't think much of what you are about to do, though it won't make much difference as I'm innocent.

Thus, as the days slipped by to the preliminary court hearing, there were a number of pieces of prosecution evidence which appeared to fuse together: the 'gun' conversation with Slack, the 'back seat' conversation with France, the '36A bus' conversation with William Nudds. Then there were the identifications of John Skillett and James Trower. Finally, of towering importance, there was the evidence of Valerie Storie – which consisted not solely of her identification, but also of what she recalled of the gunman having said about himself during those harrowing hours in the Morris Minor. Much of it seemed to fit Hanratty.

Yet however much the prosecution evidence appeared to dovetail, the defence, for its part, could point to the absence of vital corroborating evidence, the total lack of a motive and the fact that Hanratty had at least the prospects of an alibi.

The prison prevented the letters to Slack and France from being sent; Hanratty was informed that they had been confiscated by the Home Office, presumably because it was viewed as an attempt to influence Crown witnesses (although Slack never was a Crown witness). Hanratty was, however, allowed to write to his aunt and mother:

Brixton Prison
16 November 1961

Dear Auntie,
Just a few lines to let you know that I am in the best of health. I was very pleased to see Eileen on Tuesday. She cheered me up a great deal and when you see her I would like you to thank her for me. Though we never had long together, it made my mind more at ease. Well, Auntie, I bet when you got to hear about this trouble, it was a great shock to you; but you know that I couldn't do a terrible thing like that. Though I am a bit of a crook, I wouldn't hurt a mouse. I suppose you've read articles about this case, and if I don't speak up, I will find myself in serious trouble. I am lost for words now. Give my love to Uncle Fred and Eileen,
Your loving nephew, Jim

Brixton Prison
21 November 1961

Dear Mum,
Just a few lines to let you know I am keeping well. I don't want you to worry about me. I know you can't help worrying, things might look bad at the moment, but please do not worry too much. I don't think that Dad and I will be able to do anything towards the case. I gather that Mr Acott has found some more witness statements against me.
By the time you receive this letter I will be in court. This is going to be a very long case, and the newspapers aren't doing me any justice, but you and I know it is not in me to commit such an awful offence.
I am going to speak up for myself when the time comes, because if I don't, Mr Acott will do all he can to convict me. But I have got faith in my defence. Mr Kleinman and Mr Sherrard are both very intelligent men. Without any doubt, they know that I am innocent. When the time comes, I want you and Dad to be present at the big court, so you can hear this ridiculous charge. As I said before, please have faith in me. I will soon straighten this terrible thing out.
Give my love to all, From your loving son,
Jim

FOR TWO WEEKS from 22 November, the small market town of Ampthill in Bedfordshire became the focus of national attention. In those days, committal proceedings took the form of an exhaustive pre-trial hearing before magistrates who would decide whether the case should be sent for trial.

By the late 1960s, this seemed an unnecessary duplication for the Crown, which had to present all its evidence at two stages of the trial process. Nor did the defence endorse the system. The some-times melodramatic reporting of the preliminary proceedings could seriously damage a defendant's chances of securing justice at the actual trial. So a token hearing was substituted for the full one. The evidence was usually presented in document form. Reporting restrictions were usually imposed, so that only the bare bones of the case were published. Without much ado, the case would then be sent for trial at the Crown Court.

Naturally, Hanratty's committal took place under the old system, which allowed the proceedings to be fully reported. Equally naturally, there was scant prospect of less than saturation coverage in this case. Scores of press correspondents tried to shoehorn themselves into the small courthouse.

For the duration, Hanratty was transferred back to Bedford Prison; the governor of Brixton had said it would be difficult to provide an escort from London every day. Originally, Hanratty was charged solely with the murder of Michael Gregsten. Now, two additional charges were added: of attempting to murder Valerie Storie; and of raping her. The rape aspect of the case had, previously, been virtually suppressed. Now that the matter was raised in open court, newspapers were not slow to exploit the even more salacious aspects of this horrific story. That same day, the *Evening Standard* headlined its report from Ampthill:

VALERIE RAPED THEN SHOT FIVE TIMES

The Crown case was put by Mr E. G. MacDermott, for the Director of Public Prosecutions. Most of his opening speech consisted of a narration of the details of the crime. After this preamble, the magistrates heard evidence (or, in one or two cases, depositions) from seventy-one witnesses, which gave an early indication of what a protracted and complex case this was destined to become.

Many of those seventy-one either made formal statements about their own peripheral role in the case, or simply had little relevance to it. From the outset, the Crown's strategy seemed to be to hope that the sheer mass of the evidence would camouflage its want of substance. While there were abundant witnesses to Hanratty's movements before and some time after the crime, what he may or may not have been doing over most of that vital August week was simply a blank page in the prosecution script.

Nor was that all. Louise Anderson sobbed loudly the moment she entered the witness-box. Similarly, the France family witnesses – Charles, Charlotte and Carole – appeared distressed when giving evidence; in fact, Charlotte broke down under cross-examination and was led weeping from the courtroom.

There was, in fact, a particular reason for Charlotte's distress, as she explained in a statement that she later made about what had happened to her at the magistrates' court:

'The police told Carole and I that we would travel to Ampthill by police car with another witness named Louise Anderson. At 8.30 a.m. on Tuesday, 28 November, a car arrived at our flat with Louise Anderson and a police driver. When we arrived, we were all shown into a witness room where we sat together. Although I knew who Louise Anderson was, I am certain she did not realize who I and Carole were. In the middle of the afternoon, Carole was called out of the room to give evidence. Louise Anderson and I were left sitting together with no other witness near us. I told her I was scared because I had never had to give evidence in a criminal case before. Louise said she was scared too. She went on. "Those poor people. They didn't know he had the gun, but I did." I asked her, "Who are those people then? Can you tell me?" She said, "It was Dixie's place, in St John's Wood." I asked her, "Where did he have the gun then?" She said, "He used to keep it in a cupboard at the top of the stairs in a carrier bag among the blankets."

'In order to see whether it was my house she was talking about, I asked her, "What was the colour of the blankets?" She said, "They were pink. He used to keep the gun in a screwed-up carrier-bag which had the name Tomkins or Timkins on it." I said, "Did these people know he had it there?" Louise said, "Oh, no, he used to take the blankets from the cupboard and make his bed himself and put them back in the cupboard when he got up in the morning."

'At that moment, another woman witness said to me, "You're looking white, are you all right?" I said to her, "She's just told me that he had a gun and it was in my house."'

At that point, Charlotte was called to give evidence. 'A police officer gave me a chair because I was feeling so bad. When I was called into the witness-box, I felt in a terrible state and can hardly remember giving evidence because all I could think of was the awful news Louise Anderson had told me. At the end of my evidence I had to be taken out of court and attended to.

'The morning I travelled with Louise Anderson to Ampthill in the police car was the first time I had ever seen her and I did not know her. I have not met her before or since.

'It is a fact that my butcher is Tomkins of Hampstead Road, NW1, and every Friday my brother brings my meat to me in one of their carrier-bags. It is also a fact that at the top of the stairs on the first floor of our house is an airing cupboard, on the top shelf of which I store my blankets. When Hanratty first began to stay and sleep on a settee in our living-room, I took two blankets from the cupboard and put them for him to use. After that, he always took two blankets from the cupboard himself and returned them to the cupboard himself next morning. This he continued to do until the last time he stayed here for the night.

'No other member of my family would have had reason for going to that cupboard during the summer months. I have been so ill and upset about this whole case but especially about the news given to me by Louise Anderson that I didn't know what to do. I talked it over with my husband and went to see our solicitor. On his advice I sent for you to tell you the whole story.'[1]

Acott and Oxford took down this lengthy statement on 12 January 1962. It was never disclosed to the defence. Yet it was of the utmost significance, for a number of reasons. First, it explained Charlotte France's disposition in the witness-box, which could have created the impression that Hanratty was a malevolent force in their lives.

Second, irrespective of whether as a whole it is credible or not, what is simply incredible is that Louise Anderson did not realize who Charlotte and Carole were. It is certainly true that they had never met before, as Charles always kept a rigid demarcation line between family and what he and Hanratty termed business. Louise certainly knew, however, that Hanratty frequently spent time with Dixie, his wife and daughters in St John's Wood. Yet when the police car drew up at a flat in St John's Wood, she didn't put two and two together? Utterly implausible. This, then, suggests that the conversation was directly engineered in order to disconcert Charlotte immediately before she was due to give evidence.

Third, if it was true, then it was highly relevant, probably admissible and certainly persuasive evidence. So why was it never given in evidence by Anderson herself, either at the magistrates' or the assize court?

The explanation can only be that the Crown did not regard it as true. (Ironically, the essence of the story could well have been true, albeit without in any way incriminating Hanratty; it seems at least possible that Charles France may have been used as the conduit to pass the weapon to the murderer.) Certainly, Acott privately described Louise Anderson in the most disparaging terms:

'Mrs Anderson is a neurotic woman, and unreliable as regards dates. There is little doubt that although she has not been convicted, she has been a receiver of stolen property. This is made clear from her accounts of transactions with Hanratty during those weeks when we know he was actively engaged in housebreaking. From the lists of property taken possession of from her flat, they include no less than fifty items of jewellery, furs and other valuable property.'[2]

Since the hunt for Hanratty, Louise had been having a traumatic time. First, the police arrived for Hanratty's suitcases, and then, shortly afterwards, they returned to clear her premises of those items of stolen property. One of the curiosities of the case is that she was never charged with receiving stolen goods, despite Acott's 'little doubt' over the matter.

Possibly, the police let her know that they were keeping that option open. Certainly, Anderson buckled under something, whether or not it was police pressure. Over a matter of weeks, she made a series of increasingly damaging statements against Hanratty. In one, she indicated that she'd missed a pair of nylon gloves after one of his visits; in another, her sixth, that he had 'defaced' a *Health & Efficiency* magazine, and that 'his general conversation was on sex'.[3]

This material is interesting because it is precisely the sort of evidence that the prosecution case conspicuously lacked. Hanratty never wore gloves for his burglaries – which is why he obligingly left his prints all over the place. Yet the gunman had worn gloves. Anderson's was the only suggestion ever put forward that Hanratty may have had a pair of gloves.

Second, there was absolutely no motive for the crime – why on earth would Hanratty have wanted to commit such a terrible offence? There was no explanation whatever. The prosecution could merely infer that the murderer was a sex-starved fiend. There was nothing to suggest that this in any way fitted Hanratty – or, at least, there was nothing until Louise Anderson produced her scurrilous sixth statement.

Yet however much the Crown might have wished to accommodate these statements, they didn't. Again, one can only assume it was because they were thought too fantastic even for prosecution purposes.

Central to the prosecution case was, of course, the critical testimony of Valerie Storie. Without her survival it was hard to imagine anyone at all having been apprehended for the crime. On 24 November – which, to compound the sadness of the occasion, was Valerie's twenty-third birthday – the court itself moved to the archery wing of Stoke Mandeville hospital to allow her to give evidence in camera.

The legal process inflicted such an array of dirty tricks on Hanratty that many have been tempted to see another here. Why, at a public hearing, was this crucial part of the evidence suddenly heard in camera? On this occasion, though, the decision seems to have been determined solely by practicalities. By allowing her to give her testimony in private, the magistrates were able to limit the numbers at the hospital and thus forestall an unseemly ruckus with the press, legal observers and sundry others all jostling for position.

It was an immense pity that she could not have given her evidence in public; as can be imagined, it was intensely gripping. Further incidental details emerged about what had happened that evening in the car:

'The man was not carrying a suitcase, holdall or anything of that kind ... I told the witness Kerr that the man had brown hair. I said it wasn't a dark brown. His hair was medium brown, definitely not dark brown. It appeared to be swept straight back without a parting...'

She spoke also about her identification of Hanratty: 'I identified one man as the man who shot and killed Mike and shot me. I see him here sitting opposite me. Having listened to a man talking for nearly six hours, it's very hard to forget a voice. It's very hard to forget a face.' Having been reminded that she had also identified someone else, at her first parade, she encapsulated her evidence, saying, 'I had no shadow of doubt that I had got the correct man this time.'[4]

Acott himself was the last of the seventy-one to give evidence, on Monday, 4 and Tuesday, 5 December. He had to endure a lengthy cross-examination; the questioning was far tougher than senior police officers would usually expect, especially at committal.

However, his testimony was electrifying – at least so far as Sherrard and the defence were concerned. They had hitherto been kept completely in the dark about the progress of inquiries concerning the Liverpool alibi. Now Acott was saying, 'I took all the notes from the solicitor [about Hanratty's alibi] and sent them to Liverpool. The information was that he had gone into a sweet-shop in Scotland Road and spoken to a woman in the shop, that there was a child in the shop and that he had asked the way to Carlton or Talbot Road. That information has been substantiated by our own inquiries.'

Acott was forced to admit that, if Hanratty had committed the murder, the timetable was difficult to gauge. He agreed that if Mrs Dinwoodie had seen Hanratty, then she could not have done so on the Monday, the 21st, 'because we know from the evidence where he was on the 21st' [in London].

Nor did the episode of the gun on the bus appear to fit in. 'I don't say he got rid of the gun on a bus in London on the 24th and then went off to Liverpool that day so that he could send a telegram saying he was having a nice time and would be back the following day. I cannot say who put the gun on that bus. I do say that probably the defendant abandoned the gun on the bus on the 24th and then tore off to Liverpool. But if that is when he went then he could not have seen Mrs Dinwoodie and she could not have seen him. If Mrs Dinwoodie saw him, it must have been on 22 August. I had Mrs Dinwoodie's statement double-checked by a further inquiry. Mrs Dinwoodie is a perfectly respectable and responsible citizen.'

Sherrard would have liked to hear of all this much earlier on; nevertheless, it all seemed wonderfully encouraging.

One of the strongest aspects of Hanratty's defence was the baffling absence of forensic science evidence. Yet there was a chink in this armour: the loss of his suit jacket. Even without labouring the point, the Crown could hint that there may have been a very good reason why Hanratty had discarded the jacket of the suit he was so fond of. Certainly, suggested the prosecution, his own explanation was deeply suspect: not only had the coat disappeared, but there hadn't even been burglaries at Trevone and The Wheelhouse, the two houses Hanratty had mentioned. 'I did inquire whether there had been any breakings and enterings in Stanmore,' said Superintendent Acott. Not only had there not been any; it didn't even seem as though those houses existed. 'I did not come across the name of a house, Trevone, in my inquiries in Stanmore.'[5]

From the outset, Acott had recognized the importance of the evidence regarding the housebreakings at Stanmore. At the very first interview in Blackpool, Hanratty mentioned them to Acott, who said, 'I'll check these housebreakings and try and recover the jacket from the park.' That afternoon, when the interview resumed, Acott straightaway told Hanratty, 'We've had inquiries made at Stanmore and surrounding districts and we are unable to find any record respecting the housebreakings you mentioned, nor to find any trace of your blue jacket.'

In the witness-box, he confirmed to Sherrard that this remained the position. Then, on Tuesday morning, while Acott was still in the witness-box, an officer came into court and handed him a piece of paper. Acott then informed the court that he had tendered incorrect evidence. 'I have just learned that on 1 October this year a house named Trevone of Dennis Lane, Stanmore was broken into, but no property was stolen.'

Despite what Acott had been saying for the past six weeks, the housebreakings had occurred. Hanratty had been right all along; and the police wrong. Moreover, the police were wrong because they hadn't bothered to carry out the most basic checks. On the Sunday afternoon immediately following the burglary, the owner of Acorns, the third house on that ground, noticed the upper windows of Trevone flapping open in the wind. He went round to check, saw the broken glass and called the police to report a break-in. They investigated the matter that afternoon, and both families were informed straightaway.

Although Acott had to admit that the police were wrong about that, he continued to insist that the most pertinent part of Hanratty's story was untrue: no jacket had been stolen.

Sherrard delivered a robust summing-up, in which he emphasized that everything which Hanratty had told the police had turned out to be true.

'On Monday, Superintendent Acott said he knew nothing about a house called Trevone being broken into. You will understand me, I am sure, when I say my heart leapt this morning when the prosecution confirmed that the house was burgled. My client had stuck to his story all along that he broken into that house and ripped his jacket, and it was for that reason he got rid of it. If there had been blood on the jacket, he took a very long time to get rid of it.

'There is no forensic evidence. The Crown says that the assailant was blood group O secretor, and the defendant was blood group O secretor. But so was Peter Alphon, the original suspect. The evidence is that 40–50 per cent of the population was blood group O, and of them 80 per cent are O secretor.

'Every other clinical test has yielded a nil result.

'The case comes down to identification. Yet there have been two cases mentioned in *The Times* in the past fortnight alone, in which, despite positive identifications, mistakes were made.'

He concluded by submitting that there was simply insufficient evidence to send Hanratty for trial on any of the charges. 'It may have crossed your minds that this has been a case which might fairly be described as flimsy – one in which the prosecution has indeed attempted to scrape even the underside of the bottom of the barrel.' He asked the court to release his client. 'I do not want him held in jeopardy a moment longer.'

Despite's Sherrard's eloquence, despite rumours in legal circles that the whole case was so weak it would be dismissed, the magistrates determined that there was a case to answer, and that Hanratty should be committed for trial.

Sherrard did score one important victory, however. The prosecution applied for the case to be heard at Bedfordshire Assizes; Sherrard argued that the inevitable local prejudice after such a horrific case made it inappropriate for the case to be heard there. The magistrates, being local people themselves and better placed than anyone to understand the force of the argument, readily assented. They ordered that Hanratty should stand trial for his life at the Old Bailey in London.

· III ·
THE TRIAL AND
THE EVIDENCE

CHAPTER ELEVEN

ON THE OPENING day of the magistrates' court hearing, when the attention of almost the entire nation was directed towards Ampthill, two interesting developments in the case occurred elsewhere. The defence was contacted by a lady who said that she was Mrs Rouch (by no means a common name), and that she was telephoning from Marble Arch. She was calling, she said, because 'I know who the real killer is. And the real killer knows Alphon. I went to Scotland Yard with this information, but was turned away.'

The woman said that she was living with a man whose baby she had just had, but that he had warned her not to get involved. She added that if he went to work the next day, she would go to Wembley Park underground and try to phone again from there, to make arrangements to meet someone from the defence. She did not phone again.

That same day, a remand prisoner who was being returned to prison from a day at court in central London was overheard telling a fellow inmate that Hanratty had confessed to him. The man who overheard the conversation, Alfred Eatwell, was a hospital officer attached to Brixton Prison who was escorting the prisoners. He immediately reported it.

The following week, on 30 November, the prisoner who had made the remarks, Roy Langdale, was invited by Acott and Detective Sergeant Harry Heavens to make a statement. 'In the ordinary way,' he began, 'I would never tell you anything about another prisoner. This is different; it's a serious case of murder. I'll tell you what I know now because you ought to know the truth about this job.'[1]

Langdale said that when he was on the hospital wing of Brixton Prison, throughout November, Hanratty was there also, in a single cell. They met during daily exercise.

'The first time I saw [him] on the exercise yard I noticed he was walking on his own. He stood out because of his funny coloured hair which was dyed bright ginger. We talked to each other. I asked him who he was and what he was in for. He said, "I'm James Hanratty, the A6 killer." I asked him what he thought his chances were. He said, "It wasn't me, they'll get nothing on me. I've got chances."

'During the next three weeks I was in Brixton Prison Hanratty and I always walked together twice every day on exercise. We would never walk with anyone else and if another prisoner came up to us, we would always stop talking. All the time I knew Hanratty in Brixton I never saw him talk to another prisoner.

'In the first few days, Hanratty spent most of the time asking me about myself. In those days he always denied that he had anything to do with the A6 Murder. He would say very little about it and when I asked him questions he would change the subject. I was his only friend in prison, however, and we became quite pally.'

According to Langdale, Hanratty confided in him how he had committed the crime. 'Hanratty said, "I went up to the window and put the gun through and said, 'This is a stick-up.' I got in the back of the car and kept the gun on the man all the time and just talked to them. Gregsten pleaded with me to take their money and the car and just drive away but I didn't want that, so I shot Gregsten and told the girl to get in the back seat."'

Two days later, according to Langdale, Hanratty, entirely of his own volition, resumed the narrative. '"She made love to me directly she got in the back seat. She was frightened and she knew what I was going to do to her. She enjoyed it as much as me."'

Langdale continued, 'He told me Gregsten's blood was all over the front seat so he made the girl drag him out of the car and lay him down on the opposite side on a grass verge. "When she done that", Hanratty said, "I made her lay down on the grass beside him and I shot four or five times."'

The next morning Hanratty said to him, '"Somebody's been phoning the hospital and threatening Valerie. If they keep phoning it will leave me in the clear because I can't phone from in here." He added, "I wish she had died. I can't understand it. I put enough bullets in her."

'They were the main things I can remember. After I'd been exercising with him for a few days he seemed to get confidence in me. He came to trust me because I was the only one he'd talk to and he wanted to talk to someone to get this off his chest and that's when he began to talk to me about the murder. He kept going over and over again about the murder he had committed. Whenever I asked why he had done it, he always said, "It was the woman I wanted. I couldn't have done it with him there, could I?"

'I told the others I thought Hanratty must be a nutcase to do the murder and then talk about it. When he's not talking about the murder he spends most of his time talking about women and sex. I think he's sex-mad. The last time I saw him was on 21 November. He told me he was being moved to Bedford for the hearing of his case.'

Simultaneously, on 30 November, Detective Sergeant Oxford took a statement from Eatwell. The latter explained that he and other officers were escorting a group of eleven prisoners back from court at Middlesex Appeals quarter sessions at the Guildhall, Westminster (on the opposite side of Parliament Square to the Houses of Parliament). They left at about 6.30, and arrived half an hour later at Pentonville Prison, where seven of the prisoners and all the other accompanying officers alighted. It was there that Eatwell, who was sitting directly behind, heard Langdale telling one of the remaining prisoners about his conversations with Hanratty. 'I heard Langdale say that Hanratty had walked with Langdale when on exercise at Brixton and told him what he [Hanratty] had done. The gist of this conversation was that Hanratty had told him that he, Hanratty, had shot the man and raped the girl whilst the dead man was still in the car, in the front.'[2]

Langdale also said that he well understood the gravity of the case. 'I know that this is a capital murder and Hanratty can be hanged if he is found guilty of it. I know that his life might depend on what I have told you today. That is why I have been so careful to tell you the absolute truth in every detail as far as I can remember.'

The way in which testimony emerged to fill gaping holes in the Crown case must have seemed, to a legal novice, remarkable chance occurrences: pure serendipity. The murderer had worn gloves, but Hanratty never used gloves. Suddenly, Louise Anderson revealed that a pair of hers went missing after one of his visits. The murderer appeared to be sexually maladjusted, whereas Hanratty was known to enjoy regular and normal relations with the opposite sex. Suddenly Anderson and Langdale indicated that he had repressed sexual appetites. Finally, here was someone to fracture the last redoubt of the defence, Hanratty's utterly consistent protestations of absolute innocence.

Who was this man who inflicted such damage? Roy Langdale had to admit straightaway that he was not an ideal source. He told

Acott that, 'I admit I have twelve convictions recorded against me, which is a bad record for a man of my age.' Langdale was twenty-four, having been born on 5 April 1937; but, to the average citizen, his would seem a bad record for a man of any age.

There was, however, something odd about it: it wasn't merely a bad record; it was a near-impossible record. How could anyone accumulate twelve convictions for offences such as theft by the age of twenty-four? In the overwhelming majority of cases, those convicted would be imprisoned, and thus unable to add to their criminal tally. Hanratty was, at twenty-five, a year older than Langdale, and had only four convictions, precisely because he'd been prevented from re-offending by being imprisoned. Yet in contrast to Hanratty and thousands of others, Langdale had managed to recommit offences without suffering custodial consequences. He seemed to enjoy a degree of leverage with the judicial authorities.

On 14 June 1958, for example, Langdale was on trial at West London Magistrates' Court. At the time, he was already serving a sentence for car theft. This fresh case arose out of offences committed by Langdale in Wormwood Scrubs Prison, which led to an internal inquiry. According to the prosecution, he had carried out 'a sustained act of bullying' on Frank Dean, an eighteen-year-old inmate who had the severe misfortune to be sharing Langdale's cell. Langdale had first of all shaved off his eyebrows, before setting about him with a belt. He then ordered him to sing what was presumably one of the prison anthems of the time, 'Jailhouse Rock'. Langdale decided that the youth's performance did not measure up to Elvis Presley's – 'Sorry, boy, you failed' – and renewed his assault on him, scratching him a dozen times across the chest with a serrated knife.

Naturally this behaviour called for the sternest reprimand, and the magistrate duly delivered it. But not to Langdale. It was the prosecution that felt the lash of the magistrate's tongue. He upbraided Oliver Nugent, counsel for the Director of Public Prosecutions, on the grounds that the case had taken such a long time to reach court (a full two months); it was grossly unfair that it should have been 'hanging over' Langdale's head. 'It really is disgraceful that a man should have to wait this long,' the magistrate continued, 'I see no justification for it whatever.'[3]

Turning at last to the prisoner, the magistrate sentenced him to one month's additional imprisonment. He added comfortingly to

Langdale, 'It means that, with the normal remission, you will get out at the usual time.'

Langdale continued to benefit from a judicial indulgence towards his misdeeds. At this time, in November 1961, he was remanded in custody on two charges of forging Post Office Savings Bank books – an offence which the authorities were accustomed to view sternly.

Wednesday, 22 November was the date not only of the opening of the committal in Hanratty's case, but also the day on which Langdale's forgery case was due to be heard. That was why he was on the coach, being escorted from prison to the quarter sessions and back, when his conversation about Hanratty was overheard. However, Langdale's case was not dealt with that day. It was heard the following day – i.e. straight after the authorities had been appraised of his new 'evidence' in the A6 case. Once again, Langdale's luck was in. Despite his string of convictions, despite the seriousness of the offence, despite the fifteen other cases that had to be taken into consideration, he was put on probation.

In subsequent years, even the highest authorities seemed prepared to look benevolently on him. On 18 May 1962 he was jailed for six months for receiving a stolen car – again, a lenient sentence for a man with his record. The police had put in a good word for him. A detective told the magistrates, 'Normally, he is very helpful.'[4]

In 1971 one errant judge, presumably believing that he was there to administer the law, did hand down an eighteen-month sentence for theft. Langdale got out of that as well: on appeal, the Lord Chief Justice, Lord Widgery, ordered that the term of imprisonment be halved.

In early December 1961, however, Langdale's statement constituted new evidence and the defence had to work out how to counter it. The first thing was to assess its veracity. When they first mentioned the name 'Langdale' to Hanratty himself, he couldn't immediately think of who they were referring to. So they made inquiries to discover who Hanratty had regularly exercised with. The names they received back did not include Langdale. They quickly realized that where checks could be made on the most basic of Langdale's assertions – 'All the time I knew Hanratty I never saw him talk to another prisoner'; 'I was his only friend'; 'I was the only one he'd talk to' – they turned out to be false.

In this most tortuous of cases, finding prisoners with whom Hanratty had exercised in October and November was just about the defence's most straightforward task. There was the twenty-one-year-old Nicolai Blythe, who informed the defence that after about three weeks, he'd begun talking to Hanratty. 'He frequently discussed his case with me and consistently maintained his innocence. On no occasion did I have the impression that he was in fact guilty.'[5]

Blythe pointed out, however, that Hanratty was more friendly with a man named David Emery, who was subsequently convicted of manslaughter and given a six-year sentence. Emery said that he always exercised with Hanratty: 'Everybody in the prison, including the officers, knew I always walked with Hanratty.'[6]

The defence also contacted William Aldred, who was facing an arson charge. He exercised with Hanratty 'practically every day' during December 1961 and January 1962: 'I found him to be a very nice and social person. I am absolutely convinced of his innocence regarding the murder of which he is accused.'[7]

All those were mentioned by Hanratty as people he spoke to in prison; and, when contacted, they immediately confirmed Hanratty's story. By now, Hanratty had managed to recall who Langdale was. 'It took me two days to place him. I have walked with him at the most four times, for very short periods. He made the conversation. Langdale told me his missus had a greengrocer's shop. I did not say I'm the A6 killer – everybody in here knows I'm innocent of this charge.'

Hanratty concluded, 'I would not say such a thing after speaking two or three words to him.' As usual, he made the critical point, perhaps not articulately, but as bluntly as he could. Inmates, especially those who have some experience of prison life, are well aware of the presence amongst them of 'grasses' or informers. Accordingly, they do not vouchsafe details of their criminal activities to any but the most trusted colleagues. The idea that, in such a septic environment, they would be indiscreet with transient acquaintances is fanciful. Moreover, even that assumes that an inmate is guilty and does wish, as Langdale claimed, to 'get this off his chest'. In this instance, the notion that Hanratty might have confessed to someone he barely knew, while maintaining his total innocence to all those with whom he generally socialized, is simply an affront to reason.

In dealing with Langdale's devastating evidence, however, there was yet another mystery: what was Langdale doing in the hospital in the first place? He wasn't ill. Hanratty was there because, as the country's most notorious remand prisoner, he had to be specially confined. But why Langdale? This was his own explanation: 'I was

transferred to the hospital wing at Brixton Prison because I was
worried about being separated from my wife who was on her own.'[8]

Beggars belief, doesn't it? In the circumstances, the suspicion that
the authorities deliberately placed a known informer in Hanratty's
vicinity is irresistible. The informer, of course, fully understood
what vileness was expected of him.

Yet the Langdale evidence had a sour-sweet taste for the defence.
While they acknowledged that it created a considerable problem
for the forthcoming trial, at the same time it provided reassurance:
again, Hanratty's credibility was put to the test; again, of two
diametrically opposed accounts, his emerged as the plausible one.

On 11 December, another part of Hanratty's account fell
smoothly into place. Kleinman, beavering away at any and every
lead, was so dissatisfied with the police investigations into the
Stanmore burglaries in Dennis Lane, Stanmore, that he telephoned
himself.

Walter Mills, the owner of Trevone, explained what happened:
'Mr Kleinman said his client had said he took a jacket but not the
trousers because they would be too big for him. He then asked me
whether or not I'd lost a black jacket. I said, "Not to my knowledge,
but I'll go upstairs and look." I examined my suits in the cupboard.
I found then that a black jacket was missing, only the waistcoat was
on the hanger. The trousers were still there. The last time I can be
positive I saw my black jacket was some time in the late summer. I
did not tell Mr Kleinman that the jacket was missing. I said I would
make sure and let him know if he would telephone me this evening.'

Thus Walter Mills telephoned police to report the loss of a black
barathea coat. He explained that although he had examined his
clothing in response to police requests, they had always asked him
about a missing *sports* jacket or coat: 'It was only when the solicitor
made a specific reference to the black jacket that I [found] it was
missing.'

At the magistrates' hearing, the police had disdained Hanratty's
account. Even when it was partly established, they still declined to
concede that it was fully accurate. Now, on another critical point, it
was demonstrated that it was Hanratty who was telling the truth.

In the light of Acott's revelations at the magistrates' court, Joe
Gillbanks set energetically to work examining the Liverpool alibi
afresh. With regard to the left-luggage office, Hanratty had spoken
of the man who served him having 'a turned or withered hand'.
Gillbanks discovered that two employees who may have worked
in the left-luggage office that day were physically impaired. The

regular attendant there was William Usher. He had a disfigured left hand, with the middle finger amputated. He was on duty, in the week beginning Monday, 21 August, from 6.00 a.m. to 2.00 p.m. He fitted the description Hanratty had given. Gillbanks discovered that the police hadn't bothered to take a statement from him.

The other employee with a disability was Peter Stringer, whose left forearm was artificial. That week, he was on the 2.00–10.00 p.m. shift. He was normally employed as a toilet attendant, although he would frequently help out in the left-luggage office towards the end of his period of duty, from about 8.45 p.m.

The information didn't, on the surface, appear to benefit Hanratty. He certainly did not arrive until after 2.00 p.m., and was not there at 8.45 p.m. Also, he may have picked up that kind of information from previous visits to the city. Nevertheless, even on this least favourable analysis, there appeared to be some semblance of confirmation of his story.

Then, with regard to the sweet-shop, Gillbanks went over the ground again. In particular, he talked to the thirteen-year-old Barbara Ford, who had been comparatively neglected in previous inquiries, because of her age. Interviewed in the presence of her mother, she said: 'I stayed with Gran until she finished at the shop, and did not go there on Tuesday because I went to the shops in town with my friend Linda. On the way back from town I called in at the shop about a quarter to five and Mr Cowley's brother was there with Gran. We stayed for about half an hour, but we were not behind the counter.'

So, she *was* there on the Tuesday.

This illustrates how deficient even the most supposedly thorough inquiries can be. No one had previously even asked Barbara whether she was in the shop at any time on the Tuesday as well.

This, then, nullified the *only* reason Mrs Dinwoodie had for placing the incident on the Monday rather than the Tuesday. Liverpool police, in concluding their investigation, had acknowledged this; similarly, Superintendent Acott, at the magistrates' court, had testified that the presence of the child was the solitary criterion.

Although Barbara was not asked to assist on the Tuesday, it was clear that she would do so whenever necessary. Her friend Linda Walton stated: 'When Barbara goes into the shop, she goes behind the penny counter to serve. She did it on that day. She was standing in front of the counter most of the time with me, but when children wanted serving she went behind the counter to serve them.'

If the 'Tarleton Road' inquiry did occur on the Tuesday, then the timing would fit. The investigators – whether police or lawyers – had that day's railway timetables printed out several times and exhaustively analysed. It must be stated that Hanratty's own timings were frequently awry. He did not have a watch of his own; the winder of the stolen one he was carrying was broken. The train which he said arrived at Lime Street Station at about 3.30 in fact probably pulled in at 4.54, having left Euston at 11.37 and reached Crewe at 3.38. The trains prior to that one had departed at 10.20 (a direct through train) and 10.35. Thus no other timing would fit at all. If Hanratty had arrived at Euston at, say, 9.30 (which, in any case, must be too early) he'd have had a long wait, but then caught a through train which was non-stopping at Crewe; if he'd caught the next one, he'd have stopped at Crewe but wouldn't have had a long wait. The only train which fitted the circumstances and the timings was the 11.37.

He would then have reached Liverpool at 4.54, and would probably have arrived at the sweet-shop by about 5.15, which fits in with Barbara Ford's timings. It could not have occurred, as Mrs Dinwoodie calculated, as early as 3.30–4.00, as Hanratty could not have arrived by then (and, indeed, Mrs Dinwoodie subsequently gave a later timing).

If the incident did occur on the Tuesday, then the problem of witnesses having placed Hanratty simultaneously in London and Liverpool evaporated. But in that case, could Hanratty have committed the murder? For all practical purposes, the answer was an emphatic 'No'.

Further parts of Hanratty's story were checked. What about his contention that he stole a Jaguar Mark VII on the evening of 6/7 October from near Portland Place in order to flee north? If true, that in itself would establish his driving credentials. Kleinman asked Mr. E. G. MacDermott, the Assistant Director of Public Prosecutions, who had presented the Crown case at Ampthill, whether he had any information about that.

From the DPP's office, McDermott pedantically replied that 'There is no record of a Jaguar Mark VII car being stolen during the early hours of 6 October from Portland Place, W1.'

Well, no, but what the defence actually wanted to know was whether a Jaguar Mark VII was stolen from *near* Portland Place in the early hours of *7 October*.

The DPP responded: 'Between 11.00 p.m. on 6 October and 8.00 a.m. on 7 October a black Jaguar Mark VII was stolen from

Hallam Street [the road running north–south adjacent to Portland Place]. The vehicle was fitted with floor gear change, overdrive and maroon upholstery.'

Once again, Hanratty's account was confirmed down to the last detail.

The police were still trying to demonstrate that Hanratty could have come into possession of a gun. Laurence Lanigan had made a statement to Acott in which he asserted that, in prison, he and Hanratty had hatched a scheme to steal cash collected as rents from an estate office opposite the Torch public house in Wembley. They decided that they'd need a couple of guns to carry out this robbery.

This was highly tendentious. Of course there may have been discussion along those lines; but prison dreams, whether licit or illicit, are rarely accomplished on the outside. There is nothing to suggest that either of them ever intended to put this idea into operation. For his part, Lanigan said, 'On my release from prison, I got myself a job with a good wage and was quite satisfied.' The essential point was that there remained no evidence that Hanratty had ever had a gun, or had actively sought one. Michael McCarthy, who knew both Hanratty and Lanigan in prison, affirmed, 'As I remember it, any talk about guns which took place between [them] was brought up by Lanigan. He is a small chap and tries to be very tough.'[9]

In a different area of evidence, Lanigan was helpful, confirming that there was nothing untoward about Hanratty's attitudes to women: 'All the time I have known him, I have never known him to be unduly familiar towards women. If he felt sexually inclined, he would go with a prostitute. In my opinion, he is definitely not the type of person who would attempt to rape a woman.'[10]

Hanratty himself had been angered by the press reports, just prior to his arrest, of his relationship with Mary Meaden. He disputed her suggestions that he had proposed to her. 'I took her home and had a kiss and a cuddle – I said "I love you" and that – she seems to have taken it seriously. She was a decent girl. I took her home twice, but nothing happened between us. She has told lies about me, and I do not like her now.' In fact, he need not have taken umbrage. When the defence took her statement, she was totally loyal: 'At all times he was quiet and shy and blushed very easily. He only kissed me once, and always behaved quite properly towards me.'[11]

Indeed, Kleinman regarded his client with increasing respect. He wrote, privately, in his records, 'Hanratty is cooperative, does as he is told, never puts a foot wrong.' The sentiments were not wholly appropriate – Kleinman didn't know that he was still being kept in the dark about the alibi – but his concern for Hanratty's predicament became so strong that he appears to have overstepped the mark. He went to Liverpool to liaise with Joe Gillbanks and to meet Mrs Dinwoodie. After they visited her, Olive Dinwoodie and her husband, John, both made additional statements in which they complained about the 'bullying' manner of the defence; and the way in which Kleinman tried to slip in the phrase 'I am not sure whether it was a Monday or Tuesday that the man called' to a statement he had drawn up for her. Quite correctly, she refused to sign it. In frustration, Kleinman blurted out, 'There is a man's life at stake.' His professional detachment seemed to be slipping; he was warming to his client's cause.

It was clearly important for the defence to be able to prove that there was nothing distinctive about Hanratty's speech, other than the fact that he was a cockney; and that, accordingly, he was unfairly compromised on the critical identity parade. The issue was particularly interesting because Acott had, bizarrely, alluded to Hanratty's speech 'impediment'. Thus, Kleinman arranged for Hanratty to be examined by Professor Dennis Fry, head of the Phonetics Department at University College, London, probably the most respected man in the field at that time. He had spent his whole professional life in the study of speech and language. What was his view of Hanratty's diction?

'In my opinion his speech is in every way typical of a man with his background and upbringing; his pronunciation is that of a boy of low educational attainment brought up in London. I could not detect any feature in his pronunciation which could be regarded as a personal peculiarity. His mode of speech was shared by very many thousands of Londoners.'[12]

Another small brick of the defence wall was safely in place.

On 14 December, Hanratty had to undergo an especially important psychiatric examination. This was a prerequisite in a capital murder trial. If a murderer was not of sound mind, then, under the 1957 Homicide Act, he would not be executed. In this respect, Detective Superintendent Acott's own contemporary comments, written in his report dated 10 November 1961, are illuminating. He believed that Hanratty had committed the crime;

and he also believed that the murderer was deranged. Accordingly, he did not think that Hanratty would have to face the possibility of execution.

'From 9 p.m. on 22 August until 3 a.m. on 23 August, Hanratty behaved like a psychopath, and this behaviour and his known mental and medical history should be sufficient grounds for him to gain a verdict of diminished responsibility. Dr Keith Simpson describes a schizophrenic as a person "usually in his twenties, often a bad mixer, sensitive and introspective and emotionally cold, whose crime may be skilfully covered up". How well this fits the Hanratty we have come to know.'[13]

The views of Dr Denis Leigh, of the Maudsley and Bethlem Royal Hospital, did not accord with Acott's. After a thorough examination, he concluded that Hanratty was 'perfectly sane and fit to plead'.

Over the New Year period, the defence case was being assembled with some confidence and with gathering prospects of ultimate success. Kleinman asked the DPP whether it might be possible for the defence to carry out its own scientific testing on the clothing. The DPP replied, 'I regret I have no authority to allow your expert to examine any of the exhibits. I would suggest that you communicate with the clerk of the CCC who now has custody of [them].'

The CCC was the Central Criminal Court, the official title by which the Old Bailey was known. At this moment concerns over the forensic science evidence became marginal, as an Everest of a problem loomed. To start with, the letter from the DPP seemed just a procedural one: 'The clerk of the CCC has asked me to inform you that an application will be made on 2 January for a date to be fixed for the time of trial.'

Then came the bombshell: 'The clerk also informs me that on the application the Court will consider whether the case should be remitted to the Bedford Winter Assizes.'

This was shattering news. The whole matter of the location of the trial had already been fairly and properly determined. On what basis was it now being reconsidered?

The reason the prosecution gave, at the 2 January hearing, was that the trial would come on more quickly at Bedford. This was a feeble argument. The Crown was not even able to support it with detailed points about the exceptional delays then being incurred by cases due for trial at the Old Bailey. Of course, no such delays existed.

The incontestable facts about the A6 case were as follows:

It was the most high-profile contemporary case, one of the most significant criminal cases since the Second World War. The natural venue was the Old Bailey.

It was likely to prove a difficult and protracted case, with intense media interest. Again, the natural venue was the Old Bailey.

A considerable part of the evidence – the abandoned car, the gun on the bus, the discarded cartridge cases in the hotel room – concerned London. Of all the witnesses, only two civil and three police prosecution witnesses were from Bedford. The overwhelming majority of those involved came from the London area. So, the natural venue was the Old Bailey.

The case was not an appropriate one for the area in which the crime had occurred because of the intensity of local feeling about the crime. This was what the magistrates, local people themselves, had recognized. That was why they had sent the case to the Old Bailey in the first place.

The arguments were more than powerful: they were unanswerable. There could only have been one reason for the Crown's determination to remit the trial to Bedford: with the defence case appearing buoyant, the prosecution needed to take advantage of the perceived prejudicial atmosphere there. There were two aspects to this. In Bedford, the town where Valerie Storie had been hospitalized, the jury would inevitably reflect the antipathy and outrage of the populace. In that locale, too, a man of Hanratty's stripe would be seen as virtually an alien interloper. A metropolitan jury would have been able to recognize his small-time criminal ways and assess what relevance, if any, they bore to a crime of this wickedness. A Bedfordshire jury would have no such understanding of the gradations of criminal mores.

On 2 January, notwithstanding Sherrard's eloquent arguments, the Recorder, Sir Anthony Hawke, redirected the case from the Old Bailey to Bedford. There is really no margin for ambiguity here. This was a profoundly disgraceful manoeuvre by the Crown. This was dirty tricks *in excelsis*.

Trawling through court documents, thirty years later, I came across the following memo, written at Leighton Buzzard on 7 December 1961, within forty-eight hours of the end of the magistrates' court hearing:

Attending Mr McDermott on [*sic*] telephone, who said it appeared that trouble had arisen over the committal of this case to the Old Bailey. He said that he had been called upon by the DPP to explain how it came about the case had been sent to the Old Bailey. Mr McDermott informed the Director that Mr Simpson [Clerk to the Ampthill Justices] had telephoned the Old Bailey and *had been assured that they could take the case* . . . [my italics].

We gathered from Mr McDermott that the Old Bailey might now refuse to take it, and he promised to let me know the outcome in due course. He said that the Lord Chief Justice had been on to the Old Bailey, but exactly what the trouble was, he, Mr McDermott, did not know.

I can take the issue no further. The memo goes on to reiterate the point that the Old Bailey, when first approached, indicated that there would be no problem with its taking the case. It accordingly appears to bear out that the argument used by the Crown in the 2 January court hearing was not merely flimsy but bogus. The almost immediate, behind-the-scenes intervention of the Lord Chief Justice is astonishing. (Nor was it to be his only involvement with the case: he was the senior judge who heard the appeal.) The impression that the mightiest powers in the land had closed ranks against Jim Hanratty becomes ever more palpable.

Nor, even there, did Hanratty's misfortunes end. He also lost his barrister, or the man who would have been his barrister. Michael Sherrard had represented Hanratty superbly at the magistrates' court; but he was young, and up-and-coming. He hadn't then, as the jargon is, taken silk. In normal circumstances, he would move on to become junior counsel at the actual trial. In a major case like this, the defence would always be led by a heavyweight senior barrister, a QC. For the trial, therefore, Kleinman chose the eminent silk, Victor Durand.

In those days the Metropolitan Police used to have an important reference system, the Black Book, which contained the instructions of the ACC (Assistant Commissioner: Crime) to all CID officers. Included in the book was a list of lawyers – solicitors and barristers – of whom the police had to be especially wary: in other words, those who were likely to defend their clients effectively. (At that time, police officers could take cases to court themselves; but if any of the listed lawyers was acting for the defence, then they had to pass the case over to DPP lawyers.) One of the names on the list was certainly that of Victor Durand. At that time, when police evidence tended to be unquestioningly accepted, he was one of the few barristers who had no hesitation in saying the police were lying, if that's what he thought.

It looked as though Kleinman had made an excellent choice for Hanratty. Unhappily, at just this juncture, Durand was caught up with a problem of professional etiquette, having over-zealously fought a libel case. The Bar Council suspended him for a year, and he had to withdraw from the case.

Hanratty himself had no doubt about what course of action to take. He had enormous faith in Sherrard, having witnessed his combative performance at Ampthill. He wanted him to be elevated to lead counsel.

It was virtually unprecedented for the defence in such a case to be the responsibility of a barrister who was not yet a QC. (Sherrard, of course, became one later, in August 1968.) Almost all of those advising Hanratty – including, prominently, Sherrard himself – tried to talk him out of it; but, on this matter, he was uncharacteristically resolute. Ultimately, what probably weighed in Sherrard's favour was his own thorough grasp of the case, and the lack of time available to brief a fresh lawyer. So Sherrard moved up to the top position, with Anthony Ellison coming in as his No. 2.

Kleinman was still desperately trying to gather as much information as possible about the case. 'To save public funds,' he wrote to the DPP, 'I would be grateful if you were kind enough to let me have copies of statements made by all those persons who were not called before the magistrates.' Was the DPP kind enough? No, he certainly wasn't.

In the days of full committal hearings, virtually nothing was disclosed to the defence by the Crown because all the prosecution evidence was presented in open court at the preliminary hearing. In this instance, the DPP kept strictly to the legal rules as they then applied and was prepared to supply only a list of names and addresses of witnesses from whom unused statements had been taken. If this was a complete list, it would have contained many hundreds of names.

The defence were working blind. They could have no idea of whether any of those statements were pertinent to their client's cause. Nor did the system make much sense for witnesses, who had no doubt made statements out of a sense of civic responsibility. The only way the defence could assess the import, if any, of their testimony was to go and interview them all over again. If the bare information which the DPP supplied was inaccurate, then the defence task became absurdly time-consuming. In this case, for example, the defence was told merely that one of those who had witnessed the escape of Mrs Dalal's attacker on 7 September was the window-cleaner, Philip Dyson. In fact, his name was Philip Dyerson.

The difficulties were exacerbated if evidence for the Crown was adduced subsequent to the magistrates' hearing, as happened in this case. A bundle of fresh statements was supplied to the defence on 15 January – just a week before the date fixed for the start of the trial.

Tendered as part of this late evidence was a fresh statement from Valerie Storie – in effect, her sixth, although the defence had no idea of this since no one had shown them the previous five. The new statement read as follows:

'I thought the man was in his mid-twenties. He did say he had been to prison and since he was eight he had been to remand home, Borstal, CT, and his next one coming up was PD. He did say he had done five years for housebreaking, he had done the lot. He said he had now been on the run for four months and every police force in Britain was looking for him.'[14]

The gunman said a great many things ostensibly about himself during the car journey. As it developed, the case against Hanratty hinged more and more on Storie's identification of him and her account of what the gunman said about himself in the car. At this juncture, the prosecution was in the process of discarding the pieces of information which could not possibly apply to Hanratty, and emphasizing those which, with some manipulation, just might. In being so unethically selective, one of the pieces of testimony which they sidelined at an early stage was Valerie Storie's telling statement that 'We didn't know whether he was telling the truth or not.'

Other formal statements which the defence now saw for the first time included those of Langdale and Eatwell, the prison officer who said he had overheard the conversation in which Langdale told a fellow-prisoner that Hanratty had confessed to him. There was also one from Peter Stringer, the toilet attendant at Lime Street Station. This was another prosecution smoke-screen. Almost certainly, Stringer was not the man whom Hanratty had seen in the left-luggage office. The Crown was rebutting a point which the defence was not making. Of the two men, it was Usher who more closely fitted Hanratty's description. The prosecution did not even take a statement from him until 19 January, the last working day before the trial. They never disclosed it. In fact, it was of no assistance.

Usher seemed to be one of those kind-hearted individuals who was only too ready to assist. In trying to be helpful, he seemed to assent to whatever suggestion was put to him.

For the defence, Liverpool, and the battening-down of Hanratty's alibi, remained the priority. In this respect, they had encountered disappointment. Kleinman wrote: 'The difficulty with this case is that although Hanratty pleads an alibi he refuses to disclose the names and addresses of his four chief witnesses with whom he said he was staying during the period the murder was committed.

'However, he gives sound reasons for withholding information with regard to these witnesses, although not such good reasons as would lead a man to endanger his life on a capital charge. They might, however, be quite good enough reasons for a criminal who is convinced of his innocence and the fact that the case against him cannot be established.'

Whether or not the case against him could be established was now to be put to the acid test.

CHAPTER TWELVE

TRADITIONALLY, ON THE first day of the assizes, the High Sheriff would throw a lavish lunch, inviting past High Sheriffs, prospective future High Sheriffs, and indeed all local dignitaries. Trial barristers and court officials would usually be tapped on the shoulder; yes, they would be pleased to accept an invitation to lunch. The one man who was not invited was the judge. For the duration of the assize, he lived a solitary existence, in a kind of purdah, and every day would be escorted back to his lodging for lunch and dinner.

In Bedford, the assize judge that year was the notoriously implacable and punitive Sir Melford Stevenson. However, Hanratty's case was a late annex to the Winter Assize, so there was a different judge: the infinitely more emollient and humane Mr Justice Gorman. Hanratty may have had a plethora of valid complaints about the judicial system, but he could have had none about this unfailingly courteous and considerate judge.

Counsel for the prosecution were Graham Swanwick QC and, as his junior, Geoffrey Lane. The former became a High Court judge; the latter was subsequently Lord Chief Justice from 1981 to 1992 and presided, not at all comfortably, over one of the most turbulent periods in the history of the English criminal justice system. E. G. MacDermott was representing the Director of Public Prosecutions.

The courthouse in Bedford was the elegant red-brick Shire Hall, in front of which stood a statue of John Howard, the penal reformer. For this trial the Shire Hall was completely full; crowds had been congregating since first light. Although the whole atmosphere was more subdued than it had been at Ampthill, there was inevitably an air of intense interest and expectation.

MONDAY – FRIDAY, 22 – 26 JANUARY 1962: **The First Week**

The first matter of note was that the two charges added at the magistrates' court – the rape and attempted murder of Valerie Storie – were now withdrawn. Hanratty was again charged simply with one count of murder. Officials would have wanted him committed on all possible charges, so that they could choose which to proceed with for the trial. This suggested that the prosecution didn't settle on the thrust of its case for some months.

Hanratty, then, was charged with the murder of Michael Gregsten. He pleaded not guilty. The twelve members of the jury were informed by the Clerk of Assize that 'It is your duty to hearken to the evidence.' Graham Swanwick QC rose to his feet.

As is the custom with prosecutors, Swanwick went through the crime in detail, stage by harrowing stage. Although the account was neither sensationalized nor over-graphic, it nevertheless proved too traumatizing for one male juror who was momentarily overcome. Mr Justice Gorman halted proceedings and solicitously asked if he felt able to carry on; the juror replied that he had recovered.

Swanwick then outlined the main points of evidence against Hanratty: the identification by Valerie Storie; the details which the gunman had revealed about himself in the car that, by successive processes of elimination, ultimately pointed to only one man – the defendant; the identifications of Skillett and Trower; the gun found on a bus in the exact location where Hanratty had said he liked to dump things; the cartridge cases from the murder weapon, left behind in the hotel room in which he had stayed; and the confession to Roy Langdale. According to Swanwick, this all added up to a compelling case.

The final point was the lack of a solid alibi. Swanwick elaborated on the lengths to which the prosecution had gone to try to substantiate it.

'Very extensive inquiries have been made. Lists of names have been supplied, and I hope you will be satisfied that everything that can properly be done to assist the defence in this matter has been done.

'[Hanratty] refused to give the names of the three men who could establish the alibi, stating that he had been kicked out by them when they knew he was wanted for the A6 Murder; that the flat was full of stolen jewellery, and adding, "There is a lot of jelly there", meaning a load of gelignite. He then gave more details of this man supposed to be wanted by the police. He said he was wanted on a warrant for non-payment of a fine for having televisions on hire purchase – not, you may think, a tremendously serious matter which would prevent his being produced as a witness for a murder alibi.

'All warrants outstanding in the Liverpool area (something over 3,000) were checked, including around Scotland Road, which is an area that abounds in thieves. No trace was found of a man who had a warrant outstanding to do with television or hire purchase. So there was no trace of the three men.'[1]

All inquiries – whether prosecution or defence – had foundered on the lack of detail. Hanratty was being just too cryptic about his activities that summer evening. In this respect, his disingenuousness counted against him. Yet was the Crown's account, for all Swanwick's frequent protestations of absolute fairness, itself immune from accusations of disingenuousness? After all, it started off by withholding material information from the jury. The reason given for Gregsten and Storie having been in the cornfield in the first place ('They discussed the rally that they were planning together') was, to say the least, elliptical.

Parts of Swanwick's address seemed inspired less by exhaustive analysis of the evidence than by blind confidence in his own case. For example, the 'roadworks' evidence:

'By now, you will hear, he seemed to know his way pretty well, all through the Harrow area. At one point he even warned Gregsten to go carefully, "Just round the corner you will find some roadworks." Sure enough, the car turned the corner and there were the roadworks. Members of the jury, that is very important, you may think, in this case because that area lies very close to a place called Kingsbury ... One of the postcards [sent from Ireland] was for Mrs Hanratty of 12 Sycamore Grove, Kingsbury. [That] verifies what I was suggesting to you that he would know the Kingsbury and Harrow area very well.'[2]

In the public gallery, members of Hanratty's family – his father and brother Michael attended the whole trial – knew that James had not been seen at home for several weeks before the murder, and hence his knowledge of local roadworks in late August was likely to be less than encyclopaedic.

Finally, there were three areas of evidence where the prosecution case became so hazy one suspected that Swanwick wasn't sure of it himself. First, there was the description which the gunman had provided of himself in the car – some of which fitted Hanratty, and some of which didn't:

'You may think some of what he said betrayed a knowledge of various matters, some of which may have been genuine, some exaggerated, and some of it of course may have been designed to put her off the scent or impress her by some form of boastfulness . . .

'He told her he had been to prison, he told her that since he was eight he had been to a remand home and to Borstal, and to CT, corrective training, and that the next one coming up was PD, preventive detention. That might well follow after a sentence of corrective training, but not in a man of the age of the accused. He told her he had done five years for housebreaking, and had done the lot, meaning, you may think, that he had served the whole sentence without remission; that he had been on the run for four months and every police force in Britain was looking for him . . .

'It will be true of James Hanratty to say that he had been to prison. It would not be true to say he had been to remand home or Borstal. It would be true to say he had done corrective training. It would not be true to say he had done five years for housebreaking, but he had in fact been sentenced to imprisonment for house-breaking, to two years for housebreaking. He had "done the lot" not on that occasion, but when serving the sentence of corrective training.'[3]

Then there was the mystery of the missing jacket:

'The [suit] jacket was disposed of *possibly* – and I only say *possibly* – for fear that there *might* be some bloodstains on it . . . Although the location of the bloodstains in the car coupled with the use of the rug for the seat *may, you may think, indicate* that the assailant *may have* escaped without any bloodstains upon him at all, nevertheless it is *possible* – again I emphasize that the prosecution put this forward only as a *possibility* – that he *might have* either known or feared that the jacket *might have* bloodstains on it and have got rid of it for that reason [my italics].'[4]

There is solid evidence, and less solid evidence; this was just gossamer.

Vaguest of all, it seemed, was the answer to the most basic question, of why this crime had ever been committed. The motive, Mr Swanwick, what was the motive?

'Gregsten was shot through the head – twice, deliberately and in cold blood, for no better reason than that that man wished to possess himself of Gregsten's companion in that car, Valerie Storie.'[5]

Swanwick mentioned that the gunman asked for their watches, but then handed them back: 'That, you may think, possibly supports the view that the principle motive for this crime was perhaps sex rather than money.'

Towards the end of his opening speech, Swanwick got vaguer still.

'The gunman said that he had got scared because Gregsten had moved too quickly. I suppose that might be true. Or was he lusting after Miss Storie at this time and did he want Gregsten out of the way? Or was the urge to use his new and exciting toy to shoot someone for the first time too much for him? Or did he think that Gregsten had seen him and might recognize him?'

There was a variety of possible motives there, none of them very plausible. Bizarrely, the last thought introduced a completely new idea (that the gunman might have been known to them) from which he, Swanwick, recoiled straightaway. After all, that simply wasn't the prosecution case.

Altogether, such tentative and unconvincing suggestions (they would be flattered to be described as theories) only highlighted the fact that there was a black hole at the centre of the case. For all the individual pieces of evidence, there was no coherent framework. The Crown simply had no viable explanation as to why this man had ambushed those two people, or this extraordinary crime had ever taken place.

By the start of the second day, it was clear that the distressed juror would be able to hearken to the evidence no longer. Mr Justice Gorman referred to him as being 'in obvious discomfort'. The juror told the judge that '[after] the description of the shooting, I started to go hot. I tried to stop myself by putting my head down between my knees. Normally, when blood is mentioned I faint. I cannot stop myself.'[6]

The 1925 Criminal Justice Act allowed a trial, where any member of the jury has to be discharged through reasons of ill-health, to be continued with eleven, or even ten, fit members. So the judge ruled that this man should, 'without the slightest criticism of the court', be relieved of this, for him, intolerable civic duty. Thus, in these exceptional circumstances – everything about this case seemed exceptional – one of the jurors walked outside and was immediately interviewed by the press. He was named as twenty-eight-year-old Philip Taylor. He explained: 'I even fainted when I read about Douglas Bader. I have tried to overcome it, but nothing I seem to do can overcome this dreadful fainting.'[7]

The hearing of the evidence then began with a number of police witnesses giving what were supposed to be purely formal statements regarding the various locations in the case, and drawing of plans and taking of photographs.

Even here, however, there was immediate controversy and a suggestion that someone was being highly selective in the presentation of evidence. Under cross-examination by the defence, a senior photographer at Scotland Yard conceded that some photographs showed fingerprint marks on the windows of the abandoned Morris Minor car; and, much more importantly, that a further twelve photographs not presented in evidence showed suspected fingerprints.

Swanwick hastened to repair the damage by pointing out that he would not in any case be suggesting that any fingerprints on the car had been matched with Hanratty's. However, even at this early stage, serious shortcomings had emerged in the prosecution case. The jury might have found those omissions informative. On whose instructions were those other photographs withheld? And whose were those unidentified fingerprints? Were they matched with other suspects? – Peter Alphon's, for example? The jury was never told. To this day, the information has never been publicly revealed.

Janet Gregsten did not have to go to court to give evidence as a witness (although she did attend, once, sitting in the public gallery) and everyone accepted that her deposition could simply be read. Once again, it appeared purely formal; once again, it incorporated the lie that underpinned the prosecution case ('Michael Gregsten and Valerie Storie were going to plan a rally').

After that, the stage was set (the whole business of the courtroom is so intrinsically histrionic that the clichéd theatrical analogies are always apposite) for the arrival in the witness-box of Valerie Storie herself. Amidst mounting press excitement, she had been brought from Stoke Mandeville by ambulance, taken into court on a stretcher, and was able to give her evidence quietly from a wheelchair. Everyone there clearly felt overwhelming sympathy for her and, as the central character, the miraculous survivor of this grievous ordeal, she made a compelling witness.

Almost straightaway, Swanwick asked about her association with Gregsten:

Swanwick: How long had you known him?
Storie: Since the middle of 1958.

Swanwick: Did you know him well?
Storie: Yes.
Swanwick: How well was your relationship with him?
Storie: We were very fond of one another.
Swanwick: Did you take an interest, you and he, in any particular
    pastime?
Storie: Motor rallying in particular.[8]

So for reasons of discretion, and to avoid personal embarrassment, a veil was drawn over this relationship from the outset. It
was something in which all those who knew the true situation
colluded. In subsequent years, the liaison between Gregsten and
Storie became one of the key components in the public understanding of the case; yet the jury was told nothing about it.

However, everyone knows the judicial ground-rules; witnesses
are enjoined to tell 'the truth, the whole truth and nothing but the
truth'. Whenever that injunction is not adhered to, then the judicial
process is imperilled. If there is an arrangement, even for the
putative best of reasons, to suppress a little area of the truth, then
the chances are that that area can never be self-contained.

Further, the passage quoted above contained not just the overall
deception but also a specific one.

Storie, as befitted a diligent civil servant, was never vague about
matters like dates. On 11 September 1961, Superintendent Acott
asked her about the start of her relationship with Gregsten. She
replied: 'We first met through the laboratory, 1957. I liked Mike
and he liked me. That was as far as it went, and in Christmas 1957
we went out for a drink together; it was at the Pineapple at Dorney.
That was the first time I went out with Mike.'[9]

On 2 June 1962, Valerie Storie's life-story was serialized as a
first-person account in *Today* magazine. She wrote that 'Our first
date was at a dance just before Christmas . . . I was nineteen.' That
would have been 1957.

In the witness-box at Bedford, on 23 January 1962, she gave this
reply:

Swanwick: How long had you known him?
Storie: Since the middle of 1958.[10]

One may speculate that once the decision was taken (by whom,
we know not) to mislead the jury about the liaison, then it would
presumably have been implausible to date the start of the associa-

tion from December, a time of year when there were unlikely to have been car rallies that needed organizing; it became better to place it in 'the middle' of the year to fit in with the cover story.

Storie's evidence was obviously lengthy and was heard over two days. Sherrard, of course, had a hugely difficult task in cross-examining her. If he appeared to be unkind towards her, and over-critical of her testimony, then he risked alienating sympathy for his client. For example, he did not take issue with her over her lack of candour about her relationship with Gregsten. At the same time, however, her evidence was the kernel of the prosecution case. So he had to negotiate a difficult razor's edge: he could afford to show her neither too much respect nor too little.

He did challenge her testimony in a number of other key areas, particularly highlighting inconsistencies between what she had just told the Bedford court and what she had previously said in evidence at the magistrates' court hearing. (The general public was not aware of the fine detail of the latter which, of course, was given in camera.)

The first area of dispute concerned the gunman's remarks as they were starting the journey. This was Storie's evidence before the magistrates:

'He said, "Where does that [road] go to?" and we said, "To Maidenhead or Slough." At that point, he said he didn't want to go to Slough.'

And in the assize court:

'We said that was the Bath Road which went either to Maiden-head or to London. He said he did not want to go to London.'

At the first hearing, Sherrard pointed out, Storie had referred to Slough; now, she had substituted 'London'.

Sherrard: When you said in the magistrates' court on several occasions that he did not want to go to Slough, that whenever you said that, that was an error?

Storie: I do not think I ever actually said that he did not want to go to Slough. I said he did not want to go to London.

Sherrard: I will be corrected if I am wrong, but apparently there was no reference in the [magistrates' court transcripts] to his not wanting to go to London.[11]

At this point Mr Justice Gorman intervened to ask Storie, 'What do you say about that?'

Storie: I do not remember saying he did not want to go to Slough; I
   thought it was London.

Sherrard: There are other references, too, because when I cross-
   examined you, you again confirmed that it was Slough.

Storie: I do not remember that.

Sherrard: You will recall that your deposition [of evidence before
   the magistrates] was read to you?

Storie: Yes.

Sherrard: And you were given an opportunity to correct anything
   which was inaccurate?

Storie: Yes.

Sherrard: Do you agree that you in fact made no attempt to correct
   'Slough' for 'London' or 'London' for 'Slough' or interchange
   the two? (No answer.)[12]

Sherrard then moved on to the discrepancies in her evidence
concerning the roadworks. This was her evidence at Ampthill:

'He said at one stage, "Be careful. There are some roadworks
round this corner." We said, "How do you know? Do you know
this road?" He said, "No, but I know there are some roadworks
there."'

And at Bedford:

'At one point in our meanderings through the roads he said, "Be
careful, round the corner there are some roadworks"; and sure
enough when we got round the bend there were some roadworks.
He then hastily added, "I do not know this area."'[13]

Sherrard pointed out the difference in her evidence on this point.
Which, he asked, was correct?

Storie: They are both correct.

Sherrard: The way in which you put it here was leaving out your or
   Gregsten's question to him, and indicating that it looked as if
   the man realized he had given himself away. You see the
   difference? You were not intending, I hope, to give that
   impression?

Storie: No.[14]

The third area of dispute concerned the gunman's driving ability.
At Ampthill, Storie said:

'We said, "Do you drive?" and he said, "Oh, yes."'

And at Bedford:

'I asked him if he could drive a car and he said, "Oh, yes," he could drive; he could drive "all sorts of cars".'

He asked whether she could say which response was the fully accurate one.

Storie: They were both said.
Sherrard: But you had forgotten to refer to it when giving your
    evidence before the magistrates?
Storie: I cannot remember every single word that was said.

Sherrard also asked about the gunman's apparent inability to drive a car, and the fact that Storie had to show him how it operated:

Sherrard: As I understand your evidence, it appeared to you clear
    that the man appeared to have been unable to understand
    properly how to drive that car?
Storie: He got in and drove it off quick enough. He asked for the
    gears to be explained to him and where the light switches were.

The fourth area concerned whether or not, in talking about his criminal past, the gunman had said he had 'been in institutions' since he was eight. Storie's evidence at Bedford omitted that term.

Sherrard: You referred yesterday to remand homes, Borstal, prison,
    but I do not think you said institutions. He did say, did he, that
    he had been in institutions since was eight?
Storie: I thought the full name for Borstal was Borstal Institution.
Sherrard: But you said to Mr Acott that he had been in institutions
    since was eight.[15]

Sherrard quoted a passage of testimony, and the discussion wandered off the point. The judge intervened.

Mr Justice Gorman: Mr Sherrard, you have not yet got an answer to
    your question as to whether he said he had been in institutions
    since he was eight, using those exact words.
Sherrard: I thought she had agreed that.
Mr Justice Gorman: I do not think she did.
Sherrard [to Storie]: Did he say he had been in institutions since he
    was eight?

Mr Justice Gorman: Using those exact words?
Storie (after a pause): I believe he did.[16]

The fifth area of controversy was her conversation with John Kerr. Did she remember giving him a description of her assailant which included the phrase 'light fair hair'? If substantiated, this was a highly material piece of evidence; Hanratty's hair was dyed black at the time.

Storie: I said brown hair.
Sherrard: This is a matter, as I am sure you appreciate, of great importance. This witness said that he wrote down the details which you gave him?
Storie: He may have done.
Sherrard: And indeed that he had specifically written down those words, 'light fair hair'?
Storie: I cannot remember any occasion when I said he had fair hair. I have always said brown.
Sherrard: Leaving aside Mr Kerr for a moment, this is what you said before the magistrates: 'His hair was a medium brown, definitely not dark brown.' Do you remember saying that?
Storie: I do not remember saying that.
Sherrard: That is the way in which you would describe it?
Storie: I remember saying brown hair. I do not remember qualifying it.
Sherrard: I am not at the moment concerned with what you said or what you remember. Would it be an accurate way of describing your recollection of the man's hair to say, his hair was a medium brown, definitely not dark brown?
Storie (after a pause): I think so.[17]

These were five examples of areas of evidence where Valerie Storie appeared to have varied her statement between the two court hearings. Perhaps it was coincidence, but in each case the revised version of what she said created additional headaches for Hanratty's defence. Hanratty would hardly have said he'd had enough of Slough when there was no evidence that he'd ever been there; he might, on the other hand, have had enough of London. The new variation in the driving ability evidence ('He could drive "all sorts of cars"'; 'He got in and drove it off quick enough') was particularly astonishing – because it seemed to conflict with the rest of the evidence – and particularly damaging for Hanratty. He had, in fact, boasted to Acott of his ability to drive 'almost any make' of car.

Sherrard asked Storie about the two identity parades – first of all, the one on which Alphon stood. Word had reached Sherrard that she had subsequently passed an intriguing comment:

Sherrard: Did you not afterwards say that there was a fair resemblance between Alphon and the man who attacked you?
Storie: When am I supposed to have said that?
Sherrard: Some time after that parade?
Storie: Some time afterwards, yes.
Sherrard: Can you tell us to whom you made that observation?
Storie: In the first instance I believe it was a doctor at Stoke Mandeville hospital.
Sherrard: And later? May it have been Superintendent Acott?
Storie: It may have been, but I do not remember.
Sherrard: It comes to this – that the resemblance between Alphon and your assailant was mentioned first to a doctor and, then, to get it quite accurately, to a police officer, possibly Mr Acott himself?
Storie: Yes.[18]

At the conclusion of the main part of her evidence (the part that's known as evidence-in-chief, prior to cross-examination by the opposing barrister), Valerie Storie was asked by Graham Swanwick about her identification of Hanratty at the second identity parade. Her subsequent avowal was both forceful and dramatic:

Swanwick: Who was the person who you identified?
Storie: The accused.
Swanwick: Do you see him in court now?
Storie: Yes.
Swanwick: The man in the dock?
Storie: Yes.
Swanwick: Had you any doubt at that time?
Storie: I had no doubt at all that this was the man who shot Mike and myself.
Swanwick: Have you any doubt now?
Storie: I have no doubt whatsoever.[19]

The rest of the third day's proceedings was, in the main, devoted to two other witnesses. The pathologist, Dr Keith Simpson, gave his testimony. During his evidence, it became clear that there was some confusion over the numbering of the scientific specimens. The numbers allocated to each exhibit had become detached from the exhibits themselves. Sherrard commented: 'There is no issue about that in this case, but one shudders to think what would happen if something did turn on it. It could lead to a very dangerous situation.'

Then John Kerr testified to what had happened in the lay-by. He reiterated that, in the immediate aftermath of the crime, Valerie Storie told him that the assailant had 'light, fairish hair'. As Kerr had had the presence of mind to make notes as she spoke to him, there was documentary evidence of this – or, at least, there should have been. He explained what had happened: 'At about eight o'clock I was interviewed by a police officer. I had the impression that his rank was higher than sergeant. He was wearing a flat peaked cap, similar to the inspector's cap now shown to me. I pointed out that I had made some notes on the back of a [census] form, and he said, "I'd better take that."'

At the magistrates' court, there was general surprise when it emerged that this critical document – containing the first, rudimentary description of the wanted man – was not in evidence, in any sense. It was missing. When Sherrard learned that it had disappeared, he expressed great concern and not a little incredulity. Questioned on the matter, Detective Superintendent Charles Barron, of Bedfordshire, responded, 'Since the witness Kerr gave his evidence, I have made inquiries to find any officer to whom he gave a piece of paper. I have interviewed all officers who were present at the scene that day. I have not been able to find any officer who had got such a piece of paper.'

So not merely could the document not be traced; its very existence was called into question.

In his opening address, Swanwick referred to John Kerr's evidence about having taken notes on the back of a census form, which he then handed to police: 'No such piece of paper and no such police officer has come to light ... That little mystery remains unsolved. You may think it is not of vital importance in this matter.'

He continued: 'The description which [Valerie Storie] says she gave him and the description which he says she gave him may differ in one respect particularly, namely, the colour of the hair. You will have to decide whether you accept her version or his. You will see him of course and you will form your impression of him and decide whether or not you think he was a rather frightened young man on that occasion.'

Now, when Kerr came to give trial evidence, the missing, if not non-existent, form had apparently turned up. This new exhibit – which, if genuine, should have been Exhibit 1 – now became one of the last of all, Exhibit 104.

A police officer had conducted a search of the county surveyor's office in Bedford and 'found' the document. It was, in fact, a formal letter written about the census by the surveyor and sent to John Kerr. On the back were a few scribbled notes. The car number, for example, was written; but there was no embryonic description of the gunman. Exhibit 104, suggested Swanwick to Kerr, must have been the form that he made such a song-and-dance about and which he thought he had handed to a police officer.

Kerr, politely but emphatically, repudiated this suggestion. For a start, he said, the writing wasn't his.

Swanwick: Are you really saying you do not think any of that is in your handwriting?
Kerr: That is so.
Swanwick: Can you recognize that writing? Do you know whose it is?
Kerr: I have no idea.
Swanwick: Is it anything like yours?
Kerr: No, not really. I do not do 4s like that, or Bs. My upward strokes do not taper off like the ones there do.[20]

In fact, the car number hadn't been written there anyway – or, at least, not accurately. It was written as BHN 847 (the numbers and letters were reversed). Yet the possibilities of Storie having given the registration wrongly, or of Kerr having taken it down wrongly, were equally remote. The cross-examination continued:

Swanwick: Do you remember who you handed this form to?
Kerr: I have no recollection of what happened to this. This would have been with the sheets of paper which would have been on my pad.
Swanwick: How were you feeling?
Kerr: Quite well, as well as one might expect.
Swanwick: Did you have to consult any doctor?[21]

At this point, Sherrard interjected, quite rightly. A later witness from the murder-scene, however, said he thought Kerr may have been 'agitated', and there the matter had to be left.

It may have appeared that a mountain of controversy was being made out of an insignificant molehill; yet it was really extremely important. It is not putting it too strongly to suggest that on the basis of this area of evidence alone Hanratty should have been acquitted. First, a critical piece of paperwork went missing, highly conveniently for the police, it seemed; and then a crude forgery was produced in its stead. Ultimately, the only way the Crown could repair the damage to its case was by trying to smear the witness concerned, suggesting that he was emotionally overcome by the circumstances (when the available evidence suggested that, on the contrary, he had kept a commendably cool head). In such circumstances, the prosecution did not merit the jury's trust. Its conduct stood exposed as entirely discreditable.

There were two other positive identifications of Hanratty. First, John Skillett told the court he had no doubt that Hanratty was the man they'd seen that morning. However, his passenger, Edward Blackhall, was the next to give evidence. He could remember the 'horrible expression' on the face of the driver – 'sort of half a smile and half a sneer' – but he had not identified Hanratty as the man.

In the court context, therefore, Skillett seemed the major witness and Blackhall the minor one. What was interesting about this was that these relative positions were originally reversed. There is no doubt that it was Blackhall who was regarded by police as the vital witness. He was the one who had first connected the incident with the murder and reported it to police; he was the one who illustrated his powers of observation by identifying the car at Scotland Yard, by 'three red strips on the car bumper and a small, torn green label'; he was the one who stayed calm and used more controlled language ('Get off the road'); and, whereas police had ignored Skillett's description for the photofit, they had relied on Blackhall's.

Although Blackhall became, in the prosecution's eyes, someone of no importance in the case, they still called him as a witness. This was a sly judicial manoeuvre; if they had not, then he would have been available to the defence.

The other identification witness, James Trower, explained how he had called on his way to work, at about 7.05, to pick up a friend, Paddy Hogan, who worked at the same engineering plant. After parking his car outside Hogan's flat, which was above a green-grocer's shop, he rang the bell and then stood around on the pavement waiting for somebody to answer. Because he heard the grinding of gears, he turned to see a car go past and then turn left into Avondale Crescent.

The following morning, he was approached by a plain-clothes policeman and asked if he had noticed anything suspicious. 'No, I do not think so,' he replied. It was Hogan who reminded him of the 'mad' driver he had seen the previous day, and suggested that he might have something to do with it. As a result, Trower went to the police. In court, he confirmed that he saw the driver for 'about three seconds' as he drove past. Trower's own car was, of course, between him and the Morris Minor. As the car was travelling from right to left, the driver was on the far side of his car from him.

Nevertheless, Trower, too, had made his identification:

Swanwick: Did you go to . . . Bedford to try to identify the driver of
    the car you had seen on 23 August?
Trower: Yes.
Swanwick: Did you succeed in identifying him?
Trower: Well, I identified a man there, yes.
Swanwick: Do you see that man in court?
Trower: Yes.
Swanwick: Will you point to him?
Trower: In the centre *[Indicating]*.
Swanwick: Have you any doubt about it?
Trower: No.[22]

The case continued with evidence pertaining to the 36A bus. The combination of the gun, left on the bus in London that day, and the telegram, sent by Hanratty from Liverpool that evening, created difficulties for the prosecution. So, by this stage, Swanwick had already introduced a cautionary note about the bus-cleaner:

'The prosecution would suggest that Hanratty might well have deposited the gun on the 36A bus in the early morning of 24 August, *assuming that the evidence you have of the cleaner is reliable* [my italics], have caught a train some time during that day to Liverpool and have sent that telegram in the hope that it might support some possible alibi. Because the police were able to check and test the telegram it clearly is ill-founded: it did not come off.'[23]

Because the evidence of the bus-cleaner created difficulties for the prosecution, a small question-mark had to be placed against it.

But why should it not have been reliable? There was no reason at all. Nor, when the prosecution had to abandon innuendo and rely on the evidence, could they show that it was. Edwin Cooke, the cleaner who discovered the gun and ammunition under the back seat, had once found 'two big dead rats' under the back seat, so every day he always made a point of looking underneath. He said he had checked the previous night. Was he sure? Cooke responded that he was 'positive'.

In view of this evidence, Swanwick had no option but to offer the blasé suggestion that the gun was left during the morning run ('The bus passed those parts of London about seven o'clock in the morning'). That, he said, would have given Hanratty 'ample time to catch any train to Liverpool that day in plenty of time to send a telegram at 8.40 in the evening'. So it would. Yet the Crown brought to court the bus-driver of the morning trip and the conductor of the afternoon one. If Swanwick believed his own case, then the only genuinely pertinent witness would have been Pamela Patt, the conductor during the morning. She was not called.

Swanwick then explained to the jury that 'That telegram is utterly pointless, except as an attempt to create the impression that he had been at Liverpool for the earlier part of that week ... and thereby help to build up his alibi for this murder.'

To reiterate, this is what the telegram said:

Having a nice time. Be home early Friday morning for business. Yours sincerely, Jim. The sender was *P. Ryan, Imperial Hotel, Russell Square, London.*

So this must have been the first and only time in judicial history that someone had tried to establish a fraudulent alibi in Liverpool by giving a bogus address in London. Whatever Hanratty's reasons for using a London address (partly perhaps a naive attempt to give himself social airs and partly a lack of imagination – Hanratty couldn't think of anywhere else), the essential point is that he had no Liverpool address in mind. This was actually proof not of what Swanwick alleged, but the very opposite: Hanratty had clearly given no thought at all to the notion of establishing a fraudulent alibi.

The more this aspect of the Crown case was examined, the more enfeebled it seemed. Unfortunately, however, the defence handling of this evidence was poor. Of course, they had no access to unused statements, and thus were unable to ascertain the true situation. Nevertheless, they should have been much more vigorous in probing the 'bus' testimony and simultaneously ensuring that they could place Hanratty well outside London, thus demonstrating he could not have placed the gun under the upstairs back seat.

Nor was there any logic attached to the cartridge cases. Swanwick tried to use these as one of the key prosecution points, while endeavouring to say as little as possible about them. The reason was obvious. Here was another part of the evidence which didn't make sense. Swanwick told the jury that the cases 'must have been left at the Vienna Hotel by the murderer before the gun was found'.[24] A reasonable assumption; but the problem was that, if the murderer was Hanratty, they must have been left at the Vienna *before the gun was used.* How could Hanratty have accidentally dropped the cartridge cases *before* he'd committed the murder? Whereas Alphon was linked to the Vienna after the crime, Hanratty wasn't. Faced with this difficulty, all Swanwick could offer was the vague suggestion of target practice.

Towards the end of the week, members of the France family were listed to give evidence. The case had overwhelmed them all, and Charles in particular seemed utterly distraught by the whole experience. Three days before the trial started, he was taken to Hammersmith Hospital after being found, still conscious and just in time, in a gas-filled room in Holland Park, London. A few hours after arriving at hospital he had to be restrained from jumping out of a high-level window. In consequence, he was admitted to Horton Mental Hospital, in Epsom, Surrey, where he was given electro-convulsion therapy.

On Thursday afternoon, when he was called to give evidence, he was said to be too ill to go into the witness-box. His wife, Charlotte, appeared instead, though she too was clearly in a bad way. She delivered a few sentences, which scarcely anyone could hear. She was enjoined several times to speak up. She had got only as far as giving her home address when she collapsed in the witness-box and had to be carried from the courtroom.

Of course, exactly the same thing had happened at the magistrates' court, when (as we now know) she was in a state of shock after Louise Anderson had told her about the gun being hidden at her house. On this occasion, too, she seemed traumatized. Perhaps, as Swanwick told the judge, 'the illness of her husband may have accentuated the position'.

After other evidence was heard, however, the clerk received a message that Charlotte France would, after all, give evidence that afternoon, 'as she dreads the thought of coming back another day'. She still could not raise her voice, and so was given a seat near the jury. Even then, the judge had to intervene during her brief testimony: 'Mrs France, I am showing you every possible consideration, but I do want you to speak a little more loudly, because if what you say is misunderstood an injustice may be done.'

The jury would have been entitled to wonder what the significance of all this was; her evidence seemed anything but critical. She had little to contribute, saying that Hanratty had left their flat at about seven o'clock on the Monday evening, 21 August (later than Hanratty himself estimated); and that she next saw him on Saturday, 26 August, when he produced the bill from the Vienna Hotel and explained that he had stayed there the previous Monday night.

Once again, Sherrard had to conduct his cross-examination with kid gloves. He contested some of her evidence: she said that Hanratty had given her money on only one occasion; and that, on his return from Liverpool, the family saw him on the Saturday when he was wearing a green jacket and brown trousers. Sherrard put it to her that she was given money on more than one occasion; and that his client actually returned from Liverpool on the Friday, not the Saturday, wearing his black Hepworth's suit. However, she did not accept that she was wrong.

Charles returned to court the following week, and was attended, while giving evidence, by two nurses from Horton. His testimony, albeit damaging, was hardly controversial as Hanratty had himself verified the gist of the conversation about the back seat of a bus. Also, although France appeared for the prosecution, he, in stark contrast to Louise Anderson, displayed no animosity towards Hanratty.

The prosecution would doubtless have contended that the emotional turmoil of the France family resulted from the knowledge that they had opened their family home to a monster like Hanratty. This may have had a veneer of plausibility, but the defence could have argued that it was essentially illogical. As Hanratty was arrested, what did they have to fear? As they were giving evidence against him, what did they have to reproach or distress themselves over? On the contrary, the defence might have argued, wasn't the explanation of their demeanour that they were overwrought by having to appear as prosecution witnesses at all?

The threat of fresh gaming charges could easily have been used to persuade Charles to give prosecution evidence; the family would then have fallen in line. Clearly, both Charles and Charlotte gave evidence only with intense reluctance, and neither was prepared to denigrate Hanratty (although they did minimize the extent of their relationship with him). Indeed, Charles told the court that 'I give his character the highest praise' and Charlotte was equally generous. She testified that he had always behaved properly towards her and her three daughters, and was treated as one of the family. Only Carole, it seemed, had developed any personal animosity against Hanratty.

Her testimony, which was heard on Friday morning, mainly concerned her having dyed and re-dyed Hanratty's hair. Sherrard certainly felt there had been more social contact than she was prepared to acknowledge. For example, Hanratty recalled having driven Carole to work when she was late one morning; and of her having accompanied him shopping when he wanted to buy handkerchiefs. She insisted these episodes had not occurred. She also said she had been out with him in his car only once (there had been a few times, Hanratty said), and was uncomplimentary about his driving: 'He drove zig-zagging, he was driving from side to side up the road.'

Like her mother, she also said that Hanratty returned from Liverpool on the Saturday; although, under cross-examination, she was not certain and said she couldn't remember. Nor was she sure whether or not Hanratty was wearing his suit when she first saw him after his return. At the conclusion of Carole's evidence, Sherrard remarked testily, 'I am not going to take up any more time with this. You are just not being completely frank with the court.'

On Friday morning, before the hearing of the evidence began, there were two preliminary matters. It was the judge, Mr Justice Gorman, who, having spent the previous evening assiduously writing up his notes from that day's hearing, straightaway mentioned that the evidence regarding the 36A bus was incomplete. The Crown dealt with his objection after the weekend by calling an additional witness – though not Pamela Patt; the account still remained totally unhelpful as far as the jury was concerned.

Why, having had two opportunities, was the Crown so reluctant to call Pamela Patt? Her statement was not disclosed to the defence at the time, and I only discovered it thirty years later. This was what she had to say:

'By the time we got to the Harrow Road, the bus was full and remained like this until we arrived at Victoria ... In the first journey to Kilburn the passengers were all regular ones ... I did not see anything suspicious during the whole of this journey.'[25]

The significance of this is that during the time the bus was travelling through what Swanwick described as those 'parts of London with which Hanratty was very closely connected', it was full. If the Crown had disclosed it, it would have demonstrated that the opportunities for Hanratty to have deposited the gun during the morning run were all but non-existent – and there was no other time in which he could have done so.

Then there was controversy about John Skillett's evidence. Sherrard complained to the judge that Skillett had been observed talking to a police officer just before giving his evidence. 'It is very undesirable', he said, 'that there should be discussion of any kind between police and witnesses before they are called.' The judge wholeheartedly agreed, albeit without censoring or even identifying the officer involved.

Swanwick then intervened to say that the witness had merely been discussing a matter with Mr MacDermott, who was not a police officer. This obliged Sherrard to go into further detail about what had happened.

'It was not Mr MacDermott's conversation to which I was referring. There was some discussion [between Skillett and a police officer] about not forgetting this, that and the other.'[26]

There had already been many warning signals that this was an irregular prosecution. Here was yet another irregularity.

By this stage, also, a crude prosecution tactic was beginning to emerge. The evidence of honest witnesses (Kerr, Cooke the bus-cleaner) was, being inconvenient, smeared or questioned; conversely, the evidence of dishonest witnesses was talked up. The jury was told that Roy Langdale's evidence was 'accurate in very many details'; and that Hanratty had given him 'a potted account, which only the murderer at that stage could know'. In normal circumstances, Swanwick admitted, the evidence of William Nudds, police informer and former employee of the Vienna Hotel, might well be regarded with 'considerable suspicion'. He had made one statement, rescinded it, made another, rescinded that, and was currently attesting to the absolute truth of his third. This time, however, it was 'in many respects corroborated by documents, by other witnesses and, indeed, in one very vital aspect by the accused himself'.

The validity of Swanwick's remarks could be put to the test, as Nudds himself was the next to enter the witness-box. Some small pieces of his evidence seemed circumstantially damaging to the defence. According to Nudds, Hanratty – or Ryan, as Nudds knew him – returned after leaving the hotel, and said 'he had forgotten something in his room and asked to go and retrieve it.' There was an insinuation that this could have been when the cartridge cases were dropped.

Sherrard went through this part of the statement virtually word by word – it was the only way with Nudds – and managed to tease out the fact that Hanratty had done nothing more incriminating than return to his room to collect his luggage:

Sherrard: Do you see the difference between someone who has left a hotel and then comes back and wants to go back to a room which he has vacated; and someone who is still there, still a guest, who has just paid his bill, and wants to get his luggage? You see the difference, do you not?[27]

This was one point which Nudds did concede. Otherwise, it was a gruelling Friday afternoon for all concerned. Mere logic stood little chance against a man of such fathomless perversity. To him, truth was merely a commodity to be bartered. The situation regarding the 36A bus was instructive. Nudds said that, on his departure from the hotel, Hanratty had asked directions to Queensway:

Nudds: I said, 'Turn right, walk along Sutherland Avenue until you come to the Harrow Road, where you will find a bus to take you direct.'
Sherrard: Did you tell him the number of the bus?
Nudds: Yes. 36 or 36A.[28]

There was then a misunderstanding, followed by a lengthy courtroom discussion among counsel, prompted by the unfailingly conscientious Mr Justice Gorman, about whether Nudds had actually added 36A after 36. (According to the transcript, he had.) As a result, the question was again put by Sherrard in his cross-examination. Now, Nudds answered it differently:

Sherrard: Do you say now you mentioned both buses?
Nudds: Yes. I did mention it at the time.
Sherrard: Both of them – 36 and 36A?
Nudds: Not here; not in this statement.
Sherrard: At the time it happened?
Nudds: No, I never mentioned 36A at all. I mentioned a 36 bus.[29]

Trying to make sense of Nudds's answers was like trying to build a solid structure out of blancmange. Nevertheless, the inference here (whether or not the 36A bus itself was referred to) again appears to lend a smattering of support to the prosecution case. But it actually did something different: it opened up a further contradiction in it. According to Swanwick's opening address, Hanratty could be linked to the 36A bus because he knew the area, and hence the bus-routes, well; according to this evidence, Hanratty could be linked to the 36A bus because he didn't know the area at all and had to seek directions.

Later in the trial, Nudds's 'wife', Florence Snell, gave evidence about the 'directions': 'I am quite sure I was on the steps when the accused left. He asked Mr Nudds the way to Queensway, and Mr Nudds directed him. He told him to walk to the top of the road, and from there he could get a bus to Queensway.'[30]

Sherrard was dumbfounded. 'You have not mentioned about that conversation before, have you?' he asked. She responded that she had not been asked about it before.

Sherrard: Not by anybody, at any time?
Snell: I was asked at Scotland Yard, but not here.[31]

In fact, there is a transcript of what she said at Scotland Yard to Acott – a transcript which was never disclosed to the defence. If it had been, Sherrard would have found it very useful. It contained no reference whatever to the conversation. However, Acott had asked her about Hanratty's departure:

Acott: Did you see Ryan leave the hotel?
Snell: He thanked me for his breakfast and I saw him go out. He was carrying a portable radio and a green holdall.[32]

I saw him go out. This obviously indicates that she was inside when he left, not 'on the steps' outside.

Returning to Nudds himself, other aspects of his evidence conflicted with what Hanratty had said. Nudds was adamant that Hanratty was brought across from the Broadway House hotel, in one of the company's own vehicles, between 9.00 and 11.00 p.m. According to Hanratty, by the time he went it was midnight, and he went by taxi.

Neither defence nor prosecution paid particular attention to this, but the point should not be neglected. There is some support for

Hanratty's version: a large asterisk or star was next to his name in the hotel register – Juliana Galves always put one there in the morning against the name of the last person booked in the previous evening; and, although no one knew this until the Snell transcript became available in 1991, when Acott asked her what time Hanratty had arrived, she replied, 'About 11.00 p.m., or a little later.'

If Hanratty was correct – as I believe he was – then why would Nudds have bothered to lie about that (over and above the fact that he seemed to lie about almost everything)? What was the point? The answer is perhaps that, if Hanratty were looking for a hotel sometime earlier in the evening, when he would still have been able to catch a late-night train, then it undermined altogether his stated objective of going to Liverpool that day.

In the magistrates' court, Nudds had described his first two statements with all the eloquence he could muster as 'a mixture of lies and truth, a bit bottom heavy the lies end'. Now in Bedford, Sherrard, commenting 'Before we come to the double somersault we must do the single somersault,' took him stage by stage through his second statement (see pages 66–69).[33]

Sherrard's contention was that this was the one that was actually accurate: 'These things happened and we can check them through the records and, fortunately, by other means. It was only when you realized that that was not the story which you thought would help the police that you changed it.'

This was Nudds's first attempt to explain the second statement: 'When I made this, it was referring to Ryan, and I put it on to Durrant.' As a longtime police informer, Nudds would of course be thoroughly used to 'putting it on' somebody. 'Very well,' responded Sherrard, 'let us examine it in that vein. Durrant – that is, Alphon – said he didn't like a basement room and preferred one upstairs.' According to the statement, Nudds then said, 'All our single rooms are booked, but if one should become vacant, I'll let you have it and move you into it.'

Sherrard: That is not something that could have happened with regard to Ryan, could it?
Nudds: Why not?
Sherrard: He was arriving very nearly at midnight. You were not expecting that he was going to go into that room and perhaps be moved into a single room in the middle of the night?
Nudds: No.[34]

Sherrard went on to consider the note left for Durrant, when Nudds and his wife went to bed. Nudds suggested that that applied to someone else, someone different.

Sherrard: But the contemporary records, you agree, rather seem to stand in the way of that?
Nudds: I suppose they do.[35]

When Mrs Snell came to give evidence, she, inevitably, supported Nudds. However, Sherrard asked her about how it was that the second statements, implicating Durrant, or Alphon, came to be made:

Sherrard: Why did Mr Nudds tell the second story about the man called Durrant if it was not true?
Snell: Because he was so confused.
Sherrard: Did you say 'confused'?
Snell: Yes.
Sherrard: You mean it was not a deliberate story invented just to jog along nicely and happily with the police?
Snell: No.
Sherrard: You mean that when that second story was told it was thought by both of you to be genuinely true and what had happened?
Snell: Yes.
Sherrard: Supported, as it was, by the hotel records?
Snell: Yes.[36]

So, according to her, Nudds was able to give, in utter confusion, a statement which was not only highly detailed but which was either supported, or not contradicted by, every other source of information. Further, her own confusion had exactly mirrored her husband's.

By the end of the day in court, the legal argument had been so convoluted, and so difficult to follow, that it was difficult to gauge what impression it would all have had on the jury members. Probably they found Nudds utterly unconvincing and ignored his evidence altogether. They may have found his valedictory remarks the most unconvincing of all.

'I am determined to keep straight. I have even got myself another job, and I am going to tell you this. Through your bandying my criminal record about in this case, I am going to lose this one, but I shall not throw in the towel. Somebody will give me a chance to live out my life decently. The milk of human kindness has not dried up completely.'[37]

There was a hiatus in Nudds' long stint in the witness-box, occasioned, yet again, by an irregularity in the legal process. Superintendent Acott was observed at the Bedford Hotel on the Embankment, taking a fresh statement from one of the witnesses, Louise Anderson (though she was not named at this time). As she'd already made five statements, this was most improper. Any fresh points could be put to her in the witness-box. Graham Swanwick explained to the judge that 'I was told about this and I gave instructions that pending further consideration the statement should cease.'

Sherrard commented: 'I think the least said about it the better. It does rather reinforce what I was saying to your Lordship earlier on. If there is any question of communication between witnesses and the prosecution, it is best not done by the police officers in charge.'

The judge said, 'You are absolutely right. I thank you for bringing it to my attention. I do not want anything to happen that may for one moment give the impression that a fair and proper trial is not being held. You see, in a case that has excited as much publicity as this, the limelight has the effect not only of showing the right things but also the blemishes.'[38]

For all of Gorman's good intentions, however, the blemishes were inexorably accumulating.

HANRATTY'S EXPERIENCE OF criminal trials was limited. As he'd always pleaded guilty in the past, the cases had been straightforward with no requirement to call evidence. He was probably as ignorant as the rest of the population of the below-the-belt methods that sometimes characterized contested trials.

In fact, innocent defendants have frequently been disadvantaged not primarily by the judicial process itself but by the attendant mythology – according to which British justice was now, and ever had been, the best there was. Why then should an innocent man concern himself with the functioning of the process? He was not guilty; nothing could go wrong; he would be acquitted.

The opening days of the trial must have been a shattering eye-opener for Hanratty. From the dock he must have followed proceedings with, at first, perplexity and, then, increasing trepidation. Three people had identified him with a sureness that precluded any possible doubt; and the few friends he had in the world – the France family and Louise Anderson – were aligned with the prosecution. That weekend of 27/28 January, Hanratty was a very worried man. Unusually for him, he did a lot of thinking.

When his defence team saw him at the beginning of the second week, he had a shock for them. He said he had not come clean about his alibi. In truth, that wasn't the shock; they had long suspected that. He said it was now clear that he would have to go into the witness-box to defend himself and he had to be able to tell the complete truth. Thus, for the first time, Hanratty mentioned Rhyl to his defence team, and told them that during the critical period he was staying in a Rhyl guest-house. That was the shock. The defence lawyers were distraught. They were now faced with the prospect of instigating an entirely fresh area of investigation at this very late stage.

But why had he withheld such utterly vital information, and kept for so long to his deception about the three men in Liverpool? As ever, Hanratty was so inarticulate he could hardly express himself. A combination of three reasons probably explained what had happened. The first was, as Kleinman had already perceived, Hanratty's assumption that the case against him could not be established. Consequently, he felt that he didn't even need to bother providing the information. It was a clear illustration of the point that the innocent could be in greater jeopardy from the criminal justice process than the guilty. Second, Hanratty knew that as an alibi it was very weak, because he recollected little more himself than that he had stayed somewhere in Rhyl. Since he could not give his lawyers any concrete details about the name or location of the guest-house, what he now affirmed as the truth had scarcely more substance than his previous charade of having remained in Liverpool.

The third reason, one he may have had difficulty in acknowledging to himself, was the sheer embarrassment of mentioning it. There were several aspects to this. First, he hadn't told anyone on his return to London at the time. He'd told everyone he was going to Liverpool; if he said he'd gone elsewhere, it would have entailed admitting what a fiasco his Liverpool excursion had been. In particular, he'd told Charlotte France that he was going to Liverpool to visit an aunt, so he could hardly have admitted on his return that he'd been somewhere else altogether.

Second, even by his own high standards of fecklessness, he'd spent an especially vapid time in Rhyl. People like to pretend that they lead socially successful lives, not empty and friendless ones. Hanratty's movements had been so aimless he felt awkward simply about relating them.

Third, having started off on the wrong tracks, it became increasingly difficult to switch to the right ones. This was how Hanratty himself responded when Sherrard asked him, first of all, why he had not told the truth to the police:

Hanratty: On the previous phone call [I told Acott] that I had stayed in Liverpool. At that stage, I made up a lie and, to cover the lie, I made up previous other lies to cover the lies which I had already said in the first place.

Sherrard: Why did you not tell him you had been to Rhyl?

Hanratty: Because at that point, I did not know the name of the street, the number of the house, or even the name of the people living in the house.

Sherrard: Why was it that, having told this story which was untrue, you persisted in it so long?

Hanratty: Because, my Lord, I am a man with a prison record and I know in such a trial of this degree it is very vital for a man once to change his evidence in such a serious trial; but I know inside of me somewhere in Rhyl this house does exist and, by telling the truth, these people will come to my assistance.[1]

Asked the same question (why did he lie?) by the prosecution, Hanratty supplied his own, somewhat less resonant version of Sir Walter Scott's 'O what a tangled web we weave / When first we practise to deceive': 'I had already told a lie and I had started on one and I had to cover up and cover up and cover up until eventually I made things a lot worser for myself.'

The sudden mention of Rhyl fell into the category of what the prosecution termed 'ambush alibis'. The police complained that criminals evaded justice by using associates to introduce alibis into trials at the last possible moment, too late for the Crown to be able to show how bogus they were. Ambush alibis were outlawed by the 1967 Criminal Justice Act. Had his trial been held six years later, this manoeuvre would have been denied to Hanratty.

However, it should be emphasized that this by no means fell into the general pattern of so-called ambush alibis. Hanratty was not introducing a witness to give evidence for him. He was merely stating where he had been; it was in the hands of others as to whether or not it could be supported or authenticated. Hanratty himself could play no part in that.

The defence team gave Hanratty a hastily drawn-up, handwritten document and asked him to sign it: 'I hereby instruct my solicitors and counsel to proceed on the basis of the true story about Rhyl. Please try to find the landlady there. This has been read to me. I fully understand it.' He accepted the full consequences of his actions. The defence acquired the judge's permission to take fresh photographs of Hanratty – for which he posed at the rear of the courthouse, outside on the terrace overlooking the River Ouse – to assist the identification process. Kleinman's practice contacted Joe Gillbanks, telling him apologetically that he had indeed been wasting his time in Liverpool, and could he possibly go to Rhyl instead?

MONDAY – FRIDAY, 29 JANUARY – 2 FEBRUARY:
The Second Week

Monday's proceedings concluded with an especially histrionic performance from Louise Anderson, remembered by many of those who saw her as 'that shrill woman'. Prior to her appearance Sherrard had argued, again succcessfully, for the exclusion of material contained in her latest statement (the one taken so contentiously by Acott the previous Friday). According to this, Hanratty had sometimes stayed at her flat; and, sometime during the previous five months, she had lost a pair of black gloves. Sherrard pointed out that she was saying no more than 'Somewhere, some time, I lost [some gloves], I do not know precisely where or when or in what circumstances.' The prosecution now hoped to use this as 'evidence'. The judge agreed totally with Sherrard, threw it out, and sent Mr MacDermott to warn Anderson not to allude to it in her evidence.

In an early part of Anderson's testimony, she said that Hanratty had visited her shop on Saturday, 26 August. She continued:

Anderson: I rather think about 5.30 or 5.45 ... The first thing I noticed was that his hair had been dyed and it was very dark brown and he also had scratches which I at first thought—
Mr Justice Gorman: His hair had been dyed?
Anderson: Yes.
Gorman: Very dark brown?
Anderson: Very dark brown, and he had marks down the side of his left cheek. They were very deep and I thought they were razor cuts.
Swanwick: Do you remember the last occasion you had seen him before [then]?
Anderson: Yes, it was on the 22nd, on the Tuesday morning.
Gorman: One moment—
Anderson: He said he was going to Liverpool.
Swanwick: In the morning?
Anderson: Yes. That was early in the morning, but he had not stayed at my flat that night.
Swanwick: Do you remember what he was wearing?
Anderson: It was an Italian-type suit, with more like a chalk stripe.
Swanwick: What was he wearing on the Saturday?
Anderson: Very light slacks and a light fawn pullover.[2]

The point about this astonishing passage, which took everyone by surprise, is not just that it contains three separate untruths and one massively misleading assertion, but that each of these four was deliberately injurious. They were calculated to harm Hanratty. Anderson was saying: (1) that he had visited her on the Tuesday morning before the murder; (2) that he had dyed his hair straight after the murder; (3) that his face was badly scratched when she saw him after the murder; and (4) that he was wearing his suit just before the murder but not wearing it straight afterwards.

Anderson seemed to have got hold of the wrong prosecution script. None of these assertions was particularly helpful to the Crown because each was clearly unsustainable. All were either contradicted, or not supported in any sense, by the rest of the evidence.

Prior to the two police raids on Anderson's premises – the first on her flat for Hanratty's suitcases; the second on her shop for stolen articles – relations between her and Hanratty had been wholly cordial. The assumption remains that, after the raids, she was frightened into giving evidence damaging to Hanratty on the basis that if she didn't, she herself would face a number of criminal charges.

Even though Swanwick led her solicitously through her perjury, she was in obvious emotional distress while giving evidence, and the pressure proved overwhelming. She very soon collapsed – as she had done at the magistrates' court – and had to be carried from the witness-box. It was like an encore of the France family performance. Again, the prosecution might have explained this in terms of the malevolent impact exerted by Hanratty; again, it seems more likely to have arisen as a result of feeling under duress to give evidence against him which she knew to be untrue. Certainly, it seemed significant that she collapsed at a point when she was describing Hanratty's 'Robin Hood adventures', his housebreakings; at a time, in fact, when Swanwick was about to lead her on to what she knew to be another whopping lie.

When she recovered, Swanwick asked what Hanratty had told her about his burglaries.

Swanwick: Did he tell you about anything he used?
Anderson: Yes, he said they could not possibly detect him because
    he used his gloves on these occasions.

Swanwick: When he told you about wearing gloves, did he mention any particular type of gloves?
Anderson: No, he merely used the expression 'gloves'.[3]

If there was anything that was well understood about Hanratty's modus operandi as a burglar, it was that he never used gloves. The police knew this well enough. It was because he always left finger-prints that they were able to catch him. This was merely a further example of the prosecution's broad-brush damage-maximization technique: if it appeared damaging, any tendentious evidence would do, irrespective of whether it was inherently credible.

During Sherrard's cross-examination, he did establish that Han-ratty had always behaved 'perfectly properly' towards her. But Anderson, like other witnesses, gave answers at variance with those she had given in the magistrates' court and with what she had said in her statements. Her antipathy towards her former lodger was plain for all to hear; she indicated that she was 'frightened of this man'. Sherrard concluded, in anger and bafflement:

Sherrard: Are you standing there quite deliberately to say anything you can to hurt this man?
Anderson: How absurd you are.[4]

Later that day, the court heard Roy Langdale. As if his evidence wasn't already tainted enough, he had to admit, under cross-examination, that he had approached the *Sunday Pictorial* with his story, and been paid £25; that the *Daily Herald* had offered him £20, and that he had also been contacted by the *Evening Standard*. Hardly the inducements that might be offered today; but *any* monetary payment – whether already made, contractually promised or merely anticipated – automatically undermines the integrity of testimony.

Although the evidence which Langdale brought to bear on the case supposedly emerged as a result of a conversation he had with a fellow-prisoner which was overheard by a prison warder, Alfred Eatwell, neither Langdale nor Eatwell was allowed to give evidence about this conversation at the trial. This is because it was hearsay, and therefore inadmissible.

This resulted in the matter being handled in an oblique and, for the jury, probably confusing way. However, the whole business was so spurious that the more that was known about it, the more it would actually have assisted the defence. As it was, Eatwell had to concede at trial that he was in uniform, and sitting directly behind Langdale; and that Langdale wasn't even talking to the person beside him: 'He was talking across another prisoner to one on the other side of the coach.' Moreover, Sherrard asked him 'whether, in your experience, prisoners learn how to talk without being overheard by prison warders'. Eatwell replied that they did. So the idea that Langdale was *inadvertently* overheard was clearly absurd. However, the conversation itself was not referred to.

Eatwell said that Langdale had neither come into contact with prisoners on bail, nor seen the papers. 'At no time whilst he was in my custody did he receive a newspaper nor was he in a position to obtain a newspaper.'

Langdale himself added that 'The only time I read a newspaper is to read the football report'. With regard to this case, though, he did remember 'reading in some newspaper that the murderer had thumbed a lift, and I did not know that this was wrong until Hanratty told me how the car had been stationary when he saw it'.

Questions and answers such as these helped to foster the impression that Langdale–Eatwell had to be wholly reliable because Langdale could have had no access to the details and circumstances of the crime other than through the murderer himself; QED Hanratty, who provided the information, was the murderer.

In fact, the usual reason why informers are able to display inside knowledge of the crime is that they are briefed by police officers. In this instance, however, one can set aside that argument, because it is a fallacy to suggest that Langdale had *any* inside knowledge of this crime.

Because of the special circumstances of the case – in particular the widespread reactions of shock and revulsion to the crime itself, and the unusually high-profile and protracted search for the culprit – it had received more publicity, across a broader range of media outlets, than almost any other criminal case. Altogether, a lot of detail had been published. There was no fact about the crime in Langdale's testimony that he could not have gleaned from previous newspaper reports.

More importantly, Langdale's supposedly privileged information was not even accurate. This is an extract from his first statement:

'On exercise I told Hanratty that I'd heard on the television news that he had thumbed a lift from a passing car and then had set about the man and woman after they'd given him a lift.

Hanratty said, "Oh, that's all paper talk. I wasn't thumbing a lift at all. I was coming across a field when I saw the car standing still just off the road a little way."'

The field in which the Morris Minor was parked – which today is owned by Thames Water – was extensive. However, Gregsten and Storie would have had a good panoramic view of it. The car was at that stage pointing into the field. When they were there, it was getting dark. Nevertheless, if the man had been 'coming across a field', they would have had some advance warning of his arrival – either seeing a silhouetted figure, or hearing him – and not have been taken totally by surprise.

As it happened, the corn had not been cut, so walking across the field would have presented difficulties. Valerie Storie said that she didn't believe he'd been sleeping rough because 'it had been raining very hard' and he was 'immaculately dressed'. If she'd been able to notice this, she'd presumably also have noticed whether these clothes were muddied or soiled in some way, as a result of having just walked across a wet cornfield.

Every intelligent deduction must be that the gunman approached the car, not 'across a field', as Langdale had it, but from behind, from the road, from Marsh Lane. The information which Langdale had, and which was held to demonstrate unique knowledge of the crime, was palpably incorrect.

However, eliciting such information at the trial was virtually impossible. Sherrard was given an exasperating time. The court was already wearily familiar, from the testimony of Nudds, of the slippery ways in which informers gave evidence, and Langdale merely gave a further demonstration of the technique.

Sherrard pointed out to Langdale that he had also given two different versions of the circumstances in which he first met Hanratty and of what was said at their initial meeting: one in his statement to Acott; and one in his evidence-in-chief to Swanwick. Which, Sherrard wanted to know, was accurate? Both, Langdale asserted. Cross-examination, as those of Langdale's stripe well knew, becomes pointless if the witness refuses to play to the ground-rules of logic and rational argument.

Langdale's tortuous attempts to reconcile the irreconcilable in his evidence were tedious for everybody. Towards the end of his evidence, he suddenly said that Hanratty had mentioned wanting to shoot Superintendent Acott. At that point, there was laughter in the courtroom. This offended the judge, who commented, 'I think those people who desire amusement ought to seek it somewhere else.' However, derisory laughter was actually the only appropriate response. Sherrard, almost incredulous, asked Langdale, 'Is this a bit you have made up just now?'

Detective Superintendent Acott endured an especially long period in the witness-box. He was cross-examined for part of Thursday, all of Friday and part of the following Monday. In all, his evidence lasted thirteen hours ten minutes. In those days when the weekly exploits of the incorruptible *Dixon of Dock Green* were one of the nation's television highlights, and when the probity of the police was taken on absolute trust, the fact that this very senior officer's bona fides should have been in any question at all was itself a startling reflection of the latent concern within some legal quarters about this case.

Sherrard: Mr Acott, do you agree that the care and fairness with which an investigation is conducted may be a reliable pointer to the reliability of the result?

Acott: Yes.

Sherrard: I have to suggest to you, and I want it to be quite clear, that your inquiries in this matter were neither careful nor fair, and were in many respects distinguished by inaccuracy.[5]

Of particular concern were the police records of the interviews with Hanratty. These, ostensibly, were complete. Yet the first could be read aloud, at conversation pace, in twenty minutes; the interview itself was supposed to have taken ninety minutes. Acott maintained that the discrepancy was accounted for by the length of time it took Hanratty to provide answers; there were, he explained, frequent 'pauses'. Sherrard pointed out that, in the first interview, there would have been 'an hour and ten minutes of pauses'. (Even that was making allowances for what Acott claimed was a fifteen-minute 'settling-in' period.)

Sherrard further suggested that some of these pauses occurred at very odd points in the conversation. For example, Hanratty said to Acott, 'I am glad this has come. I am relieved now this is all over. You'll see I couldn't have done this horrible murder. I know exactly where I was when it happened. What do you want to ask me about it?' (Pause.)

Any pause there, suggested Sherrard, was obviously Acott's fault; Acott maintained that he was waiting for Hanratty to say something else. Sherrard continued, reading from the interrogation record: 'You said, "Was there anyone else in that room that night?"

Defendant, "No." (Pause.) Again, he answers the question perfectly sensibly.'

Sherrard implied that all the 'pauses' in the record had been inserted both to make it appear as though Hanratty had replied haltingly, when in fact he had given confident, direct answers; and to mask the fact that this was a very incomplete record of what had been said.

Sherrard gave examples of what he termed 'inaccuracies and omissions'. He quoted Acott saying to Hanratty, 'Are you telling me that these three friends of yours in Liverpool can clear you by giving you an alibi?'

Sherrard: Where is there any reference to the 'three friends' in Liverpool before that?
Acott: I have already noticed this discrepancy.[6]

Another of Acott's questions which Sherrard quoted from the interview was, 'Are you trying to tell me you tried to get a gun from a man at Ealing?'

Sherrard: Did it not occur to you to say, What is the name of this man in Ealing?
Acott: No.
Sherrard: It was a rather important question.
Acott: I did not ask him.
Sherrard: The truth is you told him, 'I have interviewed Fisher [Donald Slack] at Ealing and he tells me you inquired about a gun in March.'
Acott: That is not true, sir, I never said that.[7]

There was an important passage in the interview which concerned the discovery at the Vienna Hotel. Acott told Hanratty, 'I can't make it too clear how desperate your position is. I must tell you now. After your leaving Room 24 on 22 August and before it was occupied again, two empty cartridge cases were found at the end of the bed you slept in that night.'

'What size were the bullets, Mr Acott?' Hanratty is alleged to have replied.

'I can't tell you that,' said Acott.

'Well, that's the end for me, isn't it?' responded Hanratty. 'I tell you I've never had any bullets and never fired a gun.'

Sherrard put this purported conversation to Acott:

Sherrard: Do you really tell my Lord and the jury upon your oath that that man's answer was, 'What size were the bullets, Mr Acott?'

Acott: I do indeed. That is one of the most remarkable statements I have ever had to record . . .

Sherrard: It brings capital murder to his doorstep, does it not?

Acott: Yes. Here were the bullets almost in his possession.

Sherrard: Bullets?

Acott: Well, cartridge cases.

Sherrard: My instructions are that in fact you did say 'Bullets' to him, that he sat there (and this was the only genuine pause) and he looked at you and then said, 'You are not kidding me, are you, Mr Acott?'

Acott: That is not so . . .

Sherrard: It was not a very fair performance on your part, was it?

Acott: I myself can see nothing unfair in it. I am the interrogator. I can stop when and where I please.

Sherrard: Including deciding the length of the pauses?

Acott: I do not decide the pauses.[8]

There was a further area of significant dispute. According to the interview record, the first session concluded, at 9.30 in the morning, as follows: 'We'll leave you now,' said Acott, 'while we make inquiries which will probably take several hours.'

'OK, I'll go to kip,' commented Hanratty.

The afternoon interview ended: 'Think very seriously about what I've told you,' said Acott. 'If you change your mind about the three men you can send for me.'

'All right, Mr Acott,' replied Hanratty. 'I'm going to have a good kip.'

'Why? Are you tired? It's only early afternoon.'

'No, I'm not tired but I can always kip any time, any place.'

The use of the word 'kip', a cockney expression then in vogue, was important because Valerie Storie said the gunman had used the term. Hanratty was adamant that he never used the word, and that this was a cast-iron example of police 'verbals' – the practice by which police attributed incriminating comments to defendants.[9] By way of comparison, Sherrard drew Acott's attention to the opening passage of one of the telephone conversations:

Hanratty: I read in the paper this morning that you and your mate slept at the Yard all night on a couple of camp beds. I'm sorry I'm causing you so much trouble, Mr Acott.

Acott: That's all right, Jimmy. I bet you slept well last night.
Hanratty: Yes, I slept all night on the train. It was very comfortable.

Sherrard commented to Acott:

Sherrard: He did not say 'kip' then?
Acott: He did not. I just used the word 'slept' right in front of him.
Sherrard: But he had used the word 'slept' before you did. Look at your note.
Acott: Can you give it to me, please?
Sherrard: Just read it.
Acott: Yes. 'Slept at the Yard all night.'
Sherrard: He used 'slept' first. It was not true that you used it and he picked it up.
Acott: No, it is quite true that he used it.[10]

Further, Hanratty had spontaneously used the word when, in the first interview, Acott had asked him about the Vienna Hotel:

Acott: Was there anyone else in that room that night?
Hanratty: No. It was a very big room with three or four beds. I slept in a small bed against the wall.[11]

This was persuasive support for Hanratty's claim that the police were using 'verbals' against him. His argument was further strengthened in that the police account – suggesting that Hanratty required sleep at 9.30 a.m. and at 2.30 p.m. – seemed, on the face of it, unlikely.

There are two further respects in which there was a clear difference of opinion between Hanratty's own memory of what had occurred and the records kept by the investigating officers. In both cases documentary evidence which subsequently emerged – in one case, almost immediately; in the other, thirty years later – goes some way to supporting Hanratty's recollection rather than the police records. Firstly, according to the police records, Hanratty said that at the Vienna Hotel he returned to his room because he had forgotten his luggage.

Sherrard: He did not tell you, I suggest, that he had forgotten his luggage?
Acott: He did.
Sherrard: What he said was that when he had finished breakfast 'I

popped down to the room to get my luggage and after that I left the hotel', and that is the way he put it.

Acott: No.

Sherrard: This little piece about 'some luggage I'd forgotten' is something, I suggest, which has been lifted really from Mr Nudds' story?

Acott: I would not lift anything from anybody's story.[12]

Subsequently the rough notes of this interview, made by Detective Sergeant Kenneth Oxford, Acott's junior partner, were disclosed. Sherrard immediately noticed that these contained the phrase: 'popped room for lug'. This appeared to be cast-iron corroboration of Hanratty's testimony. Accordingly, Sherrard questioned Oxford:

Sherrard: Is there anything there about 'I had forgotten'?

Oxford: No.

Sherrard: I had not seen that note yesterday, you appreciate that?

Oxford: Yes.

Sherrard: When Mr Acott was being asked about it, it was being put to him on the basis of [Hanratty's] memory [alone]. Hanratty's recollection was that all he had said was that after breakfast he had popped down to get his luggage and left the hotel. Your note, to that extent, bears him out completely, does it not?

Oxford: Yes.

Sherrard: There is nothing there about having forgotten the luggage?

Oxford: No. I have not got the words that he had forgotten his luggage or any such thing.[13]

Acott was also asked, again solely on the basis of what Hanratty had told Sherrard, whether he, Acott, had told Hanratty that he would help him.

Sherrard: Will you think very carefully before you answer this question because it is of some importance. One of the first things you said to this man was this, that it had been a long and troublesome inquiry and now you had got him you did not want to be hard and, if he wanted to plead diminished responsibility or insanity, you would do what you could to help him?

Acott: Not one word of that is true.

Sherrard: Not a word?
Acott: Not one word.[14]

Yet, though no one knew it at the time, Acott had privately written three months earlier that Hanratty's 'known mental and medical history should be sufficient grounds for him to gain a verdict of diminished responsibility'.

Altogether, there was extensive disagreement over large swathes of the records of both the telephone conversations and the interviews. The defence argued that there had been 'flagrant breaches of the judges' rules' – the code of conduct then in place (which had no force in law) to regulate police interviews of suspects. Acott retorted that he had 'a clear conscience on this matter'.

Under cross-examination, Acott was obliged to concede that many facets of the evidence were entirely in the defendant's favour. He agreed that – unlike what the gunman had said about himself on the car journey – Hanratty did not know the Bear Hotel, Maidenhead; hadn't been to Oxford; wasn't on the run; hadn't been locked in a cellar and provided with only bread and water; hadn't been to a remand home; hadn't been to Borstal; hadn't done five years for housebreaking; and wouldn't qualify for preventive detention next time because he was five years too young.

Acott confirmed that there was 'no doubt' in his mind that the hotel records supported Nudds's second statement; that, equally, there was 'no doubt' that Hanratty was wearing his Hepworth's suit until the end of September; that for some time after the murder he kept his hair black; that he had stolen a Jaguar car to drive north, and that he had never been convicted of careless or dangerous driving. Nor had he been convicted of any violent or sexual offence. At that time, any suspect could have declined to give specimen samples for scientific analysis; Acott agreed that Hanratty, without asking for any legal advice, immediately volunteered to give whatever samples Acott required. Finally, Acott, asked to describe Hanratty's manner, responded, 'He is unusually polite and never uses a swear word.'

Acott claimed not to be aware of previous trial evidence because, he said, he had been cloistered: 'Since before this court sat I have been locked up in a separate room until I was called to the box this morning ... I have discussed [the trial] with no one. I have not read a newspaper account of it ... Every police officer working with me in this court has been told not to approach me, and those instructions have been carried out.'[15]

Sherrard considered this remarkable, and, thinking perhaps of the Louise Anderson episode, said, 'It is not even right to say that those instructions have been carried out, is it?'

Acott replied: 'There are officers who have had to come to me on certain matters, but we have done our best to keep to those officers who have nothing to do with the evidence in this case . . . I have never had an experience like this over the last fortnight.'[16]

When Acott was followed into the witness-box by Detective Sergeant Oxford, defence lawyers considered that the latter's answers on this point were at variance with Acott's. Oxford said that Acott was sequestered only since the day he began giving evidence:

Oxford: I have had no contact with Mr Acott since noon on
    Thursday last.
Sherrard: But a great deal of discussion before that?
Oxford: There has been quite a lot of discussion about the case as a
    whole.[17]

Other highly contentious areas on which Acott was probed at some length included the fact that he found no record of the Stanmore burglaries at Trevone and The Wheelhouse until two months after they occurred, even though they were reported straightaway.

Towards the end, Sherrard questioned him about the original description of the murderer:

Sherrard: Was not part of Miss Storie's description 'hair which was
    swept back'?
Acott: I will have to refer to that. No, I do not think so.[18]

This was a curious answer. When the record of Valerie Storie's first statement finally became available, this was how she had described the hair: 'Straight, well-greased, dark brown, brushed straight back, slightly receding at temples.'

After virtually two days of intensive cross-examination of Superintendent Acott, Sherrard concluded:

Sherrard: I have to suggest to you that your note [personal case
    record] is not accurate, your inquiries were not thorough or
    careful in the respects I have specified, and that as a whole your
    recollection as well as your note is at fault and you have not told

my Lord and the jury the truth about what was said to you by this man.

Acott: I deny all those suggestions, my Lord.

Sherrard: I am afraid I have to suggest to you that you are really trying to make things mean just whatever it suits you to let them mean.

Acott: I will just say 'No' to that.

Sherrard: Rather like *Alice in Wonderland*?

Acott: If I look like *Alice in Wonderland* . . .

Sherrard: Mr Acott, you do not. On that we are agreed.[19]

MONDAY – FRIDAY, 5 – 9 FEBRUARY: **The Third Week**

There were two other matters of immense importance on which Acott still had to be examined in the witness-box: the elimination of Peter Alphon as a suspect; and the assessment of the sweet-shop evidence.

Had he been following reports of the trial in the press – and it seems as though he certainly was – Alphon would have noted allusions to Superintendent Acott's having been able to satisfy himself that he, Alphon, was not the murderer. Extraordinarily, that Monday, Alphon attended the Bedford court himself in order to hear Acott's detailed reasons why he had been ruled out as a suspect. A number of those also present on the public benches were interested to note that, compared with his appearance the previous autumn when his photograph was in all the papers, Alphon was now sporting a distinctively different hairstyle. 'He had a quarter-inch crop,' recalled Michael Hanratty. 'That was very strange.' In fact, after sitting only briefly on the public benches, Alphon moved into the well of the court to stand behind the dock where Hanratty was sitting.

Swanwick, re-examining the police officer after the long interrogation by Michael Sherrard, brought Acott back to the matter of the first suspect.

Acott: Looking back on this, I can think of a good many points, concrete points, which certainly put together, plus my feeling, eliminated him.

Swanwick: In case there might be any suggestion that he is still responsible, will you give my Lord the main points?

Acott: First, he was not Jim or James; he was Peter. He was twenty-nine. Our suspect was mid-twenties. I beg your pardon, he was thirty-one. He was 5 feet 9 inches; our suspect was 5 feet 6 inches. He has hazel eyes; our suspect had large saucer-like blue eyes.

Swanwick: Was there anything about his speech?

Acott: He pronounced the dipthong 'th' correctly; our suspect could not. Our suspect had an East London accent; Alphon did not and was well-spoken. The suspect was described as an uneducated man; Alphon was distinctly educated. Our suspect had been described by Miss Storie as hesitant and claiming time for thinking; I found not the slightest hesitancy in Alphon who readily and immediately answered all my questions. The suspect had used the word 'kip'; Alphon never used the word 'kip'. The suspect had shown great desire to stop and sleep somewhere; despite the fact that Alphon had been up all the previous day and I had kept him up all night with this interview, followed by the identification parade, the medical tests, laboratory tests, never in my presence did he show any tendency to sleep and in fact I can say that up to 5 p.m. that day, when I last saw him, he had not slept. One last point that I can recall is this. He volunteered himself for identification tests, medical tests, laboratory tests and was pleased when I arranged them.

Swanwick: Anything about his driving or power to drive?

Acott: My inquiries shows that he had not driven a motor car, but had a good many years before had some little experience with a motor cycle.

Swanwick: His dress?

Acott: Our suspect was described as immaculate; Alphon was shabbily dressed in a blazer and old grey flannel trousers.[20]

Altogether, these constitute what became the famous 'twelve points' which allowed the police to exculpate Alphon. Thus did Detective Superintendent Acott and Graham Swanwick QC between them bring great comfort to Alphon, who learned at first hand that he could now put all this behind him.

Swanwick and Acott gave the impression that the list of reasons was exhaustive and utterly conclusive. Some of those in court, like members of Hanratty's family, found the reasons less than compelling. Several observations can be made about them.

By Acott's own admission, a similarly persuasive list (assuming this one was in any way persuasive) could have been compiled of reasons to eliminate Hanratty. The inclusion amongst this list of the fact that Alphon 'volunteered himself for identification tests, medical tests, laboratory tests and was pleased when I arranged them' was remarkable: everyone in court, Acott included, knew that precisely the same point could have been forcibly made on Hanratty's behalf.

The very first reason Acott gave was the name: 'he was not Jim or James'. This had to some extent already been undermined in cross-examination:

Swanwick: When the man in the car said 'Call me Jim', you are not saying, are you, that you accepted that as necessarily being the name by which the man was known?

Acott: Not necessarily, no.

Swanwick: Otherwise it could not conceivably have been Alphon?

Acott: That is right.

Swanwick: So it really came to this, that this man is known as Jimmy or Jim and the man in the car said, 'Call me Jim'?

Acott: Yes.

Swanwick: After thinking about it apparently?

Acott: Yes, that is right.[21]

Nevertheless, the prosecution had impressed the name upon the jury. Swanwick said to them: 'He told Miss Storie to call him Jim. That is a very odd thing, because you will hear this man James Hanratty was known frequently as Jim or Jimmy. . . "Call me Jim"? Was that something that perhaps slipped out, at a time when the murderer thought that Valerie Storie might not live to tell the tale?'[22]

The prosecution side kept to themselves the only valid information on this point, which Acott elicited in his interview with Storie:

Acott: Do you remember if he [the gunman] told you what was his Christian name or his surname or his nickname?

Storie: No, he never told us his name at all, the only name he ever gave was right at the end, after he had shot Mike. I said, 'Well, look, I must call you something.' I don't know why I said this, one never knows why one says these things. I said, 'What shall I call you?' and he sort of said 'Jim'. That's the only name, obviously not his proper name I shouldn't think.[23]

The clear inference here was not that the murderer was called Jim, but that he was called anything except Jim. It provided no reason at all to rule in Hanratty, or to rule out Alphon. However, the court remained wholly unaware that, in Valerie Storie's opinion, Jim was 'obviously not his proper name'.

The next reason which Acott gave for Alphon's elimination was his age. This was also astonishing: 'He was twenty-nine. Our suspect was mid-twenties. I beg your pardon. He was thirty-one.'

Despite correcting himself, Acott still managed to get Alphon's age wrong. At the time of the crime, Alphon was neither twenty-nine nor thirty-one. He was aged thirty. No one knew it then, but in Valerie Storie's very first statement, made on the morning following the crime, she gave as part of her description: 'Age: thirty years.'

Acott further told the court that his inquiries had established that Alphon could be eliminated because he, Alphon, 'had not driven a motor-car, but had a good many years before had some little experience with a motor-cycle'. Sherrard questioned him on this point in more detail:

Sherrard: Did you know when you were interviewing Alphon
    whether he could drive a motor vehicle?
Acott: My information was that he could not drive a motor car or
    at least we had no knowledge that he could.
Sherrard: Was there any information as to whether he could drive a
    motor-bicycle?
Acott: He was in fact convicted of taking and driving away a
    motor-cycle, but the facts of that case were that he pushed it
    and was stopped I think within 100 yards or so.

At this point, the judge intervened:

Mr Justice Gorman: That was a motor-cycle?
Acott: Yes, my Lord.[24]

This point was then emphasized by Swanwick in his closing speech to the jury: '[Alphon] was not a car driver. The only thing he could drive was a motor-cycle.'[25]

In 1992 I found the information regarding Alphon's previous criminal record. He was convicted at the Guildhall in London on 6 October 1953 of taking and driving away a motor car. The fact that the judge intervened in this dialogue, virtually inviting Acott to think again about what he had just said, indicated that he, the judge, was probably appraised of the criminal records of the central figures, and thus personally understood how misleading Acott's evidence was.

The final matter of particular consequence to arise during Acott's lengthy innings in the witness-box concerned the sweet-shop. He was questioned by Swanwick about the fact that, in the first instance, Mrs Dinwoodie was shown only a solitary photograph of Hanratty before identifying him as the man who had entered her shop. Acott was highly critical of this process, describing it as 'extremely bad practice', and stating that the photograph of Hanratty should have been only one amongst a number that she was shown.

This infuriated the defence. After all, whose fault was it that critical defence evidence had been tarnished in this way? It was entirely the fault of the police.

The sweet-shop nevertheless continued to cause apprehension in prosecution ranks. On Tuesday, 6 February, at virtually the close of its case, the Crown passed to the defence yet another notice of additional evidence. This concerned the testimony of Albert Harding. Ideally, Swanwick would have wished to call Harding after the defence had called Mrs Dinwoodie. He applied to the judge in these terms, asking, in effect, that if Mrs Dinwoodie were to say such-and-such, would he then be allowed to bring forward this evidence to counter it?

The judge felt that his patience was being tried a little too far. He informed Swanwick that 'I am not prepared to say now how I might be prepared to exercise my discretion on some future occasion.' Accordingly, the prosecution had no option but to call Harding straightaway.

The sense of the absurd – with Harding being called to rebut evidence which hadn't yet been heard – was heightened by the fact that Sherrard was able to ensure that all reference to the vital conversation in the sweet-shop was excluded; it was, quite blatantly, hearsay evidence. Swanwick was in the position of trying to combat evidence which the jury had not yet heard and regarding which he was unable to enlighten them.

Harding explained that he was a supervisor employed by a roofing company. He was a good friend of the Cowley family, who owned the sweet-shop, and on Saturday, 19 August had driven Mrs Cowley to Heswall, on the Wirral peninsula, for her summer holiday. On 21 August, he drove the company's van to Carrington, on the outskirts of Manchester, to collect materials, and then returned to Liverpool. Every day after clocking off, he said, he called in at the sweet-shop on his way home. That day, the Monday, he reached it at about 5.35–5.40. What he would have gone on to say, had legal etiquette not prohibited it, was that he saw Mrs Dinwoodie, who asked him whether he knew of a Tarleton or Carlton Road because 'a man had called at the shop a short time earlier asking for directions'. He indicated that this – this matter that he couldn't refer to – couldn't have happened on the Tuesday, as on that day he hadn't reached the sweet-shop until about 7.00 p.m., when only David Cowley was present. The prosecution appended Harding's time-sheets as documentary support for this statement.

The cynical might have ventured that it had taken the Crown a very long time to unearth this evidence, bearing in mind that Mrs Dinwoodie had originally verified the conversation on 17 October. However, there was far more to bring Mr Harding's evidence into question than mere mistrust of prosecution conduct.

The time-sheets didn't support the statement at all. Harding maintained that he always called at the sweet-shop directly after clocking off; Sherrard pointed out that he had clocked off at 6.00 on the Monday, and 5.45 on the Tuesday, but reached the sweet-shop at 5.35–5.40 on the former day, and 7.00 on the latter. When this was put to him, Harding became vague: 'I am not a clock-watcher.'

Perhaps one factor which did emerge is that Harding's evidence, if it did anything at all, *strengthened the fact of the conversation*. In that respect, Sherrard could safely have withheld his objection to the use of hearsay evidence.

So the conversation had taken place, and must have occurred on either the Monday or the Tuesday. If it happened on the Tuesday, could Hanratty then have been in a different part of the country a few hours later to be able to commit the crime? Sherrard asked Acott about this:

Sherrard: If the defendant went to Liverpool on 22 August and had that conversation at some time a little after 4.30, do you say that it is possible that he could have returned south and been at Slough by 9.00 or 9.30?
Acott: I still think it is possible.[26]

Swanwick subsequently revived consideration of this point.

Swanwick: You said it was possible.

Acott: Yes, I think it is possible, but I do not think it happened and I never have thought it happened.

Swanwick: We have particulars of the trains. Is there any other way of travelling from Liverpool?

Acott: One can go by road; one can fly.

Swanwick: Is there a regular service?

Acott: There is a service.

Swanwick: My Lord, if necessary, I can have evidence directed to that matter.[27]

Some observers consider that, of all the disreputable manoeuvres deployed by the prosecution in its handling of this case, this moment was the nadir. Sherrard believed it 'the most extraordinary series of questions and answers which could be given in a case of this kind'. *There is a service.* Although Acott did point out that he didn't think this had happened, he nevertheless colluded in the suggestion that it could have.

'What a fantastic attitude,' commented Sherrard. 'Is the truth that [Hanratty] got to Liverpool at about half-past four, dashed up Scotland Road, ran into a sweet-shop, had a bogus conversation with a woman he hoped would recognize him again, rushed back down Scotland Road, got to the nearest airport, flew somewhere, London Airport if you like, and then – presumably he would need a helicopter to do it – just after nine o'clock got to a field in Dorney Reach just in case Mr Gregsten and his girlfriend should decide to drive there? This is absurd. This is fantastic. What happens to our common sense?'

In fact, Acott had already asked Liverpool police to examine the times of flights from Speke Airport, Liverpool to London Airport. The last flight left at 5.00 and arrived at 6.15. Given that the conversation in the sweet-shop probably occurred within thirty minutes either side of that time, then, if it occurred on the Tuesday, Hanratty had not committed the murder. It was that simple.

CHAPTER FOURTEEN

IN THOSE DAYS, the defence barrister still made an opening speech at the outset of his case. Sherrard took full advantage of this, to emphasize to the jury, with great forcefulness, what he viewed as the weak and even shameful nature of many of the prosecution arguments.

'The greatest thing about this case is the fact that it is trial by jurors, trial by strangers; not, thank God, trial by police or trial by the press because, if it were trial by either, then justice, liberty and life would be in danger ... How would you feel if [Hanratty] was your brother or son and it was sought to condemn him to death on the sort of evidence you heard from Nudds, the sort of evidence you heard from Langdale, and the sort of performance that was given by Superintendent Acott?'[1]

He outlined Swanwick's five main planks of the prosecution case: the positive identifications; the factors derived from the Morris Minor conversations which fitted Hanratty; the gun on the bus; the cartridge cases in the hotel; and Langdale. 'If those are the main planks, are we not justified in saying that most of them are of rotting timber?'

He examined in turn these pieces of rotting timber.

The factors which supposedly fitted Hanratty? But the prosecution was being disgracefully selective in saying, That fits and that fits, but that doesn't so it can be ignored – 'Can a man in England be so imperilled?'

The gun and ammunition on the bus? 'It almost looks as if somebody wanted these things to be found.'

The cartridge cases? Left *before* the murder? All the Crown could suggest was that Hanratty had wanted 'target practice' – according to Sherrard, 'an improbability bereft of evidence'.

And then there was Langdale.

'The Crown itself has been driven to presenting a wretch like Langdale as evidence. You may wonder why it was that we did not hear Langdale give evidence before the magistrates. It may be that you will come to the conclusion that they could hardly bring themselves then to rely on him. But, as the case for the defence developed and as it turned out that more and more of the things that [Hanratty] said could be established, they were driven to the last ditch and to say, "Let us call Langdale, There is nothing to lose".[2]

That left only the identifications, and here too the Crown was guilty of shabby conduct.

'An Oxford undergraduate, minding his own business, comes across this and has the good sense to make a note. Oh well, there is only one way to handle him, say the Crown; we will have to put it around that he was so upset and distressed that he took leave of his senses. Light fairish hair! But what about Dr Rennie? Miss Storie, according to him, picked out a man with light fairish hair.'[3]

Sherrard also pointed out that if Hanratty had gone north to arrange a bogus 'Liverpool' alibi, as the Crown alleged, then the circumstances were more than curious – because he would have been setting up an alibi before a murder could even have been contemplated, bearing in mind Valerie Storie's evidence that no one could possibly have known that she and Gregsten would go to the cornfield that evening.

He informed the court that although the defence believed they now had a clear idea of Hanratty's whereabouts during that vital period, 22–24 August, he was pessimistic about the chances of producing fresh evidence in consequence: 'Rhyl is being combed for some trace of the boarding-house. Whether [landladies] will remember a casual visit in August in the holiday season is very, very speculative.'

The unexpected, however, often seemed to happen in this case. Now, Sherrard sprang a surprise by announcing that the defence would be calling Hanratty straightaway, 'so that you can see whether he is a monster'. (Acott had written in his own report that the possibility of Hanratty going into the witness-box was 'extremely doubtful'.) With the press and public benches even more packed than usual, Hanratty took the stand.

There were those who formed negative impressions. Jeremy Fox, the barrister who had taken an interest in the case and would later play a major role in the campaign, thought him not at all a savoury character, and assumed that he must have committed the murder. Nevertheless, others in court felt that it was difficult to think of this pleasant, apprehensive and very smartly dressed young man (he wore a blue suit, white shirt and blue tie with a triple handkerchief in his top pocket) as a monster. Hanratty himself believed he could not 'frighten anybody with a gun, because I have not got that appearance'.

Many were struck by his deference, his general mildness of manner and what appeared to be his essential openness. Dr David Lewes, a consultant surgeon at Bedford General Hospital, took annual leave so that he could attend virtually the entire trial ('I am an Australian, and naturally was keen to see at first hand the great wheel of British justice turning'). He commented, 'Hanratty may have been educationally deprived, but throughout that long period in the witness-box, he was able to give a good account of himself and, I thought, created a favourable impression.'

During long questioning by Michael Sherrard, and particularly under the strain of a much longer cross-examination by Graham Swanwick, Hanratty sweated a great deal in the witness-box. It was a formidable ordeal for him. He knew he was standing trial for his life, and that the bulk of his testimony was, as Sherrard said, 'terribly, terribly important'. In moments of agitation, or when he was striving to get a point across, his large blue eyes did seem to be almost protruding from his head, which was unfortunate in view of Valerie Storie's utter certainty that her assailant could be identified by his 'large, icy-blue staring eyes'.

No one could have described Hanratty as naturally articulate. He had no facility with words, and was frequently thwarted by his lack of understanding of plain English, as this dialogue illustrates:

Sherrard: Did you see either of those two officers [the ones who arrested him in Blackpool] again?
Hanratty: Yes.
Sherrard: When?
Hanratty: On two previous occasions in the evening—
Mr Justice Gorman: He does not mean 'previous'.
Sherrard: No. (*To the witness*.) You do not mean 'previous', but afterwards, after you had been arrested?
Hanratty: Yes.[4]

At other times, he stumbled over his sentences, or the use of everyday words, or asked for the question to be rephrased; sometimes he tried to adopt the erudite vocabulary of the lawyers, with what in other circumstances would have been comical results:

'These houses in Rhyl are all semi-attached'; 'If I had thought there was blood on a jacket, I would expose of the suit.' Yet, for all his ungainliness of speech, he evinced at every opportunity a blazing determination to affirm his absolute innocence of the charge.

Sometimes, his keen awareness of his plight induced an affronted, albeit understandable, asperity in him. He said to Swanwick: 'For twenty days I have sat in that box, twenty days, and listened to the trial ... It was quite obvious to me inside that I never committed this crime and I had nothing at all to fear. But – let me finish – as this case went along, I got so frightened with the evidence what was being brought forward, with the lies and such things as have happened in this witness-box – well, it is disgraceful to talk about them ... This is the only chance I have had to explain and now you are trying to pull me to pieces.'[5]

There was another momentary loss of equanimity. Swanwick suggested that the sweet-shop conversation could have occurred on the Monday, and that Hanratty had returned to London directly afterwards:

Swanwick: There is a 5.15 train from Liverpool which gets in about 9.15?

Hanratty: How about Mrs France? I did not leave them until seven o'clock. I thought you had more intelligence, sir.

Swanwick: Thank you.

Mr Justice Gorman: Mr Hanratty, I do not want to interrupt, but do not say things like that.[6]

Nevertheless, Hanratty, his composure taxed to the limit, continued: 'I must put this quite clear. This man is suggesting he knows where I was. The Frances have given evidence. He has heard what their evidence is. I left their flat at seven o'clock on the Monday. It is quite obvious. Why put this to the court so that the press can print it and disgrace my character?'

His counsel then intervened: 'It really is a matter of very considerable embarrassment to the defence if they are presented with a case for the prosecution seeking to establish certain dates; and then, when one calls one's client, suggestions are put to him on the basis that the prosecution wants to abandon the reliability of its own witnesses.'[7]

At another juncture, Hanratty bluntly asked Swanwick: 'Are you trying to suggest to the court that I went out on 22 August to do a stick-up with a gun?'

Swanwick: Indeed I am.

Hanratty: It is quite obvious if I did that I would not be looking for
   a car in a cornfield, as you put it to the court. I will be looking
   for some cash, a bank, a shop, something to that effect. I would
   not be looking for a car in a cornfield for some cash for a stick-
   up.[8]

As he faced some aggressive questioning, Hanratty almost irrit-
ably reminded the court of the conditions under which his evidence
was given: 'I have a lot to remember in this case. I have got no
notes in front of me.' (Other witnesses, like the police, were allowed
to refer to their notes while giving evidence.) With the scales of
justice seemingly loaded so heavily against him, Hanratty underlined his feeling of isolation: 'In this case now I have got three
friends: that is my counsel and my family. The rest of the world are
against me. The papers have seen to that.'

He was clearly angered by the press reports of the trial. Sherrard
had sensibly, if unconventionally, decided to lay Hanratty's complete criminal record before the court; usually, a defendant's
previous convictions are withheld, lest the past pollute the present.
Although this tactic resulted in some unflattering publicity, Sherrard
wanted to demonstrate both that Hanratty was hiding nothing and
also that there was a pattern to his criminal behaviour – a pattern
of thieving, certainly, but a pattern which precluded any kind of
violence. Hanratty was matter-of-fact about his way of life: 'I know
I am not a man the court approves of, but I am not a maniac of
any kind. The man who committed this is a maniac.'

Probably he also gained credit for conceding points which, on
the surface, appeared detrimental – like the conversation with
France about the back seat of a bus ('a very common hiding-place
to a man in my position'); and also parts of the Acott interviews.
Had he said to Acott, 'What size were the bullets?'

Hanratty: That is what I did say, but I should mention there was a
   little bit more which should go with that. I said to
   Superintendent Acott, 'That is the end for me now. I have had
   no gun or bullets at any time', and at that stage I asked what
   size the bullets were. I was flabbergasted, and I knew at this
   stage that matters looked very, very serious against me.[9]

And had he made enquiries about a gun?

Hanratty: Half-way through the interview Superintendent Acott
    put it to me this way. He said, 'Jimmy, I have interviewed a
    man at Ealing called Fisher, and he tells me that you have
    enquired about a gun.' This was a very big shock to me.
Sherrard: What did you say?
Hanratty: I did not deny it because it was the truth, my Lord . . . it
    was just a phrase of talk, my Lord.[10]

Under cross-examination, he added: 'If I wanted to get a gun, it
would be quite easy to get one. You can get a gun for £10 or £15
any day of the week. Anywhere in Soho. Teenagers are getting
them today.'[11]

He explained why he had originally telephoned Superintendent
Acott: 'This man wanted to interview me, as I took it, about
somebody else. That is how I looked at it. I read in one paper,
one article, that I might have shared the same room, the same
hotel, as another man who caused this murder and I wanted to
straighten it up. That is why I did phone him, so that I could
help him in every way. I did not phone him just to talk to
somebody.'[12]

The police records of the interviews remained a major bone of
contention. There were many parts which Hanratty repudiated
absolutely:

Sherrard: Did you say to Mr Acott anything like this: 'One day
    you'll get the cuffs on me, but I'm all right now and I've give
    you a good run. I've got some money tucked away.'
Hanratty: No. I would not say anything at all like that, because I
    was maintaining my innocence and I would not be – well, I was
    not brought up to be cocky like that.
Sherrard: Did you say anything at all about being a really clever
    screwsman and never making a slip?
Hanratty: No, sir. I never boast like that, because it does not pay to
    boast to the police.[13]

Similarly, he was adamant that he'd never used the word 'kip' or
even thought about sleeping ('They were more tired than me
because they had been travelling down. If anybody did mention
sleep, it was Mr Acott, it was not me').

He told Swanwick about the number of things he'd said that
were not recorded by Acott.

Swanwick: Can you think of any object he would have had in
   leaving it out if you said it?
Hanratty: Well, he has put so much in that is not true, that he has
   got to take the truth out to put in the non-truth to make up for
   the truth that has been took out.[14]

After Langdale was disposed of ('It is all false, every word of it'),
Hanratty asked why would he have mentioned at all his mistake in
going to Paddington Station after leaving the Vienna hotel:

Hanratty: If I was the man who committed this crime, it is quite
   obvious I would not say I went to Paddington Station. I would
   be quite compared [*sic*] to know that the man who committed
   this crime was round the Slough area and I would say, I went
   straight to Euston; but I wanted to be frank and I told Mr Acott
   I went to Paddington.
Swanwick: What you did was to go to Paddington where you could
   dump your case and go to the Maidenhead and Slough area—

The judge intervened:

Mr Justice Gorman: When? Are you suggesting he went that
   morning? On that day? Is there any evidence to support this?
Swanwick: No.[15]

Far from having been in a cornfield just off the M4, Hanratty
explained how he had gone to Rhyl on the evening of Tuesday, 22
August and, arriving late at what was still the height of the season,
encountered some difficulty in trying to find someone to put him
up for the night. At length, after 'I had travelled in and out through
other streets', and by which time it was dark, he knocked at the
door of a small guest-house with a sign saying, 'Bed and Breakfast'.
That landlady took him in. He slept in a back room, from where
he could hear, but not see, the trains shunting. He could remember
a green bath at the top of the house, the large hallstand and potted
plant (and disputed the view of the Crown, that a coatstand and
aspidistra in the hallway would be characteristic of almost any
guest-house anywhere in Britain); and also that he paid 25s to stay
for two nights. He could recall that there was no front garden, but
a small courtyard at the back. He was vague about the geography
of the town, and could remember merely that the house was
'towards the railway, the back end of Rhyl'.

Apart from the lack of corroboration – Hanratty admitted that 'I have got to hope for a miracle, that this woman will happen to record me staying there' – all this seemed straightforward enough.

Mrs Olive Dinwoodie, the sweet-shop lady, was the next witness called by the defence. This area of evidence rested on the slimmest of chance conversations. All that had occurred was this: she had received a brief request for directions, which momentarily distracted her; she was personally unable to assist, so she asked a customer if he could help and returned to her duties in a crowded shop. The incident was so inconsequential that no one could conceivably have planned to use it as the basis of a false alibi.

It should be emphasized that this part of the defence case was adhered to from first to last. 'It is generally thought', explained Michael Sherrard, 'that Hanratty changed his alibi. Now, that's not quite right. The substance of the Liverpool alibi was maintained. When the Rhyl episode came to light, it wasn't a substitution of the Liverpool alibi, it was an extension of it.'

Swanwick's bad-tempered interjections during Mrs Dinwoodie's evidence ('Is he [Sherrard] entitled to ask that, my Lord?') was a rebuke to his insistence that the primary interest of the Crown was to analyse alibi evidence objectively. Yet, however offensive, all this was a rigorous application of the Queensberry Rules compared with what took place the following afternoon. Graham Swanwick's cross-examination of Grace Jones is one of the most shaming episodes in the history of British criminal justice.

The defence team had hoped against hope that they would be able to find the Rhyl landlady in time; that Hanratty's miracle would come to pass. Now, amidst high excitement in every quarter, they had found her: Grace Jones, who ran Ingledene at 19 Kinmel Street, Rhyl, and whom the defence team immediately dubbed Mrs Miracle Jones.

Gillbanks had found Terry Evans first – it was relatively easy to find him. Although Evans would forever associate Hanratty with the loss of his shoes, he provided valuable assistance in the seemingly thankless task of questioning the landladies of Rhyl. It was in the morning of Tuesday, 6 February that Joe Gillbanks knocked at the door of 19 Kinmel Street, and asked the lady who answered if she recognized the man in the photograph, one of those taken at the rear of the courthouse. She confirmed that she did.

At this point, Gillbanks examined the house. He noted the bed-and-breakfast sign in the window. There was no front garden, but a tiled yard at the back. There was a hallstand with a large mirror, and a prominently positioned vase containing artificial flowers. He established that she charged 12s 6d per night. Could you hear the trains shunting? Oh yes, said Mrs Jones, you could. And was there by any chance a green bath in the attic? Yes, replied Mrs Jones, there certainly was.

Mrs Jones was brought to Bedford, along with Terry Evans and Arthur Webber (who ran the bumper car business on the amusement park), and instantly became the cornerstone of the defence case. She explained that she generally took pre-booked guests by the week, but 'When someone comes for bed-and-breakfast to the door, we take those in as well.' She was asked about the man whose photograph she had identified: 'There he is, there [indicating the dock], I feel as if I have seen him at our house.' When could that have been? 'Between the week of 19 and 26 August last year.'

Swanwick was granted leave to postpone his cross-examination for a few hours, and so the judge carefully asked Mrs Jones to keep her own counsel. Just before the lunch adjournment, he brought her back to the witness-box to reiterate his warning. After lunch, as the lawyers were discussing a preliminary matter, one of the jurors interjected:

Juror: My Lord, may we ask a question? Mrs Jones, on our way to lunch, was seen talking to Mr Evans.
Mr Justice Gorman: I beg your pardon?
Juror: Mrs Jones was talking with Mr Evans on our way to lunch. We would just like to confirm, while she is on oath, as to whether anything had been mentioned, whether in fact she had discussed anything with relevance to the case.[16]

The judge was visibly shocked. He recalled Mrs Jones, to ask what they were talking about. She informed him that 'We were just talking about lunch, that is all.' He then sent for Terry Evans who was found, after some delay. He asked him the same question, but received a different answer. 'I just asked her if she recognized Mr Hanratty,' responded Evans, 'that is all.' The judge then re-interrogated Mrs Jones, who admitted she had said, 'I am almost sure of him, something like that'. In mitigation, she said, 'He was the only one I knew, you see, to talk to.'

Compared to the shiftier dealings of the prosecution, this unwitting contamination of defence evidence scarcely registered. Yet it did have a devastating impact. Mrs Jones had not only disobeyed the judge, but attempted to cover up about doing so.

Her credibility evaporated before it was ever established. Her composure was shattered and her nerves were in shreds.

Swanwick straightaway took his cue from her reply to the judge – 'That was a lie, was it not?' he said – to launch an assault on her character and reputation. Had she been one of the country's notorious villains, the cross-examination might have been justified; but she was an ordinary middle-aged woman who'd scarcely set foot outside Wales before, and it was not.

Swanwick: The winter months are pretty dead in Rhyl, are they not?
Mrs Jones: Yes.
Swanwick: And a little good publicity for Ingledene would not come amiss, would it?
Mrs Jones: Well, I do not know.[17]

This scurrilous suggestion was completely without foundation. Then he asked:

Swanwick: Has the bathroom got anything in it besides a bath?
Mrs Jones: Do I have to answer that?

The bathroom had a double bed in it. At high season, the family would use it themselves, thereby allowing them to rent out extra rooms. Sometimes, in fact, they would even rent that out to visitors. While one view of this was that Mrs Jones's hospitality was boundless, Swanwick put a different interpretation upon it: that what was boundless was her avarice.

Having heaped further public embarrassment upon her, Swanwick moved on to discuss her registers. At this point, the purpose of requesting a delay in cross-examination suddenly became apparent. How many books did she keep? What size were they? What colour? Had she by any chance brought her visitors' book with her? No, she replied. Swanwick then handed it to her.

Swanwick: Is that your visitors' book?
Mrs Jones: Yes, that is it.

The police, it seemed, had gone round to the guest-house after she had left for Bedford and taken the book. 'They said they had to have it,' explained Brenda Harris, Mrs Jones's daughter. 'Of course I didn't want them to take it, but I didn't know any better.'

Mrs Jones was bewildered; she had no advance knowledge. 'What is it doing here?' she asked. Nor was Mr Justice Gorman impressed by Swanwick's deception.

Mr Justice Gorman: I thought you asked this lady if she had brought it.
Swanwick: I did, my Lord.
Mr Justice Gorman: But you had it. You asked this lady if she had brought it and all the time you had it.
Swanwick: I did, my Lord.
Mr Justice Gorman: So she could not very well have brought it.[18]

Worse was to follow. Michael Hanratty has always remembered Swanwick handing Grace Jones the book to examine. 'As she put her hand out, he dropped it on the floor. The leaves flew out. He picked it up for her, and just shoved the pages back in. She didn't know where she was.' It subsequently became impossible to refer to anything properly, as the book was so disordered. This naturally helped to reinforce an impression of a household whose affairs were in disarray.

Mrs Jones began to display increasing signs of distress from this point. The questioning about her books went on and on. She was pitilessly humiliated because they were so muddled. Yet this was all irrelevant anyway. No one ever claimed that Hanratty had signed the visitors' book (the sort of thing he was likely to do only if expressly asked) or even been, as it were, officially registered. In subsequent years, Hanratty campaigners always alluded to an obvious contrast: the court had already heard that the Metropolitan Police books were in complete confusion so far as the Stanmore burglaries were concerned – but it seemed that the professional lapses of the police were excusable, whereas the supposed short-comings of Mrs Jones were not.

In fact, on the few genuinely germane questions that she received, her evidence was perfectly clear and straightforward:

Swanwick: It would not be quite right, would it, to say that when you were shown the photograph [of Hanratty] you recognized it?
Mrs Jones: Well, no.
Swanwick: It would not. Then why did you say it in answer to my learned friend?

Mrs Jones: Well, he had different-coloured hair.
Swanwick: What?
Mrs Jones: If he had had dark brown hair, I would have known
   him straightaway.

Most of the questions seemed, to her, to concern irrelevancies.
At one point she was driven to comment, 'I have never heard such
tommy-rot.' By the end of the afternoon, Mrs Jones was left
distraught and wretched.

That weekend, Hanratty's lawyers would have been forgiven
feelings of desolation. They had wished for, and been granted, a
miracle; they had not anticipated that the miracle might be
combustible. Nevertheless, however discomfited they felt, they had
cause to be far more aggrieved than they realized.

The first the outside world knew of the putative Rhyl alibi was
on Wednesday, 7 February. The *Daily Sketch* carried a front-page
report that the town was being combed for witnesses in this case.
Other national newspapers published similar reports. There was an
almost immediate public reaction. Thirty years later, I discovered
that on Thursday, 8 February, the very next day, Flintshire police
in Rhyl had contacted Detective Superintendent Acott at Bedford
in the following terms:

> *Dear Sir,*
> **JAMES HANRATTY**
> *As a result of reports in the national press, radio and television, several
> persons have called at this office with regard to the visit of the above-
> named to Rhyl.*
>   *All such persons have been interviewed by the detective staff and the
> statements obtained, which may be of any significance, are forwarded for
> your information.*
>   *Yours faithfully,*

If only the defence team had been aware that, far from a solitary
miracle, there was a little cluster of them. Within twenty-four hours
of the first, unofficial announcement (and a full two days before the
massive publicity engendered by Mrs Jones's court appearance),
'several persons' were, entirely on their own initiative, volunteering
information to the police about Hanratty's visit to Rhyl. If a few
news items produced such an instant response, what might a proper
inquiry have yielded?

One statement was made by poultry-keeper Trevor Dutton. He went to Abergele police on 9 February. His statement read as follows:

'I thought I had better get in touch with the police regarding the fact that the man James Hanratty says that he stayed in Rhyl in August last year.

'What brought everything back to mind was when one of my customers read part of a newspaper report to me and mentioned that Hanratty claimed he had tried to sell a watch in Rhyl. I recalled on my return home that a man had offered to sell me a gold watch in Rhyl one day in the summer. I pondered over this because I could not remember exactly when it was. I then suddenly realized that I had been to the bank – Barclays Bank, High Street, Rhyl – one day in August, and this was the only time in August I had visited the bank. This morning I checked up with my paying-in book, and this visit was made on 23 August 1961.

'I usually park my car by the old Post Office and when I was offered this watch I was walking somewhere between Burton's shop and the old Post Office. This man stepped forward and asked if I wanted to buy a gold watch. He had a wrist-watch in his hand and I just glanced at it and told him I was not interested.

'I am afraid I cannot describe this man. However, I can say he was not an old man, but was probably in the twenty-five to thirty-five year age group, but seemed to look a little older than he probably actually was. This man had an accent which I cannot really place. It was more like a dialect, and was possibly Irish or cockney or a mixture of the two.

'Although I have not been able to describe this man, I think I would be able to say either that I had never seen him before or that he was the man who offered me the watch.'[19]

Having made his statement, however, Dutton was surprised to hear nothing more – not until the A6 Murder Committee tracked him down six years later.

The names and addresses collected by Flintshire police could not have included a statement by Christopher Larman, who went to Staines police on 16 February to report that he thought he had seen Hanratty in Rhyl. Nor could the Flintshire file have included the following letter that was sent direct to Scotland Yard, and arrived there on 10 February:

Dear Sir,
I am writing on behalf of James Hanratty, though I don't want my name

known on account of owing a fine. I know James was in Rhyl on the 22–23 August. I know him very well and I saw him there at the time. It is only right I should let you know. I am being honest. I met James when he was released from Strangeways. We had coffee in a Milk Bar. I am a prostitute, well known.

I was with a businessman in Rhyl at the time I saw James, though he didn't see me. The man said his wife was away for the week and asked me to stay with him as he took photos of me in the nude. I got £20 for posing. So, you see you are holding James who has nothing to do with your crime. He maybe won't remember me, only by the name 'Bet' or 'Topsey'.

So there are various statements which are additional to the Flintshire file. Individually, many are compelling; together they may well have presented an irresistible case.

The Crown never allowed the defence to become aware of the full extent of the immediate interest in Rhyl regarding, and of possible corroborative testimony for, Hanratty's alibi. Neither the Rhyl file statements nor those supplementary to it were disclosed to the defence. At some point, names and addresses only – nineteen, according to the subsequent Nimmo report – were passed on to defence lawyers. These addresses appear to have arrived piecemeal. As far as is known, all these various statements have to this day never been collated.

Ever since 1962, it has been generally assumed that Hanratty revealed his Rhyl alibi too late in the day for it to be adequately substantiated. This impression is wholly incorrect. If only the authorities had exercised their public trust with the rectitude and competence expected of them, then there was ample time, because the evidence emerged almost overnight.

Overall, the investigations into both the sweet-shop and Ingledene gave the impression that the energies of the police and prosecution were channelled in one direction only. From the very first inquiries into the sweet-shop, to Swanwick's *coup de théâtre* with the Ingledene register, it was hard to dispel the feeling that their underlying objective was not a rational evaluation of the alibi but a determined demolition of it.

MONDAY – SATURDAY, 12 – 17 FEBRUARY: **The Final Week**

Grace Jones's purgatory continued after the weekend. Swanwick brought her back for renewed questioning, and endeavoured to show that she had further deceived the court on Friday afternoon by saying that there was no other register. It now seemed that there was another. The police had appropriated that one too. Mrs Jones had to endure a second barrage of questions about the rooms that were available for letting, and which was let to whom when. She responded, 'I never thought you would be bringing things like this up. This is nothing to do with the case.'

Swanwick's tactics were designed both to destroy her credentials as a witness and to fill up the guest-house, thereby leaving no possible vacancy for Hanratty that week. He was allowed to produce additional witnesses all of whom had stayed at Ingledene that week; and none of whom had ever seen Hanratty before: Douglas Such and his wife and small child had Room 1, and Thomas Williams, his wife and daughter Rooms 6 and 8. There were two other (untraced) families in residence that week. Joseph Sayle, a trade union representative, had Room 4. Mrs Jones and her husband had Room 2, and Brenda Harris, 5. The court also heard that Brenda's cousin, Joan, regularly stayed.

Among all the questions, one highly relevant answer went unnoticed:

Swanwick: All I am asking you at the moment is was there more than one single gentleman that week. According to what you have told already there would not be room for more than one?
Mrs Jones: There would have been room for one in that attic if Joan slept with my daughter.[20]

Swanwick, of course, deftly changed tack at that point. Had Mrs Jones not been so flustered – well, petrified – she would have been able to supply the logical answer about what had happened. It was not difficult to fathom. On the first night, the Tuesday, Hanratty had stayed in the bathroom-cum-bedroom at the top, which was why he remembered the green bath; and, on the second night, Mrs Jones was able to move him into a proper room when the Such family left early, having had 'a very miserable holiday'. On the first morning, being a supernumerary guest, Hanratty had not breakfasted with the other residents, but was given his meal in the family's own room at the back – which is why Hanratty was able to recall the 'two tables' and the tiled yard. There was no reason for him to act differently the following morning.

The evidence was all there in the courtroom, had it not been so completely obscured by judicial procedure.

On the Friday of the previous week, the jury had put in a request for additional information regarding the evidence of James Trower. They wished to be given further details – photographs, and a plan with heights and distances – of the setting in which he made his identification. Arrangements were made to carry out this work without delay, over the weekend.

Despite the setbacks suffered by the defence team, all were still energetically and purposefully engaged. Emmanuel Kleinman – 'His industry in this case knew no bounds,' recalled Michael Sherrard – had taken the opportunity to carry out further investigations in this area himself. Thus it was that, by Monday, the jury's request seemed especially discerning. The Trower evidence took on an even more blemished complexion.

The original doubts surrounding this most momentary of sightings – that Trower had had only a fleeting opportunity of seeing the driver, and hadn't even recalled the incident when questioned by police the following day – were now compounded by fresh factors. It seemed that Trower had returned to the scene himself over the weekend. The defence put it to him that he was rechecking the line of sight himself. He denied that. He did, however, have to concede that the 'three-second' sighting encompassed a full view, a three-quarter view and a rear view. It further emerged that he'd picked out three faces from a portfolio of photographs, suggesting that those men looked like the driver. Scotland Yard had not volunteered this information. The judge commented: 'Now it comes out that he picked out three people. If he had not come back in the box, we should not have known it.'[21]

Fourthly, Paddy Hogan, outside whose flat the sighting was made, said that on that particular morning Trower hadn't arrived at all until *after* the Morris Minor had gone past. According to Hogan, Trower used to pick him up for work every day, but was especially late that morning.

Naturally, Hogan had to endure vigorous questioning from Swanwick. It was, indeed, to Hogan's discredit that he had not previously been involved in the case at all – he simply explained, 'I decided to keep out of it. I do not like having a lot to do with the police.' When Kleinman had told him that a man's life was at stake, however, he decided that he would go to court.

As to the remainder of the defence case, Sherrard called evidence from other prisoners, to rebut Langdale; and Annie Mills, of Trevone in Stanmore, who confirmed that Scotland Yard had telephoned asking her about a missing *sports* jacket – which explained why her husband had not appreciated, until the defence called, the loss of his formal black jacket.

Audrey Willis and Meike Dalal also gave evidence. Both had encounters with a man claiming to be the A6 murderer. He had threatened the former with a gun. Willis was shown the murder weapon in court, and commented that it was 'very much the sort of gun I remember'. Both women mentioned the mackintosh he wore. Willis described him as having 'a long thin face, sallow complexion and brown eyes'. She thought he was 'about thirty'. Dalal thought that he was younger, mid-twenties, but she too recalled 'an oval face, with dark brown hair plastered back'. The latter had picked out Alphon at an identity parade. Both had no hesitation in saying that Hanratty was not the man.

Sherrard then gave his closing speech, pointing out those factors which he described as 'a series of beacons leading to a verdict of not guilty'.

He said that cases resting on identification always created unease in lawyers, because they had so often produced miscarriages of justice in the past. 'Matters of identification are difficult enough when the circumstances are good – and in this case, they were not, not for anybody.' Witnesses to the gunman had mentioned 'a pale face', whereas Hanratty's was florid – those in the court-room could see plainly enough that he blushed easily. Then, there was his suit. 'Do you think you would notice a stripe as jazzy and as prominent as that?' Everybody who saw Hanratty in his suit noticed the stripe; none of those who saw the gunman noticed it. Regarding the most important witness of all, Sherrard concluded, 'My respectful sub-mission is that Miss Storie is honest, but wrong: not once, but twice;' on both identity parades, she picked out an innocent person.

With regard to the absence of any forensic evidence, the Crown had tried to have it both ways, argued Sherrard. Detective Inspector John McCafferty testified that the gunman would have been able to get in and out of the car without getting blood on his clothes (an opinion shared by no one else who has ever examined the case); yet a recurring theme of the Crown's case was that Hanratty had disposed of his suit jacket because it had got incriminating blood-stains on it – even though, as Hanratty affirmed in the witness-box, 'You do not get rid of something, if it is incriminating, six weeks after the event.' Nor, as he added, would an alarmed criminal dump just the jacket.

Sherrard explained that through July, August and September his client had actually exhibited a pattern of innocuous behaviour – innocuous, at least, in relation to this crime. Hanratty had displayed some anxiety over his green suit, being concerned about possible blood-spots on that. Again, said Sherrard, this is indicative of innocence: a guilty man would have known which suit he had to be worried about. Also, a guilty man, having dyed his hair, would, after the crime was committed, not redye it the same way, but try to get it back to its natural colour as fast as he could. 'This does not require the ingenuity of a Sherlock Holmes,' insisted Sherrard. 'This is a matter of common sense.'

Sherrard emphasized that during the trial every word of Hanratty's about the Stanmore break-ins had proved true, right down to the coloured candle abandoned in the wash-basin. There was similarly a dispute with the police over the Ruislip break-in in April, which Hanratty maintained that, being in Middlesbrough at the time, he had not committed. Sherrard again considered that the circumstances favoured Hanratty's account: 'If that housebreaking did take place in April, is there not something rotten in the state of Denmark that it should take five months for the Yard to match the fingerprints?'

Concluding, Sherrard implored the jury to bring in a verdict of not guilty. 'This trial is in every sense absolutely critical for him and his family and I venture to think for the public.'

Thus the case for the defence was concluded. Now, the Crown QC prepared to deliver his summing-up. One of the quaint judicial rules extant in those days was that if a defendant called a witness other than a character witness in addition to his own testimony, then his counsel surrendered the right to make the final speech. What this meant in practice was that any defendant with the effrontery to mount a proper defence of the charge against him had to contend with a very serious handicap. As Mark Antony well understood, the opportunity to be heard second confers consider-able advantage.[22]

There was a high level of polemic in Swanwick's summing-up: 'The murderer embarked on this hold-up without any forethought. Once he had committed armed robbery of course there was no retreat, and no obvious means to somebody who was not very experienced in these matters of safe escape.'[23]

Armed robbery? Here is another example: 'I have no doubt he stole, either by himself or with others, the Jaguar from Hallam Street that night and motored to Manchester, although it was found in Oldham; one of his accomplices may have taken it there.'[24]

Accomplices? On occasions such as these, the judge might have reminded him that he was supposed to be summarizing the evidence, not inventing it.

Swanwick continued, with regard to Ingledene: '[Hanratty] said that he had breakfast in the general room in which there were two tables. Members of the jury, first of all, in Ingledene there are not two tables in the general room, but five. It seems hardly likely, does it, that a person would make that sort of mistake?'[25]

This was disgraceful. Swanwick was actually misquoting not only Hanratty's response but even his own question.

Swanwick: Did you have breakfast in your room or in a general room?
Hanratty: I had breakfast in a general room. There were two tables.

Hanratty obviously didn't have breakfast in his own room; Ingledene wasn't the Dorchester, as Swanwick well knew. Nor did he ever agree that he ate in the general room, but in *a* general room; in other words, the family's own dining room at the back, where there were two tables.

At the start of his summing-up, Swanwick plaintively told the jury that the Crown 'cannot be expected to fill in all the movements of the murderer'. Perhaps not, but the court was entitled to expect a postulated scenario that was both rational and had some evidence to support it. It is interesting to set out what, if the prosecution case was correct and Hanratty had indeed committed the murder, his movements were that August week.

On the Monday, he would have had to fit in the sweet-shop in Liverpool – because Swanwick was driven to suggest that the incident occurred on the Monday, and Hanratty had merely displaced it by twenty-four hours and worked what Lewis Hawser QC later described as 'the classical false alibi trick'.

So Hanratty undertook an extraordinary trip to Liverpool. No one at all saw him, either when he was going, or while he was there; no one, that is, except this woman serving in a sweet-shop who was going to act as Hanratty's witness. In order to set up this fake alibi, he had the most rudimentary of conversations with her, which it was wholly unlikely that anyone would ever remember. Having gone to this trouble to set up such a frail but critical alibi, he nevertheless forgot at first to mention it to anybody – until he belatedly remembered and informed his solicitor accordingly. Then his solicitor, having no conception of its potential importance, abandoned it to the police to investigate.

After this solitary incident, Hanratty then returned to London, again managing to ensure that no one at all noticed him, and went to the Broadway House Hotel before going on to the Vienna.

Moreover, in order for all that to have happened, the prosecution witnesses who placed Hanratty in London on the Monday (and who were certainly believed by Superintendent Acott) must all have been mistaken. These witnesses included the man who took Hanratty's suit in for cleaning and alteration, and whose recollection was confirmed by the company's books; they included Ann Pryce, the barmaid who saw him twice at the Rehearsal Club that evening, once early and once late; and they also included the France family, and in particular Carole, whose testimony about remembering the day because of her dental treatment was borne out by the dentist's records. All those witnesses must have been mistaken.

On the Tuesday, Hanratty disappeared, and then committed the crime. On the Wednesday – again, he'd vanished from the face of the earth. Would he have been lying low somewhere in London after disposing of the Morris Minor in Redbridge? If so, he could have booked in at a small hotel or guest-house; but, despite police pleas for landlords and hotel-owners to report guests keeping themselves to themselves, and whose behaviour aroused suspicion, no one came forward to report James Hanratty. (Conversely, of course, and in exactly those circumstances, people did report Peter Alphon.)

Alternatively, he could have laid low with friends whom he trusted – which would have meant either Charles France or, more likely, Louise Anderson. If that had happened, it is bewildering that neither should have mentioned it, since they both gave evidence for the prosecution. In fact, if he had been lying low at Louise Anderson's, it is utterly inconceivable that she should not have revealed it, bearing in mind the series of increasingly bitter and damaging statements which she made against him after his arrest. The only other alternative was that Hanratty had made himself scarce.

So, from the prosecution point of view, Wednesday was a vacuum.

On Thursday, Hanratty would have had to be up early to leave the gun and ammunition on the bus without anyone noticing. There was, of course, an obvious contradiction here: Swanwick had told the jury that Hanratty used the 36A bus on which to plant the gun because it passed through familiar territory – 'parts of London with which he was very closely connected'. Yet the Crown's best guess as to why Hanratty escaped attention at this time was the direct opposite of this – that he had fled his usual haunts.

According to this theoretical log of events, Hanratty rose early to put the gun on the bus, and then went to Liverpool, for the second time that week. Once there, he seemingly did nothing at all other than to send a telegram which even the most dimwitted criminal (which Hanratty certainly wasn't) could hardly have imagined would serve as a bogus alibi (as it was forty-eight hours late). Further, having gone all the way to Liverpool for a second time that week with the sole aim of establishing that second alibi, he then ruined it by appending a London address to it.

The prosecution scenario was as bereft of common sense as it was of supporting evidence.

Swanwick having concluded his peroration, the judge painstakingly gave a thorough precis of all the evidence. His summing-up lasted Thursday afternoon, all of Friday and the first hour of Saturday morning. In the opinion of many of those who heard it, the speech, though a meticulously balanced recapitulation of the evidence, did seem to be weighted in favour of acquittal. He mentioned that one of the key points of identification of the gunman was 'brown hair combed back with no parting' – something that, although he refrained from saying so, applied to Alphon rather than Hanratty. Then, referring back to one of Sherrard's comments about Nudds, Mr Justice Gorman advised, 'This man holds the key to many locks; but, members of the jury, do not try to force the door.'

He alluded to the fact that the prosecution also theorized that the sweet-shop alibi was 'bought' or 'invented': 'Members of the jury, when it is said that this alibi is "bought", then how did he know that anyone had made an inquiry of Mrs Dinwoodie for Tarleton or Carlton Road?' He emphasized that the poor performance of Mrs Jones should not count against Hanratty. Nor, indeed, should his own performance. 'A man who is concerned with a charge of murder may not be at his very best. Do not judge too harshly a man who must not be in a happy position, at the hands of these police officers.'

Finally, at 11.22 a.m. on Saturday, 17 February, by which time the proceedings had lasted for twenty-one days and this had become the longest murder trial ever held in Britain, the members of the jury were sent out to consider their verdict.

IT MAY HAVE been the longest British murder trial on record, but it should have been a great deal longer. The jury was allowed to hear only a fraction of the evidence. Apart from those factors already alluded to, there was much concealment of material evidence. The prosecuting counsel would not personally have been party to this; as much as the defence and the jury, they would have been kept almost completely in the dark.

The most critical evidence was the three identifications. Yet John Skillett's was neutralized by Edward Blackhall's corresponding non-identification, and the jury itself had helped to tease out the shortcomings in James Trower's supposed sighting. That left just the Storie identification, the full background to which has never previously been revealed.

Any juror would naturally assume that a woman who had been in such close proximity to her assailant for such a length of time would have no difficulty whatever in identifying him. Initially, this was Valerie Storie's own belief. In her first statement she said, 'I think I would be able to identify him. In fact I am sure I would.'[1]

However, she admitted that she was shortsighted. To make matters worse, she had scarcely got a good look at the gunman, who sat in the back of the car and ordered Storie and Gregsten to keep facing the front. When Acott re-enacted the drive himself, he noticed that, for some stretches on the main roads, the street lighting was first-class. He wondered whether that had helped her to see him.

Acott: In those well-lit roads, there is a fair bit of light coming in the car. Did you have a good chance of looking at him then?
Storie: No.
Acott: Why, because you were looking forward?
Storie: He wouldn't let us turn round.[2]

At Deadman's Hill it was, as Storie bleakly confirmed, 'dark, completely and utterly dark'. Even after she had been raped, the opportunities of seeing her attacker properly were not good. 'At the time he was out of the car, I only had a glimpse of him. In any case, I'd got my glasses off. They were in my right-hand coat pocket. I can't see very clearly without them.'

In all those six hours, she only once obtained a proper sighting of him. This was how she first of all said the opportunity arose: 'I did have a good look at him when I was in the back of the car when I was trying to soften him up.'[3]

And this was how she later told Superintendent Acott it had happened: 'Well, the point is, the only time I saw him to get a look at him was after he'd shot Mike, when he was still in the back seat of the car and I was in the front, when he pulled me round to face him, and a car came from behind as it were, and lit up his face.'[4]

According to her first statement, the critical moment came when she was in the *back* of the car; according to her long interview with Superintendent Acott, it was when she was in the *front*. It is not easy to see how this ambiguity arose. The moment was of such overwhelming significance that one would have expected her to have a clear and consistent recollection of how it occurred. She made the former comment within hours of the crime, when her memory was at its freshest, and at which time the supervising doctor was 'amazed at the coherent manner in which she related events'. The latter version was the one she provided in court.

Whatever the explanation of this discrepancy, it is clear that by the time of Storie's interview with Superintendent Acott on 11 September, her early confidence about being able to identify the gunman had evaporated. She twice told him about her apprehensions. The first time was at the outset of the long interview: 'My memory of this man's face is fading.'[5]

Towards the end, she reiterated her doubts, and said that the prospect of trying to identify him had been 'worrying' her: 'I am so afraid that when confronted with the man I may not be able to pick him out.'

However, she did pick out somebody on 24 September: an entirely innocent man. During the trial, Swanwick emphasized that at the time she had recently undergone an operation – though he glossed over the full circumstances of that.

In fact, the operation, for the removal of two bullets which were near the surface, was a minor one, performed under local anaesthetic. Forty-eight hours would have afforded ample time for recovery. Her doctor, Dr Ian Rennie, considered that she was 'in a fit condition' to go through with the parade, and 'quite clear in her mind'. Further, the very next day, Valerie Storie's condition was thought comfortable enough for her to be transferred from Guy's Hospital in central London to Stoke Mandeville Hospital in Buckinghamshire.

Nevertheless, Storie, together with Skillett and Trower, did pick out Hanratty at an identity parade. Many legal experts, however, believe that there are two fundamental grounds on which this parade, the most notorious in British legal history, should have been ruled invalid.

The first is that everyone was asked to speak. The complaint here is not simply that anyone guilty of the crime would have tried to disguise his locution; it is that in this respect the whole concept of an identity parade was negated. The men making up the parade were commandeered from nearby bases. The majority were on National Service. They were not local men; they came from all over the British Isles. Of the nine men whom we traced in 1991, most came from the Midlands, the north-east and Scotland; none came from London. From among the rich variety of accents, anyone should have been able to discern a cockney dialect.

But Hanratty was more critically compromised even than that. There had already been references in the daily press reports to the fact that police were hunting a man with dyed hair. At that time it was rare indeed for men to dye their hair, so these reports would have aroused particular fascination. On the parade, the one man with tinted hair would not have been difficult to spot. Even Kleinman, whose performance at this critical stage was not one of the landmarks of legal representation, noted that Hanratty's 'dyed hair showed up very badly' under the harsh glare of the artificial lighting of the hospital's medical inspection room. Antony Luxemburg, one of the parade members, clearly remembered that 'His hair was the outstanding feature – very vivid, orangey hair, which was obviously dyed.' Another, Brian Oliver, readily recalled this aspect of the parade. 'I've never seen hair like it. Very strange, carrotty. The nearest thing I've seen to it was Wee Willie Harris.'

At the trial, Sherrard asked Trower about Hanratty's hair:

Sherrard: Practically all colours of the rainbow, was it not – most peculiar?
Trower: You could put it like that.

Mary Hanratty, with James in 1941.

James Hanratty.

Michael and Janet Gregsten with with their son, Simon, in 1953.

William Ewer and Janet Gregsten attending trial at Bedford.

(from left)
Peter Alphon, Valerie Perkins and Jeremy Fox.

Jean Justice.

Paul Foot (*centre*), Michael Hanratty (*left*) and Mary and James
Hanratty (*backs to camera*) campaigning in 1969.

Justice and Fox revisiting the Old Shire Hall, Bedford, where the
trial was held in 1987.

Mary and James Hanratty in 1971.

Sherrard: There was nobody else there with that sort of hair? Be sure.
Trower: No.[6]

He also raised the point with Valerie Storie:

Sherrard: Would I be putting it, possibly colloquially but accurately, that his head of hair must have stood out like a carrot in a bunch of bananas?
Storie: That is right.[7]

Hanratty had been fully aware of this handicap from the moment of his arrest in Blackpool by Detective Constable Stillings and Detective Constable Williams: 'Mr Williams made a remark at the station to me about the description which was given to him by the police, and he said, "Jimmy, it was your hair that give you away."'

He was apprehensive before the parade, as he told police constable Jack Braybrook, who was guarding him: 'His greatest concern appeared to be the colour of his hair. He remarked that it was "a dead giveaway". With no prompting from us, he then stated, "You'd think that the girl would know the bloke after being with him for six hours. But she made a mistake last time, didn't she?"'[8]

Another officer, Sergeant Christopher Absalom, saw Hanratty later that day, after the parade had taken place. 'When I first saw Hanratty in his cell at about 6.00 p.m. on 14 October, I said to him, "I don't like the colour of your hair." He then said, "Neither do I. I got it done in Liverpool. I read that the police were looking for a dark-haired man. I'd had mine dyed black so I went into a hairdresser's in Liverpool and said, 'I've dyed my hair black. I want you to change it for me. I'll see you all right.' Well, you know what happens when you say, 'I'll see you all right.' The chap said, 'It'll be a long job, sir.' I had it bleached and it cost me thirty bob." Hanratty then put his finger on his hair and added, "This hasn't done me any favours."'

This matter was brought up by Hanratty in one of the comments which, according to him, had been omitted from the police records: 'I explained to Mr Acott, "Was that fair, putting me on an ID parade with my hair like that?" His reply was, "I did not ask you to get your hair dyed, Jimmy. If you have got any complaints, you can tell the judge." Those were his exact words.'[9]

Acott denied this at trial.

Sherrard: Are you saying that nothing whatever was said to you
about his concern with the colour of his hair and these parades?
Acott: I am saying I had nothing to do with that.[10]

One of the police documents which I discovered in the files at
Bedford thirty years later was a message recorded as being from
Superintendent Acott, then in Blackpool, to Detective Superintend-
ent Barron, of Bedfordshire police. It reads:

> Please make arrangements ... for witnesses to attend an identifica-
> tion parade at Bedford at 3.00 p.m., 13 October ... Also make
> arrangements with Aylesbury police for identification parade to be
> held at Stoke Mandeville Hospital at 11.30 a.m. 14 October. Men
> required for parade to be aged in the region of 25 years, 5′7″,
> respectably dressed. Skull caps to be obtained – suggest those worn
> in operating theatres in hospitals would be suitable.

The key part is astonishing: *Skull caps to be obtained*. This suggests
that the police were fully aware that the two parades would be
unfair because Hanratty would be prejudiced by his dyed hair,
unless the hair was hidden. They had already made contingency
arrangements.

Yet Superintendent Acott gave no hint at the trial that he had
personally taken these advance precautions to ensure the fairness
of the parade – precautions which were then never put in place.
Kleinman, of course, raised no objection himself, and indeed
assented to the parade. I believe that he made the wrong decisions,
but it is easy to be wise after the event, and one should not
underestimate the dilemma that he faced. Although unaware that
skull caps were ready for use, he certainly knew that Hanratty's
hair-colouring was distinctive. Yet he would have faced a problem
if he had insisted that the hair of the men on parade be covered to
the eyebrows. This might then have made the men's eyes much
more prominent. With Storie now insisting that it was the gunman's
'large, icy-blue staring eyes' that were his most notable feature,
Kleinman clearly wished to avoid anything which might have
drawn greater attention to Hanratty's eyes.

Accordingly, he adjudged that it was better to let the parade
go ahead. Storie had already made one erroneous indentification.
In the event that she did pick out Hanratty, then he believed it
would be a weakness in the prosecution case that she had picked

out someone whose hair looked *strikingly different* from that of the murderer.

Despite all these factors, it may nevertheless be thought that a rape victim could not possibly be in error over the identity of her attacker. Criminal justice history, however, can throw up abundant examples of mistakes having been made in such circumstances. One of the most extraordinary sequences of mistaken identity occurred in the John McGranaghan case (see Appendix 1).

With regard to Storie's identification evidence, it is now known that she was shown a number of photographs and picked out particular ones – 'This photograph is most like him.' The defence would have wished for access to those, so that they could compare likenesses. More than that, they would have wished for access to the man she did pick out on the first identification parade.

What, Acott was asked, did this man look like?

Acott: I can give you a full description of the man who was picked out on that parade.
Sherrard: Would you tell me whether he was, as Dr Rennie has told us, a fair-haired man?
Acott: No, he was not. I have his full description. I have had this man physically examined . . . I can tell you this from my own knowledge: 5 feet 9 inches, dark short-cropped hair, about twenty-seven years of age, and he was heavily built. Anything else, sir?
Sherrard: Is the man available, by any chance?
Acott: He was some time ago, but I cannot say off-hand.[11]

In the event, there was no opportunity for the defence to be able to test the differing descriptions of the man given by Acott and Rennie; or to compare his likeness with that of the other man picked out by Storie, Hanratty.

Over the years, there was considerable mystery regarding this missing man. There were rumours that he was a Spanish sailor. Like most rumours surrounding this case, that was entirely false. The man was an airman serving at Northwood in Middlesex, Michael Clark. On the face of it, it seems unlikely that there would have been any impediment at all to his attending the trial. Yet the information concerning the misidentified man was never released to the defence.

Thirty years later, Clark proved infuriatingly impossible to trace.

He left the country in 1965 and emigrated. However, I did locate his closest surviving relative, an aunt living on the Welsh borders. She recollected his hair as being of a 'general mousey colour' – which appeared to corroborate Rennie's description, and not Acott's.

It has never been appreciated just how tenuous the overall identification evidence in this case was. The police organized a number of parades, and brought along a number of witnesses to them. The final tally worked out as follows:

Peter Alphon: two identifications
James Hanratty: three identifications
Others: seven identifications.

Other parts of Valerie Storie's evidence concerned the ostensibly self-revealing information which the gunman vouchsafed during the car journey. The prosecution tried to suggest that Hanratty fitted the description that the gunman had given of himself. In reality, this didn't fit him at all, other than when the remarks became completely vague, and then they could have been applied to almost anybody. Among other things, Storie recollected the following points:

'He did say that he had been in prison for five years for house-breaking, and that the next time he was caught he would get PD, and that would mean going to the Isle of Wight. He also said that when he was in prison he had been on thirty days' bread and water. He also said he had been in and out of prison since he was eight years ... He told us he hadn't had a chance when he was a kid. He'd been locked up in a cellar for days, and beaten and had bread and water ... When we asked if he had any family, he said, "No." '[12]

Many of these remarks could not possibly have applied to Hanratty. He had never lived in a house with a cellar, let alone been locked in one and given only bread and water. He came from a stable family background. He wasn't coming up for PD (which applied to those thirty or over). Hanratty had not served five years for housebreaking. However, perhaps the most revealing comment of all is the gunman's suggestion, 'that would mean going to the Isle of Wight'. The clear inference is that this would entail a new severity of punishment for the gunman. Accordingly, this could certainly not have applied to Hanratty, who had, of course, already been imprisoned on the Isle of Wight.

The most intensely damaging of these allegedly self-incriminating remarks, however, was the gunman's suggestion that he had 'done the lot'. Not, on the face of it, very significant. However, the Crown argued that 'done the lot' was, in criminal argot, a very specific phrase. It referred to having served a complete prison term. At this time, that could have applied only to five people in the country, four of whom could safely be eliminated from inquiries. The fifth was Hanratty. Swanwick questioned Storie about this at trial:

Swanwick: With reference to what did he say that he had 'done the lot'?

Storie: I presumed that he had done all sorts of crimes and had been imprisoned for them. What he actually meant, I do not know.[13]

Thus Storie herself helped to foster the belief that 'done the lot' was a phrase of some cryptic significance. What the jury did not know was that Acott had asked her about this point in particular during the interview.

Acott: I believe he said he had done five years for housebreaking and he'd done the lot. What do you understand by 'he'd done the lot'?

Storie: We asked him why he'd been in prison, and he said, 'I've done five years for housebreaking' and we said, 'What else?' and he replied, 'I've done the lot.'[14]

It was significant that, having received this reply, Acott abandoned that line of questioning.

By the way he framed his question to Storie, Acott seemed to be wondering whether the phrase 'done the lot' could have the significance that was indeed later attributed to it. Yet Valerie Storie's response clearly indicated that it did not have that connotation. The phrase 'done the lot' must have referred to something other than the 'five years for housebreaking' because the gunman used it in response to the question '*What else?*' Also, the way the original question was put – we asked him *why* he'd been in prison – makes it clear that the reference was to crimes committed, not prison terms served. (Moreover, of course, Hanratty had never

served five years for housebreaking.) Subsequently, the matter was
not raised at all during the magistrates' court hearing. Then,
ominously, it emerged as part of additional evidence tendered by
Valerie Storie and served on the defence just prior to the start of
the trial.

Here was what might be termed creative forensics – the process
of kneading meaningless testimony into damaging evidence. It was
a sure sign that the prosecution found it hard to put its case
together. A similar technique was employed on the 'roadworks'
material. This evidence in full was actually even stranger than it
originally seemed.

Swanwick told the jury that '[The gunman] even warned
Gregsten to go carefully, because he said, "Just round the corner
you will find some roadworks." Sure enough, the car turned the
corner and there were the roadworks. You may think he was
somebody who knew that area very well indeed – well enough to
know that the road was up as you came to a particular corner in
that journey and when you came round it you would find the
roadworks there.'[15] Swanwick suggested this was proof that
the gunman 'knew the Harrow area', where the roadworks were
located, 'particularly well'; indeed, 'very intimately'.

No one told the jury that these roadworks had moved during the
course of the inquiry. This is what Valerie Storie told police about
them:

'He appeared to know all about the Stanmore area and the
roadworks.'[16]

'Near Stanmore, he said, "Just round the corner there are some
roadworks."'[17]

'I recall that at some stage, and I believe it was near Stanmore,
the man said, "Mind, there is some roadworks round the corner,"
and as we travelled there were some roadworks.'[18]

'We went through, I think it was while we were going in the
region of Stanmore. He did say, "There are roadworks round the
corner, watch out" and in fact when we went round the corner,
they were there.'[19]

Then, in her trial evidence, Storie said:

Storie: At one point in our meanderings through the roads he said,
'Be careful, round the corner there are some roadworks' and
sure enough when we got round the bend there were some
roadworks. He then hastily added, 'I do not know this area.'

Swanwick: In what area were the roadworks?
Storie: In the Harrow area.[20]

A complete reading of the 'roadworks' testimony from start to finish reveals that it was only when giving evidence at the trial that Valerie Storie framed the remarks in what was, for Hanratty, a damaging context. Much more importantly, she located the road-works in the Stanmore area the first four times she referred to them; it was only when giving evidence at the magistrates' and the Crown Court that they became relocated in the vicinity of Harrow. By the time of Swanwick's summing-up, their location was fixed as close to the Kenton Road junction – damaging for Hanratty, certainly, because that was near where his family lived, but some way south of Stanmore, where they started off.

Faced with an absence of bona fide evidence, the prosecution simply manufactured it.

There were further indications provided by Valerie Storie of the gunman's apparent knowledge of the area through which they passed: 'We continued up the A5 until we got to St Albans. We said, "Oh, this is St Albans." He said, "No, it isn't, it's Watford." We said, "No, it isn't," and he said, "We passed St Albans a long time ago. This is Watford." We didn't argue.'[21]

Hanratty, having been brought up not far from Watford, would hardly have mistaken it for St Albans.

The third geographical clue was that the gunman was familiar with the Bear Hotel in the centre of Maidenhead. Storie made this point several times. But there was no evidence that Hanratty had ever been to Maidenhead, let alone that he had been a patron of the Bear Hotel, which was hardly likely in any event. Hanratty, being a non-drinker, rarely used pubs.

If one were asked to review these strands of evidence, and place them in order of weight and importance, one would probably say that the apparent knowledge of the Bear Hotel was the most significant clue, the lack of knowledge of Watford and St Albans was the next strongest, and the roadworks evidence was the weakest.

For the trial, this evidence was turned on its head. The more compelling evidence was ignored, because it didn't fit Hanratty; while the vaguest evidence was distorted to make it appear as though it did fit, and then presented as of major importance.

The gunman, it was clear, knew little about cars and driving.

Storie herself, through her professional and social interests, was especially knowledgeable in this field, so what she said carried particular authority. In fact, each of her statements makes at least some reference to his ignorance in this respect. She told Superintendent Acott: 'He kept on asking where gears were, where reverse was, and he often said to Mike, "What gear are you in now?" He said at one stage, "You go down into first now," and Mike said, "No, it's third," and he didn't seem to cotton on to the fact quite where the gears were . . . He said, "Turn the back light off as well." He never actually called it a reversing light, he always referred to it as "the back light" . . .

'I said, "Look, it's nearly three o'clock, dawn will be breaking soon, you'd better go or let me give you a lift somewhere, or let me take you somewhere. I am probably a better driver that you are . . ."

'I started the car up. He wanted me to start the car for him, and tell him where the gears were, which I did, and he said, "How do the lights work?" and I showed him. The car was ticking over and I sat down on the ground, and he sort of got into the car and you know how when a car's been standing and it ticks over it sometimes cuts out after a few minutes. Well, the car cut out, and he got out again. So, I started it up again, and I said, "You'd better go, it's nearly daybreak" . . .'[22]

(Once again, the impact of this evidence was distorted at trial, when Storie said, 'He got in and drove it off quick enough . . .')

Nor did he understand much about driving conditions, even about motorways which were then of particular interest to all drivers, if only for their novelty value:

Storie: I had the impression that he didn't know what a motorway was.
Acott: He knew that the motorway went under that bridge?
Storie: He knew that the motorway went under that road, but he didn't seem to realize that you couldn't get on to the motorway from the road we were on. I couldn't sort of get that over to him.[23]

Astonishingly, Gregsten and Storie were able to deceive the gunman into believing that the car, which had half a tank of petrol, needed refuelling – thus forcing him into a potentially perilous situation. ('It was going about forty to the gallon,' said Storie, 'but he wasn't to know that.') Anyone used to driving would have been at least partly aware of the capacity of the car, and in any case could have checked for himself by looking at the gauge. It was obviously hazardous for the gunman to pull in at a garage.

All that Storie perceived about the gunman's driving limitations was, of course, buttressed by what those witnesses in Redbridge the next morning saw for themselves.

So there is a consistent pattern of evidence there. None of it fits Hanratty, who loved the thrill of cars and driving. He was not someone who was inexperienced, or who would be unable to grasp the gear-change mechanism of the humble Morris Minor, nor who would be unfamiliar with contemporary driving situations. He did have a minor collision in Ireland, which the prosecution used to his disadvantage; but, as usual, they could only do so by resorting to disturbing tactics – in this instance by withholding the statement from John Dowling, the policeman who attended the scene and assessed the damage as so slight that the incident wasn't even worth reporting.

Despite all this material, it is the apparently inconsequential remarks about the gunman's watch that forms the most bewildering part of Valerie Storie's record. This is what she said:

'He [the gunman] kept looking at his watch and the final time he said it was 2.50 a.m. I told him it would be light at 3.30.'[24]

'We then told him he could take anything he wanted – money, the car, but to leave us alone. Whenever we said this he would look at his watch and say, "There is plenty of time." '[25]

'During the journey the man kept looking at his watch and he kept saying it is not much longer to daybreak.'[26]

Storie: He merely sat there and kept looking at his watch.
Acott: Where was his watch?
Storie: On his left wrist.[27]

There was consistency in her testimony about the fact that he had a watch, and, indeed, that he kept looking at it. Partly because it was so mundane, this information was unlikely to have been invented or misremembered. When giving evidence at Bedford, however, her evidence suddenly departed from this clear and consistent line:

Swanwick: Had he got a watch on – do you remember?
Storie: He may have, I cannot remember.[28]

Her evidence on this one mundane subject is so startling, one naturally is led to wonder whether much faith could have been placed in the remainder of it. Superintendent Acott, however, expressed no doubts at all: 'I did depend on her from the day of the murder until today. I stand firm on her. She has never altered one scrap.'[29]

Irrespective of whether one would endorse this assessment *in toto*, one of the particular matters on which Valerie Storie definitely never altered one scrap – indeed, probably the single matter on which she was at her most utterly consistent – concerned the garage at which the car in which she, Gregsten and the gunman stopped for petrol. This is her testimony on that point:

'We stopped for two gallons of petrol at a garage along the Great West Road near London airport – travelling towards London.'[30]

'Eventually we drove to the A4 and stopped at a Regent garage which was the first garage after the Colnbrook by-pass opposite London airport ... At no stage did any of us get out of the car.'[31]

Acott: Now what makes you sure that the garage where you called for petrol was a Regent garage and the first one after the Colnbrook by-pass opposite London airport?

Storie: Well, when we started to go, he asked us how much petrol there was. There were a couple of gallons in the car and Mike said there was only one gallon, mainly to sort of say we can't go far, and he said, 'How far will it go?' I said about thirty miles. In fact, it was going about forty to the gallon but he wasn't to know that, and he said, 'Well, we'd better get some petrol then.' We went through Slough, we stopped opposite Neville and Griffins, and we said, 'Let's get some milk if you want something,' and we discovered that none of us had got any sixpences and we said, 'Shall we go and ask?' – thinking that we could get an opportunity of doing something, and he said, 'No, it doesn't matter, I know a café near Northolt airport.' I think he said, 'On Western Avenue.' I can't remember whether I said, 'On Western Avenue' or he said, 'It is Western Avenue.' He said, 'Near Northolt airport.'

Acott: During the whole journey, Valerie, did you ever see a policeman or a police car?

Storie: I don't remember seeing one. Can I just say about how I know it was a Regent garage?

Acott: Yes.

Storie: Because as we drove into the garage I looked at the pumps and I thought, Oh, Lord, it's Regent petrol. Mike doesn't like Regent in his car.[32]

'Just past the airport on the left-hand side there is a Regent garage. He said "Go in there." He said, "Get two gallons." He said, "Don't forget. Don't get out and don't say anything to the man at all. Don't pass him any notes. Just say what you want." We drove in. The garage attendant came up to Mike. Mike opened the window and asked for two gallons. When the car had been filled Mike handed him the £1 note. The attendant brought back a 10 shilling note and a 3d piece ... After leaving the petrol pump we carried on towards London.'[33]

Storie: We drove on through Slough and near London airport we saw a Regent garage on the left-hand side of the road. He said to Mike, 'I want you to go in and get two gallons of petrol. You are to stay in the car. You can wind down the window and ask the man for two gallons only ...'

Swanwick: Then did you drive on?

Storie: We drove on.

Swanwick: In which direction?

Storie: Towards London.[34]

It was not only very easy then to locate the garage to which Valerie Storie referred, it is still easy to locate it today. The Regent company was taken over by Texaco in 1965, and a petrol station remains on exactly the same site (although it has been rebuilt several times in the interim). A statement was obtained from the attendant on duty, who was John Ward, of 128 Linkfield Road, Isleworth, Middlesex. He was unable to assist the inquiry.

'About 150 vehicles called at the garage for petrol between 10.00 p.m. and midnight on 22 August. About 40 per cent of the customers required only two gallons of petrol. We charge 9s 9d for two gallons of Regent Super Mixture. I would estimate that about thirty to forty customers would have handed me a £1 note on purchasing two gallons of fuel ... I cannot remember seeing any Morris Minor that tour of duty containing a man and a woman, or a man and woman with a third person.'[35]

That should have been the end of the matter. There was no

evidence to be obtained there. However, Superintendent Acott took to two identity parades an attendant, Harry Hirons, from an entirely different garage. At the trial, Acott gave the following testimony in relation to this:

Sherrard: Was there a person who was called to the identity parade on which Hanratty stood, called Hirons?
Acott: There was.
Sherrard: Was that man a garage attendant?
Acott: He was.
Sherrard: At which garage was Mr Hirons working on the night of the 22/23 August last year?
Acott: Kingsbury Circle.
Mr Justice Gorman: On which night?
Acott: On the night of 22 August.
Sherrard: Kingsbury Circle is broadly speaking in the Harrow–Stanmore area, is it not?
Acott: Yes. It is Kingsbury.[36]

Harry Hirons made three statements altogether. He worked at the 584 garage at Kingsbury Circle, a garage which served Shell petrol then (and still does today) and which was close to the Hanratty family home. It was approximately 12 miles from the Regent garage opposite London (Heathrow) airport. Mr Hirons said that one of the people travelling in the Morris Minor which he noticed had got out of the car.

So there are three stark differences between the Hirons account and what Valerie Storie said: the location of the garage; the brand of petrol that it served; and whether all three remained in the car throughout.

The exchange from the hospital interview is quoted at length because it shows how, even when the conversation had drifted off the point, Valerie Storie was particularly concerned to get the information across to Acott and explain why she had a definite reason for remembering ('Can I just say about how I *know* it was a Regent garage?').

The location of the Hirons garage, the 584, may have seemed further to incriminate Hanratty, in much the same way as the 'roadworks' evidence was deemed to have done. It was close to his family's home, and in an area he would have known. However, it was definitely not the garage at which the car had stopped.

In fact, Hirons never identified anyone and thus did not give evidence at trial. Nevertheless, Acott continued to give the impression that he had been called as a bona fide witness. The Crown colluded in this misleading of the jury:

Swanwick: Mr Hirons, who was called to the identification parade –
on which date was it?
Acott: For this defendant?
Swanwick: Yes.
Acott: 13 October.
Swanwick: You said [he] had not identified Gregsten or Miss
Storie. Had he identified the car which he served as being the
same car or not?
Acott: He had.[37]

Acott cannot have it both ways. Either Valerie Storie is an entirely reliable witness, as he testified. In that case, it was dishonest of him to have pretended that Hirons could ever have been a genuine witness (and what would have happened if Hirons had picked out the 'right' man – Alphon in the first instance, and Hanratty in the second?).

On the other hand, if Acott felt that even her totally consistent evidence relating to this – a matter on which she was particularly well informed and unlikely to err – could not be trusted, then how much weight could be placed on the rest of her evidence?

In regard to the Vienna Hotel evidence, there were two further aspects in which the wool was pulled over the jury's eyes. The first concerned the hotel records.

The sequence of events at the Vienna Hotel was obviously of critical importance. In which room had Hanratty stayed? Where had Alphon stayed? Would anyone else have stayed in or had access to the all-important Room 24? It was thus hardly surprising that a lengthy time at trial was spent going through the register and associated documentation to ascertain precisely what could be established from them. In view of William Nudds's three controversial statements, this was particularly important. It was vital to establish that no one had had the opportunity of interfering with the evidence. During cross-examination, defence counsel Sherrard naturally put this matter to Superintendent Acott:

Sherrard: Let me ask you about that at once. The Glickbergs
[Nudds and Florence Snell] had not had access to the hotel
records, so far as you know, from 11 September 1961 when

they were dismissed . . . They had no access to the records,
which would have enabled them to tamper with them?

Acott: No.

Sherrard: They were always, from 11 September, in your
  possession?

Acott: Yes.[38]

Superintendent Acott's testimony would appear to be directly
contradicted by a hitherto undisclosed statement made by his
colleague, Detective Sergeant Kenneth Oxford: 'On 20 September
1961 I went to the Vienna Hotel, Sutherland Avenue, Maida Vale,
W9, when Detective Superintendent Acott interviewed the manageress, Mrs Galves. I took possession of the Hotel Diary, the
Letting Sheet, sheets from the hotel register and a specimen receipt
card.'[39]

In the light of this, it appeared that Superintendent Acott had
misled the court with regard to a significant area of evidence, and
also that there was a vital nine-day period during which the hotel
records could indeed have been tampered with.

Secondly, at the trial, Swanwick tried to make sense of the
retraction of the second statements of Nudds and Snell, and
the subsequent restoration of the thrust of the first ones. He
told the jury: 'All the probabilities point to the fact that the first
and third statements are true and there is no truth in the second
. . . That position is in fact confirmed by the documents . . . the
hotel diary shows Durrant in Room 6, never in Room 24, there is
no "Durrant 24" ever in that book . . .

'The only entry in those documents on which [the defence] can
rely is the word "deposit". That, appearing where it does in
connection with Durrant, is in fact . . . utterly meaningless. It
disappears, in my submission, from the case.'[40]

Swanwick's argument is fallacious firstly because there was a
possibility of the records having been altered; and secondly because,
even if they had been, there remained surviving entries in the hotel
records (which Swanwick tried to dismiss) to reinforce the second
statement. There was also the documented testimony of the
manager, Juliana Galves. She said: 'I do not understand that part
of the entry "£1 7s 6d deposit" because if the guest Durrant had
telephoned this hotel in the morning he could not have paid a
deposit before his arrival. If he telephoned this hotel in the morning,
there was no need for him to call at the Broadway House before
coming here. If he had come direct to this hotel without calling at

the Broadway and had paid for his room here he would have been given a receipt signed by the Glickbergs or myself, and there would have been no need to show in the hotel diary that he had paid a deposit of £1 7s 6d.'[41]

The word 'deposit' is not utterly meaningless, as Swanwick suggested; it is absolutely critical. As Galves said, there is no explanation for it. In fact, the only conceivable explanation is the one which Nudds did give in his second statement: that Alphon made a telephone booking, called at the hotel at lunchtime, and was shown into a larger room which he didn't like and for which, furthermore, Nudds intended to charge him extra (thus, 'deposit'). Although he left his case there, Alphon made it clear that he preferred a single room. None was available at that stage. One did indeed become available later that evening, as Juliana Galves, later in her statement, made clear: 'I remember at about 11 a.m., on the morning of 22 August, Mrs Glickberg told me that she had received a telephone call for a man who had booked a room for one night and who said he would be arriving at the hotel late that night. Somewhere about 9 p.m., Mr Pichler telephoned and informed us that Mr Bell had cancelled his booking. I crossed out the entry in the diary referring to Mr Bell's booking and at about 10 p.m., just before I went to bed, I told the Glickbergs that their guest, who was expected to arrive late, could occupy Room 6.'

This second Galves statement directly confirmed the veracity of the second statement (which incriminated Alphon) and, therefore, indirectly demonstrated that the first and third (which incriminated Hanratty) were fabrications.

All of this was more than vital background evidence. It was completely critical to an understanding of the case itself. None of it was passed to the defence. The jury members heard not a word about it.

The judge, Mr Justice Gorman, told them that the 'credibility' of Superintendent Acott was 'of tremendous importance in this case'. Yet Acott had misled the court over the previous conviction of Peter Alphon, and the safe custody of the records of the Vienna Hotel. He had not told the court that the roadworks had moved, nor that he'd taken to two identity parades a petrol attendant from the wrong garage, nor that the man whom Valereie Storie had misidentified could easily be brought to court. Nor did he mention the gathering support for the Rhyl alibi.

Graham Swanwick concluded his summing-up by listing the factors which pointed to Hanratty: 'The factors about the assailant that fit Hanratty ... narrow down ... until there is only really one person ... How many do you think would be called Jim? And how many would have been to prison and "done the lot"? And how many would know the Harrow–Kingsbury area so intimately that they knew where there were roadworks to be found round the corner? And how many would use the phrase "I want a kip"?'[42]

None of these points, which 'narrow down' to Hanratty, has any validity whatever.

In such circumstances, what hope did the jury have? What chance of being able to make ultimate sense of the bewildering array of half-truths, bogus prosecution claims, partially disclosed witness testimony and the dissimulation of police informers like Nudds and Langdale? When juries are provided with the correct information, they usually arrive at the correct verdict; it is when aspects of the evidence are withheld from them that justice miscarries.

On Saturday, 17 February, having been sent out to consider their verdict, the jury members went upstairs to the first floor of the Shire Hall, and to the red-carpeted old Grand Jury Room overlooking the Ouse. They were served lunch (game soup, cold meat and salad, as virtually every paper diligently reported).

Some six hours later, they returned – not with the verdict, but with some specific questions, and a general request for further guidance from the judge: 'May we have a further statement from you regarding the definition of reasonable doubt? Must we be certain and sure of the prisoner's guilt to return a verdict?'

David Lines, Under-Sheriff of Bedfordshire, was among those in court who felt that for the jury even to ask that question was particularly telling: 'To me, as a lawyer, it meant they clearly weren't sure.' The judge, it seemed, thought along similar lines, saying to them, 'If you have a reasonable doubt, then you are not sure. You understand that, do you not?'

The jury had also asked a further question about the cartridge cases. The judge told them, 'Those cartridge cases, it is said, were left before 24 August. They were not found until 11 September. You have heard that another person used that room, that there were other people in the hotel, that there was a way outside from this bedroom, and you must not jump to the conclusion that the mere finding of those cartridge cases there denotes that they were left there by the prisoner.'

Hanratty had to be brought up to hear what was said; nothing could be done in his absence. He had steeled himself for the verdict, only to learn that no verdict was available.

At 7.30, the jury returned again – and again, not with the verdict. On this occasion, Sherrard did manage to forewarn Hanratty. This time, the jury put in a request for further refreshment. 'The judge was furious,' recalled David Lines. 'He thought all this was putting too much strain on Hanratty. It was difficult for the judge as well, he too showed the strain.'

Nevertheless, Mr Justice Gorman ordered that their wishes be attended to (once again, the gastronomic details were faithfully recorded: the jury received tea and tomato sandwiches). Naturally the court was packed with people milling about, just waiting for the verdict – members of the public, the press, the police, the family trying to comfort Mrs Hanratty. By now, there was a groundswell of opinion that the verdict must be in Hanratty's favour.

Finally, at 9.10 p.m., the court refilled for the third time, nearly ten hours after the jury had first filed out and after one of the longest retirements on record. Everybody resumed their seats. As the hubbub died down, there was great tension and anxiety. The jury was ready with its verdict: Guilty, my Lord. Was that the verdict of them all? It was.

Sherrard looked completely drained. In the corridor outside Mary Hanratty, who had not returned into court, collapsed. Hanratty himself fell against the rail at the front of the dock, his face crumpled in disbelief. He was asked if he had anything to say. Those present vividly recall his exact words:

'I am not – innocent.'

No one considered this a belated admission of guilt. In his state of terrible distress, Hanratty once again faltered, as one thought overwhelmed another. He never could find the right words when he needed them most. Yet only someone in absolute and unanticipated turmoil could have made such a potentially catastrophic mistake. His words, 'I am not innocent', came to be recognized as a heart-rending declaration of innocence.

After some momentary hesitation – no one believed he was happy with the verdict, but there are times when even a judge must feel impotent – Mr Justice Gorman, the black cap now over his wig, sentenced Hanratty to death.

· IV ·
THE EXECUTION

JEAN JUSTICE WAS born in Dublin on 6 October 1930. He was the third child and first son of a Belgian diplomat. His father, a vice-consul at the legation in Eire, had met Jean's mother, who came from Oxford, in Folkestone while on leave during the First World War. Justice is an unusual Belgian name, and the family acquired it in unusual circumstances. Jean's father's grandfather was, as a small child, found abandoned on stone steps in the centre of Leuven, just east of Brussels. He was beautifully dressed, and well wrapped up against the cold. No one had any idea who he was; a card pinned to him read, *Appelez cet homme Justice.*

From Dublin, the family moved the few miles south to Dun Laoghaire (then called Kingstown) where Jean and his sisters and younger brother enjoyed a prosperous and, according to all family recollections, blissful upbringing. Jean attended schools in Glasthune and Dublin, but the family was inevitably wrenched from its domestic idyll with the outbreak of war in 1939. Jean's father was promoted, going briefly to Warsaw before becoming consul-general in Alexandria. Jean attended the Victoria College there. He finished his schooling in Belgium, and then read law, initially at Leuven University, before taking up a place at St Catherine's College, Oxford.

Although he did have a keen interest in the law, excellent language skills and enormous natural intelligence, these advantages were, in academic terms, vitiated by a gregarious and high-spirited nature. Those post-war years were supposed to be the age of austerity, but there was nothing austere about Jean's lifestyle. He loved japes of any kind, and generally carried them off with impunity. He got away with a great deal because few who met him were not captivated by his debonair presence, personal charm and conversational gifts; although, certainly, there were also those who found him overbearing and loud – even friends called him 'Boomy'.

He didn't complete his degree, and after Oxford purchased Fairley Farm, near Okehampton in Devon, where he thought he might compose quartets and indulge his other main interests – painting and drinking. He was irresponsible in most senses of that adaptable word, having by this time twice changed his nationality in order to avoid military service. He enjoyed the financial means to be able to eschew conventional career paths. Academic failure scarcely mattered; he successfully pulled off some shrewd property deals. After disposing of the Okehampton farm (having discovered, to no one's surprise but his own, that he missed the revelry of metropolitan life) he bought a flat in Half Moon Street, Mayfair.

Jean was then absorbed into a London society from which, in other circumstances, his homosexuality and disdain for upper-class proprieties might have alienated him. With his cosmopolitan upbringing, he had no truck with traditions of deference or the mores of the British establishment.

One evening in 1955, at a gay club in Knightsbridge called Dorothy's, he met Jeremy Fox. The two discovered to their mutual surprise that they lived virtually next door to each other. Fox was, like Justice, sociable, of independent means, and dedicated to enjoying his salad days. Unlike Justice, he had a real job: he was a barrister. His father was the headmaster of Sunningdale Boys' Preparatory School, which Jeremy himself had attended. He then got a scholarship to Eton and, subsequently, another to King's College, Cambridge. His academic progress was halted by National Service, and he became a sergeant in the education corps, attached to the Enniskillen Fusiliers in Omagh, County Tyrone. Then he completed his law degree and was in 1952 was called to the Bar at Lincoln's Inn. He found chambers at 5 New Square.

Of the two, Justice was the taller, more dominant man. It took almost two years, however, for him to prevail upon Fox to move in with him. 'I did have my doubts at first,' explained Fox, 'he was rather militantly gay, whereas I liked keeping a low profile. Of course, in the end, I was glad I did.'

Together, they indulged their every appetite: they dined in fashionable restaurants, drank in exclusive clubs, and had the best seats at the Royal Opera House, Covent Garden. Then they purchased a weekend cottage – first of all, Smuggler's Cottage in Lamberhurst, Kent; and subsequently a luxurious bungalow in Newdigate, West Sussex, not far from Gatwick airport. Jean immediately, if improbably, christened it Laudate, after his favourite *Laudate Dominum* passage (of Psalm 117) from Mozart's Vespers. It had a lake and landscaped gardens, which Jean filled with a variety of animal life, including a caged bear he'd bought at Harrods.

It was at Laudate that Fox and Justice suffered the first of what became a series of scandals. Jean had invited an eighteen-year-old, William Dart, to spend some time with them. After two weeks, Jean, having exhausted his carnal desires, sent Dart on his way. The latter felt cheated by such treatment, and returned, with a friend. As a result of this visit, Dart was charged with seeking to obtain money by menaces.

Justice had felt so betrayed and angered by the incident that he instigated proceedings, in a roundabout way, by talking to his friend Captain David Brown, who owned a gay club, the Candy Lounge, in Soho and thus fostered cordial relations with the local police in Savile Row.

In November 1960, Leo Abse's bill to legalize homosexuality was still to come. So the decision to press charges of this kind could have been interpreted as commendably brave; it turned out, almost inevitably, to be disastrously foolhardy. The Dart trial provided a ready supply of lubricious copy for newspapers eager to lift the counterpane on the homosexual activities of the young and privileged. Justice, who described himself in court as an 'art designer', could scarcely admit that Dart had been invited down in the first place as a rent-boy. So, the prosecution witnesses – closely questioned by defence counsel about who had been sleeping where, and with whom – all had to perjure themselves. The jury wasn't fooled, the case quickly collapsed and Dart was acquitted.

To the chagrin of Fox, the tabloids had a field-day. Justice, however, was unabashed. 'When the *News of the World* described Laudate as "a sink of iniquity"', recalled Fox, 'Jean was absolutely thrilled. He revelled in publicity. For my part, I was terribly upset. The whole case was severely embarrassing for my family in the Home Counties, because the whole world then knew that I was gay. I remember my mother telling me that I'd be an outcast.'

Some had thought that Justice himself might be prosecuted as a result of the case, but nothing happened. However, charges were brought after an unruly incident on a train from Gatwick airport. After what was, even by their standards, a heavy drinking session, Jean and Jeremy and friends were returning to London. The party became particularly boisterous and at some point Fox histrionically flung open a train door. Then someone pulled the communication cord. When the train finally pulled into Victoria, a contingent of police was waiting. Fox and Justice found themselves in Bow Street Magistrates' Court.

The magistrate found their behaviour reprehensible. 'He said that opening a train door and endangering the lives of the public was a very serious offence,' remembered Fox. 'And so it was, of course. He said he had a good mind to commit us for trial to the assizes.' However, Fox and Justice had secured the services of a good solicitor, David Jacobs, the location of whose offices – in Pall Mall – indicated that, for those who could afford to pay for it, there would always be a better class of justice. 'He defended us very well,' said Fox, 'and mercifully we were let off with a fine.'

By this time, Justice was himself doing occasional pieces of work for solicitors, before his equal enthusiasm for the serious business of the law and the frivolous business of japes and wheezes nearly precipitated further disgrace. Early in 1961, the Portland Spy Trial began. This promised to be one of the most sensational for many years, and Justice was enormously excited by the prospect of the case. He had a habit of issuing peremptory demands which, however burdensome, he expected others to carry out. He told Fox that he simply had to attend this trial.

Fox could think of only one way to get Justice into the Old Bailey. He took a wig and gown from his chambers, and Jean made his entrance into court disguised as a barrister. At the time, the ploy worked perfectly; in a courtroom otherwise crammed to the rafters, Jean sat undisturbed and in splendid isolation through an engrossing day in court.

Unfortunately, the scheme had a rather obvious flaw. The press was also out in force for this trial. It didn't take the more observant among the reporters long to begin to wonder about this oddly superfluous barrister. And didn't he look like Jean Justice? The 'art designer'? The man who, in drunken high jinks, 'endangered the lives of the public'? The next day's papers carried scarcely veiled stories about the phantom barrister of the Old Bailey.

Fox, who at that time was engaged on contributing a number of titles to the third edition of *Halsbury's Laws of England*, was invited to provide an explanation of the wig-and-gown affair: 'The Treasurer of Lincoln's Inn was surprisingly lenient, but he did suggest that I should get away from the company I was keeping.' Fox understood the sense of that. 'We had a playboy image and were living a crazy life. By the time the A6 case came along, Jean and I must have been two of the least credible personalities in London.'

When the A6 Murder took place, Jean Justice was, ironically, one of the few people in England not in the least interested. However, three months later, on Wednesday, 22 November 1961, he emerged in the late afternoon from the Barrington, a drinking club in Jermyn Street, and noticed the newspaper placards blazoning the news of the opening day's proceedings from Ampthill. He bought an *Evening Standard*, and started reading. The more he read, the more fascinated he became.

He'd got nothing on – well, he'd had nothing on for a year or two – so he asked his chauffeur, Gordon Perkins, to drive him to Ampthill. There, he had to endure an unfamiliar experience – queueing – but did eventually manage to squeeze into the tiny court. From that day, he rose early to make sure of his place.

He noticed the prison van arriving, its windows covered with brown paper, and the crowd outside yelling, 'There's the A6 killer.' In court, he saw Janet Gregsten burst into tears after giving her evidence. That was entirely explicable; but then he saw Mrs France collapsing in the witness-box, and Louise Anderson collapsing also. Hanratty, he felt, surveyed proceedings more as an interested onlooker, someone who joined in the moments of light relief, rather than the man in the dock. Justice himself was mostly baffled by the fact that the evidence seemed to have very little to do with the crime; and there was no mention at all of a motive.

Then came the electrifying moment when Sherrard suddenly raised his voice: '"Missing", "missing", what do you mean, "missing"?' Sherrard had just been told about the absence of John Kerr's contemporaneous notes. 'There was an adjournment,' remembered Justice, 'but then they still hadn't found it. That really opened my eyes: a vital piece of documentation had been mislaid. It was obvious that something was going on here, something I couldn't quite grasp.'

By the time that Hanratty was committed for trial, Justice was utterly fascinated. He tried to encourage a similar interest in Fox, but the latter was preoccupied with his work on *Halsbury's*, and anyway, he told Justice, 'Murder isn't my field.'

Nevertheless, he was prevailed upon to lend occasional assistance. Prior to the start of the trial, he and Justice, together with the latter's brother, Frank – the Half Moon Street Irregulars, as it were – did make a few desultory inquiries. They went to the Rehearsal Club, and asked about the case among those who they felt might have some familiarity with the Soho underworld. The gossip they picked up served only to reinforce Justice's inchoate impressions, of Hanratty as a sneak thief, a very minor crook and by no means a significant or dangerous criminal.

Justice tried to see Hanratty's family – Michael still remembers that tall commanding figure, in his overcoat, briefcase under his arm, striding down the path – but the ever-vigilant minders from the *Daily Express* ensured that he got no further than the front door. Undaunted, he and Fox went to see Emmanuel Kleinman. However, Sherrard got to hear of their somewhat cavalier investigations. He, mindful of their reputation, was alarmed; he understandably regarded them with a circumspection that bordered on hostility.

Then the trial began. Justice was there every day, attentively listening to the evidence. He heard Valerie Storie's testimony, and began to understand 'how bits and pieces of evidence had been woven into a web by the prosecution'. Justice recalled being 'shocked by the dishonesty of a senior detective like Inspector McCafferty' (who said that it would have been possible for someone to get in and out of the car without getting blood on them and that the jacket was more likely than the trousers to have been bloodstained).

He was impressed with Hanratty. 'I thought he came over well. He was quite clear about everything, about his thieving activities and his criminal past, but he made it clear that he had nothing to do with the murder. And that rang true.'

Two moments utterly transfixed Justice: when Swanwick suggested to Hanratty that he might have caught a train from Paddington, and the judge asked if there was any evidence about this, and Swanwick had to admit that there was no evidence at all; and when Acott said, 'There is a plane service.'

'I thought, this is just fantastic – taking a plane from Liverpool to a cornfield?' Justice recalled in 1990. 'Lord Russell said later that it was difficult to believe that all this happened in England in the latter part of the twentieth century and not in the land of Oz – and that was my feeling too.'

Justice decided to try to find the first suspect, Peter Alphon. 'I'd missed all the public interest surrounding the nationwide search for him; but people who knew far more about the case than I did said he was an intriguing character. I wanted to see if he knew anything; I thought he might be able to help.'

Fox was issued with another of Justice's peremptory orders: find Alphon. This, too, was no easy task, but Fox accomplished it because Alphon had issued a writ against Superintendent Acott, on which he had had to give his address.

His address was the Ariel Hotel, an expensive, newly built hotel, perfectly circular in shape, stuck out on the Bath Road near

London airport. On Thursday, 8 February Justice telephoned, but was told that Alphon was out. He called again at 1.00 a.m., and was put through to him. Alphon was wary, but agreed to meet Justice later that day, at noon, at the offices of his solicitor, H. MacDougal, in Barnes, south-west London.

Justice arrived with his brother, but was disappointed. After they'd waited some time, MacDougal arrived to say that his client didn't want to see them. It was intensely frustrating, especially as Justice had missed the most sensational day of the trial so far (the first part of Grace Jones's testimony).

Justice tried again that evening and on Saturday to contact Alphon, but without success. On Sunday, 11 February, he went to the hotel. Alphon agreed to talk to Justice if the two of them could go for a drink somewhere. So they walked along the Bath Road to a pub.

'I was struck by his manner. He seemed polite, but aloof and shy. He had a curiously gliding gait when he moved, there was something reptilian about him. He seemed weary, but became animated when talking about his political views, the state of the country, that sort of thing. I soon learned that he was a puritan and a fascist. He also told me that he hated homosexuals. I did mention the case, and we talked about it in very general terms. At one point, he said, "They can't pin it on me, now," which I thought was strange.'

Two days later, Justice met him again, at seven o'clock at the Ariel. Again, they talked in a pub until, at 10.00, Jean's driver took them to a Chelsea restaurant, the Ox-on-the-Roof, where Jeremy Fox joined them. Afterwards, Alphon accompanied them back to Half Moon Street. At such times, Justice would pump Alphon about the case, questioning him all the time. He didn't seem to mind; he was, as Jean put it, 'quite affable'. In these early days, Justice and Fox established that Alphon had an especially detailed knowledge of the case; that he fitted the description of the gunman originally put out by Bedfordshire police; that he had a great enthusiasm for dog-racing; and that his lifestyle was nocturnal. Certainly, they were intrigued enough to want to pursue the relationship.

Fox and Justice saw him again at the Ariel Hotel, on Thursday, 15 February. 'I remember Alphon was generous in buying Jean and myself drinks,' Fox wrote in a contemporary memo, 'and he appeared to show no resentment at Jean's cross-examination.'

Still somewhat supercilious about the whole matter, Fox attended only four days of the trial (whereas Justice missed only the one), but he did drive Justice to Bedford for the final day – which, for those present, meant little more than hours of waiting. Justice paced up and down in the corridor, as nervous as anyone. At one point, Sherrard, who by now appreciated that their interest was genuine and well-meant, went over to them to express his gratitude for how much they'd tried to help the defence.

Then they all filed back into court for the verdict. It is, as Ludovic Kennedy remarked in *The Trial of Stephen Ward*, a shocking thing when justice miscarries before your eyes. Jean now found himself in that position; he was stunned. 'I thought, this is incredible – that anybody could be relying on the word of Nudds and Langdale. All I could think was, he'll have an excellent chance at appeal. I thought it was inconceivable that he would actually hang.'

The previous day, Justice had telephoned the Ariel, to be informed that Alphon had moved from the hotel and left no forwarding address. On Tuesday, 20 February, Alphon telephoned Justice; he was now installed at the Regent Palace Hotel, just off Piccadilly Circus. This bewildered Justice: 'I thought, why, with the trial at an end, does he suddenly move from this hotel in the middle of nowhere to one at the centre of everything?' However, together with his brother Frank, Justice went to see Alphon at about midnight that same evening. He immediately asked him for his views on the verdict. He never forgot Alphon's chilling reply: 'Yes, I was at the White City [for the dog-racing] when I heard. It surprised me a little bit, but Hanratty's expendable.'

CHAPTER SEVENTEEN

IMMEDIATELY AFTER THE end of the trial, even before the official and unofficial units of Hanratty's defence corps had been able to gather their thoughts and plan their tactics for the appeal, the case unfurled its most bewildering development of all.

When a major trial is finally over, the press, partly in a spirit of exhilaration at being able to cast off its long-borne shackles of sub judice, will publish not just reports of the verdict and the concluding proceedings but also background features unravelling the truth about the whole affair.

In the A6 Murder case, this didn't apply. Some would perhaps have suggested that this was because the truth had been buried so effectively that it would now take years, not days, to excavate it. Certainly, in the wake of the jury's decision, the public would have looked in vain for newspaper articles which explored and explained the intricacies of this baffling case. There were none.

Yet there was one backgrounder which did throw fresh light on the case, albeit in ways which no one immediately understood. The trial had finished late on the Saturday evening so that the Sunday papers were able to include only the bare details about the verdict. However, that Monday, 19 February, the *Daily Sketch* announced on its front page that 'Second sight led her to killer'. The back page carried the story, which was written by Peter Duffy. This is of such significance in the context of the entire case that it must be quoted in full:

Mrs Gregsten's amazing intuition
SHE SAW HIM AT THE CLEANERS

The amazing intuition of Janet Gregsten, widow of A6 Murder victim Michael Gregsten, helped to put James Hanratty on trial for his life.

This intuition and two fantastic coincidences which set detectives on Hanratty's trail were revealed last night – 24 hours after he was found guilty of the A6 Murder.

But only eight days after the murder – when Scotland Yard were without a positive clue to the killer – Mrs Gregsten pointed to Hanratty and said: 'That's the man the police are looking for.'

Mrs Gregsten's 50-year-old brother-in-law Mr William Ewer, had taken her to his antique shop in the station arcade at Swiss Cottage, north London, to try to help her to get over the tragedy which struck her life.

Mrs Gregsten had been shown an identikit picture of a man the police wanted to interview in connection with her husband's killing.

Her brother-in-law's shop was 21 miles from Dorney Common, where the A6 murder nightmare began. It was 50 miles from Deadman's Hill, near Bedford, where the horror climaxed.

Far enough away, anyone would think, to dull the memory of tragedy.

But then came COINCIDENCE No. 1.

On the morning of 31 August, Mrs Gregsten was standing in the shop window helping Mr Ewer to hang a picture – a Wilson Steer interior.

Suddenly she clutched at Mr Ewer's arm and pointed through the window to a man with jet black hair walking into a Burtol cleaners shop only two yards across the arcade.

'That's the man. He fits the description,' she said. 'But it's more than that. I have an overpowering feeling that it is him.'

Said Mr Ewer last night, 'I calmed her down and told her she was overwrought.

'But she was so convinced about what she had seen that I went into the cleaners later and talked to the manageress.

'She told me the man had bought a green suit in on 21 August to have a tear in the coat mended and the trousers tapered.

'He had called in that day to ask if it was ready. He gave the name J. Ryan and an address in St John's Wood.'

Neither Mr Ewer nor the police knew then that Jimmy Ryan was an alias of James Hanratty and that, immediately after the murder, he stayed in the road named with his friend Charles 'Dixie' France – only a mile away from the cleaners.

Said Mr Ewer: 'So convinced was I about what Janet had seen that I vowed then to search for the man myself. I had to find him again.'

Then, almost miraculously, came COINCIDENCE No. 2.

Next day Mr Ewer walked 47 paces from his shop to the Fal a Fal café in Finchley Road.

As he sat drinking a cup of tea and pondering the almost hopelessness of the A6 murder he spotted a pair of hand-made Italian shoes.

'My eyes travelled upwards to a well-cut blue suit. Then I found myself staring into those blue eyes again. It was the same man.

'As I recognized him he got up to leave and walked out. I let him go but followed discreetly.

'I was just in time to see him cross Finchley Road and go into a shop in Northways Parade.

'I thought it was a photographer's. I raced over. But the photographer, an ex-policeman, said no one had been in.

'I used his phone to ring Scotland Yard. That is how much I was convinced by Janet's intuition.

'A Squad car arrived. I introduced myself and told the police the story.

'They made inquiries at all the shops on the parade until they came to Cater's, the florists.

'The man had gone in there.

'He had placed an order but vanished before we got there.'

The florist, Mrs Dorothy May Morrell, said:

'The man came in on 1 September and said he wanted to send some roses to his mother.

'He ordered a dozen and asked us to send them to a Mrs Hanratty in Kingsbury.

'He bought a 3d greetings card to go with them and wrote, "Don't worry – everything's all right".'

'I thought there was something strange about him. I asked him, "What have you been up to?" He muttered something and walked out.

'When the police made inquiries I looked back through my records and found the same man had sent a bunch of gladioli to his mother during August.

'This was before the A6 murder. I remembered then that he wanted to send roses but could not afford them.'

A report was made to Scotland Yard. But the Murder Squad had never heard of Jimmy Ryan. They had never heard of the address in Kingsbury, which was the home of his mother.

But Bill Ewer could not rest. Almost daily he went out looking for the man with the staring eyes.

He walked into the shop of a business associate – 58-year-old Mrs Louise Anderson, who has an antiques business in Greek Street, Soho.

He chatted with her for a while, discussing the A6 murder.

He did not know that Hanratty, whom Mrs Anderson had befriended, had been in the shop only that morning.

As he spread his search further to the West End and the Elephant and Castle, Mr Ewer went one morning to Petticoat Lane.

He said, 'The police said the killer was a cockney. I thought that was a reasonable place to look for the man with the staring eyes.

'The police must have thought so too, for I recognized plain-clothes detectives posing as street photographers in the market but obviously looking out for the man.'

Yet on that very day Hanratty was in Petticoat Lane buying himself a new suit, shirt and tie.

He said, 'It only came out in court when Mr France was giving evidence. I checked my diary and found that I was there too looking for him on that very day.'[1]

That was the story. It was not, however, an isolated report. There was one, too, in the *Daily Mail*:

> A face made her gasp . . . Had she seen the killer?
> The face in the crowd that caught the eye of Janet Gregsten left her gasping. Was it, could it be, the face of the man who only eight days before had cold-bloodedly murdered her husband?
> She saw the blue, staring eyes when she looked suddenly out of the window of a tiny antique shop in Swiss Cottage.
> It was a flash of intuitive recognition.[2]

The report, written by Bernard Jordan, was a rather thin version of Duffy's, and contained virtually no additional information.

In subsequent years, both William Ewer and Janet Gregsten independently attempted to dismiss this story as an invention of the gutter press. According to *Who Killed Hanratty?*, Ewer told Paul Foot that he did recall 'chatting to the *Sketch* and *Mail* journalists after the conviction of Hanratty at Bedford', but described the story which appeared as 'a farrago of nonsense'; similarly, Janet Gregsten bluntly told me, 'I say that is absolute total nonsense . . . It's come out of Duffy's imagination, Bill [Ewer] wouldn't say that because there isn't any basis on which to say it.'[3]

However, if one thing is certain about this curious episode, it is that the press did not invent it. Years later, I tried to establish precisely what had occurred. It did not originally concern the *Sketch* journalist – ironically, Peter Duffy was not one of those involved – nor did it take place after the conviction. Early one evening, in the last week of the trial, George Hollingbery, of the *Evening News*, and Bernard Jordan were having a drink together in the King's Head, the pub affectionately known to all its patrons as the Merry Widows. Unusually, there were no other reporters present. William Ewer walked in and buttonholed them. 'We'd noticed this man at the outset,' said Hollingbery. 'He was always fussing, and taking a very keen interest in the trial the whole time. He was always there, and so that evening in the pub when he came up we knew who he was, but this was the first time that we'd actually spoken to him.'[4]

Hollingbery bought him a drink, and Ewer then regaled them with this tale. 'This came completely out of the blue. It was something totally new, and quite dramatic,' explained Hollingbery. 'Neither of us made a move, to make notes or anything, because we thought it might frighten him off. We just let him speak. When he'd gone, I said to Bernard, "We'd better get this down quick."

'Of course, being "top reporters", neither of us had a note-book at the time, so I can remember making a shorthand note of everything that he'd said, all over this cigarette packet. Then, we went straight back to the hotel and each of us wrote it out in longhand. We agreed we would keep it to ourselves; we knew we were on to a good thing.'

However, Jordan did not keep his part of the pledge. He and Peter Duffy were very good friends. They'd worked closely together on the entire A6 Murder investigation. When this happened, Jordan felt he couldn't leave him out in the cold. So he let him in on the story. Duffy was thrilled. Being a conscientious journalist, he checked it all out for himself. It seems that he asked Ewer and Janet to re-enact it for him and a *Sketch* photographer in the arcade – although Janet's role, as can be gauged from the fact that there are no direct quotes attributed to her, was a largely passive one.

(Hollingbery's own story never saw the light of day. By the time the *Evening News* was next published, on the Monday, both Sunday's and Monday's papers had already carried extensive trial reports, the story was getting stale and – the unkindest cut of all – Hollingbery's colleagues had scooped him.)

Almost five years later, Duffy was questioned by John Morgan for BBC1's *Panorama* about this story. He explained what happened, exactly as he had reported it, and continued:

Duffy: The police went back to those shops and they questioned everybody on the block. They went into the florist's and they found on that day, the day that Bill Ewer saw this man in the café, a man went into the florist's and gave his name as Ryan, Jimmy Ryan, and sent a dozen red roses to Mrs Hanratty.
Morgan: Does this seem to you an extraordinary coincidence that Mrs Gregsten, having only the identikit to go on, which doesn't really look very much like James Hanratty . . .
Duffy: Nothing like him . . .
Morgan: Should look out and discover a man who's eventually convicted of her husband's murder?
Duffy: It's something that's completely inexplicable. It's a tremendous coincidence and I've tried to explain it but I'm at a loss to explain how she was able to say, 'That was the man who killed my husband.'[5]

However strange, there was no apology there for the journalism, no suggestion that it may have been in error. Years later, Paul Foot also made inquiries; and, once again, was able to establish the accuracy of the secondary events – the police being called, the shopkeepers in the arcade being questioned. In 1971, the *Sunday Times* reported that Edmund King, the assistant in the photographer's shop, remembered Ewer going in. 'He was obviously very excited,' said Mr King. 'He was quite insistent, and asked to see in the back. I took him into the studio at the back. I'm a reasonably public-minded chap.'[6]

Yet, in one fundamental sense, the story is wholly misleading. Whatever happened in the Swiss Cottage arcade, nothing that occurred there set the police on Hanratty's trail. When the cartridge cases turned up at the Vienna Hotel, the one name the police had to link with the discovery was Durrant/Alphon. At that stage, Ryan/Hanratty did not feature at all, even though Nudds tried to lure the police in that direction. When Alphon was eliminated, the police were in the dark about the identity of Ryan.

The contemporaneous police inquiries that were conducted in response to Janet Gregsten's 'sighting' would have been carried out by local police, simply following a lead that, in their view, took them nowhere. Police records make it clear that during this period, within the first two weeks of the murder, sightings of possible suspects were being reported the length and breadth of the country. In some of these, police officers, hoping for that elusive break-through, would take statements which would then be passed on to the inquiry team; but it is doubtful whether many of these were ever considered significant enough to warrant the personal attention of Superintendent Acott.

The Swiss Cottage incident didn't even reach the stage where statements were taken. The suggestion in the *Sketch* report that 'a report was made to Scotland Yard ... but the Murder Squad had never heard of Ryan' may well be accurate; but the essential point is that no significance was attached to this incident at the time. Whatever happened at Swiss Cottage made no impact on the inquiry itself.

Whether or not the family *thought* they had put the police on to Hanratty: well, that's a different matter.

There are three other points of astonishing interest to emerge from this. First, it was remarkable that Mr Ewer knew one of the most controversial prosecution witnesses at the trial, Louise Anderson. They were in the same field of business, and she was described as an 'associate' of his. He even discussed the crime with her – at a time when there was no known suspect, but when Hanratty often visited her and she would regularly put him up for the night. Second, Mr Ewer seemed to be unusually au fait with police matters. It is true that a number of local shopkeepers might have been aware that the owner of the photographer's used to be a policeman; but would the average citizen have so confidently recognized the plain-clothes detectives in Petticoat Lane? Third, Hanratty had, during this period, mentioned that he thought he was being followed – on the face of it, a bewildering and absurd perception. This account appeared to bear out that in fact he *was* being followed.

It is difficult now to gauge the exact state of contemporary public opinion when the trial ended. Certainly, there was apprehension – but this was primarily felt by those who had some close or first-hand knowledge of the case, whether they were lay observers (like Jean Justice and Dr David Lewes) or members of the press or the legal profession.

Amongst the latter, there were some who believed that there was never even sufficient evidence on which the magistrates could have committed Hanratty for trial, and considered it alarming that he should now have been found guilty and sentenced to death after a trial containing any number of bizarre features. Yet this unease was, for the most part, latent.

I also believe that there were perhaps many thousands – lone, voiceless individuals – who understood that something was seriously awry but were in no position to do anything about it. Hanratty's prison correspondence and events at the appeal and the execution to some extent bear this out. The perception and discernment of ordinary people should never be underestimated.

It was, however, unlikely that the public en masse ever harboured a moment's doubt. After all, it was widely believed that the police wouldn't arrest someone unless he'd done it, and that the trial process then worked smoothly to convict the guilty. Nor would any doubts have filtered through. One of the problems with the reporting of criminal cases is that once the verdict has been delivered and the press has run its post-trial 'backgrounders', it's as though a heavy curtain is drawn. The whole affair is instantly ignored – more so today, even, than then, when at least the post-trial stages followed in relatively quick succession. In this instance, two were scheduled: the appeal, and the execution.

In the same edition of the *Sketch* that carried the 'She Saw Him At The Cleaners' article, the paper reported Janet Gregsten's vehement opposition to hanging. She was quoted as saying, 'It's against my principles – it isn't civilized', and that she did not wish Hanratty to be hanged. The paper added that one of the factors which could influence the decision of the Home Secretary, R. A. 'Rab' Butler, in determining whether or not to grant a reprieve was 'the wide belief that the death penalty is to be abolished before long'.

Newspapers of this period regularly reported calls from Church leaders and other groups for abolition. In fact, in February 1956, on a free vote, the House of Commons passed a resolution, 'That this House believes that the death penalty no longer accords with the needs or the true interests of a civilized society'. The bill for abolition then passed all its stages in the Commons, but suffered defeat in the House of Lords.

As a result, fresh legislation was enacted in March 1957. The Homicide Act introduced the concept of 'capital murder', thus limiting the categories of murder for which the death penalty could be imposed. The type of murder in the A6 case – by shooting – unfortunately fell unequivocally within the new definition of 'capital murder'; and capital murder necessitated capital punishment.

In April 1948 – and indeed on countless other occasions down the years – the Commons was reassured that there was no possibility whatever of an innocent man being executed because the Home Secretary would invariably recommend a reprieve where there was even 'a scintilla' of doubt. Few could pretend that the doubts in this case did not amount to something considerably more substantial than a scintilla. Indeed, the press quoted 'top lawyers' as being sceptical of the need for the gallows in this case, for that very reason: 'the evidence contained an element of doubt too great to warrant execution'.

Nevertheless, Kleinman and the defence would have been more than foolish to sit back and put their trust in bureaucratic honour. They knew they had to redouble their efforts. With the end of the trial, it was now possible for newspapers to publish photographs of Hanratty; and they all did. In view of this, Kleinman was hopeful that more people might remember having seen him at the critical time and come forward to say so. He appealed publicly to the 'clerky gent', the man whom Hanratty sat next to when travelling from Euston to Liverpool, the man with the initial 'E' engraved on his cuff-links. Kleinman was disappointed in that respect – as far as is known, the man never did identify himself – but there was some consolation when Michael da Costa contacted the defence. He said he had been on the same train from Euston, albeit not in the same compartment, and remembered having seen a man he thought was Hanratty. As an actor, da Costa recognized dyed hair, and knew how uncommon it was to see a man with dyed hair.

Joe Gillbanks continued to make progress in Rhyl, speaking to and taking statements from Ivy Vincent and Margaret Walker. They lived in a small, very narrow street of newer houses behind Kinmel Street. Gillbanks established that Walker, on that fateful day, 'was in her favourite position at her front gate, surveying the street'. Her dog was with her, when 'a young man came up the street'. He asked if she could put him up for bed-and-breakfast for a couple of nights. She could not, so she sent him across the street to Mrs Vincent. She, too, had no room: 'I told him to go further up and if he was not successful to try the houses in Kinmel Street' (of which Ingledene was one).

Margaret Walker was the vital witness here. She had also gone to the police while the trial was still in progress, and it is a matter of great regret that no jury ever heard her. As a witness, she carried immense authority. Her original statement, which was sent to Scotland Yard, has never been released, but she told Gillbanks that 'I have seen the photographs of James Hanratty in the weekend papers and they are very much like that young man.' She was, in fact, naturally circumspect – no one could be absolutely sure about a fleeting event of months earlier. However, the detail which she did remember was highly persuasive. She recalled that 'his hair was dark, but there was something not quite natural about it as though it was streaky or tacky'. Also, she could be certain, by reference to a family event which occurred that week, of the precise date: Tuesday, 22 August.

Christopher Larman now came forward. Having made his statement to police before the end of the trial, he was astute enough to realize that they had no intention of doing anything at all about what he regarded, correctly, as potentially crucial eyewitness testimony. So he took the initiative of contacting the defence himself. This is what he originally said, in the statement made to police prior to the jury's verdict but first made available to defence solicitors some twenty-nine years later:

'As I left the Whynstay Hotel at approximately quarter-past seven, a man asked me if I knew a place where he could get bed-and-breakfast. He was aged twenty-eight to thirty, about one inch taller than me, which makes him 5 feet 6 inches. He was of medium build, clean-shaven, there was nothing unusual about his complexion. He was not wearing a hat and I noticed his hair was black, but as he walked away from me with the sun shining on it, his hair had a bronze effect in parts of it.

'I had met a Mrs Jones, and directed this man to her boarding-house by pointing out to him the Windsor Hotel which is painted black and white. I told him that Mrs Jones's place was right opposite. The man walked off in that direction and that was the last I saw of him. He was not carrying a bag of any kind.

'The other day I saw a photograph of a woman in the newspapers which I recognized as Mrs Jones. Up to that time, I had not been interested in the A6 Murder case, but seeing her picture started to read it. The incident of the man asking me for bed-and-breakfast came back into my mind and I decided to tell the police about it.'

Larman could also remember the date precisely – because he was in the process of leaving Rhyl, to set up home in the south, and had to take money out of his Post Office savings account. He still had the account book to provide supporting documentary evidence.

These statements amounted to important testimony which contained several mutually corroborating points. Both Walker and Vincent, for example, were adamant that the man asked for bed-and-breakfast for two nights. According to all three witnesses – Walker, Vincent and Larman – the man was not carrying a suitcase; Mrs Walker remembered him standing with his hands in his pockets.

If these people had been inventing statements to save an evil convicted murderer from the gallows (which, however risible, appeared to be the prosecution viewpoint), then they might logically have been expected to say that the man was carrying a suitcase. The fact that they said he had no luggage was a detail not likely to have been invented. Moreover, it was an accurate observation.

What had happened, as the Jones family confirmed, was that when Hanratty first called at Ingledene, he was told it was full (not surprisingly, as it was); but Mrs Jones, being a kindly soul, allowed him to leave his case there while he made further inquiries among neighbouring houses. When those proved fruitless, she could not turn him away and decided to take him in anyway. So Hanratty was for a time making inquiries without his suitcase. (It is, of course, possible that when Larman directed him to Mrs Jones, Hanratty had already found Ingledene for himself, but was characteristically too reticent to mention that.)

This area of testimony is consistent and persuasive. Further, it was clear that there were three witnesses – da Costa, Larman and Margaret Walker – who had specifically and spontaneously mentioned the unusual appearance of this man's hair. This stood in complete contrast to the testimony of the witnesses to the gunman, none of whom had noticed any unexpected feature about the hair.

A number of other statements were furnished to police. Someone at New Scotland Yard sent a message dated 18 February to the inquiry team as follows:

'May we have guidance and instructions please in respect of the following: we have received two phone calls – one from Dorset, one from Liverpool. Having seen the photo of Hanratty, they say he did not commit the murder. We also had one caller at New Scotland Yard to the same effect.'

He was told to take statements and forward them to Detective Superintendent Acott. What information they may have contained, we do not know. It is evident, however, that in the wake of Hanratty's photograph appearing in the papers there was a public response and potential witnesses contacted the police. Because the defence was never informed, the credibility or otherwise of this testimony has never been independently assessed.

*

On Wednesday 21 February Jean Justice had telephoned the Regent Palace Hotel, but Alphon told him he was unable to see him. They did, however, make arrangements to go to the dog-racing at the White City the following evening.

Alphon regularly used the phone, and often in the small hours of the morning. Even at this stage, Justice and Fox began to associate him with telephone harassment. One of those who mysteriously received a series of calls was, in fact, Alphon's own solicitor, H. MacDougal, and his wife. She was pestered with calls from someone claiming to be the barrister Jeremy Fox. When Mac-Dougal rang Fox's chambers to remonstrate, he realized at once that Fox was not the man making the nuisance calls. This was probably one of Alphon's less serious japes.

In the event, on the Thursday, Alphon went to the White City unaccompanied, but Jean and Frank Justice saw him afterwards, at the hotel at about midnight. Alphon said he had something really interesting to show Justice, 'a fantastic drawing'.

He invited them up to his room, but they declined, and asked him to bring it down to the lounge. It was very carefully wrapped in cellophane. When he saw it, Justice could at first make neither head nor tail of it. Alphon teasingly suggested that the drawing was given to him on behalf of 'Willoughby', who lived in Half Moon Street.

It was a drawing or a graphic, with black lines criss-crossing, scribbled apparently at random across a sheet of paper. However, it turned out to be a bewildering word-game, with the seeming confusion masking a message. By holding it at various angles and looking at it in a certain way, Justice eventually began to understand. 'It took me twenty minutes to see it,' he wrote. Then the confusion cleared and he could pick out words distinctly from the jumble of black lines. Held one way, it read: 'murderer' with, at the bottom, 'Bedford'; held the other way, it read 'Peter MacDougal'. Alphon had by this time abandoned the 'Durrant' pseudonym, and had booked in at the Regent Palace under his solicitor's surname.

On Saturday, 24 February, the four of them – the Half Moon Street Irregulars and Alphon – went to the White City. Afterwards they dined again at the Ox-on-the-Roof and then went back to the Regent Palace. While sitting drinking in the lounge, Justice asked Alphon to show Fox the drawing. As he put it on a table for him to examine, Justice stepped in and seized it. Justice and Fox then began to understand something of Alphon's unstable personality, and that his mood and character could change instantly; he was furious. After considering his course of action, he stood up. 'I understood him to say that this meeting would be the final one,' wrote Fox, 'and he left.' For days afterwards, Alphon would speak to neither Justice nor Fox, and refused to take any of their calls.

On Monday Justice lodged the drawing with his solicitors, but took the precaution of making photostat copies. He made an appointment at Scotland Yard for 11.00 the following morning. He and Fox were greeted by Chief Superintendent Kennedy, at that time the head of the Murder Squad, who examined the drawing from several angles. He said, 'Yes, I see it at once,' but was unimpressed. He just got angrier with them, before saying – in words which neither of them ever forgot – 'This is a lot of balls. You two men are on the fringe of interfering with the course of justice. Get out.'

Justice recalled, 'What registered in my mind was the veiled suggestion that we were rocking the boat, and that was why they were so hostile towards us.' The next day he telephoned Mac-Dougal, who confirmed that he was no longer receiving harassing calls, but asked them not to see his client again. Justice readily assented. The following day, however, he did see him again; and the next day, and the day after that. Even though Alphon affected to despise homosexuals, a relationship between the two men was developing.

'Quite unpredictably, the man whom I was leading on in the hope of extracting information gradually came to feel far more than mere friendship for me,' wrote Justice. 'I had certainly set out to pursue him, to flatter him perhaps, to introduce him to a sophisticated way of life that was completely alien to him. I had gone for walks with him and had often taken him to my flat. I had made no attempt to hide my very genuine interest in his character. There was a great deal about his behaviour and outlook that jarred on my sensibilities, but I found him so vital and versatile that I could easily forget his blemishes. I did not agree with many of his principles, but I enjoyed listening to his lively arguments.

'It was after I became aware of Peter's passionate regard for me that I began to see how I could undermine his defences. Just as a man will tell the woman he loves secrets he has never revealed to anyone else, so Peter might be persuaded to let me share some of the dark memories that I could plainly see were disturbing him from time to time. If I allowed him to think that I was wholly in his power, his "little girl" as he sometimes called me, then he might foolishly assume that he could confide in me without fear of betrayal. All I had to do was to convince him that I was as infatuated as he was.'

Justice and Fox began writing regular signed memos, to ensure that a documented record existed of all that was happening. Justice was aware that he was playing a dangerous game, by gulling someone with such an unpredictable temperament as Alphon.

On Monday, 12 March, he and Fox were disturbed by a number of telephone calls. From the other end of the line, they heard 'what could only be described as maniacal laughter – which went on without let-up for about four minutes'.

Justice had the call traced. It was made from a public call-box at Manor House underground station, which was very near Harringay dog stadium, where they believed Alphon was that evening (and, come to that, was also near the Alexandra Court Hotel, where Alphon had been staying when first questioned).

They were initially bewildered, but soon understood why Alphon may have been behaving in an especially hysterical fashion at that time. It was, after all, a very significant day in the case. It was the day that Hanratty's appeal began.

CHAPTER EIGHTEEN

> HM Prison
> St Loyes
> Bedford
> 10 March

Dear Mum,

Thank you for your lovely letter which I received today. It cheered me up a great deal. I'm looking forward to the appeal. I've waited a very long time for this day. I am a little bit concerned in the way that this appeal will be carried out. I do not know what really lies behind this case, but Mr Sherrard and Mr Kleinman have great faith as well as myself and that is all that matters. They cheered me up a great deal when I saw them. They are giving me every assistance possible.

You will no doubt wonder what I do during the day. Well, I play cards, draughts and talk to my warders. I must say that the staff has done everything in their power to make things as pleasant as possible in the circumstances.

I have been informed by the Governor that I will be leaving for London on Sunday morning, and will be staying at Pentonville prison while my appeal is heard. My clothing has been cleaned and pressed so I will look nice and smart. I will be wearing that nice white shirt you bought me for Christmas.

I'm glad that you and Dad will be at the Court with me because when a court is full of people and you know that there is someone there who has got great faith in you, it makes you relieved and confident, but I feel there will be a lot more people who will have the same feelings as ourselves.

I have had one or two letters from different people all expressing their faith in me and the outcome of the appeal. It is clear not only in here but to thousands of people that the jury has made a terrible mistake.

Before I forget, I would like you to thank Micky for the kind letter he sent me the other day. I also received some very nice letters from Eileen. Everybody has been so thoughtful towards me these last few weeks. I've *had some very nice letters and I wish you could read some of them, but I won't be allowed to hand them to you.*

I hope that this will be the last letter that you receive from me until we are all together again. Give my love and best wishes to Dad, and tell him not to look on the black side because everything is going to turn out alright.

Your loving son,
Jim

Like Hanratty himself, his family and friends had naturally invested all their hopes in the outcome of the appeal. The defence lawyers, however, would have counselled against optimism, understanding that it was unlikely to be efficacious.

The Court of Appeal traditionally sees itself as having two priorities: the first is to uphold the decision of the lower court; and the second is to move on without much ado to the next case. That might seem unusually cynical, but it is a view which most lawyers would share, at least privately. Very rarely will an appeal court interfere with an assize or Crown Court decision. In fact there is genuine surprise amongst the public at how difficult it is to base an appeal on what is seemingly the most fundamental ground (he didn't do it, my Lord). The reason is that in practice appeal court judges will always conclude that matters of fact are for a jury to determine; the appeal court exists merely to ascertain – and invariably to underline – that the law has been properly administered. When a case goes to appeal it is not, as some have claimed, that the goal-posts have been moved, but that the distance between them has been narrowed to a mere crack.

Thus an appeal at first instance will be successful only if it can be demonstrated that there has been some legal flaw in the trial process, perhaps because of some misapprehension on the part of the judge. The scandalous unfairness in capital cases, of course, was that an appellant was only going to get an appeal at first instance; not for him personally the luxury of being able to present renewed grounds of appeal in future years.

Accordingly, when the A6 Murder case went to appeal, the factor that had earlier been to Hanratty's advantage – the conspicuous fairness of Mr Justice Gorman in his conduct of the trial – now became a crushing disadvantage. The Lord Chief Justice, Lord Parker, who heard the appeal together with Mr Justice Ashworth and Mr Justice Fenton Atkinson, described the summing-up as 'not only fair, but favourable' to Hanratty. He emphasized that it was 'as one would expect from this judge, a very, very conscientious task and a job well done'. Realistically, all knew it was impossible to disagree.

The defence tried; the defence strained every nerve and muscle – Sherrard spoke in all for seven hours twenty minutes – but the arguments lacked real force. There were four main grounds of appeal: (1) that the jury's verdict was unreasonable and could not be supported having regard to the evidence; (2) that the judge misdirected the jury as to the evidence and failed to sum up on issues raised in the trial; (3) that the defence was not fully or fairly put to the jury in the summing-up; and (4) that part of Detective Superintendent Acott's evidence of interviews with Hanratty was inadmissible.

The first three were unlikely to succeed, for the reasons given. Lord Parker further ruled that one could not draw any conclusions from the length of time the jury was out considering its verdict. In rejecting the fourth point, the Lord Chief Justice made it clear that he was swayed by the force of the identification evidence: 'The vital point for the jury was the evidence of the three witnesses of identification. Assuming that Detective Superintendent Acott is not to be believed at all, the case against Hanratty is not a jot weaker.'

There was some surprise that the defence did not try to utilize the mounting evidence of the Rhyl alibi. Here again, however, the lawyers faced a genuine problem: the judges were likely merely to conclude that the jury had heard this evidence at trial and, in reaching its verdict, rejected it. Further, bearing in mind the torrid cross-examination suffered by Mrs Jones, and her consequent poor performance as a witness (albeit under intolerable pressure), there was some concern that the use of this evidence could do more harm than good.

The appeal was dismissed in decisive fashion. Lord Parker told Graham Swanwick QC that it wasn't even necessary to hear any Crown arguments in rebuttal of the appellant's points, and then proceeded to deliver a thirty-minute judgment, saying that the Court could find no reason to interfere with the jury's verdict.

The public, not unreasonably, expect more of the country's great judicial institutions. When the appeal was rejected, there was some disquiet. Allan Lofts, of the *Sheffield Telegraph*, described what happened next:

An elderly, slightly built woman wearing an olive-green coat and flowered straw hat stood up in the crowded public gallery and screamed, 'It is not true. He didn't do it. You ought to ask the conductor on the 36 bus.' The woman continued to shout as the judges rose and left the court. Then she walked out with the other members of the public and disappeared in the crowd in the street outside.[1]

This astonishing incident was reported in every paper, so it wasn't a journalistic invention. It's always been one of the most mystifying aspects of the entire case. It takes a lot of nerve and passionate commitment to stand up in the daunting setting of those courts and harangue the judges; so this woman must have had some sound reason for feeling so goaded by the judges' decision that she needed to speak out. Yet no one has ever had the faintest idea who this woman was.

Although there were slight variations in the reported comments, Lofts's piece seemed the most authoritative. The implications of the lady's remarks were that she knew that Hanratty didn't do it; and she knew he didn't do it because of something to do with the bus conductor. For years this was taken to be a reference to Pamela Patt, the conductress on the 36A's morning run. She was not called to give evidence. However, her statement contained no vital information. Others, including a number of passengers, made statements which, again, revealed nothing. So what was it that this woman in the public gallery knew? Had the conductor during the afternoon run perhaps seen something that he kept to himself?

That this individual, anonymous woman was palpably correct – at a point when the criminal justice process, the police and the press were all deluded – merely provides additional cause for wonder. The mystery, however, remains unresolved.

Lofts reported that, in court, 'Hanratty's mother, with tears streaming down her face, echoed the words, "He didn't do it."' Outside the courts, Mr and Mrs Hanratty talked to reporters. Mary again affirmed her son's innocence; and James commented, 'So far in this business Jimmy has been like a man whose luck has run out at cards. Every deal he has had was a bad one. But it isn't over yet.'

Defiant words, but in reality the grounds for optimism were wafer-thin. The problem was that the appeal was virtually Jimmy's last hope, even if that was no hope at all. At the time, the judicial process was not the interminable sequence of applications for review and leave to appeal, of references to courts in one jurisdiction or another, that it has since become in Britain and, especially, in America. The judicial process then consisted simply of trial and appeal. It was finite in more than one sense. All that now stood between Hanratty and his fate was a plea for a reprieve to the Home Secretary.

CHAPTER NINETEEN

THE RULING REGARDING the timing of executions was laid down in some dusty regulation: they took place on the first Wednesday after three clear Sundays had elapsed from the end of the last judicial hearing. Accordingly, the Home Office announced after the failure of the appeal that the execution was now set for Wednesday, 4 April.

HM Prison
St Loyes
Bedford
17 March

Dear Mum & Dad,
I feel sure things will still go in my favour. I was very disappointed last week. I feel quite sure, and I said this last week and I say it again, that somebody somewhere knows the truth and will come forward. Mum, I never knew it would end like this, what have I done to deserve this? Only you and Dad with your faith in me keep me going. How can one imagine what it is like to experience something like this? I wake up every morning and it seems like a dream and I pray that one morning I will awake and it will not be a dream any longer.

I hope you will understand why I haven't asked you and Dad to visit me, because I love you so much and it is too much of a strain for me seeing you under these circumstances.

I have just been visited by the priest, and we had a nice little talk together. He informed me that he has been in contact with my solicitor, and he has got up a petition in Bedford for me. He has great faith in me, and so have a great many more people. I am now going to write to Mr Butler, the Home Secretary, hoping he will consider my case carefully and come to a favourable decision.

From your loving son,
Jim

The *Daily Express* carried a front-page report that Joanna Kelley, the Governor of Holloway, the women's prison in north London, had telephoned Scotland Yard about the case, saying that a prisoner had information about the gun used in the killing. Detectives went to the prison and took a statement. Again, this may have been the kind of inconsequential lead that could occur in any case; what was extraordinary about this one was that there seemed a proliferating number of pieces of potential additional evidence; could they all be inconsequential leads?

In the wake of the dismissal of Hanratty's appeal, there were yet more remarkable occurrences. First, Peter Alphon wrote to the *Daily Express* saying that he would support any petition to the Home Secretary for a reprieve. 'I've studied the case very closely,' wrote Alphon, in a letter that the *Express* gladly published, 'and I believe Hanratty is innocent. There has been so much confusion and doubt in this extraordinary case that I'm prepared to do all in my power to seek a reprieve.'

Others who had studied the case closely had tentatively concluded that Alphon himself might know much more about it than Hanratty; so if Alphon was prepared to say publicly that he thought Hanratty didn't do it – well, just what was he saying?

The second development was the suicide of Charles France. The appeal was dismissed on Tuesday; it was reported on Wednesday; and on Thursday France disappeared. In the afternoon, Charlotte received a brief letter, posted that same morning, saying, 'Tell the children I was a good Dad to them.' Charlotte became understandably alarmed, contacted the police, but by the time they found France it was too late.

On Thursday evening he had taken a bed-sit in a small boarding-house in Second Avenue, Acton, west London. He went out to buy some writing-paper, returned to his room and was never seen alive again. He simply laid his head by a small gas-pipe and turned it on. He had written a great deal – the landlady said there were 'about 100 pages lying loose around the room' – but unfortunately it was the police who found him. They took away all these deathbed writings, most of which have never been disclosed to any independent source. A few have been publicly revealed (one was published in full in the *Sunday Times* a decade later). On the evidence of these it appears that, although Charles France himself may have held the key to what happened, it is unlikely that these last letters did.

The *Sunday Pictorial* that week published a lengthy interview with Charlotte France. Earlier in the year, France had twice attempted suicide. On this occasion, one of the matters apparently causing additional heartache was the article he was contracted to write for the *Pictorial*. So this piece, in which Charlotte attempted to explain why her husband had found the emotional strain too much, had particular poignancy:

> The ordeal of that horrible trial was bad enough. But what came afterwards was Hell on earth. There were the nightmares. My husband seemed to see Hanratty's pale, leering face in every room. Wherever he went, the shadow of the killer was there. He couldn't stop talking about him. In the night he would cry, 'Why did I let him into my home?'
>
> Something happened to Dixie when he discovered the truth about Hanratty. He became a different man. He could not sleep, could not rest. He kept on talking about the killer. He felt guilty about inviting him into our home. He thought he had done us all a terrible injury. We pleaded with him that it was not his fault. But he would not listen.[1]

The problem with this was that, like the presumed content of his letters, it didn't convincingly explain why Dixie had been so stressed. 'When he discovered the truth about Hanratty': what truth was this? After all, whether he had committed the crime or not, Hanratty had done no injury at all to Charles or his family (it was unlikely that France knew anything of the escapade with Carole); on the contrary, relations always seemed to be convivial. All had spoken up for his character in the witness-box. The article, however, did offer one clue: 'There were the threats. Voices on our telephone that we didn't recognize. They said, "If Hanratty dies, you die."'

This was intriguing, bearing in mind that someone closely associated with the case – someone who, unlike Hanratty, actually did have a pale, leering face – was fast developing a reputation for telephone harassment. In fact, Justice rang Alphon to tell him the news that France had committed suicide. Alphon immediately responded, 'That's made my day.' Yet even those who did not perceive these undercurrents of the case should have recognized that this event, which the *Daily Mirror* headlined as 'A6 Witness Death Riddle', added yet another perplexing feature to an already tortuous case.

Several of that Sunday's newspapers expressed unease, for a variety of reasons, about the forthcoming execution. The *Observer* carried much material about Hanratty's mental capacity, revealing that at the age of fifteen doctors had thought him a mental defective. Ironically, if Hanratty had committed the offence then he would have been able to run this as a defence, and would almost certainly have escaped the ultimate penalty. Yet he had instructed his lawyers that he was to be defended on the basis that he had not carried out the crime; accordingly, his mental capacity was not raised at any stage of the judicial process.[2]

The *Sunday Express* had an interesting exclusive. Father John Hughes, of the Church of the Holy Child Jesus in Bedford, had visited Hanratty in the condemned cell, and taken his confession. Although such matters should remain strictly confidential, Hughes made it ringingly clear that Hanratty did not feel the need to confess anything to do with the A6 crime: 'He could confess to me in absolute privacy, knowing that what he said would be a secret for ever. But knowing him and on the evidence of the trial, I do not believe it can happen because I firmly believe in James Hanratty's innocence. We can only pray that justice will still be done.'[3]

Hughes added that Hanratty was fit and well, and 'talks intelligently'. He explained that he had declined to see a number of visitors, including his mother. 'He tells me that she would become upset and he, naturally, would want to comfort her, and that would be impossible through a glass screen.'

There was a second story that week in the *Sunday Pictorial* – the only interview that Janet Gregsten ever gave for publication. She had spoken to Harry Ashbrook, a journalist who was in fact a longstanding family friend. Even at this stage, the piece was a public relations job, designed not to reveal the truth but to present a still delicate situation in the least damaging light. It did, however, contain the first public acknowledgement of friction in the Gregsten family, with the admission that Michael had spent two periods living apart from his wife and children.

He loved me and he loved his children, but the demands the outside world made on him were too heavy. But I did not lose faith in him. I felt that our marriage could withstand this, that it was strong enough to outlast temporary infatuations. I knew that all the time he was away, Michael was trying to break free from his commitments and come home. Michael's motor-rally friends came at weekends to see us because it was so difficult for me to get out of the house with the young children. Valerie Storie was one of those friends. We had a long talk. I told her frankly of our troubles and difficulties. I felt I had to protect the children from any hint of scandal.

Michael and I decided that we would make a clean break. We would leave Abbot's Langley and set up a new home in the north. And there would be no more distractions. We would have a fair chance to reshape our life together, and our children would grow up in a secure and loving home. And then this cruel blow. As our plans were maturing, Michael was savagely murdered.

It was said that Michael was having a clandestine affair at the time of the shooting. This was a cruel lie. I deplore the methods used and the liberties taken to publish such untruths. Michael and I had come to terms with each other. We were united in our love and marriage.[4]

This account was, I regret to say, composed essentially of untruths. It's always easy enough to accuse the newspapers of publishing falsehoods. The 'cruel lie' to which Janet Gregsten referred was, of course, the absolute truth.

As these various stories were appearing in the Sunday newspapers, there was another bewildering incident involving Alphon, who had returned to his hotel in the early hours of Sunday morning after a long Saturday evening at Half Moon Street. 'He left about two,' remembered Justice, 'he'd had a few Guinnesses, but he certainly wasn't drunk, yet he was behaving in a most peculiar way.' Although it's not clear what happened, he was involved in an incident with a chambermaid, who fainted. The hotel representative who was called, Cyril Potter, tried to attend to her and asked Alphon to leave. He replied, 'I'm fucking well going, but you don't know who I am.' Alphon went downstairs to the lobby. Two policemen arrived, apparently in response to a call from Alphon himself, and found him in a telephone booth, trying to speak to Superintendent Acott at Scotland Yard. He then telephoned his solicitor, and told him that he was being beaten up by two policemen. The officers had not laid a hand on him; but they then marched him to the door and arrested him outside in Glasshouse Street, on a drunk-and-disorderly charge. (You couldn't be drunk-and-disorderly indoors, only outside.)

He appeared at Bow Street on 19 March, when he was remanded on bail. He appeared again on 27 March, when the police requested another adjournment, to 3 April, the day before Hanratty's execution was scheduled to take place. It then became clear that the charge could not be sustained, as two doctors testified that Alphon was not drunk at the time. The magistrate accordingly dismissed the charge, but was clearly not happy with what he described as Alphon's 'completely lunatic and unstable behaviour', and told him he had to pay his own costs.

HM Prison
St Loyes
Bedford
21 March

Dear Mum & Dad,
How are you both keeping? I hope you are both in good health, as with this weather which we are having now there are plenty of colds about.

The Governor has stopped my papers, as the news that was being published in them was causing me some disturbance, as it is bad enough being in here without reading articles which upset you and make things much worse. I didn't know about Mr France until I read it in your letter, as I am away from the other fellow men and the officers that are present with me are not allowed to discuss matters that refer to my case.

I am a little bit anxious about my concern, and I would never have learnt about Mr France if you had not told me, so please forgive me for not writing such a pleasant letter this time.

Give my love to all the family,
Jim

HM Prison
St Loyes
Bedford
22 March

Dear Mum,
I said yesterday I would write you a nice letter today and not talk about the case. There isn't a lot I can say. Yesterday was a bit of a strain. After washing my hair regular in here, my hair is nearly back to its normal colour, though it's falling out. It's enough to make any man's hair fall out, what I have been through. Last night I had a very nice half-hour listening to the football match between Spurs and Benfica. I don't know what I would do without my little wireless. You know I don't care much for reading. I don't think I mentioned it in my letter to you yesterday, but I wrote to Sister Catherine and also a letter to the Pope in Rome. I sent it by air-mail as I feel it would reach there much quicker this way.

Your loving son,
Jim

Jean Justice was always scheming, probing, and attempting, with an increasing sense of urgency, to understand what had happened. Though their relationship was decidedly mercurial, there was a deepening affection between him and Alphon. Justice wrote: 'I used to meet him at one o'clock in the King's Arms at Shepherd Market. He would be sitting there on his own, reading the *Greyhound News*. He would invariably buy me a large Amontillado. Then, hands clasped in token of the deep bond between us, we would talk.

'From the King's Arms, we used to stroll down to Piccadilly and make for Fortnum and Mason, where we always ordered the soup.' Then, in the evenings, 'Night after night in my flat, Peter and I would listen to his favourite pop records, drink Guinness and go over the details of the A6 Murder.'[5]

Justice hit on a new plan. He and Fox decided to take Peter Alphon to the area where the crime had started. Accordingly, in the early evening of Tuesday, 20 March, the three of them headed west out of London. On the way there, Alphon insisted on stopping for a drink. 'The first thing that struck me', recalled Justice, 'was that he seemed to know his way round Slough. He said to us, "Don't park here, there's a pub round the corner." The pub was near the Uxbridge Road, where the Slough greyhound stadium was. Alphon gave the impression that he knew both the pub and the stadium very well.'

From there, they went to the Old Station Inn at Taplow. Fox ordered a Tio Pepe sherry and Alphon had a Guinness. As they were leaving, Justice managed to linger behind to have a discreet word with the landlady, Mrs Lanz. He asked if she recognized either of his two friends. Yes, she said, she did: 'the one with the Guinness'. She recognized him, she said in a statement to police, as 'a man who had previously been in the bar. I cannot remember when I have seen him previous to this; I just know that I have seen him before.'

They then went for dinner at the Hindshead Hotel in Bray, although by this time Justice was overcome with a sense of foreboding and had lost his appetite. Nevertheless, he determined to stick to his plan, and afterwards they headed back towards Dorney Reach. It was completely dark, but Justice became aware that it was Alphon who was providing directions: 'He would say, "Go right here, now there's a horseshoe, it's a winding road." And suddenly: "Stop here."' Fox, who was driving (and always maintained that he could never be totally certain which of his passengers had said that), turned into an opening. 'There was this vast field before us,' explained Justice. 'I just had a terrible feeling about the way Alphon was acting. He had sort of come alive, and was in a very peculiar mood.'

It was nearly midnight. Fox got out of the car and, bizarrely, set out to stride across the field, saying, 'My mother said I should take more exercise.' Alphon tried to drive the car, but crashed the gears, didn't succeed in moving it and soon gave up. He then went to join Fox.

Justice was overcome. 'Terror gripped me. I sprinted along the road until I reached a small cottage (the one, I found out later, where Valerie Storie saw the bicycle being put away). I banged on the door again and again, but nobody appeared. If the occupants of the next house had not answered my frenzied knocking, I think I should have blacked out.' The owner took out his dog and escorted Justice back, trying to calm him down. Fox remained unflustered: 'I have no idea what sort of help he thought we needed; we weren't in any danger.'

Retrospectively, however, he understood the reason for Justice's alarm. 'I'm sure it was while we were there that he became utterly convinced. As I drove back to London, he was obviously very depressed. He sat in the back and didn't say a word.'

At that moment, they had no real idea of exactly where they had been. No outsider knew exactly where the A6 crime had originated; there were no photographs in the papers. Prior to running off, Justice had had the presence of mind to place a Guinness bottle under the hedge by the car. Afterwards they made contact with Tony Mason, the local freelance journalist who had assiduously reported the case from the locality. He was one of the few people apart from the police who did know precisely where the Morris Minor had been parked. On the following Sunday, 25 March, he met them for the first time and took them to the field. They had been in the right spot; the Guinness bottle still under the hedge confirmed it.

Justice had initially considered Alphon a strange and immature personality. He further reckoned that he might well know something about the crime. Now it all added up to a much more disturbing picture. 'It was a combination of three factors: there was the drawing; his patterns of behaviour; and then that evening. On a misty March evening in the dark, he was able to direct Fox and myself without difficulty to the exact location, which hardly anyone was aware of. I thought, this really is weird.'

Two other factors were almost immediately added to those. First, when they met him, Mason had an interesting story to relate about Michael Fogarty-Waul, a local man, who lived in a caravan at Pecks Farm, Marsh Lane. He told Mason of his surprise that, when the photograph of the convicted man (Hanratty) was finally published in the press, it was not that of a man he had seen in Marsh Lane, Taplow.

Fogarty-Waul said that on a Tuesday evening about two weeks before the murder – or, actually, since it was about 1.00 a.m., a Wednesday morning – as he turned from the Bath Road into Marsh Lane, he saw a man walking down the lane. He offered him a lift. The man was wearing a blazer, and also a short raincoat; he said something about going to the dogs. When they reached the farm, the man got out and continued walking down Marsh Lane, in the direction of the cornfield. Fogarty-Waul formed the opinion that he was 'a nut case'.

Later, he thought on the evening of 27/28 February, after he had been fishing in the river at the bottom of the cornfield, Fogarty-Waul noticed a man acting suspiciously by his car, and chased him off. He thought it was the same man he saw that evening in August. He noticed a kind of distinctive gait and further suggested that the man resembled the then popular actor, Sidney Tafler. This was interesting; others had commented that Alphon reminded them of Tafler.

Second, it emerged that the occupants of those two cottages who were disturbed by Justice's alarming behaviour went to see the police. They were told that it could not have been Alphon who was involved, because at the time he was in prison on a drunk-and-disorderly charge; even the Chief Constable of Buckinghamshire denied that Alphon was in the field. Yet that incident had happened on Sunday morning, and Alphon was not remanded in custody. The police, of course, knew how easy it was to discredit Justice and Fox. But Justice himself was perplexed: 'I was supposed to have been drunk, and Alphon not there at all. These are the sort of things that convinced me. Why was it important that Alphon wasn't there? Why did it matter? Why the lies?'

HM Prison
St Loyes
Bedford
27 March

Dear Mick,
Well, Mick, time is getting very short. I'm very worried about what my solicitor is doing on my behalf. I am not very impressed with the way he

is making his inquiries. I have got so much at stake. I would have felt
much better if Mr Sherrard had been my solicitor.

I am writing you this short note Mick to ask you if you would like to
have my car, as there is no one I would prefer to give it to other than you.
As you know, it is a lovely car. I am sending you a letter which I received
from the car-dealer enclosed with this. You will find the log-book in the
dashboard compartment. If you do have the car, it will please me very
much knowing that I left you with something, just to show how much you
really mean to me.

With that, Mick, I will close now, so please give my love to Mum,
Dad, Pete and Rich, and tell them I love them all.

From your brother,
Jim

During that last full week before the scheduled execution,
everyone concerned with the defence continued to behave, publicly,
with great dignity. In private, there were escalating feelings of
anxiety and horror. On Wednesday, 28 March, James and Mary
Hanratty took to the Home Office a bundle containing a 23,000-
signature petition and a collection of 300 personal letters to the
Home Secretary. They said that these were accumulating every
day, but that they could wait no longer to hand in the material.
Mary told reporters who gathered to report the event, 'Nearly
everyone we ask believes our son is innocent.'

Was this true? I think it probably was. There was at this stage,
over a month after the end of the trial, a clear dichotomy in
perceptions of the case. The judicial authorities, Parliament, the
police and, to some extent, the press: all were ranged against
Hanratty, and unquestioningly considered him guilty. Ordinary
people, however, seemed to have a more sophisticated understanding of the crime; open-minded members of the public put the pieces
together and realized that it did not add up to the same picture
that the authorities perceived. Tony Mason was one of those who
discerned this striking distinction at the time, and wrote: 'Although
those who are closely connected with the case, such as staff
journalists, say they are satisfied with Hanratty's guilt, there are
many people in the general area of Slough and Maidenhead, where
interest is high, who seem to take the view that Hanratty is innocent
of the crime.'

This is not to suggest that the press was clamouring for a
hanging. Far from it. For the widely acknowledged reasons (the
areas of doubt in the case; and the perception that state executions

were going, going and almost gone), the press advocated mercy.
'Every national newspaper that commented editorially', wrote Louis
Blom-Cooper, 'recommended a reprieve.'

So in those last days, popular support for Hanratty may have
been welling but it barely rippled the surface of public affairs.
Those actively working to stop the execution on the grounds of
miscarriage of justice were pitifully few. Apart from Hanratty's
family and his legal team, there were the Half Moon Street
Irregulars. They had co-opted Tony Mason, who in turn had
managed to enlist the support of his local MP, who happened to be
Fenner Brockway, one of the most ardent campaigners for the
abolition of capital punishment. He understood almost immediately
that the case was riddled with uncertainty, and that it was an ideal
focus for his particular preoccupation. The fact that even such a
natural ally as Brockway was recruited late in the day only
reinforced the impression that, however high-profile this case had
been for over seven months, there was consummate ignorance
about it in Government and parliamentary circles.

At a time when Hanratty's execution was less than a week away,
those actively campaigning for him could have comfortably fitted
into two London taxis.

There was, however, another lone voice who was furiously
active. This was Dr David Lewes, the consultant from Bedford
General Hospital who had excitedly gone to see the full majesty of
British justice in action and come away having witnessed a process
which he felt shamed the country.

From the outset, he was aware of a great pall of prejudice
hanging over the community. 'I was struck by the fact that a
number of highly intelligent men and women, including fellow
consultants, seemed to regard Hanratty as the murderer even
before he came to trial.' Bedford, he knew, was already notorious
as the town which had imprisoned John Bunyan for twelve years
for preaching without a licence. Lewes wanted to do all he could to
galvanize local opinion, to prevent another historic injustice for
which, he felt, the townspeople of Bedford would be to some extent
responsible.

Lewes wrote a lengthy memorandum, based on his eye-witness
analysis of the trial, and obtained permission to hold a meeting in
the hospital grounds. The event generated considerable interest
locally; Lewes sent out invitations to a wide range of professional
people. Then, at the last minute, he was told he had to cancel it.
No very good reason for the volte-face was ever given: 'It was

forbidden ostensibly because it was in hospital grounds and concerned a matter which was sub judice. Well, I didn't think it was sub judice, when Hanratty had already been condemned to death. It may well have been stopped on orders from the Home Office. We had no direct proof, but that was what many people believed.'

Lewes, in fact, was instructed to neither go ahead with the meeting nor make any statement at all regarding the case. Fortunately, he was unable to comply with the latter, having already dispatched a letter to his local newspaper, the *Bedfordshire Times*. This was published on Friday 30 March, and stands for all time as a document of extraordinary power and prescience:

> The Hanratty trial, the longest murder trial in British criminal history, lasted for 21 days. The transcript of the proceedings exceeded 620,000 words, and more than 60 witnesses appeared for the Crown. The judge's summing-up took 10 hours and the jury considered its verdict for more than nine-and-a-half hours. The reliability of the two most important Crown witnesses, Valerie Storie and Superintendent Acott, was questioned; other key witnesses had criminal records and Nudds was a self-confessed liar.
>
> To discover where the truth lay, amidst this vast array of deliberate distortion and frank perjury, honest but possibly mistaken recollections of months past and evidence of identification based on transitory recognition of an individual during brief moments of intense emotional disturbance must, for judge and counsel, have been a formidable task indeed. For the jury, the task must have been almost insuperable.
>
> After the preliminary hearing at Ampthill, certain newspapers by innuendo and a more vocal public by outspoken comment appeared convinced of Hanratty's guilt even before he came to trial. But a number of discerning and interested observers, who not only followed closely the local and national press reports but also attended the trial and heard the evidence, remain unconvinced of Hanratty's guilt.
>
> Whatever Hanratty's ultimate fate, it is confidently predicted that controversy about the correctness of the verdict will continue for months and years to come. Maybe vital fresh evidence bearing on the A6 murder will come to light; should this happen, one trusts it will not come too late as it did in the tragic case of Timothy Evans.
>
> If Hanratty be removed from the scene irrevocably and miscarriage of justice be subsequently proved, there will be no turning-back, no redress, no recall: only the heavy load of conscience

and remorse which every member of society will have with shame
to bear.[6]

After being rebuffed by Scotland Yard, Justice and Fox took
Alphon's drawing to the leading barrister, Christmas Humphreys
QC, who said he thought that it could be construed as a confession.
With this encouragement, they bundled it up, together with a
number of their statements and other material, and sent it all, via
their solicitor David Jacobs, for consideration with the mass of
Hanratty documentation now accumulating at the Home Office.
They naturally explained what they considered to be the significance of the Alphon drawing. The officials ignored it, but what
especially exasperated Justice was that, some weeks later, he
requested the return of the drawing. The Home Office responded
that this would not be possible as the drawing now formed 'part of
the records of the Department'.[7] Justice's view was that if the
document was trivial and irrelevant, then it could have been
returned; if it could not be returned, then that suggested that it was
neither trivial nor irrelevant and, as such, should have been heeded.

The main thrust of the last-ditch efforts naturally came from
Kleinman and Sherrard. They pointed out to the Home Secretary
that 'There is no class of evidence more liable to fall victim to the
frailties of human judgment than that relating to identity.' Such
evidence was made more difficult to evaluate 'by reason of its
coming from honest, unprejudiced witnesses'; and that the 'honest,
but mistaken' witness was a central problem for the criminal justice
process. As with so much else that was argued on Hanratty's behalf,
these remarks proved prophetic, as public disquiet about wrongful
convictions in identification cases escalated in the 1960s and 1970s.
Sherrard concluded his entreaties to the Home Secretary by saying,
'If my endeavours here are regarded as insufficient, would you
please be good enough to allow me to see you personally?'

Sherrard was invited personally to the Home Office.

As far as can be ascertained, Home Office case officials were
influenced by two particular areas of information. The first was the
'done the lot' phrase which was held to have that very specific
meaning, one which could have applied only to Hanratty. If they
did consider this information as of any significance at all, it could
only be because they hadn't read the background evidence for
themselves, otherwise they would have understood how meaningless, in reality, it actually was.

The other area was also remarkable. It was apparently believed that Langdale–Eatwell was reliable and credible evidence. Once again, they can only have reached this conclusion by not examining the material with the requisite thoroughness. Even more remarkably, however, they accorded it greater value as additional evidence which buttressed the Crown case *precisely because it had not been fully heard by the jury*. That was an extraordinary situation. Material not adduced at trial – inadmissible evidence, in fact – was being weighed in the scales against Hanratty. Nothing better illustrated the failings of the administrative process of reviewing criminal cases.

> *HM Prison*
> *St Loyes*
> *Bedford*
> *28 March*

Dear Mum,

Before I go any further, I would like to wish you a very happy birthday and also a very enjoyable Mother's Day. I have bought you a nice box of chocolates. I know your birthday is next week, so I have taken the opportunity of sending the card with the chocolates.

You and Dad have been working so hard. I would like to say I am so pleased with the way you have shown your courage all through this. I'm sure that no one could have done more than you and Dad. I feel that one day my name will be cleared without any doubt. With that knowledge there is no need for you and Dad to be ashamed of any gossip or any remarks of any sort. When eventually the truth does come to light, people will regret the remarks they have made about me.

I have sat here for the last three weeks and I still can't imagine that this is really true. I pray at nights that I will wake up and find that it is all over. When I lay here at nights, hour upon hour, night after night, and knowing that somewhere the person knows what I am going through. People today don't seem to have any conscience at all.

So, Mum, keep that old chin up and say that little prayer. I'm sure between the two of us our prayers will be answered.

From your loving son,

Jim

Kleinman wrote to the Hanratty family on Friday, 30 March. 'This weekend must be a great ordeal for you. I feel that not only has Jimmy acted courageously and with dignity, I also think that each of you have, and I know will continue to do so. Let us pray the Home Secretary will urge Jimmy's reprieve. I am sure the vast majority of people in this country will join with this.'

HM Prison
St Loyes
Bedford
1 April

Dear Mum,

Well, Mum, as you said I'm trying my utmost to keep myself together and this is the first time in my life I have acted like a man. I will do so until my name is cleared. I have only kept myself together knowing that I had you and Dad with me all the way and that I was innocent.

The wireless is on and I am listening to Family Favourites now, and I can just imagine you and Auntie Annie getting the dinner ready. The two officers who are with me now, when they were off duty, they went to the Bingo, the first night they had ever been, and they won £13 between them. They don't come from Bedford, they are special staff from other prisons. I feel, Mum, that they won't be with me much longer, and they will be going home to their wives and children.

I hope you and Dad are keeping your spirits up and not worrying too much. No matter what happens we know that the country has made a terrible mistake. If I was given the opportunity whilst the trial was on to explain in more detail, I'm sure that the verdict would have been different. I was in the witness-box for 10 hours and I answered every question truthfully and correctly, but it was a waste of time because they had already made their minds up. I knew in my own mind that was going to happen before I ever went up to Bedford, and I prayed at night that my case would be dealt with in London.

God bless you all,
Jim

1 April

Dear Mick,

Well, Mick, keep your chin up and whatever you do don't give up because it doesn't matter how long you wait, the truth will always come out. Look after Mum and Dad, as I have been so silly in the past. Me being the eldest son I should have had more sense. You will have to take care of them now.

Love
Jim

Was there mercy? Was there clemency? There was not. The prayers of those whom Kleinman described as 'the vast majority of people in the country' were not answered. On Monday, 2 April, there was an official announcement from the Home Office, to the effect that the Home Secretary, R. A. Butler, 'has most carefully considered all the circumstances of this case, but regrets that he has failed to discover any sufficient ground to justify him in advising Her Majesty to interfere with the due course of law'.

The timing of the Home Secretary's decision itself only further fuelled the controversy dogging the case. According to all media reports, the Home Secretary spent the weekend soul-searching about the case before reaching his decision. The *Daily Express* reported that he read the lessons at St James' church at Greenstead Green, near his home in Halstead, Essex. However, Justice and Fox, if not others, knew prior to the public announcement of the decision. A letter which reached Justice's solicitor by first post on Monday, informing him of the decision, was dated 31 March, and must have been posted on Saturday morning.[8]

By this stage, Justice was seeing Alphon daily. His grand plan, of course, was to secure a full confession from him. 'The sands were fast running out. We were working endlessly to save Hanratty from the gallows, but in spite of all our efforts, Peter made no move to confess.'

That day, something extraordinary happened. Audrey Willis, of Knebworth, Hertfordshire, the lady who was held up in the aftermath of the A6 crime, and who gave evidence about it at the trial, was ambushed again, by the same man, in entirely parallel circumstances. The once-in-a-lifetime incident had happened again.

She told police that at 12.50 p.m., he called again with a gun. 'I had to take off his shoes again. It was the same man – absolutely, definitely. One of the things that was so unnerving was that he knew his way around, he knew where the stairs were. I can remember my clothes going up and down because my heart was beating so fast.'

He again asked for a drink, but on this occasion wanted not milk but sherry. He again asked for money, and she was forced to leave Hugh, her baby son, downstairs with him while she went upstairs to get some. This time, she found £3 8s. 'He never made any sexual advances, or did anything inappropriate like that. He was much more sure of himself the second time, he was slightly showing off. The gun – he kept waving it in Hugh's direction – wasn't wobbling.'

He made sure that she washed and dried his glass very carefully. He then left, but as he was leaving said to her, 'You and I will have a smile on Wednesday morning, knowing that it is the wrong man. You and I know who did it, don't we?' He then added, 'Look into my eyes – they are blue, aren't they?' He then disappeared.

If nothing else, the timing of the incident seemed especially intriguing. There was something else that puzzled the alert Hertfordshire police officer who conducted inquiries into this incident. As he reported, 'I reminded Detective Superintendent Elwell that as far as I knew the first release to the public that Hanratty's reprieve had been refused was given on the 1.00 p.m. BBC News today, so how does Mrs Willis account for the remark made by the man at 12.50?'

Audrey Willis was initially anxious, lest this gunman was the murderer, and wondered whether the country was about to hang the wrong man. The police, however, set her mind at rest. 'I do remember two quite senior officers coming. I can remember them standing in front of the fireplace; one was quite fatherly towards me. They assured me that they hadn't got the wrong man, they were quite certain they had got the right man. And I was convinced by them.'

So, was the returning intruder Peter Alphon? It was certainly true that Alphon disappeared early that morning. Justice recalled that 'He said he had to see someone on business.' Of course, if the re-enacted incident was designed in some way to forestall the execution, it might have seemed more pointed to carry it out the day before; Alphon, however, would have been unable to do that as he was bound to answer his drunk-and-disorderly charge in court that day.

The whole matter clearly created some perplexity at Scotland Yard. The Willis file was not immediately available – by some quirk of bureaucratic efficiency (for which the case was not otherwise noted) it had been sent back to Hertfordshire constabulary on 6 March. Bedfordshire officers found a file, however, and arranged to *post* it to Sergeant Oxford at Scotland Yard.

HM Prison
St Loyes
Bedford
2 April

Dear Dad,
I am very sorry that things have turned out like this, but I know that you have got the courage and strength to bring back the family good name, and you have been such a good father to us all.

I am writing this letter, knowing that this is my only chance to thank you and Mum for all that you have done for me. The only way I can pay my respect to you and the family is to show what kind of man I really am. Though I am about to take the punishment for someone else's crime, I will face it like a man, and show both courage and strength and try to make you proud of your son.

Thank you, Dad. Your courage was really wonderful and I will never forget the way you controlled yourself. You can't understand just how much that really meant to me. The time is nearly here, and I will be thinking of you.

God bless you all, Your ever loving son,
Jim

On the Tuesday there were a number of last-ditch attempts to prevent the onrushing tragedy. The family sent a telegram to the Queen. Christopher Larman spiritedly rang every daily newspaper: 'I was pleading for them to stop the execution, because I'm sure that boy was innocent. I'm sure it was he who asked me for lodgings in Rhyl.'

Also, Superintendent Leonard Elwell clearly perceived that the incident at Knebworth was so exceptional that it had to be properly considered by the appropriate authorities. He acted conscientiously, and ensured that the new Willis statement was rushed to the Home Office.

But the criminal justice process moved implacably to its denouement. The hangman and his assistant, having arrived at Bedford prison, conducted rehearsals to ascertain the weight of the body, and the kind of noose needed. Since the failure of the appeal, Hanratty had been watched over by prison warders specially brought in from outside the area, as he mentioned in his letter of 1 April to his mother. The family went to see him for the last time. James said to his mother, 'Mum, you must always remember that I didn't do it.' Mary Hanratty told reporters outside the prison, 'I'm more convinced than ever of his innocence. I told him I would try to clear his name for as long as I live. Those were my last words to him.'

The Hanrattys received a reply to their telegram: 'On the Queen's Command, your telegram has been forwarded to the Home Secretary who is constitutionally responsible for advising Her Majesty in this matter.'

The whole problem was that constitutional channels didn't seem in the least efficacious; they were leading inexorably to disaster.

Ironically, later that day, Alphon told Justice that he had done
certain things to let them know that Hanratty wasn't the murderer,
and that he had employed 'unconstitutional' means. Justice understood him to be referring to three particular initiatives: the drawing;
the letter to the press; and the re-enacted Willis incident.

It was a traumatic evening. Justice and Fox had kept in contact
with Fenner Brockway, who averred that, even at this late stage, it
wasn't too late to get a reprieve if Alphon could be persuaded to do
something more definite. At about seven o'clock, Alphon arrived at
Half Moon Street. 'We played some records. The atmosphere was
rather tense,' recalled Justice. 'An hour later, a Home Office official
and an officer from Scotland Yard arrived. Brockway had persuaded them to visit. They asked where Alphon was. I said he was
upstairs. They said, "Can we make a call?" "Yes, but the telephone's on the landing, he'll hear you," I explained. They
responded, "We'll make one from outside and come back." They
never came back.'

The presence of a Home Office official appeared to suggest that
the case was, belatedly, causing a high level of concern in the upper
echelons of the administration. Nevertheless, one imagines that the
priority was not to re-examine the case but to ensure that the law
took its course as smoothly as possible.

Justice, his brother Frank and Alphon went out for a meal at the
Mayfair Hotel. Jean was beset by total gloom; Alphon said the floor
was moving underneath him. They left almost straightaway. 'At
that time, I noticed two detectives shadowing us. They were always
there, when I looked back. We walked into Soho, and then back to
Half Moon Street, and they followed us all the way.'

Back at the flat, Justice phoned Brockway again, who reiterated
that if they could get something in writing a reprieve might still be
possible. Until three o'clock in the morning, Justice tried every plea,
every entreaty; but to no avail. Alphon's attitude was clear. 'One
day I will admit it to the world,' he said, 'but just now my life is
more important. We will get Acott together. Hanratty is only a
common thief, he is expendable. I stand for something far more
important; I have my mission.'

Justice did succeed in getting a message through to Bedford
Prison which he hoped would reach Hanratty. The message read:
'I've done everything possible to save your life, I know you're
innocent and I'll do everything possible to clear your name.' Fox
recalled his friend's emotional state: 'Jean was in tears. I was
amazed that he felt so strongly about someone he'd never met.'

HM Prison
St Loyes
Bedford
3 April

Dear Mum and Dad,

I am finding this letter very hard to put together. You have all been so brave all the way in this case, and to show my gratitude to you all I am going to face up to it, and am going to be a son that you and Dad can be proud of. I have not been much of a son to you in the past, but Mum, what I am about to say to you comes from the bottom of my heart. I have always loved you and Dad and all of my family.

Though I will never see you again, through the fault of others, I will know in my own mind, as my love for you is very strong, your love for me will be just as strong. I was very pleased in the way you and Dad had great courage on your visit. It must have been a great strain on both of you. As I tried my utmost best to keep hold of myself, where I failed, you showed your courage in every way. I am sitting here and you have been on my mind all evening.

I still find it very hard to believe what is about to happen, but Mum, I promise you that I will face it like a man. I am sure that it is the way you and Dad would want it. And I hope that this will open the eyes of many people. And what I have said will one day be proved to the world.

Well, Mum, though I have been in trouble at certain times in my life, it was only my own fault to blame. From the family I came from, there was no need for me to turn to crime, every man makes mistakes some time or other in his life, and my bad mistake was dog-racing. I feel that's what really put me on the road to crime. If I had had any willpower to stop, I would not have been away from home so much, and a man has everything he needs in our home.

Many a man would be glad to have the home you and Dad gave to me, but it was my own fault for not taking it, and if I had taken it and stayed at home, my life might have been different. Because I would have had every chance in the world to settle down and lead a good, clean and honest life.

You know I am not very good at putting these letters together, and I am trying my utmost. I only hope there is nothing I forgot to say, but before I close, Mum, the time is getting near, and when it comes I will be thinking of you and Dad. That will give me lots of courage and strength.

I was visited by Father Keogh from Brixton. He is a fine gentleman, and I am going to see him any hour now. He stayed with me and Father Hulme on Tuesday from 6 until 10 p.m. We talked together. They will help me to keep my courage and my spirits up. But I would do it on the *courage alone that you and Dad have shown, so Mum and Dad until we meet again, you will always be in my thoughts.*

So God bless you all, Your ever loving son,
Jim

                                                  3 April

Dear Mick,

Well, Mick, I am going to do my best to face the morning with courage and strength and I am sure God will give me courage to do so.

Mick, now you are the eldest in the family, I am counting on you to look after the family and I know that I could not count on anybody better than yourself. Mick, we always got on well together and we had many good times together over the years. But I am going to ask you to do me a small favour, that is I would like you to try and clear my name of this crime. Someone, somewhere is responsible for this crime and one day they will venture again and then the truth will come out, and then Mick that will be the chance for you to step in. I feel the police will try to hush it all up if they get the chance.

Well, Mick, with that as time is drawing near, it is almost daylight, so please look after Mum and Dad for me, as you just could not wish to have better parents than the ones you have got. I only wish I could have the chance all over again, as I don't know what I have done to deserve this.

Thanks for all the trouble you have been to, I can assure you that you have not been wasting your time, as it will all help to bring out the truth in the end, and Mick don't let anyone say a bad word about me. I feel I will have to say goodbye for now. Give my best wishes to Mum and Dad and all the family.

Your loving brother,
Jim

PS. I hope you will like the car. I wish I had paid the full amount and had given it to you as a gift before now. But please Mick remember it is a very fast car, and whatever you do take care when you drive it. With a car of this standard it is very powerful. I know you are a very good driver and that you will take care of it. Keep smiling, Mick. Jim.

In Bedford, early on Wednesday morning, the upper floor of the nearby multi-storey car park which gave a view of buildings inside the prison wall was closed at the request of the prison authorities. Three Oxford University students – Flavia Lunn, Peter Jackson and Gordon Ray – had held an all-night vigil outside the prison.

David Lines, the Under-Sheriff of Bedford, arrived at the prison at about 7.25. He was an official witness, and was in the formal dress of his office – morning coat and top hat. When he was shown into the office of the prison Governor, Reginald Llewellyn, the High Sheriff, Humphrey Whitbread, was already there, together with Dr Rhys Oliver, the prison medical officer, and Canon Anthony Hulme, Catholic chaplain to Bedford jail: five witnesses in all. They had 'a nip', which all felt was much needed, and then Oliver went to examine Hanratty. He returned to say that he'd offered Hanratty a drink, but the reply was, 'No, doctor, I've not touched alcohol in my life, and I'm not going to start now.' Hulme went to see Hanratty. When he returned, the party moved off around the perimeter road back towards the front of the prison, to the execution block. They went in, and lined up on a sort of mini-platform.

Outside, a crowd of men and women on their way to work, estimated by the *Daily Telegraph* at 'more than 300 people', gathered outside the gates. The crowd included Audrey Willis and two plain-clothes police officers. 'They said that the gunman in my house was a nutcase, and they thought he might be outside the prison when Hanratty was hanged,' she explained. 'So they asked me to go there. We walked around; he wasn't there.'

Inside the prison, the moment was at hand. 'It was a very fraught moment,' explained David Lines. 'The platform with the gallows was five yards away. Opposite was the door through which the condemned man came. Hanratty marched in with the executioners at either side. Marched is not quite the word – strut, I would say, was more appropriate. He didn't flinch at all. He was clearly putting a very, very brave face on it.

'At that point, they had already bound his hands behind his back. One executioner put what appeared to be a flour sack over his head, while the other bound his legs. The first man then put the noose around his neck, and adjusted it. He then stood back, and pulled a lever, a little like an old-fashioned signalman's lever. The trap fell away.

'Someone, not me, had timed this, and the whole process from the moment he appeared at the door to the moment he disappeared from view took forty-five seconds.

'The doctor and priest went down to certify that Hanratty was dead.'

'There were a couple of steps to go down into the pit,' Hulme later recalled, 'and that is what I was concentrating on, and making sure I did anoint his wrists. Hanratty did have dignity. At the end, he was very brave. He died like a soldier. It made an impression on all those who were there.'[9]

Ray Miles, a local Bedford man who helped to collect signatures for the petition, laid a wreath of daffodils and irises outside. The message with them read:

> These flowers are for James Hanratty who, like Evans and Bentley, has been murdered by our so-called civilized state. One day the executioners and the accusers will have to answer to their crime – On behalf of the many people who believe in his innocence.

Yet again, the pellucid perception of ordinary people stood in absolute contrast to the blind judgment of the authorities.

'It was pretty gruesome,' said David Lines. 'It was something that stayed with me vividly for about three months. I just hoped to forget it soon, but I never have. You never forget something like that.

'Llewellyn, the Governor, was a very sensitive man. He was clearly distressed. I could tell he was deeply upset by the whole business. After it was over, he led us back not the way we'd come in, but back in through the prison. Off to one side was the condemned man's cell. We walked past. There were his pyjamas on the bed, and his empty cup of tea on the bedside table. It was such a domestic scene. That really brought it home: we'd just killed this man.'

The duty log of the police officer in charge outside read as follows:

07.30 Men in position. All in order.

07.47 All correct, 80–90 people present, including a large number of press and photographers.

08.21 Crowd dispersed. Man who placed flowers has been photographed.

08.35 Coroner's officer has received official confirmation from the Governor HMP Bedford to the effect that the sentence had been carried out.

· V ·
THE CAMPAIGN

IN THE DAYS immediately following the execution, Jean Justice remained in inconsolable distress. He felt an acute sense of personal failure. He had a finer understanding of the case than anyone else (and, for the rest of his life, would remain its pre-eminent authority); as an enthusiastic dilettante, he had displayed greater detective acumen than several police forces could muster between them; yet it had all been unavailing. He was utterly wretched.

On the day of the execution itself Jeremy Fox rang him to say that, all through the city, as he went to his chambers, the newspaper placards had just two words: *Hanratty hanged*. That evening, Alphon turned up at Justice's flat, where the Half Moon Street Irregulars and a few other friends were gathered for an impromptu wake. Alphon feigned surprise that everyone was so downcast. Justice angrily denounced him as the real murderer and told him to leave. To general surprise, there were no histrionics and Alphon, though displeased, submitted. Frank Justice saw him down the stairs. As he was hustled outside, Alphon turned and reproached him, 'Murder is one thing, manners are another.'

Jean and Jeremy had seats at Covent Garden for the day afterwards. The tickets had been booked weeks earlier, in anticipation of a small celebration. It was a performance of Beethoven's *Fidelio*, with the great maestro Otto Klemperer conducting, and Sena Jurinac singing the part of Leonore. However, there was no balm for Justice's grief. His mind was on only one matter. As the second act was about to begin, Jean, from his seat at the front of the Royal Circle, brought the production to a momentary standstill with a loud and searing cry of 'HANRATTY!'

Controversial executions occurred from time to time; but apprehension beforehand about the fate of the condemned man never persisted afterwards; there were too many injustices to the living to allow attention to linger on those to the dead.

The Hanratty case was entirely exceptional because the

execution itself acted as no kind of punctuation in the evolution of the case; it was not a full stop, nor even a comma. The simmering public anxiety continued. The only change was that the disquiet which, prior to the execution, had been located outside the newspaper columns began at last to be reflected within them.

At the inquest into the death of Charles France, the Ealing Coroner said that the deceased had left a letter which would not be read out as it would not be in the public interest to disclose its contents. The *Observer* immediately declared that this was plain nonsense:

> In trying to unravel all the evidence about this crime, it becomes abundantly clear that what was heard in the Bedford courtroom was not the whole story. It most emphatically is in the public interest that the contents of France's letter should be known in order to allay the suspicion that something is being kept back which might materially alter the whole aspect of the case.[1]

A few days later, the *Bedfordshire Times* reported the closing of the inquest on the victim, Michael Gregsten, and added its voice to the general concern:

> But is the story concluded? Since the hanging of Hanratty, discussion about the case has been hardly less than at the time of the trial. It is clear that throughout the country many people are disturbed about aspects of the affair.
>
> Our correspondence columns have already reflected the view of people who, after making a close study of the evidence, and in particular the evidence relating to identification, are unconvinced of the accused man's guilt.
>
> The law operates in the name of the community, and it is public opinion that shapes the law. For that reason, public opinion on this issue should be enlightened by a full knowledge of the facts.[2]

Unhindered by *Daily Express* gauleiters, Justice and Fox were now able to meet the Hanratty family at last. They understood straightaway that the parents were both terribly upset and they promised to do everything they could to redeem the pledge that all of them had individually made to Jimmy. The family was impressed with Jean's passion and dedication to the cause.

Alphon's feathers did not remain ruffled for long. Friendly relations between him and Jean were quickly restored. Within a few days, together with Frank, they were back at the White City. The little group – Jean, Jeremy, Frank and Alphon – saw each other practically every day; Alphon occasionally went to stay at Laudate, sometimes with the others, sometimes on his own. The relationship between Jean and Alphon grew particularly close. Alphon was now prepared, it seemed, to drop occasional indiscretions about the case. On one occasion, he said, 'When I let Gregsten out of the car for cigarettes, I half hoped he might make a break for it.' Another afternoon, Alphon suddenly said to Jean, 'If I'd known you a year ago, this terrible murder would never have happened.'

However convincing Justice personally found such heartfelt utterances, he kept pressing and pressing for something more tangible; something that smacked of documentary proof. Alphon, seemingly becoming prone to bouts of depression, said he would write something out. On Tuesday 15 May, in the lounge of the Imperial Hotel, Alphon suddenly produced a few pages of handwritten confession notes. 'You probably can't read them,' he told Justice, 'but you can keep them.'

There would be many elaborate compositions produced by Alphon over a thirty-year period from 1962 to 1992. There is little point in labouring their significance, because they have scant credibility. They are rambling fictions. However, these were the very first, so they are interesting for that reason, and it would be perverse to omit them. They start off methodically, listing a set of points. They are often difficult to read, as Alphon anticipated, and are frequently scrawled, with many crossings-out, as if written in a state of some emotional tension. Here they are, in full:

1. Obtaining the gun. Reasons for this. Name of person George.

2. Frame-up in Vienna. How I knew Nudds. Reasons for this frame. Altering the register (alibi with my mother). Planting cases in Room 24 when 'R' [it looks here as if 'H' has been altered to 'R'] was out. Asking Nudds if Ryan had left.

3. Slough. Had gun but hoping not to commit murder at that time but well in mood for it. The dogs. Bookmaker who might know me. Going out after Mentals Only Hope. Walking out into the country. Stopped at [The Dumbbell] pub opposite Old Station Inn. On to Marsh Lane. Couple in car fitted my mood and my main plan.

4. From the moment I went in, imitated working class person with voice and background although I had never met Ryan. But a

lot of what I said which could be interpreted as Ryan's hatred of ordinary middle class people stemmed from my heart and was my own hatred of them.

5. I played with them as cat and mouse – but all the time I was tense and being an extrovert. I showed it and exaggerated and a lot of my nervousness was communicated to them.

6. When I killed him and she said, 'Oh, you swine, you bastard, you've shot him,' I felt the need to give her some explanation and I said, 'He shouldn't have tried to turn the tables on me.' She said, 'He wasn't, you swine. You are mad.' I said, 'He moved too quickly.'

I knew I must kill her but first I might as well rape her. I felt tense and overwrought and I felt that even fleeting love would help me. She said, 'Do what you like now. Nothing matters any more.' We went in the back of car. She was crying and sobbing all the time but relaxed when we had intercourse. At the end she said, 'What are you going to do?' I said, 'I must kill you now. It is either your life or mine and I have a messianic mission.' She said, 'Please don't hurt me! I'll do anything for you and won't give you away.' It was then that I said, 'One day you will see me on an identification parade but you will not identify. Remember and listen to me now, Valerie, and one day I will come back for you and we will be happy together.' She swore she would not identify me. I knew all along that I would have to kill her but I liked the drama and felt touched by her repeated assurances that she would not identify me. I said, 'Goodbye Valerie. You will stay here.' But as I walked away I turned and shot her ? times. She fell and lay on the ground. I went over and fired more shots into her. She lay absolutely still. I believed she was dead.

7. Meeting the drivers on the road. Driving badly.

8. Meeting my friend at Southend. Disposal of gun.

9. All my interviews with police (Finsbury Park and Acott) can be found from my papers with MacDougal.

10. If they had been other sort of people I wouldn't have killed them.

11. When I reproached them on their illicit love, Gregsten said, 'That is nothing to do with you.' I became heated and said that everything which happened was my business. That I could see civilization slipping into vice and decadence. He laughed and this antagonized me more. As I spoke with them more and more his mentality emerged and I came to detest and despise him and knew he would be no loss to the world.

1. Car passed. Lights lit up face twenty minutes after Gregsten's death.
2. I arrived in car about 9.30.
3. Left about 11.30.
4. Drove to lay-by by roundabout route.
5. I said, 'Shut up, I'm thinking my plan out.'
6. Fired about ten times at her.
7. Drove off about 3.00.
8. Raped Valerie about twenty minutes after Gregsten's death.
9. Fired shots at Gregsten at point-blank range.
10. Said, 'Kiss me' before raping her when she was in front seat.
11. .38 Enfield revolver
12. Past attempt at cornfield.[3]

Justice sensed that Alphon, having finally discharged his promise, seemed relieved of a burden; he had made his confession. However, Alphon was nothing if not shrewd. He was as aware as Justice that the evidential value of his handiwork was very limited. From the outset, he understood that he could achieve complementary aims with such writings. On the one hand, he could use them to claim the 'credit' for not only having carried out such an extraordinary and notorious crime, but also having duped Scotland Yard and got away with it: the perfect murder, no less. On the other hand, Alphon could also safeguard himself against prosecution by colouring his account with palpable falsehoods.

The writings are so full of inaccuracies that it is futile to try to disentangle the supposed nuggets of truth. Much of the incidental detail is the product of a fervid imagination. Here, one can almost visualize him becoming engrossed in his own story and giving free rein to his own appetite for adventure ('I knew all along that I would have to kill her but I liked the drama') and to narrative powers ('Valerie, one day I will come back for you and we will be happy together') that – who knows? – could even have been put to more constructive use as a thriller-writer.

Nevertheless, perhaps there are more bits of the truth scattered throughout this, the prototype, than there were in subsequent versions. The form they take is especially interesting.

These notes are the first, written to honour a personal pledge to Justice for whom, at the time, Alphon seemed to have a deep affection. On close examination, they seem to lose any association with reality, particularly at the first Point 6. Accordingly, Alphon jerked himself back to the matter in hand, his promise to Jean, and *started again*, with a fresh list of numbered points. This second list of twelve points may well be accurate. There is an all-too-obvious exception, the reference to Storie having been raped in the *front* seat (which is not only known to be wrong but is even contradicted in the first section of the notes). Having planted the essential inaccuracy, Alphon is then free to return to the truth with '.38 Enfield'.

If this evaluation is valid in any sense, then 'Past attempt at cornfield' is extraordinary. It indicates that the couple in the field were deliberately targeted. It illuminates a critical feature of the crime that the entire judicial process completely omitted. This was an aspect of the case that simply never crossed the minds of those who prosecuted and hanged Hanratty.

The early part of the notes also introduced the idea that Hanratty had been framed. Here was another element of a pre-arranged plan; that Alphon had 'imitated' the kind of working-class criminal he assumed Hanratty to be. Moreover, Scotland Yard couldn't turn round and denigrate this as total fantasy, because this had crossed their minds; they had suggested it first, albeit the wrong way round. According to the *Daily Mirror* of 4 October, 'one of the theories being considered by detectives was that the A6 killer had spotted Alphon and tried to frame him'. This was reported in several papers. Now, in his notes, Alphon was saying that there was indeed a framing, which had been worked out in advance.

Some other points in the notes – 'a lot of my nervousness was communicated to them' – have a ring of authenticity. The proximity of Slough dog stadium meant that an earlier reconnaissance trip (or 'Past attempt') could have been conveniently dovetailed with a session there.

The references to the Vienna Hotel – 'How I knew Nudds. Altering the register' – are on any level intriguing, even if (one cannot make the point too often) not necessarily true. However, what does make these remarks utterly tantalizing is the fact that at the time the only publicly available information – the evidence given at the trial – was that there was no opportunity for the records to have been altered. Alphon could not, of course, have known that this aspect of his confession notes would be given credence by confidential police documents only released thirty years later, indicating that there was indeed a nine-day interval during which the records could have been tampered with.

There were other respects, too, in which the A6 story was continuing to cause perplexity. In the early morning of Tuesday,

22 May Carole France was rushed to New End Hospital, Hampstead, north London, after taking a drugs overdose. Happily, the *Evening News* was able to report that her condition was 'satisfactory'.

One Sunday morning, the *News of the World* proclaimed a major exclusive: the last letters of James Hanratty (extracts from which have already been placed in context in the narrative). Jean Justice was astonished:

'These were fantastic. Any lingering doubts anyone had would have been laid to rest by reading these letters. They reek of innocence. And think of the prominence the *News of the World* gave them. These are the last letters of "the A6 monster", a man convicted of a terrible murder. What do they reveal about the crime? Or about the character of the man which led him to commit it? Nothing. He just states and restates his innocence in such a way that it is impossible to believe that he could be fabricating it. Compare all this with Alphon's protestations of guilt, as they developed over the years. Is it really possible that the first police suspect who protests his guilt is not to be believed, and the second police suspect who protests his innocence is also not to be believed?'

In June, there was a fresh blow for those hoping the case might now be quietly forgotten. Over three weeks, Valerie Storie's own account of the tragedy was serialized in *Today*. This was the only occasion, apart from the court hearings, in which Storie has ever attempted to explain everything from her point of view. The authorities may well have wished that she had kept her own counsel completely. This sole published account of her story contained two glaring departures from what might be termed the authorized version of events, both of which the ever-alert Half Moon Street Irregulars were quick to seize upon.

First, the serialization was headlined: 'Once I Had a Secret Love'. The account dwelt at length on her relationship with Michael Gregsten: 'I was in love with a married man for four years.' This in itself was devastating. It exposed Janet Gregsten's 'cruel lie' of three months earlier as a complete fabrication. It made clear that the jury at Bedford had been presented with a very incomplete picture of the background to these events.

Second, as has already been noted, Storie gave a different time for the start of her association with Gregsten to that she had offered on oath at the trial.

There was another, entirely separate point. Valerie Storie wrote, in respect of her identification of Hanratty: 'I said quietly, "Number 6". In a second the door of the room had slammed shut behind me as I was quickly wheeled out into the corridor. Superintendent Acott gripped my arm, and said, "Well done." I knew I had settled my score with Hanratty.'[4]

There was nothing wrong with Acott's behaviour, as the rules stood at that time. (They have been thoroughly revised since.) Officers were allowed to be present, albeit as mere observers. Providing that Acott made no comment until it was all finished, and he appears not to have done so, then no rules of procedure would have been breached. However, in the light of Valerie Storie's account, it seemed that her belief that she had picked out the right man could only have been reinforced by Acott's instantaneous reaction. She said at the trial that she had 'no doubt whatsoever' that Hanratty was the gunman. But to what extent was her certainty due to her own identification alone? Or to what extent was it buttressed by Acott's confirmation? Fiercely contested identification evidence lay at the heart of this conviction. If it was beset by doubts before, then in the wake of the *Today* article it looked even more dubious.

Justice appreciated as keenly as Alphon the illusory value of the confession notes. He still hoped to provoke him into a more obvious indiscretion and as such tried to put him under emotional duress. After acquiring the notes, Justice left the country for Brussels, where Ann Wyllie, an old friend, and Jeremy joined him; Alphon was left behind, isolated, at Laudate.

They soon relented, and Alphon was invited to join them in Paris. They were at Le Bourget airport to meet him. If it had been a trial of emotional strength, then Alphon emerged the victor.

'The old excitement possessed me as I watched him leave the plane. He was wearing black trousers and a black jacket fastened up to the neck with brass buttons. I had been looking forward to seeing him, but suddenly I felt afraid. His military swagger as he marched over to Customs sent a shiver up my spine. Peter still fascinated me, but at the same time I was terrified of him.

'For the next few days I endured Peter's boorish behaviour in cafés and restaurants, his unpredictable moods and his sudden lapses into violence. I was now seeing the real Peter Alphon: the fascist, the psychopath, the pervert, the man who lusted for power. He thought, I suppose, that now that I knew the worst, there was no further point in putting on an act.'[5]

It was about this time that Fox finally began to endorse Jean's opinion. From his particular viewpoint, he'd always found it difficult to believe that the judicial process could have gone quite so disastrously awry: 'As a barrister and member of the establishment, I couldn't really believe this sort of thing could happen. I knew Hanratty had been convicted of the murder and his appeal had been turned down. I was meeting Alphon daily, he struck me as a reasonable person, and I was highly sceptical of Jean's claim that he was the murderer.'

Fox noticed, though, that at times when he was getting excited, Alphon would lapse into cockney, saying 'fink' and 'fr'pence'. Then he made a confession.

'One evening in June in the Blue Angel Club in Berkeley Square, Alphon asked me to look him straight in the eye, and he said to me, "I did that murder." He said they were obviously an immoral couple and he had a mission to stamp out vice and immorality. I was not completely convinced by this, but I did become convinced later in July when I said to him, "You know how badly Mrs Hanratty feels about her son being hanged for a crime he didn't commit." The look of anguish that came over his face at that moment finally convinced me that he was indeed the A6 killer.'

It was also evident that Alphon was certainly not courting police attention. One evening at this time, as their party was returning late from Overton's in St James's Street (one of London's most expensive restaurants), Justice was struck by his old temptation, his zest for high jinks. An irresistible opportunity presented itself. Parking meters were just being installed across London. Someone amongst the company noticed one that had not been properly bedded into the pavement. With some manoeuvring, a bit of brute force and a few dexterous twists, they managed to uproot it. They put it in the boot of Fox's car, and then carried it in triumph up to Jean's flat where it was displayed for a couple of days until discretion dictated that it be moved under Jean's bed. Those present realized afterwards that as soon as it became clear that the merriment was crossing into dangerously illegal territory, Alphon had disappeared into the night.

At first, the jape was accounted a huge success. It's hard to understand today, but the introduction of parking meters was a minor social revolution, and a matter of national interest; the theft of one was a serious news topic. The next day's papers carried photographs of a stunned London traffic warden: 'I couldn't believe it – I looked, and it was gone.' Those in Jean's circle all found it a matter of enormous amusement. Just after eight every morning,

Captain David Brown would ring Jean: 'Have you put sixpence in the meter yet, Boomy?'

It may have been Brown, with his need to maintain close relations with the police, who, whether deliberately or inadvertently, mentioned it to them. At any rate, three of those involved – Jean, Gordon Perkins and James Bride-Hennessey – were charged, prosecuted and fined for the theft of a parking meter. The saga, however, had a tragic outcome. Bride-Hennessey had a wife and small child. The police cruelly questioned him at his home, in front of his family, who naturally knew nothing of this side of his life or his homosexual proclivities. Immediately afterwards, Bride-Hennessey committed suicide.

With Alphon again at Laudate, Justice decided he needed to take a break and went to Vienna, before moving on to Budapest for a few days. In retaliation for being deserted, Alphon had, prior to Justice's departure for Budapest, assailed him with a series of telegrams. Now, on his return to Vienna, Justice received a particularly threatening one: 'EN ROUTE TO VIENNA WITH ENFIELD. A FRIEND.'

Justice panicked. At the central police station in Vienna, he applied for a licence to purchase a gun. He used the telegram to explain that his life was in danger, and also showed the police the material he was assembling on the Hanratty case to convince them that this was no idle threat, because Alphon was a dangerous murderer.

They were polite and understanding, but Justice was made to wait, on the pretext that his licence was being prepared. He became alarmed when he began to realize that it was he himself who was under scrutiny. The police had indeed checked the contents of his briefcase, and then contacted Scotland Yard. At length, Justice was informed that he was ill, and had to be detained for his own safety: 'You – sick.' His protestations were in vain. He was forced into a police car, and taken to the Klinik Hoff, an asylum for the criminally insane. He wrote:

> The long arm of the English law stretched even as far as Vienna. It was obvious to me that the Viennese police were merely acting on instructions they had received from Scotland Yard. At all costs I had to be stopped from spreading the truth about the manner in which James Hanratty had been framed. I was an innocent tourist;

but I was about to undergo a spell of false imprisonment, thanks to
the combined efforts of the Austrian and the English police.[6]

Justice kept insisting that he needed to see the British consul, but
nobody listened. It emerged afterwards that the consul had signed
the order for Justice's detention without ever having seen him. As
soon as he heard what had happened, Jeremy Fox paid for Ann
Wyllie to fly out. After strenuous efforts, she managed to get him
out. Justice had by then been held against his will in a locked ward
of the hospital for five days.

The arrangement was that he had to be put on a plane and
escorted back home. When they arrived at London airport, Justice
almost expected to see medical staff from a psychiatric hospital, or
a contingent of British police, ready to apprehend this returning
madman. There was no one at all, only the other Half Moon Street
Irregulars, the faithful Frank and Jeremy.

The entire affair had been one of the most bizarre twists that
even this saga could produce. There had been no medical tests, no
psychiatric examination. Justice was simply committed to a mental
asylum, the Austrian officials having seemingly taken their instructions direct from the British authorities. 'It was absolutely sinister,'
he commented. 'Obviously, they were putting the wind up me –
teaching me a lesson.' Could it have been coincidence that on the
morning of 24 July, the day of Justice's detention, Jeremy Fox had
gone to Scotland Yard to hand in the confession notes and other
interim results of their continuing A6 investigations?

Back in England, Justice discussed the matter at length with his
solicitor, David Jacobs. The British consular authorities appeared
to have neglected all their responsibilities for the well-being of
British citizens abroad. It was also abundantly clear that the
Viennese officials had broken most of their own rules, most
significantly the habeas corpus provision that a court had to be
informed within twenty-four hours if anyone was held against their
will. But what was Justice to do? He comprehended the judicial
possibilities only too clearly: the British legal process was slow,
painful and, even for a man of his means, expensive. He would be
able to rely on no cooperation whatever from the British authorites.
He wisely decided that there were more important matters on
which to expend his energies.

Within a few days of returning to England, Justice left again. To
recover from the experience in Vienna, he decided to spend a few
days in his favourite city, Brussels. He took a party of friends, and,

against his better judgement, invited Alphon. However, because of the latter's increasingly loutish behaviour, they abandoned the trip half-way through. On the way back Justice reached two firm decisions: to sever all relations with Alphon; and to marry Ann Wyllie.

By this point Justice thought he was close to a nervous breakdown. The whole saga had exacted a profound psychological toll. After the original stress of trying to prevent the execution, the emotional turbulence had only swelled. There were the traumas of the relationship with Alphon ('the impact of his powerful personality was considerable, even an hour in his company left me drained'); the parking-meter incident and its aftermath; and Vienna.

Justice needed a rest from such nerve-racking episodes. He also knew that a heterosexual relationship would help him to present a façade of normality to the outside world. Ann was a loyal and long-standing friend who was cheerfully prepared to enter into this marriage of convenience (which instantly provided Jean with two stepdaughters, Vivienne and Clarissa). He then felt better able to concentrate on the main issue, the Hanratty case.

He and Fox visited Rhyl for the first time; yet there was no respite from the pressure. On their return journey they suffered further police harassment. They stayed overnight in Stratford. As they were breakfasting in their hotel the following morning, two plain-clothes policemen insisted that they had to accompany them to the station. As Fox remembered, 'I said, "What's it all about?" and their reply was, I think, "False pretences."' They were held at the station for some thirty minutes before it emerged that they wanted to question Fox about some cheques that he had had stolen and reported missing about two years earlier. They were allowed to leave, but only on condition that they called in at Oxford police station on their way home.

The professional advice of David Jacobs was again sought. He told them they could have nothing to worry about. At Oxford, Fox was made to take a handwriting test after which he was shown the recovered cheques – which, clearly, were not in his handwriting. They were finally allowed to leave.

'I think it was done to frighten us,' remarked Fox. 'If the police really thought I had issued those cheques myself, why did they wait two years before questioning me about it? And why apprehend Jean at all, because he had nothing to do with it? It was certainly an unnerving experience – I was very frightened at the time. I believe the police probably thought we had uncovered something in Rhyl and were coming back to London to spill the beans.'

Ironically, they had accomplished nothing on their visit. Terry Evans could not be found and Grace Jones wouldn't speak to them. With memories of the trial still haunting her, she had no wish to risk further mortification.

The first anniversary of the murder was eventful. On the morning of 22 August, Justice rang Alphon to deliver the news that he no longer wished to see him. He did, however, arrange a final meeting for the following afternoon.

After receiving Jean's telephone message, Alphon paid an extra-ordinary visit to the Hanratty home in Kingsbury. Mr Hanratty asked if it was right that he had written a confession. Alphon replied that he had, and produced the original notes from his pocket. He then said, 'I am very sorry that all this has happened. I never thought they would hang your son. I know he did not do the murder.' He then astonished the family by taking out his cheque-book and suggesting that he recompense them for Jimmy's death. James Hanratty was understandably livid; he threw Alphon out of the house. He and Mary then contacted Justice, and they arranged a meeting for the following day to discuss this sudden development.

On the Thursday, Justice was surprised to receive a telephone call from Chief Superintendent Kennedy at Scotland Yard. He said, 'Listen to me, Justice, if you don't drop the A6 business, loony bin for you and no mistake.' Justice, who had recent first-hand experience of just what that involved, acquiesced. 'I take the hint,' he responded. Kennedy commented, 'That's the first glimmer of light you've seen.'

That afternoon Justice, along with Jeremy, Frank and Gordon Perkins, went to the Barrington Club for his confrontation with Alphon. He told him squarely that he didn't intend ever to see him again. Alphon became angry and abusive, arguing, 'Since when do you take orders from the police?' (A good point, thought Justice, as he reflected anew on the perverted intelligence of the man.)

Frank went on ahead to meet James Hanratty at Green Park underground station; then the others left. Alphon, growing angrier and more voluble, pursued them down Jermyn Street. He yelled, among other things, 'Tonight, Justice, there will be no cigarettes for you.' (The intimation here was that Gregsten was offered a chance of escape; but there would be none for Justice.)

Mary Hanratty joined them, but at Green Park a fracas

developed. Alphon hurled himself down the steps, grabbed Justice and then, as Mary tried to intervene, gripped her by the throat and pushed her against a wall. She slapped him across the face. A few of the rush-hour passengers tried to intervene, and a ticket collector lent assistance. Frank arrived with James Hanratty, and shortly afterwards the police came. By then Alphon had fled.

Mary Hanratty, her neck bearing red weals as proof of the attack, determined to sue for assault. On Monday, 27 August, she took out a summons at Bow Street. Alphon's address was given as the Rembrandt Hotel, South Kensington. Justice recalled the reaction of the police: 'Although there was never any doubt that Alphon had assaulted both me and Mary Hanratty, although there were plenty of witnesses to his attack, although it took place in a public thoroughfare and inconvenienced tube passengers, although we pressed for a prosecution, the police, for some mysterious reason, were most reluctant to summons Alphon.'[7]

During September, Justice was abroad again, on a month's holiday with Jeremy. When he returned, he was amazed to learn that the summons had not been served. The police explained that they couldn't find Alphon.

It took ten minutes for Justice to find him. He telephoned to arrange a meeting at the Grosvenor Hotel in Victoria. He also arranged for detectives to be there, so that, finally, the summons was served. Alphon was enraged by Justice's duplicity, and told him so; but Justice no longer cared. This proved to be the last face-to-face meeting between the two men.

'The police did their best to dissuade me from going to Bow Street,' wrote Justice; but he did testify when the assault case was finally heard one Saturday afternoon, 27 October. In the witness-box, the barrister asked Justice his opinion of Alphon. He replied: 'I think he's a criminal lunatic.'

'And guilty of the crime for which Mrs Hanratty's son was hanged?' continued the lawyer.

'Yes,' replied Justice.

He then dramatically produced the confession notes from his inside pocket, telling the court that both the Home Office and the police had seen the material, but ignored it. He was informed by the bench that he could not refer to this in court.

In the event, the magistrate averred that his mind was not sufficiently clear of doubt about the offence, and so Alphon was acquitted. Afterwards the latter telephoned Justice, saying, 'Isn't it funny? Whether there is no doubt at all in their minds, or whether their minds are not sufficiently clear of doubt, it always goes in my favour.'

The hearing, however, resulted in another burst of publicity about the case. What Justice had been able to say in court was protected by privilege, so several Sunday newspapers reported that 'company director' Jean Justice had announced that he had a confession to the A6 crime.

Deprived of Justice's company, Alphon began telephoning him regularly, over a period of some seven months from October 1962 to May 1963. The calls were invariably late-night, and always exceptionally lengthy: thirty minutes would be a short conversation. Many were made from call-boxes where Alphon (having reversed the charges) would often spend half the night.

Justice fully comprehended that 'in the hands of a cunning madman, a telephone could be a terrifying instrument'. It already had sinister associations in this case: Valerie Storie having been plagued by a telephone caller while in Stoke Mandeville, Alphon's solicitor having received a series of calls, and Charles France having been to some extent hounded to his suicide by telephone calls. So Justice had some idea what he was letting himself in for. Yet it could be worthwhile. He had previously begun to suspect that his efforts to ensnare Alphon were always going to be thwarted; now the telephone seemed to open up fresh possibilities. Could Alphon be hoist with his own petard?

After meeting Fenner Brockway and Martin Ennals, general secretary of the National Council for Civil Liberties, it was decided to tape all these calls, in case Alphon was incautious enough to say anything that would incriminate him. At first the technology was makeshift: Justice simply placed a microphone as near as possible to the ear-piece. Later, he was able to get hold of equipment that was, for its time, state of the art.

The result was boxes and boxes of tapes – reel-to-reel and later cassettes. Alphon regularly alluded to the crime, and continued to discuss it in a semi-hysterical fashion. Justice wrote that the transcripts showed him to be 'a psychopathic boaster'; but that the written version unfortunately lacked 'the accompanying tone of voice – the cockney whine, the sudden outbursts of screaming gibberish'.

Although Justice never stopped prodding and leading in attempts to extract information, and although Alphon had no notion that the calls were being tape-recorded, Justice was the first to acknowledge that most of what was collected on the mounting piles of tape-recordings was 'wild inventions'. Alphon never revealed any piece of actual evidence, or any bona fide information which only the murderer could have known. This gives some flavour of the dialogue:

Alphon: I don't think talking makes things clear. Hitler talked a lot before the war, but no one took any notice of him till he struck; then they did not know what to do.
Justice: Like in the car you mean?
Alphon: Yes, that's right. I will just tell you one thing. No, I had better not. About the car.
Justice: Yes.
Alphon: Yes. Anyway, I can tell you Gregsten did not take any notice at all. Did not take any notice at all of talk. You know what happened to him. It is not easy to terrorize anyone by talk, you know. Don't think it was all terror in the car because it wasn't.
Justice: I quite agree.
Alphon: It was after the shot was fired, but not before. He was quite cocky.
Justice: Who?
Alphon: Gregsten.

However, Alphon did consistently portray himself as a kind of moral vigilante who had committed the crime: 'There's only one thing in the world that means anything to me, and that was Hitler. When I say that Hitler lived again in the cornfield that night, you know what I mean.'

During this period, Justice and Fox knew little of Alphon's circumstances. Although the generosity of Justice and Fox was boundless, there was only one occasion (when Fox paid a hotel bill for him) on which they supported Alphon financially. The tape transcripts show that Alphon was now making demands for money:

Alphon: I want £250, and don't fuck about with me. I have told you what I want. I want £250.
Justice: If I cannot get it?
Alphon: Then I am going to kill you.

The only piece of news they found out about Alphon came in December 1962 when they read that he had been arrested by railway police at King's Cross station and charged with attempting to steal money from Mrs Fadzuk, a Hungarian lady. Although by then Alphon appeared to assume that he could commit any crime, whether trivial or serious, with impunity, this was one occasion when he was disappointed. Charges were pursued, and he was successfully prosecuted. He was enraged by the affair, and accused Justice of having instigated it.

Alphon also used to make regular calls to the Hanratty family. Sometimes, when one of the family picked up the phone, there would just be silence at the other end; at other times, he spoke and made threats. Once, when Mary Hanratty answered, he said, 'I am the A6 killer, and I'm coming to get you.' On 17 May 1963 he spoke at some length to James Hanratty, during which the latter let slip that the calls to Justice were being tape-recorded. Alphon's reaction – the abrupt silence – indicated that this came as a complete shock to him. Afterwards, he berated Justice for this further deception.

The first book about the case was published in June 1963. It was written by Louis Blom-Cooper, the distinguished barrister and legal commentator. The unwieldy title of the book – *The A6 Murder: Regina v James Hanratty: The Semblance of Truth* – hinted at its somewhat unwieldy aims. Blom-Cooper had envisaged taking a case to illustrate what he felt were the shortcomings of the English judicial process. The book suffered from an overwhelming handicap: despite having attended the entire A6 trial, despite having studied the case assiduously, despite recording his suspicion that even the judge 'disagreed with the verdict', Blom-Cooper had somehow concluded that Hanratty was guilty as charged. A critique of the system which adjudged that, its many faults notwithstanding, the right outcome had been reached was clearly going to be less pertinent than one observing that the correct result had not been achieved.

Yet the book is not without interest or merit. His major concern was what he termed 'the straitjacket of the English trial system' and 'the limitations on our knowledge of the crime' which this dictated. The fact was that no one engaged in the process was searching for the truth. Thus the police could not be blamed for their role: 'The process of selectivity is imposed by the system, and is not a malicious act by the police to pin the crime on someone they think committed it.' The end-product, he averred, was 'a system of criminal justice which left the community more perplexed at the end of the process than at the beginning'.

Blom-Cooper was also spot-on about several aspects of the trial itself. He was perhaps the first to point out that the crime could hardly have been as random as the prosecution maintained: 'Was Hanratty *sent* to the cornfield in Buckinghamshire with a gun in his hand?' He also discerned significance in the sad end of Charles France. Blom-Cooper considered his 'almost overweening guilt complex', and asked, 'Did France, in fact, play some part in the events which led to the A6 killing?'

He analysed other points of evidence, showing, for example, how ludicrous the 'roadworks' evidence was. He also impugned Valerie Storie's entire testimony, arguing that 'No trained judge could have placed much weight on her evidence.' So what did that leave? 'Once Storie's evidence was discounted, the only other evidence of great moment was Langdale's.' Finally, like the Home Office, he seemed to make the elementary mistake of failing to see through the prison grass.

Dr David Lewes was one of those who communicated with Blom-Cooper almost immediately – pointing out a number of errors, notably his assertion that Hanratty had described the back seat of a bus as 'a good hiding-place for a gun'. Hanratty had, of course, said no such thing.

'I was very depressed about Blom-Cooper's book,' recalled Jeremy Fox. 'I thought that when that came out, we had virtually no hope of making progress. His book appeared at a time when we were preparing to raise the case again with the authorities. This seemed like the final nail in the coffin, which would prevent the case being reopened.'

For some time, Fox himself had also been finding the whole business a great emotional strain. He was under tremendous pressure, from both his family and within the Bar, to resolve what was held to be the problem of his private life. In the end, in June 1963, he decided to break with Jean, a decision made somewhat easier by the fact that Justice was now, technically at least, married. Fox took a flat in the Old Brompton Road with another friend, Donald Stephenson, and thought he'd opted for a more settled and less emotionally draining lifestyle. Tragically, a few weeks later, Stephenson committed suicide. For homosexuals in Britain, those were still times of terrible stress.

When Fox left Justice, he gave him a significant leaving-present: his memorandum on the A6 Murder case. At that time, the campaigners had no access to transcripts of the trial; their primary source of information was the thorough reports carried by the *Daily Telegraph*. Fox's paper was the first material casting doubt on the conviction written by a member of the Bar. Coming so hard on the heels of the Blom-Cooper setback, it was particularly valuable. Justice was immensely grateful, and considered the Fox report the real foundation of the posthumous case for Hanratty's innocence. It certainly made breaking up a little less hard to do.

Fenner Brockway now assembled the material he had – as well as the Fox report, there was a detailed memorandum from Dr David Lewes, the confession notes, transcripts of telephone conversations, and voluminous material provided by Justice – into a complete dossier of evidence, *Was Hanratty Guilty?* He sent it to the Home Office in July 1963. He also put down an early day motion, demanding an open inquiry into the conviction and execution of James Hanratty, which was signed by over 100 MPs, including Chuter Ede, the Home Secretary who had, in 1950, sanctioned the execution of Timothy Evans. In addition, the Speaker granted Brockway time for an adjournment debate, which was held on Friday, 2 August, the first time the matter was debated in Parliament.

Brockway opened the debate himself, arguing that there was now 'a prima facie case for an inquiry'. He said that he had been engaged in investigating the case for over a year. Contrary to what might have been expected, this work was, he explained, 'a somewhat disagreeable experience; it has necessitated associations which I would not normally choose'. He was clearly referring here not to his discussions with the Hanratty family, whom he described as 'the best type of the working class'; in fact, he was alluding to Justice and Fox, and their circle of rampantly homosexual acquaintances. Clearly, he felt that their extrovert personalities made his whole case vulnerable.

Brockway observed that 'No murder takes place without some exhibitionist making a confession'; but pointed out that this situation was entirely different. Although Alphon was not named (he was described as Mr X), Brockway went through the confession notes in some detail, and used extracts from the telephone tapes, explaining that Alphon's voice would sometimes be tinged with cockney (thereby nullifying one of the points by which Acott had eliminated him). He then read out Hanratty's last letter, with its injunction to his brother to 'clear my name'. He added, 'In the light of the evidence which I have presented, it will be on our conscience if we do not respond to his appeal to find the truth.'

Eric Fletcher, MP for Islington East, reinforced the request for 'a completely impartial inquiry'. The Gravesend MP Peter Kirk also argued along those lines, referring in particular to the Fogarty-Waul evidence, and 'the nightmare-like tape-recordings of those astonishing telephone conversations'. In conclusion, he hoped that any hearing would be in public. 'We have had the experience of the Scott Henderson inquiry [into the Evans case] which, because of the way in which it was handled, did not carry an enormous amount of conviction. If this particular matter is to be cleared up, it should be cleared up as publicly as possible.'

The Home Secretary, Henry Brooke, who had replaced Butler in July 1962 after Prime Minister Harold Macmillan's so-called Night of the Long Knives, himself put the government's position. He explained that the Home Office had devoted 'a tremendous amount of careful thought to the details of this case' and made it clear that 'If there is reason for thinking that there has been a miscarriage of justice, no effort must be spared to get at the truth.'

Brooke then itemized the exhaustive efforts of the authorities to get at the truth. For example, he told MPs that the Home Office knew that Alphon could not have committed the murder, because he was not a car-driver:

'At the time of the murder, [Alphon] could not drive a car. He had never held anything more than a provisional driving licence, and that was a number of years before. He had held no driving licence. He had no driving licence at the time. It is *quite inconceivable* that [Alphon] could have been the man who drove the car that night after the murder. There is, of course, *no question* about Hanratty's ability to drive a car [my italics].'

He pointed out that the timetable didn't fit. If Alphon had seen a greyhound called Mentals Only Hope racing at Slough (at about 9.05), he would not have been able to reach the cornfield for 9.30.

Alphon's supposed confession was, he said, worthless.

'In March 1962 Hanratty's solicitor brought to the Home Office statements made by that businessman [Justice] and that barrister [Fox] about meetings and conversations with Mr X, who had been cleared of suspicion and who had, in fact, a *complete alibi* [my italics] for the night in question ... Naturally, those suggestions [that Alphon was the murderer] were at once examined, and exhaustively examined, on [Butler's] instructions by the police, but they were found to be groundless.'

He added: 'It was established that newspapers and newspaper cuttings, with references to the case marked in red ink, had been seen strewn about [Alphon's] room, together with what was evidently the confession which was later produced.'

He then reinforced the point about the substantiation of Alphon's alibi: 'I said that he had a complete alibi. It is *beyond challenge* [my italics] that [Alphon] was occupying a room at the Vienna Hotel in London at the time of the murder and, therefore, could not have been at Dorney Reach or Deadman's Hill. The main thing about the evidence of Nudds is that he made three statements. The jury accepted, and I have *no reason whatever* [my italics] to doubt that the first and third statements were true and the second statement, which he admitted was a fabrication, was untrue. There is also the evidence from the hotel register, and so forth, very convincing evidence.'

Finally, to complete the rout of the campaigners, he launched a swingeing attack on the character of Jean Justice:

'The businessman said that Mr X had confessed to the murder of Michael Gregsten and had threatened his life on a number of occasions. He made a similar statement at a police station in Vienna. The result of that call was that he was sent to a psychiatric hospital from which he later returned to London. I think it right for me to say – the Hon Member for Eton and Slough [Brockway] did say that his investigations had led him into queer ways and among queer people – that both [Alphon] and [Justice] are people of precarious mental balance and there is evidence of [Justice] being a heavy drinker.'

In conclusion, he rejected all calls for an inquiry: 'The memorandum has been exhaustively examined and the arguments and alleged evidence have been found to be of a very flimsy kind ... We must keep a sense of balance and proportion in these matters. I have found nothing to cause me to doubt that Hanratty was rightly convicted. I cannot agree to reopen the case because I believe it is *impossible* [my italics] that [Alphon] could have committed the murder.'

Alphon must have smiled to himself when the Mentals Only Hope point came up, as he realized just how easy it was to dupe those in the higher ranks of government. In fact, Justice himself, checking through the card for Slough greyhound stadium for the evening of the murder, had come across this dog with the extraordinary, and somewhat apposite, name. It had become something of a regular joke between them all. So it was almost inevitable that Alphon would include a reference to it in his notes. It was undoubtedly another of his deliberate mistakes, included to give the authorities the excuse (which they readily accepted) not to take his confession seriously.

What is more astonishing, however, is the blinkered reasoning of the Home Office. After all, if the Mentals Only Hope point eliminated Alphon, then the sweet-shop point must have eliminated Hanratty – rather more comprehensively, in fact.

Then there was the 'complete alibi', sensationally revealed to MPs. It must be recalled that, at Hanratty's trial, Acott had given twelve reasons for the elimination of Alphon. If the latter had had a 'complete alibi', then it would have been extraordinary, not to say misleading and dishonest, for Acott not to have included it. It would have been a far more cogent reason than any of those he did give.

Was this, then, new evidence? No, just the same old evidence. The Home Secretary was only too happy to accept the testimony of William Nudds – the liar, thief and police informer, the man who gave a different story each time he was asked to tell it, who'd been in and out of prison for over thirty-five years, and who was at that very moment back inside, serving a six-year sentence, having been convicted of various offences of fraud and theft within eight months of telling the Bedford jury that 'Since I left prison I have been going straight.' As soon as the Home Secretary examined the file, he was able to determine that this man was a paragon of truth – or a paragon, at any rate, of occasional truth: the first and third statements were 'true', and the second 'untrue'. It was 'beyond challenge'.

The attack on the character and reputation of Jean Justice (which Brooke would have been unable to make outside Parliament) probably served, as intended, to discredit the campaign by discrediting the principal campaigner. It was wholly objectionable. It also made the affair in Vienna seem in retrospect even more sinister than it had at the time.

Virtually nothing of what the Home Secretary told MPs that day about the case was true. Would he have known that himself? Probably not (although the car-driving point was so idiotic that he should have had more sense than to make it). A minister is dependent on his officials, just as officials are dependent on the police for first-hand investigations. It must be for others to decide where the lies start and the buck stops.

CHAPTER TWENTY-ONE

IN THE EARLY months, because of the absolute priority of halting the execution, the A6 campaigners were preoccupied with only one question: had Hanratty committed the crime? As that was resolved, so it was subsumed by an alternative puzzle – had Alphon, in fact, done it? Incipient feelings that he probably had crystallized into near certainty, and then different questions began to emerge. Why had this crime happened? What lay behind it?

Immediately after the execution the inquest into the death of Charles France, and the refusal to make his last letters public, had fuelled suspicions that this was a more complex affair than had originally been supposed. All observers of the case – whether or not they believed that Hanratty had committed it – no longer felt comfortable with the view expressed at trial by the prosecution that the crime was the work of a 'moon maniac'.

Louis Blom-Cooper publicly raised such thoughts for the first time in his book, asking, Was Hanratty *sent* to the cornfield? The idea that the gunman might have been hired was beguiling. So, a more sophisticated understanding of the crime began to emerge. People looked for some sort of coherent plan, and wondered whether Gregsten and Storie were deliberately targeted, and if the liaison between them had any relevance to the crime.

Alphon, the man who saw civilization slipping into vice and decadence, didn't scotch this idea but neither, to begin with, did he encourage it. In his confession notes there were veiled suggestions of some larger scheme ('How I knew Nudds', 'Past attempt at cornfield', and the notion that Hanratty was framed), but Alphon could not at first permit anyone else a share of the glory for what he clearly considered a solo achievement.

In November 1963, after a hiatus of some months, he resumed his calls to Justice. Even though he now knew they were being tape-recorded, he maintained contact. After some months, on 18 March 1964, he suddenly dropped the name of the man whom he described as the central figure – the man who had initiated and organized the crime. In fact, Alphon spat out the name with such venom that Justice and others monitoring the case found it (bearing in mind that Alphon's credibility rating rarely moved above zero) unusually convincing. From this point, references to the Central Figure, who is still alive today, featured routinely in Alphon's diatribes.

Justice moved from Mayfair to Belgravia. Having been deeply wounded by the Home Secretary's comments about him in Parliament, he gave up drinking and became a teetotaller for the rest of his life.[1] He set to work on a book about the case. Its central tenet was that Hanratty had not committed the murder, but that Alphon had. Much of the book explored the mesmerizing relationship between Justice himself and Alphon. No British publisher, perhaps inevitably, was willing to accept the book. All considered it a high-risk venture, both because of the naming of Alphon and consequent libel difficulties and because of Justice's own chequered reputation.

So Justice took it to Paris, and to Maurice Girodias, a man who believed, as W. L. Webb wrote in the *Guardian*, that 'freedom to publish was not to be qualified'. Girodias derived equal relish from publishing works of outstanding literary merit and ones of pure pornography. If a work was difficult to place elsewhere – for whatever reason – the Olympia Press, in the Rue Saint-Severin, would often provide sanctuary. Amongst his notable successes, Girodias began with Nikos Kazantzakis's *Zorba the Greek*, and then enthusiastically published Samuel Beckett, William Burroughs, Jean Genet and Vladimir Nabokov's *Lolita*. He was certainly keen to take on board Justice's book, *Murder vs Murder: The British Legal System and the A6 Murder Case*.[2]

He published it on 16 October 1964. So Alphon, whose identity was scrupulously disguised for the parliamentary debate, was publicly named for the first time (there was, of course, no mention of the Central Figure – that would have been too foolhardy), even if few in Britain were aware of it.

At about that time, the case attracted a fresh supporter: Lord Russell of Liverpool. He, too, had followed the case, and become increasingly concerned about it. He considered that Henry Brooke's reasons for turning down the pleas for an inquiry were spurious. He told the press he now intended to write a book about the case.

As soon as this was publicized, Lord and Lady Russell began to suffer a series of nuisance telephone calls. At one juncture, they received sixty in ninety minutes. Within a year, they had received hundreds of calls, both at their London flat and at their farmhouse in Plaistow, in the Sussex countryside. Since Russell had an international circle of friends, he was reluctant to change the number. Lady Russell said that what always haunted her about the calls was the man's 'diabolical laugh'. She added, however, 'All I usually hear is heavy breathing and then he rings off. Every time the phone goes, I expect it to be him.'[3]

What especially angered Lord Russell was the attitude of the police. The threats being made against him were clear enough. '[The caller] has said my life hangs by a string and he can cut it whenever he likes.' All of this was reported to the police; yet no action was taken. When Lord Russell pressed the matter, and asked for an explanation, he received a reply from Sir Joseph Simpson, Chief Constable of Police at New Scotland Yard. He made the astonishing suggestion that, if prosecuted, the caller would be able to mount a persuasive defence on the basis that 'you [Russell] had enlisted police assistance primarily to gain publicity for your forthcoming book on the A6 Murder'. Russell termed Simpson's argument 'impertinent'.

Like Justice, Russell experienced some difficulty in finding a publisher bold enough to want to go ahead with his book. Gollancz, having orginally agreed to take it on, withdrew. Russell then took it to Secker and Warburg. No sooner had they agreed to publish it than the telephone harassment of the Russells ceased, and Fred Warburg started receiving calls at his London flat. The caller, who described himself as a fascist and went on at some length about Hitler, was clearly trying to dissuade him from publishing the book. Fortunately, this only strengthened Warburg's resolve, and the book, *Deadman's Hill: Was Hanratty Guilty?* appeared on 21 October 1965.

Although the book indicated that the reasons given in court for Alphon's elimination were very peculiar, it otherwise ignored him. Instead, Russell concentrated on the weaknesses in the Crown case at the trial, and marshalled the arguments that he believed were powerfully suggestive of Hanratty's complete innocence: nothing to connect him with the cornfield, or even that part of the country, no motive or reason at all for his having been in the area; the fact that his behaviour in the weeks following the murder was entirely inconsistent with guilt; no evidence that he was a sex maniac, and overwhelming evidence to suggest that he wasn't; no evidence that he ever possessed a revolver.

Russell's diligent research uncovered the fact that Superintendent

Acott had described Hanratty as 'a typical gunman'.[4] He commented:

> It must be admitted that [Acott] should know better than anyone what makes 'a typical gunman'; but unless he is in possession of some information which has not yet been disclosed, the fact that he so described Hanratty must raise considerable doubts as to his power of judgement. Hanratty was never 'a typical gunman', nor did the A6 murderer behave like one, whoever he may have been.[5]

The book reignited public interest and received complimentary reviews from, among others, Hugh Trevor-Roper (now Lord Dacre), Regius Professor of Modern History at Oxford, one of a growing number of academics who were disturbed by the case. Others included Stan Cohen, later Professor of Law at the Hebrew University of Jerusalem; and also Terence Morris, today Emeritus Professor of Criminology in the University of London. While engaged on a research project in 1958, Morris got to know Hanratty through working alongside him in the prison laundry at Maidstone. He wrote a long submission to the Home Office in 1962 when Hanratty was under sentence of death. 'I was deeply troubled by the whole thing,' he recalled. 'It was so totally out of character.'

After personally offering them financial compensation for Jimmy's death, Alphon continued to behave in an erratic and eccentric way towards the Hanratty family. One Saturday evening he telephoned several times; Michael told his mother not to get distressed and tried to calm her. The following morning he drove off to get the Sunday papers. He then saw Alphon close to their house, so he jumped out of the car – he was still driving Jimmy's Sunbeam Alpine – to confront him.

'He hadn't shaved, he was in a terrible state,' recalled Michael. 'I just saw red and said, "What are you doing here?" "It's a free country," he replied. He was raving, his eyes were sticking out of his head – and that's not my imagination. He said, "I might have done the murder, but the establishment murdered your brother." I remembered what Lord Russell always said to me, which was never to touch him. I just jumped back in the car, drove to a phone box and rang up Scotland Yard. I said, "If you don't come and pick him up straightaway, there's going to be another murder." Within three or four minutes, the local police came. They also said to me, "Don't touch him, you'll spoil your case." They added, "It doesn't matter what he does, we've been told to put him on a train back to West End Central [Bow Street]."

'The next day, my father and I went to Scotland Yard. We told them, "This has got to stop." The Superintendent replied, "Don't take any notice, Michael, he's just a crank." I said, "If he's just a crank, can you prove to me he didn't do the murder?" He just lost his temper then, and said, "You think you've fucking had enough? I'm up to here with it." He said, "Do you know where he gets his money?" I said, "No, I expected you to tell me." We thought at the time that Scotland Yard was the best police force in the world, and all they could say to us was, "Have patience." I thought, Is this man blackmailing them or what? They seemed terrified of him.'

Monday, 8 November 1965 was a watershed in post-war British social and judicial history: the bill to abolish capital punishment was enacted. There have, in recent years, been suggestions that concern over the Hanratty case played some part in achieving this. I believe this is a reinterpretation of events which owes everything to hindsight. During the debate, one of the main proponents of abolition, Barbara Wootton (Baroness Wootton of Abinger), said: 'There is the appalling risk, human beings being fallible, that we may hang an innocent man, and in the minds of many of us is a very grave doubt – certainly in two cases in the last twenty years, possibly in more – that this very thing may have happened.'

The two cases she referred to would have been those of Timothy Evans and Walter Rowland. Hanratty was embraced, if at all, in her 'possibly' category. Only Fenner Brockway actually mentioned the A6 case. The police, and many others, remained overwhelmingly convinced of Hanratty's guilt – it was at this time that Madame Tussaud's was preparing an effigy of him for their Chamber of Horrors. By that time, the moves to abolish capital punishment were already well advanced; the Hanratty case was not yet popularly established throughout the country as a cause célèbre, and, on this occasion, made scant difference to the outcome.

When the bill was debated earlier in the year, the then Home Secretary, Sir Frank Soskice, had promised that if it did become law, he would consider sympathetically any application to remove the remains of executed men from inside prison grounds for private burial outside. Once the bill became law, the Hanratty family was the first in the queue to take advantage of this. On 17 February 1966 the new Home Secretary, Roy Jenkins, signed the licence allowing the family to remove the remains of their son from

Bedford Prison. At noon on 22 February 1966 Jimmy was reburied in Carpenders Park, Watford.

One of those attending the funeral was the journalist Paul Foot, who became interested when Richard Ingrams, editor of *Private Eye*, told him that a man called Jean Justice seemed to have some very interesting material. *Private Eye*, then as now, was in the vanguard of reporting issues that impugned establishment attitudes. Foot's involvement gave the campaign a critical stimulus and, over the years, his contribution became priceless. Media interest in the case as a miscarriage of justice was slowly being kindled.

Lord Russell had maintained his close links with the campaign, and on Thursday, 4 August 1966, almost exactly three years after the case had last been debated in Parliament, managed to arrange a debate in the House of Lords. He put down the following motion:

'To ask Her Majesty's Government whether they will set up an independent commission to inquire into the confession of the said murder made by Peter Louis Alphon, and to consider any further information which may have become available since the conviction of James Hanratty, and to report whether, in their opinion, there are any grounds for thinking there has been any miscarriage of justice.'

Russell referred to the then Home Secretary's remarks (quoted earlier) about the three Nudds statements, and rebuked him, albeit in the most courteous of parliamentary language, for saying that it was 'impossible' for Alphon to have committed the murder. He suggested that it was astonishing for the Home Office to set so much store by Nudds's evidence. Even the Crown QC, Russell pointed out, 'had told the jury, "Do not rely on Nudds unless there is documentary corroboration available." The only documents available corroborated statement No. 2. That should dispose once and for all of the complete alibi, beyond challenge.'

Russell went on to tell the House about the long series of harassing calls he had received from the man whom, beyond any possible doubt, he knew to be Alphon:

'The man who made these calls certainly fitted the description by Superintendent Acott of the murderer as being erratic and excitable; for he frequently threatened me, shouting "I will come and do you in," and at other times he spoke in a quiet voice. He told me on several occasions, "I got away with murder, didn't I?"

'On another occasion, he asked, "Who do you think committed the murder?" I said it was not for me to say, but I was sure that

Hanratty had not. He replied, "There is no third party, don't you know – it is either him or me. At any rate, Hanratty was expendable." He also said the police would not take any action against him because he was protected by them.'[6]

Having abandoned their earlier excuse that it might all be viewed as a publicity stunt by Russell, the police had now reverted to their original one: Alphon couldn't be traced.

Ironically, the main protagonists of the earlier duel in the Commons – Fenner Brockway and Henry Brooke – were now both ennobled, and both ready to resume their former roles (the latter by making his maiden speech in the Lords). The latter said, 'On all the information available to me as Home Secretary three years ago, I was entirely satisfied that there was nothing which pointed to a miscarriage of justice.' On the other hand, Lord Brockway commented, 'If we are to take pride in our society it must be because we take infinite care that justice is done to any individual. That is the test of a liberal and civilized society. If there is any reasonable doubt that James Hanratty was executed when he did not commit the murder, then the duty of holding an inquiry cannot be shirked.'

The Government case was put by Lord Stonham, Parliamentary Under-Secretary of State at the Home Office. He informed the peers that, 'This is an exceptionally complex case, and I have studied it carefully.' He went on to illustrate just how complex: 'In this case the material is of such magnitude that it would be impossible to bring all the files over here tonight, though I assure your Lordships that the resources of the Home Office are such that arrangements have been made to refer to the files, should any point requiring this have been made.'

In rebutting Russell's points, he said, 'The [Nudds] statements were not the first evidence the police had in support of Mr Alphon's alibi. He was seen by them, first on 27 August, four days after the murder, when he said that he was with his mother on the evening of the 22nd, the fatal evening, and then went to the hotel. This was verified with the hotel at the time and with his mother.'[7]

He also gave an explanation in response to the inability to trace Alphon: 'There continues to be great difficulty in tracing the man who makes these calls. He is believed to be in north London and inquiries are being made in this area. His exact whereabouts are unknown. It is an extremely difficult matter, and the police have tried very hard. But I would assure the noble Lord that . . . renewed and vigorous efforts are being made to trace the man. At this stage, we do not accept categorically even that the man making the calls is Alphon. Certainly, it seems likely but it is a fact which would have to be conclusively established.'

When making this point he was, unfortunately, in error. Not only was it crashingly obvious that the man making the calls *was* Alphon, but the police, presumably aware that their feeble efforts to track him down were going to be heavily criticized in Parliament, had finally located him. No one had bothered to tell Stonham. On the following Monday, 8 August, he had to return to the Chamber to inform the Lords that Alphon had in fact been interviewed by police on 2 August, and a report forwarded to the DPP; and to apologize to the Lords for giving them incorrect information.

It was altogether an extraordinary business. A man who kept making scarcely veiled confessions to one of the most appalling crimes in post-war Britain seemed to enjoy the full protection not only of the police, but also of Parliament, whether the Commons or the Lords, with ministers – even ones who had, or so they claimed, 'studied the case carefully' – prepared to disseminate untruths on his behalf; and all this, moreover, happened irrespective of party: the first occurred during a Conservative administration, the latter under a Labour one.

Having been so belatedly apprehended, Alphon was brought to trial by Chief Inspector Henry Mooney at Marylebone Magistrates Court on 25 August, and charged with making annoying telephone calls not only to Lord Russell but also to Frank Justice. As ever, he was treated indulgently, and merely fined £5. However, he was additionally bound over to keep the peace in the sum of £50. This marked the start of a significant sub-plot in the saga.

In the aftermath of the Lords debate and the Alphon court hearing, media interest was beginning to percolate again. Paul Foot's first significant contribution was commissioned by Jocelyn Stevens and appeared in *Queen* magazine on 14 September.[8] Unusually for such an accomplished journalist, Foot experienced difficulty in persuading more mainstream publications to take the story. Perhaps, though, this was understandable: Foot named Alphon as the A6 murderer – the first time this had happened other than in Justice's Paris-published book, or outside the protection of parliamentary privilege.

One result of the publicity was that, on 20 September, Joan Lestor, Brockway's successor as MP for Eton and Slough, put down a Commons motion asking the Home Secretary to institute an inquiry into the conviction. A second was that *Panorama*, the BBC's prestigious current affairs programme, set to work on the case; and a third was that *Queen* magazine began receiving a series of silent, and potentially distressing, telephone calls.[9]

The *Panorama* programme was broadcast on 7 November 1966.[10] Alphon agreed to be interviewed and, perhaps to his surprise, was played extracts from the tape-recordings of the telephone conversations, which Justice had supplied to the BBC. The reporter, John Morgan, asked Alphon for an explanation; the latter responded that he and Justice had merely been rehearsing ideas for a book based on the case – although it was not only Morgan who found it hard to conceive of a book being planned in quite such a hysterical fashion. There was also an interesting moment when Alphon, who seemed unable to resist talking about the crime, gave his own, supposedly hypothetical version of what had happened in the car that night: 'He did try to separate them. He sent Gregsten away to get some cigarettes, didn't he, and Gregsten came back . . . I think that perhaps if he hadn't come back things would have turned out very differently.'[11]

Thus he twice referred to Gregsten having 'come' back to the car. Anyone not personally involved would logically have said that Gregsten had 'gone' back to the car.

Nevertheless, for those heartened by the notion of the infallibility of British justice, the programme was ultimately reassuring. First, Alphon, publicly confronted with his confession, had disavowed it. Second, Morgan had also spoken to Peter Duffy, who gave his first-hand account of the 'She Saw Him at the Cleaners' episode. Despite being in personal possession of one of the most cryptic parts of the A6 story, Duffy persisted in his belief that Hanratty was guilty. Third, Valerie Storie gave what is to date her most recent television interview (she has declined all requests ever since), and declared that she had no misgivings: 'Of course, Hanratty's the man. I was there, I saw him. There's no possible doubt whatsoever.'

Valerie Storie's certainty was shared by a diminishing number of people. *Panorama* also commented at length on the Rhyl alibi. Grace Jones was now fully prepared to re-affirm her trial testimony and insist that Hanratty had stayed at Ingledene at that vital time. *Panorama* also produced a fresh witness, Charlie Jones (also known as Charlie White), a newspaper-seller.

Jones said that one evening in August, he thought it was a Tuesday, he had set his papers on the wall at the Crosville bus station. Someone came up to him, and asked, 'Where does Terry live?' Jones knew a few Terrys, and didn't immediately know who was being referred to; the man then said, 'Where's the fairground?' so Jones told him. After a little while the man returned, and asked where he could get digs. According to Jones, 'I told him the only place I knew was 19 Kinmel Street, at Mrs Jones's.'

Some time afterwards, after the trial, Charlie Jones saw a photograph in one of the evening papers and recognized the face 'as that of the young man who had spoken to me at the bus station'. He kept the photograph, and showed it to Terry Evans, saying, 'I'm sure this is the lad who asked me for Terry.' Evans replied, 'Well, it's all over now.'[12]

When *Panorama* arrived in Rhyl in the autumn of 1966, the producer approached Terry Evans for assistance. He mentioned this story to them, although they couldn't at first locate Charlie Jones. Then, when Evans was with an assistant producer in a café in Windsor Street, just across the road from Ingledene, Jones walked in. Evans said to the BBC man, 'That's the chap who I was looking for who might have seen him.' Jones's cup of tea immediately went down on *Panorama*'s expenses.

Jones and Evans both appeared on the programme, receiving 10 guineas each for their troubles. Jones's testimony subsequently became the subject of fierce dispute, with both the *Sunday Telegraph* ('Paper Seller Disclaims TV Alibi for Hanratty') and the *News of the World* arguing that he was an unreliable witness who had now contradicted his televised statements.

In the wake of the *Panorama* broadcast Jones, like Grace Jones before him, became an instant celebrity and, again like Grace Jones, fared poorly in the glare of publicity. Nevertheless, he did make a statement to Rhyl police towards the end of the month, on 25 November, clearly putting everything into perspective: 'I am really sorry I have got mixed up with this matter, I can't understand how I have been dragged into it. I have told you the truth, I did not know Hanratty, I have never seen him before that day in Rhyl and again I tell you I cannot say what day it was he spoke with me.'

Altogether, the *Panorama* programme generated considerable publicity. After the *Sunday Telegraph* had demolished its main witness (by now, television and newspaper journalists relished the opportunity to scupper each other's stories) the *Daily Telegraph* dispatched a reporter of its own to Rhyl to build on its stablemate's success. His visit didn't work out to plan; he found only witnesses wishing to substantiate Hanratty's alibi. 'Inquiries in Rhyl yesterday revealed that at least three other people who were not called at Hanratty's trial claimed to have seen him in the town during late August 1961.'[13]

It was in this way that the testimony of Margaret Walker and Ivy Vincent first came to public attention.

The Rhyl alibi having been extensively thrashed out in the media in *Panorama*'s slipstream, the Government accepted that the issue had to be addressed. On 30 January 1967, Roy Jenkins, the Home Secretary, announced the appointment of Detective Superintendent Douglas Nimmo, of Manchester City Police, to undertake an inquiry. Jenkins told the Commons that Nimmo would 'investigate the claim that James Hanratty was at Rhyl on 22/23 August 1961; take statements from all relevant witnesses; and make a report to the Home Secretary'.

The Hanratty family was delighted. James Hanratty imagined that this might well be the prelude to the full re-opening of the case. It didn't take long for this mood of optimism to be soured. The rumours reaching them about the course of the inquiry became less and less promising. Superintendent Nimmo stayed in Rhyl from 9 to 15 February to interview witnesses, none of whom was legally represented, or accompanied by independent observers.

On 22 March the *Evening News* reported that the report was complete and had been passed to the Home Office. It was thought that Jenkins would make a statement in Parliament after the Easter recess. However, there was no official word; only unofficial leaks. Disturbingly, Percy Hoskins, the experienced and well-informed crime correspondent of the *Daily Express*, reported that Nimmo had found nothing to support the contention that 'Hanratty was in Rhyl on the night of the murder'.

With the case receiving continuing publicity, Alphon, who became petulant if he wasn't the centre of attention, was not inactive. He continued to regard himself as above the law. Despite the court judgment in August 1966, he ignored the injunction laid upon him and, as early as September, simply resumed his telephone harassment of Lord and Lady Russell.

On 10 February 1967 Russell took out a private summons against him. Nothing happened for a little while, but, finally, on 27 April, eleven weeks after it was issued, the police served the summons on Alphon. He was told to appear at Marylebone Magistrates' Court on Friday, 12 May. Having so blatantly disregarded the terms of a court order, he now faced the very real prospect of a prison sentence.

Alphon doubtless enjoyed a particular frisson from having as his adversary a bona fide member of the aristocracy. When they were on opposite sides in the courtroom, however, there was in theory little doubt whom the magistrates would choose to believe. Even with his ability to escape the legal consequences of his actions, Alphon must have sensed that he'd at last crossed the Rubicon.

Instead of answering the summons, he went to Paris, and announced his intention of holding a press conference. So, on Friday, 12 May, just as a warrant was issued for his arrest in London (as a result of his failure to answer the summons), he was holding court in a different sense. At the Hôtel du Louvre, he told the handful of journalists present that he had committed the A6 Murder. According to *The Times*, he said, 'I have been so persecuted, but now I want to drag British justice through the mud . . . I did in fact do the A6 Murder. I killed Gregsten and half-killed our friend Miss Storie . . . The police are now trying to hush up the fact that they hanged an innocent man.'

The *Evening News* carried a full front-page report of the bizarre event: 'At one point when reporters began firing questions at him, Alphon became rambling and incoherent. He referred to Russians, Nazis, Bertrand Russell and mini-skirts in Britain, which he said showed a moral decadence.'[14]

The Times further reported that proceedings were observed by a Metropolitan Police inspector, stationed in Paris on Interpol liaison duties, and a detective sergeant sent from Scotland Yard. The latter had instructions to report back to Sir Joseph Simpson, by now rejoicing in his new title of Commissioner of the Metropolitan Police.[15]

Paul Foot didn't attend the conference, but later that day he did manage to reach Alphon by telephone, at the Hôtel Ste-Anne where he was staying. This was the first time that Foot had spoken to him. From their lengthy conversation, Foot was able to piece together the Alphon confession, as it then stood. This was it, as reported in that week's *Sunday Times*:

I first met [the Central Figure] in the White Bear Inn in Piccadilly Circus about two years before the murder. He pretended to be an extreme right-wing fascist and we agreed on a lot of things, especially about immorality among married people. [The Central Figure] talked a lot for months before the murder about Michael Gregsten and the affair he was having with a girl in his office.

I knew he had a plan to stop the affair once and for all. He approached one or two people in Soho to see if they would help, but no Soho tiddler could do what he wanted. Anyway, I used to boast a lot about how easy it would be to frighten Gregsten. One day he said, 'If you're so clever, why don't you do it?' and I said, 'I can do almost anything.' 'Like use a gun?' he said, and I replied, although I had never used a gun before, 'Of course, you would have to use a gun.'

Then he talked about the money, and he offered me £5,000. You can check on this and as far as I am concerned, the bank manager has my permission to disclose all the facts about my account. The money was paid into my account at the Law Courts branch of Lloyds Bank – £5,000 in five or six instalments, I think starting in October 1961.

Charles 'Dixie' France was a mutual friend of me and [the Central Figure] and Hanratty, especially of Hanratty. France was very broke at the time and he got money to get the gun and he gave me the gun a week before the murder. I wasn't very good with a gun and I had to have some practice so I shot two bullets into a cushion in a chair at the Cumberland Hotel, Marble Arch. I took the two cartridge cases and gave them to France.

[The Central Figure] had shown me the cornfield where Gregsten and Valerie used to go after work. I'd been there twice before the murder on a reconnaissance.

On the day I was at Slough dog-track and there was a bookmaker there who knows me and who can confirm this, although I don't know his name. I left the track at about eight o'clock and I walked all the way down through Taplow cross-country to the cornfield. I know the area well because I was brought up there in the war. It's about seven miles and it took me about an hour and a half. When I got there the car was in the field.

I climbed into the back of the car and stayed there for five hours. Two hours in the field and three hours driving about. My plan was to persuade Gregsten to get out of the car and run away. And then I would take the girl and rape her, and then she might feel, what sort of a man is he to leave me like that?

But that didn't work. Gregsten had two chances to go, when he got out for cigarettes and milk, but he kept coming back. When I complained to them about their immorality they laughed and told me to mind my bloody business. There was an awful lot of talking in that five hours in the car. Gregsten was cocky the whole time, trying to take the mickey. I knew that the only way to break up the affair was to kill them.

When I shot him it was more in self-defence. If I hadn't shot him I would have had it. He turned very quickly. But it wasn't accidental because I was going to kill them anyway.

I knew the way from Bedford to Slough but I didn't know the way back to London, and I got lost down a lot of side roads trying to find the A5. I left the car at Redbridge and walked to Ilford Station. I got the train there, changed at Stratford on to the tube, changed again at Oxford Circus and went to Warwick Avenue, which was near the Vienna Hotel where I'd booked in the night before. I went into the hotel and went up to my room, had a wash, came down and had breakfast about 9.40.

I went to Paddington Station and left my case there. I was still wearing the same suit, but there was no blood on it and I had the gun in my pocket. I took the tube to Oxford Circus, changed and went east to Southend. I met France at Southend and gave him the gun. We had drinks and a meal and then we left separately about five o'clock. I came back and booked in at the Alexandra National [Alexandra Court] Hotel, Finsbury Park.

I was still staying there on the Sunday when the police came to interview me. They said it was a routine check-up because the hotel manager had reported my strange behaviour. But I don't believe it. I think I was shopped. They interviewed me for five hours, but I had a good alibi and there was nothing they could pin on me. The grey suit and the dark glasses I had worn for the murder I had put in a locker in Leicester Square tube station and destroyed the ticket.

They let me go then but were obviously out to get me. I gave myself up on 22 September after the police had started a nationwide hunt for me. I was pretty sure I would be all right because Valerie wouldn't recognize me. She didn't recognize me. She never saw my face once in the car.

When I was in the clear I began to realize the plot against Hanratty. [The Central Figure] had suggested to me that when I was in the car I could pretend I was Hanratty whom we all knew as a stupid little crook. That's why I said my name was Jim and I was on the run and had done time.

What I didn't realize was that they meant to get Hanratty for what I had done. France put the gun on the bus where Hanratty had told him it was a good place to hide loot. And France put the cartridge cases in the Vienna Hotel. [The Central Figure] first put the police on Hanratty's trial.

I couldn't understand why they were so keen to fix Hanratty. I mean, we had got away with it. But France took money from the press to give evidence against his friend and he went into the witness-box against his friend. I can tell you that I put pressure on France.

I used to ring him again and again after Hanratty was convicted telling him to retract his evidence and threatening him that if Hanratty died, I would see he died too. I think I had something to do with his suicide, but I don't want that on my conscience as well.[16]

That last paragraph rings absolutely true, which is more than can be said for the rest of it. Now that more is known about the case, Alphon's confessions take on a clearer perspective. As I have already made clear, I believe it is wrong to assume that these are a mixture of truths and falsehoods; they're essentially a collection of falsehoods. Wherever anything is verifiable, wherever it can be checked against documentation or known facts, it turns out not to be true. Paul Foot reached a parallel conclusion. 'Key facts were swapped and replaced with malevolent abandon,' he wrote. 'The more I tried to construct a coherent story from Alphon's conversations with me, the more his story crumbled.'

The devil is in the detail, and all Alphon's details are wrong. In just about every confession that he made, he mentioned returning to the Vienna Hotel and having breakfast there. It's an absurdly trivial point; but it isn't true. He did not have breakfast. The testimony of the Vienna staff is unanimous on this point (even Nudds fell in line).

The description of how he made his way to the Vienna from Redbridge was untrue, and also illustrated how plausibly inventive he could be. The story is feasible – but only theoretically. In practical terms, it is nonsense. It was unimaginable that he should have walked all the way from a tube (underground) station at Redbridge to a British Rail (overground) station at Ilford. It was far too dangerous for him, a stranger, to walk that far through residential streets. It would have vastly increased the risks of his being seen, and of someone providing an accurate description of him. Conversely, as the whole world must have known, the best way to effect an escape in London was to be absorbed into the crowds on the tube. In fact, the car was abandoned where it was precisely because it was close to a tube station.

Also, if Alphon had done the journey which he now posited, then the timing wouldn't fit. It would have taken at least thirty minutes longer, and he'd have risked being noticed by staff and guests when arriving at the hotel. The Redbridge tube station was, conveniently, on the Central Line, and took him straight into the centre of London, and Oxford Circus, from where he could change to the Bakerloo line to reach Warwick Avenue. That was a straightforward journey. (Hanratty's lawyers did check the timing before the trial, to show that Alphon would have reached the hotel at 8.00 a.m., and thus slipped into his room while the guests were either still rising or having breakfast, and when the staff were preoccupied in serving them.)

Today, other lies leap off the page: Shooting practice in the Cumberland Hotel? One way or another, I expect they'd have noticed; and in any case, Alphon wasn't staying in hotels of that standard before the crime. The notion that he went to Southend to meet France to hand him the gun is absurd; Alphon was seen in London towards 5 p.m. that day. There is no evidence at all that Alphon was brought up in the Slough area during the war. The family then lived in west and south London (and the young Peter was evacuated to Horsham in West Sussex).

Finally, it is very instructive that, although Alphon is supposed to be providing a clear account of why the crime took place, that's precisely what he doesn't do. He says the Central Figure had a plan to 'stop the affair once and for all'; he mentions the need 'to frighten Gregsten'. Why? What business was it of the Central Figure's? Out of sympathy for Janet Gregsten? But no mention is made of her. And how would he have known the scene of Michael and Valerie's trysts?

Then the account gets really confused. Although Alphon said that 'my plan was to persuade Gregsten to get out of the car and run away', he contradicted this by saying, 'I was going to kill them anyway.'

If the plan had been to separate the couple, so that Gregsten ceased his immorality and returned to the family home and his wife and children, thus bringing comfort to Janet, then Alphon wouldn't have been contemplating killing him, and wouldn't have been negotiating a handsome fee for doing so.

If, on the other hand, the Central Figure's objective had been, for whatever reason, to kill Gregsten, then it is certain that he could have got the job done more efficiently and less expensively (despite Alphon's laughably vainglorious comment about this being a mission for 'no Soho tiddler'). Altogether, the first full confession raised a myriad of questions and answered none. Even so, one particular reaction remained: Alphon was the sort of psychopath who lied so convincingly that it was dangerous to place faith in anything he said; and yet he was also the sort of psychopath who could have committed a crime of this cruelty.

In the immediate wake of this confession, James, Mary and Michael Hanratty went to the Home Office, where they spent two hours the following morning discussing developments in the case with an official.

Two days later, Wednesday, 17 May, an entire edition of *Dateline*, ITV's current affairs programme, was devoted to Alphon. Interviewed lolling on his bed in his Paris hotel room, he reiterated what he'd said at the press conference. Confronted by an interviewer who, notwithstanding his other journalistic credentials, had little more than a rudimentary grasp of this case, Alphon was thoroughly at ease, and clearly enjoying himself enormously.

Interviewer: Are you or are you not the A6 killer?
Alphon: Well, I've stated that at the press conference, and when I say something, I stand by it.
Interviewer: Now there seem to be three different opinions of you. People think you're either a liar, a killer or that you're mentally disturbed and unbalanced. Which are you?
Alphon: Maybe it's all three.
Interviewer: Why do you think the police haven't arrested you?
Alphon: I think they'd like to arrest me, and I don't think because of the A6 Murder. I think they would if they could trump up another little charge to get me, and it may take a little time for them to get themselves together, because they're very stupid, you know.
Interviewer: Isn't it the fact that the police haven't arrested you because they are satisfied you are not the killer, and you've been able to make your confession because you know they know you're not the killer?
Alphon: The real reason why I've confessed, and I said it at the press conference, is that I want to drag the name of British justice through the mud – where it belongs. I think I neglected to say that at the press conference, in the mud where it belongs . . . I'm saying now that I've done it, but I don't like other people saying it – does that make sense to you?
Interviewer: No.
Alphon: Well, let me put it this way. I've done it, and now I want to forget about it. If you'd done a murder, you'd want to forget about it, you wouldn't want to go on thinking about it the whole time.

Interviewer: But you've confessed here in Paris?

Alphon: This is the first time in six years, I've been forced to do it by the actions of these people, to bring it out into the open.

Interviewer: I don't understand why you should confess to the killing if you were the killer, because you might be inviting a possible life sentence.

Alphon: I might be inviting a lynching. You see, the thing is, this murder happened six years ago, and they've hanged someone, wrongfully, they've hanged him wrongfully.

Interviewer: If you were charged, how would you react to that?

Alphon: I should be delighted – well, this may be a bit hard for your audience, the general public, to appreciate. But as I have been charged with so many things I haven't done, I would at last like to see the British police charge me with something I have done.

Interviewer: Can I get some impression of you? How do you regard yourself?

Alphon: I'm a Nazi. That's the beginning and end of my life. My faith is in common decency. I felt I knew my aim in life all along. Let's say it was a messianic mission.

Interviewer: Well, I don't understand that.

Alphon: Do you want a dictionary? Everybody knows what a messianic mission is.

Interviewer: So you had a crusade of some sort?

Alphon: Exactly. My crusade was against indecency and immorality. Those two things. That's enough, isn't it?

Interviewer: How have you lived since the A6 Murder?

Alphon: How do you mean, how have I lived? Just breathed the air in . . .

Interviewer: What have you done for money?

Alphon: Oh, I see, got a private income.

The interviewer subsequently put to Alphon the points by which he had been eliminated at the trial:

Alphon: You've just put Acott's 12 points to me, which have been destroyed by people, who are not my friends, admittedly, but they've destroyed them adequately. So what you're saying is absolute rubbish.

Interviewer: What about the cockney accent?

Alphon: Let's put it this way. I can put a certain veneer on my voice when I want to.

Interviewer: You're not Jim or James?

Alphon: The killer would hardly give his real name unless he was a complete idiot, and I don't think even Hanratty was that, and I'm certainly not.

Interviewer: You haven't got 'large icy-blue staring eyes'?

Alphon: No, I don't think anybody has. That sounds like a police formula to me.

Interviewer: How did you feel when you knew Hanratty was going to be hanged?

Alphon: I didn't feel too good, nor for some time before. I tried my damnedest, in ways that were unconstitutional, to stop it. France committed suicide, need we say more?

Interviewer: But you framed [Hanratty]?

Alphon: I didn't frame him, it wasn't me.

Interviewer: Are you simply a mentally sick exhibitionist?

Alphon: I'm hardly going to go along with that. If I'm sick, then Lord Russell is sick, and Mr Justice is sick.

Interviewer: Would you like to kill again?

Alphon: Certainly not. I'm not a pacifist, but private murder is out. We've got no blood-lust on us.[17]

Despite, or perhaps because of, the naivety of the interviewer, it was fascinating television. Alphon peppered his account with inaccuracies (for example, he said he'd fired only one shot at Michael Gregsten), making them particularly glaring so that the interviewer could not fail to notice. Alphon then smiled indulgently; he'd got television and the newspapers dancing to his tunes.

But perhaps because the lies are so blatant, there are other moments when he appeared utterly credible – as when the interviewer asked how he felt as the time for Hanratty's execution drew near. His answer in response to the garbled question about whether he was a liar, killer or was mentally unbalanced – 'maybe it's all three' – demonstrated that here was a fine intelligence at play.

From Paris Alphon flew to Dublin and stayed in Dun Laoghaire, the delights of which he probably knew about from Jean. At this point, he seemed unsure whether he'd be able to return to Britain. It quickly appeared unlikely that the authorities were taking the A6 confession seriously (Acott, picking up the baton just as Alphon had intended, told the *Daily Express* that if he'd ever had any doubts, he no longer had. Alphon couldn't have committed the murder because his description of it was at variance with the known facts);

but there was certainly a warrant out for his arrest on the telephone harassment.

The following Sunday, the *People* reported that Alphon had withdrawn his confession.[18] On the following Thursday, Alphon, still in Ireland, telephoned Paul Foot at the *Sunday Telegraph* to repudiate the *People* story. He subsequently wrote to Foot, saying, 'I shall stand by my Paris confession whatever happens. I cannot do more!'[19]

Sometime late in July, Alphon simply came back to Britain. He wasn't apprehended at the airport; nobody arrested him. A few days later, on 5 August, he resumed his nuisance calls to Lord Russell (which were all meticulously logged). Again, Russell reported the matter. The warrant for Alphon's arrest, which had lain dormant since 12 May, was re-activated. The issue was resolved when Alphon surrendered himself at Scotland Yard on Saturday, 2 September – as before, just after midnight. He was taken to Paddington Green police station, where Chief Inspector Mooney arrived at 1.45 a.m. (Alphon rejoiced in getting senior officers out of bed in the early hours.)

He appeared in court later that morning. It was another extraordinary hearing. Alphon had no legal representation, but Mooney, who was prosecuting him, explained that he had taken a statement from Alphon during the night, and that this now cleared up any uncertainty: Alphon could not have done the A6 Murder. Mooney told the court, 'I am satisfied Alphon did not and could not have done it and I know where he was at the time of the murder.'

Alphon was convicted of breaking his promise not to make annoying telephone calls. The magistrate, David Wacher, was understanding. 'It is quite clear that what you have been doing has been done under a sense of grievance which appears to have some foundation in fact. I hope that what has been said in court today will finish for good all these stories that have been put about saying you had a hand in the murder. I can see no reason why anybody from now on will have cause to say you did the murder.'

Once again, British justice, as applied to Alphon, could not have been more fair. He was fined £11, and lost just a mere £10 of his original £50 recognizance. Lord Russell was mystified. 'In fifty years' legal experience I have never seen such a gentle cross-examination. What happened this morning makes me more certain than ever that there should be a public inquiry.'[20]

The timing of Alphon's surrender achieved its twin aims: of

causing the maximum possible inconvenience for the police; and of creating the maximum possible publicity. Any events that took place on a Saturday were bound to be given generous space in the Sunday papers, simply because little else newsworthy would be happening. So headline after headline in the following day's papers recorded Scotland Yard's assertion that Alphon could not have done the murder. The *Sunday Express* was one of the few which tried to explain why not. 'I understand that Yard detectives have interviewed witnesses who say they saw Alphon in a Paddington hotel at a time on the night of 22 August that would have made it impossible for him to have got to Dorney Reach just after 9.00 p.m.'[21]

The *Sunday Times* (10 September) gave further details of the new alibi. It seemed that, on Tuesday, 22 August, Alphon went from the Volunteer pub in Baker Street to the Broadway House Hotel to book a room. He then went to Streatham to meet his mother, before going to the Vienna where he was let in by the manager's wife and stayed the night. However, according to the *Sunday Times*, Alphon himself was unusually taciturn. He said the police would shortly make known the full details of the alibi. 'If I tell you now, and the police tell a different story later, well, I'm not going to look a gift-horse in the mouth.'[22]

No elaboration or explanation of this new alibi was ever produced. The stories that were 'finished for good' in August were flourishing again in September, having been resurrected by none other than Alphon himself. The gift-horse was indeed spurned. On 28 September he wrote to the Home Secretary, saying, 'I hope that I never again witness a major trial where the prosecution is so unsoundly based.'[23]

While all this was going on, Hanratty's parents, still very anxious about the conclusions of the Nimmo inquiry, had gone to Rhyl themselves over the weekend of 3/4 June. They took statements which were published in the *Sunday Times* the following week. On 13 July, after three months' delay, came a bombshell. Roy Jenkins announced what he intended to do about the Nimmo inquiry: he was sending Nimmo back to Rhyl to conduct another one. This development was especially puzzling: if the inquiry had been as diligent as it should have been, why was it necessary to ask Nimmo to repeat or clarify the work? If it hadn't been diligent in the first place, then why was it being entrusted to Nimmo again?

In fact, there was now much ill-feeling in Rhyl towards Nimmo. Witnesses already felt their integrity slighted by what they had read in the press of the first report. The second inquiry was a brief, tense and bad-tempered affair. As total despondency settled over the campaigners, James and Mary Hanratty returned to Rhyl over the last weekend in July to take further statements.

Finally, on Wednesday, 1 November, in a belated response to the speculation that had been mounting from the time of the transmission of *Panorama*, almost exactly a year earlier, Roy Jenkins announced his decision. He turned down calls for an inquiry. The Home Secretary told the Commons: 'I have considered with great care the representations made to me about this case. Peter Alphon has withdrawn his earlier confession. Neither his confession nor other allegations about his part in the case are supported by new material of substance.

'Material has been submitted about Hanratty's claim that he was in Rhyl on 22/23 August. At my request Detective Chief Superintendent Nimmo of Manchester City Police, who had not previously had any connection with the case, has made detailed and exhaustive investigations covering all possible lines of inquiry into the alibi.

'Mr Nimmo's thorough investigations have ... found nothing to strengthen the evidence called at the trial on Hanratty's behalf, and no further evidence which, if put before the jury, might have influenced the verdict.

'I have accordingly decided that there are no grounds for taking any further action in this case.'

What were these decisive conclusions based on? Campaigners at the time had no idea. However, the contents of the Nimmo report (detailed in full at Appendix 2) show that the various statements were collated in a haphazard fashion, with no coherent chronology, and with even statements concerning distinct parts of the field of inquiry scattered at random throughout the report. This report was supposed to be an independent analysis by a disinterested police force. Yet even its structure was bewildering.

There was much extraneous material, some of which seemed to have been included merely because it was prejudicial to Hanratty's case. Nothing, however, was quite so extraneous as a statement from Ruby Philpotts, regarding a possible sighting of the gunman on the evening of the murder in the vicinity of the cornfield. What was the point of including that? How had Nimmo acquired it in the first place? (It is scarcely conceivable that all the case documentation had been passed over to him.) Logically, his task precluded examination of the cornfield evidence.

The report began with the original police instructions of 16 October 1961 relating to the alibi which Hanratty put forward when first arrested. Hanratty had, of course, rescinded aspects of that alibi. There was no argument about that; and thus no purpose was served by resurrecting it. The point was not whether he'd changed his alibi, but whether what he replaced it with – the Rhyl part of the story – was credible.

Nimmo included a statement from Joe Gillbanks, the man conducting inquiries on behalf of the defence: 'I conducted extensive and careful inquiries in both Liverpool and Rhyl in late 1961 and early 1962 and I have no hesitation in saying that I found no reliable person in either place which would convince me as an ex-police officer that Hanratty had been in either place on 22 and 23 August 1961.'

This was, to say the least, unhelpful; but Gillbanks was in a difficult position. He was perhaps wary of the implication that an innocent man might have been hanged when he, Gillbanks, should have done more to prevent the execution.

But was his statement to Nimmo true? I don't believe it was. Gillbanks was, as he pointed out, an ex-police officer. On this occasion he was, it seems, just telling the police what he thought they wanted to hear. What he told Nimmo in 1967 was not borne out by what he said at the time, in February 1962. In his 'Résumé of Inquiries, Interviews and Statements made in Liverpool', he reported:

Olive Dinwoodie [assisted in the shop] on 21 and 22 August, but was taken ill and did not return for several weeks. She remembers Hanratty asking for directions to 'Tarleton Road' and has no hesitation in identifying his photograph. She fixes the day as Monday 21st only because of the alleged remark of Hanratty that a girl was serving in the shop at the time ... Mrs Dinwoodie could easily be confused over the Monday or Tuesday, and if in fact the question of the girl in the shop could be made more plain, she would be happy ...

   Barbara Ford, aged 13, also called in the shop on Tuesday 22nd. She has no clear recollection of Hanratty calling at the shop. She did, however, identify a profile photograph of Hanratty and whenever she does visit the shop and there is an opporutnity of serving behind the counter she does so.

So what Gillbanks found at the time and what he told Nimmo over five years later do not tally. However, there is another point here. This isn't actually evidence. Gillbanks himself hadn't seen Hanratty, or anybody else; he was not in Rhyl at that time. Nimmo should have been concentrating on the first-hand, primary testimony of those who were there.

It is not until page 49 of his report that we get to the whole point of the exercise and reach some primary evidence, with the statement of Grace Jones, one of the critical witnesses. Back in February 1962, she had protested to Gillbanks that she had no wish to attend the trial in Bedford and give evidence. According to her new statement, 'My daughter remonstrated with the man, but he was insistent.'

This doesn't sound like the authentic voice of Mrs Jones to me; but, to continue, here is the pith of her statement:

'I have thought and thought about this case ever since. I cannot say if Hanratty ever stayed at my house although I have a feeling he may have done. If he did stay, I could not honestly say when it was. If Hanratty stayed at my house on 22 and 23 August, he could only have stayed in the attic bathroom . . .

'To put my position quite clear it is as follows: both I and my daughter remember a young man coming to the door one night and asking if we could take him in for bed and breakfast. This man may have been Hanratty but I do not know for certain.'

Mrs Jones's daughter, Brenda Harris, said:

'We could not identify the photograph but we both had a feeling that we had seen the man before. That was the highest we could put it at the time and the position is still the same now . . . At some time, and it may have been around that period in August 1961, a boy did stay in the attic and he had his meals in our living-room at the back of the ground floor which was furnished as it is now with the settee, armchairs and the television set.'

This gives an interesting insight into how statements can be written selectively, so that they conceal as much as they reveal. What else was this back room furnished with? The answer was (and has been ever since) two tables. Had the statement referred to this, however, it would have provided a direct link to Hanratty's testimony at trial. It's intriguing that this point is omitted, especially as I am sure that Mrs Harris would have wished to mention it. At almost the same time as she was interviewed by Nimmo, she told defence representatives:

'I have already made a statement to Mr Nimmo. During the

week 19–26 August 1961, all the bedrooms were occupied. The only room we had vacant with a bed was the attic, which contains a green bath. We offered this to a young man about twenty-five years with dark hair, who I feel sure was James Hanratty. The reasons why the guests in the dining-room never saw him was because he had his breakfast in our general room. That's how he knew the back yard was tiled.'

The Nimmo file included Margaret Walker's original statement, made on 8 February 1962. She particularly remembered the man, and she particularly remembered the date: 'I was standing by the gate of my home when a man came up the street and asked me if I could put him up for a night or two nights. He said he didn't mind sleeping anywhere, settee or anything.'

A fresh statement was taken from her:

'On Tuesday 22 August, between 7 and 9 p.m. a young man came up to me. He was about 20-odd years old. He asked me if I could put him up for a couple of nights but I told him I could not. I sent him across the road to No. 21, but he could get no answer there, so I directed him to Mrs Vincent's, No. 23 . . .

'Some time later, the following year, there was a lot of discussion – someone said Mrs Jones had to go to a murder trial. Something made me think, I wonder if this is the man who called at my house that day. I went to Rhyl police station. They took a statement from me. That is the statement you have read to me today. It was a true statement and still is . . .

'I have been bothered by a lot of newspaper reporters. Although some of them are all right, others try to put words in your mouth and some of the things they have printed are not correct.'

Ivy Vincent's original statement, of 19 February 1962, seemed helpful: 'I have seen the picture of James Hanratty in the *Sunday Pictorial* and I seem to recognize his face.'

Nimmo returned to her to take a fresh, expanded statement. She recalled the incident as having happened when Mr and Mrs Barnett, an elderly couple from Leek, Staffordshire, stayed with her. The Manchester police officers then called on the Barnetts, and took a statement from them; they had not been at Rhyl at all that year.

The Barnett statement was flourished as a card to trump Ivy Vincent. Why? All it proved was that, in 1967, Mrs Vincent could not remember which guests she had taken in during August over five years earlier. This did nothing to invalidate the fact that in 1962, when her memory was much fresher, she made a statement about someone asking for lodgings, in just the way Hanratty described.

Margaret Walker was a witness whose testimony carried such intrinsic authority (I met her in Rhyl in 1991 – one could tour the country and not meet as honest and straightforward a woman) that it couldn't be undermined; yet, by getting her statement to finish with a condemnation of some of the press reports, the officers made her evidence appear less supportive than it was.

There were negative statements from a number of people, like those who worked in Dixie's Café (where Hanratty said he had enquired about Terry Evans), who could not recollect having seen Hanratty in Rhyl. Then there was an extraordinary statement from a hairdresser, who said he did not recognize the photograph of Hanratty 'as anyone I had seen previously who has had a haircut or a shave in my establishment'. This statement was included in the report; no doubt it was all grist to the mill of making the alibi seem without substance.

But shouldn't Nimmo have been rather more thorough? Shouldn't he have interviewed more than just the one hairdresser? In fact, another Rhyl barber, Gerald Murray, later made a statement saying that he thought he had given a haircut to Hanratty. This does not correspond with Hanratty's own evidence (he said he'd had a shave in Rhyl), but that isn't the point. The point is that this man should have been seen and interviewed and his witness testimony properly assessed as part of Nimmo's 'thorough' inquiry. The fact that Nimmo hadn't seen him merely highlights another shortcoming in the report.

Several witnesses seemed to feel under pressure. Where previous statements existed, these would be read out to witnesses beforehand – a reminder, perhaps, not to 'improve' their evidence. One man came in for especially unfriendly treatment. That was the newspaper-seller, Charlie Jones. He was in many respects the key figure: it was his fresh testimony on *Panorama* which had set the ball rolling and led to the setting-up of the inquiry. Jones was taken into Prestatyn police station. Nimmo had some further questions for him. The report includes a transcript of what took place:

Nimmo: I have made some more inquiries. I am not at all satisfied that the statement you made on 12 February 1967 is the truth.
Jones: Oh dear, what, sir, me? Not tell the truth? What do you mean, sir?
Nimmo: I'll be quite blunt about it, Jones. That story you told on

the *Panorama* television programme and the story you told me
about some man coming to you in 1961 and asking for Terry
was just a pack of nonsense.

Jones: Oh, oh dear. I don't know – I don't tell lies, sir. Oh, I knew
this would happen.

Nimmo: Just listen to me. You said on the television that a man had
come to you outside the bus station in August 1961, asking for
Terry. Firstly, I don't think you would remember an incident
like that for five days, let alone five years, even if it had
happened, which I don't believe. Secondly, if it had been
Hanratty who approached you, he would not have asked for
Terry because he didn't know Evans as Terry then.

Jones: Evans said – Oh, I don't know. Why am I being blamed? I
didn't say it was Hanratty, did I?

There was more questioning. Then it was recorded that 'Jones
sat quietly for a moment, and then he shook his head.' The dialogue
continued:

Jones: I can't carry on with this, sir. I've been scared to death – the
worry won't let me sleep. I wish from the bottom of my heart I
had never got into it.

Nimmo: Let's have the truth now.

Jones: It's that Evans that made me do it . . . The whole lot came
from him, sir.

Nimmo: I was right, wasn't I? The whole story is nonsense. There
was no man asking for Terry – no man with bad shoes – no
man sent to Mrs Jones, and of course you did not approach
Evans after Hanratty's photograph appeared in the press and
tell him that the man had been looking for him.

Jones: That's about it, sir – I didn't mean no harm at all. I never
realized it would come to this. It was just that Evans said there
might be some money in it and I was broke at the time – my
rent was overdue and I was in debt. I couldn't see no harm in it
– I do send people to Mrs Jones and people coming asking me
questions, but I can't remember people like that.

Nimmo: Jones, do you wish to put what you have now told me into
a written statement?

Jones: I'm ashamed to admit it, sir, but I can't write.

Detective Chief Inspector Charles Horan (Nimmo's assistant): Shall I write
it out for you?

Jones: Please, sir.

With a fresh statement having been taken from Jones – 'That story I told on the BBC and the story I told you when I saw you is not true' – the Manchester police were able to report back to the Home Secretary that the alibi story had collapsed.

Nimmo also reinterviewed Evans, but this time there was a different result. Evans didn't resile from his testimony. He stood firm.

Nimmo: Evans, I have now almost finished my inquiries in this case and I returned to you and Charlie Jones because I am satisfied that the story Charlie Jones told on that *Panorama* programme was an invention and, what's more, you were the inventor.

Evans: I wish you'd do me a favour. Who gave you this?

Nimmo: Well, I've seen Charlie Jones for one – he says you made suggestions to him about various points in his story . . . You were responsible for getting this man on to a television programme.

Evans: Yes, you could say that, this Jo Menell asked me if I could find some witnesses to go on the programme.

Horan: You were going round Rhyl canvassing for witnesses for the *Panorama* programme and you saw Ernest Gordon [proprietor of Dixie's Café]. If he had been as vague and foolish as Charlie Jones, he'd have finished up on *Panorama*, reciting a lot of nonsense.

Evans: Look – you think what you want – I know you don't believe me, but you're wasting your time talking to me. I'll tell you another thing – I'm not sorry I was on that *Panorama*. I knew Hanratty and from what I saw of him, he didn't do this murder.

Nimmo: You saw him for about half a day, didn't you?

Evans: Yes, but he wasn't a bad lad.

Nimmo: One thing I must warn you about. Keep away from Charlie Jones.

Evans: Have you finished? I'm going.

Thus although Jones had retracted his testimony, Evans' complementary evidence remained intact. This is what Evans had stated: 'When I got back from giving evidence at the trial in 1962, I was walking down the front one day, it was after Hanratty's photograph had appeared in the papers, and Charlie stopped me and said, "I'm sure this fellow came up to me looking for you."'

Although nothing happened for some years after that, Evans relayed that conversation to the *Panorama* team, and as a result they were already on the look-out for Jones when he bumped into them in the café in Windsor Street.

So when Nimmo had said to Jones, 'I don't think you would remember an incident like that for five days, let alone five years,' he was missing the point: Jones was not casting his mind back five years, because he had discussed the incident with Terry Evans some little while after it occurred. Further, at the time they discussed it, they could have had no possible mercenary motive for doing so. Nimmo also seemed to have overlooked the fact that Jones had re-affirmed what he originally said in a statement to police, on 25 November, at a time when he was under some pressure from the press.

Jones was undoubtedly wrong about several aspects of his evidence – the timing, for a start (as Hanratty wouldn't have arrived in Rhyl until 8.15), although, on long summer evenings, that's not too surprising. Also, in trying to identify the day of the week as a Tuesday, he was certainly guilty of trying to be too helpful.

As Nimmo pointed out, Hanratty certainly wouldn't have asked for 'Terry' as Hanratty did not then know his proper name. Yet Nimmo had overlooked another important point here. Jones was able to relay the chance meeting with this man back to Evans – so, if it was Hanratty, the two of them must have worked out some way of establishing whom he was looking for (perhaps by reference to the tattooed star between Evans's eyebrows).

Overall, this is another fleeting encounter which, individually, would mean little. Yet it fits in with what Hanratty said. Yes, Jones got the time wrong – but he got the place emphatically correct, because the bus station is precisely where Hanratty would have arrived in Rhyl, on the Crosville bus from Liverpool.

The fatal flaw at the heart of the Nimmo inquiry was the process of examining each piece of testimony as a discrete entity; and then perceiving some fault in it (a technique which could demolish just about every area of witness evidence in every criminal investigation).

What mattered (and what the Nimmo inquiry neglected even to address) was the cumulative weight of the testimony, which is considerable. Further, this would have been only strengthened if Nimmo had taken the trouble to interview all the witnesses. The report contained a list of names and addresses 'provided to the defence after 6 February 1962'. There were nineteen names on this list. Of these, eight were interviewed in the course of the Nimmo inquiry; there are no statements from the remaining eleven. Presumably when Roy Jenkins, the Home Secretary, told

•

Parliament that one of the briefs of the inquiry was 'to take statements from all relevant witnesses', he had imagined that statements would be taken from all relevant witnesses.

Some of the original statements of those missing eleven witnesses are not helpful. However, the statement of Trevor Dutton, whom Nimmo hadn't interviewed, was very helpful. Nor did Nimmo see Christopher Larman, whose name had been featured in the press in connection with the alibi but who was at that time in Australia. The original statements from Dutton and Larman were precise and persuasive; not to have interviewed them is a bewildering oversight.

The core of the alibi evidence is demonstrably strong: with Hanratty having spoken to people who directed him to Mrs Jones (Charlie Jones, Larman), having asked at her house (Mrs Jones, Mrs Harris), and then made inquiries elsewhere (Mrs Walker, Mrs Vincent, Mrs Davis) before returning to Ingledene; and then listlessly trying the next day to get a price for the watch (Dutton). It all logically fits together. Could all of these people have been lying or mistaken, or getting Hanratty confused with someone else?

Further, what is especially persuasive are the little details: trying to sell a watch, certainly; indicating his willingness to sleep on the settee (as if Mrs Walker could have known how precisely that dovetailed with Hanratty's sleeping arrangements over much of the previous two months); and Walker and Larman's spontaneous statements about noticing something strange about his hair-colouring.

There are two further points to make about the Nimmo report. The first concerns that list of names and addresses provided to the defence 'after 6 February 1962'. But of course; it could not have been supplied before because the Rhyl alibi was not publicly known until then. What we needed to know from Nimmo was the exact opposite of the information he gave: the date *before* which they were supplied to the defence: while the trial was still in progress? In time for the appeal? Prior to the execution? We have no way of knowing for sure, although Nimmo's perverse way of dating doesn't inspire confidence.

On page 76 of the Nimmo report, he included what he termed an 'extract' from the report of Chief Inspector Elliott of Liverpool City police. This report was drawn up because Acott had asked Elliott to recheck the sweet-shop alibi. This is the extract:

During the conversation with Mrs Dinwoodie she said that after feeling ill about 5.00 p.m. on Tuesday, 22 August, she went to see her doctor on Wednesday, 23 August.

In an endeavour to test her accuracy, we saw the doctor concerned, Dr Kinsella of Liverpool 5. He allowed us to examine the record card in respect of Mrs Dinwoodie, which showed that on Tuesday, 22 August she had visited Dr Kinsella's partner, Dr Ryan, at the surgery.

This discrepancy was later pointed out to Mrs Dinwoodie and she then agreed that she may have been mistaken regarding the date upon which she did visit the doctor.

So this woman appears a bit muddled, and it would hardly be safe to put much weight on her evidence. However, Elliott's original report was very thorough. It ran to seven pages, the first four pages of which were entirely concerned with the sweet-shop. Why wasn't this document included in full? It's not as though paper rationing was in force and, as it was, Nimmo saw fit to incorporate a huge amount of otiose material.

These are the two paragraphs of the Elliott report which come *immediately* after the ones which Nimmo cited:

At this stage, I would draw attention to the fact that Mrs Dinwoodie, although confident that the man who called at the shop asked for Tarleton Road, would not have known which particular day it was when the man called at the shop, but the day is pinpointed when it was said she was accompanied by a child.

As mentioned in my previous report, Mrs Dinwoodie appears to be a genuine and conscientious type of working-class woman. Mrs Cowley, a particularly sensible woman, did say that if Mrs Dinwoodie's conscience would allow it, she would be extremely relieved to say that she had no knowledge of the incident whatsoever.

This puts a completely different complexion on the sweet-shop alibi. Mrs Dinwoodie was under enormous pressure – she would have liked to be relieved of this responsibility but *her conscience wouldn't allow it*. This only helps to reinforce the credibility of her evidence. Secondly, there is the critical point that it could only have occurred on the Monday or the Tuesday; and she could only pinpoint which of those days *by when the child was in the shop*.

This should be set alongside three other points: (1) when she was specifically asked about this point, the grand-daughter (the 'child') made it clear that she was in the shop on the Tuesday as well as the Monday; (2) this report, by Liverpool police, was only being undertaken at all because Acott telephoned the office personally saying that his inquiries 'showed Hanratty to be in the London area between 3.30 to 10.00 p.m. on Monday 21st'; and (3) if the incident occurred on the Tuesday, then Hanratty could not have reached the cornfield by 9.30 and could not have committed the murder.

Thus these two paragraphs alone, which Nimmo omitted, gave Hanratty something close to a solid alibi.

The Liverpool part of the alibi, which was adhered to from start to finish, was, perhaps, outside Nimmo's remit. He chose to incorporate it, however, and so should at least have pursued it to its irresistible conclusion.[24]

In the months to come, the whole status of the report became increasingly confused. On 1 November 1967 the Home Secretary had told the Commons that the Nimmo investigations were 'detailed', 'exhaustive' and 'thorough' and 'covering all possible lines of inquiry'. Twelve months later, the Home Office was itself referring to Rhyl alibi statements made before *and after* the investigation by Detective Superintendent Nimmo – a tacit admission that the much-vaunted thoroughness of those inquiries was indeed illusory; and, accordingly, that the terms in which the Home Secretary described them to the Commons were erroneous.

Despite the setback of the Nimmo report and the Home Secretary's parliamentary statement, the campaign went on regardless; and media attention continued to run at a high level. On Friday, 17 November 1967 *The Frost Programme* was devoted to the case. In those days, an invitation to appear on one of David Frost's programmes was not declined (the Beatles made their last-ever British TV appearance on his show), and Alphon, too, agreed to take part.

However, as the day drew near, Alphon began to have second thoughts. The show went out live. Its journalistic standing was high. David Frost had a long-standing interest in miscarriages of justice: Though he has grown more emollient down the years, at that time he enjoyed a reputation as a tenacious and occasionally fierce interviewer. All this clearly spelt trouble for Alphon. This wouldn't be an occasion in which the interviewer would be easily hood-winked. Just before transmission, Alphon pulled out.

As Paul Foot has written, this was instructive. Those who have disregarded Alphon's confessions have generally argued that he made them for publicity or financial gain or both. On this occasion, a generous helping of each was available: a fee had already been negotiated, and Frost's programme enjoyed more prominence than most others; yet Alphon refused to do it.

The following month Alphon wrote to James Callaghan (who had just become Home Secretary) reiterating his own call for an inquiry: 'I must deny the validity of the statements obtained from me by the police upon my return from Paris, and produced in evidence at Marylebone Court.'[25]

By this point, the A6 Murder Committee – a loose assembly of campaigners, centred round the Hanratty family, Paul Foot, Jean Justice and Jeremy Fox – was active. During the Whitsun Bank Holiday in 1968, James and Mary Hanratty paid a third visit to Rhyl with several other members of the campaign team. The visit was carefully planned, with adverts taken out in advance in the local press:

> Can You Help Mr and Mrs Hanratty clear their son's name?
>   They will be staying at the Westminster Hotel, and can be contacted this Saturday (25 May) or Sunday (26 May).
>   For the sake of justice, please come forward.

Again, this visit sparked considerable media interest. By the Sunday evening, the campaign team held a well-attended press conference to disclose new evidence relating to the alibi. In the course of this, someone asked whether the family would be seeking compensation for the death of their son. James Hanratty, who had taken a back seat until then, spoke out: 'I want to make it clear that I'm interested only in justice. I'm not interested in compensation, and wouldn't take a penny even if it were offered. It's not possible to be compensated for the death of your son. All we are seeking is justice.'

The family was able to report that the weekend had yielded five new witnesses. Of these, by far the most important was Trevor Dutton. Despite his statement to Abergele police on 9 February 1962, the Hanratty campaign had not previously been aware of his evidence. James and Mary took these fresh statements to the Home Office in person on Wednesday, 29 May. It then took officials a little over three months to evaluate this information and respond to the family. On 10 September the Home Office at last replied:

> *Mr Callaghan wishes to assure you that your further representations, and the five statements which you presented, have received the most careful and thorough examination.*

The statement made by Mr Dutton (whose name and address were given to the defence at the time of the trial as those of a possible witness) refers to an attempt by a man to sell him a gold watch in Rhyl High Street on 23 August 1961; but your son's evidence at the trial did not include any reference to an attempt to sell a gold watch in Rhyl. Even leaving aside this consideration, there is nothing in Mr Dutton's statement to suggest any reliable identification between your son and the man who offered Mr Dutton the watch in Rhyl.

In the circumstances, the Home Secretary is sorry to have to say that he sees no grounds for causing further inquiry to be made or taking any other action.

That autumn James and Mary took possession of all their son's defence papers, which until then Kleinman had retained. Thus it was that for the first time the A6 Murder Committee became aware of Christopher Larman's evidence.

Paul Foot explained the background to his evidence in the *Sunday Times*. After seeing the photographs of Grace Jones attending the trial in February 1962, Larman recalled a chance encounter from the previous summer, and went to what was then his local police station in Staines. The head of the CID, Detective Inspector Robert Fields, recalled Larman's visit and the statement he took from him: 'I realized the urgency of this matter because the trial was on. So the following day I sent a message by telephone to Acott saying that the statement had been made to me.'[26] No one was sure when this was passed on to the defence, although a statement from Larman was taken by defence agents on 21 February – after the end of the trial.

Alphon himself always reacted uncomfortably when the Rhyl alibi was receiving attention. There were probably two explanations for this: he resented the spotlight moving away from himself; and he was probably concerned lest the alibi were properly established. It was clear that he could now only continue to generate publicity on his own behalf, and to receive due attention from the authorities, by revealing something more each time.

So he wrote to the Home Secretary with an entirely unambiguous confession. 'I killed Gregsten, the establishment murdered Hanratty and have since acted against me as though they knew I was guilty.' That had little impact, so a few months later he wrote again, and this time supplied the name of the Central Figure, the man who, he said, had engineered the murder plot and the framing of Hanratty.

Jean Justice published his second book on the case, *Le Crime de la Route A6*, which this time he wrote in French specifically for publication, again by Girodias, only in France.

Despite these developments, fresh entreaties for Government action were dismissed by an obdurate Home Office. In the course of his answer, Lord Stonham revealed to the House of Lords that by that stage the Home Office casework on the A6 Murder amounted to 198 files. In the wake of this, some MPs expressed renewed concern about the inaction of the authorities. William Hamling, Labour MP for Woolwich West, said, 'I am worried about two aspects. First, identity parades. Second, I'm worried about the habit of holding police inquiries and not publishing reports – which enables the authorities to sit effectively on any evidence which might upset the cosy picture they want us to look at.'[27]

From the summer of 1969, the campaign committee despairingly adopted new tactics. On most Sundays for the next two years, James Hanratty, Jean Justice and the others went to Hyde Park in central London and took it in turns to get on the hustings and tell the crowds at Speakers' Corner about the case, and the long-standing cover-up by the British Government. They also displayed posters and placards in which they named the murderer, Alphon, the Central Figure, and others. They were hoping to attract writs for libel or to be prosecuted for criminal libel. In the *Guardian*, Justice explained that their aim was 'to provoke legal actions which will lead to a virtual retrial of the Hanratty case. We are showing that the truth is in our hands. It is the best hope left to us.'

On 27 August 1969 Commander Bob Acott, one of the prime targets of this campaign, retired from the Metropolitan Police after thirty-four years' service. He vowed not to discuss the A6 Murder. He told Paul Foot on 14 December that 'I have decided to have nothing to do with that case, and on that I am adamant. Three months after retiring I am more than ever convinced that my decision is the right one.'

On 25 March 1970 James and Mary received a reply to a letter they had written to the Prime Minister, Harold Wilson:

The Prime Minister has asked me to reply to your letter. He has consulted the Home Secretary who has advised that both he and his predecessor have considered representations received from yourself and others with the greatest care. On many occasions consideration has been given to the Rhyl alibi that your son put forward at his trial, to the involvement of Mr

Peter Alphon and to all other aspects of the case; but the Home Secretary has concluded that there are no grounds for any further action. I can assure you that the Home Secretary would have further inquiries made if he considered that they were necessary.

All this was disheartening, but at least the campaign had secured the enthusiastic support of one of the most fêted people in Britain, John Lennon. On 10 December 1969 he held a press conference (with what the film-maker Tony Palmer described as 'typical haste and lack of forethought') at the London Apple offices in Savile Row.[28] The *Guardian* reported that 'Mr Lennon called reporters together to announce that he was joining the A6 Murder Committee in its campaign for a new inquiry into Hanratty's conviction, and that he would make a documentary film about the campaign.'[29]

Lennon was certainly concerned about the injustice. At the highly publicized film première of *The Magic Christian* (the film of the Terry Southern book, starring Peter Sellers and Lennon's colleague, Ringo Starr), Lennon held aloft a 'Britain Murdered Hanratty' placard. During meetings held by the campaign throughout 1970, at which Jean Justice, Paul Foot and members of the Hanratty family all spoke, the film cameras were in constant attendance. Lennon kept his promise to the family. On 3 November 1971 they were able to hold a press showing of the completed forty-minute campaign film. (The first public showing was held on 17 February 1972, in the crypt of St-Martin-in-the-Fields, Trafalgar Square, London.)

James, Mary and Michael Hanratty had made their enduring promise to Jimmy on the day before his death that they would fight to clear his name. Nearly nine years later, they had made almost unbelievable progress in their efforts to unravel and rectify the case – only to have them all dashed on the rock of administrative intransigence. Even their staunch faith in the integrity of the executive process was exhausted. Failing to discern any other possible course of action, they then took out a writ for negligence against 'Rab' Butler – by now, Lord Butler of Saffron Walden – the Home Secretary who had sanctioned their son's execution.

The writ was served on 4 December 1970. They argued that he had negligently considered the arguments for a reprieve, and claimed damages for grief and agony. The family's case, argued by Gershon Ellenbogen, was that 'The Home Secretary had before him material not before members of the jury when they reached their guilty verdict. That material should have been the subject of an inquiry, such as that conducted in *R* v. *Rowland* (1947). An inquiry would have cast such doubts on the verdict that a reprieve would have been almost inevitable.'

After preliminary hearings, the case was heard in full in the Court of Appeal on 13 May 1971 by Lord Denning, Lord Justice Salmon and Lord Justice Stamp (a very senior constitution, illustrating the importance of the case). The judgment was unambiguous. 'No action for damages for negligence can lie against the Home Secretary,' declared Lord Denning, 'nor can the courts inquire into, let alone pass an opinion on, the way the Crown prerogative is exercised.' Of course, one must add that, especially in the climate of the time, it would have been unthinkable for them to have found otherwise.

Denning further added that it was a pity that the case had ever been brought. That comment especially rankled with Jeremy Fox. He considered it a calculated and public censure of this very honest family who had fought so tenaciously and so honourably to secure those very ideals which the country's senior judges should have been doing their utmost to defend.

Shortly afterwards, one of Lincoln's Inn grand dinners took place. Lord Denning was among those present. After grace was said, there was a moment of silence. Jeremy Fox spoke out: 'I think everyone here should know that an innocent man, James Hanratty, has been hanged in this country, and ever since the Government, the police and the judiciary have been engaged in covering this up. Thank you.'

'I raised the case in that somewhat unorthodox manner', he explained, 'because Denning had said what he did. If you examined Ellenbogen's argument, well, in my view it's correct and even unanswerable. Today, of course, people regularly bring actions against the Home Secretary, and he regularly loses them.

'In view of what was felt to have been my disgraceful outburst, I received a letter from the Treasurer, Mr Justice Goff, and had to go to see him, at a quarter to ten in his room. He did say something to the effect that there was nothing whatever in my allegation – I of course was in no position to disagree with him – and said he had a good mind to suspend me. In fact, he didn't. I just got a good ticking-off, and was able to continue in chambers.'

CHAPTER TWENTY-TWO

THE FOURTH BOOK on the A6 case, Paul Foot's *Who Killed Hanratty?* (perhaps the most pertinent question of all) was published on 6 May 1971. This was an absolutely comprehensive, utterly enthralling account of the crime and its aftermath. The book was responsible for instilling a zealous interest in the case among many thousands, myself included, and deserves to be remembered as one of the non-fiction classics of the post-war years.

In the book, Foot unearthed one area of entirely fresh evidence. Alphon, having mentioned in May 1967 that his bank accounts would be available, indeed asked his bank in the Strand to disclose them to Foot. These revealed that in the months after the A6 Murder, about £7,500 was paid into Alphon's account – an enormous amount of money (even quite comfortable houses could be purchased for less than £1,000 at the time), especially in view of the fact that Alphon didn't have a job or any discernible source of income.

The bank accounts were authentic. The sums of money were paid into the account over a relatively short time and, as Foot observed, it was all spent at an equally fast rate. Alphon was living extravagantly from the autumn of 1961 until at least the summer of 1962. His living expenses would have been considerable.

On a number of occasions, he was asked how he managed to survive. He invariably replied – as he did on the *Dateline* programme – that he had a small private income. This, like so much else, was complete fantasy. (His father was an immigrant whose desk-job at Scotland Yard would barely have earned him a living wage.) When Alphon referred to his 'small private income', what he actually meant was that he lived by sponging off his mother, although one could understand why a man in his mid-thirties would be coy about admitting that.

So where did all this money come from? About £2,500 of the £7,500, Foot reckoned, came from the proceeds of payments from various newspapers in the wake of the publicity surrounding his arrest and subsequent release as the first suspect. £2,500 is almost certainly the absolute maximum he would have received from such sources; after all, if he wasn't the right suspect, then his wasn't a story worth buying.

That left about £5,000. A few successful days at the dogs? Very unlikely. Even if he did have a regular flutter and the occasional win, he, like the majority of punters, would have been gambling relatively small amounts which he would not have bothered to put through his bank account.

It is difficult, in fact, to put forward any explanation at all of this exceptionally large sum other than the one which Alphon himself supplied: that he received it after carrying out the A6 Murder. Certainly, if Alphon were, hypothetically, ever to be prosecuted for the crime, this would be itemized as a piece of very powerful prosecution evidence.

Who Killed Hanratty? made a tremendous impact and received, in the main, outstanding reviews. Louis Blom-Cooper, writing in the *Observer*, was generous in his assessment, and conceded that his own earlier conclusion had been 'rash'.[1] There was just the rare dissenting voice – like Dick Taverne QC, MP, who was Parliamentary Under-Secretary at the Home Office when the Labour administration declined to hold an inquiry. In his review of Foot's book, he averred that 'There are no convincing grounds for believing that Hanratty did not kill Michael Gregsten.'

That weekend, because of the book's publication, interest in the case was again at a crescendo. The Hanratty family booked a theatre in Rhyl, and held their first public meeting there.

From the moment he had become editor of the *Sunday Times* in 1967, Harold Evans, who had equally passionate interests in pursuing investigative journalism and overturning miscarriages of justice, had encouraged Foot et al. in their coverage of this story and provided generous editorial space for their regular reports. On Sunday, 9 May, to reinforce the impact of *Who Killed Hanratty?*, the *Sunday Times* carried two major pieces about the case.

The first of these concerned Charles France. Although the Home Office had always withheld his last letters, Charlotte France now made a number available to the *Sunday Times*, in an endeavour to show that his suicide could be explained purely by 'his horror and remorse at having introduced a sex murderer into his home where he became a friend of the family'.

This is the text of the one letter which the paper reproduced:

My Darling Wife,

*One day you will understand that what I have done this night I have
done for you and my darling children. They are going to crucify us all.
You in your innocence of anything wrong. As for Carole, my heart bleeds
to think what I am leaving you to face. But I sincerely promise you it will
be much better than having the stigma of bearing the fact that I have done
what was honestly right, but will be so twisted as to make it look as
though I was an associate of this filthy act.*

*My petty acts of wrong will be magnified to make it look as though I
knew all along that this man who I took to be a friend, as [sic] turned
into a monster and should pay a just penalty. Oh my darling family,
forgive me, if you think that I have taken the easy way out, you are so
wrong. I want you to find peace with your dear family, who I know will
stick by you all the way. While I am here nobody wants to come near,
but now you will find some happiness.*

God bless you all, Daddy

*Bobbie xxx Brenda xxx
Carole xxx
Mummy xxx*[2]

Superficially, it indeed appears that France killed himself for fear
that his 'innocent involvement' in this crime should bring 'shame,
humiliation and suffering' on his family. But what was the background to provoke such feelings? To all appearances, France had
acquitted himself honourably. If Hanratty was indeed the A6
murderer, then France had performed his civic duty and given
significant evidence against him; in the witness-box, he had not
spoken spitefully or maliciously about the man who was once a
family friend. He'd played it, it would seem, on the level. Why
should this bring 'shame and suffering' on his family? His involvement might well have brought the reverse: a modest sort of passing
celebrity and opportunities for financial gain – opportunities that
were in fact underway, with the *Sunday Pictorial* negotiating to buy
the France family's story once the appeal was turned down.

So what did he have to reproach himself for? Why are 'they
going to crucify us all'? What is the meaning of 'I have done what
was honestly right, but will be so twisted as to make it look as
though I was an associate of this filthy act'? The crime was carried
out by a lone gunman – a moon maniac; wasn't that the received
wisdom at that time?

An alternative reading is that France was indeed an associate in a very filthy act: the framing of Hanratty. His involvement may have been unwitting, it may have been involuntary ('I have done what was honestly right'), but, if Hanratty *was* framed, then France must have played some role. It must have been he who supplied the information about the back seat of a bus being regarded by Hanratty as a handy dump for unwanted articles.

Down the years, some of those placed in France's position – of giving perjured evidence which leads to the conviction of others – have found the burden of conscience so great they have committed suicide. France had even greater reasons for being overwhelmed by mental torment: in the first place, Hanratty faced not merely imprisonment, but execution; secondly, one can make the reasonable speculation that France was subject to countervailing pressures – from the Central Figure, threatening fearful consequences if he revealed anything; and from Alphon, promising absolute perdition if he didn't.

Faced with all this, suicide may have seemed the only escape. Because of his deep and touching concerns for his family, as illustrated by this letter, France emerges as a more sympathetic figure than he otherwise would have done. Nevertheless, the irony was that, in order to protect his family from the 'stigma' of his own involvement, he still had to continue to implicate Hanratty.

The other report was headed, 'How Did The Trail Lead To Hanratty?' The police had never disclosed how they first discovered that Ryan was Hanratty, yet it was an issue of great significance. The main reporter, Lewis Chester, examined it in the context of the 'She Saw Him at the Cleaners' story, reported in the *Daily Sketch* and *Daily Mail*, and the 'intuitive sighting' of Hanratty by Janet Gregsten, almost a full month before the police identified Hanratty as their man. The intuition prompted William Ewer to try to track him down, and caused him to report the matter to the police. Chester pointed out that the story strained 'the limits of credulity'.

Ewer had started up a small antiques business in the Swiss Cottage arcade. Janet Gregsten recalled that previously he had repaired umbrellas. 'When Bill moved his business there, he continued doing the umbrella repairs,' she said. 'The shop was antiques-cum-pictures-cum-umbrellas-cum-all-sorts-of-junk.'[3] By 1971, Ewer had a stall in an antiques market just off Oxford Street. The *Sunday Times* explained that, 'After the tragedy, Mr Ewer took Mrs Gregsten and her two young boys under his wing. They still live with Mr and Mrs Ewer at their home in Golders Green.' Neither Ewer nor Janet Gregsten would comment on the original stories, other than to say that they were 'inaccurate'.

Chester then went to see the now retired Bob Acott. As usual, Acott refused to comment – almost. He did, however, say briefly, 'To us it always seemed a simple gas-meter case.' A mere ten-word comment from the prosecution side instantly made the case for the defence stronger.

In former times, people would often report the theft of money from their gas-meters. In police eyes, there was always just the one suspect in such cases: the householder or resident himself, stealing money from the nearest and easiest available source at times of hardship. No burglar would ever steal just from the gas-meter.

So, in police terminology, a gas-meter case meant an inside job, a crime carried out by someone on the inside, a close member of the family. If this was so in the A6 case, why had the Crown case contained not a single solitary reference to this?

William Ewer responded to the article of 9 May with a full statement clarifying his own role in the case. On 16 May, the *Sunday Times* published the statement in full. With one or two minor abbreviations, here it is.

This is the true record of my involvement with the A6 Murder case.

1. Some time after the murder it became public that the police were looking for a suspect with staring eyes. One day, it was probably early in September 1961, I was sitting in a cafe on the Finchley Road, about 50 yards from my umbrella shop in the Swiss Cottage arcade. As I was sitting there, I noticed a young man making some transaction at the counter ... He was young, smartly dressed and had quite unusually staring eyes. The eyes were as distinctive as if he had a carbuncle on his face. It occurred to me that there might just be a possibility that this was the man the police were looking for in connection with the murder and answered the description I had been given of the man with staring eyes.

2. I hesitated for a few seconds and in point of fact started to walk back to my shop. As I was doing so I saw the man cross over the road and go into a photographer's shop. I decided to follow my instinct and have another look at him. I went directly over to the photographer's myself. I was surprised to find that the man with staring eyes was not there, and when I asked the photographer

whether he had seen such a man he was rather dismissive of my enquiry. This made me rather irritated.

3. On emerging from the photographer's, I looked into the window of a florist's shop next door. It occurred to me that I just might have been mistaken and that the man had gone into that shop. Unfortunately, the windows of the florist's shop were rather steamed up and I was unable to see anything of interest. I returned to my own shop.

4. On arrival I decided to ring the local police and relate this incident. This was the last I heard of it. I do not know whether this lead was important to the police or whether the man I saw was Hanratty ... I saw Hanratty at the trial myself but would not swear that he was the man with staring eyes I saw in Finchley Road. I would have to be 100 per cent sure to say that.

5. Some time after this incident when it became public that the police were looking for a man called Ryan, I did go into Burtol's, a cleaners opposite my shop, and enquired about whether a man called Ryan had ever been in there. They confirmed to me that a man of that name had done so.

6. Apart from the sighting incident my only other contact with the police before the trial was when I approached Scotland Yard for permission to attend the trial. This permission was granted. My first contact with Detective Superintendent Acott came after the verdict. I remember him saying something to me about Hanratty's remarks immediately after the verdict was announced.

7. My first statement of any kind to the police was made after the trial. I believe it arose because of some articles that had been printed in the newspapers. The second was made some years later to a policeman called Chief Inspector Mooney.

8. I did not know or have any business dealings with a woman called Louise Anderson. However, as we were both in the antiques business it is possible that she may have had some glancing acquaintance with me as a result that she did know me.

9. I only met Charles France once in my life. I remember he came into my shop after the trial was over. He came in to offer his apologies for Mr Gregsten's death. He said it had all been most regrettable. I remember calming him down and saying that justice had been done in a fair and open trial. He had no reason to reproach himself. I told him to go home to his wife and lead a normal life. I later heard that he had committed suicide.

10. I would like to place on record that I never at any time met

James Hanratty or Peter Louis Alphon. After the trial, Mr Alphon, who appears to be a raving lunatic, made my life intensely disagreeable with persistent telephone calls, some of them of a threatening nature.

11. My sister-in-law, Janet Gregsten, never at any time claimed to have made an intuitive sighting of Mr Hanratty.

12. I attended the trial regularly and would like to say that I thought Hanratty was convicted by the weight of solid and substantial evidence against him. I do not believe any purpose would be achieved by instituting a public inquiry into the case. But if the Home Secretary saw fit to open one, so be it. However, I know of no new evidence that could be brought.

13. I am not myself in favour of capital punishment which is not necessary in a civilized society. I am therefore extremely sympathetic to the Hanratty family, but the continuance of these wild fantasies do not credit to anybody.

14. I have heard some of the so-called Alphon tapes, any [sic] of which suggest that I was involved in the sequence of events that led to this awful crime. They are complete fantasy.

15. This statement is a full and accurate record of my involvement with the A6 Murder case. All published versions that contradict this statement are inaccurate.[4]

So, it ends with a Nixonian flourish, the suggestion that all previous statements are inoperative. What is one to make of all this? For the second time, Mr Ewer had exploded a bomb under the case. It was all utterly extraordinary.

With regard to point 7, why did he make a statement to police after the trial? Why did he make a statement some years later to Chief Inspector Mooney? What was in these statements? Nor was it even true that his first statement was made after the trial. It was actually made on 11 September 1961. It was noteworthy mainly for the lack of emotion with which Ewer viewed the murder of his brother-in-law: '[Michael Gregsten] was not a robust person and always a bit of a mother's boy ... There was talk of separation [from Janet] which was discussed with us ... There were no great scenes and rows, but Gregsten had a guilt complex about his association with Valerie, and on occasions said that he wondered why he had not been struck down.'[5]

In 1971 Chester contacted other witnesses, like the photographer's assistant, who disputed Ewer's recollection of events. Louise Anderson (if one can believe her) stated that 'she did know

Mr Ewer before the murder'. And why had Ewer sought permission to attend the trial? Trials are heard in public, anybody can go. Why should the police 'grant' permission for him to attend? Why did he say he 'knew of no evidence' that could be brought? Would he have been expected to know anything of the case? According to this fresh statement, Alphon had been harassing Ewer, too. But why, especially as Ewer 'placed on record' the fact that he had never met Alphon?

However, the most amazing part is Point 9. The scenario here is astonishing. Why would France, a man he had never met, go into Ewer's shop to offer his apologies for Michael Gregsten's death? Why would he do so several months after the event, and not more immediately? Why would he need calming down? What was he reproaching himself for? Admittedly, there may be answers to some questions; what we do not understand is why France was behaving in this way in the company of someone he didn't know.

With the publication of Paul Foot's book, Patrick Gordon Walker, the former Foreign Secretary, put down an early day motion calling for an inquiry into the case. This attracted signatures from 140 MPs, among them Dr David Owen, who wrote to the Hanratty family, 'After reading Paul Foot's book, I do believe there is a need for an inquiry into all aspects of this whole case.' Lord Goodman, the prominent lawyer, was among those who echoed the parliamentary call for an inquiry.

In a debate on Thursday, 20 May, Phillip Whitehead was among the MPs who asked the Home Secretary, Reginald Maudling, to institute an immediate inquiry. Maudling responded that he would institute a preliminary inquiry, a departmental analysis of the case. The former Home Secretary, James Callaghan, then intervened to say, 'If he reaches a conclusion that there should be a fresh public inquiry, I, speaking from my past study of the case, should not want to dissent from that merely because a different conclusion was reached earlier.'

As early as the following week, Thursday, 27 May, there was a fresh Commons debate. The Under-Secretary of State at the Home Office, Mark Carlisle, responded that, 'All the matters that have lately been raised are being carefully analysed.'

By the end of June, hopes were not high. On 24 June, Joan Lestor, a tenacious parliamentary advocate of the Hanratty family's cause, questioned Maudling again. The Home Secretary made it clear that it would be some time before he would be able to reach a decision. 'The available documents went into millions of words and he was not going to make a decision until he had satisfied himself that he had gone into every possible particular.'

As irritation grew with the Home Office's all-too-familiar ploy of procrastination, the *Sunday Times* ran another front-page story, bringing to public attention the fresh evidence of Mary Lanz, landlady of the Old Station Inn, Taplow. According to this, she maintained that Peter Alphon was in the bar on the night of the murder. He was accompanied by 'a blonde woman in her early thirties'; and that about thirty minutes after Gregsten and Storie departed, 'Alphon left with the blonde lady by the back exit.'

Unfortunately, this couldn't have been true, because it wasn't what Mary Lanz told police straight after the crime, on 24 August 1961, when her memory would have been at its freshest. Although she had said then that 'there were quite a number of people in the bar, many of them strangers', she had singled out for mention, 'two strange men in the saloon bar, who left either shortly before or shortly after [Gregsten and Storie]'. The *Sunday Times* itself commented that the trial took place 'in an atmosphere of only partial disclosure'. So much documentation had been withheld that it was hardly surprising if journalists were sometimes misled.

On 21 July Paul Foot and Jonathan Cape were served with libel writs by William Ewer. He also sued the *Sunday Times* in respect of the series of articles published over three weeks, on 9, 16 and 23 May, which naturally dampened its ardour, for the next eighteen months or so, in pursuing the case. Everything was settled out of court. Ewer received £1,000 from Jonathan Cape, although the publishers were able to continue publishing the book without alteration. He ultimately won a much more substantial settlement from the *Sunday Times*.

On 28 October, Maudling told the Commons that Paul Foot had not 'had full access to all the available material' and that there would be no new inquiry. Explaining his decision, he said: 'For two reasons, I have concluded that a public inquiry would not help to resolve the issues. I do not believe that any judicial tribunal can be expected to arrive at a convincing opinion as to the facts on the basis of the recollection of witnesses as to specific details ten years after the event. Secondly, there are fundamental objections to the use of such a procedure as a means to the informal trial of some other person outside the normal processes of law which would be inevitable in this case.'

Once again, Alphon basked in the full protection of the Home Office, which deemed it unfair to hold an inquiry from which one could infer that he was responsible for the murder. As Alphon had taken the trouble to go over to Paris and arrange a press conference for the express purpose of proclaiming himself culpable of this crime, one would have imagined that in this instance the 'fundamental objections' to his being 'informally' incriminated might have been set aside.

Secondly, on this occasion as on others, there is understandable anger at the automatic tactics of the bureaucracy in situations of potential political embarrassment – delay, delay and delay again – which enables it, when a decision finally has to be reached, to use the passage of time as an excuse for inaction.

There was widespread dismay. 'The ghost will not be laid by this decision,' said Phillip Whitehead, 'and the concern of many members in all parties will not be allayed.' That weekend, the *Sunday Times* ran another leader on the subject.

The Home Secretary reproaches Paul Foot with not having considered all the material. It was the Home Office which refused him the opportunity.

The *Sunday Times* has itself raised two main doubts about the trial. One relates to the quality of the evidence advanced; the other to the general context in which the evidence was set. Mr Maudling has dealt with neither of them.

Anyone who has followed the case must feel frustratingly fobbed off. Maudling could have stilled the doubts if he had made a full and detailed statement to the House, quoting at least some of the documents which his department has so far sedulously withheld. He chose not to do so; and he has thereby made certain that public unease will persist.

The A6 file is not closed.[6]

Lord Goodman, a redoubtable figure in legal and political circles, became greatly concerned about the manner in which the case had been dealt with by successive Home Office ministers. He arranged for a House of Lords debate, which took place on 14 June 1972, in which both the Hanratty and the Derek Bentley cases were raised. Lord Goodman said: 'I am completely unapologetic about the suggestion that has been made that it is an injustice to the survivors in the individual cases to rake up the matter again. Well, it is not I who may cause injustice, but the circumstances. Hence, the justice

to these people is to see whether the cases can be finally disposed
of by a system of examination and inquiry which will be finally
reassuring to the parties concerned . . .'

Lord Foot – the uncle of Paul Foot – suggested that the doubts
in the public mind arose directly from the secrecy and would never
be allayed 'until the public know that some impartial authority has
been allowed to see all the evidence'. The Earl of Arran additionally
made the point that 'Evidence suppressed at the time of the trial is
in fact new evidence.'

The Home Office response on this occasion came from Viscount
Colville of Culross. 'The whole procedure would not be a trial of
somebody else,' he said, 'it would be an attempt to exonerate
Hanratty which in the process would have the effect of putting
somebody else on trial . . . It must be apparent that I have put
forward some serious practical difficulties, one of convention and
constitution and others of practice, practicality and fairness to
people who might be involved. The ingenuity of the British is well
known. If Lords or MPs can think of a completely new piece of
machinery which would be suitable for dealing with this matter . . .
then I am sure the Government would consider it.'

On this occasion, the Government seemed to be throwing its
hands up in the air, and simply saying they had no idea how to
resolve this issue.

What no one knew at that moment, and did not know for
another twenty years, was that in view of this debate – Lord
Goodman being someone not to be lightly dismissed – the Home
Office asked Scotland Yard to prepare a special background report
on the case in advance of the debate. The policeman in charge
wrote to a colleague: 'The Home Office has asked us to do some
quick research to try and establish why the original description
circulated by police of the suspect, i.e. having brown eyes, was later
changed to suspect having blue eyes.'

In the course of this mini-investigation, the police examined the
various descriptions provided of the gunman. This retrospectively
raises a number of questions. First, and most obviously, the
apparent change in the description had been one of the factors
regularly raised in Parliament during the previous decade. If the
Home Office was only now, in the summer of 1972, asking for an
analysis of the various descriptions, what had they been doing for
the past ten years when, on innumerable occasions, ministers had
reassured Parliament – in these or similar words – that they or their
officials had 'devoted a tremendous amount of careful thought to

the details of this case'. At the very least, the commissioning of a new report demonstrated an extraordinary duplication and waste of bureaucratic resources.

Second, in the course of this report, Scotland Yard went through Valerie Storie's first statement and, en passant, reported to the Home Office, that 'She said the murderer had told her his name was Jim, although she did not believe this was his true name.'

Third, this report contained a serious error. The penultimate paragraph read: 'The basic description given by Miss Storie has never varied and although subsequently enlarged upon was never changed. Furthermore, the identikit picture she compiled does in fact compare extremely well with the features of Hanratty when comparing it with the photograph on his file.'

In fact, Valerie Storie, as her trial testimony makes clear, was responsible for the left-hand identikit picture (which looked like Alphon); not the right-hand one (which did more resemble Hanratty) and which represented the combined recollections of Edward Blackhall and James Trower. To those familiar with the case, this mistake would have come into the category of schoolboy howler; but nobody noticed at the Home Office.

CHAPTER TWENTY-THREE

ON 1 MARCH 1973 Jean Justice stood for Parliament. He was the candidate of the Hanratty Inquiry Campaign at the by-election in Lincoln. This was called after Dick Taverne resigned his seat in protest at being deselected because of his strong pro-European views. He immediately stood again as an independent Labour candidate.

At this time Shirley Williams was the darling of the Hanratty campaigners, while Taverne had long been their *bête noire*. Shirley (now Baroness) Williams said on BBC Radio that she felt the case for an inquiry 'was now made out'. She was Shadow Home Secretary at that point, so campaigners were heartened. Taverne, meanwhile, had supported the call for an inquiry in 1963; but, after becoming a member of the Wilson Government, he was part of the Home Office team, as Under-Secretary of State, which rejected demands for one. In 1971, reviewing *Who Killed Hanratty?* for the *Sunday Times*, he wrote that the book caused him to have no doubts at all about the case.

Jean Justice told reporters, 'Although I am standing against Dick Taverne as a parliamentary candidate, I can assure you it isn't to get into Parliament; it is to show up Mr Taverne's insincerity.' On the hustings, Justice told the electors: 'With your help I hope Mr Taverne will be banished from Lincoln. You need a man of integrity, not a turncoat.'

At a packed public meeting, with the five candidates speaking, Taverne naturally rejected Justice's views. He explained that he had indeed originally endorsed the view of the campaigners. 'I sent for the papers in the case because I wanted to support the call for an inquiry,' he explained. 'On looking at the papers, some of which have not been seen by Mrs Williams or Mr Justice, I came to the conclusion that the case against Hanratty was overwhelming.'

Taverne was successfully elected (albeit only until the general election of October 1974); Justice received eighty-three votes.

On 17 December 1973 the *Sunday Times* re-entered the fray. Lewis Chester had conducted fresh research into the description of the murderer provided by Valerie Storie and the identikit which was drawn up to her instructions.

Chester took this identikit picture to Hugh McDonald, the American expert who had invented this police identification technique and then trained British police officers in its use. It was a simple matter for him to establish that both photofits (not just Storie's, but the other one also) 'unquestionably depict dark eyes'. This was strange. Storie had, of course, publicly insisted that one of the most obvious facial features of the gunman was his 'large icy blue staring eyes'. By the time of the trial, indeed, the colour had assumed such an overriding significance that Graham Swanwick told the jury, 'The blueness of the eyes left a deep imprint on her mind.'

The use of dark eyes could not have been the result of any deficiency in the system or misconception about its use; a transparent sheet depicting light eyes was as readily available as the one with dark eyes. There is in fact no record of Storie ever having remarked or suggested that the gunman had 'brown' eyes, even though this formed part of the original circulated description. This point, which I believe was simply a mistake by Bedfordshire police, misled campaigners for many years.

Chester's point about the identikit is probably more interesting than even he appreciated. According to the statements which I have seen, Valerie Storie first mentioned 'icy blue eyes' on Monday, 28 August. However, according to the secret police report put together for the Home Office in June 1972, Valerie Storie first mentioned 'icy blue' eyes at 6.07 a.m. on Sunday morning, 27 August. If this is so, then it means she fixed on the idea of blue eyes four days after the crime – but almost straight after she had, on the Saturday afternoon, approved an identikit portraying dark eyes. One cannot necessarily deduce anything from this other than that, in such circumstances, it is difficult to understand how absolute reliance could be placed on her identification.

McDonald's report was passed to the Home Office. Campaigners, however, began to feel more buoyant once a Labour Government had again been installed. Jean Justice told *The Times*, 'We have now got the broad-based support that is always essential in these cases. It took fifteen years and an all-party delegation before the Timothy Evans case was rectified. The precedents in that case are encouraging for us.'[1]

On 5 April it was announced that the Home Secretary – no, not Shirley Williams, but Roy Jenkins again – had asked his officials to prepare a report on new developments in the case. While they were still doing this, the *Sunday Times* acquired a few documents as a by-product of its attempt to defend the libel action brought by William Ewer. Among these, astonishingly, was the first statement of Valerie Storie, taken down on her behalf in the immediate aftermath of the crime by Detective Sergeant Douglas Rees and Woman Detective Constable Gwen Woodin. After all the years of frustration, this was suddenly a major breakthrough.

Bearing in mind recent developments, what was immediately astonishing about the 'eyes' evidence was that she hadn't mentioned the colour at all. Much more significant, however, was the fact that the statement destroyed, at a stroke, two of the notorious twelve points by which Acott eliminated Alphon. Firstly, according to the statement, Valerie Storie estimated the gunman's age at 'thirty' – older than Hanratty, but spot-on for Alphon.

Then, critically, it revealed Valerie Storie to have said, 'After he shot Mike, he told me to call him Jim, *but I don't think that was his name* [my italics].' All parties to the prosecution had fostered the impression that (unlikely as it was) the gunman had told Storie his real name. This was the first time that the defence knew that this claim wasn't supported by the original evidence.

After the long, twelve-year process of bringing to bear new evidence, and fresh interpretations of old evidence, this was the point at which the Home Office's finger-in-the-dyke policy at last had to be abandoned. An inquiry was set up. In answer to a parliamentary question from Phillip Whitehead on 20 June 1974, Roy Jenkins said, 'I am not at present persuaded that it would be right to institute a public inquiry into the case. I intend, however, to invite a Queen's Counsel to make an independent assessment of the representations and of any other relevant material, the result of which I will publish.'

It was disgraceful that this one document, the first Storie statement, had remained hidden for so long when, once it was made public, the Government was forced into an immediate U-turn. Only two years earlier, the secret police report had recognized the significance of the point by alluding to it. Yet, even then, no one had breathed a word to the Hanratty family or their lawyers.

However, this new inquiry, would at least, according to Jenkins, 'have all the documents available to it'.

'This is a very big day for the family,' commented James

Hanratty. 'Since Jimmy was hanged, we've lived with this terrible thing every day, every hour, every minute. We've thought of nothing else but clearing his name.'

The elation was indeed short-lived. Doubts set in very quickly. For a start, it took a month to announce the name of the man who was going to conduct this inquiry. To Lewis Hawser QC fell the task of attempting to reach a considered judgment on this case which had so sharply divided public, political and judicial opinion. Whether or not the job was a poisoned chalice is a moot point; he certainly turned it into one.

Initially, he seemed an excellent choice: a liberal man, highly regarded as a barrister, who was vice-chairman of Justice, the well-respected law reform organization. However, it soon emerged that Hawser intended to conduct this important inquiry in a strangely blinkered way. He simply stayed in his chambers at 1 Garden Court, The Temple, and read through the papers – well, some of the papers. He didn't wish to hear any evidence. At the beginning of his final report he emphasized that, although he had once met Jean Justice, 'no discussion of the case occurred on this occasion'. So Hawser went out of his way *not* to discuss the case with the one man who knew most about it.

By August the Hanratty family was becoming apprehensive. There were no arrangements for anyone to be legally represented. James Hanratty commented, 'It will just be a sham and a whitewash unless I am represented.' In the event, Barney Berkson, who had represented the family's interests since 1968, felt unable to continue under these conditions. Thus, in October 1974, the Hanratty family affairs were brought under the aegis of Geoffrey Bindman's practice. He became their solicitor, represented them throughout the remainder of the Hawser inquiry, and has continued to represent them – assiduously, energetically, and with scant prospect of financial reward – ever since.

On 30 January 1975 Bindman forwarded a full submission on behalf of the family. Several supplementary submissions were also compiled. In fact, further correspondence was sent to Hawser on 9 April. By that time the Hawser report, which had been completed on 26 March, was already at the printers; no one had bothered to inform the family. It was suddenly published on 10 April.

Its stark conclusion was that 'The case against Mr Hanratty remains overwhelming and that the additional material set into the framework of the case as a whole does not cast any real doubt upon the jury's verdict.' Mary Hanratty collapsed when she heard. John

Ezard reported that 'The family's shock was worsened because they had not been told officially that the judicial report was due to be released yesterday. They had believed that Mr Hawser was still taking evidence until they were asked for an interview by a journalist who had received an advance copy of the report.'[2]

The whitewash that the Hanratty family feared had indeed come to pass. *Private Eye* headlined its appraisal of the report, 'Hung, Drawn and Hawsered'. One can easily imagine in due course the verb 'to hawser' entering the English language – meaning, obviously, to cover up injustice and maladministration in the interests of what is thought to be judicial and executive convenience. It is baffling: why should people like Hawser allow themselves to be remembered with obloquy? Why would they wish to leave such a miserable legacy to their family?

The periodical *Justice of the Peace* carried a perceptive, but unsigned, article about the Hawser report. These are extracts:

> As Mr Hawser acknowledges, Hanratty's conviction was based on evidence of identity which was not conclusive, evidence of other items of circumstantial evidence which are capable of other explanations, and implausibilities which are explicable in the context of his situation. There was no scientific evidence to connect him with the murder, and no direct evidence which is not capable of a different explanation . . .
>
> In 1975, in the light of all the evidence now available, could James Hanratty reasonably be arraigned and tried *de novo*? In our submission, such a proposition would be outrageous . . .
>
> Alphon's confession may be a bizarre story as Mr Hawser describes it, but it is far less bizarre than the crime attributed to Hanratty . . .
>
> Justice is an ideal which transcends the expedience of the State, or the sensitivities of Government officials, or private individuals. It has to be pursued whatever the cost in peace of mind to those concerned.[3]

Had Hawser done this? He certainly had not. In seeking to protect the legal establishment, he had betrayed everyone. The *New Law Journal* condemned 'the ingenuity with which distinguished lawyers' managed to turn a blind eye to 'a possible miscarriage of justice of that magnitude'. It concluded a trenchant editorial by saying, 'Sustaining James Hanratty's conviction now in order to avoid embarrassment is, we suggest, carrying fraternal solidarity to unacceptable extremes.'

The irony is that, in attempting to bury for ever the truth about this shocking injustice, Hawser may have read the runes wrongly. Perhaps a whitewash report was not, after all, what was needed this time. Certainly, his career nose-dived shortly afterwards. When, in April 1990, he retired as senior official referee, a judicial post at the circuit judge level, Marcel Berlins wrote in the *Guardian*: 'His appointment in 1978 came as a shock, because everyone expected him to be a High Court judge. On every known ground, he was superior to many of the barristers appointed to the High Court bench during that period. No one knew why he had been overlooked. I tried hard to find out at the time, but to this day I still don't know.'

So why was the Hawser report such an abject betrayal of both fundamental judicial principles and common sense?

Virtually all the evidence alluded to in this book was available to Hawser. We know that he saw the lengthy hospital interview of 11 September 1961 with Valerie Storie because he quotes her concern that she would not be able to identify the gunman – 'my memory of this man's face is fading'. This occurs on page 1 of the interview. Whether Hawser was enterprising enough to turn over to page 2, or indeed to examine any of the other seventy-three pages, is not so clear.

If he had done, he was bound to notice a number of startling evidential points: the reiteration of her doubts; the reinforcement of the fact that she didn't think the gunman's name was 'Jim'; the disparities about the roadworks evidence; the fact that the 'done the lot' evidence was not based on witness testimony and was effectively faked; et cetera. None of this, however, was addressed by Hawser in his report.

The single most astonishing aspect is his treatment (or, non-treatment) of the 'Call me Jim' issue. He referred to it when describing the features of the case (para 35); but failed to mention it again. Even when listing the distinctive points of the prosecution case (paras 72–93), he did not allude to it.

Yet this was the factor which had prompted the Home Secretary to set up the inquiry in the first place. The evidence to which Hawser alone had access merely underlined Valerie Storie's perception that 'Jim' was not his real name. It was a fundamental point, and the Home Secretary had every right to anticipate that it would be authoritatively addressed in the final report.

Hawser failed to investigate the crucial identification evidence with any rigour. He did not consider at all the fascinating point that Valerie Storie constructed an identikit that looked like Alphon, yet then didn't pick him out on an identity parade; but conversely did pick out Hanratty, who didn't look like her identikit. Moreover, her original description of the gunman's hair – 'straight, well-greased, dark brown, brushed straight back, slightly receding at temples' – was wrong for Hanratty; but would have been entirely accurate for Alphon.

He blithely accepted the identification evidence of the Redbridge witnesses, and dismissed that of the Rhyl witnesses. However, if they are going to be compared, the Rhyl witnesses all had far better opportunities of seeing the man, and thus identifying him afterwards, and, unlike the Redbridge witnesses, provided incidental details to support the identification.

Hawser referred to one of the points raised by campaigners at the time – the fact that Hanratty's suit had a distinctive stripe, but that no one who ever saw the gunman mentioned the stripe. Hawser swiftly rebutted this point by arguing that none of the Rhyl witnesses had mentioned the stripe in the suit either.

If Hawser was deploying this argument, he should have been intellectually consistent. A parallel, but more persuasive, point can be raised about Hanratty's hair. It was probably looking unnatural by then (a few days later, Carole France told him that the dye was growing out and redyed it for him) and thus likely to be especially noted by people. None of the 'gunman' witnesses noticed anything strange about his hair. Some of the Rhyl witnesses, however – Margaret Walker and Christoper Larman, for example – certainly did. This obviously telling point for the defence was ignored by Hawser.

Moreover, in trying to make this area of evidence seem incriminating, Hawser wrote: 'On 3 October 1961 (at a time when he knew the police were looking for a dark-haired man) Hanratty had the tint removed from his hair restoring it to its original auburn.' At this point, Hawser was no longer examining the available evidence from his particular standpoint; he was simply inventing it. The hairdresser responsible said in her evidence at trial: 'The hair when he left my shop was much darker [i.e. than it was at trial] – a real mahogany colour.' The hair certainly wasn't 'restored to its original auburn'. The point is not insignificant, because it helps to underline how compromised Hanratty was at his identity parades.

Trying to deal with the evidence concerning the gunman's driving abilities, Hawser gave great weight to the evidence of Carole France (she said that he 'drove from side to side zig-zagging up the road'). However, in order to make a separate point – about the sweet-shop – Hawser dismissed her evidence and, indeed, that of the whole France family. Either her evidence is reliable or it isn't; Hawser cannot rely on it and reject it at whim.

Also with regard to the driving, Hawser, apparently unconvinced by his own arguments (and no wonder), suddenly added, 'There is, of course, the possibility that the gunman was putting on an act.'

Isn't it wholly illogical to suggest that the gunman might have been putting on an act about his lack of car-driving acumen in view of the following points: that was the one factor which emerged clearly and consistently from the evidence of the entire journey; at the very end, when he wanted to get away as speedily as possible, and when he must have made up his mind to shoot Storie, he was hardly going to delay matters by putting on a pointless act of pretending to be unable to drive, and asking her to show him how the gears worked; and was he was really putting on an act about that, but still – according to the Crown – giving his correct Christian name?

Regarding the roadworks, Hawser wrote: 'Mr Hanratty's family lived in the Kingsbury area and the remarks about the roadworks *certainly* [my italics] indicated a familiarity with that sector of the outer suburbs.' Certainly? All one can say here is that Hawser's remarks certainly indicated an unfamiliarity with the evidence he was supposed to be examining.

Hawser also displayed his inadequate grasp of the case in considering the ballistics evidence. Once again, the evidence itself had the merit of consistency. Valerie Storie said:

'He stopped firing. I then heard the click of metal believing he was reloading the gun. He then fired three more shots at my head and missed me.'[4]

Storie: I think I heard five shots.

Acott: And how many misses?

Storie: I heard five straight off, then I heard a click, then another click as if he'd reloaded the gun, then he fired three more shots and I don't think they hit me, I think they went over my head.[5]

'I heard a clicking sound as if he was reloading the gun. He fired three more times. He didn't hit me this time.'[6]

'After he reloaded he fired three shots at me. In all I believe he fired eight shots at me.'[7]

The evidence is unambiguous. Hawser cited all these figures, and based his report on them:

'The man fired *two* shots in very quick succession at Mr Gregsten's head (para 29) ... [Storie] was in fact hit by *five* [my italics] bullets (para 33) ... Then he fired another *three* shots which she thought did not hit her (para 33)'.

Hawser continued: 'From Miss Storie's account, and the number of bullets and cartridge cases found, it seems clear that when the murderer left the scene there would have been *three* [my italics] spent cartridge cases in the gun.'

It seems clear, does it? Hawser has enumerated *two* plus *five* plus *three* shots: *ten*, by my calculations. If there had been ten shots, then there would have been not three but four spent cartridge cases in the gun, and two unused bullets.

This was the evidence given throughout the trial: Gregsten was shot twice, then Storie five times, then the gunman reloaded, subsequently firing over her head. But for this to have happened, there would have been seven bullets in the chamber of a .38, which only held six.

In his book, *Forty Years of Murder*, Professor Keith Simpson, the distinguished pathologist who gave evidence in the A6 Murder case, described in detail the two bullet wounds suffered by Gregsten and, then, the five by Valerie Storie: 'one in the neck and four drilled-in holes in over the left shoulder and down over her arm. I thought probably that all five shots, which were in a line, had been fired in quick succession and from beyond arm's range.'

Simpson believed that all five shots were fired in the same salvo. Perhaps confused by this aspect of the evidence, he then recorded that the gun used was a .32 – which could have fired seven successive shots. However, if the gun were a .32, then all the ballistics evidence in this case was wrong – the gun on the bus wasn't the murder weapon, the cartridge cases in the Vienna had nothing to do with the case, et cetera.

So Professor Simpson must be wrong. The gun must have been a .38, and it is the trial evidence relating to the shots that must be wrong. I do not know the solution. One explanation, however, is that the gunman partly reloaded the gun in the car, taking out the two spent cartridges. Valerie Storie did not notice, which would have been natural in her immediate shock and grief at the shooting of Gregsten.

This area of ballistics evidence certainly doesn't shed light on who the murderer was. It is interesting because it is one of the areas of evidence in this case that has been uncritically accepted throughout – and there is something glaringly wrong with it. It may not be important. What is important is that Hawser, who was supposed to be submitting this case to some high-calibre forensic analysis, totally failed to notice.[8]

But Hawser could get more myopic yet. With regard to the sweet-shop, Hawser had to concede both that the incident happened; and that if it happened on the Tuesday, then Hanratty could not have committed the murder ('This is so unlikely that it can be ignored' (para 209)).

How did he resolve this? 'My assessment is that the incident occurred on the Monday.' One of the most compelling reasons for believing that the sweet-shop inquiry took place on the Tuesday was the weight of Crown evidence placing Hanratty in London on the Monday – evidence that Superintendent Acott, among others, had found persuasive. There was no subtle examination here. Just a blunt assertion from Hawser that the incident occurred on the Monday. He couldn't fit that in with any of the surrounding testimony; so he simply ignored the swathe of Crown evidence placing Hanratty in London on the Monday.

His assessment of the Rhyl alibi followed closely the path marked out by Nimmo. In other words, Hawser adopted the fallacious forensic technique of examining each statement in isolation, finding some marginal fault in it, dismissing it, and thus disregarding the evidence *in toto*. There was not a moment when Hawser attempted to assess, as he should have, the cumulative weight of the evidence.

In his report, Hawser considered Langdale–Eatwell:

> The jury was cautioned strongly about Langdale's evidence. And rightly; for this type of evidence is always suspect; particularly when there is evidence to the contrary ... but, coupled with the evidence of Eatwell, I do not think it can be dismissed out of hand ...
>
> Langdale seems to have had a rather remarkable knowledge of the details of the crime and it is not easy to see how he could have acquired them by the evening of 22 November 1961. I have read the reports in the *Evening Standard* and *Evening News* of 22 November. Both newspapers very fully reported the opening of the case by the prosecution, although both said specifically that Miss Storie was

sitting when the first shots were fired at her and that the man had to help her get Gregsten out of the car. It seems to me unlikely that Langdale would have got these two important details wrong if he had read a report in the newspaper on that day and then invented the story that he told the fellow prisoner in the coach on the way back to prison. The differences are more likely to be due to faulty recollection by him of something told to him some time previously or perhaps faulty recollection on the part of the person who gave him the details. I do not think [Langdale's evidence] can be totally ignored. I think it is entitled to some weight as part of the total picture.

This evaluation doesn't stand up to the slightest scrutiny. If Hawser actually thought that Langdale exhibited 'a rather remarkable knowledge of the details of the crime', then his study of it must be even more superficial than I have so far indicated. Also, one hardly needs to point out that – another time, another occasion – if there had been incorrect details in witness evidence, Lewis Hawser QC would have been saying that this proved it was invalid; here he said that because there were inaccuracies, that proved its validity.

Hawser went on to say that Langdale 'did not obtain any direct advantage' from providing his evidence. Yet he had to admit that the outcome of Langdale's court case was 'favourable'. It certainly was. Hawser simply didn't consider the obvious behaviour pattern of a police informer who, time and again, reaped great advantage from his unethical activities.

Considering Mrs Dalal and the two Mrs Willis incidents, Hawser wrote:

These incidents suggest that one or it may be two other persons were claiming to be the A6 murderer and that this person or one of these two was not Mr Alphon. They are illustrations of the effect which highly publicized crimes of this nature may have on persons of an unstable character.

There was one thing of which Mrs Willis was absolutely certain: it was the same man on both occasions. If it was Alphon the first time, it was Alphon the second time; if it was not Alphon the first time, it was not him the second time. So, there was not necessarily more than one person involved in these three incidents. Once again, Hawser's technique rested on blunt assertion. Had he spoken to any of the witnesses, he could not have reached the conclusions he did; so he refused to talk to any of them.

One could go on and on, pointing to shortcomings in the report. It was extraordinary that anyone should present this to the Home Secretary of the day as a credible examination of the case. Perhaps, after all, it's not so surprising that Hawser never made it beyond the level of official referee.

Nevertheless, faced with the Hawser report, Roy Jenkins felt there was little more that he could do. He told Parliament that 'As far as I am concerned, I am afraid that must be the end of it.'

The grief of the Hanratty family, which Phillip Whitehead described in Parliament as 'profound', should never be underestimated. Michael Hanratty shook his head sadly at the recollection. 'The Hawser report,' he said, 'that just broke my father's heart.'

Despite the renewed shock and distress, James Hanratty never resigned himself to failure. He tried three more forays in his attempt to honour his promise to his son. The first opportunity occurred in 1976, as a result of escalating public concern about the widespread number of wrongful convictions obtained through disputed identification evidence. During the trial, Michael Sherrard had mentioned that such doubts had been intermittently expressed throughout most of the century, but had never been tackled. However, the issue reached a particular crescendo in the mid-1970s, after a number of high-profile miscarriages. One of those who recognized identification as a major problem area was Lewis Hawser himself, as he defended Peter Hain, now MP for Neath and Under-Secretary of State at the Welsh Office, against a trumped-up charge based on erroneous identification evidence.

The concern prompted Roy Jenkins to establish a committee under the eminent judge Lord Devlin to examine the whole issue. His report was published on 26 April 1976. Devlin recommended that a person should not be convicted on eye-witness evidence unless the circumstances of the identification were 'exceptional', or the eye-witness evidence was supported by 'substantial' evidence of another sort. James Hanratty immediately pointed out that if such safeguards had been in place in 1961, then the case against his son would probably have been thrown out at Ampthill, at the magistrates' court. Roy Jenkins, however, responded that 'There can be no question of the recommendations having retrospective force.'

Indeed there could not; if they had, the Home Office would have had to arrange the annulment of convictions in probably thousands of cases. The Devlin report led, the following year, to the Court of Appeal adopting fresh guidelines, known as the Turnbull rules, for cases in which evidence of identification was put forward. (This did not ensure that the problem of miscarriages of justice was resolved or diminished in any way. It just resulted in the police securing wrongful convictions by alternative means.)

The second development occurred when the family, still desperately pursuing all possible leads, managed to obtain Jimmy's blood donor card. Their son was rhesus negative. Geoffrey Bindman wrote to his parliamentary contacts that 'the discovery of the card had given hope to Mr and Mrs Hanratty. I am very anxious that any chance it might give us of establishing the innocence of their son should be explored as thoroughly and effectively as possible.' He realized, however, that the chances were slim. He had already taken advice from a consultant haematologist who told him that the rhesus factor was never present in seminal fluids. Subsequently, and somewhat inevitably, the Minister of State at the Home Office, Alex Lyon, closed the matter by saying that the discovery of the blood donor card 'did not throw any new light on the case'.

So the family tried another tack. Bindman asked for further information from the Director of Public Prosecutions (DPP) with regard to the non-disclosure of Valerie Storie's original statement; he wanted to know just who had seen it. On 21 May 1977 Marcel Berlins reported in *The Times*, 'The DPP has said that the statement formed part of the papers given to prosecuting counsel ... This letter is the first indication that it was available at trial.'

In this new situation, the *New Law Journal* commented:

> Mr Hawser concluded that if the jury had been aware of the 'discrepancies' between Miss Storie's original statement and the evidence she gave in court, it would have made no difference to the verdict. This is of course pure conjecture, and in the circumstances of the Hanratty case particularly, such a conjecture is not really to be relied upon ... The statement was not formally disclosed. However, the DPP makes the point that it may have been disclosed to the defence *informally*. This is simply not good enough.
>
> The question the DPP letter leaves unanswered is: did the prosecution disclose the existence of Miss Storie's original statement for the benefit of the defence, either informally or at all?[9]

The whole problem of non-disclosure of evidence is that it precipitates these kinds of unseemly, irresolvable and futile disputes about who saw what when. With regard to the vexed issue of the first statement, we have no way of knowing, although the overwhelming presumption is that the defence never saw it, otherwise they would have made effective use of it. However, the question, limited as it is to one document, is simply immaterial, because we do know that a mountain of valuable material was never disclosed to the defence. This is just one of the litany of examples which illustrates that the withholding and non-disclosure of documents is simply an unacceptable practice; it creates and perpetuates injustice. Meanwhile, the *New Law Journal* placed on record its astonishment that these questions were now being asked at all, and that 'they were not brought to light in the course of Mr Hawser's recent inquiry'.

James Hanratty died at his home in Cricklewood on 31 August 1978. He had always insisted that he would fight to clear his son's name 'until I die', and he had done exactly that. His great achievement was that by the time of his death he was a public figure; everyone knew who he was and the name 'Hanratty' sparked a chord of instant recognition with the British people. Moreover, he had reached this position of public pre-eminence without ever seeking publicity on his own behalf; indeed, the more that well-known names appeared at campaign meetings, the more that James himself was likely to take a back seat. He had achieved it all through his utter determination to win justice for his son, a reward that his courageous and tenacious work alone merited (never mind the contributions of everyone else), but which the intransigence of the British establishment and the perfidy of the wretched Hawser denied him to the end.

The case might have rested there, were it not for the enduring influence of Jean Justice. At the end of the 1980s he got in touch with me as a result of my book, *Miscarriages of Justice*. I found him, as all others had, charming, cultured, mischievous – a delightful man. We discussed the case several times at his flat on the Hallfield estate in Bayswater. (He was, by then, living in rather reduced circumstances.)

I was working at Yorkshire Television, making documentaries for the *First Tuesday* series, and promised him that I'd see whether a television programme might be possible. Michael Hanratty and Geoffrey Bindman generously gave their enthusiastic support, and Paul Foot was equally encouraging. Channel 4 commissioned a documentary on the whole A6 story for its *True Stories* strand. Jean was delighted. However, there was a delay because we wanted to do the programme for the thirtieth anniversary in 1992, and I had another film to make in Spain first.

I could begin to set wheels in motion, however. I thought Florence Snell might have been able to throw some light on Nudds's contacts and behaviour, but discovered that she died, seemingly of natural causes, in 1963. I did find Juliana Galves back home in Spain, where I went to interview her, and she was able to fill in some details about the Vienna Hotel.

We also tracked Roy Langdale to Thetford, Norfolk. We hung around all day for him, and finally intercepted him at the offices of the small minicab company that he ran. After only momentary hesitation, he declined to speak to us.

Because we also wanted to track down as many original documents as possible, Geoffrey Bindman and myself approached Bedfordshire police. They were kind enough to provide facilities for us to examine, over a period of some weeks, the voluminous documentation which they held – although even that, I am convinced, is dwarfed by what is retained at Scotland Yard.

Sadly, Jean was never able to see this material for himself. By the spring of 1990 it was clear that he didn't have long to live. Though he had made a characteristically spirited recovery from a heart by-pass operation, cancer was diagnosed in 1990 and he underwent a course of chemotherapy. I came back to London and we spent all day interviewing him at home. It was an arduous process for everyone, because he was so ill; but he was utterly determined to do it, to leave for posterity a filmed record of his own involvement in and understanding of the case. Afterwards, someone told my editor how much film we'd shot; he thought I was out of my mind, and I had to keep out of his way for the next few days.

Jean was soon back in hospital, and I visited him just before I flew back to Spain. He was still discussing the case with anyone who'd listen, pointing out that the character and personality of Hanratty meant that he couldn't have committed the crime; whereas the character and personality of Alphon meant not only that he had committed it, but that he couldn't bear to be publicly absolved of it: 'the more that the authorities said it couldn't be him, the more he hit back, as if he were saying, "No, I won't be treated like that, I did it, I take the credit."'

I was in Almeria when, at five past eight in the evening, the call came through from London. He died on 2 July 1990.

Schopenhauer wrote that, 'The deep pain that is felt at the death of every friendly soul arises from the feeling that there is in every individual something which is inexpressible, peculiar to him alone, and is therefore absolutely and irretrievably lost.' That is the deep and enduring sadness which applies to many of those who feature in this long saga, and which applies quintessentially to Jean. When my editor heard the news, his first reaction was, 'Thank goodness we've got that film in the can.' A little victory over authority: Jean would have enjoyed that.

• VI •
THE RESOLUTION

CHAPTER TWENTY-FOUR

ON 22 SEPTEMBER 1961 the police told the entire country that Peter Alphon was the man they wanted to interview in connection with the A6 Murder. They took statements from members of his family, and from some of those who knew him. (There was no one, it seemed, who could actually be termed a friend.) Others came forward to give information in direct consequence of the police appeal and the extensive publicity.

Although he was at Mercer's public school, both in London and when it was evacuated to Horsham during the war, Alphon actually finished his schooling, from January to December 1945, at a state school, Quintin Kynaston, in St John's Wood. This was very close to where the France family lived, and was also within a few minutes' walk of Swiss Cottage. Alphon did National Service in the RAF from January 1949 to July 1950, at Marlow in Buckinghamshire. He left early because of a 'mental or nervous disorder'.

On 18 September 1961 his aunt, Isabella Jordan, gave police her assessment of him:

'He is my sister Gladys's son. The last time I saw him was about four years ago. He was with his mother in Putney. He was crying. I only said, "Hello, Peter"; he didn't reply. At this time his mother was staying with us, to keep away from Peter. I expect it was a Saturday and she was probably giving him money. His mother has given him every penny she had. Peter has had all her money. He was putting much of his money on the dogs. As far as I know he has never had a proper job, although I believe he worked as a waiter once.

'I wouldn't have him at my house. Peter was the cause of my sister and her husband parting. I remember on one occasion she came and told me that Peter had talked of committing suicide. That was about four and a half years ago.'[1] From 1942 Felix and Gladys Alphon had lived at 24 Agate Road in Hammersmith. Alfred Fielding and his wife were also there: 'About three or four years ago, the family broke up and they left. Whilst they were here, there were always rows and upsets. Peter did little work, but at one time he was a guard on the railway.'[2]

Derek Boulton was another who had rooms there at 24 Agate Road:

'My wife and I lived in the same house as Mr and Mrs Fielding and Mr and Mrs Alphon and their son Peter. I did not know Peter very well, but enough to know that he was continually quarrelling with his mother and doing little or no work. I never saw him with a girlfriend. He always wore a sort of gaberdine mac. Normally his hair was all roughed up, but sometimes when he went out he would have his hair brushed straight back flat.

'In or about the last week of July this year I was in the garden when my wife called me to the side entrance. I saw a man standing there selling *Old Moore's Almanacs*. I recognized him as Peter Alphon. I said to him, "Don't we know you, you are Peter Alphon." He denied he was and hurriedly left. I know that the man was Peter Alphon. He speaks in a queer way, like a grown-up acting like a child, his voice sounds slightly slurred and he doesn't seem to sound his last letters and whines when he speaks.'[3]

The rift between the parents seemed to be healed once Peter was out of the way. While they took rooms in Streatham, Peter found digs at 99 St George's Drive in Pimlico, central London. He stayed there from 19 January 1960 until 1 February 1961. The landlady, Josephine Hayes, had good cause to remember him:

'He still owes me about £7 rent. He gave no notice of his intention to leave but left behind a note saying that he had gone. Whilst he stayed with us, we never found out exactly what he did for a living, but he told us and other residents that he was a student. He also mentioned that he was a wine waiter. I had several complaints from other residents about a tapping noise from his room. We queried a typewriter, but I never saw him with one.

'He had no mail except towards the end of his stay. Several large parcels of books arrived addressed to him. He never had a visitor but said that his mother and father lived in a flat in Streatham and that his father worked as a clerk at Scotland Yard. He told me that he often met his mother in Ebury Street and that he used to go to lunch with her to the Domestic Science College in Buckingham Palace Road.

'I have never known him to go to work in the mornings. Sometimes he stayed out after lunch and sometimes he came back.

He used to burn a light in his room very late, often until the early hours of the morning. He never smoked while I knew him, I have never seen him with a cigarette and I never saw tobacco ash in his room.

'Whilst living at this house I had no complaints about him from any of the girls here. In my opinion he was rather effeminate and liked gossiping as women do. I have no evidence of him being a homosexual. He was always polite and clean in his habits and his room was orderly. I can recall that he always paid his rent regularly on a Friday, mostly new £1 notes and silver.

'A peculiarity of his was that he kept brown paper neatly folded, quite a lot of it. He also collected the racing books, the ones that are issued at the course, either horses or greyhounds. He had two suitcases, I think. At least one was always locked. He used to have library books in his room on mystical subjects with varying religious tendencies. He would argue about religion, particularly with another resident, Anthony Pimenta, who is now a science master at a girls' school in Northampton.

'About the spring of 1960 he came down to the kitchen, it was late at night, and he looked dreadful, his face and head were bleeding and black and blue. He told me he had come off his motor-bike; up till then I didn't know he had a motor-bike, and I still haven't seen him with one.

'While he was here he was always dressed in a black or navy blazer, white shirt with a black bow-tie, dark trousers, a fawn or grey mackintosh. His hair was always smoothed back. After he left in February 1961, it was discovered that the visitors' signing-in book was missing. This book contained his signature and his Streatham address. We have never found this book.

'Since Mr Alphon has been gone in February, I have seen him once, about three or four weeks ago, about 9 p.m. in the fish-and-chip shop in Lupus Street. He left before I got near him. He looked tidy, was wearing a white shirt and a dark jacket. I have also learned since he left here that he has visited Speaker's Corner and often used to go up there.

'I considered Mr Alphon an odd type, his temper easily aroused, although he was always pleasant to me. I have formed an impression that outwardly he pretended to be a man of high morals, but that he wasn't as good as he pretended to be.'[4]

On Monday, 21 August, between noon and 2.30 p.m., Alphon went to a pawnbroker's at 105 Uxbridge Road, Shepherd's Bush,

The manager, Victor Reader, said: 'I know this man, a Mr Alphon, a regular customer, he will always argue over price. He has two pawns here at the moment.

'On 21 August he brought in three pairs of grey trousers, all appearing new. He got £2 5s. Usually when he pawns with us, the goods, mostly clothing or shoes, are new. He has always redeemed his goods. Mr Alphon is about 5 feet 7 inches, dark hair, sleek, thin face, rather pallid, staring eyes, quick nervous manner. He usually wears dark clothing, often a black blazer.'[5]

On 24 September the police took a statement from Geoffrey Ferguson, a dog-racing enthusiast who frequented Slough stadium.

'I can recall first seeing this man about six months ago. Since that time I have seen him occasionally. I have spoken to him, but do not know his name. He has not been by for the past fortnight. He knew a lot about out-of-town dogs and was without doubt a keen racing man. It was at the time when open heats were held, that would have been about three to four weeks ago, when I last saw him, but I remember seeing him about two weeks before that on a Tuesday.

'I would describe him as about 5 feet 8 inches, thirty years, slim build, wearing a dark brown or black suit, three-quarter length off-white "shortie" raincoat with vivid red lining. I got the impression that he was a waiter wearing a stiff white short with black dickie-bow. He spoke to me on one occasion when he said, "Ain't got a chance," referring to a dog. The way he said it, he sounded like a gypsy spoke, but he certainly was not one. He had well-kept hands, dark brown hair brushed back.'[6]

On the night of 22/23 August, when the murder occurred, Alphon stayed at the Vienna Hotel, and was either in by midnight (Nudds's statements 1 and 3) or in at 8.00 the following morning (Nudds's statement 2). That afternoon, however, Paul Davey, a car salesman from New Malden, Surrey, saw him at Victoria station.

'I have known Peter Alphon since 1942. He used to live next door to me at Agate Road in Hammersmith. I moved away in 1951, when I got married, and lost track of Peter Alphon until Wednesday, 23 August 1961, at about 4.50 p.m. when I met him by chance inside Victoria Station.

'I recognized him and said, "Hello." He turned round and said, "Hello," shook hands and asked after my parents, and I did his. We asked each other about mutual schoolfriends. I asked him what he was doing now, but he said, "Nothing much," and he passed it off. I could see he didn't want to tell me. He had the smell of drink on him, but faintly. I got the impression he wasn't doing well.

'He had an open-necked white shirt, no tie, blue blazer, double-breasted, grey flannel trousers, which needed a press. Black shoes, they looked as if they needed a clean. I asked if he was married, and he said, "No." His manner appeared just the same as he was when I knew him before, quiet, timid and diffident. I said I was going to the pictures. He said, "I have got to meet my mother at 5.30 p.m. from work." The conversation was then about schoolfriends and old times. One of us mentioned it was nearly 5.30. We said goodbye, and I walked across to the coach station, and he walked towards the opening that leads to the Monseigneur News Theatre. That is the last time I saw him.'[7]

Alphon went to the Alexandra Court Hotel where Anita Sims, the wife of the manager, thought he checked in between 5 and 6 p.m. The hotel was about 300 yards from Finsbury Park tube station, and slightly further from the Manor House underground. Alphon signed the register as F. Durrant, of 7 Hurst Avenue, Horsham, Sussex. He just arrived without having previously booked by phone, and did not enquire about the cost (well, it hardly mattered as he wouldn't be paying anyway). He was given Room 97.

Between 11.00 a.m. and noon the following day, he went to the reception desk and asked if he could stay until Monday, 28 August. Anita Sims said, 'I think I saw him on one or two occasions subsequently, passing through the lobby by the reception desk. I cannot say when these occasions were, but would be when the hotel was quiet.' Anita Sims described him accurately and noticed his 'slight cockney accent'.[8]

Mary Perkins, a fifty-three-year-old schoolmistress, was staying at the hotel throughout August. Alphon moved in to the room next door to hers. She described him accurately, and mentioned that he had 'either a cockney or south country accent'. The first night that Alphon was there, 'he played his wireless very loudly. Colonel Guiton went to his room and spoke to him.'

Lieutenant Colonel Reginald Le Hardy Guiton, who was retired and also occupied a room at the hotel, saw him shortly after he arrived on the Wednesday. He knocked on the door of 97. 'He agreed to turn the wireless down, he closed the door and did turn the volume down.' Le Hardy Guiton described him as 'rather a rat-faced man with sharpish features and straight dark hair, he was clean shaven but had not shaved recently'.[9]

Mary Perkins continued to be disturbed, however. 'I spent a great deal of time in my room. The wireless in 97 was almost permanently operating until almost midnight. At various times of the day I could hear squealing sounds and movement of furniture. One evening in particular he spent most of the evening moving things. I thought he was moving his bed or other furniture. I also heard the clinking of coins as though he was counting coins. On occasions I heard him go to the toilet and take the key from the lock of his room door.'[10]

Le Hardy Guiton visited Miss Perkins on the following days. 'My attention was drawn to a thumping noise coming from Room 97,' he recalled, 'and also a squeaking from a wardrobe door.'

On Friday evening, 25 August, at about 5.45, Alphon went into Burton's on the Seven Sisters Road and purchased a new raincoat. The shop manager, Paul Alexander, remembered that he paid cash, in single £1 notes. When the receipt was being made out, he said that his name was Taylor and he lived in Birmingham.[11]

At the hotel, Mary Perkins was still perturbed. 'On the first Saturday following his arrival I spoke with Dolly, the chambermaid.' Dolly told her that the staff felt there was something suspicious about the man in 97; since his arrival, he had never gone down for meals. 'One of us said', recalled Mary Perkins, 'that he must be in hiding.'

That Saturday evening, they alerted Peter Sims, the hotel manager, to the situation. Sims then realized that he hadn't so much as set eyes on this guest since his arrival three days earlier. When he again failed to appear for breakfast on Sunday morning, Sims went up to his room.

'The occupant opened the door slightly and looked round the edge of it. I explained who I was and asked him if he would like to have coffee or breakfast served in his room, or if he would come down to the dining room. He firmly refused any, but gave no reason. So far as I know, he had not left the hotel up to this stage, nor had he eaten in the hotel. In view of his behaviour and the complaints from Room 96, I communicated with the police at Highbury Vale.'[12]

Anita Sims remembered seeing Alphon go out at about noon – 'I remember the time because we were expecting the police to call' – and was at reception when he returned at about 7 p.m. His key was not on the board – not surprisingly, as the police, who had already visited the hotel at lunchtime, had returned after learning that the name and address were false, and were searching his room.

Alphon was taken down to the station in Blackstock Road, where he made a statement.

Later that evening, he returned to the hotel, having been told by Sergeant Kilner to sign the register using his correct name and address. 'He said the reasons he had given the false name was a matter of principle,' Peter Sims explained. 'He had not told the police the reason for doing this, but it was because he was mixed up in Finnish politics.'

After he returned that Sunday evening, Anita Sims heard him say that 'It had certainly taught me a lesson.' She noticed that 'He seemed quite happy.' Peter Sims also noticed an immediate change in his behaviour after he had been seen by police: 'The very next morning he started to come down for breakfast in the public dining room.'

Anita Sims said that Alphon was supposed to leave on Wednesday, 30 August, but he said he wished to stay until 3 September. Her statement continued:

'I gave him the bill which was made out for the week. It came to £8 15s. He said he would pay the following Saturday when his money came through ... On Sunday, 3 September, he paid his bill up to and including 30 August with two £5 notes. He said he could not pay the extra, and wanted to stay on until the following Wednesday, 6 September. We made it clear he could not remain in the hotel after that date.

'On the morning of 6 September, I sent the housekeeper to his room to make sure he was leaving. He came to reception with his suitcase. He said he would leave the suitcase with me as he was going to the bank to get the money to pay his bill. He said he would be gone for two hours. He did not return.

'About 1 p.m. a lady came in and said, "I have come to pay Mr Alphon's bill." She paid it, and asked me for a receipt for that and the previous bill. I suggested she would want his suitcase. She did not appear to recognize it. She suggested that he would want to return here, but finally she took the case.'

So Alphon left the Alexandra Court Hotel on 6 September. The following day, Meike Dalal was attacked after a man had telephoned enquiring about a room. She identified Alphon as the attacker. Astonishingly, on these days – Wednesday and Thursday – Alphon telephoned his old school, Quintin Kynaston, seeking employment. The secretary there, Martha Harman, remembered: 'He was enquiring whether we had any vacancies at the school for a teaching position. I asked him what his subjects were and he mentioned English. The deputy headmaster told me to tell him to write to us giving details of his qualifications. The next day, he telephoned again, making the same enquiry. I recognized his voice at once and told him this. He then made some excuse about getting the telephone numbers mixed up and rang off.'[13]

On Monday, 11 September, the cartridge cases were found in the Vienna Hotel, and the police renewed their interest in Alphon as the A6 suspect. On 13 September Acott, accompanied by Detective Chief Inspector Taylor and Detective Inspector Holmes, went to 142 Gleneagle Road, Streatham to interview Gladys Alphon to ascertain, among other things, whether she corroborated her son's statement of 27 August. According to that, Alphon said that he saw her on the evening of 22 August: 'My mother arrived at 9.30 p.m. and we met on the corner of Gleneagle Road as I do not get on with my father. I was with my mother for about ten minutes and she gave me a suitcase.' The interview with Gladys Alphon was recorded and transcribed.

Acott: Is [Peter's] relationship with you and your husband cordial?
Gladys Alphon: Well, he doesn't get on with Father because they
  had a row about four years ago and they haven't met since.
Acott: Have you given any money to your son in the last three months?
Gladys Alphon: Yes, many times.
Acott: When do you normally meet him and how often?
Gladys Alphon: He usually rings me at my place of business and I
  meet him at lunchtime several times a week, but recently it has
  been a lot less.
Acott: When did Peter last come to your address here at Gleneagle
  Road?
Gladys Alphon: He hasn't been into the house but I saw him a few
  weeks ago and gave him a cheap grey fibre suitcase with a red
  metal handle. I met him down the road near Streatham
  Common station, after arranging to meet him when he
  telephoned the office, or it may have been when I met him one
  lunchtime.
Acott: Can you be precise on the day you met him?
Gladys Alphon: No, I can only say it was Tuesday, Wednesday or
  Thursday.
Acott: When you handed him the case did he have anything with
  him?
Gladys Alphon: No, but he might keep his clothing or other stuff at
  the left-luggage office of a railway station or at his lodgings.

Acott: Does he do any work?

Gladys Alphon: No, he has not worked for over a year and I've been giving him regular money, sometimes £3 or £4 a week, to pay his board and lodgings.

Acott: Was there any reason for the heavy payments of £10 and 10 guineas that you mentioned earlier?

Gladys Alphon: Well, I suppose he gambled it away. He goes to the dogs at Wembley, Harringay and West Ham.

Acott: Does he drive a motor vehicle?

Gladys Alphon: I don't know if he can drive a car but he had a motor-cycle a few years ago.

Acott: Has he been in the Services?

Gladys Alphon: Yes, he was in the RAF doing National Service in 1949 for about eighteen months or two years, and was stationed at Marlow in Buckinghamshire.

Acott: Can you remember any regular work that he has done?

Gladys Alphon: Well, soon after his National Service he obtained work on the Underground, first as a porter and then as a guard, but he only stayed there for about twelve months as he said the trains made him dizzy and sick.

Acott: Are there any other jobs he has had?

Gladys Alphon: Well, I know for periods he has done odd jobs as a barman. I know he was at the Brewmaster public house in Leicester Square for a time.

Acott: Have you ever suspected that he may be suffering from some mental illness?

Gladys Alphon: No, never.

Acott: Is there anything that he says to you that may have caused you some worry?

Gladys Alphon: Well, there have been occasions when he has said that he was afraid to leave this world too early before he had time to do good and he has said that one day he would do it.

Acott: Has he any interest in girls or women?

Gladys Alphon: No. When I talk to him about getting married, he always says that it would impede his good work if he did so.[14]

The more evidence they assembled, the more it must have seemed that Alphon was their man. Eventually, all that stood in the way were the statements of Nudds and Florence Snell. Once they were taken in to Scotland Yard and questioned about them a second time, they narrated a very different version of events –

according to which Alphon did not reach his room at the Vienna until the following morning.

After the police appeal, Alphon walked into Scotland Yard just before midnight on Saturday, 23 September. Acott and Oxford were called in. They began interviewing Alphon at 2.15 a.m. This interview, too, was recorded and transcribed. These are the key parts:

Acott: Why have you come here? Is it because you think you can help us?

Alphon: No, I don't think I can. I'm not particularly interested in your case.

Acott: Why not?

Alphon: I've already made a statement at Blackstock Road. You know all about that, don't you?

Acott: Supposing you tell me what you told Sergeant Kilner?

Alphon: I can't remember now.

Acott: Why not?

Alphon: I can't go over all that again. I wouldn't remember it. Anyway, I had nothing to do with it.

Acott: Nothing to do with what?

Alphon: The murder.

Acott: What murder?

Alphon: The A6 Murder.

Acott: What makes you think it's the A6 Murder?

Alphon: I read it in the papers tonight.

Acott: You weren't very truthful when interviewed by Sergeant Kilner, were you?

Alphon: Not particularly, but the bit about the alibi for the murder was the truth. You haven't had much success so far and time is being wasted.

Acott: Can you help us in any way to catch this murderer?

Alphon: No. On principle I'm not on the side of law and order, but it's quite clear to me that you'll never catch him now. It's over a month old now and if you haven't caught him now, you never will.

Acott: I want you to begin by telling me your movements for the whole week, beginning 21 August this year.

Alphon: I thought I had an alibi. I gave it to that chap Kilner – as I say, I have an alibi, but I think the onus is on you to prove it.

Acott: I want you to go through the whole of that week again telling me, day by day, where you stayed, who you met and when you worked.

Alphon: Work – now that's something I don't like to discuss.

Acott: Why not?

Alphon: Well, I try never to work if I can help, that's one of my principles.

Acott: When did you last work?

Alphon: Just over two years ago. I worked in the Blue Anchor as a barman for about two weeks.

Acott: How have you managed for money all these years?

Alphon: I depend on the dogs for my money. I go nearly every day, and I am pretty successful.

Acott: Have you any other means of income?

Alphon: Well, I don't like telling you this, but I can always get money out of my mother.

Acott: What do you mean by that?

Alphon: Well, for years now she's been paying for my hotels and giving me some pocket money.

Acott: Does she do this regularly?

Alphon: Yes, she gives me nearly £5 every week, but she'll always give me more if I ask for something extra.

Acott: Have you done any work in the past fourteen months?

Alphon: I'm not going to tell you.

Acott: Why not?

Alphon: It's got nothing to do with the murder.

Acott: It may have.

Alphon: I'm not prepared to discuss my private affairs with you, it's a political thing.

Acott: What do you mean?

Alphon: I am a fascist, and we can't talk to policemen.

Acott: How can your political leanings have anything to do with the investigation of a murder?

Alphon: The whole thing's political – the murder and your investigation, the murderer was a Communist – what are you?

Acott: Let's talk about the almanacs. When did you last buy any to sell?

Alphon: I'm not going to answer that. I have told you I'm a fascist and I don't like questions about my private affairs. You get on with your own job.

Acott: It will pay you to answer my questions. If you answer my questions truthfully, although you can't see it now, it may turn

out that I shall be able to clear you of this murder which is
something you can't do at this moment, and which apparently
you won't even try to help me to do. Now then, where do you
sell and how do you sell these almanacs?

Alphon: Northolt, Wembley, Watford, Hammersmith, Manor
House – all over London.

Acott: How do you sell them?

Alphon: I go from door to door in different districts each day. I
know my London very well. Sometimes I sell them for sixpence,
sometimes a shilling, it depends on the district.

At this point, there was a break for tea.

Acott: Where are you staying at present?

Alphon: I'm not going to tell you.

Acott: Why not?

Alphon: If I tell you, you'll go round there and I've got some
private papers I don't want you to see . . . I always stay in good
hotels for bed and breakfast, but I never have any other meals
in the hotel.

Acott: How much have you earned in the past three to four
weeks?

Alphon: About £2.

Acott: How have you existed for nearly a month on only £2?

Alphon: I'm not saying.

Acott: If you have been getting money regularly from your mother
for the last few years, why haven't you seen her for the past
three or four weeks?

Alphon: Last time we met we had a terrible row.

Acott: When did you last see your father?

Alphon: Over four years ago.

Acott: Why is that?

Alphon: It's political and he's mad anyway.

Acott: Where did you sleep last night?

Alphon: I'm not saying.

Acott: Your clothes look quite smart.

Alphon: Well, they're Terylene.

Acott: How many other shirts have you?

Alphon: About seven or eight.

Acott: Where are they?

Alphon: I'm not saying.

Acott: Have you any other clothes anywhere else?

Alphon: Yes, but they're in hotels and pawnbrokers and I'm not telling you where they are.

Acott: I shall have every pawnbroker visited and I shall probably find them . . . Have you got any bags or cases?

Alphon: No.

Acott: None at all?

Alphon: Well, I have got one cheap case where I'm staying, but I'm not telling you where that is.

Acott: Do you drive a motor-car?

Alphon: No, I used to drive a motor-cycle and had a provisional licence.

Acott: When did you go to the Alexandra Court Hotel?

Alphon: I can't remember.

Acott: You went there on Wednesday, 23 August and left on Wednesday, 6 September. Is that right?

Alphon: You've obviously checked – you must know.

Acott: Who paid the bill?

Alphon: My mother.

Acott: Were you with her?

Alphon: No, I waited outside.

Acott: So you registered in a false name and address at that hotel?

Alphon: Yes . . . I don't like answering questions. I don't like anybody knowing anything about me, that's my principle.

Acott: These questions are an important part of my investigation.

Alphon: I didn't commit any murder. I never have anything to do with women. I'm frightened of them.

Acott: You went to the Alexandra in the name of Durrant on the afternoon of 23 August? Where did you come from?

Alphon: The previous night I was in the Hotel Vienna.

Acott: What was the number of the room you stayed in?

Alphon: Room 6.

Acott: Who did you pay?

Alphon: The hotel at Baker Street. They sent me to the Vienna which was an overflow hotel.

Acott: How did you find that first hotel?

Alphon: I looked it up in an ABC railway guide.

Acott: What was the name of it?

Alphon: Some house hotel.

Acott: How did you get to the Vienna?

Alphon: I left Mother at Streatham and then went to Victoria where I left a case in the left-luggage office. From there I caught a Circle Line to Baker Street and from there to Maida Vale.

Acott: How did you find the hotel?

Alphon: I asked a policeman.

Acott: What time did you get to the hotel?

Alphon: At about 11 p.m.

Acott: Did you register?

Alphon: Yes, and a girl showed me to my room.

Acott: Had you ever been to the hotel before?

Alphon: No.

Acott: What time did you get up?

Alphon: Before they finished breakfast.

Acott: Did you have breakfast?

Alphon: Yes – bacon and egg.

Acott: Who served you?

Alphon: The woman who booked me in, I think.

Acott: Did you get a receipt?

Alphon: No, I don't think I did. If I did, I threw it away.

Acott: Do you remember your room in the Vienna?

Alphon: I've told you my alibi for the Tuesday.

Acott: Did you go into another room, a bedroom which backs on to a garden?

Alphon: No.

Acott: It has been suggested that you changed your bedroom that night.

Alphon: That's quite wrong. I only had one room at that hotel.

Acott: Do you remember anyone else at the hotel who might help to prove you were there that night?

Alphon: No, I only remember the girl who booked me in. I think it was her who gave me breakfast next morning . . . I can't remember seeing any man in that hotel.

Acott: Supposing I tell you there are two witnesses willing to say you booked in at midday, were given a basement room and you left the hotel saying you would not be back until late, had not returned by 2 a.m. and was left a note and key of Room 6 on the first floor and you were found in Room 6 just before 10.00 the next day?

Alphon: You're trying to trap me . . . they must be lying, it couldn't possibly be a mistake. I only had one room in that hotel and that was No. 6.

Acott: This is a most serious matter. Can you suggest why two witnesses should lie on such a serious matter?

Alphon: No, it's beyond me. I can't fathom it out at all.

Acott: Now tell me the hotels and offices where your luggage is, so I can find it and examine your clothing.

Alphon: No, I don't want my private papers scrutinized. They are political. How do you think that's going to help? Do you think I've got bloodstained shirts?

Acott: Have you got bloodstained shirts?

Alphon: Of course not, but I don't want to produce them to you.

Acott: Why did you want to buy a mac so soon after leaving the Vienna? Was it to change your appearance?

Alphon: No, I think it was raining and I wanted to go out for a walk.

Acott: Do you know where the murder happened?

Alphon: No, I don't know Bedfordshire at all.

Acott: Have you been in any fights recently?

Alphon: No, only about eighteen months ago, at Speaker's Corner. I get into arguments about politics and religion sometimes. You won't understand this, but I am not a normal person. I'm described as a Christian, but I don't follow any of your religions, I have gods of my own.

Acott: When you left the Vienna, did you go straight to the Alexandra?

Alphon: Well, more or less, I think I was reading in a library for a long time. Perhaps it was funny when I didn't have breakfast on two or three occasions at the Alexandra, and stayed in my room for those first few days, but I often do that. I suppose you'd call me a strange fellow. I know they complained about me and called the police, but I'm telling you the truth.

Acott: Are you frightened of anything?

Alphon: I wouldn't say I am fearless, but I am a fascist, so I'm not frightened of anything.

Acott: Do you know Slough?

Alphon: I know it a little, I was stationed in the Air Force at Marlow, and I used to go to the dogs at Slough.

Acott: Are you keen on greyhound racing?

Alphon: Yes, I go every day if possible, it's my only real interest in life.

Acott: Can you think of anybody who can verify your statement?

Alphon: Only my mother. I met her at about 9 p.m. at Streatham that night.

Acott: I've seen your mother, she's not certain of the day.

Alphon: No, she's got a very poor memory, but I saw her several times about then to get money from her and I cashed a few cheques but I can't remember the days.

Acott: Can you give me details of the cheques so that I might verify the dates?

Alphon: Well, there's a difficulty there – we use different names . . . it's a personal matter, it's got something to do with an annuity.

Acott: Did you change bedrooms in the Vienna?

Alphon: No, I've told you my alibi. The statement I gave to Kilner is true and he verified it. Someone must be telling lies but it's certainly not me. Anyway, I can make all the mistakes in the world, but I am still innocent of the murder.

Acott: Can you think of anything else which will help to establish your innocence?

Alphon: No. My difficulty is I'm a wanderer and nobody knows me. You're the only person who can help me if only you'll believe what I'm telling you.

Acott: Can you tell me where you were on 7 September this year?

Alphon: No, I couldn't. I can never remember where I was on any day.

Acott: Let me help you. You left the Alexandra on the morning of 6 September. The assault at Richmond was at 1.00 p.m. the next day. Where were you that day?

(PAUSE)

Alphon: No, I've no idea. I can't remember where I was. I was probably selling almanacs somewhere.

Acott: If you will give us permission for one or two tests, it may help to clear you positively of suspicion in this case.

Alphon: Certainly, I will give you permission for anything if it's going to clear me, except my luggage. I won't tell you where that is.

Acott: Have you any objection to being examined by a doctor?

Alphon: Certainly not. I may be queer in some ways, but no doctor will say I am insane.

Acott: This will not be a medical examination, but purely to take blood samples, and a physical examination.

Alphon: Oh, that's all right. I suppose you want my blood to see if there's any of it on some clothing. Well, that will clear me, 'cos you won't find my blood anywhere else.

Acott: We shall do everything possible to clear this matter up.

Alphon: I don't know how all this started but I reckon I must have a double. Anyway, I feel a lot better now. I apologize for saying you were trying to trap me. I can see you're trying to do what I couldn't do, that's clear me . . . I know I'm hard up now, but it's not always like that. Round about the time of the murder I was at the Great Northern Hotel and I won about £1,000 on the dogs. I lost every penny of it within a few days, so I had to leave the Northern without paying my bill and I've been hard up ever since.

Acott: We have a lot of checking and arrangements to make, so you can go to sleep if you want to because we'll be a long time before we are ready to see you again.[15]

The interview concluded at 5.15 a.m. As a result of both that and the non-identifications, Alphon was cleared of involvement in the A6 Murder. It was a remarkable outcome, particularly considering the way he conducted himself and responded to Acott's questions – with a characteristic mixture of insouciance, arrogance and insolence – which would usually have had precisely the opposite effect and inflamed, rather than stifled, suspicions.

By turning up outside Scotland Yard at midnight, however, Alphon had shrewdly maximized his own advantages in his confrontation with the police. Under such conditions he was mentally sharp, and easily a match for Acott.

The ironic outcome was that, at the time that they eliminated Alphon from inquiries, the police had a mass of evidence to implicate him in the crime. Three overwhelming areas of suspicion emerge from this transcript of Acott's interrogation of Alphon.

The first concerned Alphon's general truthfulness. Even though he brazenly admitted lying in his first police statement, this didn't appear to arouse Acott's interest. Acott should have comprehended that although he was rarely able to pin his suspect down, whenever Alphon did give information which could be checked it was invariably false. In the statement to Kilner, Alphon said: 'I have been asked by police to give details of my movements since Monday, 21 August . . . I spent the weekend at Southend but did not stay at any address as I slept under the pier . . . on Monday, I left Southend at about 5 p.m. . . .

'. . . On Friday I went to the Astoria cinema in Finsbury Park . . . That was about 3 p.m. and I stayed there until 7 p.m.'

Each of these assertions can be checked against other witnesses; both are untrue. On Monday lunchtime, Alphon was at a pawnbroker's in Shepherd's Bush. Late on Friday afternoon he was buying a new mackintosh.

Similarly, although he provided few opportunities for Acott to check his answers (saying he was 'a wanderer and nobody knows me'), wherever checks were possible he was clearly not telling the truth. He didn't arrive at the Vienna casually, late at night; he had pre-booked in the morning; he didn't pay for his room at the Broadway House Hotel; he was not shown to his room by a 'girl', as Juliana Galves, the only 'girl' there, never saw him until nearly noon the next day; nor did this 'girl' serve him with his breakfast; indeed he didn't have any breakfast. Alphon could have mentioned meeting an old acquaintance on the Wednesday afternoon. That wouldn't have compromised him in any way; yet he lied there as well.

Alphon also said he couldn't 'remember seeing any man' – which means that there are extraordinary discrepancies with Nudds's statements 1 and 3. According to those, Nudds said, 'I saw him and stood by while my wife dealt with him ... I didn't see him again until the following morning when I went to his room to see if he wanted breakfast. He told me he didn't want breakfast.' Either Nudds was lying, in which case Alphon's alibi went up in smoke; or Alphon himself was lying.

Secondly, there is no doubt at all that in the A6 case the forensic science should have comprised a particularly revealing area of evidence. Valerie Storie said at the magistrates' court, 'I suppose the body of Mike was pretty well covered with blood.' PC Reg Edwards, who saw the car when it was abandoned in Redbridge, specifically drew attention to the amount of blood in the car. In the wake of the crime, all police reports said that the suspect's clothing would be 'undoubtedly bloodstained'. Nor was this all; the gunman had draped the rug over the driver's seat in what would have been a vain attempt to prevent blood-spots getting on his clothing. The only result of this would have been the additional transfer of fibres from the rug to his clothing.

So was Alphon's clothing examined? No; he repeatedly told Acott that he wouldn't let him have anything for forensic examination. During the night, one astonishing exchange passed apparently unnoticed:

Acott: Now tell me the hotels and offices where your luggage is, so I can find it and examine your clothing.

Alphon: No, I don't want my private papers scrutinized. They are political. How do you think that's going to help? Do you think I've got bloodstained shirts?

Acott: Have you got bloodstained shirts?
Alphon: Of course not, but I don't want to produce them to you . . .

When police fixed on Hanratty as their suspect, he told Acott exactly where his clothes were, so that the police could retrieve them. He gave immediate permission for them to conduct whatever scientific tests they wanted. Michael Sherrard emphasized to the jury just how important that was.

However, Hanratty gained no advantage from this at trial, basically because Acott assured the jury at Bedford that precisely the same applied in the case of the other suspect, Alphon. According to Acott, Alphon 'volunteered himself for identification tests, medical tests, laboratory tests, and was pleased when I arranged them'. In view of the many occasions when Alphon demurred on just that point, it is hard to understand why Acott felt able to give this unqualified testimonial.

Thirdly, there was the important matter of the alibi. One of Acott's priorities was to obtain an account of Alphon's movements. He never seemed to notice that, because Alphon nimbly changed the subject, he didn't receive one.

Alphon had suggested two possible alibis – one with his mother, and the other at the Vienna Hotel. Neither stood up to examination. Acott certainly knew that the alibi was not corroborated by his mother. Mrs Alphon did indeed mention a meeting when she gave her son a suitcase – but in particularly vague terms. It almost seemed as if she, a doting mother, knew that she was meant to be giving him an alibi and so was deliberately keeping open as many options as possible: 'I can only say it was Tuesday, Wednesday or Thursday; or it may have been when I met him one lunchtime.' There was no concurrence on *when*; nor even on *where*: Alphon said the meeting was on the corner of Gleneagle Road; his mother said it took place 'down the road near Streatham Common station'.

Without Mrs Alphon, there was only the Vienna Hotel. But the one reliable witness there, Juliana Galves, had not seen him: 'The only time I saw the man who occupied Room 6 was about 11.45 a.m. on the day he left.'[16]

That just left Nudds. After Storie failed to identify Alphon, Acott's subsequent tactics in trying to establish where the truth lay in the contradictory Nudds–Snell statements were disastrously inept. He had made a major miscalculation in taking their second statements on consecutive days; for the third statements he interviewed them in circumstances which did not allow them to collude on a story.

This time, his blunder was not to speak to Nudds first. Had he done so, he could have found out the truth; he could have established whether his account was subsequently corroborated by Florence Snell. But he interviewed her first. She appears to have had no idea of how to react. She was frightened, and out of her depth. Should she be supporting Nudds in his first statement? In his second? Should she be telling the truth? She simply didn't know. She jumped back to the first story.

By the time that Nudds was brought in, the die was already cast. This is what happened:

Acott: Now I want to deal with your evidence. Which of your two statements is true?

Nudds: The second one. I told you I was confused when I made the first one. It's all clear now and I have told you all I know.

Acott: We've seen Mrs Snell today and she now tells us that the second statements made by you and her are completely false. What do you say about that?

Nudds: Did she say that?

Acott: She said that, and she also said that you rehearsed her so that her second statement to us would agree with your second statement.

Nudds: I'm confused. I must have time to think.

Acott: This is not the time for confusion. I'm investigating a murder, and a man's life may depend on your evidence. All I want from you is the truth.

Nudds: Yes, but I've told you so many lies you won't believe anything I say now. Give me time to think.

Acott: Take your time, but make sure you tell me the truth this time.

Nudds: I'm in a tight spot. It wasn't a case of rehearsing, we went over it a few times. If she's gone back on her story, she's scared. I've got mixed up.

Acott: Is your second statement true or false?

Nudds: Well, it's obvious you know now it's false. That lets Durrant out, doesn't it?[17]

When he went in to be interviewed, Nudds had one priority, which was to save his own skin. Consequently he told the truth straight off. The second statement, he told Acott, was the genuine one. That, indeed, is the one corroborated by other documentation and testimony. Acott clumsily talked him out of it, so that his story once more dovetailed with Snell's.

When he interviewed Florence Snell on that Monday morning, Acott should have realized that her second statement was unusually detailed for one that she now disclaimed, that it included some plausible detail that wasn't in her husband's, and that in any case it was borne out by the testimony of the one honest witness at the Vienna, Juliana Galves.

On 18 September Peter and Anita Sims telephoned the police from the Alexandra Court Hotel to say that they had found a bloodstained pillow-case in Room 97, which Alphon had used. This was sent to Scotland Yard for examination, where Lewis Nickolls, the director of the forensic science laboratory, found that the blood-spots were 'a human blood stain on one side of the pillow'. It was, however, too small to group. I'm inclined to doubt whether this was relevant.

What was absolutely relevant, however, was what Juliana Galves saw when she opened the door of his room at the Vienna at 11.45 to tell him he had to leave by noon. Alphon was by the wash-basin, washing his hands. The suitcase was lying open on the bed. As soon as the door opened, Alphon moved to close the suitcase. As he did so, Galves noticed that it contained 'very dirty clothing'. What particularly caught her eye, however, was the pair of black ladies' gloves lying on top.

After he had satisfied police at Highbury, Alphon was obviously buoyant. His mood changed straightaway; Anita Sims described him as 'quite happy', and he began appearing for breakfast. Likewise, after his elimination by Scotland Yard, he was particularly elated, even though he was remanded in custody on the charge of assaulting Meike Dalal.

(Roy Brooks, the former Detective Sergeant on the Scotland Yard inquiry team, recalled, 'I think by then Acott thought they'd got the wrong man. He was very relieved when the CID at Putney agreed to take him off his hands and charge him with the Dalal offence.')

So, despite being held, Alphon was bubbling, and talked 'almost constantly'. The two constables guarding him made statements about everything he said. Among other things, he said to Police Constable Glyn Davies that 'I didn't think I would be charged with this case at Barnes. What will I get for it, there was no sexual assault and they must take into account that I'm a first offender. I didn't mean that I did it, but if I'm found guilty the Court must treat me for a first offence. I am not interested in women, some men go mad for them.

'I saw in the paper that the girl in the A6 case was still very ill, but when I saw her today she had quite a good complexion. She couldn't move, she couldn't point so all the men in the parade held numbers in front of them. I was No. 10. I thought that if I took up a position in the middle when they took the screens away she would be looking straight at me so I stood at the end. I came out in a cold sweat but she picked out another man, No. 4, I think. I don't think much of these identification parades.

'I realize that I do look like the man who did it but it wasn't me. They tried to say that I had one of those shortie macs, but I've never had one. One of the witnesses said I had bought one like it but it must have been a mistake.

'I can't understand how that girl in the A6 case couldn't pick out the man. She must have been close to him for a long time and when he raped her his face must have been a few inches away from hers. Still, I'm clear of that.'[18]

PC Davies's colleague, Ian Thomson, also recorded what Alphon told him:

'I expect the bloke shot the man so that he could rape the girl. I don't think they can hang someone for rape. I imagine the bloke then drove off, I can't drive so it couldn't have been me. There can't have been any fingerprints in the car otherwise mine would have given me away.

'Something I can't understand is why they didn't ask me if I ever used gloves although they are not the sort of things you throw away, are they? At the identity parade regarding the A6 Murder, all the witnesses seemed to look at me for ages, much longer than anyone else, anyway the woman could not move much so I expect it was very hard for her to pick out the right bloke. Anyway, I am clear of that murder. All I hope now is that I can get a good lawyer for this Richmond job.'[19]

This information, from Davies and Thomson (the latter was good enough to contact me to confirm his statement), was never in any sense 'verbals'. By this stage, the police were not interested in Alphon in connection with the A6 crime; he'd been eliminated from inquiries. So there was no ulterior motive for making these statements; they can be taken as a straightforward and accurate record of what Alphon said. Men have been given life sentences on evidence a lot less unambiguous than 'There can't have been any fingerprints in the car otherwise mine would have given me away.'

After he was cleared of this second case, Alphon was in all senses a free man, but about to suffer what in other circumstances would have been his fifteen minutes of fame. The press were after him. Alan Williams, one of the *Daily Express* reporters, recalled, 'He was in the news, so we wanted him. It was a reflex action. As long as the *Mirror* or *Mail* didn't get him, it didn't matter whether there was any story there at all.'

Alphon went to his parents' house in Streatham, where mayhem broke out, with reporters scrambling over the house to try to reach him first, and get their exclusive. 'The *Mail* had a ladder up to his bedroom window, but we'd got him by then,' said Williams. 'One of our team pushed the ladder away. The *Mail* reporter landed in the flower-beds. His parents were screaming, "Get out, get out, you're ruining the garden."

'We got him out of the back, and in our car and back to Fleet Street. I remember his sallow face. He was very shifty, and for three days he was hanging round our offices in this dirty raincoat. He gave us all the creeps. Finally, I remember the news editor, roaring, "Get this psychopath out of here."'

The Express paid £1,000 for Alphon's story, but what did they get for it? Very little. 'He was no use to us, they hadn't charged him with anything.' With regard to the Acott interview, Alphon told the paper, 'I can tell you it was an ordeal. On and on the questioning went until nine o'clock in the morning. The more I tried to help clear up this dreadful mess, the blacker things looked for me.'[20]

None of this was true. Whether it was the police or the press, Alphon just provided his inimitable string of lies. Almost everything that Alphon ever said, whether in statements to police, the press or in casual conversation, was full of untruths. In particular, he clearly lied about his whereabouts and activities in the week of the crime.

Had all the evidence ever been properly assembled and analysed, then the case against Alphon – long before he ever started confessing to the crime – would have been overwhelming. Remarkably, the statements regarding Alphon were never collated and properly assimilated. Many were made, by concerned and conscientious members of the public, directly after the public appeal for Alphon – which was also, ironically, directly after his elimination.

Yet those statements together constitute a compelling portrait of exactly the kind of man that police were searching for in connection with the unusually violent and seemingly motiveless A6 crime. He looked like the first identikit; one witness referred to his 'staring eyes'. Valerie Storie's description of the murderer's hair fitted Alphon, her original estimate of the man's age was exactly right for him, and her photofit very much resembled him. Three witnesses who saw him around the time of the murder referred to his 'cockney' accent (and another to the fact that he 'sounded like a gypsy', suggesting that he sometimes feigned a more colloquial speech). There was unanimity about the fact that he didn't smoke. That trait – something of a rarity for a period when smoking was considered virtually a social necessity – was considered one of the earliest clues to the gunman.

It seems astonishing that Acott should have told the jury at Bedford that one of the reasons for Alphon's elimination was his dress: 'Our suspect was described as immaculate; Alphon was shabbily dressed.' Yet Acott himself said to Alphon, 'Your clothes look quite smart.'

When Alphon was leading a normal life, he seems to have been invariably well dressed; the witness testimony bears that out. In the days after the crime, he seems to have been a little shabbier. He then adamantly refused to surrender his clothing or to allow it to be forensically tested. There are a number of references, in what both he and his mother said, to his habit of leaving a suitcase in a left-luggage locker. According to one of his confessions, that was what he did with the clothes he wore when carrying out the murder; this is where the 'undoubtedly bloodstained' clothing, the dirty clothing that Juliana Galves noticed, together with the women's gloves, was all assuredly deposited.

Something else is quite extraordinary. Alphon had a characteristic off-white, three-quarter length 'shortie' raincoat with a bright red lining and epaulettes. Everyone who knew him then knew that he was rarely seen without it. He had it on Thursday, 24 August when he accosted Audrey Willis (*if* that was him).

Evidence was tendered that on Friday, 25 August Alphon purchased what the salesman described as 'an off-white three-quarter length raincoat, known as a shortie, with a bright red lining and epaulettes'. Alphon had very little money at that stage (the raincoat cost £5 3s 6d; Mrs Willis had given the gunman £4). Why was it necessary to strain his financial resources by buying a new raincoat now, *in August*? What had happened to the previous one? And why was it necessary to replace it with something exactly similar? Why did he give a false name and address (a *different* false name and address)?

Had he disposed of the previous raincoat (in a left-luggage office, perhaps?) lest it revealed scientific traces that might be associated with a gun and bullets? Once again, the parallels with the case against Hanratty are stark. Hanratty disposed of his suit jacket six weeks after the crime, and this was held to be incriminating evidence against him. Alphon disposed of his raincoat straightaway. The circumstances were infinitely more incriminating, yet were completely overlooked.

Storie also referred to the gunman's continual conversation. This was a characteristic utterly at odds with the ill-at-ease and naturally reticent Hanratty, but which completely fitted the garrulous Alphon. What the gunman said was also highly revealing: not the information which was obviously spurious ('Call me Jim,' 'I've never been in the Services'), although the police fell for it, but the attitudes. The remark about the petrol-station change ('You can have that as a wedding present') is so wholly extraordinary that there has to be some explanation. Similarly, Valerie Storie said that, 'He asked us if we were married, and we said "No" ... but after that he kept referring to Mike to me as "your husband".' In isolation, these remarks made no sense. In the context of the messianic mission against indecency and immorality, they have the chilling irony which Alphon clearly intended.

Alphon had some knowledge of the locale, as he was stationed in the area while on National Service. Someone who looked like Alphon was seen in the vicinity of the cornfield not only on the day itself, by Stanley and Elsie Cobb and Frederick Newell, but prior to the event as well, by both Newell and Michael Fogarty-Waul. Then, Alphon was almost definitely seen at the adjacent Slough greyhound stadium earlier that evening. (In fact, it is intriguing how the Ferguson statement ties in with Alphon's confession notes, about the man 'who might know me' and 'past attempt at cornfield'.)

His behaviour immediately after the crime was so strange that hotel guests reported him to police. When he was being investigated, police found at the bottom of his suitcase a cutting about the A6 crime. This is important because those who later disregarded his confessions usually suggested either that they were inspired by a desire for notoriety, publicity and money; or attributed them to an obsession with the crime after becoming inadvertently caught up in it.

The former was clearly not an adequate explanation, because of the occasions on which Alphon spurned opportunities for money and publicity; and this cutting exposed the fallacy of the latter argument. The crime must have held some particular attraction for him straightaway.

On the evening of the murder, not even Alphon's mother could provide an alibi for him. The Vienna Hotel staff certainly couldn't. Once it was appreciated that Nudds's second statement was fully accurate, then the case against him became all but conclusive. Used as evidence, that statement would have sealed the case against him. Alphon was missing from the hotel throughout the night; and when he returned was in a nervy state. In contrast to Hanratty, who was composed, 'and left our hotel like a normal man would who had had a breakfast after a full night's sleep', Alphon was 'in a bit of a flurry – he told me that he was going out and would not be back until late; he said, "Do not wait up for me."' The next morning, Alphon was 'hurried and agitated' and 'very different from the man of the day before'.

Finally, there was the money and the lifestyle. Here was a man without visible means of support, who was accustomed to living on occasional £2 handouts from his mother. How was he suddenly able to enjoy the lifestyle he did – and spend approximately nine months living it up in some of London's best hotels? In any orthodox police investigation, this would have been regarded as utterly conclusive.

We do not know what other evidence there may be against him. In particular, we do not know whether the fingerprint tests carried out on the Morris Minor car and Mrs Dalal's house fitted him. The results have never been revealed. This, after all, was the man whom Scotland Yard went to such lengths to protect during the 1960s, during the years when he was freely confessing to the crime.

It is true, of course, that Valerie Storie didn't identify him when he was standing in front of her. I must add that Audrey Willis told me that the man who accosted her was not Alphon. She also saw the man years later, probably in 1967, in Stevenage: 'I was walking in the main street. Suddenly, you have an instinct that someone is looking at you, something you notice out of the corner of your eye. I looked round and he was standing in a doorway. I behaved completely irrationally, I was so frightened, absolutely terrified. I just ran back to my car and drove home. But I know that was him.'[21]

She was certain that this wasn't Alphon: 'my man was a weedier specimen, I have the distinct impression that he really looked quite undernourished – he was very sallow.' It is interesting to note what Roy Brooks told me. He was assigned to take Alphon from Cannon Row police station to the identity parade at Guy's Hospital. Brooks remembered, 'He struck me as a weak, insignificant man. I took one look at him, and thought, They've got the wrong man – he was looking very small, crumpled, shabby. I got him a cup of tea. I went with him, still thinking this isn't the man. I wasn't surprised when he wasn't picked out.'

The Willis mini-saga remains fascinating. The first incident would certainly fit Alphon. In the immediate aftermath of the crime, he seems to have been afraid to leave his hotel room, but he began to need sustenance, as well as money. He'd have been able to reach Knebworth easily by the overground train from Finsbury Park. Certainly, Audrey Willis's description would fit him. Mrs Willis further said that she was 'powerfully reminded' of her accoster by listening to what Alphon said (I played her a videotape). What was especially reminiscent was the way in which he was so contemptuous of the police. 'It is extraordinary that he is very similar,' she said. 'I do get a weird feeling listening to what he says. But I think Alphon has better brains.'

If it was Alphon, then he could have come back into London, and deposited the gun on the bus at Victoria in the afternoon. The second incident, on Monday, 2 April, also fitted because Alphon was missing that day. He did hint in later years that this may have been one of the ways in which he tried, indirectly, to prevent the execution of Hanratty.

However, there is something, even aside from Audrey Willis's non-identification, which does not fit. If he had the gun the first time, and then left it on the bus, how did he acquire an exact replica or very similar in order to repeat the incident months later?

If the Willis situation is intriguingly unresolved, the question of who carried out the A6 Murder is beyond logical dispute. Alphon not only displayed many of the characteristics of the gunman, but was the sort of personality who was ripe for study by a team of forensic psychologists: as someone who loathed his father and was unnaturally close to his mother, he was undoubtedly a repressed homosexual. He was unstable, certainly a loner, was prone to sudden mood-swings, and there was regularly an air of suppressed violence about him.

Valerie Storie's comment that 'we didn't know whether he was telling the truth or not . . . he kept contradicting himself . . . he was slightly round the twist' could have been echoed by anyone who knew Alphon during the 1960s. Acott had already noted the definition of a schizophrenic as someone 'usually in their twenties, often a bad mixer, sensitive and introspective and emotionally cold, whose crime may be skilfully covered up'. He mistakenly thought this applied to Hanratty. Apart from the age, it was completely wrong for him, but absolutely accurate for Alphon.

Alphon, however, was not a schizophrenic, but a psychopath. He exhibited all the usual signs (one of which is that psychopaths generally stabilize in their mid-thirties, and are not thereafter a public danger) – and one of the classic symptoms of a psychopath is high intelligence. How he gave Acott a series of highly incriminating answers, and still managed to throw him off the scent completely, will doubtless be remembered as a prime example of the criminal mind outwitting the authorities. It is fascinating that it was he, in this interview, who seems to have introduced the idea of a 'double'. It stuck in Acott's mind, and in due course he used it as an explanation of how Alphon had become involved in the case; he should have realized that it was Hanratty who had become entangled in someone else's plot.

CHAPTER TWENTY-FIVE

WHEN PRODUCTION OF *Hanratty – The Mystery of Deadman's Hill* got underway in 1991, it obviously became essential to find Alphon, if only to establish what his current attitude was towards everything that had happened. No one, however, had heard anything of him for almost twenty years, since Jeremy Fox met him by chance in Brighton in 1972.

We traced him to a small hotel in Argyle Street, King's Cross, which was, by a superb irony, within a hundred yards of where the offices of Bindman & Partners then were. Ros Franey and I went to see him. The hotel manager sent us straight upstairs to his room. We knocked on his door. I have to say that he was friendly and hearty. 'Hang on a minute, will you?' he called from inside. Although it was the middle of the afternoon on a brilliant summer's day, he was just getting dressed; clearly he still clung to nocturnal habits. He opened the door; it was recognizably Alphon. He was momentarily open and inquisitive, but as soon as he realized what we wanted, his face dropped. He instantly turned angry, slamming the door and loudly threatening to call the police unless we left immediately.

Since that unpropitious beginning, he has adamantly refused to see me. Subsequently, however, Jeremy Fox was helpful in arranging to renew his acquaintance with Alphon, so that we were able to communicate through him. Alphon did offer, entirely voluntarily, to provide a fresh confession for the film. Although this included the phrase, 'I, the killer', he still cloaked the plausible confession in a mass of increasingly implausible detail. His story on this occasion was highly imaginative, and clearly borrowed from the 1971 Mary Lanz statement in its references to a blonde woman at the Old Station Inn:

I arrived outside the Old Station Inn at dusk; Gregsten's car was there. I did not enter the pub, but waited at some distance away outside.

There were other cars there, and from one on its own parked furthest from his I had already noticed some movement. When the pub doors opened and two people emerged, almost immediately by my side was a woman who, I realized, had strode swiftly from the isolated car that I had previously observed.

She was blonde(-wigged); had her coat collar fully turned up; and carried in her hand a pair of dark glasses. She stood close to me, keeping her back toward the couple who had come out of the pub.

'Are you who I think you are?' she asked. I froze; I had a loaded gun in my pocket, and I thought for a second that I had been set up. I just looked at her, but she must have felt that her question had been answered. 'That's them now,' she said, with a slight toss of her head to indicate the couple. She continued, 'Do you need any help? I have a car.' I declined her offer, and then for a brief moment she nestled her body to me, gripped my arm, and whispered, 'Do your best – do it.'

This gives a flavour of his inventiveness. The woman in the story was supposedly Janet Gregsten, against whom Alphon appeared to have developed a particular animus. Yet one had only to recall the severe financial straits in which, in August 1961, she was actually living, and her need to look after two very young children, to understand how absurd it was.

Ros Franey and I did see Janet Gregsten, on 22 October 1991, at the house of Roy and Jean Catton, her longtime friends and former neighbours. She earnestly repudiated any suggestion that she was involved in the crime at any point. Almost all of what she said was borne out by the contemporary documentation.

Nevertheless, I felt that she was not completely candid about three matters: her hospital visits to Valerie Storie (she had contacted police on 6 September, asking if she might visit Storie, but at that point permission was refused. Altogether, she made three visits, including two in three days in the week when Alphon was named); about She Saw Him at the Cleaners; and about the exact state of affairs with her husband. She told us that the marriage was an enduring one; despite his infidelities, she and Michael always patched things up, if only for the sake of the children. However, according to the statement which she made on 23 August, in the immediate aftermath of the crime, he did appear to be making a more permanent breakaway:

It seemed that Valerie was pressing him to do something about leaving me. I had her over to see me and tried to explain to her that although Mike was searching for something he seemed to have his roots at home as he felt secure there. This was to no avail and my husband left me again. He returned to me just before Christmas 1960. Matters didn't improve and about three weeks ago he said he was leaving again and got himself a room at Maidenhead. On Tuesday, 22 August, my husband left home ... he did not return home and I was surprised because earlier he had said he would not be leaving me till the weekend.[1]

Yet I do not intend to imply by this that she was in any way culpable of either instigating or colluding in this terrible train of events.

Sadly, this lovely woman endured a most miserable life. She told us about her 'really crappy childhood', and about her two major relationships. 'What I had with Mike,' she explained, 'maybe because there were no great passions involved, one was just content to jog along every day. Mike was a good conversationalist when he was around. What we didn't have was this great sexual thing which causes so much angst in people's lives and leads to so much malevolence.'

She tape-recorded her thoughts about the other relationship:

Bill [*Ewer*] and I did have an affair. It happened in fact because of our close proximity and my sadness. I cannot describe my emotions after Mike died: a mixture of guilt, despair, loneliness and fear to say the least. I don't think I've ever felt so lonely in my life before or since. My sister Val came and stayed with us in Hertfordshire. I couldn't control myself at all, I just used to cry quietly to myself. After some weeks Val went back to London. I was almost glad because then I could cry as loudly as I wanted.

Bill came down one weekend and stayed. One night he heard me crying and came in to talk to me. He put his arms round me and cuddled me and for the first time since Mike died I felt a warmth which I needed. Before I really realized what we were doing, we were making love. For the first time in my life I really knew what all the fuss was about. I completely abandoned myself. It was the most spontaneous thing I'd ever done in my life, and I seemed to fall instantly in love. Bill's and my liaison helped in part to relieve the distress and unhappiness at Mike's death, but I know now that basically it stopped me from grieving properly for Mike.

It was one of those things that happened which I wish hadn't happened. It took away my, if you like, freedom to be honest and open with the world because having an affair with your brother-in-law is not an acceptable situation.[2]

She stayed with Ewer until 1969, and then moved with her children to Cornwall. She was, though, never able to escape what happened or achieve any peace. 'A murder has ripples,' she said. 'All sorts of people get affected. Everybody's life was changed by it.' The crime was always there; and the state's punishment had only magnified its legacy.

'I didn't then and don't now approve of hanging. To me, it's legalized murder. I don't think the death penalty is ever appropriate. I don't think someone has got the right to take someone else's life. Justice is frequently wrong, and of course if you hang somebody, you can't say sorry afterwards and put it right. Hanratty's execution brought no comfort to me, no comfort at all.

'If I were the Hanratty family, I would have done exactly as they did. I would have done exactly the same if I thought my child was innocent.'[3]

After the transmission on Channel 4 of *Hanratty – The Mystery of Deadman's Hill*, Geoffrey Bindman and I set to work on what eventually amounted to a 400-page submission on the case.

The first thing that we established, in consultation with Michael Hanratty, was that we certainly did not intend to ask for a pardon. Nor did we seek a public inquiry.

A pardon would by then have been a wholly objectionable way of rectifying the case. Pardons are offered to absolve a guilty person of punishment for crimes committed. They were the currency of the Truth and Reconciliation Commission, dealing with those who committed horrifying offences during the apartheid years in South Africa; likewise, Gerald Ford, on taking office as president of the United States, gave a full pardon to his predecessor, Richard Nixon.

Lindy Chamberlain, the mother wrongly convicted in the dingo baby case in Australia, was offered a pardon. She told the authorities she had no intention of accepting one. What she wanted was both the quashing of her conviction and a clear and public acknowledgement of her innocence. Being a resolute woman whose determination was only intensified by the grievous wrong she had suffered, what she wanted was what she got.

In fact, for reasons such as these, and even on semantic grounds, the Home Office had itself put forward the view, in a white paper in April 1983, that the 'pardon' mechanism was inappropriate.

Up to that time, campaigners had naturally sought a pardon as there was no other apparent means of redress in execution cases.

So how could the wrongfully executed be posthumously cleared? In researching the Hanratty case, I had noticed an interesting exchange in a House of Lords debate:

Viscount Dilhorne: The question asks about a public independent commission. Will the noble Lord confirm that, should there be any credible evidence to show that the jury was wrong, and the Court of Appeal was wrong, the Home Secretary has power to refer the matter again to the Court of Appeal?
Lord Stonham: My Lords, most certainly the Home Secretary has that power.[4]

It seemed to me that this was much the most sensible course to pursue. This was quickly confirmed when the appeal court dealt with the case of the Maguire family – in which a group of seven innocent people was wrongly convicted of explosives offences – and considered the legal position regarding one of the seven, Giuseppe Conlon, who had died in prison in January 1980. The appeal court judges determined that it was a correct judicial procedure to quash the conviction of a deceased person. Thus the avenue to go down in this instance was clear: we had to ask the Home Office to refer the case back to the Court of Appeal.[5]

I finally completed the submission to Geoffrey Bindman's satisfaction, and it was sent to the Home Office in July 1994. The Home Office then asked for a confidential report on the case from Scotland Yard. This was carried out by Detective Chief Superintendent Roger Matthews. The conclusion of his report first emerged through the somewhat unlikely channel of the *News of the World*:

WE HANGED AN INNOCENT MAN ADMIT POLICE
Hanratty shouldn't even have been charged with A6 killing

As Geoffrey Bindman explained, 'Mr Matthews concluded that James Hanratty was entirely innocent and had been wrongly hanged. He said that his enquiries had led him to change his mind about capital punishment, of which he had previously been a supporter, and to which he was now opposed.'[6]

The *News of the World* accompanied their story with a trenchant editorial arguing against any restoration of capital punishment:

James Hanratty died protesting his innocence and begging his family to clear his name. Now, following an extensive review of the case, Scotland Yard have done just that. They have uncovered a disgraceful package of discrepancies, fabricated evidence and suppressed facts which has led them to conclude there was a grave miscarriage of justice. It is a terrible indictment of the criminal justice system at that time.

Our criminal justice system is not infallible and probably never will be. One of the strongest arguments against restoration has always been the danger of hanging the wrong man. Hanratty was the wrong man. We shall never know how many others there were.[7]

The *News of the World* actually published that prior to the delivery of the Scotland Yard report. Meanwhile, the Home Office had asked Geoffrey Bindman for clarification of a number of further points; we sent that clarification, in a fresh mini-submission, on 24 April 1996. The completed Matthews report was then sent to the Home Office in May 1996. On 29 May, the Home Office confirmed that they had received it. The official dealing with the case wrote to Geoffrey Bindman:

We shall now give full consideration to all of the material with a view to establishing whether grounds have emerged for the Home Secretary to take action. I would hope that this stage in the process would not take too long – three to four weeks at the very most. The conclusions will have to be considered at both a senior official and ministerial level and I can therefore make no commitment as to the overall timetable.

On 5 July, the Home Office wrote again:

Initial consideration of the case has now been completed. Senior officials and ministers would want also to give consideration to the recommendations and that is the stage we have now reached. The timescale for this is beyond my control, but hopefully it will now be only a matter of weeks before we are able to provide you with a full reply.

On 6 August:

We hope to be in a position to inform you of the Home Secretary's decision before too much longer.

There was then a fresh burst of publicity in September, when the *Sunday Mirror* and *Sunday Express* followed up the earlier *News of the World* story that the Matthews report had determined that Hanratty was innocent. On 26 September, the Home Office said that they hoped the Home Secretary would be able to come to a decision 'before too much longer'.

On 3 December, the Home Office apologized: 'Despite best intentions and a recognition of the priority which it rightfully demands, this task has still not been completed'.

By now, there was a definite deadline in sight. A new body, the Criminal Cases Review Commission (CCRC), was due to take over the Home Office's function of reviewing contentious criminal cases on 1 April 1997 – so the Home Office had to complete the review of all its residual cases before then.

On 27 January 1997 there was fresh speculation, as a result of a front-page headline story in the *Independent*, that Hanratty had been 'found innocent' by both Scotland Yard and the Home Office. It was widely assumed that the case was on the point of being referred back to the Court of Appeal. However, this was not yet to be. Finally, on 19 March, the Home Office wrote again to Geoffrey Bindman:

> Unfortunately, we remain unable to bring the case to a conclusion. We have had to concede that it will not be possible to do so before the responsibility for considering alleged miscarriages of justice transfers to the CCRC at the beginning of April. This means that the papers on Mr Hanratty's case will shortly be sent to the Commission so that they can decide what action, if any, is required.
>
> I am afraid that this inevitably means that there will be yet more delay. I am sorry to have to pass on such disappointing news.

At this point, the internal reviews conducted by both the police and the Home Office officials had concluded that the case should be referred to the Court of Appeal. These conclusions were reached in abundant good time – seemingly by the previous summer – for the Home Secretary to have been able to act upon them. When the case was baulked at the last, therefore, the widespread assumption was that it had been thwarted by the intransigence of the Home Secretary himself, Michael Howard. This view appeared to be confirmed when it was learned that before the case papers could be passed on to the CCRC, officials had to delete all references to the recommendation made to the minister. In a press statement, Geoffrey Bindman responded:

The failure of the Home Secretary, Michael Howard, to implement a recommendation made 10 months ago calls for an explanation. All Mr Howard was required to do was to refer the case to the Court of Appeal. The continued distress of the family at the inexcusable delay in clearing James Hanratty is now a public disgrace.

So there was widespread dismay at the prospect of further delay: the CCRC would have to reassess the case in its totality, and in any event would need some time to come on stream. Even so, just how much delay could not then have been envisaged.

By the autumn, a breakthrough appeared to have been achieved. On 20 October 1997, the chairman of the Commission, Sir Frederick Crawford, told the House of Commons select committee on home affairs that the CCRC had been making a 'very intensive effort' on the case and 'dredging up a lot of information'.[8] He added that a decision would be announced by the end of the year.[9] With speculation mounting, the Commission then sought to clarify matters on 27 November, issuing a press release to state that it hoped to reach its decision 'within the next two months'.

Nevertheless, there was no official word, only unsubstantiated reports. In January 1998, the *News of the World* told its readers that DNA evidence had finally cleared Hanratty of the crime;[10] and in March the *Daily Mail* informed theirs that DNA evidence had re-inculpated him.[11] In the wake of this, there were reports that Hanratty's body might need to be exhumed.

Another year went by. It wasn't until December that *The Times* reported that the CCRC would indeed refer the case to appeal.[12] On 11 December, the Press Association 'confirmed' that this decision would be announced 'in the next day or two'. In the event, the case was finally referred to appeal on 29 March 1999, almost exactly two years after the CCRC had taken over responsibility for the case.

By then, it was nearly three years since Michael Howard, as Home Secretary, had been advised to refer the case to appeal. In the interim, a number of those involved with the case had died. Brenda Harris, the daughter of Grace Jones of Ingledene, whose evidence was one of the key components of the Rhyl alibi, and David Lines, the last surviving witness of the execution, both passed away in January 1997. Sir Charles Cunningham, who, as permanent under-secretary of state at the Home Office in 1962, had advised the Home Secretary not to grant a reprieve, died in July

1998. (In 1991, he had politely declined my request for an interview.) Sir Kenneth Oxford, who had later become chief constable of Merseyside (and who steadfastly declined all requests to be interviewed about the case) died in November 1998.

Shortly after the case was referred, Jeremy Fox died of a heart attack at his home in Ealing, west London. An unfailingly courteous and unstintingly generous man, he had without demur provided whatever funding was needed to pursue the case in the sixties. After the collapse of his investments in the volatile industrial atmosphere of the early seventies, he was made bankrupt. Even so, when he acquired fresh financial means in the nineties, he readily offered funding to carry out fresh forensic science – DNA – work. (As it happened, private funding was never required.) It was a matter of immense sadness that he would not be at the Court of Appeal to witness the denouement of the case.[13]

However disappointing the reference to the CCRC was, from one perspective the idea was welcome; campaigners had always believed that the case should be subject to a fundamental inquiry. This was indeed what the CCRC had conducted, under the overall direction of Baden Skitt, formerly assistant commissioner of the Metropolitan Police and chief constable of Hertfordshire. The conclusion that the case should be referred back to the Court of Appeal was made on three primary grounds: lack of disclosure: flawed identification evidence; and police conduct.

As a result of the CCRC's investigation, it now seems that the car was not, after all, parked at Avondale Crescent, east London, during the day. It was probably not left there until the early evening, shortly before Allan Madwar noticed it and reported it to police at about 6.45 p.m. There appear to have been three areas of evidence which led the CCRC to this conclusion: statements from those who saw the Morris Minor elsewhere in the country; statements from witnesses in the vicinity of Avondale Crescent; and the overall mileage of the car.

Of the statements giving details of other sightings of the car, one of these, which I alluded to earlier, is immediately convincing. It was provided by a milkman, Charles Drayton, who saw the car at 5.25 a.m. in Bedford. As he was crossing the junction of Ampthill Road and St John's Street, a car coming from the direction of London Road shot the traffic lights. Drayton had to stop suddenly to avert a collision. He made a mental note of the registration number: 'I remembered this so well because I have always regarded 8 as my lucky number and 47 was my round number in Norwich and also the number of my house there. The letters BHN stick because they remind me of a racehorse named Bahrain owned by the late Aga Khan which I used to back each time it ran. I am quite certain about this vehicle and the index number. I did not notice the driver, but can say there was no passenger.'

The statement provides further information to buttress what was already known about the gunman's driving. It confirms that he was an inept driver; here he was, at 5.25 in the morning when there can have been little traffic, almost causing an accident with a milk-float. It additionally underlines his lack of road sense. If the car was still within four miles of Deadman's Hill over two hours after leaving it, then it was being driven on a bizarrely circuitous route.

Other statements purporting to place the car in other parts of the country do not carry the same degree of credibility. However, what was of overriding importance was the fact that another woman, who worked in the City of London, routinely parked her car in Avondale Crescent during the day. Her car was a grey Morris Minor, and it seems that this may have been confused by some witnesses with the murder car.

In the wake of the CCRC's referral of the case to appeal, several press reports noted that the car had been sighted as far away as Derbyshire. However, this was plainly wrong. There was 'missing' mileage on the car, but it was not sufficient to get the car north to Derbyshire and back south to London.

Nevertheless, the 'missing' mileage was certainly too great for the car to have arrived in Redbridge by 7.00 a.m. Acott had written the 'before' and 'after' mileages of the murder car in his pocket notebook, so he should have been aware of this. He should therefore have been aware of the corollary: that the identification evidence of John Skillett and James Trower was invalid. They could not have seen the right car, let alone the right driver. (There is nothing to suggest that they even saw the same car.)

Another area of the case that was coming into focus was the involvement of William Nudds. His role now began to seem more central than had hitherto been supposed. There was compelling evidence from a fellow prisoner (this was good evidence, not the contemptible prison grass type) that Nudds had told him that Hanratty was innocent. It also now seems that Nudds himself had access to firearms, and indeed had obtained a gun three years earlier after being robbed when he was working as a bookmaker.

Also, in his capacity as a police informer, he was passing on information about illegal dealing in guns.

The more the Liverpool alibi was tested, the more watertight it appeared. It was clear from an examination of all the relevant evidence that Hanratty had mentioned that a small girl was also in the sweet-shop (not necessarily serving behind the counter); and that the girl in question, Barbara Ford, was not only in the shop that Tuesday but was there at the time when Hanratty would have made his inquiry about Tarleton Road. Further, Barbara's mother, Stella Cowley, stated that Mrs Dinwoodie indeed remembered a man asking for Tarleton Road. There were also notes on Kleinman's file to the effect that Mrs Dinwoodie felt certain that the man was Hanratty: 'I am sure that [the man in the photograph is] the man who came into the shop.'

In making the original submission to the Home Office in 1994, we had requested that DNA work (which, when the technology was first developed, was known as 'genetic fingerprinting') be carried out on surviving exhibits. These had been found in the basement of what was then the Metropolitan Police forensic science laboratory in Lambeth. We had hoped that state-of-the-art forensic analysis might be able to provide a DNA profile of the gunman which could then be matched with a putative profile for James Hanratty (to be obtained from his mother's and brother's DNA).

At that time, we were frustrated; the tests did not yield meaningful results. The CCRC spent much time and resources in trying to get DNA results from the surviving materials, although the results, at the time of writing, remained equivocal.

However, every area of evidence against Hanratty had now been demolished. The identification evidence, the bulwark of the Crown case, had been thoroughly discredited. Although one of the original identikit pictures had vaguely resembled Hanratty, it had been drawn up by the Redbridge witnesses – and it was now clear that they could not have seen the murder car. Hanratty's alibi withstood the closest examination. There was nothing left to suggest that he had committed this crime.

On the basis that the identification evidence was hopelessly flawed; that there had been massive non-disclosure of vital evidential material (there are thought to have been altogether sixty-one 'potentially important' witness statements that were withheld from the defence); and that there were numerous examples of serious misconduct by senior police officers in their handling of the case, the A6 Murder was finally sent back to the Court of Appeal.

CHAPTER TWENTY-SIX

IT HAS LONG been believed that the A6 Murder occurred as a result of an attempt to sunder the Michael Gregsten–Valerie Storie liaison, so that Gregsten would return to his wife and children. In my opinion, this theory is untenable. If there had been some family impulse to separate Gregsten from his lover, then less dramatic warnings would firstly have been given.

Gregsten and Storie had indeed received many, many warnings about their extra-marital relationship – but only at work. They were trespassing upon contemporary codes of civil service conduct, and were upbraided accordingly. The inquiry statements of their colleagues make that resoundingly clear. There was nothing more; the matter went no deeper than that. It is, of course, unthinkable that those thoroughly strait-laced civil servants would have withheld information from the police.

At the time, everyone wondered what they themselves would have done in Gregsten and Storie's position. Would they have been able to devise some ruse to get the gunman out of the car and effect an escape? This was one of the intriguing factors about the case, and one of the reasons why it fired the public imagination so much.

It was because Gregsten and Storie literally had no idea of why the gunman was in the car, of what he was seeking, that they were unable to deal with him. If they had previously received warnings or threats about the relationship that they had ignored, then they would have fully appreciated the danger they were in. The fact that they could not comprehend the situation themselves demonstrated that they had not been in any way forewarned.

Acott asked Storie the all-important question:

Acott: Have you any reason at all to suspect that Mike's wife, or any other relative or friend or associate of any of you three persons could be in any way connected with this crime?
Storie: No, none at all.[1]

That seems conclusive. Storie herself was hardly going to shield the murderer. In any case, the concept of a family plot to send an errant husband back to his family would have stretched credulity in 1961 (although today, with the problems resulting from arranged marriages in Britain's Asian communities, the idea would seem less implausible). And what did Alphon say? In one of those rare moments when, I believe, he was being perfectly straightforward, he said in a telephone conversation to Justice: 'I think you ought to look for a more mundane motive in that murder.'

Exactly. (Admittedly, Alphon went on to talk about breaking up the relationship, but he was not the person to admit that he himself had been duped.) The motive in this case was the most 'mundane' and time-honoured of all: the passion of a man for Janet Gregsten. He became more and more obsessed with her. She was demure, delightful, intelligent, articulate and wonderfully attractive. He yearned for her. Yet not only was she married; she resolutely refused to leave her husband, even though he treated her despicably. How unbearably frustrating for a would-be lover.

One surmises that, as Alphon talked so heatedly of his mission against immorality, the man saw and seized his opportunity. The latter mentioned a particularly immoral couple and dared Alphon to put his mission into practice.

There was no strict plan but, whatever happened, the man would reap some advantage: either the business would result in publicity and humiliation for Gregsten (perhaps the gunman would catch them *in flagrante delicto*), in which case Janet would finally leave him; or Michael would be placed in a position whereby, through protecting Valerie, he became fully committed to her. Add to this rationale a touch of spite against Gregsten – a man who was so demonstrably having his cake and eating it – and there were the grounds for a malicious jape that went disastrously wrong. Alphon himself didn't really know why he was in the car, or how he was supposed to pursue his mission. That was why events took such a protracted and unpredictable course. Probably, the man never imagined that shots would actually be fired.

The man's motivation was thus the very opposite of the one which has been assumed for so long: he didn't want to break up the relationship so that the marriage stayed intact; he wanted to break up the marriage so that Janet became available. Far from wishing to reduce the amount of indecency and immorality in the world, the man wanted to supplement it with some of his own.

There was just one tragic problem and one enduring irony. The problem was that he fatally underestimated Alphon's dangerous personality; the irony was that it may all have been unnecessary as, only five days later, Michael Gregsten actually was leaving Janet for good.

Now that we have knowledge of a great deal of case material, it must be conceded that this enduringly baffling case retains its central mysteries: Why did Alphon happen to stay at the Vienna Hotel the day after Hanratty? How did the cartridge cases come to be there? And how did the police discover that 'Ryan' was Hanratty?

The answers to these questions have a bearing on, amongst other matters, whether there was a deliberate attempt to frame Hanratty. I don't believe there was. Perhaps, however, there was a deliberate attempt to put Hanratty in the frame. The concepts are not the same.

There are clearly ways in which the gunman, Alphon, appears to have thought himself into the role of a small-time criminal and may have used Hanratty as his model; hence, 'call me Jim', the (only slightly) exaggerated cockney accent, and the fact that Alphon probably suited up for the occasion.

Was he also shadowing Hanratty, so that their movements would be confused? Certainly, on that August Tuesday, Alphon checked into the Vienna, just as Hanratty had done the day before. He was shown into Room 24, just as Hanratty apparently was. Although, characteristically, Alphon complained about it, he did leave his case there ('When we entered Room 24,' said Nudds, 'Durrant chose the single bed which is in the alcove and put his suitcase on the seat of the arm-chair ... Durrant left his case in Room 24, the key of which he had already been given'). Probably he left immediately afterwards for the cornfield, and arrived in the area shortly after 2.00 p.m. As a man who always had time on his hands, he'd have been happy to wait. In the early evening, the lure of the dog-track may have been irresistible, but he'd have been able to leave in good time to return. Having recce'ed the area, he knew more or less where he was going.

Valerie Storie told the Bedford court that the gunman 'could not have known' that the car would be there that night. However, it was frequently there, and there was a good chance that Michael, having just returned from holiday with Janet and the children, would want to get back with Valerie on his return. Although it would have been relatively easy to establish the vicinity in which the trysts took place, it was certainly true that Michael and Valerie moved around and didn't keep to one particular spot. Already that night they had moved from Huntercombe Lane South, probably because they were disturbed there, to the cornfield. It was a large area, and in the dark it would not have been easy to locate them. This is another factor that precludes the possibility of a hired hitman, and suggests instead someone like Alphon: someone who was used to walking and was engaged on a messianic mission.

The fresh light now shed on the case in no respect eliminates Alphon as a suspect. Having committed the crime, he drove back to London, eventually. There is no reliable sighting of him until 11.45, when Juliana Galves saw him in Room 6 of the Vienna and noticed a pair of woman's gloves on top of his suitcase.

The car travelled further than we originally thought, and arrived at Redbridge much later in the day. The most plausible conclusion to be drawn from this information is that the car was brought back to central London, parked discreetly or hidden during the day, and then taken in the evening rush-hour to Redbridge, a place that had no connection with the crime, in the hope of throwing the police off the scent. The car is unlikely to have been on the roads outside London during the day. By midday, the registration number was being broadcast in news bulletins; the car would have been spotted and there would have been reliable reports of it. The sighting by Drayton, the Bedford milkman, suggests that much of the additional mileage can be accounted for by the car having been driven round in circles in the early morning.

After Alphon left the Vienna on Wednesday 23 August, he probably intended to lie low. There were no plans in existence for what happened afterwards – naturally, because neither Alphon nor the man anticipated what was going to happen or knew what kind of crime, if any, would take place. So, afterwards, Alphon probably just telephoned and harangued the man: What was he to do with the car? What was he to do with the gun?

There is literally no information about the dumping of the car. It now seems that the car was left there sometime between 5.30 and 6.30. It is unbelievable that no one saw the car being parked, especially as, with two wheels on the pavement, it was parked inexpertly. It was a late summer's afternoon; there were sure to have been people about.

Once again, the explanation of this gaping hole in the case is the ineptitude of the police investigation. No door-to-door inquiries were ever made along Avondale Crescent to establish whether anyone had caught sight of the person who abandoned the car. If inquiries had been undertaken, of course, then the police may have swiftly realized their fundamental misconception about the car being dumped there at about 7.15 a.m.

Thus, the sheer ineptitude of the police investigation becomes clear. Unbelievable as it may seem, much of the rudimentary work was never undertaken. There were no on-the-ground investigations in the cornfield area (not, at least, in the immediate aftermath of the crime); no door-to-door inquiries in Avondale Crescent; and there was no attempt to contact any of the other Vienna Hotel guests who stayed there on the critical nights of 21 and 22 August.

Before disposing of the gun, Alphon had a further use for it. He was hungry – he was unable to go down to breakfast at the Alexandra Court Hotel, or be seen in public for any length of time. As the money from Monday's visit to the pawnbroker's would have run out, he also desperately needed ready cash. He would have been temporarily unable to call on his usual source of funding (his mother), and he certainly couldn't go selling almanacs door-to-door.

So, I believe, he went on the train from Finsbury Park to Knebworth, to hold up Audrey Willis, to get cash and some sustenance.

There are two reasons for supposing that, when he went to Knebworth, Alphon had not been in touch with anyone else. Firstly, the gun and ammunition must at that time have been in separate places – he would have been unlikely to have carried the heavy, bulky boxes with him. Secondly, if he'd met anyone else, who could presumably have given him a few pounds, there would have been no need to undertake such a potentially dangerous hold-up at all.

On his return to London he met an intermediary, and was given the extra boxes of ammunition – the man didn't want any incriminating evidence on his own hands. It could have been relatively easy to board an unattended bus at Victoria while the driver and conductor chatted at the front; Alphon was cool enough to do the job with the requisite efficiency, wrapping the loose bullets in his handkerchief to prevent them rattling about.

The additional information now unearthed suggests that Nudds may have been more heavily involved than has been previously suspected; perhaps he even provided the gun and ammunition. He is the one man who seems to have understood the significance of key aspects of the case: linking Hanratty to the crime by way of

Room 24, and through the conversation about a 36 bus. The cartridge cases were found in Room 24 within a few hours of he and Florence Snell having been told to leave (but then allowed to return to the hotel for a further night as they had no alternative accommodation). So: did Nudds plant the cartridge cases? If so, what was the objective?

Down the years, many have suspected that it was the police who planted the cartridge cases. Of course, police officers have planted evidence in serious cases. In this instance, however, it is highly unlikely. This police inquiry was only ignited *after* the discovery of the cartridge cases. It was then, with the realization that this was the first bona fide clue, and that the Vienna Hotel had already been brought into the case by Peter Alphon, that those pieces were fitted together; beforehand, the police had no genuine leads.

Were they, then, left accidentally? When Alphon arrived back sometime during the morning, he was still officially booked into Room 24 and needed to transfer to Room 6. Perhaps, in his haste, the cartridge cases dropped out of his pocket. If they had, they may well still have been there on 11 September; from what we now know, it is hard to believe that anybody would have bothered to clean the room in the interim. Overall, this theory still seems possible, even if, I admit, unlikely.

The most compelling explanation must be that they were put there as part of an attempt to bring Hanratty into the frame and in so doing divert attention away from Alphon. Already, Alphon had been taken in for questioning and had provided a statement. At the Vienna, Juliana Galves had been asked, purely as a matter of routine, to verify this. There may have been concern that the police were hot on Alphon's trail. (In reality, they certainly weren't.) Consequently, the cartridge cases may have been put there – and Nudds was the ideal person to have done so – to divert attention away from Alphon and towards Hanratty. Ironically, this had completely the opposite effect to that intended although, once Alphon had allayed suspicion on his own account, they eventually served their purpose.

Any other effort to implicate Hanratty was merely a panic-stricken attempt to shield Alphon. It is essential to remember one key point: in those days few people understood how fallible the police were. The myth of police expertise was still strong, even in criminal circles. It is highly likely that the man believed Hanratty would muddy the waters, so making the crime harder to solve and providing Alphon, and thus himself, with an escape-route. Even he probably didn't appreciate the extent to which the telling pieces of prosecution 'evidence' ineluctably followed the formation of a police mindset.

Alphon was able to shatter the police mindset by doing the unexpected and presenting himself for interview. Conversely, Hanratty did what was expected – he fled, although even he made contact with the Yard – and thus reinforced the police mindset.

The day after Alphon left the Alexandra Court, he assaulted Mrs Dalal. At that precise juncture, the police had been holding a suspect for questioning for about 16 hours – this was headline news in the lunchtime editions of the papers. Possibly, the attack was an early indication of Alphon obliquely trying to tell the authorities they had the wrong man. If so, it was the first sign of a pattern of behaviour that Alphon continued to exhibit.

After his release from prison on the Dalal charge, Alphon, with his sharp intelligence, would soon have comprehended that the man had used him for his own purposes; there was no mission against immorality. Perhaps in response to this, Alphon decided to reap some pecuniary advantage from the situation. He named his price for silence: £5,000. Doubtless the man would have found it extremely difficult to raise such a substantial amount of money. Through a series of menacing telephone calls, Alphon made sure he got it. (Even so, he characteristically found it impossible to remain silent.)

It is certain that he got the money as blackmail, not as prearranged payment. If the crime had been 'commissioned', he'd have received something in advance and thus wouldn't have needed to go to a pawnbroker's immediately beforehand and wouldn't have had to hold up Mrs Willis immediately afterwards. More obviously, if the man had wanted to hire a hitman, and had £5,000 available for the purpose, he was unlikely to have hired a novice like Alphon.

Alphon himself probably overestimated the nature of the 'plot' to frame Hanratty. Certainly, Charles France's role in any of this is likely to have been marginal. Nevertheless, Alphon used his usual effective weapon (the telephone) to prick, not to say lacerate, France's conscience and hound the poor man to suicide. Nudds, of course, would have been impervious to such treatment; his conscience had long since atrophied.

There have been abundant revolutions in world affairs since 1962, but the Hanratty case is still with us, lingering testimony to Britain's unimaginably feeble record in the administration and dispensation of justice.

All miscarriages are serious injustices on three levels: the innocent are punished; the guilty go unpunished; and the victims and bereaved are betrayed. The victims in this case – notably Valerie Storie and Janet Gregsten – had to endure much, much more suffering because of the maladministration of justice than they otherwise would have done.

Michael Hanratty always maintained that, even apart from the fraudulent nature of the prosecution case, there were two particular reasons why he, as a brother, knew that Jimmy was innocent: because he would never have used a word like 'Institutions' as, Valerie Storie had to concede at trial, the gunman had done; and, secondly, because whenever he was confronted with his wrong-doing, Jimmy couldn't avoid blushing with shame. His unembarrassed reaction when these charges were put to him confirmed to Michael that he was as innocent as he claimed.

Meanwhile, there was the mountain of unassimilated and disregarded evidence against Alphon. Of all the difficulties which the defence encountered during the trial, one of the most fundamental was that it was not their job to incriminate Alphon. The more they brought him into the case, the more it may have seemed to the jury that they were behaving irresponsibly – that, in fact, it was they who were engaging in dirty tricks. Thus, one of their strongest cards was denied them. Considered in conjunction with all the masses of highly relevant material which the Crown withheld from them, this demonstrates the impossible task that the defence faced.

Emmanuel Kleinman, who died some years ago, acted throughout with the utmost determination and dedication, but was not the most formidable lawyer in the country at the time. Even if he had been, however, the outcome may not have been different. By the time the case reached trial, and was in the hands of Michael Sherrard, who is today director of advocacy at Middle Temple (one of the Inns of Court), Hanratty was being expertly represented. Once the adversarial system has been set in motion, with one side competing against the other, then truth somehow disappears down the gulf between them.

Perhaps the real scandal of the Hanratty case is that the prosecution relied predominantly on criminals and police informers; the defence relied on ordinary, honest citizens, like John Kerr, Olive Dinwoodie and Grace Jones. The latter were traduced for their troubles, while all kinds of official excuses were made for the perjured testimony of Crown witnesses like Nudds and Langdale.

However, it should be remembered that the majority of the evidence now brought to bear on this case and assembled here in this book has been available to the authorities from the outset. This is the evidence on which the Crown convicted and executed Hanratty; and on the basis of which successive governments have seen fit to reassure members of parliament and the general public that he was correctly convicted and there was no possibility of miscarriage of justice.

Hanratty himself had recognized the root problem of dishonesty – it was self-perpetuating: 'I had already told a lie and had to cover up and cover up until eventually I made things a lot worser for myself.' His mistake was held to be the foolish reaction of a young man of inadequate mental capabilities. Intriguingly, however, his comments could be equally applied to the instinctive reactions of the highest political and judicial authorities in the country: they had covered up and covered up until eventually they made things a lot worser for themselves.

The key point about non-disclosure is that the judicial process is undermined from the outset. Allowing the police to decide what material should be passed to the defence is a recipe for disaster. Police officers are logically not in a position to ascertain the merits of material that threatens to be detrimental to their case. Acott may genuinely have believed that the material he was withholding from Hanratty's lawyers was immaterial. He was wrong, tragically wrong; but, having perceived the case in a certain light, he was incapable of shifting his focus.

Sadly, Janet Gregsten died on 19 January 1995. Just before her death, she said that she was keen to assist inquiries into the case in any way, if this was going to benefit the future administration of justice. What was most important, she considered, was this issue of disclosure:

> The defence has the right to have all the information. That's very important, because that's a part of the justice system which is all wrong in this country. If the defence has access to all the information, then maybe the end result would often have been different. I think the legal system stinks, and what the police are doing stinks. If I can be involved in helping to put that right, I would be happy to do so.[2]

She would have been dismayed to learn that after her death the Home Secretary, Michael Howard, brought forward a new bill, which became the 1996 Criminal Procedure and Investigations Act. This was brought in to nullify a series of appeal court judgments, in which the court had stressed the importance of the disclosure of material to the defence. The new act, which came into force on 1 April 1997, allowed the police once again to decide what information they were going to pass on to the defence, and what they would retain and not disclose. The act was brought in – or so the police said – partly to aid the position of informers: the Nudds and Langdales of the criminal justice process.

Many legal observers considered that this act was one of the most detrimental and inexplicable developments in the history of British criminal justice; and that, as a direct result, the reputation of British justice would sink still further. But we all know that those who will not learn from their mistakes are compelled to repeat them.

CHRONOLOGY

1961

AUGUST

7   James Hanratty and Charles France go to Hendon dog-track, and have a conversation about the upstairs back seat of a double-decker bus.

18   Hanratty collects his new suit from the tailor's, Hepworth's, in Burnt Oak.

21   Hanratty stays at the Vienna Hotel.

22
(11.30 a.m.)   Hanratty catches a train to Liverpool.

(1.00 p.m.)   Peter Alphon goes to the Vienna Hotel to book a room for the night; and expresses dissatisfaction with the one he is allocated.

Scotland Yard identifies fingerprints from robberies in Northwood on 2–3 August as Hanratty's.

(4.15 p.m.)   Michael Gregsten leaves his home in Abbot's Langley and drives in his aunt's Morris Minor car to meet Valerie Storie as she finishes work.

22/23   A gunman abducts Gregsten and Storie in their car from a cornfield at Dorney Reach, Buckinghamshire. In the early hours of the morning, at Deadman's Hill, Bedfordshire, he shoots Gregsten dead and rapes and shoots Storie.

23
(6.45 a.m.)   Valerie Storie and the body of Michael Gregsten discovered by Sydney Burton and John Kerr. Thomas Reay telephones the police.

(7.10 a.m.)   Morris Minor observed being driven erratically at Redbridge, east London.

(1.45 p.m.)   Janet Gregsten arrives at murder scene to identify body.

(3.20 p.m.)   Detective Superintendent Bob Acott and Detective Inspector John McCafferty arrive at murder scene.

(5.30 p.m.)   Postmortem conducted by Dr Keith Simpson at Bedford mortuary.

(6.30 p.m.)	Morris Minor car found at Redbridge, east London.
24	
(11.00 a.m.)	Audrey Willis held up by gunman in her house in Old Knebworth, Hertfordshire.
	Police issue first description of the man they want to interview.
(8.40 p.m.)	Hanratty sends telegram to France family from Liverpool.
(8.45 p.m.)	Murder weapon and sixty rounds of ammunition found under back seat of a 36A London bus.
26	Carole France redyes Hanratty's hair black.
27	Hanratty family told by police that James is wanted for housebreakings.
	Peter Sims, manager of Alexandra Court Hotel, telephones local police to report the suspicious behaviour of a guest, Peter Alphon.
	Alphon interviewed at Blackstock Road police station in Finsbury Park.
29	Two identikit pictures issued by police.
31	Valerie Storie moved from Bedford to Guy's Hospital, London.
	Police issue revised description of their suspect.

SEPTEMBER

4	James Hanratty flies to Ireland to obtain driving licence.
6	Juliana Galves makes statement confirming Alphon's alibi at the Vienna Hotel.
7	Police hold first suspect for more than sixteen hours and interview him before releasing him.
	Mrs Dalal attacked at her home at Barnes, south-west London.
	Hanrattty's hired car in collision with another hired car in Castlemartyr, County Cork.
11	Two cartridge cases from murder weapon found at Vienna Hotel, Maida Vale.
	Valerie Storie gives five-hour interview to police.
12	Second Juliana Galves statement confirms that she did not see Alphon at the hotel until nearly noon on 23 August.
13	Felix and Gladys Alphon, Peter's parents, interviewed by police.
15	William Nudds makes his first statement.
20	Hanratty purchases cream Sunbeam Alpine car.
	Janet Gregsten visits Valerie Storie in Guy's hospital.
21	William Nudds makes his second statement.
22	
(2.30 p.m.)	Gladys and Felix Alphon seen again by police.

(3.30)	At Scotland Yard press conference Acott names Peter Alphon as the man wanted for interviewing in connection with the A6 Murder.
(7.30)	Janet Gregsten visits Valerie Storie again.
(11.30)	Alphon surrenders himself at Cannon Row police station.
23	
(12.40 a.m.)	Acott arrives at Scotland Yard.
(2.15 a.m.)	Acott begins interviewing Alphon.
(3.10 p.m.)	Alphon placed on two identity parades.
24	
(11.00 a.m.)	Alphon placed on third identity parade before Valerie Storie at Guy's Hospital.
	Storie 'identifies' RAF airman, Michael Clark, as the A6 murderer.
	Alphon ruled out as an A6 suspect, but remanded in custody on the charge of assaulting Mrs Dalal.
25	William Nudds makes his third statement.
26	Acott and Oxford visit home of James and Mary Hanratty in Kingsbury, north London.
29	
(11.00 a.m.)	Alphon placed on third identity parade, and then brought before Mortlake magistrates and released on bail.
	Acott and Oxford go to Dublin in pursuit of their second suspect.
(8.30 p.m.)	James Hanratty learns from the press that his son is the new A6 Murder suspect.
30	Hanratty breaks into two houses at Stanmore and tears his suit jacket.

OCTOBER

1	
(6.10 p.m.)	A mystery caller from Windsor telephones Stoke Mandeville Hospital and threatens to 'finish off' Valerie Storie.
3	The case against Alphon is dropped.
	James Hanratty goes to Scotland Yard with birthday card from his son.
	Hanratty tries to have the dye washed out of his hair at a barber's in Kilburn.
4	Hanratty's twenty-fifth birthday. He leaves his suitcases at Louise Anderson's.
5	Hanratty learns that he is wanted for the A6 Murder, and telephones Charles France.
	Acott and Oxford fly back from Dublin.
6	
(12.15 a.m.)	Hanratty telephones Acott at Scotland Yard, and promises to call again later.

(11.45 p.m.) Hanratty telephones Acott a second time.

7

(midnight) Hanratty steals Jaguar car from central London and drives to Manchester.

(2.30 a.m.) Police pick up Hanratty's belongings from Louise Anderson's flat.

(5.26 p.m.) Hanratty makes a third telephone call to Acott, this time from Liverpool.

9 Acott and Oxford visit Hanratty home again.

Hanratty sends flowers to his mother from Liverpool.

10 Hanratty goes into barber's in Liverpool and asks to have his hair bleached.

11

(11.10 p.m.) Hanratty arrested in Blackpool.

12 Acott interviews Hanratty twice at Blackpool.

13 Hanratty taken to Bedford.

Hanratty placed on identity parade.

14

(11.00 a.m.) Hanratty placed on second identity parade before Valerie Storie at Stoke Mandeville Hospital.

(11.00 a.m.) Scotland Yard fingerprint bureau tells Acott that none of the prints on the Morris Minor car are Hanratty's.

(6.15 p.m.) Hanratty charged with murder.

17 Olive Dinwoodie makes statement about 'Tarleton Road' inquiry in Liverpool sweet-shop.

NOVEMBER

22 Magistrates' court hearing begins at Ampthill.

Roy Langdale overheard by prison officer Alfred Eatwell talking about 'confession' of Hanratty.

24 The court adjourns to Stoke Mandeville Hospital to allow Valerie Storie to give evidence.

30 Langdale makes statement to Acott.

DECEMBER

5 End of magistrates' court hearing; Hanratty committed for trial at the Old Bailey.

14 Hanratty examined in prison by psychiatrist Dr Denis Leigh and found 'perfectly sane and fit to plead'.

1962

JANUARY

2 Hearing relocated to Bedford.

22	Trial begins in Bedford.
23	One of the twelve jurors is discharged.
29	Hanratty tells his lawyers of his Rhyl alibi.

FEBRUARY

6	Grace Jones, landlady of Ingledene in Rhyl, tells defence that she recognizes photograph of Hanratty. Start of defence case at trial.
7	National newspapers carry prominent reports that defence are searching for potential witnesses in Rhyl.
8	Flintshire Constabulary write to Acott, informing him that 'several persons' have contacted them with regard to Hanratty's visit to Rhyl.
9	Trevor Dutton makes statement to Abergele police.
11	Jean Justice meets Peter Alphon for the first time.
12	Christoper Larman makes statement to Staines police.
17	Hanratty found guilty and sentenced to death.
19	*Daily Sketch* and *Daily Mail* carry 'She Saw Him at the Cleaners' report.
19	Margaret Walker, Ivy Vincent make statements about Rhyl alibi.

MARCH

12	Hanratty's appeal begins.
13	Appeal dismissed.
14	Home Office announce execution date: 4 April.
15	Peter Alphon letter, saying that he believes Hanratty is innocent and supporting moves for a reprieve, published in *Daily Express*. France commits suicide.
18	Alphon charged with being drunk and disorderly at the Regent Palace Hotel. Catholic priest in Bedford speaks out publicly about his belief in Hanratty's innocence.
28	James and Mary Hanratty deliver petition of 28,000 signatures to the Home Office.
30	Letter by Dr David Lewes published in *Bedfordshire Times*: 'If Hanratty is [executed], it is confidently predicted that controversy about the correctness of the verdict will continue for years to come.'

APRIL

2	Home Secretary turns down pleas for a reprieve. Audrey Willis held up again in Old Knebworth.
3	James and Mary Hanratty send a telegram to the Queen.

Alphon acquitted at Bow Street on a drunk and disorderly charge, but ordered to pay costs.

Statement by Mrs Willis rushed to the Home Office by Hertfordshire police.

Christopher Larman telephones national newspapers, asking them to stop the execution: 'I'm sure it was that boy who asked me for lodgings in Rhyl.'

4
(8.00 a.m.) Hanratty executed at Bedford.

MAY
15   Alphon gives Justice his first set of confession notes.
21   Carole France takes overdose.

JUNE
2, 9, 16   Valerie Storie's own account serialized in *Today* magazine.

JULY
24–28   Justice incarcerated for five days in lunatic asylum in Vienna.

AUGUST
22   Alphon goes to the Hanrattys' home and offers to compensate them for the death of their son.
23   Justice tells Alphon he will not see him again.
       Fracas at Green Park station between Alphon, the Hanrattys and Jean Justice.
27   Mary Hanratty takes out summons for assault against Alphon.

OCTOBER
27   Green Park assault case heard at Bow Street; Alphon acquitted.

1963

JUNE   Publication of *The A6 Murder* by Louis Blom-Cooper.

AUGUST
2   First debate on the case in House of Commons.

1964

OCTOBER
16   Publication of *Murder vs Murder* by Jean Justice.

1965

OCTOBER
21   Publication of *Deadman's Hill* by Lord Russell.

1966

JANUARY
27   Hanratty's body exhumed and reburied in Carpenders Park cemetery, Hertfordshire.

AUGUST
4   Debate on the A6 Murder case in the House of Lords.
25   Alphon convicted at Marylebone Magistrates' Court of making harassing telephone calls to Lord Russell and Frank Justice.

SEPTEMBER
14   Publication of first Paul Foot article on the case in *Queen* magazine.

NOVEMBER
7   *Panorama* (BBC1) television programme on the case.
14   Statements of Margaret Walker, Ivy Vincent revealed publicly for the first time.

DECEMBER
14   Investigation into the case by Brian Moynahan and Peter Laurie published in *Sunday Times*.

1967

JANUARY
30   Roy Jenkins asks Detective Chief Superintendent Douglas Nimmo to conduct inquiry into the Rhyl alibi.

MARCH
22   Nimmo's completed report delivered to the Home Office.

APRIL
27   Alphon summoned to appear at Marylebone Magistrates' Court on 12 May to answer charges of telephone harassment.

MAY

12 Alphon calls press conference in Paris to confess to the A6 Murder.

15 James, Mary and Michael Hanratty discuss the case with officials at the Home Office.

17 *Dateline* (ITN/ITV) interviews Alphon, who reiterates his confession on television.

JUNE

3–4 James and Mary Hanratty visit Rhyl for the first time and take statements.

11 New alibi statements published in the *Sunday Times*.

12 In the House of Lords, Home Office minister responds to questions on the case put down by Lord Russell.

JULY

13 Home Secretary sends Nimmo back to Rhyl to conduct a second inquiry.

SEPTEMBER

2 Alphon convicted at Marylebone Magistrates' Court of breaking his promise not to make further telephone calls.

28 Alphon writes to the Home Secretary, restating his confession to the crime.

NOVEMBER

1 Home Secretary rejects demands for an inquiry.

17 *The Frost Programme* (London Weekend TV/ITV) examines the case.

1968

MAY

24 James and Mary Hanratty go to Rhyl again and take further statements.

OCTOBER

Publication in Paris of *Le Crime de la Route A6* by Jean Justice.

NOVEMBER

28 Home Secretary turns down further calls for an inquiry.

1969

MARCH
7   Alphon writes to the Home Secretary naming the Central Figure as the man behind the crime.

AUGUST
27   Commander Bob Acott retires from the Metropolitan Police, vowing never to discuss the A6 Murder.

DECEMBER
10   John Lennon holds press conference to announce that he is to join the A6 committee and that Apple, the Beatles' film company, will make a documentary film about the A6 campaign.

1970

MARCH
25   The Prime Minister writes to the Hanratty family: there are no grounds for further action.

DECEMBER
4   James and Mary Hanratty serve writ on R. A. Butler, Home Secretary at the time of their son's execution, alleging negligence in his consideration of the case.

1971

MAY
6   Paul Foot's *Who Killed Hanratty?* published.
9   *Sunday Times* publishes one of Charles France's last letters.
13   Court of Appeal dismisses action for negligence against R. A. Butler.
16   *Sunday Times* publishes rebuttal statement from William Ewer.
20   Case debated again in the House of Commons.
23   *Sunday Times* publishes further analysis of the case.
27   Case again debated in the Commons.

JUNE
24   In the Commons, Joan Lestor again asks the Home Secretary to hold an inquiry.

OCTOBER
28   Home Secretary turns down demands for an inquiry.

1972

FEBRUARY
17   First public showing of John Lennon-backed A6 campaign
        film, at St-Martin-in-the-Fields, Trafalgar Square, London.

JUNE
14   Lord Goodman raises the case in a debate in the House of
        Lords.

1973

MARCH
1   Jean Justice stands for Parliament as the Hanratty Inquiry
        Campaign candidate in the Lincoln by-election.

DECEMBER
17   Fresh doubts over the identification evidence raised by Lewis
        Chester in the *Sunday Times*.

1974

APRIL
5   Home Secretary asks officials to prepare a fresh report on
        the case.

JUNE
7   First publication of Valerie Storie's original statement.
20   The Home Secretary accedes to fresh Commons demands
        for an inquiry.

JUNE
19   Lewis Hawser QC is appointed to conduct the inquiry into
        the case.

1975

APRIL
10   Hawser inquiry report published.

1976

APRIL
26   Devlin inquiry report on identification evidence published.

1978

AUGUST
31   James Hanratty dies at his home in Cricklewood.

1990

JULY
2   Jean Justice dies in St Mary's Hospital, Paddington.

1992

APRIL
2   Transmission of *Hanratty – The Mystery of Deadman's Hill* (Yorkshire TV / Channel 4).

1994

JANUARY
18   Grace Jones, landlady of Ingledene in Rhyl, dies.

JULY
13   Full submission on the case sent to the Home Office.

OCTOBER
9   *Hanratty – The Mystery of Deadman's Hill* transmitted again.

1995

JANUARY
18   Janet Gregsten dies in Horsham, Sussex.

FEBRUARY
8   Home Office agrees to allow DNA testing of surviving exhibits.
25   *A Break in the Silence* by Paul Foot published in the *Guardian*.

JULY
4   DNA testing fails to produce conclusive results.

AUGUST
   10   *Hanratty – The Mystery of Deadman's Hill* shown a third time.

NOVEMBER
   16   Geoffrey Bindman again asks the Home Office to consider
         the case in the light of the new evidence raised in the
         submission.

1996

FEBRUARY
   14   Home Office requests further clarification of points raised in
         the submission.

APRIL
   14   *News of the World* reports that Metropolitan Police inquiry on
         the submission has concluded that Hanratty was innocent.
   24   Geoffrey Bindman sends supplementary submission to the
         Home Office.

MAY
   29   Home Office confirm that police report on the case has been
         received.

JULY
    5   Home Office confirm that examination of the case has been
         completed and that they hope to provide the response to the
         submission in 'a matter of weeks'.

SEPTEMBER
   15–23 Further publicity confirming the police report concluded that
         Hanratty was wrongly hanged.

1997

JANUARY
   26   Brenda Harris, of Ingledene, Rhyl, daughter of Grace Jones
         and ardent Hanratty supporter, dies.
   27   Under the headline, 'Wrongly hanged: Hanratty is found
         innocent', the *Independent* reveals that Home Office officials
         have concluded that the case was a miscarriage of justice.
   28   David Lines, last surviving witness of Hanratty's execution,
         dies.

MARCH
19   Geoffrey Bindman informed that case will not be dealt with by the Home Office, but will be considered afresh by the Criminal Cases Review Commission.

1998

NOVEMBER
23   Death of Sir Kenneth Oxford.

1999

MARCH
29   Hanratty's conviction referred to the Court of Appeal by the Criminal Cases Review Commission.

MAY
26   Jeremy Fox dies at his home in Ealing, west London.

JULY
15   Mrs Mary Hanratty dies in a nursing home in south London.

WITH REGARD TO the process of identification and the possibility of error, it is instructive to compare Valerie Storie's experience with that of three women who were victims of serious sexual attacks committed by the same man. The case led to the conviction of a Scottish man, John McGranaghan, who was sentenced to life imprisonment. McGranaghan had protested his innocence throughout and, after ten years' imprisonment, his case was referred back to appeal. As a result, his conviction was quashed on 30 October 1991. These are extracts from the judgment of Lord Justice Glidewell, Mr Justice Hodgson and Mr Justice Buckley, in which they outlined the case against him at his trial:

'On 14 May 1978 Mr and Mrs G were in bed together when between 2.00 and 3.00 a.m. a man broke into their home, came into their bedroom, threatened them and struck Mr G with some metal object. He then indecently assaulted Mrs G ... He told her not to look at him. He demanded money and jewellery and became aggressive as he could not find anything. He then blindfolded them both and raped Mrs G ...

'Mrs G had three sights of him, her initial sight when she woke up as he came into the room – there was no light in the room but a street light outside shines on that part of the room, she said; secondly, when she raised her head as he put his penis in her mouth and, finally, when he instructed her to do the same to her husband.

'Nineteen months later, on 12 December 1979, a man broke into the home of Mrs L ... She was awoken at about 2.00 in the morning. The intruder told her to keep her head down. He asked for money. She gave him money ... He spent some time looking at articles which might have been of value, and then he said that as there was nothing to steal he must have a satisfying night and he wanted sex. He put his penis in her mouth and she had to fellate him twice ... The whole incident took a considerable time ... She had seen his face, again with the street light shining outside and through a glass panel on the front door . . .

'Five months later, on 20 May 1980, Mrs F was woken at about 3.00 in the morning by a noise in her home. A man forced his way into her bedroom just as she was starting to dial 999 . . . He made her lie on the bed and forced her to suck his penis . . . He told her not to look at him . . . He then sucked her vagina, tied her arms together and then brought her child into the bedroom and made the child witness the mother being forced to fellate him and finally raping her and putting his penis into her mouth . . .

'It has never been denied that the rapes and other offences took place . . .

'After the appellant [McGranaghan] was arrested he attended three identification parades . . . The first woman who was brought in was Mrs F. She walked along the line and half-way back and then said, "I can identify someone. I think it would be fairer if they all spoke." She then pointed to the appellant. He was asked to speak, and he did. Mrs F then said she identified him. Nobody else was then asked to speak. In her evidence to the trial court, Mrs F said, "I knew him immediately by his eyes" . . .

'She was followed immediately by Mrs L. After walking up and down the line twice Mrs L said she could not identify anyone by appearance. Three men, including the appellant, were then asked to speak. Of the three, the appellant was the only one with a Scottish accent. He also stuttered badly. Mrs L then pointed at the appellant and said, "I identify the voice and also by the features." In her evidence she said, "I could stake my life on the man's voice" . . .

'On 30 October 1980 there was another parade . . . Not surprisingly, on this occasion the appellant objected to being asked to speak. Mrs G asked if she could hear the man speak and she was told she could not. According to the inspector conducting the parade, when she was asked if she could identify any person Mrs G said, "I am not absolutely sure." The inspector asked her, "Is there any person you think may be the person?" She said, "Yes," and touched the appellant. "You only think this is the man?" "Yes, I would be absolutely sure if he could speak" . . .

'In her evidence at trial Mrs G said she was sure it was Mr McGranaghan almost as soon as she went into the room. She denied that she had shown any hesitation. She said she went straight to the appellant and identified him. She had not said that she was not sure.'

In his summing-up the judge cautioned the jury with the

Turnbull guidelines, introduced in 1977 after the Devlin report. The appeal judgment continued:

'[The judge] reminded the jury of the effect which a victim's terror might have on her reliability as a witness of identification . . .

'It is clear that the semen on the bedcover and the sheet taken from Mrs F's home cannot be that of this appellant. This appellant was not that assailant . . . We conclude that the conviction of this appellant on counts relating to Mrs F are wholly unsafe and unsatisfactory and must be quashed . . . The whole prosecution was based on the hypothesis, the acceptance indeed, that the same man committed all three groups of offence . . . It follows that the appeal against these [other] convictions is also allowed and the appellant's convictions on all counts are therefore quashed . . .

'The identification by Mrs F of the appellant as her assailant was most probably mistaken and the identifications by Mrs G and Mrs L cannot safely be relied upon as being accurate . . .

'We add a postscript. We think it desirable to make some brief observations about how what can only be seen as a miscarriage of justice came about . . .'

McGranaghan had been convicted and sentenced to life imprisonment even though a routine scientific analysis of the semen stains on the bed would have proved that he could not possibly have committed those offences. (This was not something determined by sophisticated forensic work such as DNA analysis; McGranaghan's blood group was different from the offender's.) The appeal court judges, having freed McGranaghan, thus concluded by condemning equally the work of defence and prosecution lawyers.

The points of similarity between this case and Hanratty's scarcely need underlining. In each instance, the victims of these sexual assaults were with their assailant for a considerable period, in conditions of prevailing, although not unbroken, darkness. Although the identifications were made after a longer interval than that which applied in the A6 Murder case, it is clear that the opportunities which these victims had of seeing their assailant were in some respects more favourable than those which Storie had had. The first woman, for example, enumerated three separate occasions on which she saw him. Further, the first two women believed that the voice of the assailant provided an additional means of identifying him correctly. Moreover, the first victim even referred, as Valerie Storie had done, to the indelible impression that the assailant's eyes had left on her. As it happened, all three women were totally mistaken.

APPENDIX TWO

ON 30 JANUARY 1967 the Home Secretary appointed Detective Superintendent Douglas Nimmo, of the Manchester City police, a completely independent force, to investigate the strength of Hanratty's Rhyl alibi. His report was delivered to the Home Secretary on 22 March 1967. On the basis of that report, and a subsequent shorter one, the Government determined that it could take no action regarding the case.

This inquiry work has never been published, or made public in any way. However, I discovered a copy of the main report at Bedfordshire police headquarters. It is headed 'James Hanratty: Investigation of Rhyl alibi'. These are its full contents;

Just by glancing through the contents, a confusing picture begins to emerge. The whole thing was a muddle. The essence of the Rhyl alibi, the matter that Nimmo was supposed to be have been investigating, was addressed on pages 21–72, 86–104, 108–29, and 138–55 (those passages marked in bold above). In total, about 72 per cent of the Rhyl alibi report actually dealt with the Rhyl alibi.

The Ingledene statements are on pages 49–61 and 125–6. The witnesses who best dovetailed with Grace Jones are Margaret Walker (86–92) and Ivy Vincent (99–104). Charlie Jones (108–17) maintained that he had directed a man who could have been Hanratty to Ingledene. Statements relating to the contemporary inquiries by defence agents occur on pages 28–48, and 92–5; statements appertaining to the July visit of Hanratty to Liverpool, and his subsequent first visit to Rhyl, can be found on pages 10–20, 84–5 and 105–7; statements regarding the Liverpool sweet-shop alibi are on pages 5–9 and 73–6.

Altogether, this was a genuinely bizarre report.

THE BASIC SOURCE material for this book has provided a more complete record of the case than has ever previously been assembled. Michael Hanratty generously lent me all the family papers; Geoffrey Bindman provided his complete files on the case, and Jean Justice bequeathed to me his own extensive archive. In addition, much material was obtained from Bedfordshire police headquarters. I also managed to get hold of the complete magistrates' court transcript which, again, had not previously been available.

The full trial transcript is also available. The trial lasted for twenty-one days, and so the reference given is to the particular day (in Roman numerals) and then the page of the volume. If phrases such as 'no answer' or 'after a pause' are incorporated in quotations, that is because they are indicated as such on the trial record.

Valerie Storie made a number of statements which, for ease of reference, have been abbreviated as follows:

VS1: the interview given from 8.45 a.m. on Wednesday, 23 August 1961 to Detective Sergeant Douglas Rees and Woman Detective Constable Gwen Rutland (now Woodin).

VS2: the statement made from approximately 5.30 – 7.15 p.m. on the same day to Detective Chief Inspector Harold Whiffen.

VS3: the statement given to Woman Police Constable Margaret Walters, recording what Storie had said to her, on Thursday, 24 August.

VS4: statement of Monday, 28 August.

VS5: the interview at Guy's Hospital with Detective Superintendent Acott, timed from 2.40 to 7.30 p.m. The transcript was signed by Valerie Storie.

VS6: Storie's statement of Wednesday, 18 October.

VS7: Storie's testimony given in the magistrates' court, again signed by her, on Friday, 24 November.

VS8: Storie's statement supplied to the defence on Monday, 15 January, just a week before the trial was due to start.

Finally, there is her lengthy trial testimony.

I: THE SUSPECT

CHAPTER ONE

1. *Maidenhead Advertiser*, 3 February 1961.
2. VS5, 12.
3. Valerie Storie always said she could not remember the exact words.
4. VS4.
5. Trial, II, 50.
6. Ibid.
7. *Today*, 9 June 1962.
8. Trial, III, 3.
9. Trial, III, 6.
10. Ibid.
11. Ibid.
12. The solitary source for all of this narrative is, of course, Valerie Storie herself.
13. Interview with John Kerr, London, 26 September 1991.

CHAPTER TWO

1. Janet Gregsten, in conversation with Paul Foot, 30 December 1994.
2. Statement of Roy Bigmore, 13 September 1961.
3. Interview with Roy and Jean Catton, Abbot's Langley, 18 July 1995.
4. At the time of his death, Michael Gregsten was engaged on research into improving the visibility of road-signs at night. An article he'd written on the subject appeared posthumously in the technical magazine, *Traffic Engineering and Control*.
5. VS5, 6.
6. Interview with Janet Gregsten, Abbot's Langley, 22 October 1991.
7. Statement of officer at Road Research Laboratory, 11 September 1961.
8. VS5, 7.
9. VS5, 6–7.
10. Statement of telephonist at Road Research Laboratory, 8 September 1961.
11. Paul Foot, 'A Break in the Silence', *Guardian*, 25 February 1995.

CHAPTER THREE

1. Interview with Gwen Woodin, Bedford, June 1991.
2. Statement of Dr Andrew Pollen, 25 September 1961.
3. Interview with Tony Mason, Cambridge.

4. Interview with John Kerr, London, 26 September 1991.
5. *Daily Telegraph*, 24 August 1961.
6. Here I can only reiterate a footnote originally made in *Miscarriages of Justice* (page 348 of the hardback edition): 'This proved an extraordinary example of the power of media myth. For years afterwards, it was commonly believed that Gregsten and Valerie Storie had been a hitch-hiker's victims. I remember it cropping up regularly in conversation during my own hitch-hiking days.'
7. Trial, III, 19.
8. Arthur Koestler and C. H. Rolph, *Hanged By the Neck*, Penguin, 1961.
9. Interview with Janet Gregsten, 22 October 1961.
10. Report of Det. Supt Bob Acott, in the case of James Hanratty, 10 November 1961.
11. Professor Keith Simpson, *Forty Years of Murder*.

CHAPTER FOUR

1. Statement of Roy Bigmore, 13 September 1961. Bigmore died in a tragic boating accident in the 1970s.
2. VS5, 21–2.
3. Ibid.
4. Statement of Mary Lanz, 24 August 1961.
5. Statement of David Henderson, 10 September 1961.
6. Statement of Ruby Philpotts, 2 September 1961.
7. Statement of Elsie Cobb, 30 August 1961.
8. Statement of Stanley Cobb, 30 August 1961.
9. Statement of Frederick Newell, 30 August 1961.
10. Ros Franey and I did go to see Mr and Mrs Cobb in 1991. They were very hospitable; but could, of course, add nothing to the statements they had made at the time.
11. Interview with Brian Hilliard, 31 October 1996.
12. Testimony of Rex Mead, magistrates' court.
13. Testimony of Ronald Chiodo, magistrates' court.
14. Statement of John Smith, 5 September 1961.
15. Testimony of Edward Blackhall, magistrates' court.
16. Statement of Ada White, 1 December 1961.

CHAPTER FIVE

1. Statement of William Halcro, 31 August 1961.
2. Statement of Alfred Hance, 31 August 1961.
3. Trial, XV, 21.
4. Interview with Audrey Willis, 10 February 1997.
5. Trial, IV, 52.
6. Statement of Sydney Moorcroft, 26 August 1961.
7. Statements of Ernest Brine, 25 and 26 August 1961.
8. *Daily Telegraph*, 26 August 1961.

9. Ibid., 29 August 1961.

10. Statement of Mary Perkins, 15 September 1961.

11. Police message, logged at 7.50 p.m. on 27 August 1961.

12. Ibid.

13. Statement of Det. Sgt Arthur Kilner, 18 September 1961.

14. Statement of Det. Con. Anthony Dean, 20 September 1961.

15. Statement of Det. Sgt Arthur Kilner, 18 September 1961.

16. Statement of Peter Alphon, 27 August 1961.

17. *Daily Telegraph*, 31 August 1961.

18. Statement of Dr Ian Rennie, 8 September 1961.

19. VS4.

20. The extract was deliberately incorporated into *Hanratty – The Mystery of Deadman's Hill* so that viewers could see this for themselves.

21. Interview with Janet Gregsten, 22 October 1991.

22. VS2.

23. *Evening News*, 5 September 1961.

24. *Daily Telegraph*, 7 September 1961.

25. Statement of Harry Hirons, 2 September 1961.

26. *Daily Telegraph*, 7 September 1961.

27. Statement of Meike Dalal, 8 September 1961.

28. *Daily Telegraph*, 8 September 1961.

29. *Slough Observer*, 8 September 1961.

30. *Daily Telegraph*, 9 September 1961.

CHAPTER SIX

1. Interview with Juliana Galves, Spain, 9 November 1991.

2. Trial, VI, 9.

3. *Sunday People*, 1 December 1974.

4. Report of Det. Supt Acott, 10 November 1961.

5. *Daily Telegraph*, 12 September 1961.

6. Statement of Robert Crocker, 11 September 1961.

7. Statement of Juliana Galves, 6 September 1961.

8. Ibid., 13 September 1961.

9. Ibid.

10. In 1998, the Criminal Cases Review Commission discovered to their surprise that the police had made no attempt to trace other hotel guests who had stayed there at that time.

11. Statement of William Nudds, 15 September 1961.

12. Trial, V, 26.

13. Paul Foot, *Who Killed Hanratty?*, 58–9.

14. 'Wandering abroad' (and lodging in the open air) was an offence against Section 4 of the Vagrancy Act. Post-war convictions for the offence were comparatively rare. Police recruits were advised to avoid the charge on the grounds that it was difficult to prove in court. It was necessary to prove both that someone had been directed to a place of shelter, and

had then refused to go. Even in central London, however, places of designated shelter were few and far between.

15. Statement of William Nudds, 21 September 1961.
16. Statement of Florence Snell, 22 September 1961.
17. *Daily Telegraph*, 4 October 1961.
18. BBC News report, 22 September 1961.
19. Interview with Peter Woods, London, June 1991. Peter Woods died at his home in Somerset on 22 March 1995.
20. *Daily Express*, 22 September 1961.
21. *Evening News*, 22 September 1961.
22. *Daily Mail*, 23 September 1961.
23. *Evening News*, 22 September 1961.
24. *Daily Mirror*, 23 September 1961.
25. *Daily Express*, 4 October 1961.

II: THE ARREST

CHAPTER SEVEN

1. Interview with Michael Hanratty, 1 October 1996.
2. Deposition to defence solicitors.
3. All Hanratty's quotes are taken from his lengthy depositions to defence solicitors.
4. Statement of Laurence Lanigan, 11 October 1961.
5. *Sunday Times*, 18 December 1966.
6. Charles France, magistrates' court.
7. The traditional view is that Carole France dyed Hanratty's hair over the early August Bank Holiday, and then redyed it on 26 August. However, Hanratty himself was adamant that she had treated his hair more times than that, and had done so earlier: 'It was not August, it was late July.'

   When Arthur Webber gave evidence about seeing Hanratty in Rhyl on 25 July, when the latter briefly worked on his dodgem cars, he was asked what colour Hanratty's hair then was. Webber, who had only ever seen him on that one occasion, replied, 'His hair was black.' This indicates that, once again, it was Hanratty's account which was the accurate one.
8. Charles France, magistrates' court.
9. Deposition to defence solicitors.
10. Statement of Ann Pryce, 10 October 1961.

CHAPTER EIGHT

1. Trial, XII, 2.
2. Letter from HPM Reay, solicitor, 30 August 1974.
3. *Evening News*, 2 October 1961.
4. Paul Foot, *Who Killed Hanratty?*, 92.

5. *Daily Telegraph*, 4 October 1961.
6. Statement of Det. Con. Donald Langton, undated.
7. *Daily Telegraph*, 10 October 1961.
8. *Daily Express*, 11 October 1961.
9. Interview with Antony Luxemburg, June 1991.
10. Statement of Jack Braybrook, 23 October 1961.
11. Interview with Brian Oliver.
12. Message logged at murder headquarters from Supt Squires, 11.05 a.m., 14 October 1961. Whether Alphon's fingerprints were ever checked against those found on the car is something else which Scotland Yard has never disclosed.

CHAPTER NINE

1. *Daily Express*, 16 October 1961.
2. Statement of Det. Chief Insp. Reginald Ballinger, 24 October 1961.
3. *Bedfordshire Times*, 27 October 1961.
4. Telephone call by Det. Supt Acott to Liverpool City police CID, 10.30 a.m., 1 November 1961.
5. Report by Det. Chief Insp. T. Elliott, 4 November 1961.
6. Statement of John Dowling, 20 September 1961.
7. Statement of Laurence Lanigan, 11 October 1961.
8. *Daily Express*, 11 October 1961.
9. Testimony of Jean Rice, magistrates' court.
10. *Daily Mail*, 19 February 1962.
11. Statement of Donald Slack (Fisher), 26 October 1961.

CHAPTER TEN

1. Statement of Charlotte France, 12 January 1962.
2. Report of Det. Supt Acott, 10 November 1961, p. 80.
3. This was the statement of Louise Anderson taken under such controversial circumstances during the trial itself (see page 197), 12 February 1962.
4. Testimony of Valerie Storie, magistrates' court.
5. Testimony of Det. Supt Acott, magistrates' court.

III: THE TRIAL AND THE EVIDENCE

CHAPTER ELEVEN

1. Statement of Roy Langdale, 30 November 1961.
2. Statement of Alfred Eatwell, 30 November 1961.
3. *The Times*, 14 June 1958.
4. *Daily Express*, 18 May 1962.
5. Statement of Nicolai Blythe, 19 January 1962.
6. Trial, XV, 29–30.

7. William Aldred, 20 January 1962.
8. Statement of Roy Langdale, 30 November 1961. By the time of the trial, he'd thought of a diffferent reason for being on the hospital wing. When asked about it, Langdale said that, as a potential suicide risk, he was on special watch: 'I expected a visit from my wife . . . they did not let her in . . . I sort of lost control of myself and sort of pretended – well, I sort of just did not want to live any more and they put me in the hospital wing for protection against myself in case I done any harm.'
9. Statement of Michael McCarthy, 16 December 1961.
10. Laurence Lanigan, statement to defence solicitors, 22 December 1961.
11. Statement of Mary Meaden to defence solicitors, 19 December 1961.
12. Statement of Professor Dennis Fry, 20 December 1961.
13. Report of Det. Supt Acott, 10 November 1961, p. 121.
14. VS8.

CHAPTER TWELVE
1. Trial, II, 21–2.
2. Trial, I, 6.
3. Trial, I, 13–15.
4. Trial, II, 7 and 10–11.
5. Trial, I, 2.
6. Trial, II, 2.
7. *Daily Sketch*, 24 January 1962.
8. Trial, II, 40.
9. VS5.
10. Trial, I, 13.
11. Trial, III, 13–14.
12. Trial, III, 14–15.
13. Trial, III, 16.
14. Ibid.
15. Trial, III, 17.
16. Ibid.
17. Trial, III, 19–20.
18. Trial, III, 22–3.
19. Trial, III, 12.
20. Trial, III, 33.
21. Ibid.
22. Trial, IV, 39.
23. Trial, II, 7–8.
24. Trial, XVIII, 23.
25. Statement of Pamela Patt, 26 August 1961.
26. Trial, V, 3.
27. Trial, V, 37.
28. Trial, V, 21.
29. Trial, V, 22.

30. Trial, VIII, 10.
31. Trial, VIII, 11.
32. Transcript of interview of Florence Snell by Det. Supt Acott, 25 September 1961.
33. Trial, V, 43.
34. Trial, V, 44.
35. Trial, V, 50.
36. Trial, VIII, 7.
37. Trial, V, 60.
38. Trial, V, 30.

CHAPTER THIRTEEN
1. Trial, XIII, 33.
2. Trial, VI, 42–3.
3. Trial, VI, 50.
4. Trial, VI, 56.
5. Trial, IX, 55.
6. Trial, IX, 56–7.
7. Trial, X, 19–20.
8. Trial, IX, 62–3.
9. The practice was significantly circumscribed by the 1984 Police and Criminal Evidence Act, which required the tape-recording of interviews in police custody.
10. Trial, XI, 16–17.
11. Interview with James Hanratty, Blackpool, 12 October 1961.
12. Trial, XI, 12.
13. Trial, XII, 5.
14. Trial, IX, 62.
15. Trial, XI, 22.
16. Ibid.
17. Trial, XI, 61.
18. Trial, IX, 70.
19. Trial, XI, 33.
20. Trial, XI, 48.
21. Trial, XI, 27.
22. Trial I 18/XVIII 31.
23. VS5, 29.
24. Trial, X, 29.
25. Trial, XVIII, 24.
26. Trial, X, 48.
27. Trial, XI, 52.

CHAPTER FOURTEEN
1. Trial, XII, 44.
2. Trial, XII, 45.

3. Trial, XII, 55.
4. Trial, XIII, 34.
5. Trial, XIII, 65.
6. Trial, XIV, 14.
7. Trial, XIV, 16.
8. Trial, XIV, 37.
9. Trial, XIII, 44.
10. Trial, XIII, 42.
11. Trial, XIV, 14.
12. Trial, XIII, 66.
13. Trial, XIII, 41.
14. Trial, XIII, 64.
15. Trial, XIV, 55.
16. Trial, XV, 33.
17. Trial, XV, 36.
18. Trial, XV, 40.
19. Statement of Trevor Dutton, 9 February 1962.
20. Trial, XVI, 51.
21. Trial, XVI, 25.
22. This legal provision allowing the prosecution to sum up after the defence was finally scrapped in the 1967 Criminal Justice Act, since when the defence has always had the right to the final speech.
23. Trial, XVIII, 34.
24. Trial, XVIII, 43.
25. Trial, XIX, 3.

CHAPTER FIFTEEN

1. VS1.
2. VS5.
3. VS1.
4. VS5, 59.
5. VS5, 1.
6. Trial, IV, 42.
7. Trial, III, 24.
8. Statement of PC Jack Braybrook, 23 October 1961.
9. Trial, XIII, 45.
10. Trial, XI, 21.
11. Trial, IX, 68–9.
12. VS5.
13. Trial, II, 50.
14. VS5.
15. Trial, I, 5.
16. VS1.
17. VS3.
18. VS4.

19. VS5.
20. Trial, II, 52.
21. VS7.
22. VS5.
23. VS5.
24. VS1.
25. VS2.
26. VS2.
27. VS5.
28. Trial, II, 45.
29. Trial, X, 26.
30. VS1.
31. VS2.
32. VS5.
33. VS7.
34. Trial, II, 50–51.
35. Statement of John Ward, 25 August 1961.
36. Trial, X, 49–50.
37. Trial, XI, 52.
38. Trial, X, 26.
39. Statement of Det. Sgt Kenneth Oxford, 28 September 1961.
40. Trial, XVIII, 46.
41. Statement of Juliana Galves, 20 September 1961.
42. Trial, II, 24.

IV: THE EXECUTION

CHAPTER SEVENTEEN
1. *Daily Sketch*, 19 February 1962.
2. *Daily Mail*, 19 February 1962.
3. Interview with Janet Gregsten.
4. Interview with George Hollingbery.
5. Transcript of *Panorama*, 7 November 1966.
6. *Sunday Times*, 27 May 1971.
7. Statement of Christopher Larman, 16 February 1962.

CHAPTER EIGHTEEN
1. *Sheffield Telegraph*, 14 March 1962.

CHAPTER NINETEEN
1. *Sunday Pictorial*, 18 March 1962.
2. This was really not relevant. From all that we know of him, Hanratty may have had limited mental faculties, but was in full possession of those that he had.

3. *Sunday Express*, 18 March 1962.
4. *Sunday Pictorial*, 18 March 1962.
5. *Murder vs. Murder*, 97.
6. *Bedfordshire Times*, 30 March 1962.
7. Letter from the Home Office, 10 April 1962.
8. *Private Eye*, 24 December 1965.
9. *Bedfordshire Times*, 14 May 1987.

V: THE CAMPAIGN

CHAPTER TWENTY

1. *Observer*, 8 April 1962.
2. *Bedfordshire Times*, 13 April 1962.
3. These are also reproduced in full in both *Murder vs. Murder* and *Who Killed Hanratty?*.
4. *Today*, 9 June 1962.
5. *Murder vs. Murder*, 121–2.
6. Ibid., 125–7.
7. Ibid., 134.

CHAPTER TWENTY-ONE

1. After Justice's death in 1990, Dr Rodney Long, his GP, wrote to the *Independent*: 'It was an astonishing fact that he ceased drinking, absolutely and permanently, in December 1963. He enjoyed twenty-seven years of total abstinence. I kept in close touch with him. Despite the stress of his eventful life thereafter, and during his distressing terminal illness, he never once resorted to alcohol. This was a remarkable achievement' (12 July 1990).
2. Maurice Girodias, coincidentally, died on 3 July 1990, less than twenty-four hours after Justice.
3. *Brighton Evening Argus*, 26 August 1965.
4. *The Medico-Legal Journal*, January 1963.
5. *Deadman's Hill – Was Hanratty Guilty?*
6. House of Lords (Hansard), 4 August 1966.
7. Ibid.
8. Sir Jocelyn Stevens is today Chairman of English Heritage.
9. *The Times*, 21 September 1966.
10. The producer of this programme was Jo Menell, who in 1997 produced a documentary about the life of Nelson Mandela; and the editor was Jeremy Isaacs, later founding Chief Executive of Channel 4 and subsequently General Director of the Royal Opera House.
11. Quoted in *Who Killed Hanratty?*, 357.
12. Statement of Charlie Jones, 25 November 1966.
13. *Daily Telegraph*, 14 November 1966.

14. *Evening News*, 12 May 1967.
15. *The Times*, 13 May 1967.
16. *Sunday Times*, 14 May 1967.
17. Transcript of *Dateline*, 17 May 1967.
18. *The People*, 21 May 1967.
19. *Who Killed Hanratty?*, 372.
20. *Sunday Times*, 3 September 1967.
21. *Sunday Express*, 3 September 1967.
22. *Sunday Times*, 10 September 1967.
23. Ibid., 1 October 1967.
24. The supplementary Nimmo report has never been disclosed.
25. *Sunday Times*, 17 December 1967.
26. Ibid., 29 September 1968.
27. Ibid., 9 March 1969.
28. *Spectator*, 8 May 1971.
29. *Guardian*, 11 December 1969.

CHAPTER TWENTY-TWO

1. Louis Blom-Cooper has since reverted to his original assessment of the case: 'Privately, I and others present thought that there was not much, if any, doubt that the perpetrator of the crime had been James Hanratty ... Whatever doubts any observer of the trial might have entertained, they were not shared in legal professional circles of the time ... the [Hawser report] should have quietened, if not extinguished, any lingering doubt' (*Spectator*, 8 February 1997).
2. *Sunday Times*, 9 May 1971.
3. Janet Gregsten in conversation with Janet Freer, 18 January 1995.
4. *Sunday Times*, 16 May 1971.
5. Statement of William Ewer.
6. *Sunday Times*, 31 October 1971.

CHAPTER TWENTY-THREE

1. *The Times*, 17 March 1974.
2. *Guardian*, 11 April 1975.
3. *Justice of the Peace*, 12 July 1975.
4. VS2.
5. VS5, 64–5.
6. VS7.
7. Ibid.
8. At trial, Swanwick was astute enough to notice the discrepancy, telling the jury that: 'That confirms the story of two bullets fired at Gregsten, four remaining in the six-shooter revolver discharged at Miss Storie, the gun reloaded, and three more fired at Miss Storie making nine in all.' He carefully glossed over the fact that although this made arithmetical sense, it didn't accord with the scientific evidence that the prosecution

was presenting. According to that, the five bullets which hit Storie were fired in the same salvo; and, in any case, she consistently said that the three extra shots all passed over her head.

9. *New Law Journal*, May 1977.

VI: THE RESOLUTION

CHAPTER TWENTY-FOUR

1. Statement of Isabella Jordan, 18 September 1961.
2. Statement of Alfred Fielding, 19 September 1961.
3. Statement of Derek Boulton, 20 September 1961.
4. Statement of Josephine Hayes, 18 September 1961.
5. Statement of Victor Reader, 27 September 1961.
6. Statement of Geoffrey Ferguson, 24 September 1961.
7. Statement of Paul Davey, 26 September 1961.
8. Statement of Anita Sims, 15 September 1961.
9. Statement of Lt. Col. Reginald Le Hardy Guiton, 22 September 1961.
10. Statement of Mary Perkins, 15 September 1961.
11. Statement of Paul Alexander, 21 September 1961.
12. Statement of Peter Sims, 14 September 1961.
13. Statement of Martha Harman, 25 September 1961.
14. Interview of Gladys Alphon by Det. Supt Acott, 13 September 1961.
15. Interview of Peter Alphon by Det. Supt Acott, 23 September 1961.
16. Statement of Juliana Galves, 13 September 1961. Her husband was also honest and reliable – there is no doubt about that – but his English was limited, and he spent most of the time working in the kitchen, and so did not figure in the inquiry.
17. Interview of William Nudds by Det. Supt Acott, 25 September 1961.
18. Statement of Glyn Davies, 24 September 1961.
19. Statement of Ian Thomson, 24 September 1961.
20. *Daily Express*, 4 October 1961.
21. Interview with Audrey Willis, 10 February 1997.

CHAPTER TWENTY-FIVE

1. Statement of Janet Gregsten, 23 August 1961.
2. Janet Gregsten, in conversation with Janet Freer, 18 January 1995.
3. Interview with Janet Gregsten, 22 October 1991.
4. House of Lords (Hansard), 12 June 1967.
5. In the intervening years, the convictions of two executed men, Mahmoud Mattan and Derek Bentley, have been quashed at the Court of Appeal.
6. Roger Matthews, now retired, has remained a committed supporter of the Hanratty cause. See his article, 'They Hanged The Wrong Man', *Daily Mail*, 8 May 1999.

7. *News of the World*, 14 April 1996.
8. *The Times*, 21 October 1997.
9. *Guardian*, 21 October 1997.
10. *News of the World*, 11 January 1998.
11. *Daily Mail*, 11 March 1998.
12. *The Times*, 11 December 1998.
13. *Guardian*, 31 May 1999; *Daily Telegraph*, 1 June 1999.

CHAPTER TWENTY-SIX
1. VS5
2. Interview with Janet Gregsten, 22 October 1991.

BIBLIOGRAPHY

Louis Blom-Cooper, *The A6 Murder: Regina v James Hanratty – The Semblance of Truth* (Penguin, 1963)

Paul Foot, *Who Killed Hanratty?* (Cape, 1971; revised, Panther, 1973; revised, Penguin, 1988)

——'A Break in the Silence' (*Guardian*, 25 February 1995)

Jean Justice, *Murder vs. Murder: The British Legal System and the A6 Murder Case* (Olympia, Paris, 1964)

Lord Russell of Liverpool, *Deadman's Hill – Was Hanratty Guilty?* (Martin Secker and Warburg, 1965; Icon, 1966)

Professor Keith Simpson, *Forty Years of Murder* (Harrap, 1978; Grafton, 1980)

Bob Woffinden, *Miscarriages of Justice* (Hodder & Stoughton, 1987; Coronet, 1989)

INDEX